It Was a Lover & His Lass by Margaret Oliphant

Margaret Oliphant Wilson was born on April 4th, 1828 to Francis W. Wilson, a clerk, and Margaret Oliphant, at Wallyford, near Musselburgh, East Lothian.

Her youth was spent in establishing a writing style and by 1849 she had her first novel published: Passages in the Life of Mrs. Margaret Maitland.

Two years later, in 1851 Caleb Field was published and also an invitation gained to contribute to Blackwood's Magazine; the beginning of a lifelong business relationship.

In May 1852, Margaret married her cousin, Frank Wilson Oliphant. Their marriage produced six children but, tragically, three died in infancy. When her husband developed signs of the dreaded consumption (tuberculosis) they moved to Florence, and then to Rome where, sadly, he died.

Margaret was naturally devastated but was also now left without support and only her income from writing to support the family. She returned to England and took up the burden of supporting her three remaining children by her literary activity.

Her incredible and prolific work rate increased both her commercial reputation and the size of her reading audience. Tragedy struck again in January 1864 when her only remaining daughter, Maggie, died.

In 1866 she settled at Windsor to be closer to her sons, who were being educated at near-by Eton School.

For more than thirty years she pursued a varied literary career but family life continued to bring problems. Cyril Francis, her eldest son, died in 1890. The younger son, Francis, who she nicknamed 'Cecco', died in 1894.

With the last of her children now lost to her, she had little further interest in life. Her health steadily and inexorably declined.

Margaret Oliphant Wilson Oliphant died at the age of 69 in Wimbledon on 20th June 1897. She is buried in Eton beside her sons.

Index of Contents

CHAPTER I

There stands in one of the northern counties of Scotland, in the midst of a wild and wooded landscape, with the background of a fine range of hills, and in the vicinity of a noble trout-stream, a great palace, uninhabited and unfinished. It is of the French-Scottish style of architecture, but more French than Scotch—a little Louvre planted in the midst of a great park and fine woods, by which, could a traveller pass, as in the days of Mr. G. P. R. James, on a summer evening when the sun had set, and find himself suddenly face-to-face with such an edifice amid such a solitude, the effect even upon the most hardened British tourist would be something extraordinary. There it stands, white and splendid, raising its turreted roofs, such a house as a prince might live in, which would accommodate dozens of guests, and for which scores of servants would be needful. But all naked, vacant, and silent, the glassless windows like empty sockets without eyes, the rooms all unfinished, grass growing on the broad steps that lead up to the great barricaded door, and weeds flourishing upon the approach.

Round about it are avenues of an exotic splendour, like the building, tall araucarias of kin to nothing else that flourishes in Scotland, blue-green pines of a rare species, and around these, in long-drawn circles, lines of level green terraces, upon which you can walk for miles—terraces more fit for Versailles than for Murkley, where the grass is generally wet, and promenades of this kind not very practicable for the greater part of the year. The pines have taken hold of the soil, have thriven and flourished, the araucarias are unequalled in Great Britain. Nature and the landscape have assimilated them, and made them free of the country in which they are to stand for ages. But the house, being due to human-kind, cannot be thus assimilated. No kindly growth, naturalizes it, no softening of years makes it fit into its place. It is too big and imposing to be run over by honeysuckles and roses like a cottage; it stands like a ghost among all the paths that lead to its blocked-up door. The rows of melancholy openings where windows ought to be glare out in their emptiness, in contrast with that door which never opens, and makes all natural access to the place impossible. An army of tramps might clamber in at the windows, and make carnival in the vacant rooms, but the master of the house could not without an organized assault find admittance in the recognized way. At night, or when the evening glooms are falling, nothing can be more startling than to stray into the presence of this huge thing, which is not a habitation, and which seems, all complete yet so incomplete, to have strayed into regions quite uncongenial and out of sympathy with it, where it stands as much out of its element as a stranded boat.

But all the same there is nothing ghostly or terrible about Murkley Castle. It involves no particular mystery of any kind—nothing but the folly of a man who built a house without counting the cost, and who found himself without means to complete, far less enjoy, the palace he had constructed. Not the less is it a strange feature in the landscape, and it would be still stranger if popular superstition did not see sights and bear sounds in it of nights, for which the wiser persons in the country declared they could not account, though of course they did not believe in anything supernatural. This was the reason given by the driver of the gig from the "George" at Kilmorley for the round he wanted to make on a certain June night in the lingering daylight, as he conducted the gentleman reckoned as No. 5 in the books at the 'George' to Murkley village, where this ill-advised person, not knowing when he was well off, as the "George" was of opinion, meant to establish himself at the village inn, which was no better than a public-house.

"It's no from ony superstition," the driver said. "I'm no a man, I hope, to be feared for ghosts; I'm mair feared for flesh and blood. I've a good watch in my pocket, and life's sweet, and if it's tramps, as is maist likely, that have a howff in the auld castle, and mak' a' thae noises to frichten the countryside, the mair reason, say I, to gi'e the auld castle a wide berth."

"But it's daylight," said the traveller; for, after all, as in the days of Mr. G. P. E. James, it is a traveller of whose early impressions the historian avails himself; "and there are two of us; and that beast of yours could surely show a clean pair of heels—"

He spoke with a slight accent which was foreign, but which the countryman took to be "high English:" and had certain little foreign ways, which Duncan was not clever enough to understand. He responded, cautiously,

"Oh, ay; she'll gang weel enough—but a mare ye see's a flighty creature—they're mair nervous than a fine leddy—and, if they think they see something they canna account for—"

"But, man alive!" cried the stranger, "you're not afraid of ghosts in broad daylight."

"I'm no speaking about ghosts—and ye ca' this braid daylicht! It's just the eeriest licht I ever saw. Do you ken what o'clock it is? Nine o'clock at nicht, and ye can see as plain as if it was nine in the morning. I come from the South mysel', and I'm no used to it. Nor it's no canny either. It's no the sun, it's no the moon; what is it? Just the kind of time, in my opinion, that ye might see onything—even if it wasna there—"

This lucid description gave our traveller great pleasure.

"I had not thought of that," he said, "but it is quite true. Here is a half-crown for you, if you will drive by Murkley—is it Murkley you said?"

"You kent a' about Murkley when you made up your mind to make your habitation there," said Duncan, with a glance of suspicion. "If you ken the village, ye maun ken the castle. They're ower proud to have such a ferly near them, thae ignorant folk."

"You don't mean to win the half-crown," said the other, with a good-humoured laugh.

Duncan, who had slackened his pace when the offer was made, and evidently, notwithstanding his ungracious remark, contemplated turning, which was not so easy in the narrow road, here suddenly jerked his mare round with an impatience which almost brought her on her hind quarters. "It's of nae consequence to me," he said.

But this clearly meant not the half-crown, but the change of route. They went in through a gate, to which a castellated lodge had been attached, but the place was empty, like the castle itself. A slight uncertainty of light, like a film in the air, began to gather as they came in sight of the house, not darkening so much as confusing the silvery clearness of the sky and crystalline air. This was all new to the stranger. He had never been out in such an unearthly, long-continued day. It was like fairyland, or dreamland, he could not tell which. The evenings he had known had been those rapid ones, in which darkness succeeds day with scarcely any interval; this fairy radiance gave him a strange delight, the pleasure of novelty mingling with the higher pleasure of a beauty which is exquisite and has scarcely any parallel. It seemed to him the very poetry of the North, the sentiment—far less glowing and passionate, yet, at the same time, less matter of fact than that to which he was accustomed—of the visionary land into which he had come. He did not know Scotland, nor yet England, though nobody could more pride himself on the quality of an Englishman. He knew Ossian, which had delighted him, as it delights the fancy of those who know nothing about its supposed birthplace. To be sure, storm was the Ossianic atmosphere, and nothing could be more completely removed from any indication of storm than this. The sky was like an opal descending into purest yellow, remounting into a visionary faint blue, just touched with gossamer veils of cloud. It was not like the glories he had read of a midnight sun. It was like nothing he had ever read of. And into this strange, unearthly light suddenly arose the great white bulk of the palace, with its rows upon rows of hollow eyes looking out into space. Lewis Grantley started, in spite of himself, at the sight, and, what was more remarkable, the mare started too, and required all the efforts of her driver to hold her in.

"I tellt ye!" Duncan said, with a smothered oath, directed at the horse or his companion, it would be difficult to say which. He did not himself so much as look at the great house, giving his entire attention to the mare, whom he held in with all his might, with a lowering countenance and every sign of unwilling submission, when Grantley bid him draw up in front of the castle. Two or three minutes afterwards, the stranger waved his hand; and the animal darted on like an arrow from a bow. She scarcely drew breath, flashing along through the avenue at full speed, till they reached the further gate, which was opened for them by a respectable woman, neat and trim, as one under the eye of her master. Lewis could only perceive among the trees the small tourelles of an old house as they darted out of the gate.

"I'll no get her soothered down till she's in her ain stable," Duncan said. "Your half-a-crown's hard won. She'll just pu' my hands off on the road hame, with her stable at the hinder end, and this pawnic in her. And now ye have seen it are you muckle the better for it? That's what I aye ask when folk risk their necks for the pleasure of their een."

"My good fellow," said Lewis, "are all Scotchmen, I would like to know, as uncivil as you?"

A spark of humour kindled in Duncan's eyes.

"No—no a'," he said, with a somewhat perplexing confusion of vowels, and burst into a sudden laugh. "And even me, my bark's worse than my bite," he added, with an amused look. Then, after a pause, "You're a gentleman that can tak' a joke. I like that sort. The English are maistly awfu' serious. They just glower at ye. You've maybe been in this countryside before?"

"Never before. I have never been in Scotland before, nor in England either, for that matter," said the young man.

"Lord sake!" cried Duncan, "and where may ye belong to, when you are at hame?"

But the stranger did not carry his complacency so far as this. He said, somewhat abruptly,

"Do you know anything about the family to whom that place belongs?"

"Do I ken onything about— It's weel seen you've no acquaintance with this countryside," said Duncan. "What should a person ken about if no the Murrays? Was it the Murrays ye were meaning? I ken as much about them as ony man, whaever the other may be. My sister cam' frae Moffatt with them— that's my caulf-ground—and my little Bessy is in the kitchen, and coming on grand. I can tell you everything about them, if that's what you want."

"Oh, not so much as that," said Grantley; "I am not so curious. Do they intend to finish the Murkley Castle?" he asked.

"Finish it! Oh, man, but it's little you ken. I'll tell ye the haill story, if you like. You see there was old Sir Patrick. He was the man that biggit yon muckle castle; but his siller failed, and he took a disgust at it;

then he gaed abroad, and things turned, and he got his money back. But do ye think he was the man to do like other folk, to let it go to them that had a right? Na, na, ye're out of your reckoning. He was an auld fool—him that had a son, and grandchildren, and a' that—what must he do but take up with some urchin he picked out of the streets, and pet it, and make of it, and set it up for a gentleman, and leave all his siller to that."

Lewis Grantley had started again at this description. He said, hastily,

"How do you know that it was out of the streets? How do you know—" and then he stopped short, and laughed. "Tell the story, my good fellow, your own way."

"I'll do that," said Duncan, who despised the permission. "Out o' the streets or no out o' the streets, it was some adventurer-lad that took the fancy o' the auld man. True flesh and blood will not aye make itself over agreeable, and the short and the long is that he left all his siller to the young fellow, that was not a drap's blood to him, and left the muckle castle and the little castle and twa-three auld acres mortgaged to their full valley to his son. He couldn't help that, that was the bit that was settled, and that he couldn't will away."

The young man listened with great interest, with now and then a movement of surprise. He did not speak at first; then he said, with a long breath,

"That was surely a very strange thing to do."

"Ay was it—an awfu' strange thing—but Sir Patrick was aye what's ca'ed an eccentric, and ye never could tell what he wouldna do. That's Murkley down yonder, on the water-side. Ye'll be a keen fisher, I'm thinking, to think o' living there."

"And the son?" said the young man. "I suppose he had behaved badly to his father. It could not be for nothing that he was disinherited. You people who know everything, I suppose you know the cause too."

"The general?" said Duncan. "Well, he wasna a saint: and when an auld man lives twice as long as is expected, and his son is as auld as himself, there's little thought of obedience to him then, ye may weel suppose. The general had a way of pleasing himself. He married a lady that was thought a grand match, and she turned out to have very little; and syne when she was dead he married anither that had nothing ava, and I suppose he never asked Sir Patrick's consent. If it was that, or if it was something else, how can I tell? But you'll no find many men to beat the general. They're a' very proud of him in this countryside."

"I thought he was dead," said the young man, hurriedly.

"Oh, ay, he's deed: and now it's the misses that has it. I have the maist interest in them, for, as I tellt ye—but ye were paying no attention—Moffatt, where their little bit place is, is my caulf-ground. They're living in the auld castle, just by the gate we came through. Lord, if he had been content with the auld castle, it would have been better for them a' this day. But 'deed I shouldna say that matters. It would have gane in every probability to yon creature I was telling ye of, the foreign lad."

"You don't seem," said the stranger, with a laugh, "to have much charity for this foreign lad. Are you sure he is foreign, by the way?"

"Ye'll maybe ken him, that ye ha'e a doubt," said the sharp-witted countryman.

"How should I know him?" the young man replied, with a peculiar smile.

"I say foreign, for nae Englishman—or maybe rather nae Scotchman, for I am no so clear of the other side—would do such a dirty trick. Take a doited auld man's siller that had kith and kin and lawful progeny of his ain. Fiech! I couldna do it if I was starving. And I ha'e a wife and bairns, which are things that are aye craving for siller. The Lord haud us out o' temptation! But I wouldna do it—no, if I was master of mysel'."

"I did not know," said Grantley, with a forced gaiety, "that you were so scrupulous in Scotland. It is not the character you usually get in the world. But you are harsh judges all the same. Perhaps this unfortunate fellow did not know the circumstances. Perhaps—"

"Unfortinate! with the Lord kens how mony thoosands! I dinna ca' that misfortune, for my part."

"But then to balance the thousands he has not the privilege of possessing your esteem," Grantley said. He had an air of anger and pain under the pretended lightness of his tone, and meant to be bitterly satirical, forgetting evidently, in the warmth of the feelings raised by these animadversions, that the critic by his side was not very likely to be reached by shafts of this kind.

Duncan gave him a stolid stare.

"Ye'll be joking?" he said.

The young man perceived the ludicrousness of his attempted sarcasm, and burst into a laugh which was somewhat agitated, but betrayed no secret to Duncan, who joined in it quite good-humouredly; but, growing grave immediately, added,

"That's a' very weel. What I'm thinking of him's nae importance, nor what's thought in the countryside; but for a' that it's an ill thing to scandaleeze your fellow-creatures, whether they're folk of consequence or no. Yon's the 'Murkley Arms,' and Adam at the door. Ye maun be an awfu' keen fisher, sir, as I was saying, to leave a grand house like the 'George' for a country public, for it's no to call an inn—just a public, and no more. Here, Adam, here's a gentleman I've brought you; you'll have to give me a good dram for handsel, and him your best room, and as many trout as he can set his face to. He deserves it for coming here."

The person thus addressed was a tall man, with a red beard, revealing only about a quarter of a countenance, who stood smoking and leaning against the doorway of the "Murkley Arms." He looked up, but somewhat languidly, at the appeal, and said,

"Ay, Duncan, is that you?" with the greatest composure without deranging himself. Thereupon Duncan jumped down, throwing the reins on the mare's neck, who was much subdued by her rapid progress, and besides had the habit of standing still before the door of a "public."

"And hoo's a' wi' ye, and hoo's the fushing?" Duncan said, plunging into an immediate conversation with his friend, at which Grantley, first in consternation, afterwards in amusement, listened with only partial understanding, but a most comical sense of his own complete unimportance and the total want of interest in him of the new world into which he was thrown. He sat for about five minutes (as he thought) quietly surveying from that elevation the village street, the river in the distance, the homely sights and sounds of the evening. Cows were coming home from the riverside meadows, and wondering no doubt why night and milking-time were so long of coming; the children were still about in the road, the men in groups here and there, the women at the doors. They said to each other as a chance passenger went by, "It's a bonnie nicht," interrupting the quiet now and then by a scream at Jeanie or Jackey adjuring them to "come in to their beds." "They should be a' in their beds, thae bairns; but what can ye do when it's sae lang light?" the mothers said to each other.

Young Lewis Grantley in the leisure and surprise of his youth, still fresh and pleased with everything novel he saw, was well enough occupied in contemplating all this, and in no hurry to assert his own consequence as a visitor. But by-and-by he got tired of his eminence and jumped down from the dog-cart; the sound disturbed the lively conversation at the inn door.

"Lord, we've forgotten the gentleman," said Duncan.

Long Adam took no notice of the gentleman, but he put his hand to his mouth and called "Jennit!" in a sort of soft bellow, thunderous and rolling into the air like a distant explosion. In a minute more quick steps came pattering along the brick-paved passage.

"What's it noo?" said a brisk voice. "A gentleman. Losh me! what am I to do with a gentleman?—no a thing in the house, and the curtains aff a' the beds. I think ye're crackit, Duncan Davidson, to bring a gentleman to me."

"He's crackit himself to want to come, but I have nae wyte o't," said Duncan. "Would you have had me tak' him to Luckie Todd's? They'll take him in, and welcome there."

"No, I wouldna be so illwilly as that," said the woman, with a laugh: and she advanced and looked curiously at the neat portmanteau and dressing-bag, which no one had attempted to take down from the dog-cart. "Ye'll be for the fushin'," she said, dubiously; but the absence of all a fisherman's accoutrements struck Janet with surprise. She added, with a slight sigh of care, "I can give you a good bed, sir, if you're no particular about your curtains; the curtains is a' doon on account o' the hot weather; and something to eat, if you can put up with onything that's going for the night. I'll promise you a fine caller trout the morn," she said, with a smile. "But, ye see, it's rare, rare that we have onybody here by the folk of the town; and it's drink that's a' they're heeding," she added, with a shake of her head.

"I am not hard to please," said Grantley, with the little accent which Duncan had taken for "high English."

Janet, better informed, made a little pause, and looked at her visitor again. The lingering light had got more and more confused, though it was nothing like dark. Janet's idea of "a foreigner," which was not flattering, was that of a dark-bearded, cloak-enveloped conspirator. The light, youthful figure, and smooth face of the new arrival did not intimidate her. She took down the bag briskly from the dog-cart, and bid her husband give himself a shake and see if he had spirit enough to bring in the gentleman's portmanteau; then at last, after so many delays, beckoned to him to follow her, and led the way upstairs.

CHAPTER II

The village of Murkley next morning bore an aspect wonderfully different from that of the enchanted dreamland of the previous night. In that wonderful light, everything had been softened and beautified— a sort of living romance was in the air; the evening softness and the strange magic of the lingering light had given a charm to everything. When Lewis Grantley looked out next morning, the prospect was not so idyllic. The "Murkley Arms" was in the centre of the village, where the street widened into a sort of place by no means unlike that of a French country town of small dimensions. The house exactly opposite was an old one, with a projecting gable and outside stair, washed with a warm yellow, such as the instincts of an earlier age found desirable, and with excellent effect, in a climate never too brilliant. There were two or three of these old houses about, which gave a quiet brightness to the grey stone and blue slate which, alas, were in the majority. The road was partly causewayed and partly in a state of nature—and mud: though the dryness of the weather about which everybody remarked, though it had not especially struck the stranger, had kept this in check. A handful of hay dropped here and there, a few stalks of straw or other litter, gave a careless look to the place, which otherwise was not disorderly. The little stone houses, with the blue-slated roofs, had a look of comfort. It was not half so pretty, but it was a great deal more well-off than many villages the stranger knew, and he recognized the difference. He could scarcely, by craning his neck, get a glimpse from his window of the river, which, with one or two rare bits of meadow on its bank, disappeared immediately below underwoods and over-hanging cliffs.

The room from which Lewis Grantley made these observations was immediately above the front-door, where he had stood so long, with amused astonishment, watching the leisurely proceedings of his hosts, downstairs. It was an old-fashioned parlour, with a red and green carpet on the floor, a red and blue cover on the table, furniture of mahogany and black haircloth, and a large sideboard like a catafalque. A slight mustiness, as of a place long shut up, was in the air, but this was counteracted by a huge bouquet of hawthorn thrust into a large jug which stood upon the sideboard. The blossom of the thorn is not May in Scotland: were it to take the name of a month, it would be June. There was not much refinement in the manner of this decoration, but it was fresh and fragrant; and the windows were open, and the "caller trout," for which Mrs. Janet had pledged herself, cooked as fish can only be cooked when it is newly out of the water, was on the table, along with the tea, "masked" to Janet's own taste, black and bitter, but with a jug of mollifying cream by the side of it, "baps" and "scones," by no means to be despised, and sweet butter, free from any suspicion of salt, furnished forth the table. Grantley did not disdain these dainties. He made an excellent breakfast; and everything was so fresh and new to him, that to look out of the window was enough to amuse him, and the absence of a newspaper, and of various other accompaniments of breakfast in town, did not disturb his comfort in the least. Grantley did not know anything about town indeed, and had no regrets when he found himself in the silent atmosphere of this strange little place. He had a very serious purpose in coming, but apart from that it was pleasant enough to see new sights, and breathe an air to which he was unaccustomed.

His upbringing had been of a curious kind. He was the son of English parents, born (let us say for the sake of brevity, and according to the fashion of our country) "abroad," which may, of course, be anywhere, from one side of the world to the other: but was, in the present case, on the European continent, and amidst the highest civilization. He had grown up there rather in the subjection and quiescence of a French boy during his school-time, than in the freedom of an English one, and at seventeen had been left orphaned and penniless amid people who were very kind to him, but who did not know what to do with the desolate boy. It was at this crisis, in his mourning clothes, his eyes dim with watching and weeping, that he attracted the attention of a desolate old Englishman, wandering vaguely about the world, as it seemed, with nothing to interest or attract him. It is not necessary to be good in order to be kind, and old Sir Patrick Murray, though he had cast off his own family, and cared nothing for his flesh and blood, was not without a capacity of love in him, and was as desolate in his old age as any orphan could be in his youth. He was appealed to, as being an Englishman, in favour of the child of the English pair who were dead. They were not of exalted condition; the father was a clerk in the Vice-Consul's office, the mother had come "abroad" as a nursery governess, no more. Their child spoke English badly, and though he was furious in defence of his nationality, knew nothing about the habits of his race, and had never been in England in his life. Sir Patrick took him as he might have taken a puppy in the same desolate circumstances. The lad was about his house for a month or two, reading for him, arranging his papers, fulfilling offices which were only "not menial," as the advertisements say. He was browner than an English lad, and more domestic, with no pressure upon him of games to be played or athletic duties to fulfil, and perhaps more soft in his manner, with warmer demonstrations of gratitude and youthful enthusiasm for his benefactor than an English youth could have shown. By degrees he got into the old man's heart. They left the place of young Grantley's birth, and thus cut all the ties he had of human association. There were some relatives at home he had never seen, and one of them had written to say that his sister's son should not want while he had anything, and that the boy "of course" must come to him; but none of the others took any notice, and even this open-hearted person was evidently very glad and relieved in no small degree when he was informed that a rich old Englishman had taken his nephew up.

"I hope you will do nothing to forfeit his kindness," this uncle wrote, "for, though you should have come to us and welcome had you been destitute, we are poor people, and it is far better that you should have to depend on yourself."

This was all Lewis had in the world out of old Sir Patrick's favour, but that favour was bestowed upon him all the more liberally that he had nobody, just as the old man declared he had nobody, to care for him.

"We'll stand by each other," Sir Patrick said. And no doubt there is a standing ground upon which old age and youth can meet which is wanting when one of the two involved is an old man and the other a middle-aged one. Sir Patrick scarcely remembered his son, who had been away from him by far the greater part of his life, and had shown very clearly, when they met, that a man of fifty is on too great an equality with another man of seventy-five to leave much room for filial feeling. The general thought his father (frankly) an old bore, and could not forgive him for that ridiculous palace, the new Murkley, which Sir Patrick had built in his youth. But to Lewis Grantley his noble patron was no old bore, but the most gracious of gentlemen and the kindest of fathers. The lad looked up to him with a kind of adoration. What did he know about the Scotch relations? and, if he had known, he would not have cared. It seemed natural to him that a man should know nothing about his relations. It was his own case.

They travelled about everywhere, the old man and the young one, the tie between them growing closer every day. When Sir Patrick got too weak to travel, Lewis nursed and served him like the most devoted of sons. It was only when a letter came with prodigious black borders, about a year before Sir Patrick's death, announcing that of General Murray, that the young fellow became aware that his old friend had a son. But except that a dinner-party was put off, and a hatband put on, no other notice was taken of the loss, and it faded out of the favourite's mind as a matter of no importance either to himself or any one else. When Sir Patrick died, Lewis mourned as sincerely as ever child mourned a parent, and was as much startled to find himself the master of a large fortune, left to him by this second father, as if he had been seventeen instead of twenty-five; for all this time, eight long years, had passed since his adoption by the kind old man to whose service he had devoted himself with an insouciance more characteristic of the country of his birth than of the race to which he belonged.

During Sir Patrick's life he had received an allowance which was enough for his wants, and he had scarcely begun to awaken out of his grief to the consciousness that he must do something else for his living when the extraordinary intimation was made to him that he was a rich man. It may be thought strange that a young man of five-and-twenty should continue, without a profession or any further apparent hopes, devoted to the service of an old benefactor who had never made him any promises, and taking no thought as to what his future was to be, when that old benefactor in the course of nature should be taken from him. But such things are possible enough. The young man was not afraid of the future. He had never expected anything but to face it when the time came. He was of an easy temperament, not troubled about what would happen to-morrow. And why should Sir Patrick die? He did not forestal that event, nor make sure of it till it came. Afterwards he must do what he could—he was not afraid.

But it overwhelmed the young man when he was told of all he had gained by the death of his old friend. He had not even known how rich Sir Patrick was. His income might have ended with him for anything Lewis knew; he had never inquired what his means were. When this astounding news suddenly burst upon him, he was so much touched and overwhelmed by so great a token of the old man's love that no other circumstances had much weight with him. But by-and-by he began to inquire and understand. The will was a very curious will. It began by enumerating the property which was settled and out of his power by his son's marriage settlement, and which would naturally go to his son's daughter; to other daughters mentioned as the elder and the second, but without names, which probably had been forgotten, he left each a sum of money, two thousand pounds, the residue being entirely for "the use and benefit of my beloved young friend, Lewis Grantley, who has been a true son to my old age."

This will, as we have said, came upon Lewis like a thunderbolt. That he himself should suddenly be turned into a rich man was wonderful enough, but that his old friend had relatives so near was still more wonderful. After the first shock of sensation, which was naturally excited by his own personal share of the revelation, the mind of the heir turned with a vague curiosity to those unknown personages. It did not for a long time occur to Lewis that he had in any way wronged them; indeed, it is very doubtful whether it would ever have done so, had not the suggestion been thrown into his mind by the lawyer who had the management of Sir Patrick's affairs. When the agent and the heir met some time after the old man's death, the former congratulated his client significantly that "the family" did not seem to have any idea of disputing the will.

"The family—disputing the will!" Lewis said, with astonishment. He was bewildered by the suggestion. The agent had come from Scotland on purpose to give the young man full information concerning his fortune.

"They might, you know, have pleaded undue influence, or even that Sir Patrick was old, and unfit to judge for himself: that he had been bullied into it, or coaxed into it."

"Bullied into it—or coaxed into it!" Lewis echoed the words in utter amazement and dismay, with that slightest touch of foreignness in his accent which in the circumstances made the lawyer's blood boil, for he was an old family lawyer, who had managed the Murray property for generations, and his indignation was unspeakable, as may be supposed.

"Just so," he said, coldly. "I was consulted on the subject; but I could only say there was no evidence—nothing that had come under my observation; so you need not fear any opposition on that point."

"But this is very mysterious," said Lewis. "Why should they entertain such an opinion of me?"

He asked the question in all innocence, fixing his eyes upon the lawyer's face; and Mr. Allenerly, though so prejudiced, could not help being moved by this entirely straightforward regard.

"You see," he said, a little abashed, "they know nothing about you."

"That is true enough," said Lewis, reassured.

"They know nothing about you; all that they know is, that somebody has stolen into their grandfather's regard, and got all their money—somebody that has nothing to do with the family. That's rather a bitter pill, for they're not rich. You might be an angel from heaven, and yet as you are not a Murray the family would feel it; but you may make yourself easy on the subject. There will be no opposition."

The insinuation and the re-assurance were alike astonishing to Lewis.

"If there is any ground on which to oppose it, I should wish that there should be opposition. I did not want Sir Patrick's money. I never thought of it—never knew he had any."

"You couldn't suppose," said Mr. Allenerly, with some disdain, "that all this was kept up on nothing?"

They were in Sir Patrick's rooms, where the young man had remained.

"That is true. No, surely it could not be kept up without money—and there was plenty of money—of course, I must have been aware of that; but I never thought of it—not for myself."

The lawyer was very prejudiced and extremely unwilling to allow himself to say anything, but after a little hesitation he burst forth, as if the confession had been forced from him, "I believe that."

"Then why should they think so badly of me?" Lewis said.

He did not make any rash proposal to give up the property, as perhaps a hot-headed young Englishman might have done. People who have been brought up abroad have more respect for money in itself than we have. If they do not seek after it so enterprisingly, neither do they separate themselves from it so lightly. There was no indignant flash of a proposal to undo Sir Patrick's will, and prove his disinterestedness beyond a question, in what Lewis said. That would have been foreign to all the habits of his mind. But he grew very grave from that time forth, a mood which suited well enough with his mourning. An intention formed itself in his mind almost immediately, which he did not at once carry out for a number of petty reasons each entirely unimportant in itself, but mounting up together into a certain reasonableness. It was not his grief, for he was young and his patron old, and the natural tears were wiped soon; nor the necessity of settling all his foreign affairs, getting rid of the house, selling or storing up the furniture and pictures, providing for the servants; but there were a number of other small things, including an illness which very naturally followed his long devotion to a sick old man.

At last, however, but not till Sir Patrick had been dead nearly a year, he set off for Scotland to carry out his intention. He was not seduced to London on the way, or to make any acquaintance with the wonders of England. London, to be sure, was growing empty and the season near its end. He came direct from one of the Dutch ports to Leith, and without any pause proceeded to the town which was the nearest, so far as he could make out, to Murkley. One night he had reposed himself in Edinburgh, and one in the "George." It was but three days now since he had crossed the sea, and here he was in Murkley, in the native place of his benefactor, on the very estate which had been his, near the house in which he was born. All this had produced a great effect upon the young man, and so did the conversation with Duncan and the new view of himself and his own conduct suggested by that worthy. Passing gusts of anger and uneasiness had crossed his mind, which were neutralized indeed by the amusing circumstances of his arrival and the novelty of the scene around. But when he had found himself alone that first evening, and the outer world shut out, it could not be denied that the usual peace of his mind was much disturbed. He no longer felt sure of himself, and that tranquil consciousness of having done and of meaning to do his best, which gave serenity to his character, failed him almost for the first time in his life. It was a painful experience to go through, but there was a satisfaction in the thought that he was now on the spot at least, and in the way of ascertaining exactly what the state of the matter was, and how he could best amend it, or if amendment was possible.

This cheering thought and the influence of the morning restored his satisfaction in the external world, and his hopes for what was before him, and the sense of being surrounded with novel circumstances in a new country with everything to learn and to enjoy, restored his spirits. One thing gave him a momentary annoyance, which, however, ended soon in the half mischievous, boyish pleasure which he felt in the expedient he thought of to meet it. The annoyance was his sudden recollection that the name of Lewis Grantley was no doubt well known at Murkley Castle. To allow himself to be known as that detested personage would baffle him in all his intentions. The way of eluding this was a sufficiently simple one, that of dropping his own name. Accordingly he took the first step in conciliating the family by doing the thing of all others at which they were most indignant—assuming the name of Murray, as Sir Patrick had wished. Sir Patrick had expressed a wish on the subject, but it was not mentioned in the will, nor was there any such stipulation made. And Mr. Allenerly had thought it inexpedient. Therefore it had been understood that Grantley he should continue to be. The best disguise he could assume, he felt, was to take the name which would be supposed to be the most unlikely he could hit upon, and yet to which he had a certain right. The idea of doing so amused while it annoyed him. Sir Patrick would have liked it. It would have been a pleasure to the old man; and to himself it would be a shield in this country of the Murrays where every third person to be met with bore the name. If at the same time a sense of deception and unreality crossed the young man's mind, he put it away as a piece of folly. He had nothing but a good meaning in this visit to his adversary's country, to the neighbourhood of the people whom he had wronged without knowing it, most innocently because altogether unawares.

This serious background of thought occupied his mind much while he lay awake in the stillness of the night. But the stillness did not continue long. The darkness was not much more than the twinkling of an eyelid, he thought, and the birds were all awake in a multitudinous chorus, and the sun shining into his room before drowsiness overcame him. At five and twenty, however, a great deal of noise and tumult is necessary to keep sleep away from the eyes, and Lewis, when he got the tangle of his cares unloosened, soon lost consciousness of the birds. And when he woke in the morning and found himself in a new world, with everything about him novel and unfamiliar, amusement and pleasure got the upper hand with scarcely an effort. Let the countryside think what it would of him, he knew himself better, and it would go hard with him, he said to himself, if he did not conquer even the countryside.

CHAPTER III

"Ye'll be for the fushin', sir? Adam, that's my man, will give ye a' the information. He's fell at the saumon; and muckle need to be fell at something," added Janet; "for a mair fusionless man about a house doesna exist. He's no made for an innkeeper. I'm aye telling him that; but I might just as weel keep my breath for ither purposes. It never does him ony good."

"It is all the more to your credit, Mrs.—"

"Oh, you needna fash your head about the mistress. I've aye been Janet, and Janet I'll be to the end o' the chapter. If there had been ony pith in the man, we might, maybe, have risen like the rest of the world; for he's no ignorant, nor yet a gommeral, though ye might think sae to see him: but no pith in him—you would call it spirit, maybe, in English. That's 'the stalk o' carle-hemp in man,' that Robert Burns speaks about. You'll maybe mind? Na, he's no an ill man, but there's nae carle-hemp in him. Sae I have a' upon my shoulders. And, if everything shouldna be just as you wish, it'll be real kind to name it, Mr. Murray. So you're Murray, too? there are a hantle Murrays hereabout. Ye'll be of the Athol family, or—"

"I have lived abroad all my life," said Lewis, "and I have been an orphan since I was very young—so that I know very little about my relations."

He felt very self-conscious as he made this little explanation, and thought it so awkward that he must be found out, but Janet was entirely unsuspicious, and accepted it as a matter of course.

"Eh, that's an awfu' pity," she said, sympathetically; then added, "If ye've been abroad so lang as that, ye'll maybe have met with auld Sir Patrick about the world. That's the grandfather of our misses here—a real grand-looking auld gentleman as ever I set eyes on—but, I'm feared, sir, no sae good as he looked. He's been aye abroad sin ever I mind, and the general and him didna gree; and he has left every penny of his siller that he could meddle with, away frae his family. It's an awfu' hard case," Janet said.

"I have heard something of that: and I think—I have met Sir Patrick."

"I wonder," said Janet, "if ye've seen the lad that did a' the mischief!—a young Frenchman or foreigner he was—that creepit into the auld gentleman's heart, and turned him against his ain flesh and blood. I wouldna have that man's conscience for a' the siller."

"I've seen," said Lewis, colouring in spite of himself, "a young man—to whom Sir Patrick had been very kind—and who loved him as if he had been his father. They were like father and son for years. I don't think he knew anything about the money."

"Eh, that's mair nor I can believe," said Janet, shaking her head. "What was a' that for, if he kent nothing about the money? I canna believe that."

"Do you think foreigners, as you call them, are such canaille—I mean, such brutes and dogs—"

"I ken very well what canailye means," said Janet. "Well, I wouldna be uncharitable. There's maybe some that are mair high-minded, but the most of them, you'll allow, sir, are just for what they can get—'deed the English are maistly the same, in my opinion;—and twa-three Scots, too, for that matter," she added, with a laugh.

"You are entirely wrong in that," said Lewis, with some heat. "Don't you know, in other places, it is the Scotch who are said to be so interested and greedy—always grasping at advantage, always thinking what is to pay."

"Weel," said Janet, "that just shows what I'm saying, how little we ken about our neighbours. Murkley folk canna bide the Braehead, and Braehead has aye an ill word conter Murkley. That's just the way o' the world. Me that's a philosopher's wife, if I'm no philosophical mysel'—"

"Are you a philosopher's wife?" said Lewis, restored to good-humour, as she probably meant he should be, by this statement.

"Oh, sir, do you no ken that? That shows you're little acquaint with this countryside," said Janet. "And yonder he is, just starting for the water; and if I was a fine young gentleman like you, instead of 'biding in the house this fine morning, I would just be aff to the water, too, with Adam. Ye'll find him a diverting companion, sir, though it's maybe no me that should say it. He has a great deal to say for himself when he is in the humour. Hi!" she said, raising her voice, and tapping loudly on the window, "here's the gentleman coming with you, Adam."

This way of getting him out of the house amused Lewis greatly. He did not resist it, indeed the sun was shining so brightly, yet the air was so cool and sweet, a combination little known to the stranger, that he had already felt his blood frisking in his veins. Adam was going leisurely along, with his basket slung around him, and a great machinery of rods and lines over his shoulder. He scarcely paused to let Lewis come up with him, and all he said by way of salutation was, "Ye've nae rod," said somewhat sulkily, Lewis thought, out of the depths of his beard and his chest. And it cannot be said that the description of Janet was very closely fulfilled. Adam was much intent upon his work. If he could be "diverting" when he was in the humour, he was not in the humour to-day.

He led the way down the riverside with scarcely a word, and crossing the unsheltered meadow which lay along the bank, with only a few trees on the edge, soon got within the shelter of the woods. Tay was smooth and smiling as he passed by the meadows and the village; a few yards up the stream there was a ferry, with a large boat, intended to carry horses and carriages over the water, but here, where the fisherman established himself, the placid reach ended abruptly in rapids, rushing among huge boulders, through which the water foamed and fretted, with cliffs rising high on the opposite bank, and an abundance of great trees bending over the water's edge and on the bank, and nodding from the cliff that looked like a ruined tower.

"I was about to ask you if you had much boating here," Lewis said, with a laugh; "but Nature seems to have stopped that."

"You'll no boat much here," said the philosopher, grimly, which was not a profound remark.

He came to a pause upon a green bank, a little opening between the trees opposite the great cliff which reared itself like a great fortification out of the water. The village, the bit of level meadow, the stillness and serene air of comfort seemed to have passed away in a moment to give place to a mountain torrent, the dark water frowning and leaping against the rocks. Adam took some time to arrange all his paraphernalia, to fit his rod, and arrange his bait, during which time he did not deign to address a word to his companion, who watched him with curiosity, but, unfortunately, with a curiosity which was that of ignorance. After he had asked several questions which made this very distinct, the philosopher at last turned round upon him with a sort of slow defiance.

"You're no a fisher," he said. "What will have brocht ye here?"

This was to Adam the most simple and natural of questions; but it somewhat disturbed Lewis, who was conscious of intentions not perfectly straightforward. Necessity, which is the best quickener of wit, came to his aid. He bethought himself of a little sketch-book he had in his pocket, and drew that out.

"There are other things than fishing to bring one into a beautiful country," he said.

"Oh, ay," said Adam, "if you're o' the airtist class—" Perhaps there was a shade of contempt in his tone. But, if so, he changed it quickly, with a respect for his companion's feelings, which was the height of politeness. "There's mony comes this way, but to my mind they should a' gang a wee further. We're naething in comparison with the real Highlands."

For nearly an hour he said no more; the little click of the reel, the sweep of the water, the occasional leap of a fish, the multitudinous hum of insects were all the sounds about. Lewis seated himself on the grass, and began to justify his title of artist by beginning a sketch at once. He had a pretty amateur talent, and could accomplish without much difficulty the kind of sketch which seems to promise great things. The promise was never fulfilled, but that mattered little. The bold cliff opposite, the mass of rock half way across the stream, which at that point lashed the rapid water into fury, the deeper shadow under the bank, the blaze of light where the trees opened, and flickering intermixture of light and shade where the foliage was thicker, gave exactly the picturesque effect necessary for such a composition as amateurs love.

As he sat on the grass, sketching this unfamiliar landscape, with the silent figure by his side, manipulating his line, and the rush of the water in his ears like a new language, Lewis could not but smile to himself at the strange revolution in his own thoughts and surroundings. His connections had been entirely urban. Old historical towers, churches, and palaces had been the shrines at which he had paid his devotions. Of Nature he knew next to nothing, and to think that his first acquaintance with her should be made on the banks of the Tay was strange indeed. The Tiber would have been more likely, that yellow stream to which its sons paid a most undeserved compliment when they hailed the noble Tay as its resemblance. But there was something in the coolness and sweetness of this still hour which moved Lewis strangely. He had been more used to the cicali in the trees than to the endless twitter of the northern woods, the perpetual concert in which "the mavis and the merle were singing," and to avoid the grass as perhaps full of snakes, and to fear the sun as it is feared where its fury gives sudden death. He sat in the full blaze of it now with a pleased abandonment of all precautions. It was altogether like a pleasant dream.

"Is that a house behind the cliff high up among those trees?" he said. He could not help thinking of a similar corner of old masonry peering through the olive groves on a slope of the Apennines; but how different this was! "And who may live there, I wonder?" he added, pausing to look sideways at his sketch, in the true artistic pose.

Adam was very busy at that moment; he gave a sort of oblique glance upwards from the corner of his eyes, but he was struggling with his first fish, which was far too important a crisis to be mixed up with talk, or vain answers to useless questions. It was not till he had pulled out his prize, and deposited the glistening, gasping trout upon the grass with a grunt of fatigue and satisfaction, that he took any notice of what his companion said. Lewis got up to look at it as it leaped its last in a convulsive flutter. He was no sportsman—indeed, he was so little of his race that the sight of dying was painful to him even in this uninteresting example. But he knew better than to show this.

"That's a fine ane," said Adam—"no so big as mony, but a strong creature; he has most strained my wrist wi' his acteevity. Ye were asking what house is yon. It is old Stormont Tower, a bit poor place, but as old as the hills themselves. You that makes pictures, did ye ever see a bonnier picture than that?"

"Is it for the value of the fish or the pleasure of catching it," said Lewis, "that you put a stop to its enjoyment? That's a more pleasant picture, I think," and he pointed to the sudden gleam of a salmon leaping in the middle of the stream.

Adam cast a glance at him of mingled curiosity and disdain.

"I said ye were nae fisher the first look I got at ye," he said. "And ye find more pleasure in making scarts upon paper than in sport?" he added, a minute after, in a solemn tone.

"At least, the scarts on the paper do no one any harm," said Lewis, laughing. But he acknowledged the ineffectualness of his occupation by forthwith putting away his sketch-book.

Adam saw this too with the corner of his eye, and apparently was mollified by the withdrawal of that peaceful competitor Art from the regions sacred to a stouter occupation. After a while, he spoke again,

"Sport," he said, "I'll no deny, is a mystery. That ye should take your pleasure in what's pain and death to another poor creature, maybe just as good as yoursel'—it's a real funny thing when you come to think o't. I can gi'e no explanation. I've taken mony a thought on the subject mysel'. That's how we're made, I suppose—to see the thing fecht for its life, that's your pleasure, and to battle wi' 't and get the upper hand. I canna be sorry for a trout," he said, casting a slow glance at the fish; "it's just made for a man's dinner, and that's the short and the long of it; but a deer, now—a grand creature, carrying yon muckle horns like a king his crown, and a wheen skulking murderers lying in wait for him, letting fly when the poor beast comes up unsuspecting! I'm not a deer-stalker," said Adam, with more simplicity than philosophy, making up

"For sins he was inclined to
By damning those he had no mind to,"

"and I just canna bide yon."

Upon which he cast his line once more, and Lewis, though he did not feel any pleasure in the sight of the last convulsions, began to watch with interest, which gradually grew into excitement, the skill with which Adam plied his trade, the cunning arts by which he beguiled a wary old Tay trout, up to a great many things, into acceptance of the fly which dangled before his nose. The trout was experienced, but the man was too much for him. Then there ensued that struggle between the two which strained the fisherman's skill and patience to the utmost. The little drama roused the spectator out of his calm and almost repugnance. He followed it to its conclusion with almost as much real, and considerably more apparent, excitement than Adam himself, and scarcely repressed a "hurrah!" of triumph when the prey was finally secured.

"I tell't you sae," said Adam. "That's just the way with man; ye canna get the pleasure without the killing o' the creature. It's a queer thing, but most things are queer. You'll have been at the college, and studied pheelosophy, nae doubt? but you'll no explain that to me: nor me, I can give no explanation, that have turned the thing o'er and o'er in my head. Life's just a long puzzle from the beginning o't to the end o't, and if you once begin to question what it means, ye'll never be done, nor ye'll never get any satisfaction," Adam said.

Lewis did not take this bait as perhaps a young scholar, one of the Oxford men to whom Adam was accustomed, who haunted these banks in the autumn, or still more keenly an argumentative youth from Aberdeen or St. Andrews might have done. He had known no college training, and had little reading of the graver sort, but he pleased the fisherman almost as much by his conversion to the excitement of sport to which indeed he was as little accustomed as to philosophy. The hours passed on quickly in the sweet air and sunshine, with the rhythm of the quick-flowing river and the dramatic episodes of trout catching, and all the novelty and freshness of the new world which was widening out around the young man. He tried to beguile Adam to talk about matters which were still more interesting to himself, but the philosopher had not that lively interest in his fellow-creatures, at least of the human kind, which usually characterizes the village sage.

When Adam's creel was full they went back, but by a round which brought them in sight of the gate which Lewis remembered having passed through on the previous night; the turrets of the old house showed over the trees, and the young man looked at them with a quickened beating of his heart. He was strangely simple in some matters, straightforward in his ideas as Englishmen rarely are, and the secret intention in his mind which had actuated his coming here moved all his pulses at this sudden reminder. He looked curiously at the trees which hid this dwelling-place. He did not know how to get access to it, how to carry out his intention; but there it was, the aim of his journey, the future scene of— how could he tell what? The future was all vague, but yet alight with pleasant chances, he did not even know whether to call them hopes. He was standing still gazing at the old house when he suddenly heard voices behind him, kind salutations to Adam, to which the fisherman replied with some cordiality. Lewis turned round quickly, for the voices were feminine and refined, though they had a whiff of accent to which he was as yet unaccustomed. It was a group of three ladies who had paused to speak to Adam, and were looking with interest at his fish. They were all in black dresses, standing out in the midst of the sunshine, three slim, clear-marked figures. The furthest from him was shorter than the others, and wore a veil which partially concealed her face; the two who were talking were evidently sisters and of ripe years. They talked both together, one voice overlapping the other.

"What fine fish you have got, Adam!" "And what a creel-ful! you've been lucky to-day." "If Janet can spare us a couple, the cook will be very thankful." "Dear me, that will be pleasant if Janet can spare us a couple," they said.

After a few more questions they passed on, nodding and waving their hands. "Come, Lilias," they called both together, looking back to the third, who said nothing but "Good day, Adam," in a younger, softer voice.

Lewis stood aside to let them pass, and took off his hat. It was evidently a surprise to the ladies to see the stranger stand uncovered as they passed. They looked at him keenly, and made some half audible comments to each other. "Who will that be now, Jean?" "It will be some English lad for the fishing, Margaret," Lewis heard, and laughed to himself. Though he did not know much about Scotland, he had of course picked up a Scotch novel now and then, and knew well enough that what he profanely and carelessly, in the unconscious insolence of his youth, called eccentric old ladies were figures invariable in such productions. These no doubt were the Miss Grizzy and Miss Jacky of Murkley. The little encounter pleased him. He should no doubt make acquaintance with them and see the humours of the country at first hand. The third little figure with the blue veil scarcely attracted his eye at all; he saw her, but did not observe her. The blinding gauze hid anything that might have raised his curiosity. She was less imposing in every way, and when they both turned again with a "Come, Lilias," their air gave their little companion the aspect of a child. He quickened his pace to make up to Adam, who, though he seemed to plod along with slow, large steps which had no appearance of speed, yet tasked his younger companion, who was easily beguiled by any temptation of the way, to keep up with him.

"Are those village people?" Lewis said.

"Eh? What was that you were saying?"

"Are those two ladies—village people? I mean do they live hereabout?"

Adam turned slowly half round upon him. His large and somewhat hazy blue eyes uprose from between the bush of his shaggy eyebrows and the redness of his beard, and contemplated the young man curiously.

"Yon's—the misses at the castle," Adam said.

"The misses?" Still Lewis did not take in what was meant; he repeated the word with a smile.

"Our misses, the leddies at the castle," said Adam, laconically.

Lewis was so profoundly astonished that he gave a cry of dismay.

"The ladies at the castle?—Miss Murray of Murkley?" he said.

"Ay," said Adam, once more fixing him with a tranquil but somewhat severe gaze. Then after a minute's reflection, "And wherefore no?"

Then Lewis laughed loud and long, with a mixture of excitement and derision in his astonishment: the derision was at himself, but Adam was not aware of this, and a shade of offence gradually came over as much as was visible of his face.

"You're easy pleased with a joke," he said. "I canna say I see it." And went on with his long steps devouring the way.

Lewis followed after a little, perhaps slightly ashamed of his self-betrayal, although there was no betrayal in it save to himself. As he looked round again he saw the group of ladies standing at the Murkley gate. Probably their attention had been roused by the sudden peal of his laughter, of which he now felt deeply ashamed. They were going in at the smaller gate, which the lodgekeeper stood holding open for them, but had paused apparently to look what it was that called forth the young stranger's mirth. He was so self-conscious altogether that he could scarcely believe the occasion of his laugh must be a mystery to them, and felt ashamed of it as if they had been in the secret. His impulse was to rush up to them, to assure them that it did not matter, with an eagerness of shame and compunction which already made his face crimson. What was it that did not matter? But then he came to himself, and blushed more deeply than ever, and slunk away. He did not hear the remarks the ladies made, but divined them in his heart. What they said was brief enough, and he had indeed divined it more or less.

"What is the lad laughing at? Do you think he is so ill-bred as to be laughing at us, Jean?"

"What could he find to laugh at in us, Margaret?"

"'Deed that is what I don't know. Let me look at you. There is nothing wrong about you that I can see, Jean."

"Nor about you, Margaret. It is, maybe, Lilias and her blue veil."

"Yes; it's odious of you," cried the third, suddenly seizing that disguise in her hands and plucking it from her face, "to muffle me up in this thing."

"You will not think that, my dear, when you see how it saves your complexion. No doubt it was just the blue veil; but he must be a very ill-bred young man."

CHAPTER IV

This was also the opinion of Janet when she heard of the encounter on the road. Her demeanour was very grave when she served her guest with his dinner, of which one of the aforesaid trout constituted an important part. She did not smile upon him as in the morning, nor expatiate upon the diverse dishes, as was her wont, but was curt and cold, putting his food upon the table with a thud of her tray which was something like a blow. Lewis, who had not been used to the mechanical attention of English servants, but to attendants who took a great deal of interest in him and what he ate, and how he liked it, felt the change at once. He was very simple in some matters, as has been said, and the sense of disapprobation quite wounded him. He began to conciliate, as was his nature.

"This is one of Adam's trout," he said.

"Just that; if it wasna Adam's trout, where would I get it?" said the ungracious Janet.

"That is true; and a great deal better than if it came from a shop, or had been carried for miles."

"Shop!" cried Janet, with lively scorn. "It's little you ken about our countryside, that's clear. Where would I get a shop if I wantit it? And wha would gang to sic a place that could have trout caller out of the water."

"Don't be so angry," said Lewis, with a smile. "After all, you know, if I am so ignorant, it is my misfortune, not my fault. If I had been asked where I wanted to be born, no doubt I should have said the banks of Tay."

"That's true," said Janet, mollified. "But you would do nothing o' the sort," she added. "You're just making your jest of me, as you did of the misses."

"I—jest at the—misses," said Lewis, with every demonstration of indignant innocence. "Now, Mrs. Janet, look at me. Do you think I am capable of laughing at—anyone—especially ladies for whom I would have a still higher respect—if I knew them. I—jest! Do you think it is in me?" he said.

Janet looked at him, and shook her head.

"Sir," she said, but with a softened tone, "you're just a whillie whaw."

"Now, what is a whillie whaw? I don't mind being called names," said Lewis, "but you must not call me a ruffian, you know. If one has no politeness, one had better die."

"Losh me! it's no just so bad as that. I said sae to Adam. A young gentleman may have his joke, and no just be a scoundrel."

"Did Adam think I was a scoundrel? I am sorry I made such a bad impression upon him. I thought we had become friends on the river-side."

"Oh, sir, you're takin' me ower close to my word. I wasna meaning so bad as that; but, according to Adam, when you set eyes upon the misses, ye just burst out into a muckle guffaw: and that's no mainners—besides, it's not kind, not like what a gentleman's expected to do—in this country," Janet added, deprecating a little. "For onything I ken," she added, presently, "it may be mainners abroad."

"It is not manners anywhere," said Lewis, angrily. "But Adam is a great deal too hard upon me, Mrs. Janet. I did not break into a loud—anything when I saw the ladies—why should I? I did not know who they were. But afterwards when I discovered their names— You must sympathize with me. I had been looking for young ladies, pretty young ladies," he said, with a laugh at the recollection. "There is something more even that I could tell you. There had been some idea of an arrangement—of making a marriage, you understand—between a Miss Murray and a—gentleman I know;—if the friends found everything suitable."

"Making up a marriage," Janet echoed, with bewilderment, "if the friends found it suitable!"

"Just so—nothing had been said about it," said the young man, "but there had been an idea. And when, knowing he was young, I beheld—two old ladies—"

"I dinna know what you call old," said Janet, with a little resentment. "If Miss Margaret's forty, that's the most she is. She's twa-three years younger than me. Ay, and so there was a marriage thought upon, though your friend had never seen the leddy? and maybe the leddy was no in the secret neither."

"Oh, certainly not," Lewis cried.

"It would be for her siller," said Janet, very gravely. "You would do well to warn your friend, sir, that there's awfn' little siller among them; they've been wranged and robbed, as I was telling you. Not only they're auld, as ye say, but they're puir, that is to say, for leddies of their consequence. I would bid him haud away with his plans and his marriages, if I were you."

"Oh, there was, perhaps, nothing serious in it; it was only an idea," said Lewis lightly. "The trout has been excellent, Mrs. Janet. You cook them to perfection. And I hope you are no longer angry with me or think me a scoundrel, or even—the other thing."

"Oh, ay, sir, ye're just the other thing—ye're a whillie whaw—ye speak awfu' fair and look awfu' pleasant, but I'm no sure how you're thinking a' the time. When I'm down the stairs getting the collops you'll maybe laugh and say, 'That's an old fuil' to yoursel'."

"I should be an ungrateful wretch if I did," said Lewis, "especially as I am very anxious to see what pleasant surprise you have prepared for me under the name of collops."

"Ah!" said Janet, shaking her head, but relaxing in spite of herself, "you're just a whillie whaw."

When she was gone, however, Lewis shook his head still more gravely at himself. Was it not very imprudent of him to have said anything about that project?—and it was scarcely even a project, only an idea; and now it was ridiculous. He had been very imprudent. No doubt this woman would repeat it, and it would get into the air, and everyone would know. The question now was whether he should confine himself in future to the collops, or whether he should explain to Janet that he had meant nothing, and that his communication was confidential. He had certainly been a fool to speak at all. To tell the truth, he had never been alone in a totally new world without any outlet for his thoughts before, and his laugh had been so inevitable, and the explanation so simple. When Janet re-appeared with the collops, however, she was in haste, and nothing more was said; and by-and-by he forgot that he had said anything that it was not quite natural to say.

The presence of this young stranger at a little village inn so unimportant as the "Murkley Arms" was a surprising event in the village, and set everybody talking. To be sure an enthusiastic fisherman like Pat Lindsay, from Perth, had been known to live there for a month at a time during the season, and to nod his head with great gusto when Janet's merits as a cook were discussed. Most people in Murkley were quite aware of Janet's merits, but the outside world, the travellers and tourists who passed, so to speak, on the other side, had no information on the subject. This was one of the points, indeed, in which it was an endless vexation to her that her husband had "nae pith" nor spirit in him. Had the little house been furbished up and made into a fine hotel, Janet knew that she had it in her to make that hotel a success; but with a man who could neither look imposing and dignified at the head of such an establishment, nor do any of the hard work necessary, what could a woman do? She had to give up the hope of rising in the world; but, when it so happened that a guest did come, Janet's treatment of him was royal. And she felt a certain gratitude to the visitor who gave her an opportunity of showing what was in her.

"What is he here for?" she said. "What for should he no be here, if ye please? He's here for his ain pleasure. He's from foreign parts, and it's good for him to see what the life is in a real quiet, honest place. They havena ower much of that abroad. They have your gambling-tables, and music playing morning, noon, and nicht. Eh, but they maun be sick o't! A band once in a way I say naething against, and when it's a regiment marching it's grand; but trumpets blaring and flaring like thae Germans, losh me! it would send a body out of her wits in nae time. He's come away from that, and I think he's a wise man. And though he's no fisher himself he likes to see Adam catch the trout. And he's a fine lad. He's welcome to bide as long as he likes, for me."

This was her answer to the many questions with which at first she was plied on the subject. The minister, who was a man of very liberal mind and advanced views was soon interested in the stranger, and made acquaintance with him as he lingered about on Sunday after church looking at the monuments in the church-yard. Lewis went to church cheerfully as a sort of tribute to society, and also as the only social meeting to which he could get admittance. He loved to be among his fellow-creatures, to see other people round him, and, unknown as he was, this was almost his only way of enjoying the pleasure. The minister, whose name was Seton, accosted him with very friendly intentions.

"You will find, I fear, a great difference in our services from those you are used to," he said. "I would fain hope things were a little better with us than they used to be; but we're far behind in ritual. The sister Church has always held up a far different standard."

"Which Church is that?" said Lewis, with his friendly candour of mind. "I am a very great ignoramus."

"Ah, I suppose you are High," said the minister, "and don't acknowledge our orders. Of course, you cannot expect me to consent to that. The Church of England is a great institution, but apt to carry things with a high hand, and look down upon Protestant brethren."

"Ah, yes—but I don't know anything about England," said Lewis, still puzzled; upon which Mr. Seton made many apologies.

"I ought to have known—of course, your complexion and all that; you come from the land of enlightenment, where everything is subservient to intellect. How glad I shall be of the opportunity ask to your advice about some passages I am in doubt about! Your fatherland is the home of biblical science."

"I am not a German," said Lewis, "but I know the language well enough, and if I can be of any use—Oh, no, I am an Englishman, though I never was in England—unless I may call this England."

"Which you certainly must not do," said the minister; "we've fought hard enough on that account in our day. I suppose you are here for the fishing," he added, as everybody did, but with a little disingenuousness, for by this time all the world was aware that Lewis did not fish, nor pretend to fish, nor, indeed, do anything but what the good people of Murkley called idling his time away.

"I am no fisher," he said—"not a sportsman at all, and not much of an artist either. I am not very good at anything. I came here because it struck my fancy."

He laughed somewhat uneasily, because it was not true, and he was a bad deceiver; but then Mr. Seton had no reason to suppose that it was not true, and he took it with great composure as a natural reason enough.

"It is a fine country," he said. "I am free to say it, for it is not my country. I am from the south myself."

"The south!" said Lewis, deceived in his turn, and looking with a little surprise at the fine burly form and grizzled locks of the clergyman, who seemed to him of the same type as Adam, and not like anything that he realized as the south. "Do you mean of France, or still nearer the mezzo-giorno? Oh, I know the south very well. I have been through the wildest parts of Sicily and Calabria, as well as most civilized regions."

"I meant Dumfriesshire," said the minister, with a blush. He felt as if he had been guilty of false pretences. "That is south to us. You have been a great traveller, Mr.—"

"Murray," said Lewis, quickly.

"You are a Murray, too? Then I suppose you had ancestors in this district. That's very common; I have had people come here from all the ends of the world anxious to look at the tombstones or the parish register."

"I shall not need to do that," the young man said. "The name came to me with some property," he added, with his usual mixture of caution and imprudence—"from my god-father," he added, after another pause. This was so far true that it was the name by which the young dependent on his bounty had been used to call old Sir Patrick; his voice softened at the word, which he had not used for so long. "He brought me up—he was very good to me. I have lost him, there is about a year."

The minister felt that it was necessary to reply in his professional capacity.

"Ah," he said, "such losses shatter the world to us; but so long as they turn our thoughts to better things, to the land whither we must all travel—"

Lewis was not used to spiritual consolation; he gave his companion a nod of not uncheerful assent.

"He always wished me to travel," he said. "It has become to me a second nature. I am told that it is to the Highlands that tourists go, but otherwise this pleases me very much."

"And you are comfortable at Adam Burnet's? He is a character—the sort of mind that we flatter ourselves is peculiarly Scotch," said the minister. "I hope you will gratify my wife and me by taking your luncheon with us. A stranger is always welcome," he continued, leading the way after Lewis had consented with a smile and bow and flourish of his hat, which made Mr. Seton smile, "in a Scotch manse; and if you are making a long stay, Mr. Murray—"

It was thus that Lewis made his first entry into society in the village.

"You should have seen his bow, my dear," the minister said; "he is just awfully foreign, but a good fellow for all that, or else my skill in faces is at fault."

This was to prepare Mrs. Seton to receive the stranger, whom, indeed, the minister brought in with a sense of an unauthorized interference in what was not his department. He was at liberty to bring an old elder, a brother minister, even a farmer of superior description; but Mrs. Seton was particular about young men. Katie was sixteen, and "there was never any telling," her mother said. In the present case the risks were even greater than usual, for this young man was without an introduction, nobody to answer for him or his respectability, and a foreigner besides, which was at once more terrible and more seductive than an intruder native born.

"Your father is so imprudent," she said to Katie. "How can we tell who he is?"

"He looks very innocent," said that young woman, who had seen the stranger a great many times, and found him entirely unlike her ideal. Innocent was not what Miss Katie thought a young man ought to look. She followed her mother to the early Sunday dinner, which Mr. Seton entitled lunch, without the slightest excitement, but there was already some one in the room whose presence disturbed Katie's composure more. Of the three gentlemen there assembled, Lewis was the least in height and the least impressive in appearance. The two stalwart Scotchmen, between whom he stood, with vigour in every line of their long limbs and every curl of their crisp locks, threw him into the shade. He was shorter, slighter, less of him altogether. His hair was light, and not very much of that. In all probability when he was older he would be bald, and people who depreciated Lewis were apt to say of him that he was all one colour, hair and complexion. His dress had a little of a foreign cut, or rather it was elaborately English à la mode de Paris, and he was not at all indifferent about his reception here, but sincerely anxious to please and make a favourable impression, and did not in the least hesitate to show that he was so. This went against him with the party generally, but Lewis was quite unaware of that.

The other young man whom he had found there, when the minister showed him into the little drawing-room and went to report what he had done to his wife, was in reality half a head taller, and looked twice the size of Lewis. He was brown and ruddy like most of the men about, accustomed to expose himself to the weather, and to find his occupation and pleasure out of doors. He was slightly shy, but yet quite at his ease, knowing that it was his duty to talk and be friendly to the stranger, and doing his duty accordingly, though he had none of Lewis's eager desire to make himself agreeable. When the minister entered they were introduced to each other as Mr. Murray and Mr. Stormont, upon which Lewis said immediately, with a little effusive pleasure,

"Ah, I know your name very well; you must belong to the tower on the other side of the river. I attempt to sketch you almost every day."

"Oh!" said young Stormont, and in his mind he added, "It's an artist," which seemed to account for the stranger at once.

"My attempts have not been very successful," Lewis added, laughing. "I go out with Adam when he goes to fish, and when a trout is very interesting my sketch-book falls out of my hands."

"You can't see much of the tower from the other side," said Stormont. "I hope you will come and study it near at hand."

"That I will do with great pleasure," cried Lewis. It exhilarated him to find himself again in good company. "You are very kind to admit me into your house," he said, with frank gratification, to the minister. "Mrs. Janet and her husband are very interesting; they throw a great light upon the country: but I began to long to exchange a little conversation with persons—of another class."

"I am sure we are very glad to see you," said Mrs. Seton. "It must be lonely in an inn, especially if you have come out of a family. We have seen you passing, and wondered what you could find in Murkley. There is no society here. Even the tourists going out and in are a variety when you are further north, but here we are just dropped in a corner and see nothing. Oh, yes, old Pat Lindsay who thinks of nothing but his trout. Trout are nice enough things on the table, but not as the subject of conversation. Even Mr. Stormont here is away oftener than we would like him to be."

"Only for the shooting," said Stormont, "and a little while in Edinburgh in the winter, and sometimes a run up to town in the spring."

"How much does that leave?" said the lady, playfully. "But never mind, we cannot expect to bind a young man here. I think of the time when my own boys will grow up and want to be moving. Thanks be to Providence, Katie's a girl and will stay at home."

Katie's eyes, which were bright and brown like the Tay, opened a little wider at this, and gave out a glance which was half laughter across the table. Lewis, looking on with great interest, felt that the glance was winged to somewhere about that part of the table where young Stormont sat, and felt a great sympathy and interest. He met her eyes with a slight smile in his, making unconscious proffer of that sympathy, which made Katie blush from head to foot, and grow hot with indignation as well, as if she had been found out.

"Mr. Murray has been a great traveller," said the minister, "and, Katie, you should seize the opportunity to try how your German sounds, my dear. It is apt to be one thing on a book and another in the mouth. I made so dreadful a failure in the speaking of it myself the first time I tried to do it that I never made the attempt a second time. But I suppose one language is the same as another to you."

"Katie speaks it very well, I believe," said her mother; "but, dear me, where is the use of it here? We are out of the way both of books and people, and how is a girl to keep it up? There's a great deal of nonsense about teaching children foreign languages, in my opinion. But, whisht, let me think what company we have that would suit Mr. Murray; everybody is so far off. To be sure, there is one family, but then they are all ladies—the Miss Murrays at the castle. We must not leave them out, but they would be little resource to a young man."

"And perhaps they are not so kind, so hospitable as you," said Lewis. "I have already, I fear, offended them, or if not them then their admirers. It is they who are called the Misses? Then I thought that must mean young ladies, very young. It was foolish, but I did so. And when in the road with Adam we encountered these old ladies—"

"Oh, stop, stop, not old. I cannot have them called old," cried Mrs. Seton. "Bless me, Miss Jean is not much more than my age."

"And it does not matter whether they are old or young," said Katie; "we are all very fond of them."

"And I," said Lewis, putting his hand on his heart, "respect them infinitely. I am much interested in those ladies. The oldness is nothing—it does not affect me. I wish to know them above everything. I have known their grandfather—abroad."

"Bless me," said Mrs. Seton; "old Sir Patrick? This is most interesting. I never saw him; he was away before we came here. And what did you think of him? He was a tyrant, I've always heard, and a terrible egotist; thinking of nothing but his own pleasure. You know the story, I suppose, of how he left all his money away from the family; and nothing to any of them but the old house and that big folly of a new one. I wonder they don't pull that place down."

"Oh, mamma, if money was to come into the family! that is what Lilias says. If some uncle they never heard of was to come from India, or somebody they had been kind to die all at once, and leave them a fortune."

"I will not have you see so much of Lilias, if she fills your head full of nonsense," said Mrs. Seton. "Such folly! for they have no uncle in India, that ever I heard tell of; and people now-a-days don't make those daft-like wills—though, to be sure, Sir Patrick's an example. Did you ever see, Mr. Murray, the young man we've heard so much about?"

"The fellow that got the money," young Stormont said.

"What kind of a being was it?" said the minister. "Some supple foreign lad that flattered the silly old man. It has always been strange to me that there was nobody near to speak a word for justice and truth."

"You are hard upon foreigners," said Lewis. "It is not their fault that they are foreign. Indeed they would not be foreign there, you know, but the people of the country, and we the foreigners. I knew this fellow, as you say. He was not even foreign, he was English. The old gentleman was very fond of him, and good to him. He did not know anything about the money."

"Ah, Mr. Murray, you'll never persuade me that. Would a young man give up years of his life to an old one without any expectations? No, no, I cannot believe that."

"Did he give up years of his life? Oh, yes, I suppose so. No one thought of it—in that light. He loved him like his father. There was no one else to take care of him, to make him happy. I see now from the other point of view. But I do not think he meant any harm."

This Lewis said much too seriously and anxiously for his rôle of spectator, but at the moment, there being no suspicion, no one remarked his nervous earnestness. He cast a sort of appealing glance round the table, with a wistful smile.

"No one," he said, "there, thought any harm. He was the most astonished himself."

"And what kind of a fellow was he," said Stormont, "a gentleman, or just some cad the old man had picked up?"

At this Lewis grew red in spite of himself, then did his best to laugh, though the effort was great.

"I do not know," he said, "having always lived abroad, what is exactly a cad, and also what, when you come to its exact meaning, is a gentleman?"

"Oh, a gentleman—" said Mrs. Seton. "Bless me, what a question? It is just—not to be mistaken: there is no two words about it—No, no—describe it! how could I describe it? A gentleman! my dear Mr. Murray, you can be in no doubt about that."

"And a cad is just a cad," said young Stormont, "a fellow, don't you know, that's not a gentleman—just as a hill isn't a river, and can never be."

"As distinct as that?" said Lewis. "It is hard upon us who have always lived abroad. It means, to be well-educated and well-bred—"

"And well-born, Mr. Murray; you must not leave out that. Well-born, above all things; there's everything in race."

"But those whom you meet only in society," said Lewis, "even on the Continent—where every man must have ses papiers—he does not carry them about with him. He does not pin a little carnet on his sleeve. You must take him on trust."

"That is just the danger of promiscuous society," said Mrs. Seton, briskly. "That is what I always say to papa. It is so easy to be taken in by a fair exterior; and when you don't know who people are, and all about them, it's a serious thing," said the lady, shaking her head, "especially where there are young people. Oh, it is a very serious thing, Mr. Murray. I am sure I always say about ball-room acquaintances and persons of that sort, if harm comes of it, really you have nobody to blame but yourself."

There was a pause after this, and a great sense of embarrassment. Katie looked at her mother with anxious, telegraphic communications, of which Mrs. Seton either would not or did not take any notice. Even Mr. Stormont, though not very quick, saw the dilemma. Lewis was the most self-possessed.

"I must be more grateful than ever," he said, turning to his hostess, with that conciliatory smile which was so natural to him, "that you have given your hospitality so kindly to one who has no vouchers, no one to speak for him—a stranger."

"Bless me, Mr. Murray, I hope you never thought—Dear, dear, you might be sure that was the last thing in my mind. Present company, you know, of course; and then in some cases the first look is enough," said Mrs. Seton, with a gracious bow to her guest.

This little episode distracted the company altogether from the question propounded by Stormont about Sir Patrick Murray's heir, and during the rest of the meal Lewis exerted himself to keep away from dangerous subjects: which was a greater mental effort to him, perhaps, than any he had ever made in his life. For he was ready by nature to take everybody he met into his confidence. He had the most unbounded trust in his fellow-creatures, and he wanted to be approved, to have the sympathy of those about him. He, whose impulse it was to be always looking out of the window—how could he put up shutters, and retire into seclusion and mystery? It was the thing of all others most difficult to him. But he was quick and ready, and kept his wits about him, having been thus put on his guard. He betrayed something else with great and simple pleasure—his own accomplishments, which were, in Mrs. Seton's opinion, many. He showed them his amateur sketch-book, which seemed the work of a great artist to these uninstructed people, and, indeed, was full of fairly brilliant dashes at scenery and catchings up of effect, which he himself was well aware were naught, but which were very attractive to the uncritical. And it was all they could do to keep him from the piano, where he sadly wanted to let them hear one or two morceaux from the last opera. Mrs. Seton had to place herself in front of the instrument with an anxiety to prevent the desecration of the Sabbath without exposing herself to the charge of narrow-mindedness, which was highly comic.

"That will be for to-morrow," she said. "We must not have all our good things at once. No, no, we must leave something for to-morrow. The servants, you see, have prejudices—we have to consider so many things in a manse. A clergyman's family are always talked about: and then economy's my principle, Mr. Murray; we must keep something for to-morrow. And that just reminds me that I hope you will come in a friendly way and spend the evening—we have no parties, you know, here—but if you will just come in a friendly way: and then it will give us the greatest pleasure," Mrs. Seton said, nodding her head and smiling.

Thus immediate advantage sprang from the over-boldness of his foreign ways; and when he left the manse, young Stormont, though somewhat contemptuous of a man who "went in for" music and spoke all sorts of languages, yielded to the ingratiating ways of the stranger, and invited him half surlily to lunch with him next day at the tower, which Lewis accepted with his usual cordiality.

He went back with a sense of exhilaration to the parlour overlooking the village street, all so still in the drowsy Sunday afternoon.

"Me voici lancé," he said to himself, with glee. He had known the excitements of society very different from that of Murkley, but he knew the true philosophy of being not only contented, but pleased, when you cannot get everything you like, with what you are lucky enough to be able to get.

CHAPTER V

"We must ask just whoever there is to ask," said Mrs. Seton. "You see, there will be no difficulty in entertaining them, with that young man. He will play his music as long as anybody will listen to him, or I'm mistaken. Philip Stormont is coming; I had to ask him, as he was there; and you can send Johnnie over with a note to the Borrodailes, Katie, and I'll write up to the Castle myself. Then there's young Mr. Dunlop, the assistant at Braehead. He is of a better class than most of the young men: and the factor—but there's three girls there, which is a terrible band of women. If you were very good, and all things went well, and there were two or three couples, without disturbing other folk, and papa had no objection—"

"We might end off with a dance—that was what I expected," cried Katie, clapping her hands. "I'll put on my hat and run up to the Castle to save you writing."

"Stop, stop, you hasty thing!—on a Sabbath afternoon to give an invitation! No, no, I cannot allow that. Sit down and write the notes, and you can date them the 15th" (which was next morning), "and see that Johnnie is ready to ride by seven o'clock at the latest. But I would not let you go to the Castle in any case, even if it had not been Sunday, for most likely they would not bring Lilias. I will just ask Miss Margaret and Miss Jean to their tea. If there was a word of dancing, there would be no chance; they would just say, 'She's not out'."

"And neither am I out," cried Katie, with impatience.

"You—you're just nobody, my dear; there will be no grand ceremony, no Court train and feathers, for you, a simple minister's daughter. Not but what I might be presented, and you too, if I liked, and it was worth the expense," said Mrs. Seton. "Lady Lorraine would do it in a moment; but you are not an heiress, Katie. Still I think they're over-particular—oh, yes, certainly they are over-particular; the poor thing will miss all the little amusement that's going. But perhaps they'll bring her, if they think they are only asked to their tea."

"The only thing I don't like in them," cried Katie, "is tying Lilias up in that blue veil, and not letting her go to parties—that's odious! But for all the rest, that Mr. Murray—that person you are so fond of—"

"Me! fond of him! I think he will be an acquisition," said Mrs. Seton calmly; "and now that I've been driven into asking him for the evening we may as well make the best of it. Yes, my dear, I was driven into it. You wouldn't have me be impolite? And you know, if the piano had been heard going at three o'clock on a Sunday afternoon, where would your character have been, Robert? I would not say but they would have had you up before the presbytery. I have to think of you as well as of myself. Oh, well, I don't just say that I would have liked it much myself. Opera music on a Sunday is a step further than I would like to go, though I hope I'm not narrow-minded; so I was just obliged to ask him for a week night. And if you will make allowance for the difference of foreign manners I cannot but think that he looks a gentleman. Yes—yes, he looks a gentleman—and it is not as if he was going to settle here, when, of course, we would need to know a great deal more about him; but you must take something on trust in the way of society, and if he can play so well, and all that—"

"My dear, you are always blaming me for going too far, but yet you are the one that goes the farthest," the minister said.

"Toots," replied his wife, good-humouredly, "you're just an old croaker. Did any harm ever come of it? Did I ever go farther than was justified? I think, though I don't wish to seem vain, that I have just an instinct for things of that sort."

This was, indeed, the conviction of the neighbourhood in general, which profited by the impromptu parties which the minister's wife was so clever in getting up. They were frequent enough to be reckoned upon by the people within reach; her own explanation of them was quite true and scarcely flattered.

"We cannot do anything great," she said, "we have no room for it. I couldn't give a regular dance like you. In the first place it would put Mr. Seton out, for, though you would not think so, there is nobody more nervous or that wants more care taken of him, not to disturb his studies: and in the second place we have no room for it. No, no, you're all very kind making allowances, but we've no room for it. And then Katie's but a child; she is not out. Oh, I don't make a fuss of her not being out like Miss Jean and Miss Margaret, they have some reason, you know, to be particular; but to make such a phrase about a minister's daughter would be perfectly ridiculous. Yes, yes, when she's eighteen I'll take her to the Hunt Ball, and there will be an end of it. But at present she is just in the school-room, you know. A little turn of a waltz just by accident, when I have asked a few friends to tea, that counts for nothing, and that is all I ever pretend to give." All this was so well known that there was no longer any need for saying it, though Mrs. Seton from habit continued to say it pretty often, as was her way.

But the preparations made were almost as careful as if it had not been impromptu. The furniture was deftly pushed, and edged, and sided off to be as little in the way as possible. The piano was drawn into the corner which, after much experiment, had been settled to be the best; there was unusual sweeping oft-repeated to clear the room of dust. Flowers were gathered in the most prodigal profusion. The manse garden was old-fashioned, and well sheltered, nestling under a high and sunny wall. The June fulness of roses had begun, and all sorts of sweet smelling, old-fashioned flowers filled the borders.

"Oh, yes," Mrs. Seton said, "we must just be content with what we can get. My poverty, but not my will, consents, as Shakspere says. No doubt but I would have a fine show of pelargoniums, or Tom Thumbs, and a border of lobelias, and the centre calceolaria, if I could. That is all the fashion now. No, no, I don't make any grievance of it. I just content myself with what I've got—old larkspurs and rockets, and so forth, that have been there since my mother-in-law's time; but they're just good enough, when you can't get better," this true philosopher said. She had her other preparations made in the same spirit. "A cold ham at the bottom of the table, and two or three chickens at the top, and as much salad as they can set their faces to, and curds and cream, which the young ones are all very fond of, and stewed gooseberries, and anything else that may be in the garden, that is all the phrase I make," said Mrs. Seton, who was sufficiently Scotch to employ a French word now and then without knowing it; but would have resented the imputation. Katie had her little white frock, which was as simple as a child's, but very dainty and neat for all that, laid out upon her little white bed, with a rose for her belt and a rose for her hair, fresh gathered from the bushes, and smelling sweet as summer. Tea was set out in the dining-room, where afterwards the cold ham and chickens were to take the place now occupied by scones of kinds innumerable, cookies, and jams, and shortbread, interspersed with pretty bouquets of flowers. It was much prettier than dinner, without the heavy fumes which spoil that meal for a summer and daylight performance. But we must not jump at once into the heart of an entertainment which cost so much pains and care.

Mrs. Seton's note was delivered early at the Castle next morning. Truth compels us to admit that it was written on Sunday night; but it was dated Monday morning, for why should anyone's feelings be hurt even by an appearance of disrespect for the Sabbath day. ("There is none meant," the minister's wife said, who had done all her duties thoroughly, taught her Sabbath class, and heard her children their lessons, and listened devoutly to two sermons before she turned to this less sacred duty.)

"I am asking one or two friends to tea," she wrote, "and I hope you will come. A gentleman will be with us who is a great performer on the piano." It was in this way that the more frivolous intention was veiled. But, unfortunately, as is the case with well-known persons in general, Mrs. Seton's friends judged the past by the present, and were aware of the risks they would run.

"It will be one of her usual affairs," said Miss Margaret, with a glance of intelligence and warning to her sister.

"Just that, Margaret, I should suppose," said Miss Jean.

"Then it will not be worth while for Lilias to take the trouble of dressing herself, Jean—a few old ladies invited to their tea."

"That was what I was going to say, Margaret. I would not fash to go, if I was Lilias. She can have Katie here to-morrow."

"Sisters!" cried Lilias, springing up before them, "you said that last time, and there was a dance. It is very hard upon me, if I am never to have a dance—never till I am as old as you."

The two ladies were seated in two chairs, both large, with high backs and capacious arms, covered with faded velvet, and with each a footstool almost as large as the chair. They were on either side of the window, as they might have been, in winter, on either side of a fire. They wore black dresses, old and dim, but made of rich silk, which was still good, though they had got ever so many years' wear out of it, and small lace caps upon their heads. Miss Jean was fair, and Miss Margaret's brown locks had come to resemble her sister's by dint of growing grey. They had blue eyes, large and clear, so clear as almost to be cold; and good, if somewhat large, features, and resembled each other in the delicacy of their complexions in which there was the tone of health, with scarcely any colour. Between them, on a small, very low seat, not sitting with any dignity, but plumped down like a child, was the third, the heroine of the veil, whose envelope had disguised her so completely that even the lively mind of Lewis had not been roused to any curiosity about her. She had jumped up when she made that observation, and now flung herself down again with a kind of despairing abandon. She looked eighteen at the utmost, a small, slight creature, not like the other ladies in a single feature, at any time; and now, with her brow puckered, the corners of her mouth drooping, her eyes wet, more unlike them, in her young excitement and distress, than ever.

"Now, Lilias, don't be unreasonable, my dear. If it's a dance, it stands to reason you cannot go; but what reason have you to suppose it is a dance? none whatever. 'I am asking one or two friends to tea.' Is that like dancing? She would not ask Jean and me, I suppose, if that was what she meant. We are going to hear a gentleman who is a great performer on the piano. It appears to me that will be rather a dreary style of entertainment, Jean; and I am by no means certain that I will go."

"Well, Margaret," said Jean, "having always been the musical one of the family, it's an inducement to me; but Lilias, poor thing, would not care for it. Besides, I have always been of the opinion that we must not make her cheap, taking her to all the little tea-parties."

"Oh, how can you talk such nonsense, when you never take me to one, never to one! and me close upon eighteen," the girl cried. "Katie goes to them all, and knows everybody, and sees whatever is going on; but I must do nothing but practise and read, practise and read, till I'm sick of everything. I never have any pleasure, nor diversion, nor novelty, nor anything at all, and Katie—"

"Katie! Katie is nothing but the minister's daughter, with no expectations, nor future before her. If she marries a minister like her father, she will do all that can be expected from her. How can you speak of Katie? Jean and me," said Miss Margaret, "have just devoted ourselves to you from your cradle."

"Not quite from her cradle, Margaret, for we were then young ourselves, and her mother, poor thing—"

"Well, well, I did not intend to be taken to the letter," said Miss Margaret, impatiently. "Since ever you have been in our hands—and that is many years back—we have been more like aunts than sisters to you. We have given up all projects of our own. A woman of forty, which is my age, is not beyond thinking of herself in most cases."

"And, reason good, still less," said Miss Jean, "a woman of eight-and-thirty."

"So little a difference as two years cannot be said to count; but all our hopes we have put upon you, Lilias. We might have been jealous of you, seeing what your position is, and what ours is; we would have had great cause. But, on the contrary, we have put all our pride upon you, and thought of nothing but what was the best for you, and pinched ourselves to get masters and means of improvement, and taken houses in Edinburgh winter after winter—"

"Not to speak," said Miss Jean, "of the great things Margaret has planned, when the time comes, which was not done either for her or me."

"I know you are very kind," said Lilias, drying her eyes.

"My dear," said Miss Margaret, "a season in London, and you presented to the Queen, and all the old family friends rallying round you—would I think of a bit little country party with a prospect before me like that?"

At this Lilias looked up with her eyes shining through the wetness that still hung upon her eyelashes.

"It is very, very nice to think of, I don't deny. Oh, and awfully, awfully kind of you to think of it."

(Let it be said here in a parenthesis that this "awfully, awfully," on the lips of Lilias was not slang, but Scotch.)

"I think it is rather good of us. It was never done, as she says, for either Jean or me."

"I doubt if it would have made any difference," said Miss Jean. "What is to be will be; and making a curtsey to the Queen—unless one could get to be acquainted with Her Majesty, which would be a great honour and pleasure—"

"It just makes all the difference," said Miss Margaret, who was more dogmatic; "it just puts the stamp upon a lady. If you're travelling it opens the doors of foreign courts, if you stay at home—well, there is always the Drawing-room to go to."

"And can you go whenever you like, after you have been once introduced?" Lilias added, with a gleam of eagerness.

"Surely, my dear; you send in your name, and you put on your court dress."

"That will be very nice," said the girl. Her bosom swelled with a sigh of pleasure. "For of course the finest company must be always there, and you will hear all the talk that is going on, and see everybody—ambassadors and princes, when they come on visits. Of course you would not be of much importance among so many grand people, just like the 'ladies, &c.,' in Shakespeare. They say nothing themselves, but sometimes the Queen will beckon to them and send them a message, or make them hold her fan, or bring her a book; but you hear all the conversation and see everybody."

"I am afraid," said Miss Jean, who had been watching an opportunity to break in, "you are thinking of maids-of-honour and people in office. Drawing-rooms—" but here she caught her sister's eye and broke off.

"Maids-of-honour are of course the foremost," said Miss Margaret. "I don't see, for my part, why Lilias should not stand as good a chance as any. Her father was a distinguished soldier, and her grandfather, though he has not behaved well to us, was a man that was very well-known, and had a great deal of influence. And the Queen is very feeling. Why she might not be a maid-of-honour, as well as any other young lady, I am at a loss to see."

Lilias jumped to her feet again, this time in a glow of pride and ambitious hope.

"Me!" she said (once more not for want of grammar, but for stress of Scotch). Miss Jean, scarcely less excited, put down her knitting and softly clapped her thin hands.

"That is a good idea; there is no one like Margaret for ideas," she said.

"I see no reason why it should not be. She has the birth, and she would have good interest. She has just got to let herself be trained in the manners and the ways that are conformable. Silly lassie! but she would rather go to a little tea-party in the country."

"No, no, no!" cried the girl, making a spring towards her, and throwing her arms round the speaker's neck. "You don't know me yet, for I am ambitious; I should like to raise the house out of the dust, as you say—I, the last one, the end of all. That would be worth living for!" she cried, with a glow of generous ardour in her eyes.

But when Lilias watched her sisters walking away, with their maid behind them carrying their shoes across the park to the little gate and green lane which led by a back-way to the manse, it was scarcely possible that her heart should not sink within her. Another of those lingering, endless evenings, hour after hour of silvery lightness after the day was over, like a strange, unhopeful morning, yet so cool and sweet, lingered out moment by moment over this young creature alone. She had "her book" which, meaning literature in the abstract, was constantly recommended to her by the other ladies; and she had her sketch-book, and her needlework. Miss Margaret was wont to express absolute consternation that, with so many things to amuse her, a girl should ever feel dull. But this poor little girl, though surrounded by all these, did feel dull and very lonely. To go to Drawing-rooms, which Lilias innocently took to mean the inner circle of the court, and to be a maid-of-honour was a prospect which took away her breath. With that before her it would indeed be wonderful if she could not bear up and submit to being dull and lonely as every girl, her sisters told her, had to do before she came out; but, after she had repeated this to herself half a dozen times, the impression on her mind grew faint, the possible maid-of-honour, the gorgeous imagination of a Drawing-room floated away; they were so far away at the best, so uncertain, while it was very certain that she was lonely to-night, and that other people of her age were enjoying themselves very much. Lilias' thoughts ended, as was very natural, in a fit of crying, after which she rose up a little better, and, the new box from the library happening by good fortune to arrive at that moment, got out a new novel, which it was a small excitement to be able to begin at her own will before her sisters had decided which was and which was not good for her, and in that happiness forgot her trouble, as she had so often done before.

"Did you really mean yon, Margaret?" Miss Jean said to her sister, as she walked along towards the manse.

"Do you think I ever say out like that anything I don't mean, Jean? I might humour the child's fancies, and let her think the drawing-rooms were real society, like what she reads; but the other, to be sure I meant it—wherefore not?—the lust of our family, her father's daughter, and a girl with beauty. We must always recollect that. You and I were good-looking enough in our day; you are sometimes very good-looking yet—"

"That's your kind heart, Margaret."

"What has my kind heart to do with it? But Lilias has more than we ever had—she has beauty, you know. Something should be made of that. It should not just run away into the dust like our good looks, and be of profit or pleasure to nobody. I struck out the idea," said Miss Margaret, with a little pride, "on the spot, it is true; it came to me, and I did not shut my mind to it; but it's full of reason, when you come to think of it. I see a great many reasons for it, but none against it. They have a sort of a little income— just something for their clothes. They need not be extravagant in clothes, for Her Majesty takes little pleasure in vanity and dressing; and then they have honourable to their name. The Honourable Lilias Murray—it would sound very well; and then in the service of the Queen. Don't go too far forward, Jean; but it is a thing to think of, to keep her heart up with. The little thing is very high-spirited when you take her the right way."

"My heart smote me to come away and leave her, Margaret."

"Why should your heart smite you? Would you like her to be talked about as the belle of a manse parlour, and perhaps worse than that—who can tell, at her age? She might see some long-legged fellow that would take her fancy—a factor's son, or an assistant minister, or even Philip Stormont, who is not a match for a Murray."

"Say no more, Margaret. I am quite of your opinion."

"And that is a great comfort to me, Jean. We can do things together that we could never do separate. Please God she shall have her day; she shall shine, at the Queen's court, and marry nobly, and, if the family must be extinguished as seems likely, we'll be extinguished with éclat, my dear, not just wither out solitary like you and me."

It was an ambition, after its sort, of a not unworthy kind. The two sisters, with scarfs thrown over their caps, and their maid following at a few paces' distance, on their way to their tea-party, stepped out with a certain elation in their tread, like two figures in a procession, holding their heads high. They had each had experiences, no doubt, of their own, and neither of them had expected that their family should wither out solitary in their persons. But here they had a new life in their hands, a new hope. Many fathers and mothers have had the same thought—to secure that in the persons of their children which they had never been able to attain themselves, to raise the new generation on their shoulders, making themselves a pedestal for the future greatness. Is it selfishness disguised, the rapacity of disappointment? or is it love the purest, love unconquerable? Miss Margaret and Miss Jean never asked themselves this question. They were not in the habit of examining themselves except as to their religious duty. But they reached the manse with a little thrill of excitement about them, and a sort of exultation in their minds. The windows were all open, and a hum of many voices reached them as they crossed the smooth-shaven lawn. Margaret gave Jean a look.

"Was it not a good thing we left her at home?" they both cried.

CHAPTER VI

Lewis came away from the manse on the Sunday afternoon with a great many new thoughts stirring in his mind. His heart was made sore by the perpetual condemnation of himself which he heard on every hand; from Duncan of the dog-cart to the company at the manse, no one could believe that old Sir Patrick's adopted son was anything but a villain, a designing, mercenary adventurer, who had flattered and beguiled the old man into making provision for him at the expense of his family. It had never entered into the thoughts of these good people that they might be wrong, that their verdict might be unjust; they were as sure of it as if they had come to this decision upon the plainest and most conclusive evidence. Lewis knew very well that it was not so, but still he was a little cowed by the reiteration. It is terrible to appear in this light to so many, even when you have the strongest internal conviction that you are right and they wrong; after a while it comes to have a certain effect upon a man's own spirit; the right which he was so unhesitatingly sure of becomes confused and dim to him. He begins even to wonder whether it is possible that he might have had an evil scheme in his head without knowing it. Lewis had not got so far as this, but he was troubled and depressed. He could not sit still in the parlour overlooking the village. It was so quiet. He longed to see somebody moving about. If there had been a band playing somewhere, and the people walking about, even in that promenade up and down which gets so dreary when it is an imperious habit, at all events that would have been more cheerful for a looker-on. But the dead stillness oppressed him. And there were no resources inside—no books, even if he had cared much for books, no piano, nothing to do but think, which is generally a troublesome and so often an unprofitable occupation. After a while he ceased to be able to put up with it at all, and strolled out to the water-side, where he so often sat and watched Adam fishing.

The trout had a peaceful time on Sunday. The river lay as still as if it had flowed through a land unexplored. Now and then a fish would flash from the water at its ease, and sink to its pool again without anxiety. Did they know it was Sunday, Lewis wondered? It went a long way to reconcile him to the unbroken quiet which, after all, had something wonderful and beautiful in it. The cows were lying down in the meadows, their great red-brown sides rising out in the green grass and daisies with a peaceful warmth. Neither up nor down the water did he see a single living soul. The stillness moved him as he had sometimes been moved in a cathedral when all the worshippers had gone away. It was the sort of moment and the sort of place, Lewis felt, to say your prayers. He had not felt so in the morning at church. There he had gone for the sake of society. Here all was sacred and still, with something unseen giving meaning to all that was visible. He was like a child in the readiness of his emotions. He took off his hat and even said a prayer or two such as he could remember, and afterwards was silent, thinking, with a little awe upon him, in which the idea of God, a majestic old man like the Padre Eterno of many a picture, blended somehow with the idea of his personal benefactor, his friend who had been so good to him, and who also was old and majestic, a vision full of tenderness to his grateful heart.

After a while the ferryman came out from his cottage up the water with his two little children, and there was a far-away babble of their little voices in the air which, though very sweet and innocent, broke the spell. And then Lewis put on his hat, and began to think of his more particular affairs. This moment of solemn calm had soothed the painfulness of his sense of being unjustly treated. He began to comfort himself with the thought of being by-and-by better understood. When they knew that this adventurer, this schemer, was no other than himself, they would change their minds, he thought. He had never been misconstrued, but always liked and made much of wherever he had gone, and he saw no reason why now, without any cause for it, all at once his luck should change.

There were other questions, however, which had been called up by his sudden introduction to society in Murkley. He thought of the little party round the manse dinner-table with pleasure, thinking on the whole that perhaps that was better than the more limited hospitality of a curé who had nobody to sit at the head of his table, and only himself to provide all the entertainment. Lewis was not sure of himself whether he was a Catholic or a Protestant: he was very latitudinarian. He thought, if the truth must be told, that both were best, for he liked the curé too, and was more familiar with that form of clerical development than with the comfortable minister surrounded by his children. He did not know the English clergyman at all, which made a sad vacancy in his experiences. But no curé ever spoke of the necessity of being a gentleman, or ignored all other classes, as the minister's wife did. Was there no other class in England? To be sure gentilhomme meant something different; but there certainly were a great number of people "abroad" who were not gentilhommes, and yet were not nobody. This idea puzzled Lewis much. He asked himself was he a gentleman, with a smile, yet a half-doubt. His old home, when he cast his mind back so far, was a very homely one; his father had been the Vice-Consul's clerk, he himself had been now and then employed about the office. His mother had performed a great many of the domestic operations with her own hands; he had seen her making the coffee in the morning, sometimes even cooking the dinner, doing up the linen in a way, he fondly thought, that he never saw it now. They were much respected, but they were poor. To bury them even required a subscription from the community. The uncle who had written to him, and who had been willing to receive him, wrote like a shopkeeper. He remembered the aspect and superscription of his letter as if he had received it yesterday.

If he got such a letter now, he would unhesitatingly conclude it to be a bill.

Was he then a gentleman at all? Of course Sir Patrick was so—but then Sir Patrick could not confer this nobility, or whatever it was, upon him. This thought puzzled Lewis greatly. It did not distress, but rather amused him; for, with all the associations and friends of the last eight or nine years, by far the most important of his life, it was impossible for him to imagine that he was not good enough to associate with the good people at Murkley. He considered the question altogether as an abstract one, a matter of curiosity; but it was a question to consider. Then as to education, Lewis was aware that in this point, too, he failed. He had gleaned enough from the conversation of English visitors to know that a good education meant an education at an English university. No other kind of training counted. He had heard this from Sir Patrick himself satirically; for neither had Sir Patrick been "a university man." So once more Lewis felt himself out of the field altogether. Neither by birth nor education: there remained one thing, money. This he had; but was this enough to claim the position of a gentleman upon? and then they all thought the money was ill-gotten, as good as stolen from the giver's descendants. Altogether Lewis felt that, if it should be necessary for him to give up, metaphorically, "ses papiers" to enter into the question of his own birth, education, and fortune, things would go very hard with him in this little place. When he came to this conclusion he laughed; for it seemed very amusing that he, who had lived with ambassadors and knew his way about many a palace, should be found not good enough for the society of the minister and the minister's wife in Murkley. It did not even occur to him that, amusing as it was, it might come some time to a serious question enough. In the mean time it tickled his imagination greatly. Perhaps no one ever sees the ludicrous side of a privilege so completely as the man who is wanting in the qualifications to possess it. Lewis, with his non-experience, amused himself a good deal with that question about gentlemen. Gentilhomme was far more easy to understand; but this mysterious word which the English used so constantly, which they tried to build upon one foundation after another, but which sometimes did not seem to require any foundation at all, what was the meaning of it? and how was it to be defined? Young Mr. Stormont of the Tower which pushed out that angle of old masonry on the cliff opposite, had every qualification necessary, "But not I," Lewis said, and laughed to himself. The son of a poor clerk and a nursery governess, the nephew of a linendraper—but this he was not aware of—with no education to speak of, no belongings, no settled place or position, or friends to answer for him! Decidedly, if Mrs. Seton had known all this she would have closed her door most rigidly upon him.

All this amused him very much to think of as he got up from the grass, and took his way back to the 'Murkley Arms.'

By this time the world had begun to wake a little. The Sabbath seriousness had relaxed. A few groups were standing about the road in Sunday attire. The women had come out to the doors; the children were playing discreetly, but now and then rising into louder riot, which the nearest bystander rebuked with a "Whisht, bairns! mind it's the Sabbath day." Notwithstanding this apparent severity, there was a good deal of quiet pleasure diffused in the air. The softness of this pause in the working-day tenor of existence pervaded everything, and at the same time the duration of the unusual stillness and sense of monotony it brought, made the good people think with pleasure of the toil to be resumed to-morrow. Adam was standing in an attitude very unusual to him, leaning against his doorpost, when Lewis came up, and Janet, in her best gown, smoothing down a fresh white muslin apron, with many frills and decorations, stood by his side. They were not an uncomely couple. He, though he concealed under the veil of his beard all but his blue-grey eyes and well-formed nose, had a head of great rustic dignity and force surmounting his six feet of somewhat languid length; for Adam had "nae pith," as his wife said, and, but for his great gift at "the fushin'," would have been a somewhat useless personage. She was not, to all appearance, of so elevated a type. Her face was round, and her nose turned up, and she was forty-five. The roundness natural to that mature age had taken all the charm from her trim figure, but still it was trim: a little vibration of activity, as if the machinery was all in such thorough order that the slightest touch would set it in motion, was in her: and Janet's smiling countenance was all alive, ready to hear and see everything, and give forth opinions, as many as might be desired.

"It's been another bonnie day," she said. "Ye'll no tell us now, sir, that we've nae fine weather on Tayside."

"I hope I never could have been so unmannerly," Lewis said.

"Na, you never said it, but I saw it in your eye—folk from the south are a' of that opinion, but it's just lees. I hear there is mair fog and mist in London town in a single winter than will come our way in a dizzen years."

"You must be very glad Sunday is over," said Lewis, with a boldness that took away Janet's breath.

"Sir!" she cried, scandalised; then after a pause of consideration: "ye're taking your fun out of us. Them that are tired of the Sabbath day, Mr. Murray, how are they to bide Heaven, if they win to it at the hinder end?"

"Hold your tongue, Janet. We ken little enough about heaven," said Adam, who was in the humour to talk. "Whiles an unconsidered question like this young gentleman's will just let loose a thocht. I've been thinking lang that ae use o' the Sabbath is just maybe to make us feel that wark is the most entertaining in the lang run. There is nae time," he continued, with dignity, "that I think o' my occupation with mair pleasure than just about this hour on the Sabbath night."

"I wouldna say but you're a grand authority," said his wife, satirically, "such hard work as yours is! Sunday or Saturday a woman's work is never done. I havena the time to weary, for my part. There's Mr. Murray's dinner to be seen to this very blessed minute: but you that makes your day's darg out o' what the gentlemen do for pleesure—"

"Who are the gentlemen, Mrs. Janet?" asked Lewis, with all his late speculations in his mind.

"She's speaking o' gentlemen in the abstract," said Adam, "and no a high view of them; them that have plenty of siller and nothing to do."

"Well," said Janet, "what would ye have mair? That's just about your ain description, Adam, my man; but I was not meaning them that leave a woman at hame to work for them. There's different sorts, sir, ye'll understand; there's the real gentlemen that have the land: and such as have their fortunes ready-made for them are no far behind: and then there is them that can take their leisure when they please and have a' they wish for: but the grand, grand thing of a' is just what every fool kens—them that have no occasion to work for their living; ye can never deceive yourself in that," Janet said.

"So," said Lewis, "for it is information I want; one who works for his living is not a gentleman."

Janet looked up somewhat startled.

"I'm far from saying that, sir," she said.

"Keep her to it, Mr. Murray; ye'll get her to maintain just the opposite before you've done with her. That's women's way. There's naething they're so fond o' as a grand, broad assumption, and then, when they see a' it involves, they will just shift and shuffle and abandon their poscetion. I'm well acquaint with a' that. The true gentleman ye'll bring her to say is him that works the hardest and brings in the most siller, and is never free of his business from morning till night."

"And well might I say it," cried Janet, "and guid reason I would have after a' that's come and gone. It's just that, sir. The man that does the best work, him that leaves naething but what is in her share to his wife, and lays up something for his bairns, and pays his debt of every kind baith to them that are obliged to him, and them that he's obliged to, and can haud up his head before ony man on earth, and no feared even for his Maker but in the way of reverence and his duty. Weel! that's an honest man at heart, if he's no a gentleman, and a better thing than a gentleman, if it was my last word. But, losh me! if I stand havering here," cried Janet, abandoning her peroration and her excitement together, "you'll get no dinner, sir, the day."

"What do you ca' that thing the auld heathens fired as they fled, sir?" said Adam, as Janet disappeared. "A Parthian arrow? Yon's just it. It's naething to the argument, but it has its effect. It doesna convince your mind, but it makes a kind of end of your debating. It's just a curious question enough what makes a gentleman. I canna tell ye, for my part. I'm maybe mair worth in many ways than a lad like you, not meaning any offence. I've come through mair, I have pondered mair—but pit me in your claes and you in mine, and it would be you that would be the gentleman still. I canna faddom it: but that's no remarkable, for there are few things I can faddom on this earth. The mair I ponder, the less I come to ony end."

"All the philosophers are the same," said Lewis. "You are not singular, my friend Adam. But how do you know I am a gentleman, come? I might be nothing of the sort. You never saw me till ten days ago. It is not the clothes, you admit, and you feel that you are a better man than I. Then, why do you take it for granted that I am a gentleman? You have no evidence."

"Maister Murray," said Adam, somewhat grimly, "evidence has little, awfu' little to do with it. Maybe you're one of them that thinks with Locke there are nae innate ideas? But I'm of the Scotch school, sir; I'm no demanding daata daata for ever, like your Baconian lads. Let us be, and we'll come down to your facks, and fit them a' in to a miracle. It's just a brutal method, in my opinion, to demand the facks first, and syne account for them and explain them a' away."

"You are abandoning the point more than your wife did," cried Lewis. "Come! how do you know?"

"I know naething about it," said Adam, turning away. "I'll argue my ain gait or I'll no argue at all. Your personal questions are naething to a true philosopher. This I'll tell ye, if a man canna be kent for a gentleman without proving it, it's my opinion he's nae gentleman ava. And I'm for a turn before the night closes in," said Adam suddenly.

Lewis was left in the lurch, standing alone by the open door. He went in after a little pause. He was pleased by what Adam said, though he had not been at all distressed before by the doubts which he had set forth before himself as to his own right to this title. He had laughed at his own argument then, and he laughed now, but nevertheless he was pleased. It was flattering, though it was so gruffly said.

Next morning rose still fair and bright, though Adam declared it would be the last day of the fine weather. Lewis was delighted to think of his two engagements. He did not care for his own exclusive society. He set out for Stormont when the sun was high, at an hour which all the experience of his previous life proved to him to be an impossible one to walk in, and found it only bright and genial with all the breadth and hush of noon, but without any of its oppressive qualities. He went across the river in the big ferry-boat, along with a farmer's shandry-dan. He recollected to have crossed a river so near Paestum in the wildest wastes of Italy, with brigands about, and dangers. The contrast was so strange that he laughed in spite of himself.

"It's perhaps not very well-bred," said the farmer's wife, who sat in state in her vehicle, holding her horse warily in hand though he was used to it, "but no doubt it's very funny to see me up here."

"Not funny at all, madam," said Lewis, taking off his hat; "but it reminded me of a ferry abroad, where we were afraid of the brigands, and every man you met carried a gun."

"Bless me! I suppose, sir, you have been a great traveller?" Mrs. Glen said; and they talked all the way over, and she thought him "just delightful." French! No, not a bit like French—nor English either. The English, they are always condescending, and ready to explain your own countryside to you. I would say of a good race, but brought up abroad.

Lewis by this time had also found out the advantages of that word abroad. It saved all necessity for explanation. The Continent was taken in by it from one coast to the other, and even America and the East.

He went on his way to Stormont very cheerfully after his talk with Mrs. Glen. And the road was beautiful. It wound up the slope of a fine wooded bank behind the cliff, with tall trees mounting upward, the roots of one showing bold and picturesque through the feathering tops of the others, in broken, irregular lines. When he had got about half-way up he saw the house, of which one turret only surmounted the cliff. It was not large, but its small windows and the rough, half-ruined battlements showed that, at some time or other, it might have been defended—which interested Lewis beyond measure. The lower story had been modernized, and twinkled with plate glass windows receiving the full sunshine; but the building altogether was like something which had grown out of the soil, not a mere house made with hands.

Stormont led his visitor all over the place. He took him upon the bit of battlement that remained, and showed him that it commanded the cliff in reality, though this did not appear from below; and he took him into the chapel, a curious little detached piece of sixteenth century architecture, which nobody knew much about, desecrated to common uses which made Lewis shiver, though he said, quite simply, that he was "not religious."

"Don't say that before my mother," Stormont said. "I am sure you are no heathen, for you were at church like myself; but she would think you so."

"Oh, that is nothing," said Lewis, "one goes to church for company. I know nobody. It all amused me very much, and I made friends with you, and with the good pastor and his family—what do you call him, minister?"

"This is worse and worse. You must be careful not to say that you went to church to be amused," Stormont said, with a big laugh. "I don't myself find it amusing at all."

"We use the word in different senses. You must excuse me if I do so in English—which is mixed up with other idioms in what you would call my mind, if I have got one," Lewis said. "I should call it, perhaps, interested. All is interesting to me here."

"This ramshackle old place, among other things, I hope," its master said, with a little conscious pride.

"I have not the least idea what ramshackle means. The old place, oh yes, more than anything. I begin to understand how it must feel to be like this, planted here for ever and ever—in sæcula sæculorum. It is very curious. It will become a part of you—or rather, you are a part of it; not one man, but a race. For me, that have only money, the contrast is very great."

"But you think you like the money best?"

"Otherwise, quite otherwise; but this is such a novelty. I have seen great castles, of course, but this which is not great, yet the same as greatness, it amuses me. Pardon there, I mistake again—it gives me great interest," the stranger said.

Stormont's brow clouded over a little when Lewis said, "this which is not great." He knew very well it was not great, but to hear it said was less pleasant, and he was piqued by the shiver with which his visitor saw the common uses to which the chapel was put.

"I thought you said you were not religious—which is a dreadful confession to make."

"No, I am not devot—few people are, unless they have been peculiarly brought up, at our age."

"But in Scotland you are supposed to be always devout—unless you are a sceptic," said Stormont. "Sceptics are coming very much into fashion. Mr. Seton has a great respect for them. If you are a freethinker, it will be a great pleasure to him to fathom your state of mind, and do everything for you. But keep quiet about all that before my mother, who is very rigid in the old way."

"I am not a freethinker. I do not think, perhaps, at all so much as I ought," said Lewis. "One does not give one's attention, that is all. Ah, I think I understand; you have duties, a sort of anchor here. You cannot any longer do whatever you like; you must respect the house and the race. I admire all that very much, very much; but it cannot change the character; it cannot give more seriousness, more substance—I think that is the word."

"It is often a great bore," said Stormont, with a passing cloud upon his brow.

"I can understand that; but it is impressive," Lewis said. And then the two young men went into the modernized part of the building, into the drawing-room, where Mrs. Stormont, in her widow's cap, sat knitting near one of those windows which looked out upon the long rolling fields of the strath and the hills beyond. The country was rich with green corn waving thick and close, a very different landscape from that which was lighted up by the rapid flow of the river. The lady received Lewis very graciously. She made a few delicate researches to find out, if possible, to whom he belonged, but he was so ignorant of the Murrays, all and sundry, and so ready with his statement that the name had come to him as an inheritance along with money that curiosity was baffled. And Mrs. Stormont had no daughters to make her anxious. She thought him "very foreign," having more or less insight than the farmer's wife in the ferry-boat.

"But he has a very nice face," Mrs. Stormont said, when he was gone. "I like the looks of him; there's innocence in it, and a good heart. He would do very well for Katie Seton, if he means to settle here."

"There is no question, so far as I know, either of his settling here or of Katie Seton. I would not be so free with a girl's name, mother, if I were you," Stormont said, with some indignation.

Perhaps it was to call forth this remark, which afforded her some information, that his mother spoke.

CHAPTER VII

The greater part of the company were assembled when Lewis entered the manse. He had been in some doubt how to dress for this rustic party, and indeed, had not some good fairy recalled to him a recollection of English male toilet in the evening, it is probable that he would have appeared in grey trousers, after the fashion of the Continent. But his good genius interfered (it would be profane to imagine that a guardian angel took note of any such details, though indeed it would have scandalised the Setons more to see an evening coat worn over gray trousers than to know, as Stormont had suggested, that the stranger was a freethinker, or even guilty of some breach of the minor moralities). He appeared, however, with a black-silk handkerchief, tied in a somewhat large bow, under his shirt-collar, instead of the stiff little white tie with which all the other men recognised the claims of an evening party. On the other side, he kept his hat in his hand, while all the other people left in the hall their informal caps and wideawakes, thus showing that he was not at all sure of his ground as they were, but felt it necessary to be prepared for everything. Perhaps he had never seen before the institution of tea. Little cups he had indeed swallowed at various hours during the day—after the déjeuner in foreign houses, at five o'clock in English ones, whenever the occasion served in the apartments of princely

Russians—but an English tea, round a long table, with cakes and scones, and jam, and every kind of bread and butter dainty, he was totally unacquainted with.

He did not much care for the tea, and still less did he like the coffee, which was coffee-tea, a feeble decoction, and served with hot milk, as if it had been for breakfast; but, on the other hand, Lewis was quite capable of doing justice to the cakes, and not at all above the enjoyment of the new meal, which "amused" him, according to his usual phrase, greatly. And he made himself impartially agreeable to everybody, showing as strong a desire to please old Mrs. Borrodaile, in that cap which was the derision of the parish, as the youngest and prettiest of her daughters.

When the meal was over, and the company streamed into the drawing-room, where there was an unusual and suspicious vacancy, the furniture pushed into corners, betraying to all the habitués the intention of the hostess, Lewis was set down to the piano almost at once.

"Hush," Mrs. Seton said to a little group about her. "Just hold your tongues, young people. There is to be something rational to begin with; and let me see that you take advantage of your opportunities, for it is not often you can hear good music. Nonsense, Katie, not a word. Do you not see that the sooner he begins, the sooner it will be over? and I am just bound to ask him to play, after yesterday. Little monkeys," the minister's wife continued, seating herself beside Miss Jean. "They would like to have it all their own way; but I always insist on something rational to begin with. Oh, yes, yes, a great treat; some really good music. It is not often we hear it. And this is just an opportunity, you know, a most unusual chance. Well, we do not know very much about him, but he is a most well-mannered young man, brought up abroad, which accounts for various little things in his appearance, and so forth. And just a beautiful performer on the piano. I wonder what that is. It sounds to me like Mozart, or Beethoven, or some of those that you don't so commonly hear. Bach, do you think? Well, I should not wonder. You know, songs are my branch."

Lewis had gone into the first movement of his sonata before he had at all taken into consideration the character of his audience. He was, in reality, though Mrs. Seton took up the belief entirely without evidence, a very good performer, and had played to difficult audiences, whose applause was worth having. After the first few minutes, it became apparent to him by that occult communication which is in the air, and which our senses can give no account of, that this audience was not only unprepared but very much taken aback by the prospect of even half an hour of the really good music and rational enjoyment which their hostess promised. He could see when he suffered his eyes to stray on a momentary rapid survey of the side of the room which was visible to him, the excellent Mrs. Borrodaile, with her fat hands crossed in her lap, and the air of a woman who knew her duty and was determined to do it. Stormont stood bolt upright in the corner, now and then lifting his eyebrows, or lowering them, or even forming syllables with his lips in telegraphic communication with one or other of the young ladies which showed impatience bursting through decorum in a guarded but very evident way. The minister, with resignation depicted in every line, even of his beard, turned vaguely over the leaves of a book. When the movement came to an end, there was a long breath of unquestionable relief on the part of the company generally.

"That's a very pretty thing," said Mrs. Borrodaile, almost enthusiastic in the happiness of its being done with.

"Oh, hush, hush; that's only the first part. Dear me, do you not know that there are different parts in a great piece of music like that? Go back, go back to your seat," whispered Mrs. Seton, loudly.

It was all that Lewis could do not to laugh aloud behind the shelter of the piano. He thought he had never seen anything so comical as the resigned looks of the party generally, the reluctant hush which ran round the room as he struck the first notes of the second movement. Mischief began to twinkle in his eyes, he stopped, and his hearers brightened. Then he broke into the lively, graceful music of a gavotte, tantalising yet cheering—and finally, after another pause, dropped into a waltz, which was more than the young people could bear. He stood up, and looked at them over the piano, playing all the while. "Dansons!" he cried: and in a moment, despite of Mrs. Seton and her precautions, the whole party was in movement. Never in Tayside had such a waltz been played before. Mrs. Seton was an excellent performer in her way. She was unwearied, and could go on for hours on a stretch, and she knew every tune that lad and lass could desire. But young Lewis, standing, stooping, encouraging them with his merry eyes, gliding with skilful hands on the keys, now softer, now louder, giving a double rhythm to the sweep of the dance, which was formal enough so far as the performers went, but yet took an additional grace and freedom from the music—played as no one had ever played to them before. When he stopped, with a peal of pleasant laughter that seemed to run into the music, after he had tired out everybody but Katie, the whole party came crowding round to thank him. It was so kind! it was so delightful!

"Oh, play us another, Mr. Murray," cried the girls.

"Tut, tut," said Mrs. Seton, bustling in, "is that all your manners? So impatient that you made him stop that beautiful sonata, which it was just a privilege to hear, and then pestering him to play waltzes, which is a thing no good musician will do. I am sure, Mr. Murray, you have behaved like a perfect angel; but these girls shall not tyrannize over you. No, no, I'll just take the piano myself; it is no trouble to me. You will think it is bold of me, playing before such a performer, but I just never mind: and they like me as well as anyone. Come now, Katie, and see that Mr. Murray gets a nice partner. He will take a turn himself."

And with this the indefatigable little woman of the house sat down, and played waltzes, polkas, and schottisches (which latter made Lewis open his eyes) for hours on end, indicating meanwhile with her vigilant glances, and with little nods of her lively head, to her husband and children the various little offices in which it was necessary they should replace her. Thus a nod in the direction of Mrs. Borrodaile called the minister's attention to the terrible fact that one of his guests was going to sleep: while a movement of the eyebrows directed towards the factor's youngest daughter showed Katie that the young woman in question was partnerless, while a young man in another corner had escaped observation. Mrs. Seton managed to talk also all the time to Miss Jean, who sat beside her.

"I am so used to it; it is really no trouble to me. When you have young people growing up, you must just make up your mind to this sort of thing. Yes, yes, it becomes a kind of mechanical. Dear me, I must not talk; that bar was all wrong. But they're not particular, poor things, so long as you just keep on, and keep the time: but playing set pieces was always beyond me," Mrs. Seton said. And on she went for hours, with a hard but lively hand, keeping capital time, and never tired.

The "set pieces" which she thus deprecated, and which had been beyond her, meant by implication the sonata which Lewis had begun to play.

As for that young man himself, he found pleasure in everything. The country girls were perhaps a little wanting in grace, and did not valse as high-born ladies do in the lands where the valse is indigenous; but they were light and lively, and the evening flew by to his great entertainment. Then there was a reel danced, at which he looked on delighted. Katie, who was a little ashamed of these pranks, stood by him primly, and pretended to be bored.

"You must not think that is the sort of thing we care for in Scotland," she said. "It is quite old-fashioned. You see, it amuses the country people, and mamma will always insist upon having one to keep up the old fashion; but you must not think that we care for it," Katie said.

"That is unfortunate," said Lewis. "It is so much like the national dance everywhere. The tarantella—you have heard of the tarantella? It is like that. For my part, I like what is old-fashioned."

"Oh, yes, in furniture—and things," said Katie, vaguely. And she took pains not to commit herself further.

He was so good a dancer that she neglected Philip Stormont for him, to the great discontent of that young athlete, who thereupon devoted himself to Annie Borrodaile in a way which it went to Katie's heart to see. The windows stood wide open, the scent of the flowers came in; the roses and the tall white lilies shone in the silvery light. Everything was quaint and unreal to Lewis, to whom it had never happened to dance in the lingering daylight before. The strange evening radiance would have suited his own poetic valse better than the sharp, hard, unvaried music which Mrs. Seton continued to make with so much industry. When the reel was over, he went to the piano to relieve that lady.

"Let me play now. I shall like it; and you must be tired—you ought to be tired," he said.

"Mr. Murray is the most considerate young man I ever saw," said Mrs. Seton, shaking on her bracelets again. "You see he has relieved me whether I would or not. As a matter of fact, I'm never tired so long as they go on; I'm so used to it. But when somebody comes, you know, and really says to you, I would rather—though it is difficult to understand it, with so many nice girls dancing. And so you would not bring Lilias, Miss Margaret? I did hope, I must say, just for to-night."

"You see," said Miss Margaret, solemnly, "she is not out yet."

"Oh, you can't think that matters among friends. Katie is not out, the monkey. But, to be sure, as I tell her always, she is very different. Poor Lilias! don't you think it would be better for her just to see what the world is like a little before she comes out. She will be forming such high-flown ideas. I always say to mine, 'Don't be excited. Oh, no, no, don't be excited. A ball in London will just be very much like a ball at home.'"

"That is true enough in one way," said Miss Margaret. "Her Majesty, I suppose, is just like any other person: She has the same number of fingers and toes: but, when a young girl makes her curtsey to the Queen, I hope that will not be the way she will look upon her sovereign."

"Oh, if you take it like that, nobody will beat me in loyalty," said Mrs. Seton. "It was just as near a thing as possible last summer that Robert would have been sent for to preach at Crathie; and I am sure I would not have known if I was on my head or my heels. It's a thing that will come sooner or later; but there will be all the difference, no doubt, between seeing the Queen dressed up at a drawing-room, and seeing her in her own house, just as you might see a friend."

"The difference will be all in Mr. Seton's advantage—when that comes to pass," said Miss Margaret, with some satire in her voice.

"And do the wives go, too? Dear me, that will be a delightful ploy for you," said Miss Jean, who, for her part, had not the slightest intention of offence.

At this Mrs. Seton, who was very good-natured, ended the episode by a laugh.

"I am sure they ought to; for what is a man without his wife? Robert, I am sure, would never put on his collar straight, if I was not there," she said; and hurried away, intent on hospitable cares. It was then that Miss Jean found courage to address the stranger, who had left the piano for the moment, in consequence of a little bustle about supper, and was standing by, with his friendly face smiling upon the party in general, but without any individual occupation.

"You will excuse me," said Miss Jean, "but I must make you my compliment upon your music—and more than your music," she said, looking, to see how he would take it, into his face.

"There has not been very much music," he said, with a smile. "It was a mistake to begin anything serious."

"It was perhaps a mistake; for you did not know how little the grand music is understood," said Miss Jean. "But, if you will let me say it, it was very fine of you, being just a young man, not used to be disappointed."

"Indeed," said Lewis, "I am not unused to be disappointed." Then he laughed. "It was not worth calling a disappointment. It is all new here, and it amused me like the rest."

"But I call it a fine thing to change like that in a moment, and play their waltz for them," said Miss Jean. "It means a fine nature—neither dour nor hasty."

"Jean," said Miss Margaret, with an admonitory glance, "you are probably giving your opinion where it is not wanted."

"Don't say so, please!" cried Lewis, putting his hands together in a gesture of entreaty. It was one of those foreign ways which they all liked, though they would scoff at them in the abstract. "I am very glad I pleased you. That makes me more happy even than if—the company" (he intended to say you, but paused, perceiving that he must not identify these ladies with the company) "had liked music better."

"But you must not think," said Miss Jean, "that they don't like music. They are very fond of it in their way, as much as persons can be without education."

"She means," said Miss Margaret again, "that your high music is not common with us. You see, we have not Handel in every church like you. England is better off in some things. But, if you speak of education in general, it is far behind—oh, far behind! Every common person here has a chance with the best."

"And do you like that?" Lewis said.

"Do I like it? Do I like democracy, and the levelling down of all we were brought up to believe in? Oh, no. But, on the other hand, I like very well that a clever lad should have the means of bettering himself. There is good and evil in everything that is human," said Miss Margaret, very gravely.

Lewis stood before her, with the smile still upon his face, observing her very slowly, wondering, if she knew who he was, whether she would consider him as a clever lad who had bettered himself. He could not have gazed so, without offence, into a younger face; as it was, his fixed look made Miss Margaret smile. To blush for anything so young a man could do, she would have thought beneath her dignity.

"You think what I am saying is very strange?" she said.

"Oh, no; it is very just, I think," he cried; but at this moment Mr. Dunlop, the young assistant at Braehead, came forward to offer Miss Margaret his arm. Lewis offered his to Miss Jean. "This is not wrong?" he said. "One does not require to wait to be told?"

"But I am sure a young lady would be more to your taste," said Miss Jean, smiling benignly. "Never mind me; I will go in in time. And look at all these pretty creatures waiting for somebody."

But Lewis continued to stand with one arm held out, with his hat under the other, and the bow which some thought so French, but the Miss Murrays considered to be of the old school. Miss Jean accepted his escort in spite of herself. She said,

"I would like to hear you play the rest of yon upon our old piano. It was a very good piano in its day, but, like its mistress, it is getting old now."

"A good instrument is like a lady; it does not get old like a common thing. It is always sweet," said Lewis. "I will come with—happiness."

An Englishman, of course, would have said with pleasure, but these little slips on the part of Lewis, which were sometimes half intentional, were all amply covered by his accent.

"I will play to you as much as you please," he added. "I have nothing here to do."

"But you came for the trout?" said Miss Jean. "No, no, I will not take you from the trout. My sister Margaret would never hear of that. But when the fishing is over, perhaps—"

"I am no fisher. I sit and watch while Adam struggles with the trout; it amuses me. But abroad, I suppose, we are less out of doors than in England. Mr. Stormont tells me we may expect a great many wet days, and what shall I have to do? May I come and play Beethoven during the wet days?"

"We will see what Margaret says," said Miss Jean, a little alarmed lest she should be going too far.

Miss Margaret was on the other side of the table. He looked at her with a great deal of interest. She was a dark-eyed woman, looking older than her age, with hair which had a suspicion of grey in it. Miss Jean had no grey hairs. Her cheek was a little hollow, but that was almost the only sign of age in her. But they dressed beyond their years, and were quite retired among the matrons, neither of them making the slightest claim to youth.

"Miss Margaret is your elder sister?" he said, with an ingratiating openness. "Pardon me, if I am very full of curiosity. I have seen your old castle, and I met you once upon the road; but there were then three ladies—?"

"That was Lilias," said Miss Jean. "She is quite young, poor thing. We stand in the place of mothers to her, and there are some times that I think Margaret over-anxious. She will always rather do too much than too little."

"She has a countenance that is very interesting," said Lewis. Fortunately, he could not say here a face that amused him, which he might have done, had he not been very desirous of pleasing, and anxious not to offend.

"Has she not?" cried Miss Jean, triumphantly. "She has just the very finest countenance! When she was young, I can assure you, she was very much admired."

"I see no reason why she should not continue to be admired," said Lewis.

"Oh, we have given up everything of that kind," said Miss Jean with a little laugh.

But, for almost the first time, she felt inclined to ask, Why should they? A woman of forty is not an old woman. And Miss Jean was very conscious that she herself was only thirty-eight.

"Perhaps it is the charge we have. I could not really say what it is—but all that has been long over. We have not been very long in this county. I think I may say that we will be glad to see you, and show you the old house. And then there is the other place," Miss Jean continued. It was a little exciting to her to talk to "an utter stranger," there were so few that ever appeared in Murkley. "But there is nothing in that to see, only the outside. And whoever passes is welcome to see the outside."

"The country people think it is haunted," said Lewis.

"No, no; that is just a fancy. It is not haunted, it is quite a new place. If you want a place that is haunted, there is our old Walk. There is no doubt about that. We are so used to it that nobody is frightened, and I rather like it myself. We will let you see that," Miss Jean said.

She was pleased with the stranger's bright face and deferential looks, and, in her simple kindness, was eager to find out something that would please him, though always with a doubt which dashed her pleasure whether she was doing what her sister would approve.

"That will give me great happiness," said Lewis again. "It is all to me very new and delightful to see the houses and the castles. I have been to Mr. Stormont's house to-day. I have seen a great many old châteaux abroad; but here it is more simple and more strange. To be great persons and seigneurs, and yet not any more great than that."

Miss Jean looked at him with a little suspicion, not understanding.

"We have never travelled," she said, after a little pause. "Which was a pity, I have often thought: and Margaret is of that opinion too. It might have made a great difference to us."

She sighed a little as she spoke, and Lewis felt a hot wave of shame and trouble go over him. She meant, no doubt, that, if they had travelled, he would never have been thus mingled in their fate. He did not know what to say, for a sudden panic seized him lest she should find him out. Good Miss Jean had no idea that there was anything to find out. She ate her little piece of chicken daintily, anxious all the time lest she should be detaining her companion from the dancing, or from the society of the young people.

"Supper was really quite unnecessary after such a tea. It is a thing we never take."

"You must try a little of this cream, Miss Jean," cried Mrs. Seton. "It is none of your confectioner's cream, that is all just froth put into a refrigerator, but our own making, and I can recommend it: or a little jelly. The jelly had scarcely time to stand; it is not so clear as I should like; but you know the difficulty with country cooks. And, Mr. Murray, I hope you will make a good supper. I am sure there is nobody we have been so much obliged to. Everybody is speaking about your wonderful playing. Oh, yes, yes, I am inclined to be jealous, that is quite true. They used to be very well content with me, and now they will think nothing of me. But I am just telling Katie that, if she thinks she is going to get a fine performer like you to play her bits of waltzes, she is very much mistaken. Once in a way is very well—and I am sure they are all very grateful—but now they must just be content, as they have always been hitherto with mamma. They are just ungrateful monkeys. You must be content with me, Katie, and very glad to get me. That is all I have to say."

"If Miss Katie would wish me to hold the piano for the rest of the evening?—that is, when I have re-conducted this lady to the drawing-room."

"Oh, will you?" cried Katie, with tones of the deepest gratitude. "It is only one waltz. Mamma never lets us have more than one waltz after supper; and it will be so kind; and we will enjoy it so much. Just one waltz more."

"But let it be a long one," the others cried, getting round him.

Lewis smiled, and waved his hand with the most genial satisfaction in thus so easily pleasing everybody.

"But I must first re-conduct this lady," he said.

CHAPTER VIII

"Was it Murray they called him?"

This question was put to Miss Jean, who had confessed, with a little hesitation, her rashness in inviting the stranger "to play his music" at the Castle, as the sisters walked home. It was a very sweet evening; not later than eleven o'clock, notwithstanding all the dancing. The ladies had left, however, before that last waltz, and the music continued in their ears half the way home, gradually dying away as they left the green lane which led to the manse, and got into the park. Miss Jean was, as she described afterwards, "really shy" of telling Margaret the venture she had made; for to meet a stranger whom you know nothing about out is a very different thing from asking him to your house, especially when it was a young man; and there was always Lilias to think upon. So that on the whole Miss Jean felt that she had been rash.

"To tell you the truth, I cannot say I noticed, Margaret. Yes, I rather think it was Murray; but you never catch a name when a person is introduced to you. And, after all, I am not sure. It might be me she was calling Murray—though, to be sure, she never calls me anything but Miss Jean."

"If it was Murray, it will be easy to find out to what family he belongs," said Miss Margaret. "And Lilias need not appear."

"Dear me," cried Miss Jean; "but that would be a great pity, Margaret, and a great disappointment to the young man. I thought to myself to ask him to come and play was a kind of liberty with a stranger, but then, I thought, it will be a pleasure to him, poor lad, to see such a pretty creature as our Lily. It is not much we have to give in return."

"I am not fond of young men coming to stare at Lilias," said Miss Margaret. "You forget she has no mother. You and me are bound to be doubly particular; and how do we know what might happen? She is very inexperienced. She might like the looks of him; for he has a pleasant way with him—or, even if it were not so bad as that, yet who can tell? it might be hurtful to the young man's own peace of mind."

"Well, that is true, Margaret," said Miss Jean. "I thought it would have been better to consult you first— but, dear me, one cannot think of everything; and it seems so innocent for two young people to meet once in a way, especially when the young man has his head full of his music, and is thinking about nothing else."

"That's a very rare case, I am thinking," Miss Margaret said.

"It is a very rare case for a young man to be musical at all," Miss Jean replied, with a little heat—which was an unquestionable fact on Tayside.

They went along noiselessly, with their softly shod and softly falling feet, two slim, dark figures in the pale twilight, with the maid trotting after them. But for her plump youthfulness, they might have been three congenial spirits of the place in a light so fit for spiritual appearances. There was nothing more said until they had almost reached home; then Miss Margaret delivered herself of the conclusion to which she had been coming with so much thought.

"It was perhaps a little rash—considering the charge we have, and that the young man is an utter stranger—but one cannot think of everything, as you say. And I cannot see why you should be deprived of a pleasure—there are not so many of them—because of Lilias. We will say just nothing about it. We will trust to Providence. The likelihood is she will be busy with her lessons, poor thing, and she will think it is just you playing the piano."

"Me!" cried Miss Jean, "playing like yon."

"Well, well, you know I am no judge, and Lilias not much better. If he can satisfy me what Murrays he belongs to, and can stand a near inspection, she may come in; I'll make no objection," Miss Margaret said, graciously, as she opened the door.

The key was turned when the family went to bed, but the hall-door of Murkley Castle stood open all day long in primitive security. Miss Jean lingered a little upon the steps.

"It is just the night," she said, "to take a turn down the Walk."

"Oh, you'll not do that, mem!" cried Susie, the maid.

"And why not, you silly lassie? If you'll come with me, you will see there is nothing to fear."

"Eh no, mem!" cried Susie; "no, if you would give me the Castle to mysel'."

"What is that you are saying about the Walk? Come in, Jean, it is too late for any of your sentiment. And, Susie, my woman, go you to your bed. If we had any business in the Walk, both you and me would go, be you sure, and I would like to see you say no to your mistress. Come in, that I may lock the door."

Nobody contradicted Miss Margaret in that house. Miss Jean glided in most submissively, and Susie behind her, trying hard, but ineffectually, to make as little noise. But, in spite of herself, Susie's feet woke echoes on the old oak floor, and so did the turning of the key in the great door. The noises roused at least one of the inhabitants. Old Simon, the butler, indeed slept the sleep of the just in a large chair, carefully placed at the door of the passage which led to "the offices," in order that he might hear when the ladies came home; but Lilias appeared presently at the head of the fine old open staircase, which descended, with large and stately steps, into the hall. She had an open book laid across her arm, and her eyes were shining with excitement and impatience. They had wept, and they had perhaps dozed a little, these eyes, but were now as wide open as a child's when it wakes in the middle of the night. Her hair was tumbled a little, for she had been lying on a sofa, and a white shawl was round her shoulders; for even in a June night, in an old house with all the windows open, especially when you are up late, you are apt to feel cold on Tayside. She held a candle in her hand, which made a spot of brightness in the dim light.

"Oh, Margaret," she said, "oh, Jean! is that you at last; and was it a dance? I went up to the tower, and I am sure I heard the piano."

"You would be sure to hear the piano whatever it was," said Margaret, silencing her sister by giving a sudden pull to her gown. "There is always music at the manse. There was a grand sonata by one of Jean's favourites, and her head is so full of it she can talk nothing but music."

"Oh, a sonata!" cried Lilias, relieved, and she gave her head a small toss, and laughed; "that is a long, long thing on the piano, and you are never allowed to say a word. I'm glad that I was not there."

"That was what I told you," said Miss Margaret. "Now go to your bed, and you'll hear all the rest to-morrow. You should have been in your bed an hour ago at least. To-morrow you shall have a full account of everything, and Jean will play you a piece of the sonata. I am sure she has got it all in her head."

"Oh, I'm not minding!" said Lilias, lightly.

She thought, on the whole, her novel had been better.

She stood thus lighting them as they came up-stairs, and they thought her the prettiest creature that had ever been seen; her sweet complexion shining against the dark wainscot, her eyes giving out more light than the candle. It smote Miss Jean's heart to deceive her, and it was a faltering kiss which she gave to this little victim. But Miss Margaret carried things with a high hand.

"It would be just barbarous," Miss Margaret said, when they were safe within the little suite of rooms that formed their apartment, one chamber opening into the other, "to tell her all about it to-night. You can tell her to-morrow, when there's a new day in her favour. She would just cry and blear her eyes; but to-morrow is a new day."

"I cannot bide," cried Miss Jean, "whatever you may say, Margaret—I just cannot bide to disappoint the darling. I am sure it went to my heart to see her just now so sweet and bonnie, and nobody to look at her but you and me."

"The bonnier she is, and the sweeter she is, is that not all the more reason, ye foolish woman, to keep her safe from vulgar eyes? Would you make her, in all her beauty, cheap and common at these bits of parties at the manse? No, no. We had no mother either, and perhaps we did not have our right chance, but that's neither here nor there. We're in the place of mothers to her, and Lilias shall have her day!"

This silenced Miss Jean, whose mind was dazzled by her sister's greater purposes and larger grasp. She retired to her inner room with a compunction, feeling guilty. It was a shame to deceive even for the best motives, she felt; but, on the other hand, she could relieve her conscience to-morrow, and there was such sense in all Margaret said.

"Margaret is just a wonderful creature for sense," Miss Jean said to herself. This had indeed been her chief consolation in all the difficulties of her life.

Meanwhile, other conversations were going on among the groups which streamed from the manse, taken leave of heartily by the family at the gate. It was "such a fine night" that Mrs. Seton herself threw a shawl over her head, and walked, with those of her friends who were walking, to the gate.

"Oh, yes, yes, I'll not deny, though I say it that shouldn't, I think it has gone off very well," she said; "and, indeed, we have to thank Mr. Murray, for I take no credit to myself to-night. Oh, yes, I'll allow in a general way I do my best to keep you all going: but, dear me! I'm not to be mentioned by the side of Mr. Murray. A performer like him condescending to play your bits of waltzes and polkas for you!—you ought to be very proud. Oh, yes, I know fine playing when I hear it, though I never did much, except in the way of dance music, myself. In dance music I used to think I would give in to nobody; but pride will have a fall, and I have just sense enough to know when I'm beaten—oh, yes, that I am. You'll be very glad to come back to me when Mr. Murray is not to be had, I make no doubt; you are just ungrateful monkeys, but I'll trust you for that."

Mrs. Seton's voice ran on in a sort of continued solo, to which all the other murmurs of talk afforded an accompaniment. She shook hands with Lewis at the gate with the most cordial friendliness.

"And whenever you weary," she said, "be sure you just come up to the manse. Mr. Seton will always be glad of a talk, and there is nothing I like so well as to hear about foreign society and scenery and all that; and I can understand it better than most, for I have been up the Rhine myself: and Katie will be most grateful for a little help with her German; so, you see, you'll be welcome on every hand," the lady said, with a grasp of his hand which meant everything she said.

Lewis walked to the river-side with young Stormont, who was not quite so cordial.

"You've had it all your own way to-night, Murray," this young fellow said, with a laugh which was not pleasant to hear.

"They are very kind to a stranger—it is true hospitality; but I think it was you that had it your own way, for you would not listen to my music," said Lewis. Then he, too, laughed—a laugh which was to the other's like sunshine to a cloud. "I did cheat you all the same," he added, "for the waltz was Beethoven's too—and quite as difficult, if you had but known."

Mr. Stormont did not understand much about Beethoven, but he felt that it was impossible to say the fellow was stuck-up about his music; privately in his own mind he despised all male performances as things unworthy of the sex.

"Miss Seton dances very prettily with you, my friend," said Lewis. "You have practised much together, that is what one can see. I watched you while I was playing. She dances always well, but better with you than anyone. But tell me, for you know, about those ladies whom everyone calls Miss Margaret and Miss Jean."

"Oh, the old ladies at Murkley! Why, these are the people we were talking about on Sunday. You made a great impression there—we all noticed," cried Stormont, with a laugh, which this time was somewhat rude, but quite cordial, "the impression you made there."

"Yes?" said Lewis, gravely; with the thoughts he had in his mind he did not mean to allow any ridicule. "It is the Miss Margaret that is the eldest. She will have everything, I suppose, in your English way."

"Oh, if that is what you are thinking of," cried Stormont, in a startled tone; and then he stopped and laughed again, the sound this time pealing into all the echoes. "No, no, my fine fellow," he said, "if that's what you're thinking of, you are out there; when it's women, they're co-heiresses. The law has not so good an opinion of them as to make an eldest son of a woman: so you're out there."

"Out there!" said Lewis, astonished. "What does that mean? And I do not understand co-heiresses either? These ladies—no, I will not say amuse me—I am interested in them. I have heard of them before I came here—indeed, it was for that cause," he added, with one of his imprudent confidences, then stopped short, giving emphasis to what he said. "What is meant by co-heiresses, if you please?"

"It means," said Stormont, with a chuckle of mingled ridicule and contempt, "that when there are sisters they share and share alike. It was not very much to begin with, so you may judge, when it is divided, whether it is worth anyone's while now. But try, my fine fellow, try; you will not find many rivals," he added, with a scream of laughter.

Lewis looked up very gravely as he walked along by his companion's side.

"There is something which amuses you," he said; "perhaps it is that I am slow in English. I do not perceive the joke."

"Oh, there is no joke," said Stormont, coming to himself; and they walked to the river-side, where the ferryman was waiting, in a subdued condition, neither saying much. Lewis, who had been in extremely high spirits after his success at the party, had suddenly fallen into a blank of embarrassment and perplexity, which silenced him altogether. He was angry, without quite knowing why, with Stormont. But this was nothing to the confusion which had overwhelmed his mind. He walked up to his own inn in a state of bewilderment which it would be difficult to describe. It was partially comic, but it was not until he had reached his parlour, and seated himself opposite to the little paraffin lamp, which always smelt a little, and gave to his most intimate thoughts a sort of uneasy odour, that he was able to laugh at his own discomfiture; then gradually the amusing aspect of the whole business came over him; he laughed, but neither long nor loud. It was too disagreeable, too annoying to laugh at after the first realization of the dilemma. He was quite hushed and silenced in his simple mind by the discovery he had made.

For it is time now to put plainly before the reader the intention with which this young man had come to Murkley. It was with the well-considered purpose of remedying the evident mistake which his old friend and patron had made. Sir Patrick had withdrawn his fortune from his own family, and given it to his adopted son, leaving his grandchildren poor, while Lewis was rich—Lewis, who had what people call, "no claim" upon him, who had only been his son and servant for eight years of his life, giving him the love, and care, and obedience which few sons give with so entire a devotion. He had no claim but this, and he had expected nothing. When he found himself Sir Patrick's heir, and a rich man, no one was so much surprised as Lewis; but still, so it was, and he accepted his patron's will as he would have accepted anything else that happened in which he himself had a share. But, as soon as he heard of the family and their disappointment, Lewis had made up his mind that he must do his best to remedy it. It would be his duty, he thought, to offer himself and his possessions to the lady who ought to have been Sir Patrick's heir. When he had discovered that these ladies at Murkley were no longer young, it would be too much to assert that it was not a shock to him. But the shock lasted only for a moment. He had not come to Murkley with the intention of pleasing his own fancy, but to fulfil a duty; and the age of the lady, or her appearance, or any such secondary matter was little to him. In all the easy and lighthearted acceptance of the position which characterised him, he had never for a moment allowed himself to think that he was free to abandon his plan, if, on examining into it, it proved against his tastes. His tastes, after all, were involved only in a secondary degree. Duty was the first, and to that nothing made any difference. If Sir Patrick's heiress had been fifty, or if she had been deformed and ugly, he would still have laid his fortunes at her feet. It did not indeed occur to him to separate himself from the fortune, and offer the money alone. He was not a Quixote. To denude himself of all he had did not occur to him as a natural thing to do: but to share it was more than natural, it was an obligation, a call of honour. It was with this view that he had looked at Miss Margaret across the table. It was impossible not to feel that the relationship would be a peculiar one, but he felt nothing in himself that would prevent him from entering into it worthily. Lewis had none of that physical instinct of superiority which makes men despise women. He did not think, as unfortunately most men do, with a curious want of generosity, that the first object of a woman's life must be to secure a husband, and that every sense of congruity, all good taste and delicacy of liking, must succumb to this imperious necessity. This was not the least in his thoughts. When he looked at Miss Margaret, the thought in his mind was not so much any objection of his own to marry her, as the certainty that she would object to marry him. He felt that it would be a derogation, that she would come down from her dignity, give up her high estate, if she accepted what he had to offer.

He studied her face with this idea in his mind. Was it the least likely that a woman with a countenance like that would buy even justice so? Miss Jean, to whom he was talking, was more malleable. It bewildered him a good deal to look at them, and to think that one or the other of these ladies before whom he bowed so low, who looked at him with timidly suspicious eyes of middle age, might, should, must, if he had his way, become his wife. But in his own person he never hesitated; he did not know how it was to be brought about. If it could be done, as "abroad," by the intervention of an agent, the matter would have been greatly simplified. But this, he was partially aware, was not possible in England. Neither in England, according to what he had heard, would it be possible to settle it as a friendly arrangement, a piece of mercenary business. No, he knew he must conform to English rules, if he would be successful, and woo the wronged lady with all the ordinary formulas. He would have to fall in love with her, represent himself as dying for her. All these preliminaries Lewis had felt to be hard, but he had determined within himself to go through with them. He would be heroically tender, he would draw upon novels and his imagination for the different acts of the drama, and carry them through with unflinching courage. He was resolved that nothing should be wanting on his part. But it cannot be denied that Stormont's revelation took him altogether aback. Co-heiresses!—he could not offer himself to two ladies—he could not declare love and pretend passion for two! He remembered even that there was a third, the one in the blue veil, and it was this thought that at last touched an easier chord in his being, and relieved him with a long low tremulous outburst of laughter.

"Three!" he said to himself all at once, and he laughed till the tears stood in his eyes. He had been ready loyally to overcome all other objections, to bend before a beloved object of forty, and to declare that his happiness was in her hands, with the purest loyalty of heart and truth of intention; but before three— that was impossible—that was out of the question. He laughed till he was ready to cry; then he dried his eyes, and took himself to task as disrespectful to the ladies, who had done nothing to forfeit anyone's respect, and then burst forth into laughter again. Here was indeed a reductio ad absurdum, beyond which it was impossible to go. Lewis tried hard to bring himself back to the point from which he started—the sacred duty, as he felt, of restoring his fortune to the source whence it came—but he could not get past this tremendous, unthought-of obstacle. Three of them! and he could not marry more than one, whatever he did. Now, also, it became evident that injustice must be done in whatever way the difficulty should be settled. He had endeavoured to believe, it is needless to say, that the representative of the Murrays might have turned out to be young and marriageable; he had been dazzled by bright hopes that she might be fair and sweet, and everything a bride should be. When these hopes and visions dispersed in the sober certainty that the heiress of the Murrays was the eldest of three all much above his own age, it had been a disenchantment, but he had stood fast. He had not been afraid even of Miss Margaret—he had said to himself that he would respect and venerate her, and be grateful to one who would thus stoop to him from the serene heights; but to make up for the slights of fortune to three ladies at once—Lewis, with the best will in the world, felt that this would not be in his power.

When he got up next morning, the mirth of the night was over; he felt then that the position was too serious for laughter. For a moment the temptation of giving up altogether a duty which was too much for him came over his mind. Why should not he go away altogether and keep what was his? He was not to blame; he had asked nothing, expected nothing. He was guiltless towards the descendants of his old friend, and they knew nothing either of him or of his intentions. He had but to go away, to walk back to the 'George' at Kilmorley, and turn back into the world, leaving his portmanteaux to follow him, and he would be free. But somehow this was an expedient which did not please his imagination at all. The little rural place, the people about who had become his friends, the family with which he felt he had so much to do, kept a visionary hold upon him from which he could not get loose. He struggled even a little, repeating to himself many things which he could do if he were to free himself. He had never seen London—he had never been in England. The season was not yet entirely over, nor London abandoned; he could yet find people there whom he had met, who would introduce him, who would carry him to those country-houses in which he had always heard so much of the charm of England lay. All this he went over deliberately, trying to persuade himself that in the circumstances it was the best thing to do;

but the result of his thoughts was that, as soon as he felt it was decorous to do so, he set out for the Castle. One visit, in any case, could do, he reflected, no harm.

CHAPTER IX

The next day, as Adam had prophesied, the weather changed, or rather it changed during the night, and the morning rose pale and weeping, with a sky out of which all colour had departed, and an endless blast, almost white, so close was the shower, of falling rain. Little rivulets ran away down the pebbly slope of the village street towards the river when Lewis got up; the trees were all glistening; the birds all silenced; a perpetual patter of rain filling the air. The country carts that stood at the door of the 'Murkley Arms' had the air of having been boiled; the horse glossy yet sodden, with ears and tail in the most lugubrious droop; the paint of the wheels and shafts glistening, the carter, with a wet sack over his wet shoulders, looking as if the water could be wrung out of him. He was being served with a dram by Janet at the door, who had her shawl over her cap to preserve her.

"Now tak' my advice," she was saying, "and be content with that. It's good whiskey. If you stop at every door to get something to keep out the damp, ye'll be in a bonnie condition to go home to your wife at the hinder end."

"Would ye have me get my death o' cauld?" said the man.

"Eh!" said Janet, "I daurna refuse to serve ye; for ye would just gang straight to Luckie Todd's, and her whiskey's bad, and siller is a' her thocht; but weel I wat, if ye were my man, I wad rather ye got your death of cauld than of whiskey. And that's my principle, though I keep a public mysel'."

Lewis, standing at his window, with the paths and the roofs all glistening before him, and the sky so low down that it seemed almost to touch the high gable of the house opposite, listened to the dialogue with a smile. It was a new aspect under which he now saw the village life. Many of the doors were shut which usually stood open; the children had disappeared from the road; silence took the place of the small, cheerful noises, the calls of the women, the chatter of the infants; the cocks and hens, which generally strutted about in full liberty, had taken refuge beneath a cart, where they huddled together lugubriously—everything was changed. Lewis could not but think of young Stormont, with a shrug of malicious pleasure, as he amused himself with his breakfast: for he supposed erroneously that this must be one of the days of which Stormont had spoken so sadly, when there was nothing to do. But by-and-by Lewis also found that there was nothing to do. He laughed at himself, which was still more comic. Stormont was at home; he had his library, though he did not make use of it; and his mother's piano, though he knew nothing about music; and he had no doubt some sort of business concerning his small estate, and he had spoken of amusing himself with fly-making and gun-cleaning. But Lewis soon woke up to the sad conviction that, so far as he was concerned, there was absolutely nothing to occupy the heavy hours. Of the two or three books which the 'Murkley Arms' could boast, one was Robertson's 'History of Scotland' in a small form, with small print, discouraging to a careless reader, and another the 'Romance of the Forest.' He was not a great reader under the best of circumstances, and these did not tempt him. He had few correspondents, none indeed to whom he could sit down on a dreary day and unbosom himself. The only thing that offered him any distraction was his drawing. He took out his sketch-books, and selected one he had made on the water-side, in order to enlarge and complete it. But he was not enthusiastic enough to work steadily, and he was unfortunately aware that his slightest sketches were his best. When Janet came up-stairs "to speak about the denner," as she said, her compassion was aroused by his evident weariness.

"Adam's awa' to the watter," she said. "Watter below and watter aboon, he'll get plenty o't. It's a grand day for the fushin', though it's no so good for us poor mortals. Would ye no gang doon, and see how he's getting on?"

"But it pours," said Lewis, "and with water above and water below, as you say—"

"Hoot ay," said Janet, "but ye're young, and ye're neither sugar nor salt, you'll no melt. At your age a bit of a shower does little harm; and ye're just wrang biding in the house all day with nothing to do."

"That is true enough," Lewis said, but as he looked at the pouring rain and the wet roads he shook his head. "I don't see that one can gain much by getting wet, Mrs. Janet."

"Dear me! a young gentleman at your age! Weel, it's a grand thing to take care of yourself. It's just what ye canna get young folk to do. There's young Mr. Philip out on the water from the skreigh of day; he just never minds. I'm no saying it's good for him. But they say it's grand weather for the fushin', and that makes up for everything with them, the gomerals. If they had your sense, Mr. Murray."

Lewis did not think she had a very high opinion of his sense, and he was somewhat piqued by her suspicious semi-approval, and by her description of Stormont, in whom the young man had come to see an antagonistic type of mankind. The more fool he, if he had been out all the morning between the water below and the water above, all for the sake of a few fish. But the description piqued Lewis. He stood at his window, and looked out for the twentieth time, and it did not look tempting. Why, indeed, should he go out, and get himself wet and dirty to please the prejudices of Janet. He had always heard that the English went out in all weathers; that they had even a preference for mud and damp, characteristic features of their own climate. But why should he emulate this strange fancy? He sat down to his drawing again, but he did not get any satisfaction out of it. Not to be approved of was terrible to him. He could not bear that even Janet should have a small opinion of his hardiness and manly bearing. This acted so strongly upon Lewis that after a while he found himself pulling on his strongest boots and getting into his thickest great-coat. The boots were not very strong; he had never had any chance of those exposures to water and weather in which impervious coverings are necessary; but, having protected himself as well as he could, he sallied forth at last with his umbrella, and went down to the river-side. There was little or no wind, and the rain fell in a perpendicular flood, soaking everything. Lewis under his umbrella went patiently on, enduring it manfully, but unable to see any pleasure in his progress through the flood. He met Katie Seton and her brother near the church. She was covered up in an ulster, with a hood over her little hat. Her cheeks were like roses "just washed in a shower."

"Oh, we never stay in for anything," she said. "It is always better out than in."

Lewis in his courtesy would have made over his umbrella, but the girl would none of it.

"Oh, I can't bear to carry an umbrella," she said.

He went on to the river-side with a little shrug of his shoulders. And there was Adam, drenched, but glowing, pulling out trout after trout, too busy to talk; and lower down the stream, in the middle of it, amid the rush of broken water, where the river swirled round the rock, young Stormont, almost up to his middle, in great fishing-boots, with sluices of water flowing from his glazed sou'-wester.

"Jolly day!" Stormont cried through the rain.

"Grand for the trout," said Adam.

Lewis stood on the bank under the umbrella and shrugged his shoulders.

"I wish you joy of it," he said. His feet were growing wet, the rain, though there was no wind, came in his face with something like a special malice. He thought there was something savage in the gratification of the two fishers. After he had watched them for a time, he asked Adam for some of the trout in his basket, and went home, carrying, with no great delight in the office, two noble trout tied together with a string. These were cold and slimy, but he overcame his repugnance. Janet saw him return, with his wet feet and the fish hanging from his hand, with a mixture of amusement and dissatisfaction.

"Will they be for your lunch?" she said, with a contemptuous thought of the fondness for eating with which Scotland always credits the Englishman.

"Oh, no," Lewis cried, with horror; "do you think I would carry these things for myself? Put them in a basket; I will take them to the Castle, where," he added, with a little innocent pleasure in making the announcement, "I am going this afternoon."

Janet looked at him with a certain contemptuous disappointment. She thought he was going to carry the fish as a proof of his own skill and prowess.

"I'll maybe no find a basket. What ails ye at them as they are?" she said, with lowering brows: which our young man did not understand at all, for it is needless to say that such an idea never crossed his ingenuous mind.

He went up-stairs a little surprised that not even now, when he had proved his manhood by wetting his boots (which he hastened to change), did he please Mrs. Janet, as he called her, but without the slightest clue to her suspicions. And after he had got into dry apparel, and eaten his luncheon, Lewis sallied forth once more, much pleased to be able to say that he was going to the Castle, where, indeed, the sound of the bell at the door stirred and excited the whole household, which had no hope of anything so refreshing as a visitor.

Miss Margaret was seated above-stairs with Lilias in a room devoted to what was called her studies, and generally known by the title of the book-room, though there were but few books in it. Lilias jumped up and rushed to the window in the very midst of the chapter of constitutional history which she was reading with her self-denying elder sister.

"There is no carriage," she said; "it will be somebody from the village."

"Never mind who it is," said Miss Margaret; "we must finish our chapter."

When the sound of music was diffused through the house some time after, Miss Margaret had a shrewd guess as to who the visitor was, and all the objections that existed to his introduction to Lilias came up before her mind, while the girl pursued, alas! very dully, the history of parliamentary institutions. "It will be the tuner come to put the piano in order," she said by-and-by, she too speaking unawares in the middle of a sentence. She felt that it was a fib, but yet it was not necessarily a fib, for why should not it be the tuner? It was about his time, she said to herself. This took from Lilias all desire to go down-stairs, all expectation of a break in the dulness. She went on with the drone of the history, which, to tell the truth, was quite as much a burden to Miss Margaret as to herself. But duty reigned supreme in the bosom of the elder sister, and Lilias had always been submissive. She was well aware, too, of the advantage of having Margaret instead of a governess. Miss Jackson would not have permitted her to slip to the window with her book in her hand to see who it was.

Miss Jean was alone in the drawing-room, which was a large room, with a number of small windows, high set in the thick old walls, each with its own little recess. It was not light generally, but there were a great many Rembrandtish effects, intense lights and shadows in bright weather. To-day all was a sort of monotone of greenish dimness: the wet trees glistening; the expanse of the wet park throwing a vague reflection into the air. The room occupied a corner of the house, and the windows on one side looked out upon a lime-tree walk, which lay under the old enclosing wall, a high, semi-defensible erection, with a turret at the corner; and on the other looked on the park, which sloped downward towards the river. To the right hand the red-and-blue roofs of the village glistened under the rain, the tiles giving a little gleam of colour which the slates did their best to neutralize. Nothing could be more complete than the air of mutual protection and dependence which the village and the Castle bore, though the Castle was but a small and homely representative of power. Miss Jean sat alone in the window which commanded this prospect most fully. She had all her work materials there; a basket of fine silks in every shade, a case of pretty, shining silver implements, scissors, and thimbles, and bodkins, and on her lap a wonderful table-cover, upon which, as long as any of the young people remembered, she had been working a garland of flowers. It was her own invention, drawn from Nature, and consequently, as she sometimes explained with a little pride, the winter-time, which was the best time for working in general, was lost to her, since she always liked to have her models under her eyes. At the present moment, a little cluster of pansies was before her in a glass, and the colours arranged upon the table in which she was to copy them. But she was not working; her table-cover lay on her lap. She was looking out vaguely upon the rain, and the wet trees, and the village roofs. It was supposed that Miss Jean was the one of the family who leant towards the sentimental, and no doubt there had been incidents in her gentle life which justified the opinion. She was thinking, as she would have said—perhaps even so late as this the soft-hearted, middle-aged maiden was dreaming—but, if so, nobody was the wiser for Miss Jean's dreams. They never prevented her ready attention to any appeal, and she only indulged in them when quite alone. They alternated with the flowers of the table-cover in her mind, and both were emanations of the same soft and tender spirit. The room was very still around this one quiet figure; behind her the dim atmosphere was brighter with the glow of a small, but cheerful fire. It was the opinion of the Miss Murrays, as of many other comfortable people, that in wet weather an old house was always the better for a fire. The little pétillement of the fire and the soft rush of the falling rain outside were all the sounds audible in the extreme stillness. What wonder that Miss Jean should drop the embroidered pansies on her lap, and take to thoughts which were a sort of spiritual prototypes of the pansies—thoughtlets, little musings, dreamikins, so to speak; they brought now and then from her gentle bosom the softest little sigh, not a sigh that hurt, but one that soothed. There was no part of her time that Miss Jean liked better than these moments which she spent by herself, when Margaret was reading history with Lilias. She closed up a pretty little note-book, which had been in her hand, when she heard the sound of the bell. If truth must be told, she had been writing in it a pretty little verse—a pansy of still another kind; for Miss Jean belonged to the age when it was a pretty accomplishment to write charming little "copies of verses," a thing very sweet and delightful for a young woman to do.

The character of the place seemed to change at once when Lewis came in. Life, and cheerfulness, and variety came with him. He was very anxious to please and make himself agreeable. He told her of his walk to the water-side, of Stormont in the river, and Adam on the bank; water above and water below.

"You will think me very effeminate," he said. "I much prefer this nice drawing-room;" and he looked round it with an admiring air that pleased Miss Jean.

To tell the truth, Lewis was thinking that, though picturesque, it was probably damp, a suggestion which would not have pleased Miss Jean at all.

"Gentlemen are very venturesome," said Miss Jean; "indeed, the wonder is that they are not all laid-up with rheumatism—but they're used to it, I suppose."

"I am not at all used to it," said Lewis; and then he added, with one of his confidential impulses: "A great part of my life I have spent in attendance upon a dear old friend."

"Indeed," said Miss Jean, her eyes lighting up with interest. "That is out of the way for a young man. You will excuse me, but I take a great interest—not father or mother, as you say a friend?"

"No: my godfather, who took me up when my father and mother died, and who was like father and mother in one. He was lonely and old, and I never left him—for years."

As Lewis spoke there came a gleam of moisture into his eyes, as he looked smiling into the face of the sympathetic woman, who had she but known—But no suspicion crossed the mind of Miss Jean.

"Dear me!" she said; "lonely and old are sad words. And you gave up your young life to him? There are few that would have done that."

"Oh, no, there was no giving-up, it was my happiness," said Lewis; "no one was ever so kind; he was my dear companion. And then, you know, abroad"—he smiled as he said this generic word which answered for everywhere—"abroad boys are not all brought up to be athletic; to defy the elements, as in England—"

"I do not know very much about England," said Miss Jean, entirely unconscious that her visitor meant to embrace Tayside in this geographical term, "but there is too much fishing and shooting here. That is my opinion. I like a young man to be manly, but there are more things in the world than the trout and the birds. And no doubt you would learn your music to please your invalid? That is very touching. I took an interest from the first, but still more now when I know the cause."

"That reminds me," cried Lewis, "that my sole excuse for coming was to play to you."

"Don't say that, Mr. Murray. We are very glad to see you," said Miss Jean, though not without a quiver, "without any reason at all."

"That is very kind, more kind than I can say. A stranger has double reason to be grateful."

"The advantage is ours," said Miss Jean, with old-fashioned politeness; and then there was a momentary pause; for the question would obtrude itself upon her, in spite of herself, "What will Margaret say?"

And then Lewis went to the piano and began to play. Miss Jean took up her work and threaded her needle, and prepared for enjoyment, for to work and be read to, or hear music played to you was one of her beatitudes; but by-and-by the table-cover fell upon her knees again, and she turned her face towards the musician in a growing ecstacy of attention. Music is not like any other of the arts, it does not address itself to the intellect. Miss Margaret was far more clever than her sister, but she had no comprehension of Beethoven. Jean had the ear to hear. At first her mind was somewhat agitated by doubts whether her sister would approve, and even whether it was altogether prudent to have thus received a young man whom nobody knew. She thought of the text, "Lay hands suddenly on no man," and she was a little confused about the matter altogether. And, had she been like her sister, Miss Jean would have continued in this mood; she would have recognized that it was good playing, but her mind would have been able to consider the original question all through it, and her doubts, it is possible, might have been increased rather than set at rest by the proficiency of the young musician, a proficiency to which, so far as her experience went, very few gentlemen attained. But Miss Jean had a faculty which Margaret lacked. After a while she forgot everything but the divine strain that was in her ear. The table-cover slipped over her knees to the ground, and she was not even aware of it; the silks, so carefully arranged in their right shades, dropped too, and lay all tangled and mixed up on the carpet. Miss Jean did not care. She neither saw nor heard anything but the music; she sat with her hands clasped, her eyes fixed upon the piano, her mind absorbed. When he stopped, she could not speak; she waved her hand to him inarticulately, not even knowing what she wanted to say. And Lewis, after a little pause, resumed. It was some time since he had touched a piano, and his mind too was agitated and full of many questions. It was not for nought that he had got admittance here. Perhaps a little of the elevation of a martyr was in his thoughts. It had not occurred to him, so long as Sir Patrick lived, that he was sacrificing his youth to the old man. It had not occurred to him until he came here: now he seemed to see it more clearly. And he had come with the intention of sacrificing himself once more, of giving up natural choice and freedom, and returning his fortune (burdened indeed with himself) to the family from which it had come. It was only now with Miss Jean's mild eyes upon him that he fully realized all this. He kept looking at her, as he played, with close and anxious observation. Not an idea of the light in which she appeared to him was in Miss Jean's mind. That any man should be looking at her with the idea of making her his wife would have startled her beyond expression; but a young man—a youth whom she regarded as not much more than a boy! It is to be feared that Miss Jean's sentiments would have been those of resentment. She would have thought herself insulted. But, happily, there was not in anything around the smallest suggestion of such a purpose. If the ladies of Murkley considered an intruder dangerous, it was entirely on account of Lilias. To think of themselves never entered their minds; they were beyond all that. They had settled down upon their own unchangeable fortunes with great peace and tranquillity, putting themselves, so far as the hopes and happiness of life were concerned, into Lilias. She was to enjoy for them, to get advancement, to go to court, to have all the delights and honours which they had never known. Generally it is in their children that women thus live by proxy; these maiden sisters felt it a special boon of Providence that, unmarried and without succession as they were in life, they should have this special representative in the new generation. But even Lilias went out of Miss Jean's mind as she listened. She would have liked indeed that Lilias, that all she loved, should be here to share the benefit; but then she was aware that the benefit would have been much less to them. She had, therefore, a reason to herself for enjoying it alone. And the afternoon stole away while this wonderful delight went on. Lewis, though he was the performer, did not lose himself in the music as Miss Jean did. When he stopped at last, she could not speak to him; her eyes were full of tears. She made him again a little sign with her hand and was silent, waiting until she could come down from that upper region, in which she had been soaring, to common earth. Fortunately at this moment Miss Margaret came in.

"So you have been playing to Jean?" she said; "that is very amiable and very kind. She is not quite her own woman where music is concerned. I thought it best to leave the treat to her by herself, for I'm not a fanatic as she is. But I am very much obliged to you for giving my sister such a pleasure."

"The pleasure is," said Lewis, "to play to one who feels it so much."

"I can fancy that," said Miss Margaret, "that it is not just all on one side. You are meaning to settle in this country, Mr. Murray? There are many of our name hereabout. We may possibly count kin with you ourselves when we know what family ye are of."

"I fear not," Lewis said, shaking his head. He grew pale, and then he grew red. Here was a danger he had not thought of, and what was he to say?

"You must not say that. It is far more likely than not that we'll find ourselves cousins. All Murrays are sib to Murkley: they say, you know, that all Stuarts are sib to the king. I am not taking such state upon us as all that: the duke, he is the head of the clan: but still Murkley is far ben," said Miss Margaret, satisfied, but calm. "Probably, as you've been so long abroad, you are a little astray in your genealogy. I have often remarked that. But tell me your county, and I will tell you what branch you come from."

Lewis got up from the piano. He was glad to turn his back from the light, to conceal his embarrassment.

"Indeed," he said, "I can't tell you even that. My god-father had been long abroad; he spoke little of his people; his money was all in the funds. I knew only him, not his origin."

"That is very strange," Miss Margaret said. "There are no godfathers in our Scotch way; but I would have thought your good father and mother would have been particular about a man's antecedents before they made him responsible."

"Oh, my father and mother—" said Lewis—he was about to say knew nothing of him, but stopped himself in time—"they died," he said, hastily, "when I was very young, and he took me up, when I had nobody to care for me. It has all been love and kindness on his part, and, I hope, gratitude on mine."

"Indeed, and I am sure of that," said Miss Jean. "Just imagine, Margaret, a young man, not much more than a boy, and he has devoted himself to this old gentleman. It is not many that would do that. He has given up his youth to please him. He has learned to play like yon for his sake. He has been a son to him, and more. For my part, I never heard anything like it. He has not a poor mind like yours and mine to inquire was he Murray of this or that; he just loved him, and served him for love's sake. And is not that the best of all?" Miss Jean said. She was still in the rapture of the music she had heard; her heart touched, her eyes wet, her pulses all throbbing in unison. She rose up in her enthusiasm, letting the famous table-cloth drop again and walked on it, unconscious of what she was doing, till she came to the fire, near which her sister had established herself. Miss Jean leant her hand upon the high mantel-piece, which was a narrow shelf of marble, and stood up there, her head relieved against the white and highly-carved pediment. Her tall, slight figure, in its black gown, had a thrill of emotion about it. Miss Margaret, seated at a little distance in the glow of the small, bright fire, looked calm like a judge, listening and deciding, while the other had all the energy of an advocate.

"I am very glad to hear such a fine account of the young gentleman," she said.

"Your sister takes me on my own evidence," said Lewis. "It is only from me she has heard it, and I did not know I was telling her all that. What I told her was that my dear god-father was old and lonely, and that when I was with him I could not learn to wade in the water and devote myself to fishing like Stormont. It was jealousy made me say so," cried the young man. "I thought Stormont looked such a fine fellow risking his life for the trout, and me, I was sorry to get my feet wet. What a difference! and not to my advantage. So, to account for myself, and to be an excuse, I told my story. 'Qui s'excuse, s'accuse.' I had no right to say anything about it. It was my jealousy, nothing more."

"You can ring for the tea, Jean," Miss Margaret said. This was the only decision she delivered, but it was enough. She turned round afterwards and made an elaborate apology for her other sister. "You will be wondering you do not see Lilias," she said, "but she is much occupied; she has a great many things to do. Another time when you come I hope I may present you to her. She is so important to us all that perhaps we are more anxious than we need be. Jean and me, we are two, you see, to take care of her: and she is the chief object of our thoughts."

"I hope it is not bad health," Lewis said, "that makes you anxious." His idea was that Lilias must be the eldest sister, and perhaps beginning to succumb to the burdens of age.

Miss Margaret gave Miss Jean, who was about to speak, a warning look.

"No," she said, "it is not bad health; but there are many things to be taken into account. And here comes Simon with the tea," she added, in a tone of relief. If there was a mystery on his part, there was a little concealment and conscious deception upon theirs too.

CHAPTER X

Lewis was greatly elated by this easy beginning of his undertaking. Everything had been so new to him in these unknown regions that he did not know how he was to make his way, or whether it would be possible to penetrate into the circle of the ladies of Murkley at all. And now everything was so simple, so natural, that he wondered at his own fears. He was the acquaintance of the whole village, or rather "the haill toun," as they called themselves, and before he had been a fortnight in the place was taken for granted as a member of the little community. On the second rainy day he called at the manse, and for politeness sake was asked to play there, and was listened to with bustling attention by Mrs. Seton, while Katie discreetly yawned behind her work, and Mr. Seton recollected an engagement.

"I'm very sorry," the minister said, "but my time is not my own. We ministers are like doctors; we are constantly being called away."

Lewis was not offended by the good man's excuses, nor by little Katie's weariness. He played them his "piece," as Mrs. Seton called it, and then, with a laugh, left the piano. Mrs. Seton thought it was essential to ask him to go on.

"You're not getting up yet, Mr. Murray," she said. "Oh, no, no, you mustn't do that. It is just a treat, such as we seldom get. You see, there are few people that can give the time to it. You must have practised a great deal, far more than our young people will take the trouble to do. Oh, you never bound yourself to hours? That must have been because you were so fond of it, and just played on without taking count of the time. Do you hear that, Katie? That is what you ought to do, if you would ever be a performer like Mr. Murray. Just let him hear you play that last thing of yours. Well, it is not like what Mr. Murray can do, of course, but it is not at all bad for a little thing like you; and very likely Mr. Murray could give you a hint or two. A hint is sometimes of such consequence. Toots! just get up at once. When you have to be pressed, and coaxed, and all that, people expect something very grand. Now, in your simple way, you should just do it at once, and nobody would criticise."

"But Mr. Murray doesn't want to hear me play. He plays far better—oh, so much better—himself," cried Katie.

"Just never you mind that," said her mother. "Do your best, nobody can do more. When you are as old as me, you will know that the best judges are always the ones that are least hard to please. Just go at once, Katie. Perhaps you will tell her what you see particularly wrong, Mr. Murray," she added, as the girl reluctantly obeyed. "Unfortunately, we can get so little advantage of masters here. I am always telling Mr. Seton we must give her a winter in Edinburgh, just to get into the ways of the world a little; for you cannot do that here—oh, no, no, you just can't get that in the country. You must see people, and see how they behave. But a clergyman has such a difficulty in getting away, unless he really falls ill, or something of that kind; and it would be going too far, you know, to wish for that. I think myself sometimes that I see signs of overwork, but Mr. Seton will not hear of it—he just will not hear of it. Katie, Katie, that's a great deal too quick. Do you not think that was too fast, Mr. Murray? Dear, dear! you must always count, you must not trust to your ear; and don't be so strong upon the pedals, Katie. That was a little better. Take care of the time, and the tune will take care of itself. La—la—la-la-la—la," sang the anxious mother, accompanying with waving hand and head the somewhat uncertain performance.

Lewis was so sympathetic that he was quite conscious of Katie's indignation, and shamefacedness, and blinding embarrassment, as well as of the humour of her mother's remarks, which ran on all the time. He got up after a little while and went and stood behind the young performer.

"Don't be frightened," he said, in an undertone. "If you will play more slowly, and not lose your head, you will do very well. I used to lose my head, too, and make a dreadful mess of it when I was your age."

"I mean to stop at the end of the first bit," said Katie, in the same undertone, with a defiant glance. "As you did the other day."

"At the end of the andante?" said Lewis. "Yes, that will be best."

The girl looked up at him this time with astonishment. It is one thing to say that you intend to break off in a performance, but quite another when your audience acquiesces in this rebellion.

"I thought you were so fond of it," Katie could not help saying, with a little pique. So fond of it that he would have liked to prolong her performance! Lewis laughed inwardly, but outside preserved his decorum.

"When you play without your will, it is no longer in harmony," he said. "However you may be correct, it will never sound so. When you take away the consent of the heart, the chords do not strike just—you understand?"

Katie stared at him, while her fingers stumbled over the keys. She was profoundly astonished, but she was not stupid, and more or less the girl did understand.

They were left to each other, while Mrs. Seton rose to receive a visitor, and Lewis seized the opportunity of the first break to substitute conversation for music. He gave her a ludicrous account of himself in the rain.

"If you had seen me, you would have despised me," he said. "How glad I am we met only in the village, and not on the river-side! When I met you I was like one of the fowls, with all my feathers drooping, don't you know, longing to get under a cart, as they did."

"Oh, Mr. Murray!" cried Katie, with a broken giggle. She had thought so, but to assent to this description of himself was quite against the code of morals inculcated at the manse.

"Oh, it is very true," said Lewis, with his cordial laugh. "You scoffed at my umbrella, but when it is wet one always carries an umbrella where I come from. Ah, but there was worse than the umbrella, Miss Katie. Is it permitted that I should say Miss Katie?"

"Oh, yes," said Katie, with a little blush—"everybody does it here: though I am the eldest," she added, with a little dignity.

"Abroad," said Lewis, with the smile which he always permitted himself when he used that vague term, "we say mademoiselle, or Fräulein, or signorina. I know that miss is a little different in English. But I wander from my subject. When I got to the river, I felt what you call small, Miss Katie. There was Stormont in the middle of the stream—he I thought a little languid the other day, not taking much interest—"

"Oh, but that, is a mistake," cried Katie, with a vivid blush; "it is just that we're quiet in Scotland—we think quiet manners the best. Oh, he takes a great interest—" and here she stopped embarrassed; for why, indeed, should she take upon herself to respond for young Stormont? She gave an anxious glance at Lewis, lest he should laugh, or perhaps indulge in a little banter on the subject, which was not foreign to the manners of the countryside. But Lewis was perfectly serious, and answered her with the air of a judge.

"Of course, I was mistaken in that. There he was in the middle of the river, like a young Hercules, glowing and fresh, while I was so sodden and drooping. If you had heard me laugh at myself! 'What a poor creature you are!' I said, 'not fit for this robust country at all, thinking that your feet will get wet, that the grass is soaking, while he is there enjoying himself—actually enjoying himself!'"

"Oh, yes," cried Katie, proud and pleased, "it was grand for the fishing. He had such a basket of fish. One was seven pounds, they said. Mr. Stormont called on his way home just to tell papa what sport he had had," she added in explanation, "and that was how I know."

Lewis was not insensible to the fact that to call at the manse, which was on the right side of the river, on his way to the Tower, which was on the left, was a peculiar short cut for young Stormont to make: but he accepted every detail with perfect gravity.

"I," he said, with his apologetic air and his cheerful laugh at himself, "basely took advantage of Adam's skill, and got some of his fish to carry to the Castle. I did not pretend I had caught them myself—I was not quite so base as that. But Adam, too, how much he was my superior! To see him there, all brown and strong, casting his rod, the rain raining upon him, and little brooks running off his hat and his clothes. How shall I make myself like that, Miss Katie? I am only a carpet knight—I am not good for anything here."

"Oh, Mr. Murray!" repeated little Katie. She was shocked with herself not to be able to find something consolatory, something gratifying to say. At length she ventured, timidly and against her conscience, to bring forward arguments in his defence against himself. "You can play such beautiful music, such hard things—and no gentleman hereabouts can do that; and you know a great many languages."

"That is no credit to me," Lewis said. "I could not help learning them—when I was a child and knew no better," he added, with a laugh.

"We are awfully backward in languages," Katie said. "We had a German governess for a while, but I never could learn it. And as for the gentlemen, they never try. After all, it is not so much wanted, do you think, unless you sing, to teach you how to pronounce the words? that is what mamma says. If you sing, you must learn how to say your words; they are always either Italian or German, or at the least French."

"That is very important," said Lewis, gravely; "and perhaps to know what the words mean: that would help you to the appropriate expression."

"Oh, I don't mind so much about that," said Katie; "it's rather old-fashioned to put expression into them. Mamma is old-fashioned; she gives her head a little nod, and she turns it like this, and she smiles at the funny parts—I don't mean really funny, you know, for of course she never sings comic songs, but at the parts where you would smile if you were talking. But you don't do that now; it is quite old-fashioned, my music-mistress says."

"Oh, it is quite old-fashioned?" said Lewis.

"Quite. Miss Jean is ever worse than mamma. Sometimes you would think she was going to cry. Perhaps you never heard her sing? Oh, it is only the old Scotch things she sings; but some people think a great deal of them. Mamma sings them sometimes too, I don't care for them myself. What I should like best would be the German, if you were quite sure that you pronounced the words right."

"So far as that goes, I might perhaps be of use."

"Oh, would you, Mr. Murray? That would be so very kind. If I only knew how to pronounce them right, I would not care for anything else."

"Not this morning, Miss Katie; but you might be singing something you would not like to utter—"

Katie looked at him for a moment with surprise, then she added, lightly,

"What could it matter? Nobody understands."

By this time several callers had arrived, and Mrs. Seton's monologue, with occasional interruptions, was heard from the other end of the room. Mrs. Stormont was one of the visitors, and Miss Jean another; but, though the former lady was a formidable obstacle, the quickly-flowing tide of speech from the minister's wife carried all before it.

"Oh, yes, yes," she said, "that's just what I always say. If it's not good for the country in one way, it is in another; it keeps down the insects and things, and, if it's bad for the hay, it's excellent for the turnips. And, besides, it's the Almighty's will, which is the best reason after all. Sometimes it's very good for us just to be dull, and put up with it—that's what I tell the children often. Oh, yes, yes; no doubt it's hard to convince young things of what doesn't please them, but it's true for all that. There are plenty of dull moments in life besides the wet days, and we must just put up with them, Mr. Philip brought us a beautiful present of trout just the other day; the big one, what was it it weighed, Katie?—six pounds? Yes, yes, six pounds. A lovely fish—I never saw a finer. I was unwilling to take it, though that seemed ungracious. I just said, 'Toots, Mr. Philip, not me this time; you're always so kind to the manse—you should send this to some greater person.'"

"I did not know," said Mrs. Stormont, with very distinct enunciation, "that my son had got anything so considerable. The biggest one he brought home was four pounds; but at Philip's age it's seldom that the best wins as far as home."

"Dear me!" cried Mrs. Seton. "Now that was scarcely nice of Mr. Philip. I told him it was a present fit for a greater stranger; but he's just very liberal-minded, and has a great respect for Mr. Seton, which is so good for a young man. For I always say you can't have a safer friend than your minister; but, if I had thought he was depriving you of it, I would just have scolded him well. No, no, that's not my way of thinking; it should always be the best for home—oh! yes, the best should be for home. It's very fine to be generous, but the best should always be for home. I often say to the children—"

"Young men and their families seldom agree on that subject," said Mrs. Stormont. "Is it true, Miss Jean, the grand story I hear about Margaret and you and little Lilias all going up to London next spring? Bless me, that will be a terrible affair. I know what it is to go through a season in London; I did it once, and only once, myself. I said to my husband, 'We'll just be ruined,' and I would never hear of doing it again."

"It would not be for us," said Miss Jean, "but for Lilias; you see, at her age—and Margaret is of the opinion that we should give her every justice; besides, we would not stay all the season, just enough to give her a good idea; and then, you see, being once presented, she would be prepared for whatever might happen."

"We all know what that means," said Mrs. Seton, nodding her head. "Oh, yes, yes, it is very natural. When you have the charge of young people, you must look on into the future. I am always telling Mr. Seton, Katie must have a winter in Edinburgh; that will be season enough for her, for you are never rightly at your ease in society till you have seen something of the world."

"For my part, I think there's far better society in Edinburgh than you can get in London," said Mrs. Stormont. "You get the best in the one place, but it's a very different class you get in the other. A good Scots family counts for nothing among all those fashionable folk. You are asked at the tail-end of one of their great parties, and your friends think they have done their duty by you. No, no, London's not for me."

"That may be very true," said Miss Jean, "but Margaret is of the opinion that this is the right thing to do; and she always strives to carry out what she thinks to be right."

"It's just the most terrible waste of money," Mrs. Stormont continued. "I never think you get half so much for a gold sovereign as you do for a pound note; and if you ask your way in the street, or stroke a bairn on the head as you pass it, there's sixpence to pay. And the beer! nobody but wants beer. How they can stand all that cold stuff on their stomachs is a mystery to me."

"Mr. Seton maintains it's not so bad as a dram," said the minister's wife. "Oh! no, no, if you come to think of it, it is not so bad as the drams. Whisky is far worse for their stomachs. If the one's cold, the other just burns them up. I set my face against it, but it's so little you can do. And sixpence goes a far way in beer; you can always hope he'll not drink it all, but take home the half to his wife. Ah, no, you must not speak against London. It's a grand place London. You see the best of everything there. When we go up now and then, which is not nearly so often as I should wish, we have no cause to complain of our friends. They are just as pleased to see us as we are to see them, and we must dine with this one, and the other will take us to the Academy, or into the park, or to hear a concert. You would be happy there with the music, Mr. Murray. The best always goes to London. Oh! yes, yes, in London there is the best of everything."

"And the worst," said Mrs. Stormont, emphatically, as she rose. She paused to shake hands with Lewis with a certain demonstration of interest. "You are going to settle down in our neighbourhood?" she said. "I'm sure I'm very glad to hear it. There's no better situation that I know of. You're near the moors for the shooting, and close to the river for the fishing, and what could heart of man desire more?"

"Unfortunately I am not much of a sportsman."

"Well, well, there are other attractions," said Mrs. Stormont, with unusual geniality. "We can supply you with better things. A nice house and pleasant neighbours, and a bonnie Scots lassie for a wife, if that is within your requirements. Men are scarce, and you may pick and choose."

"Not quite so bad as that, I hope," said Mrs. Seton, with a heightened colour. "No, no, not so bad as that; but still, no doubt, there are some fine girls."

"Some! there are dozens," said the other, with an evident meaning which Lewis, surprised, did not fathom; "and take you my word, Mr. Murray, you are in a grand position. You have nothing to do but pick and choose."

Miss Jean rose up quickly when this was said. She was nervous and alarmed by every trumpet of battle. She hastily interposed, with her softer voice.

"I must be going, Mrs. Seton. We will soon, I hope, see you at the castle; and Katie knows how welcome she is. No, no, you'll never mind coming to the door. Here is Mr. Murray will see me out," cried Miss Jean, eager to be absent from the fray.

Mrs. Stormont, however, had delivered her shaft, and it was she who led the way, with a smile of satisfied malice.

"You must really settle among us. You must not just tantalize the young ladies," she said.

When she had been placed in her pony-carriage and driven away, Lewis took the opportunity thus presented to him, and accompanied Miss Jean, somewhat to her alarm, into the park through the little wicket. Miss Jean was still a little nervous, with a tremor of agitation about her.

"Did you ever hear anything like yon?" she said. "It was very ill-bred. You see Mrs. Stormont is a person of strong feelings. That is always the excuse Margaret makes for her. But you may disapprove of a thing, surely, and show it in a way becoming a gentlewoman, without going so far as that."

"What is it," asked Lewis, always full of interest in his fellow-creatures, "which this lady does not approve?"

"There are great allowances to be made for her," said Miss Jean. "You see Philip is her only son, and naturally, if he marries at all, she would like him to look higher. The Setons are very nice people. I would not have you think anything different; but it would not be wonderful that she should like him to look higher."

"I see; then it is Mrs. Seton who has arranged to marry her daughter to—"

"Oh, you must not take that into your head. Bless me! I would not say that: it may never come the length of marrying; it is just that Philip is always hanging about the manse. And Katie, she is very young, poor thing, and fond of her amusement—they may mean nothing, for anything I can tell; and that is Margaret's opinion," Miss Jean said, with trepidation. "Margaret has always said it was nothing but a little nonsense and flirtation between the young folk."

"It is the fashion of England," said Lewis, "I suppose—but it is strange to me, too, as to Mrs. Stormont— that Miss Katie should manage her own concerns."

"I know little about the fashions of England," said Miss Jean, slightly annoyed by this answer, "but in Scotland it is not our way to arrange these sort of things; when they come of themselves, we have just to put up with it, if we don't like it, or to be thankful, if we do. It is more natural than that French way of arranging—which comes to nothing but harm, as I have often heard."

Lewis did not stand up in defence of the French way. He said,

"Miss Katie is too young, she will think that is play; but when it is otherwise, when the lady is one who knows what is in the world, and what it is to choose, and understands what she would wish in the companion of her life—"

Here Miss Jean began to shake her head, and laugh softly to herself.

"Where will you find a young creature that will be so wise as that?" she said.

"Perhaps I was not thinking of a young creature," said Lewis, piqued a little by her laugh.

"Ah," said Miss Jean, "that is just another of your French ways. I have heard that in their very stories it will be an elder person, a widow perhaps, that will be the heroine. That's a thing which is very repulsive to the like of us in this country. You will perhaps think I am very romantic, but I like none of your unnatural stories. What I like is two young folk, not very wise perhaps, mistaken it may be, but with honest hearts towards one another, faithful and true; that is what I like to hear of—and no parents interfering, except just to guide a little, and help them on."

"Ah!" said Lewis, with an involuntary sigh, "that is one way, to be sure; but must all other ways be unnatural? Might it not be that the elder person, as you say, should have a charm greater than the younger, should be more sweet in some one's eyes, kinder and truer? All romance is not of one kind."

"I cannot abide," said Miss Jean, severely, "the woman that can begin over again, and tag a new life on to the tail of another. No, I cannot 'bide that. It may be one of my old-fashioned ways: but to everything there is a season, as Solomon, in his wisdom, was instructed to say."

"That is different," said Lewis; "but do you think, then, that the heart grows old? I have known some who were as fresh as any young girl, or even as a child, though they were not what you call young."

"Well, well!" said Miss Jean, with a smile and a sigh, "I will say nothing against that. I'll allow it's true. Oh, yes; but you're a clever young man to discern it. It is just ridiculous," she continued, bursting into a little laugh, "the young feeling that—some persons have; wrinkles and grey hairs outside, and just the foolish feeling within, as if you were still a bit foolish lamb upon the lee."

Miss Jean laughed, but there was a little moisture in her eyes.

"You have neither wrinkles nor grey hairs," said the audacious Lewis. "You choose to be old, but you are not old. Your eyes are as young as Miss Katie's, your heart is more soft and kind. Why there should be anything unnatural in a romance that had you for its centre I cannot see."

"Me!"

Miss Jean stood still in her astonishment; a soft colour passed over her gentle countenance, not so much with the emotion appropriate to the occasion, as with wonder and amazement. It was a moment before she fully realized what he meant to say, and then—

"Bless the laddie! is he going out of his senses," she cried. "Me!"

"And why not? I cannot see any reason," Lewis said. He was always ingratiating, anxious to please, seeking with a smiling anxiety for the sympathy of his companions. He looked at her now with a tender desire to set her right with herself. A respectful admiration was in his eyes; and indeed, as he looked with the strong desire which he had to find out all that was best in the modest, gentle countenance before him, it was astonishing how pretty Miss Jean began to grow. The faded colour grew sweeter and brighter, the eyes enlarged, the very contour of the face became more perfect. He could not help saying to himself that careful dressing, and a little stir and excitement, would make her handsome; and as for her age, what did a few years matter? Lewis said to himself that he had no prejudices. When a man of forty marries a woman of twenty-five, there is not a word to be said—and why should there be any difference in this case? All this was written in his eyes, had Miss Jean been clever enough to see it there.

But she was not. She considered that he was trying to please her, and make her satisfied with herself, as a child sometimes does who cannot bear to think that its mother or aunt is supposed old. Perhaps it pleased her as even the child's naïve compliment pleases. She shook her head.

"You are very kind," she said, "to try to make me think that age is as good as youth. But I'm not wishing to be young—I am quite content, and there is no question of that. What I was wanting to say was that I would never be the one to cross two young things in an attachment." A pretty colour was on Miss Jean's face; she blushed a little for the sake of the imaginary young people. "I would not part them—who can ever tell what may come of it?—I would not part them," she said, with fervour.

Lewis felt a warm glow under his waistcoat, and thought with a little complacency that he was falling in love with Miss Jean as she spoke.

CHAPTER XI

Katie Seton was not yet seventeen, but she was the eldest of her family, which has a maturing influence, and she had been the chief personage in a series of impromptu performances in the manse drawing-room, like the one at which the reader has assisted, almost as long as she could remember; so that she was familiar enough with ideas which are generally beginning to develop at seventeen, and had flirted very innocently ever since she was in short frocks. From that time Philip Stormont had been her favourite partner, her closest attendant. He was the one who walked home with her when they met at the tea-parties of the neighbourhood, following with Katie behind her father and mother in the strictest decorum, when his protection was altogether unnecessary, and finding his way to the manse on any excuse; and there are so many excuses in the country for such visits. Sometimes he had business with the minister which kept him waiting for hours, much deplored by Mrs. Seton, who would bustle out and in, and lament her occupations, which did not permit her to remain with him, and her husband's absence, which wasted his day.

"But I've sent little Robbie to see if he can find his father, and, Katie, you must just do the best you can to wile away the time," Mrs. Seton would say.

Katie did her very best on such occasions. She would give the young man a lesson in dancing, in which she was acknowledged to be the greatest proficient for miles around, or she would go over one song after another, playing the tune with one hand to teach it to him, sometimes guiding him with her own pretty little voice, sometimes breaking down in rills of young laughter at his mistakes, in which he would join. They were on such perfectly easy terms that his mistakes did not trouble him before Katie—he even went wrong on purpose to make her laugh. Sometimes they would meet out of doors and walk together, the younger children who accompanied Katie following their own devices, to the satisfaction of all parties, as soon as it was realized that Stormont had appeared, and that the previous attendants were free. In this way a great many passages had occurred, unknown, indeed, to father and mother, and in themselves bearing but little meaning, which had so linked these two young creatures together, that neither one nor the other could identify themselves apart.

There had been nothing said between them about engagement or marriage, but they felt a mutual right to pout and quarrel, if Katie danced with some one else more than civility required, or if Philip walked home with Annie Borrodaile. Annie Borrodaile was the individual whom Katie had chosen to erect into a dangerous rival; while Philip, on his side, after a marked identification of young Mr. Dunlop the assistant at Braehead, had lately fallen upon Lewis as his antagonist. They would taunt each other with these supposed preferences, in which neither believed, but up to this time nothing had happened, nothing had been said to make a reference to papa necessary on Katie's part, or to give Mr. Philip that right "to put a stop to" a certain acquaintance, which he constantly declared to be necessary. They were playing with the gravity of the matter, and thinking that nobody saw clearer than themselves. But how was it possible that anyone could see so clearly as Philip's mother, who had no one but he, and who was a widow, with her mind and thoughts continually following her son. Somehow, no one could quite tell how, and herself least of all, Mrs. Stormont got to know what her son did; where he walked; how often he met Katie; how often he was received in the manse drawing-room. None of these things were done clandestinely; the servants, the children, the neighbours, all had a part in the proceedings of the young people, who themselves were as honestly void of offence as ever young people were.

On the evening of the day on which Mrs. Stormont had made the visit we have recorded, Katie went out with her young brothers and sisters. Robbie and Jock were the next to her in age. They were fifteen and thirteen, and full of mischief, as indeed, if boys are not at their age, what is to become of them? Rosie and Minnie were younger; they were little girls who had an eye to what was going on, and were deeply aware that, if anything could make Katie indifferent to the fact that they had taken off their shoes and stockings, and were wading on the edge of the river like the boys, or had scrambled up into a tree, and there sat dangling their small legs with absolute insensibility to decorum, it was the sight of Philip coming vaguely along whistling one of the tunes Katie had taught him, and looking about everywhere to find her out. These young people offered no obstacles to Philip's search: they aided him indeed with all their powers. The direction in which they usually took their evening walk was up the water, a path which ended in a wood stretching downwards from the big, empty, unfinished house of Murkley to the river-side. This wood was their favourite resort. There were rabbits in it, and squirrels; there were oaks all twisted and gnarled, which were delightful to climb, and in which the girls found no difficulty. There was a large willow very near the bend of the river, with great branches stretching half-way across the stream, upon which they would sit and fish, perched up like a bird among the foliage, and out of everybody's way. And there was an old quarry of red earth full of pebbles, in which nothing was so easy, if wilder sports failed them, as to establish a shop, and sell mimic sweets and fruits, pretending to be customers and pretending to be saleswomen, to their hearts' desire. This latter delight was best attainable by the girls when May came too, who was only eight, and who thought nothing so delightful as playing shop. Meanwhile, the boys would be after the rabbits, or investigating the nests.

The party had set out from the manse in very good order as usual. Katie had been "upset" during the day, and her mother had petted and consoled her. There had been no direct confidences between them. Mrs. Seton had made little reference to the personal offence, though she had felt it keenly.

"It was not pretty. Oh, no, it was not pretty," she said, "to speak like yon to poor Mr. Murray, a young lad that is a stranger here, and knows nobody's character. If he had known what kind of woman Mrs. Stormont was—fond of making these kind of remarks—he would of course have understood. But, no, no, indeed it was not pretty, and it should just read us a lesson, Katie, to mind how we indulge our fancies, not thinking of other people. It was not, maybe, civil either to you or me; but we know what she is, and we never mind—no, no, we just never mind. But I feel for poor Mr. Murray," Mrs. Seton said.

As for Katie, she said, with anger,

"What right had she to speak like that? as if we were wanting him, or anyone."

"Tut," said her mother, "it was not us she was meaning. She just can't help being disagreeable; it is her way."

But Katie had been angry, and consequently "upset" and wretched all the day. It was at her mother's request that she went out with her brothers and sisters. Mrs. Seton thought the air would do her good.

"Now, Robin and Jock, you will take care of Katie," their mother said. "Play none of your pliskies, but just walk by her side like two gentlemen, and take care of her, poor thing; and, Rosie and Minnie, you are not to drag and hang upon Katie, but let her get a little quiet and fresh air. Take a nice walk, and you'll be better when you come back."

The party set off very solemnly with their charge—they respected their mother, at least, so far as they could be seen from the manse windows, if not a little further. Rosie and Minnie walked in front like two little judges, and Robbie and Jock were on either side of their sister, walking, "like two gentlemen," in quiet gravity and state. Katie, between them, had a languid air. She walked with her head drooping a little, with a pensive seriousness in her countenance. It was impressive to see this fine family taking the air. Till they took the turn to the river-side their seriousness was unbroken. Then nature began to assert itself. Robbie and Jock were startled into animation by the sudden sight of a water-rat, after which Vixen, their dog, without consulting them, but with a glance out of his shag of hair contemptuous and impatient as who should say, "You laggards, come on," had turned in full pursuit. Rosie and Minnie persevered a little longer.

"It's nothing but a rat! but boys will rin for naething!" said Miss Rosie, more contemptuous than Vixen. A minute or two after, they thought they saw a squirrel, and flew along the path. Katie grew a little less languid when she was thus left alone. She said to herself that the air had done her good already. She did not call back the boys, as she had once thought of doing, or summon the little girls, who were within reach of her voice. What was the use when here was Philip Stormont coming? He was more of her own age, she said to herself, and more a companion, and there could be no doubt that he too, as well as the young Setons, was wonderfully fond of that road by the river-side. It can no more be denied that she was glad to see him approaching than that she had confidently expected his appearance; but the first sight of him suddenly gave Katie's little soul a perverse turn, and she received him without her usual cordiality, with a preternaturally grave face.

"I have often wondered," she said, "what brings you out at this hour, and on this side of the water. It is nothing for us, because we don't dine, and we have had our tea; but I have just been thinking what becomes of your dinner, and you walking about all the evening. You must be awfully fond of walking," Katie said, looking up, with the profoundest air of philosophical inquiry on her face.

"Walking! It is perhaps something else I am fond of," said Philip.

"Something else? I never see you with your fishing-rod," proceeded Katie; "but that does not matter, for of course you have your own reasons. But what happens about your dinner, if you dine at seven o'clock?"

"We don't dine at seven o'clock. Who would go in, a night like this, for a dull dinner? No, I have just something when I go home: and in the mean time I see you."

"Oh, me!—that's not much consequence," said Katie; and then she added, "I know now why Mrs. Stormont was not pleased, if she has to take her dinner by herself. I would not stand it, if I were your mother. I wonder what you mean, all you boys. Do you think you are so much grander than women are, that you turn everything upside down for your own pleasure? Oh! if I were your mother, I would be worse than vexed! I would just not put up with it," cried Katie, stamping her small foot. The object of this assault was petrified. He looked at her with a gasp of dismay.

"How do you know," he blundered out at last, "that my mother was angry? You know I don't think myself grand at all nor anything worth speaking of," he added, in a deprecating tone. "It is you, Katie, that are angry."

"And I have cause, Mr. Stormont," said Katie, with dignity.

"Mr. Stormont! Is it a quarrel, then? You are always wanting to quarrel with me," he said, in a tone of complaint, yet conciliation; "but it takes two to do that. What is it now?"

"Oh, it is nothing," cried Katie; "if unkind things are said about me, it is none of your affair. I am not complaining. It is a little strange, however," she said, after an effective pause, "that because a gentleman does not go in at the right hour and eat his dinner as he ought, a girl that has nothing to do with him, that is no connection, should be abused in her own mother's house."

"Is it me that you have nothing to do with?" said Philip, piteously. "I think nobody can have so hard a heart."

"What have I to do with you, Mr. Philip?—we are just friends. You are friends with a great many people. There are the Borrodailes—"

"I knew that was coming," said Philip, "though I tell you six times a day that Annie Borrodaile is nothing—"

"I said not a word about Annie Borrodaile. It is just a guilty conscience that makes you name one more than another. And why should you tell me six times a day? I wonder what I have got to do with it?"

"Katie," cried poor Philip, "how can you speak to me so, when you know just as well as I do that there's no one in the world I care about but you? You have got everything to do with me. You know, if all the ladies in the world were here, it is you I would choose; you know it is for you I come here; you know I think of nobody else and nothing else." Here Philip, approaching humbly, endeavoured to draw into his own Katie's hand, which lay within reach upon her lap, for by this time the pair had seated themselves, as they usually did, upon a fallen tree which lay conveniently within reach of the road, but sheltered by the brushwood. "Nobody else, and nothing else," said Philip, drawing closer.

"Except the trout," said Katie, with a laugh, "and birds in the season, and the hunting, and the curling, and two or three hundred things, not to speak of Annie Borrodaile."

To this Philip made no reply. He was wounded, and withdrew a little to the other end of the tree. It was a scene which had been played a great many times, and they were both quite familiar with it: but it was always new to them, and always threatened for ten minutes at least a tragical severance, which, however, happily never came.

"That, however, is nothing to me," said Katie; "but when your mother comes and speaks as if—oh, as if I were the dust beneath her feet—as if I were nobody that had ever been heard of before—as if I were a girl that could be bought in the market like a slave in the 'Arabian Nights'—"

"Katie, for goodness sake tell me what she said!"

Katie continued to play with his curiosity for some time longer, until she had worked that and her own indignation into a tragic heat; then, with tears of youthful fury and injured feeling in her eyes, she unfolded her wrongs.

"Mr. Murray was there—he had come to play his piece to mamma—and Mrs. Stormont turned round and looked me straight in the face, and said to him that he must settle in Murkley. 'You'll get a nice house,' she said, 'and a wife; you can pick and choose among the young ladies—oh, yes you can take your choice of them,' and she looked at me—all the time she looked at me! She just offered me—as if she had any business with me!—to that man that is not a man, that can do nothing but fiddle on the piano," cried Katie, transported by her wrongs and her indignation. She even cried a little—hot tears, out of pity for herself and the sense of injury which swelled all her youthful veins.

Philip on his side was greatly relieved to find that it was no worse. What he had feared was that his mother had interfered definitely in his own affairs. His mind was greatly eased when he heard the extent of her transgressions. He ventured upon a short laugh under his moustache.

"That was so like my mother," he said.

"It may have been very like your mother, Mr. Stormont," cried Katie, "but if you think that I am going to put up with it—and mamma too!"

"Was Mrs. Seton angry?" said Philip. "Don't call me Mr. Stormont. Now just reflect; I have nothing to do with it; I did not make my mother. Was Mrs. Seton angry?—what did Mrs. Seton say? If you think my mother ill-tempered, Katie, I know that your mother is kind. What did she say?"

"Oh," said Katie, softened, "she said nothing at all. She said that to go out for a walk would do me good. She did not say a word; she just said it was Mrs. Stormont's way."

"I don't think it is her way," said Philip, piqued a little; "but it was like my mother," he added, "oh, yes, it was like her. She would wish to snatch you away under my very nose, and marry you to another man before I knew what she was doing. Oh, that is just what she would like to try. She would think it was no harm to you."

"And what business had she with me at all?" cried Katie, but more gently, the storm having had its way.

"Well, I suppose she guesses what you know so well," said the young lover, "and that is what you are to me, Katie: that there is nobody but you for me: that I would not care if all the world was swept away so long as I had you safe: that—"

"Oh, that is just your way of talking," said Katie, but she did not withdraw her hand; "that is just your nonsense. As if it was likely the world would be swept away, and me left! But that is no reason, if you do like me, that she should think ill of me. I have done nothing to her—why should she be so cruel to me?"

"I am all she has, you see," said Philip, "and she does not like to give me up, as she will have to do."

"I am sure I am not wanting you," cried Katie. "She is welcome to keep you to herself for me; besides, if it was not me, it would be somebody else," she added, after a moment, reflectively, with a philosophy that poor Mrs. Stormont would have done well to emulate. "At your age you are sure to have somebody. She ought to mind that. If it was Annie Borrodaile, would she be better pleased? Most likely," said Katie, "it will be Annie Borrodaile after all."

It was when Philip was employed in energetic disposal of this hypothesis, which it was her pleasure to fling at him whenever the liveliness of the conversation flagged, that Lewis Murray, emerging from the woods of Murkley, in which he had been wandering, thinking over his own urgent affairs, approached the water-side. He came down from behind the scaur by a path half overgrown with tall beeches and brushwood, which was little used. The path was clothed with mosses and covered with the brown beech-wort and the slippery droppings of the firs, and a footstep was scarcely audible upon it. In the hollow of the scaur the little girls were playing, the redness of the earth throwing up their small active figures as they performed their little mimicry of life, "pretending" to be grown-up actors in it, their voices sounding clear into the echoes. At a distance the boys were shouting to each other, and Vixen barking, all of them after the water-rat which had not yet been exhausted as a possibility of fun.

Lewis looked at the children with ready pleasure and sympathy, without thinking of anything further. He was just about to call to them, when a lower murmur of voices caught his ear. He was still on a higher level than the angle of the little wood where it ran down to the river, and, as he glanced in the direction of this softer sound, the young pair became apparent to him. They were close together now, bending towards each other, making but one shadow. Philip's head was uncovered, the light catching its vigorous reddish-brown, and Katie's blue frock made a little background for the group as Lewis looked down upon them, separating that spot from the brown of the tree's trunk and the green of the foliage. A spectator may be pardoned for looking a moment at such a scene before he makes his presence known, especially when he comes upon it by surprise. Lewis stood still in a passion of soft sympathy and emotion which he himself did not quite understand. In some things he was younger than his age. He had known none of the innocent emotions of boy and girl; darker and less lovely episodes he had heard of in plenty, but fortunately for him his absorption in the life of an old man, kind as his patron had been, had kept him apart from all such seductions, and it had never been within his possibilities to fall sweetly and innocently in love, according to what was the course of nature with Katie and Philip.

He gazed at them as they sat together with a sudden comprehension, a curious self-compassion and sense of envy. He laughed to himself softly, so softly that it did not sound in the quiet evening air, with that amusement which is everybody's first impulse at sight of a pair of lovers: and then he grew suddenly grave. This was very different from what he was contemplating for himself. He had thought of duty, not of happiness, in all his recent plans. It had been a something incumbent upon him to fulfil, a wrong to atone for, a blunder to set right, that had been his inspiration. Perhaps his foreign breeding was responsible for the fact that Lewis had not looked upon the marriage which he thought it right to make as having much to do with his happiness at all. It was a portion of life, a necessity, like another, to be accepted manfully, but not the great and crowning want of youth, not the turning-point of existence. Romance was not in it to his straightforward views: and he was not unwilling to accept Miss Jean for the partner of his life, even had she been less pleasant than he found her. He would have approached even Miss Margaret in the same spirit, and with the same dauntless simplicity, had that been the right thing to do, and would have done his duty by either without any sense of hardship or even regret. But when he saw Philip Stormont and Katie, something awoke in him which was like a new sense. Oh, yes, he had heard of love, he had read of it; there was not a novel without it, and scarcely a song. He had seen lovers before now. But somehow this soft and lingering eve, the novelty of all around him, the resolution he had taken, even the satirical advice of Mrs. Stormont, and her suggestion that he had but to pick and choose, were all working together in his mind.

Suddenly it occurred to him that here was the something more which was in life, which he had never known, which he had been vaguely conscious of, but never laid hold upon, or even divined. He laughed, and then he grew grave. He took in at a glance all the points of the situation, which were so different from any of his experiences. It is to be feared that Lewis was somewhat shocked by the facts of the case. He thought that Katie ought not to have been here meeting her lover, and he divined that it was a meeting which took place daily, and that it was to both of them the chief feature in the twenty-four hours. But it was something which would never be his. He stood very gravely, and looked down upon the group for a moment more. His wooing would not be like this; it would be all orderly, decorous, calm. He would be kind, always tender, respectful, friendly to the lady whom he married. It was not in him to fail in the regard which would be her due. But this was another thing altogether. After he had laughed, he sighed. Nature in him had made a mute protest. He looked wistfully and with an irrepressible envy at the lovers. The lovers! As for himself, that was a character which he was never likely to bear. His first idea had been to make his presence known, to warn them of his coming, that they might not be caught by his sudden appearance, or feel themselves found out. But the result of this strange, new impression upon Lewis was that, after that pause, he turned back, and went away out of sight into the woods again, and, after a long détour, found his way by another path back to the village. A sort of awe and wistful admiration was in his mind. He would not have them know that anybody had surprised their secret. This tender delicacy of sentiment was untouched by the fact that he thought the meeting wrong. But, wrong or right, it was something which was beyond him, something which he should never know or share.

"Poor Murray; if he were to take my mother's advice, you would think no more of breaking his heart, if he has a heart—" Philip was saying, as Lewis stole quietly away.

"How can you tell that? He is very nice. He waltzes a great deal better than you do, though I have tried so hard to teach you my step. And if you had only heard him play his piece to mamma! If he were to take your mother's advice—perhaps I would take her advice too."

"And I'll tell you what I should do, Katie; pitch him into the Witch's Cauldron, which is the deepest hole in the water. Play his piece! It would do him a great deal of good to play his pieces there."

And they both laughed, all unconscious of his observation, as they rose from their rustic seat unwillingly, and went lingeringly back towards the manse, and the world, out of that enchanted wood. The children had been faintly called half-a-dozen times before, but now Katie's voice had a tone in it which they felt to convey a real command. The little girls followed slowly; the boys sped on before. It was the recognized way in which, as far as the ferry, where Philip's path struck off, the procession moved towards home.

CHAPTER XII

After the conversation with Miss Jean which has been reported, Lewis felt that he had begun the undertaking which brought him to Murkley. Before this it had been in a vague condition, a thing which might or might not come to anything. But now he had, to his own consciousness at least, committed himself. What effect his words might have had on Miss Jean's mind he was of course unable to tell; but, whatever she might do, there was now no retreat for him. He had given her to understand that the aspect in which she appeared to him was one of great interest and attraction. Having said so much, Lewis felt that it was incumbent on him to say more; and indeed, there was a sensation of thankfulness in his mind when he remembered that he had done so, and so made an end of his own freedom in the matter. He was glad that he had done this before the evening on which he saw Philip and Katie together, and recognized in their intercourse a something which was lacking, and always would be lacking, in his own case. What matter? he said to himself. He had much, though not all. If Miss Jean became his wife, he would have the satisfaction of redeeming a wrong for one thing, and he would not have to blush for the good woman he had chosen. Her middle-aged calm and propriety indeed suited much better the rôle of wife, to his thinking, than Katie's youthfulness and levity. He thought of her as an Englishman thinks of home, as something to return to after the occupations and excitements of the world. What he looked forward to was not perhaps a domestic life, but a life in which it would always be good to come back after every variety of experience and personal vicissitude to the same calm, smiling presence, the indulgence and tenderness of one who would never be weary, never impatient, but always ready to hear what he had to say, and to sympathize and advise.

The more he dwelt upon this idea, the more it pleased him. What he wanted was not the inseparable companion who would share all his life with him, but rather that domestic stronghold, that something to return to. There are always these differences in life. And after a while Lewis said to himself that he would have the best of it. Kate would want a great many observances which an elderly bride would not dream of; she would no doubt insist on knowing and sharing everything—her husband's thoughts as well as his home, and this was not an ideal which suited the pupil of Sir Patrick Murray. He had not been used to women, and they were no necessary part of his life. His mother, so far as he recollected her, had taken the place which he pleased himself to think his wife would naturally take. Many women rebel now-a-days at that ideal of a woman's existence which consists in being always at home, always ready to receive the wanderer, to kill innumerable fatted calves, and look out continually for the prodigal's return. Lewis would be no prodigal, but his idea was to live his own life unfettered, and to give no very great share in it to any woman. He would go back to her when tired, when sick or sorry; he would be always tenderly careful of her and kind. He would surround her, in that home where she should be always waiting for him, with everything a woman could wish for; but clearly he meant her to stay there while he should enjoy everything and come back to be sympathized with. Such an ideal watcher is pleasant to everybody's thoughts; the mere recollection of the dweller at home, uncritical, all-believing, to whom one can return, sure of eager attention, petting, and sympathy in every emergency, is in itself a consolation. It is the primitive idea of the woman's office.

Lewis meant no disrespect to womankind in adopting it as his idea of the relations to subsist between himself and his wife; he did not know any better, and nothing could be more entirely in accord with the position which Miss Jean, he thought, would naturally take. Few intending bridegrooms perhaps allot this character at once to their brides, but Lewis meant no harm; he subdued in himself the softer thoughts which the sight of Katie and Philip had roused in his mind, and in the morning was again fully awake to a state of satisfaction with his own scheme, and ready to proceed with it.

In the pre-occupation of his mind, Adam's fishing had ceased to amuse him, and he did not want to meet Philip, whose conduct in compromising Katie, our young man highly disapproved of, even when he felt envious of his happiness. When he went out, he turned his steps in the opposite direction, going up the river, past the spot at which he had seen the lovers, and reaching, by that détour through the wood, the park of Murkley, and the neighbourhood of the great unfinished palace which had made him first acquainted with the family history. He had not returned to visit that memorial of ambition again. Perhaps there was nobody in the world who could regard it with the same feelings as those which moved Lewis. Sir Patrick had not left a good name behind him in the countryside. His tastes had never been those of a Scotch country-gentleman. The building of this prodigious and pretentious house had offended all his neighbours, to whom it was almost a personal offence that he should attempt in this way to excel all their houses and put himself on so much higher a level. When it turned out that he was not able to complete what he had begun so ambitiously, a great deal of bitterness and unfriendly humour exhaled in the pitiless laughter with which his failure had been received, and there was nobody about who did not more or less remember it against him—with a scorn of failure which is very strong in Scotland—that he had thus attempted a superiority which he was not able to maintain. His own family contemplated the stately folly with modified feelings. Such a standing proof of greatness had a certain effect upon their pride; but the failure was bitter to them, and there was the sense besides that their money had been wasted in the erection of a monstrosity which was of use to no one, and of which they could make nothing. To Lewis alone this great shell spoke eloquently of something which touched the heart. The dreams of old Sir Patrick's life, its aspirations, its pride, and hopes, all seemed to him embodied in these walls. The old man had scarcely spoken of it. It was only after seeing it that Lewis was able to recall words, incomprehensible at the moment, which he had now no doubt referred to this proud intention, this ambitious vanity. As he walked round it, he framed to himself an image of the young man, impulsive, proud, and full of a hundred hasty projects, who had turned into the old man he knew so well. If he had not been hasty, full of sudden impulses, would he ever, Lewis asked himself, have taken up the charge of a friendless orphan, and made himself responsible for the life of a stranger in whom, save for tender charity and pity, he was in no way involved?

He thought of himself as another Castle of Murkley. Sir Patrick had wronged his children for the sake of both; his generosity had been as rash as his ambition. He had trained and formed his dependent for a life entirely above his natural prospects, and, if he had left Lewis in the lurch, the case would have been an exact parallel to that of the abandoned and uncompleted house. But the old man had done more for love than he had done for pride, and it was not the part of Lewis at least to blame him that he had again wronged his family for the sake of an impulse of his own. But as he roamed round and round this pale, half-ruined palace, with all its princely avenues and foreign trees, a great tenderness arose in the young man's heart for his old patron. What sanguine dreams must have been his while he was rearing these fine walls—what intentions of liberal life! In Lewis's imagination the picture rose all illuminated with sympathy and understanding. That sanguine, hasty mind would never look at all on the other side; failure would not seem possible to him till it had come. He could imagine him over his plans, superintending his workmen, elate and dauntless. A smile came upon his face and tears to his eyes as he realized what young Sir Patrick in his pride and hope must have been, and what old Sir Patrick, exiled and disappointed, but still sanguine and prodigal, was. Lewis was the creation of his old age, as this castle was the creation of his youth, both of them in their way injustices, but the one capable of affording no compensation, the other so willing, so ready, so anxious to atone. This inspired him while he stood gazing up at the vacant windows of Sir Patrick's folly. It was wonderful to comprehend how he could ever have believed himself rich enough for such a habitation. It was a house for a prince: but this idea, which made most people angry and impatient with the rash and vain man, who had not paused to count the cost, melted altogether the heart of Lewis. Anyone but Sir Patrick would have hesitated before taking upon himself the charge of a young life; any man but Sir Patrick would have trained the orphan lad to lowlier uses. He had made a son of him, and given him the happiest, most beautiful life. Dear old Parrain! it had been wrong, perhaps, but it was not for Lewis to judge. For him there was a greater privilege left, a more delightful duty—to atone.

He was walking round this silent, shut-up, windowless, and lifeless mansion, looking up at it with moisture in his eyes, when the sound of voices suddenly made him aware that he was not the only person thus occupied. He heard them but vaguely from the other side—voices in animated talk, but not near enough to hear what they were saying. The voices were all feminine, and by-and-by he made sure that they were the ladies of Murkley whom he was about to meet. Presently three figures became visible round the angle of the great house, one in advance of the others, walking backward, with a form very unlike that of Miss Margaret and Miss Jean, apparently gazing up at the walls, a blue veil flying about her, her head raised, her light figure lightly poised upon elastic feet, not like the sober attitude of the ladies he knew. A momentary wonder crossed the mind of Lewis as to this third sister, whom he had never seen, but he was too much pre-occupied to dwell upon it. He divined that there was a little commotion among them at the sight of a stranger. He heard Miss Margaret say something about a veil, and then there came a protest in a voice full of complaining.

"Oh, Margaret, let my veil alone; there is no sun to spoil anybody's complexion, is there, Jean?"

Some word or sign, proceeding from one of the other ladies, made the speaker turn round, and Lewis had a momentary glimpse of a face which was very different from that of the other sisters; large, wondering eyes darted one glance at him, then the unknown turned again and hurried back to the group, dropping the blue veil in her hurry and astonishment. It was only a moment, and the sensation in Lewis's mind was not more than surprise. The glimpse was momentary, his mind was pre-occupied, and Miss Margaret advanced immediately to meet him, covering the retreat of the others.

"You are looking at our grandfather's grand castle," Miss Margaret said.

"It is a wonderful place to find here, out in the wilderness; it is like a palace that has been walking about and has lost its way," Lewis said, with an attempt to cover the quickened movement of his own pulses in the surprise of the encounter.

"I would not call this the wilderness," said Miss Margaret, with a momentary tone of pique. "A great deal of care was taken about the place before this great barrack was built—it's more like a barrack, in my opinion, than a palace."

"It is like the Louvre," said Lewis; "it must have been planned by some one who had travelled, who knew the French renaissance." He felt a little jealous for the credit of his old friend.

"Oh, as for that," Miss Margaret said, with a wave of her hand, "knowledge was not wanting, nor taste either. Our grandfather, Sir Patrick Murray, was a man of great instruction: all the worse for his descendants. This is how he wasted our substance—and in other ways."

"He was a collector, I suppose?"

"I perhaps don't understand what you call a collector—a gatherer of costly things that are of no use to any mortal? Oh, he was that, and more. And there are other ways in which a man can wrong his family;

but it's not a subject that can be interesting to a stranger," Miss Margaret added, closing her mouth with a certain peremptory firmness, as if to conclude the discussion. "Yon," she resumed, "was to have been the great banqueting hall: and the drawing-rooms, you see—there were to be three of them, the outer and the inner, and the lady's bouédwore—were to occupy the other side; where he was to get the lady and the banquet Sir Patrick never took thought. He was not a man to take thought; but he was very well instructed, and knew what he was doing—from that point of view. If he had known better about the money, and counted the cost like the man in the Gospel, it would have been better for them who came after him. But the Murrays were never careful at counting the cost,"—that air of pride with which prodigality in a family is always confessed came over Miss Margaret as she said this, throwing up her head and animating her countenance. Nobody ever yet made a statement of thrift and carefulness with the same proud gratification. It is unpleasant to be poor, but Nature is always more pleased with the lavish than the careful. Lewis suffered himself to be led round the further side of the building, while she talked and pointed out the position of the rooms. It was a moment full of excitement for the young man; he listened eagerly while she spoke of Sir Patrick, with the strongest sense of that link between them to which she had not the slightest clue. Nor had he the slightest clue to the motive which induced her to expatiate upon the building and lead him round by the other side. The blue veil and the wondering, youthful face it guarded had not done more as yet than touch his mind with a momentary suspicion; his interest was engaged, not in secret questionings about Lilias, as the elder sister thought, but in recollections and associations of a very different kind.

"Perhaps," he said, following out his own thoughts, "had he waited and gone more softly there would have been no imprudence."

"Waiting and going softly are not in our nature: no: I'm but a woman, with little money, and very seriously brought up—and with my youth past, and no motive; but if I were to let myself go—even now!"

A sudden flush came over her face, her eyes shone, and then Lewis perceived that Miss Margaret, if she had not made up her mind to be elderly and homely, would still be a handsome and imposing personage, whom the society he had known would have admired and followed. He thought that if she had been Sir Patrick's companion his salon might have been very different. With this view he could not help gazing at her with a great curiosity, wondering how she would have filled that place, and thinking what a pity that this, which would have ruined his own prospects, had not been.

She looked at him quickly, meeting his gaze, and her eyes fell momentarily under it.

"You think me an old fool," she said, "and no wonder. Imprudence—that is always folly when it takes the power of beginning what you cannot finish—would be worse folly than ever in a person like me; but, you see, I never let myself go."

"That is not what I was thinking," said Lewis. "I was thinking—wondering, though I had no right—why you did not go to him when he was old."

"Go to him—to whom?" she cried, astonished.

"Ah! pardon! I have met Sir Patrick—abroad."

Miss Margaret turned upon him, and made a close and, as Lewis thought, suspicious inspection of his face.

"If you met Sir Patrick abroad, you must have seen that he had no need of his natural family, nor wish for them. There was no place for us there. Perhaps you have not heard that he withdrew his property from his family and gave it to one that was not a drop's blood to him—a creature that had stolen into a silly old man's favour? But no, that would not be known abroad," she added, with a long-drawn breath. Lewis felt himself shrink from her eye; he made a step backward, with a sense of guilt which in all the many discussions of the subject had never affected him before.

"No," he said, with an involuntary tone of apology, "no, it was not known, I think, that he had—any relations—"

Miss Margaret turned on him again with indignation more scathing than before.

"Not known that he had relations!" then she paused, and gave vent to a little laugh, "that must have been by persons who were very ignorant—by people out of society themselves," she said.

To this Lewis made no reply. What could he say? It was true that he had no standing in society himself, and he now perceived that he had been guilty of one of his usual imprudences in drawing the attention of a mind much more keen than Miss Jean's, and able to put things together, to himself and his antecedents. After a moment she resumed.

"I am speaking too strongly perhaps to you, a stranger. It was perhaps not to be expected—abroad— that everybody should know the Murrays of Murkley. That is just one of the evils of that life abroad, that it is lost sight of who you belong to. In your own country everybody knows. If you put a friendly person, in the place of your flesh-and-blood, the whole country cries out; but among strangers, who thinks or cares? No, no, I was wrong there; I ask your pardon. In Scotland, or even in England, Sir Patrick Murray's relations would be as well known as the Queen's, but not abroad—that was his safeguard, and I forgot. Poor, silly old man!" Miss Margaret said, after a pause, with energy, "he was little to me. I have scarcely seen him all my days, and Lilias never at all."

It seemed to Lewis that in this, perhaps, there was some explanation and apology for the unfortunate position of affairs; but he was so glad to escape from further questions that he did not attempt to follow the subject further. They had by this time come round the other corner of the building, and he perceived that the two other ladies had not waited for Miss Margaret, but were already half-way along the broad and well-kept drive which led from the unfinished palace to the old house. The blue veil fluttering in advance caught his eye, and he said, more with the desire to divert his companion from the previous subject than out of any special interest in this,

"Your sister, whom I have not seen, is the youngest?"

Here Miss Margaret, with a little start, recalled herself to a recollection which had temporarily dropped from her mind. She fixed him with her eye.

"Yes, she is the youngest," she replied. And what of that? her tone seemed to say.

"I had made one of the ridiculous mistakes strangers make," he said, very conciliatory, his reason for this being, however, totally different from the one she attributed to him. "I had supposed—you will say I had no right to suppose anything, but one guesses and speculates in spite of one's self—I had supposed that Miss Lilias was the eldest, and in bad health; whereas by the glimpse I had she is—"

"Quite young," said Miss Margaret, taking the words out of his mouth—"that is, quite young in comparison with Jean and me: but not so strong perhaps as might be desired, and an anxious and careful charge to us. Are you staying long here?"

"That will depend upon—various matters," Lewis said. "It is your sister Miss Jean whom I have had the pleasure to see most. You will pardon me if I say to you that I find a great attraction in her society. It is presumptuous perhaps on my part, but it is thought right where I have been brought up that one should say this when it occurs, without delay, to the family—"

Miss Margaret looked at him with eyes of unfeigned astonishment.

"Say—what?" she asked, pausing to survey him once more. Was the young man out of his senses? she said to herself.

"I mean," said Lewis, with that smile with which he assured everybody that he was anxious to please them, "that in all other countries but England things are so. The head of the family is consulted first before a man will dare to speak to a lady; I understand it is not so here."

"And you mean to speak to me as the head of the family?" said Miss Margaret. "Well, perhaps you are not far wrong; but my sister Jean and I are equals—there is no superior between us. The only thing is, that being a sweet and submissive creature, a better woman than I will ever be, she leaves most things in my hands."

"That was my idea," Lewis said.

"And you wanted to speak to me of something that concerned Jean? Well, there could be to me no more interesting subject: though what a young man like you that might be her son, and a stranger, can have to say to me about Jean—"

Lewis paused. He had not considered how awful it was to confront the keen, inquiring eyes of the head of the family, who looked him, he thought, through and through, and who, if he submitted his over-candid countenance for long to her inspection, would probably end by reading everything that was in him both what he meant to show and what he wished to conceal.

"Perhaps," he said, "I am premature. What I would have said was to ask if—I may come again? What further I wish will remain till later. If Miss Murray will afford to me the happiness of coming, or recommending myself so far as I can—"

"You speak," said Miss Margaret, somewhat grimly, and with a laugh, "as if you were wanting to come wooing to our house. Now speak out, and tell me to whom. I'll allow there's good in your foreign notions, if you give me this warning; and I will warn you in your turn, my young friend."

"I hope you will pardon my ignorance, if I do wrong," said Lewis. "It is your sister, Miss Jean, whom I have seen most. I have not known before such a woman. There is to me a charm—which I cannot explain. If I might see her—if it might be permitted to me to recommend myself—"

Miss Margaret had been gazing at him with eyes of such astonishment that he was disconcerted by the look. He came to a somewhat confused pause, and stood silent before her, with something of the air of a culprit on his trial. Then she cried out suddenly, "Jean!" and burst into a resounding laugh, which seemed to roll forth over all the landscape, and return from the tops of the trees. There is no more crushing way of receiving such a suggestion. The young man stood before her, silent, his face flushed, his eyes cast down for the moment. At length, being a sanguine youth, and too entirely good-humoured himself to impute evil intentions to anyone, he began to recover. He looked up at her with a deprecating smile.

"I amuse you, it seems—" he said.

"Amuse me!" said Miss Margaret, with another peal of laughter; and then she dried her eyes, and recovered her composure. "Mr. Murray—if your name is Murray—" she said; "if you mean this for a joke—but I will not do you that injustice; I see you mean it in earnest. It is very unexpected. Do you think you have had time enough to consider whether this is a wise resolution? Do you remember that she is twice your age? No, no, I would not advise you to go that length," Miss Margaret said.

"The question is, if you will forbid me," said Lewis; "if you will say I must not come."

"Ay! And what would you do then?"

"I think," he said, with a little hesitation, "I should then adopt the English way. I should submit my cause to your sister herself. But then there would be no deception, you would know."

He met her with such an open look that Miss Margaret was disarmed.

"You are a strange young man," she said, "with a strange taste for a young man: but I think you're honest: or else you are a terrible deceiver—and, if your meaning is what you say, you have no motive, that I can see, to deceive."

"I have told you my motive," said Lewis. "I speak the truth."

She looked at him again with her searching eyes.

"Perhaps you think we are rich?" she said.

"I have heard, on the contrary, that—"

She waved her hand. It was not necessary that he should say poor.

"Perhaps you think—but I cannot attempt to fathom you," she said. "You are a very strange young man. Jean! have you considered that she's twice your age? I have no right to interfere. I will not forbid you the house. But she will never take you, or any like you; she has more sense," Miss Margaret cried.

To this Lewis only answered with a bow and a smile, in which perhaps there was something of the conqueror; for indeed it did not occur to him, as a contingency to be taken into consideration, that she might refuse him. They walked on together for some time in silence, for Miss Margaret was too much confused and excited to speak, and Lewis had no more to say to her, feeling that it was only justice to the sister he had chosen that she should have the first and the best of the plea. It might be ten minutes after, and they were in sight of the old house, within which the two figures before them had disappeared, when Miss Margaret suddenly stopped short, and turned upon him with a very serious and indeed threatening countenance.

"Young man," she said, in a low and passionate voice, "if you should prove to be making a mask of my sister for other designs, if it should be putting forward one to veil a deeper design upon another, then look you to yourself—for I'll neither forgive you, nor let you slip out of my hands."

Lewis met this unexpected address with sincere astonishment.

"Pardon me, but I do not know what deeper design I could have. What is it that I could do to make you angry?" he said.

She looked at him once more from head to foot, as if his shoes or the cut of his coat (which was somewhat foreign) could have enlightened her as to his real motives: and then she said,

"I will take upon me to give you useful information. In the mornings I am mostly occupied. You will find my sister Jean by herself before one o'clock, and nobody to interfere."

CHAPTER XIII

It was with a mixture of indignation and somewhat grim humour that Miss Margaret gave the permission and sanction to Lewis's addresses which have been above recorded. There was a smile upon her face as she left him and went indoors, which burst forth in a short laugh as she entered—a laugh of derision and mockery, yet of anger as well, mingled with a sort of satisfaction in the idea of luring this presumptuous young man to his fate. Jean to be made love to at this time of day by a young man who might have been her son! (this, of course, was an exaggeration, but exaggeration is inevitable in such circumstances).

The purely comic light in which she had at first contemplated the idea gradually changed into an angry appreciation of the absurdity which seemed to involve her sister too, and a lively desire to punish the offender. That would be best done by giving him unlimited opportunity to compromise himself, she decided, and it was with this vindictive meaning, and not anything softer or more friendly, that she had so pointedly indicated to Lewis the best time and manner of approaching Miss Jean. He partially divined the satire and fierce gleam in her eyes, but only partially, for to him there was no absurdity in the matter.

Miss Margaret's heart almost smote her as he stood with his hat off, and his genial young countenance smiling and glowing, thanking her for what she had said; but this was only a momentary sensation, and when she went in she laughed with derision and the anticipation of a speedy end to a piece of folly which seemed to her beyond parallel. Such things had been heard of as that a young man who was poor, should basely and sordidly decide upon marrying, if he could, an old woman who was rich; but when there was no such motive possible—when, instead of being rich, the suitor was aware that the woman he sought was poor, then the matter was beyond comprehension altogether.

Miss Margaret was not sufficiently impartial to pause and think of this now, but as the day went on, and especially as she sat silent in the evening, and heard Lilias prattling to Jean, there were various points which returned to her mind with wonder. Why should he wish to marry Jean? Miss Margaret glanced at her, then looked steadily, then began to contemplate her sister with changed eyes. Something was different in Jean—was it that she looked younger?—something like what she used to look fifteen years ago? Was it that new hopes, new plans were rising in her mind? For the first time there breathed across Miss Margaret a cold and chilling breath of doubt—was it so sure that Jean would teach him his place, would reject all his overtures? The thought of anything else filled her with horror and shame. A young man, young enough to be her son—was it, could it be possible that she would listen to him? A groan came from Miss Margaret's breast in spite of herself.

"What is the matter?" cried Miss Jean, wondering.

"Oh, just nothing's the matter—an idea that came into my mind—nothing that you could be interested in," said Miss Margaret.

"Am I not interested in everything that can make you sigh or make you think?" said Miss Jean, with her soft voice.

"Yes, tell us—tell us what it is," said Lilias.

And then Miss Margaret laughed.

"You will know sooner or later, if it comes to anything," she said, getting up with a little impatience and leaving them.

The new turn which her thoughts had taken filled her with dismay. She went out to the lime-tree walk which lay between the house and the high wall, all clothed with ivy, with bunches of honeysuckle hanging from its embattled height. This was the walk that was considered to be haunted, though no one was afraid of the gentle ghost that dwelt there. Miss Margaret came out hastily to cool her cheeks, which were burning, and divert her mind, which was full of uncomfortable thoughts. It was still light, though it was nearly bed-time; the trees, so silken green, kept their colour, though in a sort of spiritualized tint, in the pale clear light. The sound of footsteps (which no doubt a scientific inquirer would have decided to come from some entirely natural phenomena of acoustics quite explainable and commonplace) was more distinct than usual in the complete stillness of the evening. It was said to be a lady who had died for love—one of the daughters of Murkley in a distant age, who was the ghost of this pensive walk. She was never visible; her steps softly sounding upon the path in a regular cadence, coming and going, was all that was known of her. Sometimes, when the family was in difficulty or danger, it had been reported that a sigh was heard. But no one living had heard the sigh. And even the maids were not afraid to walk in daylight in this visionary place. There was a certain green line close by the trees which was never encroached upon, and which was coloured by patches of mosses. It was there the lady walked, so people said, without considering that no footsteps could have sounded clear from that natural velvet. Miss Margaret threw her little shawl over her cap, and went out into the mysterious stillness, broken by those still more mysterious sounds which she had been accustomed to from her childhood. It soothed her to be there, and she took herself to task with a little indignation. That she should suspect her sister! that she should think it possible that Jean could "make a fool of herself!" When she had spent half an hour in the walk, slowly pacing up and down, hearing the steps of that other mysterious passenger going and coming, she returned to the house subdued. But she did not go back to the drawing-room where Jean was. Her fears on the subject of Lilias had altogether departed from her mind with Lewis' extraordinary announcement; but even the risk of an entanglement for Lilias, though more likely, and perhaps more serious, would have been in the course of nature. It would not have affected her with a sense of shame and intolerant passion like any short-coming on the part of Jean.

As for Lewis, he went home to his inn pleased, but not agitated, like Miss Margaret. He was very much satisfied with the sanction thus accorded to him, and with the approval implied in it, as he thought. If the elder sister had been disposed to oppose him, or, indeed, if she had not approved of what he was about to do, she would not have gone so far as to indicate to him when he might come. Miss Margaret's angry enjoyment of the idea of his discomfiture, her eagerness to lead him to the point so that he might be crushed at once, never occurred to Lewis. There was nothing in his own honest intentions to throw light upon such a meaning. For his own part, he did not contemplate the idea of failure at all. He thought that Miss Jean, though she might be surprised at his proposal, could have no reason to be offended by it, and he believed that he would be successful. It seemed to him entirely to her advantage, modest as he was. Her age, he thought, would make the idea of a husband not less, but more agreeable to her. It was an advancement in life of which she had probably given up all hopes. This was his idea in an economical point of view, so to speak, and not from any overweening opinion of himself. Marriage, he had been trained to believe, was often irksome and disagreeable to a man, but for a woman it was a necessity of well-being, of dignity, almost of self-respect. It was this that gave him the calm confidence he had in respect to Miss Jean. She would be startled, no doubt. It would take away her breath to find herself, after all, still within the brighter circle of existence; but she would not throw away this last and probably unexpected chance. Personal vanity had nothing to do with Lewis' calm conviction. It was not he that would be irresistible to her; but the fact of having a step in existence offered to her—a higher place.

It was about noon next day when he set out for the Castle; and when he was shown into the drawing-room, he found Miss Jean, as before, seated over her table-cover, with all her silks arranged upon her table, and her carnation in a glass being copied. She did not get up to greet him, as she had done before. Even her old-fashioned ideas of politeness, which were more rigorous than anything in the present day, yielded to the friendly familiarity with which she was beginning to regard him. She gave him her hand with a kind smile.

"This is very good of you, Mr. Murray," she said, "to give up a bonny morning to me;" her eyes went instinctively to the piano as she spoke. This piqued Lewis a very little; but he loved music too well to disappoint her.

"The finer the morning," he said, "the more congenial it is to music." There was time enough to indulge himself and her before beginning the serious business of the matter between them, and indeed it was not even necessary that there should be anything said upon that serious matter to-day.

"And that is true," said Miss Jean, fervently; "the evening perhaps is the best of all; the fading of the daylight, and the hushing of the world, and the coming on of rest—that is beautiful with music. I like it in the dusk, and I like it in the dark, when ye can only hear, not see, and your soul goes upon the sound.

But I like it as well in the day, in the brightness, in the middle of life, at all times; it is never out of season," she added, with an enthusiasm which elevated her simple countenance.

Lewis felt a sensation of pride and happiness as he looked at her. No one could say she was unworthy a man's choice or affections. It would do him honour among all who were qualified to judge that he had made such a choice. Miss Jean was somewhat astonished by the way in which he turned upon her. It half confused, half pleased her. For a long time no man had looked so intently upon her tranquil, middle-aged countenance. She thought he was "an affectionate lad," probably being without mother or sister to spend his natural kindness upon, and therefore eager to respond to it wherever he found it. His compliments on their former meeting she had put away out of her mind, though they had startled and almost abashed her for the moment; but then compliments were the common-places of foreigners, everybody knew that they meant nothing, certainly no harm. It was just the same, she thought, as if a Scotchman had said, "I am glad to see you looking well," no more than that.

And then he began to play. He chose Mozart after their talk about the times and seasons. Lewis was not naturally given to much exercise of the fancy, but he was very sympathetic, and readily took his cue from any mind which was congenial to him. He thought that the splendour of this great composer was appropriate to the richness and fulness of the noon. Themes more dreamy, more visionary, more simply sweet would be the language of the evening. And once more he watched, with an interest and sympathy which he thought must be as nearly like love as possible, the gradual forgetfulness of everything but the music which came over Miss Jean. First her work flagged, then she pushed away the carnation which she was copying to one side, and let her table-cover drop on her knees; then she leant forward on the little table, her head in her hands, her eyes fixed upon him; then those eyes filled with tears, and saw nothing, neither him nor any accessory, but only a mystic world of sweetness and emotion which she was utterly incapable of describing, but which shone through her face with an eloquence which was beyond words. Lewis, as he looked at her in this ecstatic state, which he had the power of throwing her into, knew very well that, though he was the performer and she only the listener, the music was not half to him what it was to her. It filled her soul, it carried her away above the world, and all that was in it. When he paused she sank back in her chair overwhelmed, unable to say anything. He was fond of applause, but applause was not necessary here.

"I wish," he said, rising, and coming towards her, full of a genuine warmth and enthusiasm, "that I could play to you for ever."

She did not speak for a little, but smiled, and dried her soft eyes.

"No—no—that would be too much," she said.

"It would be too much to continue always, oh, yes—but I do not mean that. To play to you whenever you pleased, as often as you pleased; when you wished to come out of the common, to be happy; for it makes you happy?"

"I think it must be like Heaven," said Miss Jean, fervently; "that is all I can think of—the skies opening, and the angels singing."

"That is beautiful," he cried, "to open Heaven. That is what I should like to do for you—always. To have it ready for you when you pleased."

"You have a kind heart," said Miss Jean; "oh, you have a kind heart. But, if it cannot be always," she said, with a tender smile, "you must just let it be as often as you can, as long as you are here."

"I am going to stay here," said Lewis, "that is, if you will let me."

"Me! Let you! But it is little I can have to do with it: and you may be sure I would let you—and kindly welcome, kindly welcome," said Miss Jean, recovering herself.

She was a little ashamed of feeling so deeply, but the beauty of the music so completely occupied her mind that, save as "a kind lad," she did not think of Lewis at all.

"If you will make me welcome, then I will stay. It depends upon you altogether; I will stay or I will go away, as you please. It is you that must decide," the young man said.

He was standing on the other side of the little table, his face lit up with the enthusiasm of sympathy and pleasure. It was sweet to him to have made so profound an impression, and the emotion in Miss Jean's mind reflected itself in him. He admired her, he loved her for feeling so much. It threw a tender light upon everything about her; there was no effort wanting to look tenderly and speak tenderly with all the emotion of a genuine sentiment. His eyes glowed with softness and warmth, his voice took a pleading tone, he was ready to have put himself at her feet, actually as well as metaphorically, so much was he touched and moved by this sympathetic strain of feeling. Miss Jean, for her part, gathering her work into her hand, and recovering her self slowly, looked up with eyes of simple surprise at the extraordinary aspect of the young stranger.

"You are meaning—? to be sure, we will be very glad, very happy to have you for a neighbour; but, knowing so little of the circumstances, how can we, that are but strangers—"

They were both so pre-occupied that they had not heard anything but the sound of their own voices, and, when another suddenly interposed, they started as if a shot had been fired beside them.

"Jean, Margaret sent me to tell you dinner was on the table," was the peaceful intimation this voice made.

Lewis turned round with a nervous impatience, finding the interruption vexatious. He turned round and found himself suddenly in a presence he had never been clearly conscious of before. What was it? To external appearance a young, slight girl, fair as Scottish beauty ought to be, with light locks just tinged here and there with the brighter light which makes them golden, a complexion of the most dazzling purity, eyes, somewhat astonished, of deep blue, and features perhaps not equal in quality to all the rest, but harmonious enough in their youth and softness. This was what she was in actual flesh and blood; but as she appeared to Lewis, at that moment actually feeling, and with all his might endeavouring to impress upon a middle-aged woman, the fervour of his devotion, and his dependence upon her fiat, she was something more. She was Youth in person, she was Love, and Hope, and a sort of incarnate delight. He looked at her, and the words he had been speaking died from his lips, the enthusiasm he had been feeling was blown out as if it had been the flame of a candle. He forgot himself and good manners, and his position as a stranger, and stood, his lips apart, his eyes wide opened, gazing at her at once in amazement and admiration.

Lilias looked at him too with much astonishment and a good deal of curiosity. Was this the person whom Margaret had suggested to be the man from Kilmorley come to tune the piano? Though she was a very docile little girl, there were moments when she could be wilful. She made Lewis a little curtsey, and gave him a smile which went to his head like wine.

"And Margaret hopes the gentleman will come too," Lilias said.

"Oh!" cried Miss Jean with a tremor of conscience, and a questioning look towards her little sister. Could it be possible that Margaret—"I am sure," she said, "we will all be pleased if you will come and eat something with us; it is our dinner, as we are only ladies, without a man in the house; but it will do for luncheon for you."

"If you will permit me," said Lewis, with that profound bow which they all thought foreign.

He drew away from the little table, so as to leave Miss Jean room to gather together her embroidery before she rose from her chair, and waited, ready to follow the ladies. The proposal was delightful to him. He did not pause to ask whether the message had really come from Miss Margaret; he had none of Miss Jean's tremor. He thought only that he was ready to follow this nymph, this vision, to the end of the world if she pleased. Had he ever seen anything so beautiful? he asked himself: and, as may easily be supposed, said "No" with hasty readiness. Lilias was in the perfection of youthful bloom and freshness, with the down upon her like a peach, untouched by anything that could impair that dazzling, morning glory; the dark old house, and the companionship of the two sisters who in her presence became old and faded, threw up her bloom all the more, and so did her simple frock, the girlish fashion of her hair, her school-room apron, her position as Margaret's messenger.

"Come along, then," she said, lightly, and ran off in advance.

Lewis offered his arm to Miss Jean. She was very nervous, he thought, because of what he had been saying to her—but Miss Jean had by no means taken up, as he meant them, the things he had been saying to her, and was nervous because of her doubt whether Margaret really meant this invitation. What if it was a sudden thought of Lilias alone? The girl did wicked things now and then of this sort, little rebellions "in fun," audacities which sometimes vexed Margaret. But Miss Jean's instincts of hospitality would have tempted her, even without this proceeding on the part of Lilias, to invite her visitor, towards whom she felt kindly. She put her arm within his with a little tremor: and Lewis felt the quiver, and thought that he had been successful in his suit. He pressed her hand softly against his side. Though he had been so startled, shaken out of his previous thoughts by this sudden apparition, yet it did not occur to him to be unfaithful. Nothing yet occurred to him except that here was a new thing, a new glory and beauty returned into life. This fairy creature glided out of the room before them, ran downstairs like a ray of sunshine, making the dark old oak staircase bright, and darted in at the open door of the dining-room, where she evidently announced their coming with a laugh. The laugh made Lewis smile in sympathy, but it made Miss Jean tremble, for it proved that her alarm was justified, and so did the sudden, startled sound of Miss Margaret's deeper voice. What Lilias said was, with that laugh,

"Margaret, I have asked the music man to come too."

"The music man! He is no music man," cried Miss Margaret, and then she said, "Quick, Simon, quick, lay another place." There was no time for further explanations now.

Lewis thought this meal was the most delightful he had ever eaten in his life. The two elder sisters sat at the head and foot of the table, and opposite to him was Lilias, with a little flush of triumph in her face, and a mischievous smile about the corners of her mouth. She did not talk very much, and to him not at all. The other ladies maintained the conversation chiefly between them. For his own part he was content to say very little, to confine himself to replying when they spoke to him, and listening eagerly to their talk, and watching the beautiful girl whom he could not raise his eyes without seeing, and whose glance he met now and then with something of the freemasonry of youth. He did not know her, nor she him, while he was acquainted with both the other ladies, and felt himself already in a position of intimacy and sympathetic friendship, if no more, with Miss Jean; but yet instinctively, and in a moment, they two, he felt, constituted a faction, a party, youth against age.

While the elders talked, she would shoot a little glance at him across the table, a glimmer of a smile would go over her face, in which there was an appeal to him for an answering smile; a sort of unconscious telegraph of mutual understanding was set up between them. When Miss Margaret questioned him, he replied with a look to Lilias first to see if she were listening. When she spoke, though it was only a monosyllable, he paused to listen. After, when it was over, the whole scene appeared to him like a dream; the dark wainscot of the room, with the bloom of that young face against it, Miss Margaret against the light, Miss Jean, with her sweet but faded face in the full illumination of the window, old Simon making slow circles round the table. His own heart was beating with pleasure, with suspense, with excitement, the feeling that something had happened to him, something new which he scarcely understood. He did not realize that he had been suddenly stopped in his love-making to Miss Jean by this apparition, nor that it had taken from him all desire to carry on that love-making. Indeed, his mind had not taken in the new occurrence at all; he was still in this state of sensation, knowing that here was a new event which had suddenly happened to him, but not knowing what it was.

CHAPTER XIV

Lewis left the Castle like a man in a dream. There was an intoxication about him which affected his whole being vaguely, as actual intoxication might do, in which there was not the slightest self-reproach or sense of doing wrong. He was elated, delighted, happy; a sort of suffusion of sweetness and brightness was in his veins, filling up everything. It affected him like a new sensation, a new event, a revelation of new possibilities. It never had occurred to him that the world could be so sweet, or any mortal creature so happy. Why was he so happy? Because there was in existence a creature so young, so fair, so sweet, as to make life itself look beautiful. What reason was that for the happiness of one who had nothing to do with her, whose life could not be affected one way or other by her existence? But he did not at first ask himself that question. It made him glad without any reason; it affected him foolishly. He could have laughed for pleasure; he thought better of everything for her sake. She seemed to fill the fresh country with a reflection of herself. He thought of nothing else as he walked down to his inn in the afternoon. She had not cared for his society, but disappeared immediately after dinner on a sign from her sister, turning and making him a salutation which was half a curtsey and half a smiling nod of familiarity. She too, perhaps, had felt the youth in him, and had not felt herself capable of curtseying ceremoniously as she had been taught. There was a merry glimmer in her eyes, though the rest of her was so demure, and this conjunction was delightful to him. He had not known what the other ladies said to him after; a kind of golden mist had seemed to him to fill the air. The place was not desolate when she went out of it, because she left it full of herself, full of vibrations and echoes. He had heard the kind elder voices in his ears, with their long sentences and the responsive waves of their talk, and had been aware that he took some share in it, had answered them when they spoke, and was not without comprehension of their meaning. But he had felt that he was in haste to get away, to be alone, to think over this new thing. And accordingly he did think it over, or rather he walked into the unbroken enjoyment of it, into the contemplation of Lilias, when he walked out of those old-fashioned doors into the afternoon sunshine. He did not think of her, he only moved along in a current which was her, in air which was full of her. He did not understand the sensation; it was as new to him as she was—new and delightful, entrancing his soul.

Lewis moved along down the country-road and through the village with his heart full of this strange and novel flood of feeling. Her look, as, turning his head suddenly in the midst of the genuine fervour of his address to Miss Jean, he had caught sight of her, and the words had gone out on his lips: the turn of her head, the going and coming of her smile as she sat opposite to him at table, the few words she said, the simplicity of appearance and movements, only a little girl, and yet the queen of all—these were before him as he walked, and not the features of the landscape. Now it was one recollection, now another; the manner in which she turned to go out of the room, the half curtsey, the half laugh, full of a sweet malice, the glance of her blue eyes, half mocking, half ceremonious. Never had drama been so full of interest for a spectator. He went over everything. Then he went into his parlour and threw himself down upon his hard angular sofa, and went over it all again—every look, every movement, every raising of the eyelids. He seemed to himself not to have forgotten a single movement, or step, or word, or almost breath. She came in with him to the dingy room just as she had come along the road. It was all a revelation, and so full of dazzling light that it confused his mind and everything about him; the sun was not so bright, nor the world so fair, as this new creature who had suddenly made of herself a new centre to the universe.

Lewis had never in his life been so happy as he was in that curious ecstasy. He did not ask himself why he went into details, he did not say to himself that to have her, to appropriate her to himself, was henceforward to be the object of his life. Many men have declared in a moment, "This of all maids is the one maid for me." But Lewis did not go so far as this; he had not thought as yet of appropriation. What he felt was that here, in the world, was a creature more sweet, more beautiful than he had ever dreamt of, and that the place was transfigured, and mere living made into a delight because she was there. This made the blood course through his veins with a warmth and fulness he had never known before; he felt as if some great happiness had come to him. But even when he paused and asked himself what was the meaning of it, what good could come to him from it, he found no answer to give to that question. He pushed it aside indeed; he had nothing to do with it in his present mood.

Later, as it began to approach evening, Lewis met Mr. Seton on the river-side, and, having nothing better to do, walked with him for a mile or two on his way to some piece of parochial duty. The minister complained a little of his work, as everybody is apt to do.

"They expect to be visited, however far-off they may be," he said, with a pucker in his forehead and a quiver of complaint in his voice, "and instead of bringing their children to church, as is their duty, they will find some reason for a private christening. It is far too much the way in these parts. Of course, the session might make a stand on the subject, and some of my elders would be very well inclined, but what is the use of making a commotion? I am fond of peace. I always say just for this once—and that is how they come over me—rather that than make a disturbance. I am always for yielding—when the question is not vital—when the question is not vital! Of course, I make my stand upon that."

"To be sure," said Lewis, vaguely, though he had only the faintest idea what was meant.

"Better be baptized privately than not be baptized at all," said the minister, solemnly. "But, to do the people justice, they are not so bad as that. They will go to the Free Kirk, or the U. P., but they will not leave a child unchristened. It is in the great towns that you find that kind of heathenism, not in the country. The country, there is little question, is better in some ways. There is not so much scepticism. Perhaps you will say there is more indifference on all subjects, and that our ploughmen just take things for granted?"

"Oh, no," said Lewis, more vague than ever, "I certainly should not say that."

"You think not? Well, there are just very curious intellects among them, I must allow that—strange bits of thought, you know, but seldom sceptical." Mr. Seton spoke with a certain regret, for he felt himself qualified to meet the legions of infidelity, and longed for nothing so much as the opportunity of converting an unbeliever. "The doubts they entertain are upon high points of doctrine which probably a young man like you would never have heard of; but they make nothing of what is often a great difficulty to a cultivated spirit—the standards, Mr. Murray. You will sympathize with that difficulty. The Westminster confession may be a stumbling-block to me, and the like of me, but as for these ploughmen they will put-to their hand to the confession, or to a dozen confessions. They swallow the longer and the shorter catechisms without even wishing—they have very strong stomachs in the way of doctrine. It is not on that point you will ever find them wanting. The difficulties and dangers of more delicate minds—" Mr. Seton said, bending upon Lewis a benignant eye.

"I suppose go with more delicate bodies," said that young man, with a laugh, which was profoundly inappropriate. And he had to laugh alone at his own jest, the minister looking upon him with gravity and disapproval, both shocked and disappointed that he should show so little appreciation. "But the ploughmen," he said, hastily and humbly, "are not the most interesting part of the people?"

"If you think a small country-gentleman, such as we have here, is more interesting, Mr. Murray, in an intellectual point of view—"

"No, no," said Lewis, half abashed, half amused. "You must not think so badly of me; I was thinking of— some of the ladies."

At this the minister paused, and gave him a doubtful look, apprehensive that the stranger was indulging in a little satire; but as Lewis laughed with ingratiating simplicity and blushed a little, and added, "I own they are more interesting to me," the minister too unbended, and joined in the laugh, and shook his head the while.

"Ah! if we were all young men. But, to be sure, we must make allowance for those that are. And which of the ladies is it that you find so interesting, if it is not indiscreet to inquire?"

This question brought Lewis back to a perception that he was on delicate ground.

"All whom I have met with," he said. "The intercourse is different, very different from what I have been used to. The young ladies, who are so frank, who meet us so—simply."

"Ah, that is your foreign way of thinking," said Mr. Seton. "No doubt it seems strange to you, but we have every confidence in our daughters. It is rarely, very rarely that it is found to be an undeserved confidence."

"But some are not so," said Lewis. He had thought a few minutes before that it would be impossible to bring the conversation to this subject, and he could scarcely believe now in the easy success of his own bold attempt. "Some are not so. I think there is one young lady who is guarded as people do abroad. I have been here so long, and I saw her but for the first time to-day."

"How long have you been here—three weeks? That is not a lifetime," said the minister. "And who may this be that is taken such care of? I cannot call to mind—"

"It is the ladies at the Castle who interest me so much," said Lewis, "especially the less old one, she whom you call Miss Jean, and who is so susceptible to music. I have seen no one who is more susceptible. It takes possession of her; it carries her away. To see it is beautiful," cried Lewis. "I am very much interested in Miss Jean; but there is one, much more young, whom I have only seen for the first time—"

"Indeed!" said Mr. Seton. "Who could that be?" And then his tone changed in a moment. "Oh, Lilias! Yes, to be sure. The old sisters, you see, they are two old maids; they have got I don't know what ideas in their heads. Poor little thing! they will make an old maid of her like themselves. I hear my wife and Katie say that she sees nobody. Poor girl! But then the old ladies are peculiar," the minister said.

"Are they such very old ladies?" said Lewis, somewhat piqued. "I think that, on the whole, I like that—to have a lovely young lady, like a flower, kept apart from the world, that pleases me. Perhaps it is that I, too, am old-fashioned."

"Is she so lovely?" said the minister with a laugh. "Well, well, perhaps she is so. I am saying nothing against it. She is just little Lilias Murray to me. I've seen her grow up like my own. She is older though than Katie. And so you admire her very much? I must tell my wife. My wife will be very much amused to hear that somebody has seen her after all, and that she is thought to be lovely, poor little thing!" Mr. Seton repeated, with a laugh of amusement.

This annoyed Lewis more than he could say.

"It is a very distinguished family," he said, with gravity. "I find it so. The two ladies like châtelaines of the old time; and the younger one so beautiful, like a young princess who is in their charge."

"Well, that is very poetical," said Mr. Seton, but it was evident that he felt it very difficult to restrain his sense of the ludicrous. "You see we are too familiar with them," he said. "Familiarity, you know, breeds contempt. No, not contempt in the ordinary sense of the word, for two more respectable women don't exist; but I'm not sure that I would just use the word distinguished. It is a very good old family, the Murrays of Murkley—but distinguished, no."

"I used the word in another sense. It is their appearance—and manner that is distinguished: as they say in France."

Upon this the minister broke forth again into a low laugh.

"They are just two very respectable, elderly women," he said.

Lewis made no reply. It appeared to him that here for the first time he had encountered in his idyllic village the spirit of detraction, the petty scorn of limited minds for people superior to themselves. He felt that, if he spoke, it would only be to call forth the minister's laughter more and more, and raise that feeling of ungenerous opposition in his mind. Lewis did not leave Mr. Seton, as was his first impulse, for he still felt the charm of being able to talk of them, and of probably learning something more about Lilias, even though it were not in a favourable sense, to be worth lingering for. He walked on by Mr. Seton's side, saying as little as possible, and unaware that there was in his aspect that air of slightly-injured dignity which, more than anything else, amuses those who have been engaged in the congenial work of pulling down idols, and making them appear to their worshippers in a proper light. But the minister was infinitely tickled by Lewis's look. And that anybody should contemplate the Misses Murray in an exalted light was delightfully ridiculous to their neighbour, who had laughed at them and their ways, and criticised their actions more or less for years of his life.

"The ladies," he said, after a pause, "have been rather hard upon the little one, or so my wife says—and women understand each other best. They will never let her come out to a young party even at the manse. I hear they are very ambitious for Lilias, and are reserving her, poor innocent women—reserving her," Mr. Seton said, shaking his head with an expression of amused pity, "for some grand match."

"For—some—" Lewis felt as if for one moment the wheels of his being stood still; the earth was arrested in its progress. What could it mean? he asked himself vaguely. A grand match! The words made a wonderful commotion in his ears, but he said to himself that he did not understand what they meant.

"That is it," said the minister, shaking his head, and with that smile always on his face. "Poor things! they want her to build up the family again. I hear they are going to take her to court, and make a great fuss, all in the hopes that she will marry some great potentate or other, and restore the credit of the Murrays. Well, since you think her so lovely as all that," he added, with a little burst of laughter, as if overcome with the ridicule of the idea, "it may be that it's us that are the idiots after all, and that the ladies are right."

Lewis scarcely heard these remarks; his whole being was in a ferment. Up to this moment it had not occurred to him what was the natural way in which to regard this new apparition which had come into his life. He had been wooing (so to speak) her sister, the old sister who was as a mother to Lilias, when this wonder appeared to him, and it was not that his mind changed about Miss Jean, but only that something entirely new and extraordinary burst upon him, something he had never dreamt of before. His words, his thoughts, the very action of his mind was arrested. He had no longer the power of fixing upon that project or any other, his mind being entirely engrossed and occupied by the new thing presented to it. But his feelings had been entirely those of joy and delight in his discovery. It was something that lighted up the earth and made the whole world more sweet; but it had not yet occurred to him to appropriate this lovely creature to himself, or to make her the centre of his individual enjoyment. Now there burst upon him another revelation, something of an entirely different nature. That she was sweet, but not for him; that her beauty was not intended only to make the whole world happier, but to be a special fountain of joy to one, but that not himself, but some one else. Lewis did not himself understand, in the rush and hurry of his feelings, what was the sentiment which succeeded that vague sensation of happiness in his mind. But he understood that in a moment the minister whom he had been accompanying with so much friendliness on the way became intolerable, and that the very sound of his voice was irritating, and not to be borne. For the sake of appearances he went on with him to a cross-road which they were approaching, that led Lewis did not know whither; but anything was better than to go on with so heartless a companion. He broke off abruptly when he came to this unknown path, saying something about letters to write, and the necessity of getting back to his inn.

"You'll not get back to your inn that way," Mr. Seton said; but Lewis paid no attention, indeed scarcely heard him as he hurried on.

He sped along this lonely road in a totally different direction from that he was acquainted with, till he had entirely lost himself and worn himself out, which perhaps in the circumstances was as wise a thing as he could have done. For his mind was agitated with a wonderful variety of new thoughts. He became aware of what that lovely figure was which had glided across his vision, and in a moment swept everything else out of his thoughts. She was more than youth, more than mere beauty and brightness. She was love. The thoughts of last night, that sudden curious contrast which had struck him between the plans and purposes of his own life and those of Philip Stormont, flashed back again and made the situation clear to him in a moment. Here was nature, here was the secret of the world. The broken scenes and visions which had been passing before his eyes since ever he saw her took a different form; instead of only seeing her, he saw himself beside her. He saw the group of last night changed from Stormont and Katie to Lilias and himself. He walked by her side as he had walked by her sister's; but how differently! He talked to her as he had talked to Miss Jean, but oh! in how changed a tone.

All this went through his mind as he walked mile after mile, always trying a new direction, always failing to recover his ground, or come near any landmark he knew. The sun had been long set, and in any other but these northern skies night would have set in, when he found himself at last approaching the village. He could see that there was a little commotion in the street as he came along, sadly weary and dusty, and beginning to come down from those celestial circles of the imagination, and to remember that he was very hungry, and had not dined. A little group of children broke up and dashed down the road in front of him towards the 'Murkley Arms.'

"Eh, yonder he's coming!" they cried.

Janet, with a very anxious countenance, was standing in the doorway.

"Eh, sir," she said, "is this you? And what has keepit ye frae your dinner? We have had a maist anxious night looking out for ye, and wondering what could have happened. Adam's away doun to the water-side, and I've sent to the manse and the Castle, and every place I could think of, we were that alarmed."

"Why should you be alarmed?" said Lewis. "The fact is, I lost my way."

"I'm real glad to see it's nae waur," said Janet. "There's been ane here frae Kilmorley keen, keen to see ye. It was just the writer's clerk, and that gied us a fright; and he didna seem that sure about your name, and he said he had instructions just to bide and no to leave till he had seen ye. But I sent him away with a flea in his lug," said Janet. "I said you were just real respectable, as we've found you, sir, and one of the Murrays, kent folk, and taken a hantle notice of by the Murkley ladies, and how daured he come here to set your friends against ye? But for a' that I got a terrible fright, Mr. Murray. I thought maybe ye had got wit o' his coming, and had just slippit away, and we would never have heard tell of ye again."

"Why should I slip away?" cried Lewis, astonished, his conviction of innocence being too strong to permit him to entertain at the moment any alarm as to the consequences that might follow if he were found to have presented himself under a name which was not his own.

Janet gave him a confused, repentant, yet penetrating look.

"Deed, I canna tell," she said, somewhat abashed; "but how was I to ken that there mightna be reasons, and the man so awfu' curious about you, and him the writer's clerk? Gentlemen are whiles overtaken, just the same as poor folk. It might have been siller, or it might have been—But, dear bless me, what is the use of speakin', when here ye are, just your ain sel', and no put aboot at a'; and the dinner's spoilt, but nae mair harm done."

"My good Mrs. Janet," said Lewis, "I am much obliged to you, but you need not entertain any fears about me. I am not afraid of any writer's clerk. What is a writer, by the way?" he said, smiling, pausing as he was about to enter.

She gazed at him with round eyes of amazement.

"What is a writer? Well, I always said you were an innocent young man—I was aye sure there would be nothing in it—but you must ken very little indeed, sir, if you have never come across a writer. He's just a—well, maybe sometimes a terror to evil-doers, I would not say—but a great fyke and trouble mony a time to them that do well. He is one that will gather in the siller that's owin' ye, that ye canna get yoursel', and pretend it's a' for your gude, syne take his percentage and his profit, till there's more of it gangs into his pocket than yours. He is one that—"

"I see—a lawyer of some sort. You thought I was perhaps running away from my creditors," Lewis said, with a laugh.

Janet gave him a guilty glance. "Mony a grand gentleman has done that, and lived to pay them a' to the last farden, and never been a preen the waur."

Lewis laughed till all the attendant children, who had been looking on, waiting for the penny promised them for intimating his approach, laughed too in sympathy.

"I owe you more than I owe anybody else," he said; "but we'll talk of that after dinner, for I'm famishing now."

CHAPTER XV

Lewis woke up next morning a different man. His light-hearted youth and easy views had gone from him. The musings of the night had only showed him the position in which he was, without showing him any way out of it. He had all but pledged himself to one woman, placed himself at her disposal; and his heart had gone out to another. He felt that life would not be worth living, nor the world have any charm for him, unless he could secure Lilias as the companion of his existence. Yet at the same time he recognized that it was the sister of Lilias to whom so lightly, thinking, as it now seemed, nothing of it, he had offered that life as he might have offered a flower. Was there ever a more terrible dilemma for a young man? And he had not found it out at first. It had not been till the terrible prose of the minister set the case fully before him that he had recognized the complication which was so novel, so strange, yet to him so overwhelming. Love! how could he love this creature whom he had seen but once, of whom he knew nothing. But even to ask that question seemed a sort of blasphemy against her, against the strange and potent sweetness of his own emotion. Knew nothing! he knew everything; he knew her, the wonder of creation! To see her was enough. What doubt, what hesitation was possible? "There is none like her, none;" he was as much convinced of that as if he had watched all her ways for years. And to think that he had not had the patience to wait, or any instinct to tell him that she was here! This was the strange, the incomprehensible thing. It was a fatality. So it had been ordained in Greek plays and uncompromising tragedy. That everything which was sweetest should come too late—that one should be on the very verge of the loveliest road to Paradise, and all unawares should choose another which led a different way.

Lewis awoke to a sense, no longer of a world enhanced, and made infinitely sweeter and fairer, by the presence in it of a creature more beautiful and delightful than he had ever before dreamt of, but of a universe which had gone suddenly out of joint, where the possibilities of blessedness were counteracted by malign influences, and fate took pleasure in turning happiness into trouble: one way and another the calmly smiling day, the happy commonplace, the matter-of-course existence had come to an end for him. It was very summary and very complete. He looked back for a few days, and thought how easily he had made up his mind about Miss Jean, how calmly he had determined to make her a present of his existence, with a kind of horror. In reality it had been a very small part of his existence which he had resolved to give up to her: but this he did not recollect in the excitement of his thoughts. He had meant to live as he pleased, always returning between whiles to the kind, elderly, indulgent wife who, he felt sure, would require no more of him; but this now seemed a sort of blasphemy to him, a travesty of the life which a man should wish to live with the true mate and companion who would share his every thought. He rejected his former thoughts with a self-disgust that was full of anger. It was odious to him to know that he had been capable of so thinking. All that had altered in a moment; not with the first sight of love, and what it was, in the person of Lilias, but with the first clear perception that this fair creature was some one's destined bride, but not his. In the irony of fate not his; revealed to him only after it was too late, after he had mortgaged his existence and bound himself to a world so much pettier and poorer than that of which she held the key.

Up to this moment there had been in the heart of Lewis very little questioning of fate; he had taken all that came in his way with, on the whole, a cheering composure. The loss of his parents had been made up to him in a wonderful way. The loss of Sir Patrick was so completely natural that there could be no repining in the sorrow, honest sorrow deeply felt, but without any bitterness, with which his young dependent mourned him. All this had been legitimate; he had accepted it as inevitable and necessary. Some natural tears he dropped, but wiped them soon. He had taken his life in the same unquestioning matter-of-fact way, almost unconscious of any deeper necessity for satisfaction in it than that which lay on the surface, the honest discharge of such duties as he knew, the honest enjoyment of such pleasures as were congenial to him. He did not know that he wanted anything more. It was not that Lewis had not heard the murmurings of bitter philosophy in many a tone, he had heard his old patron discourse upon the deceptions of life, he had heard Sir Patrick's friends talking, snarling over the lies and delusions with which, to them, the world was full; but the youth in him had rebelled, had laughed, had attributed all this to the ill-temper of age and disappointment, sometimes pitying, always certain that to him nothing of the kind would ever come. And there had been nothing in his existence to contradict this easy confidence. Nothing had gone amiss with him; there had been no occasion for him to rail at fortune, which had always been so good to him, or to find any delusions in the brightness of his life. It had been without complications, without mystery; nothing in it that was not straightforward, until he came to Murkley; and it seemed to him that the harshest moralist could not have objected to his innocent little artifice, his adoption of a name to which he had indeed a good title, even though it was taken up with intention to deceive. And even the deception had a good reason. It seemed hard to poor Lewis that coming thus innocently, with intention to do well, to right wrong, to atone for injury, he should have been made to suffer. It seemed to him cruel. His imagination did not blame Providence, which was too far-off and too solemn to be made responsible for such matters, but he found a little consolation in recalling to his mind the old snarlings he used to hear, the complaints against fate, whatever that was. Why, why should such a malign chance have fallen on him, whose wish was to be just, to be true to everybody? It seemed to Lewis that he had good reason to complain. To be sure, he did not very well know against whom his complaint could be directed, but he felt it all the same.

He was late of getting up; he was slow to go out; he did not care what he did with himself; sometimes his impulse was to hurry to the Castle, to take advantage as long as he could of the permission which certainly had been given him, on the mere chance of perhaps seeing her again. But what was the use of seeing her? It was to Miss Jean his visit would have to be made. It was she who had been the aim of his devotion; and at that thought Lewis laid down the hat which he had snatched up, and threw himself in despair upon his seat. No, better to hurry away, never to put himself within the reach of her influence again, to do nothing at least to deepen and increase it. And then he began to say to himself, what matter? no one but himself should ever know the strong temptation which had seized him, the enchantment she had exercised unawares. It would do no harm to any one but himself, if he did see her once more; and if he suffered for it, there would be compensation in the sweetness of her presence; he would have had the sunshine at least, even if the cloud were all the blacker afterwards.

Throughout the whole of this self-discussion it will be seen that the idea of being unfaithful to his first declared object never occurred to Lewis. He believed that he had made Miss Jean fully aware of the proposal he meant to make her. He had told Miss Margaret of it. He had no doubt that they must have communicated with each other on the subject, and that the mere fact of his reception at the house was a proof that he was viewed under the aspect of an accepted lover. And, this being the case, nothing in the world would have made Lewis flinch from the position he had assumed. It seemed to him now like going from the glory of the skies and free air into the dim and shadowed atmosphere indoors. Lilias would have meant the garden of Eden, the perennial, never-exhausted idyll of human blessedness. Miss Jean meant a domestic interior somewhat dull, grey, full of dimness and shadows. But all the glory and blessedness in the world could not make that possible which was impossible, as Lewis knew; and what was impossible was to leave in the lurch the woman he had wooed. That was the one thing he could not do, however hard the price he had to pay. It did not come even the length of a discussion in his mind. It was too certain, too self-evident, for anything of the kind. He made no question about it. Thus sometimes he jumped up, thinking he would go at once to the Castle, and linger there till it was time to see her again; sometimes sat down again, saying to himself why should he do it? why should he add to his pain? Better to keep that one vision as the only one, a sort of poem, a revelation for one moment, and no more. In the lives of the saints such things have been told; how they had seen a celestial vision, sometimes printing marks in their very flesh, and had seen no more. Lewis felt that it was perhaps profane to compare with that supreme sort of revelation his sudden view of the woman whom he could never forget, who might have made of his life a something glorious and noble, altogether different from its natural commonplace. It was profane, but he could not help it: only the highest images could express what he meant. That mere glimpse of her, attended by so little self-disclosure on her part, almost without the communication of words, had it not already made such an impression on his soul as could never wear out? It had revealed another world to him, it had shown him what life might be, what it never could be, and with what a strange, lamentable misconception he had chosen the lower place!

He was still in this uncertain condition, walking to the window now and then, looking out vaguely, pacing about the room, pausing to look at himself in the dingy mirror on the mantelpiece, taking up his hat and putting it down again, not able to decide what he should do, when his attention was caught by the sound of steps coming up the stairs, and the voice of Janet directing some one to come "This way, sir, this way."

"Our young gentleman took a walk yestreen, ower long, and lost his way, so he's no out this morning, which is just very lucky," Janet was saying.

Lewis threw down his hat with an impatient exclamation. It was Stormont, no doubt, he who could do what he pleased, who had taken his own way and satisfied himself, though not as Lewis would have done: or perhaps the minister who had laughed and spoken of the queen of beauty and love as a "poor little thing." There sprang up in his mind immediately a sort of hatred of them both as thus problematically preventing him from seeing her again: for he no sooner felt that he could not do it than it seemed to him he had made up his mind to do it, and was in the very act of sallying forth. But it was neither Stormont nor the minister who was shown in by Janet. She opened the door, and put her head in first with a certain caution.

"This'll be yon gentleman," she said, and made a sort of interrogative pause, as much as to say no one should enter did Lewis disapprove. Then she opened the door wider, and added, "A gentleman to see you, Mr. Murray," in a louder voice.

To say that Janet paused after this for a moment to satisfy herself what sort of greeting passed between them, and whether or not she had done well to introduce the stranger, is scarcely necessary. She stood with the door in her hand, and the most sympathetic curiosity in her mind: but when she saw the newcomer hurry forward with a sort of chuckling laugh, holding out his hand and exclaiming, in familiar accents, "So this is you! It was just borne in upon me that it must be you," Janet withdrew well pleased.

"It's a' just as it should be," she said to Adam, who had lingered to see the result. "I'll no say our young lad is pleased: but it's a friend, it's no a spy nor a sheriff's officer."

"It's a writer from Edinburgh," said Adam; "I've seen him in the Parliament house."

"Hoot awa' with your Parliament house!" cried Janet. "It's ten years since you were in Edinburgh, and how can ye mind if he's a writer or no? Besides, I told ye, he's no feared for ony writer; he asked me, bless the callant! what a writer was?"

Adam was more sceptical, having, as he thought, more knowledge of the world. "Ye may ken the thing and no ken the name," he said.

But even he shouldered his rood and stalked away with a relieved mind; for Lewis had so moved the household at the 'Murkley Arms,' and even the village itself, in his favour, that the writer would have fared badly who had meant mischief to the kind and friendly visitor who had conciliated everybody. Janet, considering all the circumstances, was of opinion that, after the greeting she had seen, it would be natural and desirable to put in hand certain preparations for luncheon of a more than usually elaborate kind.

But if his humble friends were consoled, Lewis was taken entirely by surprise. He said, "Mr. Allenerly!" in a tone between astonishment and dismay.

"It is just me," said the lawyer, "and I had a moral conviction it was you I should find, though no one knew the name of Grantley—"

"Hush!" cried Lewis in alarm, raising his hand.

"It is not a nice thing in any circumstances," said the newcomer, "for a man to disown his own name."

There was an impulse of anger in Lewis' mind not at all natural to him.

"It is with no evil intention, and it is no case of disowning my name. My kind god-father, my patron—you are free to call him what you will—wished it to be so. I have adopted his suggestion, that is all."

"But here, of all places in the world!" cried Mr. Allenerly—"it is the imprudence I am thinking of. You have a good right to it, if you please—but here! Have they not put you through your catechism to know what Murrays you were of? That would be the first thing they would do—"

"Miss Margaret has done so, I allow."

"Miss Margaret! By my conscience, you have got far ben already! And she never found you out? and you have got footing there?"

A pleasurable sense of success soothed the exasperation and pain in the young man's mind.

"It was for that I came here," he said.

"I just guessed as much. I said to my wife, 'He's of the romantic sort; he'll be after little Lilias, take my word for it, as soon as he hears of her existence.' And so you've done it! Well, Mr. Murray, if that's what I am to call you, I congratulate you—that is, if you get clear of Miss Margaret. She's grand at a cross-examination, as I have good reason to know. If you satisfied her—"

"I think I satisfied her—I go there—I was going now, if you had not come," said Lewis, playing with his hat, which was on the table. It seemed to him that to get rid of this visitor was the best, and, indeed, only thing he wished for. "After little Lilias!" The words rang and tingled through his head; he did not wish to be asked any questions, for already he felt as if his countenance must betray him; he could not laugh as his visitor did. It was impossible for him even to respond with a smile. And that fixed gravity was something which had never before been seen on Lewis's face.

Mr. Allenerly cast a curious look upon him, and then he in turn put down his hat upon the table and drew forward a chair.

"You have made your way in what seems a surprising manner," he said, "but you do not seem very cheery about it. You will excuse me if I am pressing—it is a thing I should have been keen to push on, if I had not known that things of this kind must come of themselves; and, if you will pardon me for saying so, I wanted to know more of you before I would have put you in the way of Miss Lilias, poor thing. She is very young, and the first that comes has a great chance with a young girl. But her sisters have very high notions; they are ambitious for her, I have always heard, and whether they would have the sense to see that a bird in the hand is worth two, or any number, in the bush—"

"I cannot let you continue in a mistake," said Lewis, pale and grave. "It is not as you think; the thing is different—"

He paused, and Mr. Allenerly paused too, and looked at him with a doubtful air.

"Do you mean," he said, "to tell me that you, a young man from foreign parts, that knows neither England nor Scotland—a young man that is your own master, going where you please—do you mean to say that you come here to a small Scotch village, and settle down in a country public-house (for it's little better) for weeks with no object? I have a respect for you, Mr. Grantley, but I cannot swallow that."

"I did not say so," said Lewis, with a gravity that was exaggerated, and full of the dignified superiority of offended youth; but he could not defend himself from those impulses of imprudence which were natural to him. "It is not necessary, I suppose," he said, "that my object should be exactly as you have stated. There are three sisters—"

Mr. Allenerly made no reply at first, but gazed at him with astonished eyes. Then he suddenly burst into a peal of laughter.

"This is too good a joke," he said, "you rogue, you deceiver! Do you think it's a fair thing to play off your fun upon your man of business? None o' that—none o' that! No, but that's the best joke I've heard this year or more. I must tell my wife of that. There's three sisters, says he! Lord! but that beats all."

"I am at a loss," said Lewis, more dignified than ever, "to understand the cause of your mirth; but, when you have had it out, perhaps you will let me inform you of the real state of affairs."

"That is just what I am ready to do," the lawyer said, in his turn offended, "more than ready. The ladies are my clients, Mr.—"

"It was my godfather's desire that my name should be Murray."

"Then Murray be it!" cried the writer, with vehemence. "What have I to do with your name? If it comes to that, ye may call yourself royal Stuart, or Louis XVI., or anything ye please, for me."

"Don't let us quarrel, Mr. Allenerly; you have been very kind to me," said Lewis, suddenly struck with the absurdity of this discussion. He laughed as he held out his hand. "Come," he said, "do not be so hot, and I will tell you. But why should you laugh? I have paid my court to the second of the two sisters. She is a lady whom I respect very much. She is sweet and good. A laugh I cannot endure upon her account. I have endeavoured to do what I could to please her. I hope I may have—a little—succeeded," Lewis said. The supernatural gravity and dignity had gone out of his face; instead of these, there came a smile which had some pathos in it. There was a slight quiver in his sensitive mouth. It was not vanity, but a certain sorrowful pleasure, a sort of compassionate satisfaction which was in the smile; it checked the lawyer's laugh more effectually than any big words could have done. But he looked with great and growing surprise into the young man's face.

"Miss Jean?" he said, almost timidly, with a sudden sense of something that lay behind.

"Miss Jean," Lewis said, with a little affirmative nod several times repeated. "She loves music very much. She has a fine and tender soul. I think no one knows what she is. They think her only gentle and weak."

"That is true—that is true. She is a good woman; but—"

"I will confess to you," said Lewis, "I heard that there were three, and it troubled me. I had thought there would be one who was the heir after your English way. I was in much trouble what to do. Then it was evident that this good Miss Jean was she whom I could have most access to, and I loved her on account of the music; but I did not know," he added, ingenuously, with a sigh, "I will acknowledge it to you—I did not know that the other lady was young; I did not know she was—what I found her yesterday. Ah! I saw her only yesterday for the first time."

Mr. Allenerly, who had jumped up in great interest and excitement, and had been pacing about the room all this time, here came up to Lewis and struck him on the shoulder.

"You are neither Scotch nor English," he said, "but you're a fine fellow; I would say that before the world. You came here to restore the money to them in a real generous way without thinking of yourself; but cheer up, my lad! Miss Jean has nothing to do with it. It is Lilias that is the heir. What do I mean? I will soon tell you what I mean. Margaret and Jean have a small estate in the south country that was their mother's. They have nothing to do with Murkley. Boys are always looked for, and little thought was taken for them. But when the general married his second wife, the Castle and a bit of the old land, too little, far too little, was put in the marriage settlement—and Lilias is the heir of that—Lilias the little one, the young one, the bonnie one. You are in greater luck than you thought."

"Then it will be no restoration at all," said Lewis, his face growing longer and paler with disappointment and dismay.

"Not if you persevere in your present fancy—but that is just nonsense—you must turn your thoughts into another channel."

"You speak," said Lewis, "as if one's thoughts were like a stream of water. That is not to be considered at all; it is too late."

"Then it is all settled—Has Miss Jean—the Lord preserve us—accepted ye?" Mr. Allenerly said.

"Does that matter?" said Lewis. "I have laid my homage at her feet; it is for her to take, if she will."

"But—" cried the lawyer, in dismay, "don't ye see that all will be spoiled? that your very purpose will be balked—that everything will go wrong? If it is not settled beyond remedy, you must just do what many a man has done before. You must draw back before it is too late—"

"Draw back—and leave a lady insulted—You forget"—the young man spoke with much dignity—"that, though I am not a Murray, I am a gentleman," Lewis said.

CHAPTER XVI

General Murray, the only son of Sir Patrick, had, like his father before him, married at a very early age, so that his eldest daughter was not more than twenty-two years younger than himself, and he was, when he married for the second time a wife younger than Margaret, a man but little over forty, in the prime of his life and strength, as handsome as he had ever been, and attractive enough to take any girl's fancy. The second wife had been poor, but she had been noble, and the entail of the old hereditary estate, upon which stood at once the old Castle and the new unfinished palace, was broken in order that it might be secured to the children of Lady Lilias, whether sons or daughters. Who could doubt that so young and blooming a bride, out of a well-conditioned family, would bring both in abundant measure to the old house? Margaret and Jean, the two daughters of the first marriage, were left in the south country in possession of their mother's little estate when their father began life for the second time. They felt themselves a little injured, shut out of their natural rights, as was natural, and held themselves aloof from the new ménage, which was established joyously in the old Castle with every augury of happiness. But when, no more than a year after, the blooming young wife was carried to the church-yard, and a second poor little Lilias left in her stead, the two sisters flew, with many a compunction and self-reproach, to the infant's cradle. Margaret especially, who, though she was young, was already disposed to believe that everything went wrong when she was absent, reproached herself bitterly for not being on the spot to watch over her father's wife. It would not have happened had she been there, she felt convinced, and this perfectly visionary self-blame no doubt helped to give a certain bias to her already peculiar character. "I must do my best for the daughter. I did not do it for the mother," she acquired a habit of saying when any other career was suggested to her. She did not feel quite sure that she was not her father's elder sister, so confusing were their relations. He was broken down with grief and disappointment, and she took charge of him at once, and of his home. It would perhaps be going too far to say that this was the reason why she did not marry. Had any great love arisen in her heart, no doubt Margaret would, like other people, have considered it her duty to obey its dictates; but, when suitors to whom she was indifferent came, Miss Murray metaphorically pushed them aside out of her path, with a curt intimation that she had no time to think of such nonsense. Miss Jean, who was of a sentimental turn, had not so easily escaped the common dangers of youth, but she did so in a more romantic way, poor lady, by loving, unfortunately, a young hero who had not a penny, and who died in an obscure Indian battle when she was a little more than twenty. This was shortly after the time when the infant Lilias was thrown upon her sisters' hands, and it was enough to determine the celibacy of the gentle young woman, who was indeed an old maid born: an old maid more tender and indulgent than any mother, an old maid who is still young, and can enter into the troubles of childhood and youth not only by recollection of her own, but in the sense of actual understanding and fellowship as one who had herself never thrown quite behind her the state of youth or even childhood. The more perfectly developed are apt to smile at this arrested being, but there is nothing in the world more delightful, tender, and sweet.

Between these two, Lilias' childhood had been passed. Her father was less at home than ever after this destruction of his hopes. He held some military appointments, and saw a good deal of service. In the intervals, when he returned to Scotland, his young daughter adored and made a playmate of him, his elder daughter kept him in order. Never was a man taken better care of; when the breach with Sir Patrick happened, the ladies stood by him with all the determined partisanship of women. He was living with them then on their little estate of the south, in the little feminine house called Gowanbrae, which had been their mother's, and where they had taken the baby after her mother's death. So long as they had that independent house, which they preferred, what was the Castle of Murkley to them? When Sir Patrick died, they "came north," as they expressed it, with the general, to show Lilias her home, and to acquaint her at first hand with those glories of the family which they pretended to scorn, but were in reality very proud of.

"All that money might have been in your pocket if your grandfather had been a man of sense," Miss Margaret said, pointing to the bleached walls of the unfinished palace.

But Jean and Lilias had both a wondering awe and admiration for folly which was so magnificent. Lilias was sixteen when she saw it first. She uttered a great cry of admiration and delight.

"I should like to save up every penny and finish it and live in it," she cried.

Her father shook his handsome white head: but Miss Margaret "had no patience with such nonsense," as she said.

"Live in it!—what income do you think you would require to live in it? The Queen has not so grand a house," said the elder sister, with the pride that aped indignation, "except perhaps Windsor Castle and the palace in London. Taymouth is not much bigger. You would want fifty thousand a year at the very least penny. All we have for the whole family on both sides would not so much as furnish it."

"Unless," said the general, with a laugh, "you make a great match, my little Lily, and get your duke to do it for you—or perhaps a Glasgow man would do?"

"A child of our bringing up would not be likely to demean herself so far, I hope," said Miss Margaret, with emphasis.

"A Glasgow man!" cried Miss Jean with a quaver of horror. "No, no, Lilias will never come down to that."

The general liked to gibe at his daughters; perhaps, though they were his daughters, he was not without some of that contempt for them which men of all ages feel towards unmarried women.

"I have seen some fine fellows at Glasgow," he said, "and rolling in money. I will look out for one, and bring him for your inspection, Lilias. But, Meg and Jean, you must not prejudice my candidate—you must let the child choose."

"Do, papa—it will be fun!" cried Lilias.

Miss Margaret had a high idea of her father's rights. She would not make any direct protest, as Jean was anxious to do, but she took her little sister aside when they returned home.

"My dear," she said, "gentlemen say many things that women-folk do not agree in, and papa is fond of his joke. You must not suppose that is all in earnest, that way he has of talking."

Lilias was "as quick as a needle," her sisters said. She made a momentary pause, and then said, with a laugh,

"About the Glasgow man?"

"About any man," cried Miss Margaret. "My darling, gentlemen will be gentlemen, even when they are your father. They think those sort of pleasantries just innocent, but they are not pretty for a girl; you must remember that. Jean and I have never let you hear anything of the kind. A girl, above all things, Lilias, must be unspotted from the world."

"Unspotted from the world!" the girl repeated, with a half-startled look at her sister; and then she added, with a little emotion, "Oh, what bonnie words, Margaret!"

"Yes, they are bonnie words; and they are better than bonnie, for you know where they come from. Look at Jean, if you want to know the meaning of them. You are just our child—we would like you to be like that. Papa says nothing that is not worth your attention, but he likes his joke, and when all's said he's a gentleman, Lilias, not like you and me."

Lilias gave her sister a kiss, throwing her arms round her neck. Margaret would say, "Hoot!" or "Toot!" when thus embraced, but yet she liked it. "I understand," the girl said. But when she was by herself she laughed a little at her old sister's delicacy. She did not think there was any particular harm in the general's joke. It seemed to her in her childish self-sufficiency that she understood papa (who certainly was a man, there could be no doubt of it) better than Margaret and Jean did. She was not herself a bit shocked. She thought, on the whole, she would like to have the Glasgow man up to be looked at; it would be fun. And then the girl asked herself, with a blush, whether fun of this sort was incompatible with keeping yourself "unspotted from the world." She repeated these words over and over to herself for some time after. Yes, Margaret was right; when you looked at Jean, you could understand what that meant. Margaret herself was of much more consequence than Jean, but she was not so unspotted from the world. Lilias had in her mind a sense of the pure and perfect thing which it was her sister's ideal she herself should be, mingled oddly with a little soft derision of those sisters of which she was ashamed. They were old maids. She felt as if there might be a larger life which would not be afraid of any touch from without, and yet would be stainless: and then she grew red with indignation at herself for presuming to smile at Margaret and Jean. A lily, like her name, all sweetness and fragrance and purity, holding itself high, aloof from every soil—she understood that: that was what they wanted her to be. Her heart swelled with a touching humility, yet visionary emotion, desiring to attain, yet wondering how she could be supposed capable of so sweet a perfection; and then she laughed a little gentle laugh, which, it is to be feared, was at some little peculiarities of theirs. Was it quite impossible that the fun should be had in addition? She did justice to the ideal, but—

The general thought his lily perfect, whatever she pleased to do, and the girl knew this very well, and had a little disdain for his judgment, though she adored himself. She had thus grown already into an independent creature, with a judgment of her own, bringing them all secretly to the bar, and forming her opinion in a way which bewildered these elder people who had brought her up. She was not an echo of any one of them, as at her age she might have been expected to be. She was all herself, and took nothing now for granted. To be sure, it was chiefly Margaret who noticed this. The general was not given to analysis of character, and thought his child the perfection of everything a girl ought to be, and Miss Jean was much of the same frame of mind, though a breath of anxiety would ruffle her soul from time to time. The household on the whole was unanimous enough in the worship of Lilias. As for their father, he was something of a trouble to the ladies. The sense that he was a gentleman, a being she understood but imperfectly, gave Miss Jean a certain embarrassment in his presence. She played all her music to him with a wondering doubt, which she never solved, as to whether he liked it, or if it was a bore to him, and felt that papa was far younger than herself, and that there was no telling with so handsome a man what was the next step he might take. Margaret felt him with still more force to be her junior, and kept his house much as she might have done for a widowed nephew—that was the kind of relationship which would have been natural between them. They sometimes speculated between themselves whether there was any chance that he might marry again. He was only sixty, very young-looking, in reality very young; as active as he had ever been, a man who could ride all day, and, if need were, dance all night as if he had been twenty. "I never see the like of him wherever I go," Miss Margaret said. But then he had nothing to settle, he was himself but a life-renter in Murkley, and the fortune that had always been expected from old Sir Patrick had gone to the dogs—or, at least, to a stranger.

The subject of these questions solved them all very summarily one winter evening by dying. He had not been ill. He had a slight cold—that, and nothing more. He had taken a hot drink to please Margaret, and had put his feet in hot water when he went to rest. But the next morning he was found dead in his bed. It was a very great shock to his children; but perhaps, when the shock was over, Margaret and Jean felt, though they would have thought it dreadful to say so, that an embarrassing charge was removed from them, and that perhaps it was for the best. For Lilias, who was the chief object of their thoughts, it was scarcely to be doubted that it was for the best. There would be no longer any contention, any struggle in her life. Not that there had ever been a struggle. Margaret was too judicious and the general too good-natured for that; but still, an element so out of accord with all the principles of her education as her father, with his free and easy ways, his experiences of the camp and the world, was perhaps—better away. Margaret put it in the right way, in the only permissible way, when she said, "Providence is inscrutable. A young man, comparatively speaking, and younger in his ways than any of us. And oh, so like to live! Nobody would have thought but that he would see us all out. It is a terrible loss to us, especially to Lilias. She was bound up in him, poor thing—perhaps more bound up in him than was good for her—and a gentleman is always an interruption to education. Poor thing! we must just put her back to her work as soon as she is able. It will be the best thing to take off her thoughts."

As for Lilias, she did not want anything to take off her thoughts. For three months nearly she cultivated everything that could make her think of him, and keep up the sombre current. She retired to her own room, and would stay there for hours, weeping, and keeping herself in the atmosphere of affliction. At the end of that time the monotony of sorrow began to press severely upon her young mind, and she was glad to take to her lessons for a change; and thus gradually it came about that she grew light-hearted again by unnoticed stages. When she thought of dear papa now, it was sometimes with a little guilty sense that she had forgotten him, partly with a half-fictitious representation to herself that it was "far better" for him. Perhaps, indeed, it was so: but few of us are fully able to believe that death is an advantage. And it was very hard to realize that it would be an advantage to the general. He had liked his life in Murkley so much; everything (except the want of the money) had suited him so well. He liked his newspaper, his fishing when the weather permitted, his old friends, his native place. To think of him as denuded of all these things, and living under such different conditions, was dreadfully difficult. And it seemed hard upon him to be shut out of the house of his fathers so long, and to have so short a time to enjoy it in—to be Sir George only for a year, just to be permitted to take possession, to settle down: and then in a moment to have to resign it all for a condition in which he would no longer be Sir George, or derive any gratification from the possession of Murkley. But such thoughts as these were not the sort of thoughts that she ought to entertain, Lilias knew.

And so time went on, and the summer came back again, and happiness returned to the girl's heart. The bonds of subjection to her sisters was drawn a little closer, but it was so tender a tyranny that she never resented it. It was a little hard, indeed, to be shut out from all the innocent little parties at which Katie

Seton figured, who was younger than she; but then there was that reserved for her which would never be in Katie Seton's power. And when the clouds of grief had blown away from her sky, and she began to realize herself as the lady of Murkley, it cannot be denied that there was many a flutter in the heart of Lilias. Had Murkley been the great estate it ought to have been, and had she been a rich heiress, she probably would not have been half so much in love with her own position. There was a romance in it that charmed the imagination. An heiress of poverty, with her little old house, which was half as old as the Murrays—and what a thing that was to say!—her tiny little estate, which, though there was so little of it, was the original estate, land that had been in the hands of the Murrays since the Jameses reigned in Scotland; her great name and her small possessions delighted the girl. It did not occur to her to think that Margaret and Jean came before herself in the honours of the family. They were no competitors of hers—they were aunts rather than sisters—they were their mother's children, the Miss Murrays of Gowanbrae, in Dumfriesshire; whereas she was Lilias Murray of Murkley. It was a curious position. She was like a young princess whose youth had been confided to the care of two old ladies of honour closely connected with the royal house, yet not altogether belonging to it. Naturally Miss Margaret at forty looked an old lady to the little princess of seventeen. They had done their best all their lives to impress upon her the greatness of her position, and she took it in most innocently, most sincerely. It is so natural for a young creature to feel herself the central point, the most interesting figure, especially when this has been impressed upon her all her life. She recognized it fully, yet with a naturalness and sweet submission to the powers, which were over her, yet all subservient to her interests, which took every undesirable element out of this faith. It gave Lilias unbounded material for dreams, and it gave her a youthful visionary dignity, which, perhaps, had it been analyzed, would have been found to be a little absurd by close critics, but which was very pretty in the girl, who was so perfectly sincere in her fancy. She formed endless plans as to what she was to do with that romantic palace, which was hers, yet which was nobody's. Of course the first thing was to fit it up as it was meant to be fitted up, and live in it with graceful magnificence, holding a maiden court. And Lilias would dream of vast sums coming into her hands, of treasures found in some old chest or secret nook in the old house, of far-off, unknown cousins, who would send fabulous sums from afar to restore Murkley to its greatness. It is so easy to imagine benefactors of this kind—a novel-writer can invent them without giving himself or herself the least trouble, much more the imagination of a girl. Lilias was as indifferent to wealth as it was possible to be. A single gold piece all her own, to do what she pleased with, especially if she might spend it without putting down the items of her expenditure in a note-book, was wealth to the young creature: but she knew just so much as to know that it would require what she vaguely called, following the phraseology of her sister, "thousands" to complete the great house which her grandfather had left unfinished. If it ever should happen that she could do that! In the long summer evenings, especially when her sisters had gone out, and she was left alone, she would dream out whole histories of how the money might be supplied. What romances these would have made had she written them down! She would figure forth to herself a stranger arriving suddenly some evening in the gloaming—it was always in the gloaming, in the uncertainty of light which suits women—not a handsome or interesting stranger, not the tall hero, with dark eyes and curling hair, who, Lilias felt assured, was the only man she would ever "care for," but a shabby stranger, a man one would never look twice at, with all the appearance of a nobody. Margaret and Jean were never rude to any one: they would receive him very politely, and request him to come in to the fire, if it was winter—and somehow it was always winter in these imaginations. Then he would open his story to them, how he was a man who had been much indebted to "the late Murkley," or to old Sir Patrick; or who was a cousin-german of the old baronet, though perhaps the ladies had never heard of him; how he had hoped and struggled to pay his debt, but had never been able (this was to try them, and Lilias felt sure all along that she for one would know better). But Margaret and Jean would believe the story fully. They would be very sorry for him; they would try immediately to think what they could do for him. If he professed to be a relation, they would trace out his claim and satisfy themselves, and then they would put all their resources at his disposal.

Lilias delighted in making up the dialogues which would be appropriate to the occasion. She would picture to herself how Jean would clasp her hands and cry, "Bless me!" as the stranger piled up his agony; and how Margaret would say,

"Of course you will stay here till you hear of something better. We are not rich, unfortunately because of divisions in the family, which you shall hear about further on, but for the moment that's neither here nor there. And we have little influence; for we have lived out of the world, having our young sister to bring up, and being fond of the country; but what can be done, we will do."

Lilias pictured herself as sitting silent, seeing the dessous des cartes, and convinced in her own mind that all the time this shabby old fellow was a millionnaire, like so many people who have figured in old plays and novels, and, after a few scenes of this description, there would come a crisis, and he would throw off his disguise, and produce a pocket-book with "thousands" in it, and tell them that for all his life it had been his ambition to see New Murkley finished, and the family raised to its old grandeur. "I have neither kith nor kin but yourselves," the old gentleman always said, "and all I have shall be yours; only be as kind to me now I am rich as you were when I was poor."

It was not quite so easy to manage this scene as the first one; for Lilias could not quite assure herself that Margaret's displeasure at being taken-in might not overbalance the satisfaction of receiving so unexpected an advantage. But it ended by her own intervention and a vague tableau of happiness and union. How often she went over this story! She became, in imagination, much attached to this old cousin. She seemed to know him better than any one about her. She would even make investigations into his life abroad, and get him to tell her stories of the things that had happened to him. Sometimes he would have lost his wife and an only child; sometimes he would be an old bachelor, always faithful to the memory of some grand-aunt whose portrait was in the library. It was a lady of the time of Queen Anne whom Lilias had hit upon as the beloved of this old gentleman, but what did a century or so matter! She never found the mistake out.

This was her favourite way of finishing New Murkley, and restoring the family. But now and then, it cannot be denied, that there would gleam across her mind a recollection of her father's suggestion. A Glasgow man! In novels it was generally a Manchester man who took this part. Lilias supposed they were about the same, but her mind did not play with this idea. It flashed across her, and made her blush or made her indignant. It did not attract her as the old relation did. There is something in heiress-ship which changes a girl's feeling in this respect; the idea of getting everything from a lover, from a husband, was not pleasant to her. If she ever married, and this idea was not one that the girl did more than contemplate furtively for a moment, it would be without any thought of advantage. But the old cousin was a delightful romance. And there were other expedients besides this which now and then came in to vary the matter when she was tired of elaborating her first fancy; people whose fortunes had been founded on some help given by a Murray would step in; or even there might be boxes of treasure found in the old cellars, or buried in the ghost's walk. Who can ever tell what may happen? At seventeen everything is possible.

CHAPTER XVII

Her sisters were as great visionaries in the concerns of Lilias as she was herself, but in a different way. They had no hope of any old cousin coming in from Australia or India with a pocket-book in which there should be "thousands." Margaret and Jean knew all the possible cousins of the family, and were aware that there was no one who could be expected to appear in this accidental way. But for all that they too had their dreams. So far as themselves were concerned, they had for a long time given up that exercise. It is doubtful, indeed, whether Margaret ever had indulged in it, and Jean's visions had come to an end very sadly, as has been said. But the new castle of Murkley had taken hold of their imaginations as of their little sister's. It was their grandfather's folly which they had condemned all this time, but they were but women when all is said, and the sight of it had an effect upon their fancy which contradicted reason. Nothing could be more absurd, or even wicked, than to weight an old Scotch, almost Highland, estate in that ridiculous way, even if the money of the family had not been separated from it, which was the climax of all. But at the same time, if that grand house, that palace, could ever have been inhabited, what glory to the race, what illustration to the name of Murray! Margaret, to whom her young sister was as the apple of her eye, beheld in imagination Lilias the queen of that noble and beautiful place, sweeping through the fine suites of rooms, entertaining all the great people. To see anything so young, and slight, and ethereal the mistress of all this would be so pretty, so touching, would appeal to all hearts. Margaret was as fond of picturing this to herself as Lilias was of the aged cousin from Australia. Her fancy was captivated by it: but how to make it possible? There was not money enough in the family to furnish those fine rooms, and, if they were furnished, how were they to be lived in? She counted over on her fingers the number of servants it would require to keep them in order. As high as a groom of the chambers, and as low as the scullery maids, Margaret went. She smiled at herself, you may be sure, a hundred times when she caught herself at it. But, notwithstanding, the very next morning when she was outwardly occupied with her housekeeping, and her mind, therefore, it might be supposed, too busy to heed what her fancy was doing, lo! she would be at it again. A groom of the chambers would be necessary; there would be footmen, so many; and, as for housemaids, a regiment would be necessary, for Lilias no doubt would insist upon filling the rooms with nick-nacks which take so long to dust. Margaret pretended to care nothing for nick-nacks herself, but she furnished those great noble rooms in her imagination with everything that befitted them, and never counted the cost. When you have nothing at all to do this with, it is easier than when you have almost enough to do it. In one case the imagination may have its swing, in the other it must be sternly repressed. She saw in her mind's eye the great façade of that palace, no longer windowless, staring blankly into the daylight and night, but lighted up in every chamber, shining through the woods, and the rooms all full of fine company, and little Lilias the mistress of all. That last particular was a constant delight. She laughed to herself at the thought with the tender ridicule of a great longing. That little thing! It was just nonsense, but how sweet to think of!— and things as unlikely have happened, she said to herself. There was one way still in which miracles happened every day. It was the way which she had forbidden her little sister to look, which she had been so displeased and provoked with her father for suggesting. Certainly Lilias must never be allowed to think of it; Lilias must be kept unspotted from the world. But Lilias' seniors, Lilias' guardians, there were things which might be permitted to them.

Is it necessary to say that what Miss Margaret thought of was a great marriage? Such a thing is always possible at eighteen. Not a Glasgow man, according to her father's profane suggestion. It was a proof the General had never thought of it seriously, or he never would have said that. Glasgow men at the most were last resources, things upon which a woman who had outstayed her time might fall back. But a young girl in the bloom and glory of her youth, of an old family, with a little historical estate, General Sir George Murray's daughter—to be sure, nobody could be in earnest who put her within the reach of a Glasgow man. Margaret imagined the lover for her with a much more clear perception of what was needful than Lilias possessed. Lilias had never gone further than to imagine a handsome giant, six-foot-two at least, with wonderful dark eyes and crisp hair. But Margaret was far more circumstantial. She planned a paladin. She gave him every charm that the most fastidious could demand. It seemed to her better that he should not have a peerage; for then the race of Murray would be engulfed, and heard no more of. A commoner would do better, but then a commoner of pretensions, such as would make half the peerage look pale. She laid on fine qualities with a liberal hand; for it cost her nothing. While she was about it, she might as well make her young lover perfect. She even, though with a slight contempt of the addition, made him an amateur of music to please Jean. Why should any gift be left out? And he should come all unawares, and find Lilias blooming like a flower, and woo her—as heroes woo their heroines no longer—with a humility and faithful service and reverential devotion such as belonged to the chivalrous age; and, after having pined a little, and despaired, and considered himself all unworthy, would be raised into paradise again, and receive her hand, and, in giving his, give with it wealth enough to do everything that was wanted. It would be well that he should be a man without a great family castle of his own, otherwise perhaps he would not take to Murkley, and spend so much upon it. In her leisure moments, as she moved about the house, Margaret would employ herself in elaborating this young man, in adding to him yet another and another perfection. She would sit, while Lilias read her histories, listening to the calm young voice stumbling a little over the dates, and afraid of a reprimand, and never hear the blunder because of some new attraction she was conferring upon the lover of Lilias, the hero who was coming. Now and then, when thus employed in the girl's presence, Margaret would come to herself with a sense of the humour of the situation, and laugh out suddenly without any reason.

"What are you laughing at, Margaret?" Jean would ask.

And her sister would reply.

"At Pussy there, with all your fine silks. It will be the cat that will finish your tablecover;" which sent both her companions off in dismay to collect the skeins of silk, and left her free to pursue her occupation, though not without a slight sense of treachery in carrying on a manufacture so important to Lilias in her presence without a word of warning. Thus if the girl had her dreams, the elder sister was not far behind; and Margaret had no less warmth of imagination at forty than Lilias had at seventeen. They were both possessed by one master thought, though in a different way. Margaret all the time would scoff at New Murkley, and call it a great ruckle of stones, and wonder what Sir Patrick could be thinking when he planned it.

"He never could have lived in it," she would say. "Twenty servants would never be known in it: and to keep up a place like that on a limited income would just be purgatory, or worse."

"I wish we were rich," Lilias would say. "I would soon show you if it was a ruckle of stones. It is a beautiful palace! If there was glass in all the windows, and satin curtains, and grand carved chairs, and a grand gentleman, quite different from Simon, to open the door—"

"And a pumpkin coach, and a cat for the coachman, and two fine mice with good long tails for the footmen behind the carriage, to carry Cinderella off to the ball," Margaret would say, grimly.

Upon which Jean would step in and interpose.

"Dear Margaret, you must not abash her in her bit little fancies! Dear me, why should she not live to make something of it? It would make a grand hospital. To give our fine air, and quiet, and healing to poor sick folk would be a fine thing to do: and you would get a blessing with the rest."

"A hospital!" cried Lilias, in dismay; and then a flush of shame flew over her to think she had never thought of that. She flung her arms about her sister and gave her a kiss. "It is you that think of the best things," she said, and remembered what Margaret had said about the one who was unspotted from the world.

This Jean took very sedately, not seeing anything wonderful in it, and would then enter into details which chilled both the elder and the younger dreamer. Nevertheless, when Lilias was at church, or when she was pensive, or when she grew tired of inventing the old Australian cousin, and wanted something more definite, she turned back to this idea of the hospital with a slightly subdued sense of power. If that old man should never turn up—if nothing should happen—if she should be intended by Providence to live like Margaret and Jean all her life, which was perhaps a somewhat depressing idea, notwithstanding her love and admiration for her sisters—why, then there was this idea to fall back upon. She would make it a hospital. She would become a benefactor of her kind; she would devote herself to it like a sister of charity. There were moods and moments when this was a thing which pleased the imagination of the dreaming girl. But Margaret rejected the hospital with disdain and almost anger. She took Jean to task for the suggestion when they were alone.

"Can you not see," she said, "that to put Quixotic fancies into a young head is just criminal? They come quick enough of themselves. Next to having everything your heart can desire, what's so enticing as to give up everything at her age? You have never grown any older or any wiser yourself, my dear. I know that well enough, and I like you, perhaps, all the better. But Lilias is not like us. She is Murray of Murkley. If it had been me at her age, my word but I would have made you all stand about! But it's better as it is. She will marry, which most likely I never would have done, for I'm perhaps too much of a man myself to be troubled with gentlemen. She'll marry and raise up the old house."

To this Jean consented plaintively, yet with a little excitement.

"But who will she marry?" Jean asked; "and, if she were married to-morrow, where are they to get the money to restore New Murkley? He would be for selling it, far more likely."

Margaret had often been made to perceive before this that Jean, though she was not clever, by dint of approaching a new subject simply from a natural point of view, often threw unexpected light upon it. This was the case now. A burst or flood of illumination of the most disagreeable kind suddenly burst upon her with these words.

"Sell it!" she cried, with a kind of horror—"bless me! I never thought of that."

"Or suppose it was some person from England, that would think nothing of spending thousands—"

This was how Miss Jean always spoilt a point when she had made one. Her sister laughed.

"No person from England would spend thousands on what was not his own. As for letting it, that's out of the question in its present state. But there's truth in what you say. A man might want to sell it rather than be at the expense of finishing it. I'm glad you've put me upon my guard, for that must not be. You see," said Margaret, feeling a relief in explaining herself now that the question was broached, "as Lilias is sure to marry, my mind has been greatly exercised upon the subject. She must not marry just the first comer."

"If the first comer was the man that took her heart, poor thing—" said Jean. Her face, always so soft, grew softer at the touch of this sympathetic emotion. Lilias, who had been a child hitherto, suddenly appeared to her in a new light. It had been her own experience that the first comer was the hero.

"We must take care of her heart," said Margaret, curtly. "I will have her betrayed into no sentiment. He must satisfy me before I will let her so much as think of him. No, I'm not a mercenary person; for myself or you I would never have thought twice. Had I been a marrying woman myself, I would just have followed the drum as soon as anything else, and kept my man on his pay."

Jean did not say anything, but there came a little moisture into the corners of her eyes, and her hands clasped each other with that clasp which is eloquent, which tells of renunciation, yet of the sense of what might have been. And a sudden remorse overwhelmed her sister.

"I am just like a brute beast," she cried, "with no feeling in me. But Lilias, you will see, my dear, is different. The family depends upon her. She must marry, not for money—the Lord forbid!—but he must have plenty. I will insist upon that. I would not give her to a man that was nobody, or that was vulgar or beneath her, or that was old, or with any imperfection, not for all the gold that ever came out of the bowels of the earth. He must be a fine fellow in himself, or he shall not have Lilias; but he must have a good fortune too."

Jean looked at her sister with a little shake of her head.

"It would be far better," she said; "but you never can be certain of anything. She will make her own choice, Margaret, without thinking of either you or me."

"She cannot make her choice till she sees somebody to choose from," said Margaret, "and that will be my business. She shall see nobody that would not answer. I take that in hand."

Jean still shook her gentle head. She remembered very well where she had first seen her lieutenant—on St. Mary's Loch with a party of strangers. It was as unexpected as if he had dropped from the skies. In this respect she had an experience of which Margaret was destitute.

"How can you guard against accident?" she said. "She might see somebody—out of the window. You never can tell how these things may happen."

"There is no such thing as accident," said Margaret, with equal assurance and rashness. Was there ever a more foolhardy speech? "For those that keep their eyes about them as I will do, the things that can happen are always foreseen. Whom could she see out of the window? A tourist! Do you think our Lilias is likely to lose her heart to a tourist? No, no, there will be no risks run. I know all that is at stake. She shall see nobody that would not do."

Jean shook her head still: but she said, with humility: "You are far wiser than I am, and have more sense, and understand the world—"

"But you think you know better than I do all the same? That's very natural. In ordinary cases you would be right, and, if anybody said to me what I'm saying to you, I would think as you do. I would think there's a bragging idiot that knows nothing about human nature. But then I know what I'm capable of myself. Oh! you may shake your head, but there are not many that can watch over their children as I will watch over Lilias. Mothers have divided interests; they have their husbands to consider, and other bairns to distract them. You, my bonnie Jean, you had nobody at all to look after you, for I was not old enough."

"I am glad I had nobody to look after me, Margaret."

"I know that. You are glad of your heart-break, you innocent creature. We'll say nothing about that. But you would not like Lilias to have the same? Well, I will not brag—but if care and watching can find the right man, and bring him forward and no other—You don't know, Jean," said Margaret, abruptly, with a little broken laugh, which was her symbol of emotion, "what that bit creature is to me. She is just the apple of my eye."

"And to me too," Jean said: but so low that perhaps her sister, being moved beyond her wont, did not hear. For Miss Jean had the tenderest delicacy of soul, and would not put forth any claim that might have seemed to detract from the preeminence of Margaret's. Margaret had done far more for Lilias than she herself would do. Margaret had been the referee in everything. She had settled every particular of the girl's life. In the time of governesses she had managed them, and made everything go smoothly. She had watched over her health, she had managed her property, even, in the time of the General, taking all trouble out of his hands, as if she had been the factor instead of a daughter of the house. And now she was reading history with Lilias, and making an accomplished woman of the little girl. What were Jean's pettings and soothings, her little bit of music, her tenderness that never failed, in comparison with this? She drew back into the shadow, and respected her sister's warmer passion of motherhood. And she prayed that Margaret's cares might be successful, that no misfortune might befall her, that she might have the desire of her heart. Oh, how few people have that! but you are encouraged, Miss Jean thought to herself, to pray for it, because in the psalmist's days he did; not only what is good for you, and what is for God's glory,—such as no doubt is the first object of prayer,—but for your heart's desire. There are people who think that your heart's desire must naturally be bad for you. But Miss Jean was not one of those, neither was King David. She prayed that Margaret might have her wish. It is to be doubted whether Margaret herself had courage to do this, for she felt her own wish to be somewhat worldly. To ask from heaven a man with plenty of money to marry Lilias might have been a very honest proceeding, but not a very spiritual one. To be sure a parent or guardian is very well entitled to desire such a blessing: but to ask for it direct from God would have been a bold step. To the profane it would, no doubt, have appeared a somewhat grotesque devotion. She did not venture to do it; but Jean, who entered into no such niceties, asked with a devout simplicity that Margaret might have the desire of her heart.

Margaret, meanwhile, cast her eyes about her. Nobody in the neighbourhood was at all admissible. They were indeed dangers in her way, and nothing else. The idea of Philip Stormont made her blood run cold. A long-legged lad, with his mother's jointure to pay, and next to nothing besides. That he should be brought within sight of Lilias, or any like him, was mortal peril: and she knew that Philip was just the kind of well-looking hound (as she said) who might take a young girl's fancy. It was this, as much as concern for her complexion, which made her impose upon Lilias that blue veil: and it was this which made her so sternly determined never to take her little sister to any of the parties at the manse, where such dangers were likely to abound.

She avoided skilfully any explanation on this subject, but the natural objections of Lilias to being left behind were not to be got rid of without an equivalent. It was in this difficulty that Margaret had propounded the scheme which had been developing in her mind, and placed before the dazzled eyes of Lilias the glorious prospect which has been already referred to. That she should be taken to London, presented at court, and see society at its fountain-head, had been a prospect which took away the girl's breath, and made Jean's blood run cold. Such a privilege had not been possessed by either of the elder sisters. But then neither of them had been the reigning Murray of Murkley, the heiress and representative of the family. The little complaints to which the young creature had been tempted to give vent were all silenced by this expedient; how could she complain when this was the cause of her seclusion, when she was debarred from the little country amusements only that she should have those great and noble ones, and enter the world like a heroine, like a great lady? Lilias had been filled with awe at the prospect, as well as with delight and pride. She had not said a word more about Katie Seton and the little festivities at the manse. But Jean had ventured upon a faltering and awe-stricken remonstrance. London! And the expense of it! How was it to be done?

"You may leave that to me," Margaret said.

"Oh, Margaret," cried Jean, "it's not that I would interfere. You know I would never interfere; but where will you get the money? And do you think it will not be putting fancies in Lilias' head? It's like that dream of living in New Murkley. She will never be able to do it. Even if she had gotten my grandfather's money—"

"She has not gotten my grandfather's money," said Margaret. "You may leave the question of money to me."

"And so I will, and so I will," said Jean. "But oh, do you not think that all that grandeur, and fashion, and luxury which we cannot keep up will be bad for her. It will be just a glimpse, and then all done."

"Unless there should come something of it; and then it need not be all done," Margaret said, oracularly.

"What could come of it?" cried Miss Jean, opening wide her gentle eyes.

But Miss Margaret, bidding her ask no questions, if she did not understand, left her in her wondering. What could come of it? Margaret could not be thinking of a place at court for Lilias, as she was only a girl, poor thing; and even places at court are not things to make anybody's fortune. What could Margaret mean? But Jean had not the smallest inkling of what her sister's intentions could be.

As for Margaret, as soon as she had fully formed this determination in her own mind, her thoughts took a new impulse. She had thought over the question a great deal, but the new plan was struck out in a moment as by an inspiration. Her first idea had been Edinburgh, the metropolis of her youth, and the assemblies there which had been all the gaiety she had ever herself known. But Margaret had heard that Edinburgh was not all it once was, and the assemblies no longer the dazzling scenes they had been in her day. Besides, she reflected that there her choice would be very limited. She did not want a young advocate or legal functionary for Lilias. Many unexceptionable young men there were in these categories with good names and good blood. But this did not content her ambition. She wanted something greater, something more than an eligible parti or a good match. Such words were vulgar in comparison with the high ideal in her mind. She wanted the highest and best of all things for Lilias—a perfect lover, a husband worthy to be the prop and support and restorer of the house of Murray. She knew very well that she would not be easily satisfied. Wealth would not be enough, nor good looks, nor a good name. She wanted all together, and she wanted something more. A fool, if he were a prince, would not have done for her, nor a man of genius unless he had been a true lover, putting Lilias above all women.

It may be imagined that the quest on which she was setting out was not an easy one. She followed it in her thoughts through many an imaginary scene. Miss Margaret was a very sensible woman; there was nobody better able to guide the affairs of her family. She was not easily taken-in nor given to deceiving herself; yet, when in her imagination she went into the world of London and society there, no dream was ever more wildly unlike reality than were her thoughts. She evolved these scenes from her own consciousness, and moved about among them with a progress as purely visionary as that of Una or of Britomart. Like the one, she was in search of a true knight; like the other, ready to face all enchanters and overcome all perils; but the world into which she was about to launch was as little like the world of her fancy as was the court of Gloriana or the woods of Broceliande.

CHAPTER XVIII

The only thing which had shaken Lilias in the virginal calm of her thoughts was the example of little Katie Seton, a younger girl than herself, and whose system of education had been so different. While Lilias had been kept under the wing of her sisters, apart from any encounter, Katie had been introduced to everything their little world contained of wild sensation and adventure. She had entered upon the agitations of love-making almost as soon as she was in her teens, and her sixteenth birthday was scarcely past when she appeared one afternoon, as Lilias put away her books, evidently in all the excitement of some great news to communicate, which Miss Margaret's presence kept in, though Katie was bursting with it. Miss Margaret, as was natural, stayed in the school-room, which was still the special haunt of Lilias, much longer than was usual. It was a rainy day, and no walk was possible. Is it from perversity and desire to interfere with the pleasures of the young—pleasures now out of their own reach—that the elder people will linger and keep girls and boys on the rack when they have things to say to each other not intended for elder ears? Katie thought so as she sat biting her lips, hardly able to keep still, brimming over with her news; and Lilias, who divined that there was something unusual, almost was tempted to think so too, as Miss Margaret considered over the book-shelves, looking for she did not know what, and opened all the drawers to find an old exercise-book which was of no interest at the moment.

"Oh! if you will just leave it to me, I will find it, Margaret," Lilias cried.

"You would find it the easier for knowing what it is," said Margaret, grimly, "which is almost more than I do myself. I will know it by head-mark when I see it."

"Let me turn out the drawer," cried Katie, officiously.

Miss Margaret looked at the girl with humorous perversity.

"What nonsense are you plotting between you?" she said. "Katie, your eyes are just leaping out of your head, and you have not been still a moment since you came into this room, every flounce in motion—"

"Could anybody help it?" cried Katie. "Such a day!—and me just wanting Lilias to come out and see the garden. The lilacs are all out, and everything so sweet: and now this pouring rain will spoil them all. I am just like to cry," said Katie, the corners of her mouth drooping. But Miss Margaret knew very well it was not for the lilacs or the rain, but for excitement and impatience, that Katie was like to cry.

"Well, well," she said, "I suppose you must have your bits of secrets at your age; there will be no great harm in them. I will find my book another time. But mind you don't stay too long in this room, which is cold when there is no sun, but come into the drawing-room to your tea. You will find me there, and Jean—and sense," said Miss Margaret, with her back turned to them, calmly selecting a book from the shelves—"if you should happen to stand in any need of that last—"

"Oh, no, no!" cried Katie, when at last Miss Margaret went away, running to shut the door after her, and make sure at least of being alone with her friend, "we stand in no need of that. Oh, Lilias!" she said, rushing up to her companion and flinging her arms round her with such vehemence that the slight girl swayed with the sudden shock.

"What is it, Katie!" Lilias cried. "What is it? Tell me, but do not knock me down."

"Oh, it is you that are sense," cried Katie, with a sort of fury, pushing her friend into the big chair, and falling down herself at the side of it, with her arms on Lilias' knee. There was a degree of violence in these preliminaries; for Katie, though full of a woman's secret, was still half girl, half boy in her early development, as the sister of many brothers is apt to be. Lilias, so much more delicate and dainty, took hold of the hands which had numberless scratches upon them, nails cut to the quick, and other indications of having been put to boyish uses, and held them in her own white fingers closely clasped.

"I am as anxious to hear as you are to tell," she said. "Quick, quick, tell me! What is the matter? Have they sent him away?"

"Oh, Lily! Something far more wonderful. There is no knowing what they may do. They will do something dreadful—they will do anything to part us. Oh, Lily! you'll never, never tell anybody, not even Miss Jean—not a word! I'll never, never speak to you all my life, if you tell upon me now!"

"I tell upon you! Did I ever tell upon you?" said Lilias, indignant. "That about Robbie Bairnsfather was found out. It was never me."

"I know you will not tell," said Katie. "You are just my own Lily. You will never say a word. Lilias! I'm—oh, can't you guess? We are—engaged—It is quite true. Look," the girl cried, with a glowing countenance, opening a button of her boddice and drawing forth from under it a little ring, attached to a ribbon. Her hand trembled, though it was the hand of a tom-boy. Her face shone; tears were in the eyes which were, as Miss Margaret said, "leaping out of her head."

"Engaged!" cried Lilias. "Oh, you gave me such a fright. When I saw the ring, I thought you were going to say you were—married. Let me get my breath."

"Married!" Katie said, with a certain contempt. To be married would be the prose of the transaction. She felt herself upon a higher, more ethereal altitude. "That would be nothing," she said. "There would be no secret then. Oh, Lily, isn't it wonderful? This is a ring that is his very own, that an old lady gave him when he was a boy. Look at it! It's all turquoise, and turquoise means happiness. He put it on my finger, but I dare not wear it on my finger, for mamma would be sure to notice. She notices everything. Old people," said Katie, aggrieved, "pretend to wear spectacles, and all that, as if they couldn't see: but nothing escapes them! I can't put a pin in my collar, but mamma will see it. 'Katie, Katie!' she always says; and I know in a moment what it is. Oh, but she would say, 'Katie, Katie!' twice as loud, if she saw this! So I wear it round my neck: but I may put it on here," Katie said. "Look, Lilias! Isn't it bonnie? I always wanted a ring, but I never thought I would get the engaged ring the very first of all."

There was a little triumph in Katie's tone. Not only was Lilias far, very far, from being the proud possessor of an "engaged" ring, but she had scarcely been allowed "to speak to a gentleman"—a thing Mrs. Seton thought the worst policy—in all her life.

"But never mind the ring. Tell me about—what happened," said Lilias. "You have not even told me who it is."

"Oh!" cried Katie, red with indignation, "who could it be but him? I am sure I have never said a word, or even thought of anybody but him for—for ages," she added, with a little vagueness, sinking from the assumed superiority of her former tone.

"Well, dear," said Lilias, soothingly, "but then, you know, there was Mr. Dunlop."

"I never cared a bit about him. He was only just in the way. You have to let a gentleman speak to you when he is in your way."

"I suppose so," said Lilias, with a faint sigh. Such an experience had never happened to herself. "But how was I to know? And it is not very long since—but it is Philip? Oh, yes, I supposed so all along, especially as it is such a secret. If it had been Mr. Dunlop it would have been no secret—or Robbie—or—"

"I wish you would not speak such nonsense. I never, never thought—it was only just for fun. I never in all my life cared for anybody but him! Oh, never; you may say what you please, but it's only me that can know."

"That is true," said Lilias, with gentle conviction. "But tell me how it happened, and when—and what he said, and what you said. It will be like a story, but only far, far more interesting," Lilias said.

"It was not like a story at all," said Katie, with some indignation. "Am I that kind of person? We just happened to meet down by the waterside. Oh yes, I am fond of walking there; and the boys were after a water-rat, as they always are, and the little girls were somewhere—I am sure I never can tell where they go. Mamma scolds me when they tear their frocks, but is it likely I can run into all their hiding holes with them at my age?"

"And then?" said Lilias, conducting her penitent skilfully over this obstacle.

"And then—oh, well, nothing particular. He happens often to be that way himself. It is the prettiest walk. I was rather glad to see him coming; for, you know, neither the boys nor the girls are just companions for me. And then I asked him when he was going away, and he said would I be sorry? and I said, oh yes, I would be sorry; for he was always somebody to speak to. And he said, was that all? And I said, oh, you know that we danced the same step, and that was always nice. And then he said—oh, just nonsense; that I was always nice, or something like that; and then he said he would never go away, if he could help it. And I said, what was he going for, then? And he said, because he was too fond of somebody that never thought upon him. Of course I knew well enough what he meant, but I pretended to be very sorry, and said, who could that be?"

Katie made a very pretty picture as she told her story. She was leaning her elbows on Lilias' lap, and playing with the long chain which Lilias, after the fashion of the time, wore to her watch, and which was the object of Katie's warmest admiration. She was twisting this in her fingers, tying knots in it, occupying her eyes with it, and escaping her friend's gaze, though she sometimes paused for a moment and gave a glance upward. Her little blooming face was in a glow of colour and excitement, ready to laugh, ready to cry. As for Lilias, she was full of attention, bending forward, her face following every variation of her friend's.

"But," Lilias said, "I thought it was not he that wanted to go away, but Mrs. Stormont that was sending him."

"Oh," cried Katie, "I wish you would not insist upon everything like a printed book. I am telling you what he said—I was never saying it was all true. They never tell exactly the truth," Katie interrupted herself to say, with conviction. "There is always a little more—or just a little twist to make you believe—But you can understand that, if you have any sense. I said—who could that be? and he said, 'Oh, Katie!' just like mamma."

"And then?" cried Lilias, breathless.

"Oh, there was nothing particular then," said Katie, all one blush, "but just nonsense, you know; and fancy, he had been carrying this about all the time, always wanting to give it to me! He just put it on, and then we were engaged," Katie said.

"Oh, Katie, what a terrible thing to happen! And then did you just go home as usual, and never say a word?"

"What could I say? I would not tell mamma for all the world. She would want to make a business of it, and tell Mrs. Stormont, and get it all settled. She would want us to be married; but I don't want to be married—I want to have my fun."

"Oh, Katie!"

"Everybody says 'Oh, Katie!'" said the girl, plaintively; "but that does not make any difference. It is not dreadful at all—it is very nice. I belong to him, and he belongs to me; he tells me everything, and I tell him everything. But we don't want to make a fuss; we are quite happy as we are. Mrs. Stormont would just go daft, you know. She knows quite well that is what it is coming to—oh, I can see it in her eyes! I think she would like to send me to prison, if she could, to get me out of Philip's way."

"But, Katie, if you think that—"

"Oh, it does not make any difference to me; perhaps I would do the same myself. There's our Robbie, if he wanted to be married, I would think he was mad, and mamma would be—I don't know what mamma wouldn't do. I suppose it's natural. Everybody wants their own people to do well for themselves, and I have no money, not a penny. Mrs. Stormont would have been quite pleased, Lilias, if it had been you."

"Me!" said Lilias, with a blush, but a slight erection of her head; she laughed to carry off the slight shock of offence. "But that would not have done at all," she said.

"Oh, no, it is just the same thing; you are too good, and I'm not good enough. If it had been you, Miss Margaret would have tried to have him sent to prison; and perhaps, when there is somebody found grand enough for you, Lilias, his folk will not be pleased. That is always the way," said the shrewd Katie, shaking her head; "but it happens, all the same. Isn't it bonnie?" she added, returning to the former subject, and holding up her hand with the ring on it. "Turquoise is the right thing for an engaged ring; but, when your one comes, never let him give you an opal, Lilias—that is such bad luck."

"Oh! if anyone were to come—as you say: I should think of something else than rings," Lilias said, and blushed at the thought. It seemed to her a little breach of modesty even to speak of any such incident. When, in the fulness of time, it came, with a strange and wonderful event! but not to be profaned by anticipation. Her heart gave a throb, then left the subject in silence. "But it will have to be known some time," she said.

Katie shrugged her little shoulders.

"It will not be through me," she said. "They say a girl can't keep a secret, but just you try me. He can do what he likes, but I will never tell—never, not if I were to be put on the rack."

"But, Katie, do you think it is right? To live at home and see your father and mother every day, and not tell them—you could not do it!"

"Just you try me," said Katie. "Do you think in the persecuting days I would have told where they were hidden—or Prince Charlie?" cried the girl, with pardonable confusion. "Never!—I would never have minded either the thumbscrew or the boot."

"But I don't think this is the same," said Lilias, doubtfully. "You will be always seeing him, meeting him, and they will not know; and you will have secrets, and he will tell you things, and you will tell him things, and yet at home they will not know."

"That is just the fun of it," Katie cried.

"Oh, I cannot see any fun in that. And it will be so difficult; you will forget, you will say something when you do not intend—"

"Not me," cried Katie. "I hope I have my wits about me. I will never betray him; whoever is not true, I will always be true."

Lilias was somewhat staggered by this view of the subject, but she was not convinced. She shook her head.

"I could not do it," she said.

"Oh, you! No, you could not do it; but then you could not do any of it," cried Katie. "You have been brought up by old maids; you are never let speak to a gentleman at all; it never could happen to you," she cried, with a little triumph.

And Lilias, for her part, had to allow to herself, with a certain sense of humiliation, that Katie was right. It never would happen to her. No Orlando would ever be able to hang verses on the trees at Murkley, even no Philip meet her out walking by the river-side, and woo her in Katie's artless way. She wondered how it ever could be permitted to happen at all—or would it never happen, and she herself live and die without any other experience, like Jean and Margaret? Her heart fluttered in her maiden bosom with the strangeness of the question. She did not believe in the depths of her heart that it never could happen. In some miraculous way, as it happened to the ladies of romance, it would come to her. But it would be very different from Katie's story—everything about it would be different. The news roused her mind and affected her dreams in spite of herself. That night, in her maiden sleep, never interrupted heretofore by such visions, she dreamed that some one took her hand and put a ring upon it—a big blob of blue, far bigger than Katie's turquoise, which changed as she looked at it into the strange changing tints of an opal. She thought it very strange that she should dream of this just after Katie's disquisition on the subject. The two things did not present themselves to Lilias' mind under the semblance of cause and effect. But it vexed her that she could not in the least make out who it was that put the ring upon her hand. She was not destitute of jewellery as Katie was, though Miss Margaret discouraged ornaments; but she had neither a turquoise nor an opal in her stones.

And there were other ways in which Katie's story affected Lilias. She could not help thinking of the meetings of the lovers. She had herself gone sometimes when she was younger, with Katie to the walk by the water-side, when the boys went after water-rats or rabbits, and the little girls made "little housies" in the sand of the old quarry. In those days Lilias and Katie strolled up and down, superior to the children, talking of a hundred things. Lilias knew how it would all be. She went out herself into the Ghost's Walk, where it was always permitted her to walk when she pleased, and thought wistfully, with a little sigh, of the water-side and all its freedom, the children busy, their voices softened in the distance, and the two in the centre of the landscape, whose whispering would be—something different. What it would be, Lilias did not know. In the very secretest corner of her imagination little broken dialogues had gone on between herself and—another. But they had been too secret, too vague even to come into the legitimate and acknowledged land of visions in which the old Australian cousin had played so large a part. Katie's story dismissed that benevolent old man with his full purse from Lilias' imagination, and brought those far less perfect germs of dreaming into prominence instead.

The sunset was still blazing over the river, when it was already twilight in the Ghost's Walk, which lay on the other side of the house, and saw no sunshine later than noon. Lilias paced about under the silken foliage of the limes in the still air, which was full of dreams, and felt herself left outside of life, looking at it from a distance with a visionary pensive sadness. There was something in the air, the subdued light, the sense of evening all about, which chimed in with this mood. It was curious to think of Katie, so much younger than herself, enjoying everything, the flush of youthful sunshine, while she was thus left out. But Lilias felt at the same time a certain gentle superiority, the elevation of the pensive vestal, in delicate solitude and retirement, over the common ways of the world. She walked about in a soft dream, with a sigh, yet with a sensation of gentle grandeur which made up for and was enhanced by the sadness. As she paused under the great old lime-tree which was in the centre of the walk, the soft sounds which distinguished the family spectre were very audible. She knew the story of that gentle lady who had died for love. None of the Murrays were afraid of her. To have seen her would have been a distinction—they had heard her from generation to generation. There was even a tradition in the family that one time or other, when the wedded mistress of the house should be at the same time a daughter of the house, a Murray born, the lady of the walk would appear to her, and pace by her side, and tell her something that would be well for the race.

Lilias paused, and looked about her with pride, and tenderness, and a thrill of anticipation. She had thought often that she herself might be that destined lady; but the thought had never moved her as now. It awoke a little tumult in her bosom as she stood there in the subdued evening air full of the recollection of the love-tale that had been told her. Margaret and Jean walked in the Ghost's Walk without any such movements or beatings of the heart. Lilias felt a great awe come over her as she stood and listened. If ever these soft steps that had paced about under the limes for two hundred years should turn aside from their habitual walk, and the air above them shape into a vision, what wonderful events must happen first? She stood silent, almost without breathing for a moment, and then she drew the skirt of her dress over her arm, and fled into the house as if something had been pursuing her. It was not that she was afraid of any ghostly appearance; but she was afraid of the rustling of the wings of the coming years, and of the events that were approaching her through the silence, the things that were to shape her life. What were they?—perhaps patience, perhaps sorrow, such as women so often have to dwell with. Perhaps, who could tell, Love, the unknown, the greatest of all. She fled from them and the thought of them, whatever they might be.

CHAPTER XIX

"Did you ever hear that a turquoise was lucky and an opal an ill stone?"

Lilias was seated beside her sisters in the drawing-room in the soft darkness of the summer night. But that there were two lamps lighted, shining like two dim earth-stars in the large dim room, with its dark wainscot and faded velvet curtains, you would scarcely have known it was night. The windows were not closed, and the pale day had not altogether died. There was still light enough to read by; but Simon brought in the lamps at a certain hour, without much respect to the state of the daylight. They lighted up each the circle of the table on which it stood, but made the rest of the room darker than before. The three ladies were seated about one of these tables. Jean was knitting—a piece of work better adapted for this light than her famous table-cover; Margaret was reading the newspaper. The Times (for they indulged in the luxury of the Times, considered to be rather an extravagance in these parts) arrived at night, which was a wonder they were never tired of expatiating upon. "Published in London this morning, and here in my hands within the twelve hours; it is just a miracle," Miss Margaret was fond of saying. The large broad-sheet caught the glow of the lamp, and made a large white space in the dimness, in the midst of which Margaret's countenance was set. It made a rustling as she turned it over, and from time to time she read out a paragraph. The others were not much given to the newspaper. They heard enough of it from the bits that Miss Margaret read out. Being a person of very decided and consistent political views, she despised and detested the politics of her favourite newspaper, and would sometimes read out a leading article with a string of satirical comments, which, had Miss Jean known a little more about it, or Lilias taken a greater degree of interest, would have been amusing. But in neither case did it tell as it ought. Miss Margaret was used to a want of sympathy in this respect; but it is to be supposed that in the mere utterance aloud of her sentiments there was some pleasure, for she continued to express them without much reference to her audience. Miss Jean threw in a word now and then, mostly in deprecation.

"No, no, Margaret, I can't think that; the man will just be mistaken," she would say, or, "No, no—it's just a matter of opinion."

"Opinion!" Miss Margaret would say. "An idiot might hold the opinion that white is black—but it takes a dishonest person to say white is white one day, and black the next."

"Whisht, whisht, Margaret; how can you tell it is the same person?" Miss Jean would say.

Lilias scarcely took any notice at all. She was at the age when a young creature can carry on two mental processes at once. She was thinking all the time, dreaming her dreams, holding all sorts of dialogues within herself, but at the same time she heard every word and remembered, and could strike in when it pleased her. All her faculties were as vivid as youth and life could make them. She missed nothing and forgot nothing, yet never paid the least attention. To do this is what we all are capable of in our day.

Lilias sat on the other side of the round table with a box before her filled with trinkets. There was nothing of any great value in the little velvet-lined shelves and drawers; they were her mother's girlish ornaments, and the presents that had been made to herself from time to time, and the little nothings that gather in an old house, brooches and bracelets that had belonged to former generations, and which, found from time to time lying in a drawer, had been handed over with a "Would you like to have it?" from Margaret, or a pleased exclamation, "This will just do for Lilias," from Jean. Her mother's diamonds, which, though they were not very rich or rare, were still diamonds, were locked up securely for her against the time when she should be old enough to wear them; but the contents of the box which was now upon the table had given Lilias far more pleasure than she would ever get from diamonds. The cornelians and old-fashioned topazes and amethysts, the twisted chains and necklets and filigree brooches, had been her delight for years. She had put them upon her dolls when she was a child. Afterwards it had been one of her great pleasures to arrange and polish them, and seduce Jean into telling her over and over again the story of this one and the other. That was old Sir Claude's hair set round with a mourning border of black and a row of small lustrous pearls: the topazes? "Oh! I remember them very well; old Aunt Barbara used to wear them. She was grandpapa's aunt, and she lived to be nearly a hundred. I remember how I used to wonder—" and so on, and so on.

Lilias had heard all the stories a hundred times, but she liked them still; they were associated to her with many a cheerful, feverish hour, and many a delightful, childish convalescence. While Jean knitted her white fleecy wool and Margaret read her paper, Lilias took out and put in again the shining little ornaments, caressing them with her slim fingers. They were her earliest childish property; many of them were hideous, but she did not like them the worse for that. She had just taken out a little bracelet set with little turquoises, some of which had grown green instead of blue with age and neglect. Then it was that she made the little speech above recorded. "Did you ever hear that a turquoise was lucky and an opal an ill stone?"

"Not an ill stone," said Miss Jean, who could not bear to hear the character even of a stone taken away, "it is just beautiful; but it is a common saying that it brings ill-luck. I do not believe in any such nonsense. Long ago it had a different character. Dear me, what was the property it had? Margaret will mind."

"What are you saying about Margaret? What will I mind? You think I have room for all the trash that can be collected in my poor head, like Lilias' trinket-box. Opals! they were said to change colour when they were near poison. But we are in no risk of poison, and I'm not fond of them. Where did you hear anything about opals, or turquoise either?" Miss Margaret said.

The question confused Lilias slightly, for it brought vividly before her the great communication Katie had made to her, and the necessity for keeping it secret.

"Oh, I did not hear much about them," she said.

"It would be in some story-book," said Miss Jean. "It is just the thing to be in a story-book. But there is no luckiness or unluckiness in stones. That is just superstition."

"It is a thing you know nothing about," said Miss Margaret, "nor me either. We'll wait till we know before we pronounce judgment."

She put down her paper in one hand, so that the light and shade of the group was a little altered, and she looked keenly at Lilias through her spectacles. For she had already taken to spectacles, though all her contemporaries declared it to be affectation. She would have seen her little sister better without them, but Miss Margaret was of opinion that they increased the dignity of her appearance, and conveyed an impression of more penetrating insight. She always put them on when she had some reproof to make.

"What set Katie talking of jewels?" she said. "She has none, that I know of."

"Oh, for nothing at all," said Lilias; and then she added, "We were speaking of rings, and she said what she liked best."

"Which was turquoise? The little cutty, what does she know about such things? It will be some love-business. I hope her mother knows, or that good Christian, her father, that they just turn round their little fingers. But I'll have no talk about lovers here."

"Margaret!" said Miss Jean, with a look of distress. "Oh, I hope you are not hardening your heart, and judging your neighbours. Little Katie is a harmless thing. She is no more than a child. I suppose Lilias was showing her the things in the box. I would give her that bit bracelet, if I were you, Lily. You will never miss it, and what she wants is just a little ornament or two. Mrs. Seton takes a great deal of trouble with her dress. It does her mother great credit, Katie's dress, for they are far from rich. Since she is fond of turquoises, I would give her the bracelet: and I think I could find a locket to go with it."

"How kind you are, Jean—even though you don't approve of Katie."

"There is nobody that Jean does not approve of," said Miss Margaret, "if she thinks she has anything that they would like. As for that little thing, the best thing they can do with her is to marry her. She should marry the helper at the Braehead, who, they tell me, will be assistant and successor, for Mr. Morrison is an old man, and very frail. It would be a very suitable marriage, just in their own condition of life, and really a very presentable person."

"Katie does not think he is in their own condition of life."

"Katie is just a—cutty. I have always disliked that in a minister's family. They look down upon their own kind. Well, there is the young man that plays the piano. I am not fond of men that give themselves up to music. The piano is a fine thing for girls that have little to do. And that's well thought upon—I have not heard you practise, Lilias, for a whole month."

"I played all my pieces over the day before yesterday," said Lilias, with a little indignation.

"Oh, Lilias!" cried Miss Jean, putting up her hands, "as if it were just mechanical, to hear you speak like that."

"I see no harm in what she says," said Miss Margaret. "But when a thing has been learnt, and cost a good deal of trouble, it should not just be let down. I was saying that young man who plays the piano. He's a stranger here. If he has a good profession, or anything to live on, they might get him for Katie. I would marry her early, if she belonged to me, which, the Lord be thanked, she does not, nor any of her kind."

"There is no harm in her that I can see," said the gentler sister.

Miss Margaret answered with that monosyllabic sound which it is common to spell, "Humph," and went back to her newspaper; and then the little group fell again into soft silence, full of thinkings and dreamings. Miss Jean, indeed, did not do much beyond counting the stitches of her knitting. She was capable of refraining even from thought. She had no harsh conclusions in her mind, nor anything to disturb her. The hours slid on softly. She was happy to see the others occupied, to have no jar in the air, nothing to derange the harmony of the gentle silence. The little oppositions between her sister and herself never came to any discord. And, as for Lilias, she had begun to occupy herself, with the pleasure of a child, in stringing some pretty blue Venetian beads, which it was quite a pleasure to find loose. The girl was delighted with the task—she threaded them one by one, letting each drop upon the other with a little tinkle. This made a sort of merry accompaniment to her thoughts, and, after the foregoing interruption, she took up those thoughts—if thoughts they can be called—just where she had left them, and resumed the dialogue she had been carrying on. It was a dialogue between herself and—the other. He had just saved her life (for the hundredth time), and she was thanking him, and he, with words which meant far more than they sounded, was giving her to understand that for him to save her life was mere selfishness, for what would the world be without her? It was Katie's communication which had emboldened Lilias to carry on a conversation like this in the very presence of her sisters. She indulged generally in it only in snatches, in the uttermost retirement. Now at the very table sitting with them she ventured upon it. What would they think if they knew? This gave her a quiver of laughter and pain and pleasure all together—laughter to think how little they knew, pain to contemplate the possibility that they might find out. But in fact that did not come into the bounds of possibility. Thus the three sisters sat together, and knew just as much and as little of each other as is common with human folk.

It was about this time that Lewis first came to the house to play to Miss Jean; but of this Lilias was not supposed to know anything. She had seen him to be a stranger when they had first met on the road, and she had perceived, with a mixture of amusement and pique that whereas he looked with a good deal of curiosity at her sister, her own blue veil had been a sort of sanctuary for herself. Lilias could not but think he must be a stupid young man not to have divined. It tickled her to think that he had passed her quite over and gazed at Margaret and Jean. But he did not interest her much. Nothing could be more unlike the fine specimen of manhood over six feet high, with dark eyes that went to your very soul, who was in the habit most evenings of saving Lilias' life, than this commonplace young man who never looked at her. Lewis was not tall; there was not much colour about him. He did not seem at all like a person who could stop a runaway horse, or burst through a flaming door, or leap a wall to render instant and efficient help as that hero had now done so often that Lilias felt a little variety would be desirable. When she met him again at the new castle, she was still more amused by his startled look at her, and by the way in which he permitted Miss Margaret to swoop upon him and carry him off. There was something amiable, something nice about him, she thought. He was like a brother. Sometimes in novels the heroine will have a brother who is completely under her control, who takes his opinions and views from her, and is useful at last in marrying her confidant, as well as in backing herself up generally, whatever she may have to do. It seemed to Lilias that he would do very well for that rôle. She was seized with sudden kindness for him after that second encounter. And then it amused her much that Margaret thought it necessary to carry off this mild, colourless, smiling youth out of her way. From the moment this happened she made up her mind to make his acquaintance, and it was not in such utter innocence as Jean supposed that Lilias made that sudden appearance in the drawing-room, cutting short a proposal upon the very lips of Lewis, and interrupting the high tension of the situation. The dinner that followed, the startled look which he had cast upon herself, his silence and bewildered absorption when he sat opposite to her, and the discomfiture of Margaret, had all been exceedingly amusing to the young plotter. She meant no harm, neither to Lewis nor to her sisters. She neither meant to make a conquest of the stranger, nor to alarm her anxious guardians. She wanted a little fun. She was a girl full of imagination, full of poetical attributes: but by times an imperious desire for a little fun will overwhelm the sagest bosom of eighteen. She could not resist the impulse. To see the agitation she had caused was delightful. She could scarcely contain her laugh as she sat down opposite to him and saw his wondering looks, and perceived the efforts of Miss Margaret to keep his attention engaged. Lilias had been very demure. She had sat at table like an innocent little school-girl who thought of nothing but her lessons. She became conscious after a while that he had once or twice met her eye when she was off her guard, and probably had caught the sparkle of malice in it; and then Lilias began to feel guilty, but this was not till the meal was nearly over, and she had got her amusement out of it. She disappeared the moment they rose from table, determined to show Margaret that she meant no harm. And indeed Miss Margaret was too anxious to put "nothing in her head," to suggest no ideas to the young mind which she believed so innocent, to say a word as to this incident. It was quite natural that the child in her guilelessness should ask the stranger to come to dinner.

"I feel it a reproach on myself," Margaret said. "It's not the habit in any house of ours to let a visitor go without breaking bread. I did not do it myself because of a feeling, that is perhaps an unworthy feeling, that he came of none of the Murrays we know of, and that I'm not fond of sitting down with a person that might not be just a—"

"Oh, don't say not a gentleman, Margaret," cried Jean. "He might be an angel to hear him play."

"Ah! well, that might be: an angel is not necessarily—" Miss Margaret said, with a curious dryness. "But you were quite right, Lilias. It's what I desire that a creature like you should just do what is right without thinking of any reason against it."

Margaret's brow had a pucker of care in it even when she said this, and Lilias felt so guilty that she had nearly fallen on her knees and confessed her little trick. But to what good? Had she confessed, they would have thought her far more to blame than she really was; they would have thought she wanted to make the stranger's acquaintance, or had some secret inclination towards him, whereas all that she wanted was fun, a thing as different as night from day.

"This young man was probably saying something to you about himself," Miss Margaret said. "Lilias, you may go to your books, and I will come to you in half-an-hour or so. You have the air of being a little put about, Jean. I would be glad of your confidence, if you have no objection. I hope there is nothing that can occur that will come between you and me."

"Come between you and me!" cried Miss Jean, in astonishment. "I know nothing that could do that, Margaret; but, dear me! you must mean something. You would not say a thing like that just merely without any cause. Confidence!—I have no confidence to give. You know me just as well as I know myself."

"Is that so?" said the elder sister, looking at her with penetrating eyes.

"Why should it not be so? There must be something on your mind, Margaret."

"There is nothing on my mind. No doubt this young man was saying something to you—about himself."

"I cannot remember what he said," said Miss Jean; and then she uttered an exclamation of annoyance. "How selfish I am!" she said—"just like all the rest. We listen to what concerns us, and not a bit to what concerns another person. Yes, he did tell me something, poor lad, about settling down here. I was surprised, for what should a young man do here? and yet you do not like to say a word against it, when it's your own place. It is like saying you will take no notice of him, or that there's some reason why he shouldn't come. I was very glad when Lilias came in; it saved me from making any answer, and I did not know what to say."

"Dear me!" said Miss Margaret, still suspicious. "It must have been something out of the common if you were so much at a loss as that."

Jean looked at her for a moment with doubtful eyes.

"If it had been only me, it would have been easy enough," she said. "I would have said, 'If you settle here, Mr. Murray, we will be very glad from time to time to see you at the Castle, and if you should be going to marry, as would be natural, my sisters and me will do what we can to make the place agreeable to your young lady.' That is what I would have said if it had been only me; for to play such music as you is given to few, and my opinion is that nobody but a well-educated person, and one that was gentle by nature, could ever do it. But when I remembered that you had not that way of knowing, and were a little suspicious of the lad that he might be a common person, I was just silenced, and could not find a word to say."

Margaret had turned away to conceal a certain constraint that was in her countenance. She waited for a few minutes with her back to her sister, looking out of the window, before she ventured to speak.

"I am glad he was so modest," she said; "but what would he do settling here in this quiet little place?"

"That is just what I said," said Jean, all unconscious. "I told him he would repent. And he really is a most innocent, single-minded youth, for he said something quite plain about looking to us for society, which made it more hard for me to give him no encouragement. But I did not like to take it upon me as you were not there."

Upon this Margaret turned round upon her placid sister with a little excitement.

"You are old enough to judge for yourself, Jean. You have a good right to choose for yourself. I'm a woman of strong opinions, I cannot help it. But you're a gentle creature, and you have a heart as young as Lilias. Just do what you think best, and don't let anything depend on me."

Jean looked up with a little surprise at this speech. "I have no desire," she said, "my dear Margaret, to set up my judgment in that way. We're one, we're not two, we have always been of the same mind. Perhaps we will hear something more satisfactory about his family; for I have a real hope you will take the young man up. He has very nice manners, and his touch is just extraordinary. It would be such a good thing for Lilias, too. To see him at the piano is better than many a lesson. So I hope you will take the best view you can of him. To bring him to dinner was very startling to me, but it is fine that Lilias has such a sense of hospitality."

All this Jean said with a manner so entirely undisturbed that Margaret could not tell what to think. It was she who was abashed and confused—she who had supposed it possible that her sister could be moved by the young man's nonsense. Indeed, when she came to think it over, she felt almost a conviction that it was she herself who was mistaken. Jean evidently was totally unenlightened in respect to any intentions he might have. It must have been she who had made the mistake. She was not fond of acknowledging herself in the wrong, even to herself, but it was fortunate at least that no one else knew the delusion she had been under, and still more fortunate that now that delusion was past.

CHAPTER XX

The framework of society at Murkley was of a simple description. There were no great gatherings in that corner of the countryside. A dinner-party happened now and then, but these were very rare, for most of the best families dined in the middle of the day in a primitive manner, and a great dinner meant an overthrow of all the habits of the house. Usually friends came to tea, and remained, as in the manse, when the majority was young, to dance: or in other houses, when the majority were older people, to play a friendly rubber, with a round game for such youth as might be of the party. The routine was completely stereotyped; for human nature is very uninventive, especially in the country. Sometimes there was an attempt to vary this procedure by "a little music;" but in those days music was less cultivated than now, and a few pieces of the "Battle of Prague" kind, were usually all that were to be found in a young lady's repertoire, varied perhaps by "Sweet Spirit, hear my Prayer," and other elegant morceaux of that description. And it is much to be feared that, had the music been of a higher order, it would have been relished still less; for however little the art of conversation may be cultivated as an art, and however little entertainment there may be in it, everybody resents the stoppage of talk, and the gloomy countenance of even the most æsthetic of parties, when compelled to silent listening, continues to prove how much more attractive are our own sweet voices than anything that supersedes them. Society in Murkley would willingly put up with a few songs. It is true that it knew them by heart, but the good people were always charitable on this point, and liked, "Oh, no, we never mention her!" just as well the hundredth time as the first. And there was another thing which many of the elder ladies could do without any vanity on the subject, or even any idea that the gift was more than a convenience. They played dance music with the greatest spirit and accuracy. Mrs. Seton possessed this talent, and so to some extent did Mrs. Stormont, though she put it to less frequent use, and had not the real enjoyment which the minister's wife had in the exercise of her talent. These ladies were surprised to be complimented on the subject. It was no credit to them. It was "just a necessity where there are young people," Mrs. Seton said; a sort of maternal accomplishment which everybody took for granted. But though the entertainments and social constitution were so simple, the same schemes and hopes underlay them as were to be found on the highest levels. It was, as has been said, the dearest object of Miss Margaret's heart to keep her little sister safe, and preserve her from all youthful entanglements of sentiment. But Mrs. Stormont of the Tower had a dearest object which was entirely in opposition to Margaret's. Her dream was to secure for her own Philip this very lily of Murkley which was kept so persistently in the shade. Mrs. Stormont had been an old friend of the General; they had called themselves old friends for years with a twinkle in the eye of one and a conscious smile upon the corners of the other's mouth, which would have betrayed their little secret had not the countryside in general known it as well as they did. They had been, in fact, lovers in their youth, and all the skill of their respective families had been exercised once upon a time to keep them apart. The attempt had been quite successful, and neither Mrs. Stormont nor the General had been sorry in after-life. They had talked it over with a laugh when they met again, more than twenty years after, each with a little mental comment. It was shortly after the General's second marriage, when, in the pride and triumph of having won for himself so young and delightful a bride, he too felt himself delightful and young as in his best days.

"Good Lord! to think I might have been tied to that old woman!" he said to himself. She was some years younger than he was, and a handsome woman, but she was not like Lady Lilias at eighteen.

Mrs. Stormont's reflections were of a different order. She went about all day after, saying, "Tchich-tchich," to herself at intervals, or rather making that little sound with the tongue upon the palate which is the language of mild astonishment mingled with dismay. "He promised to be a man of sense when I knew him," Mrs. Stormont said, and the thought of what "a handful" she would have found him gave her a sense of exhilaration in her escape: thus they were mutually contented that they had not become one; but yet there was a little consciousness between them. They would laugh and look at each other when certain things were said. They had a good-humoured contempt each for the other, and yet a certain charity. And, when the pretty young wife was cut off, Mrs. Stormont was very sorry. "Poor thing, she is no doubt taken from the evil to come," she said, devoutly, with a sense that Lady Lilias too, when she grew older, might have found her handsome General "a handful."

But this was partially a mistake on Mrs. Stormont's part, for the General never did very much harm short of quarrelling with his father. She was so far justified, however, that secretly, at the bottom of her heart, it is not to be denied, Miss Margaret agreed with her. It was long before the General's death, however, that Mrs. Stormont had formed her plans. Philip was the only child left to her after the loss of many. She did not adore him in the ordinary way; she formed to herself no delusions as to his excellence, but knew him as what he was, an honest fellow, who would never set the Tay, let alone the Thames, on fire. It was a disappointment to his mother that he was not clever, but she had made up her mind to that. But she felt that he could not help more or less making a figure in the county if it could be secured for him that he should have Lilias Murray to be his wife.

Everything is relative in human society. Lilias was poor in the estimation of the people whom her sisters would have considered her equals: and they know her to be poor, they who were supplementing her importance by their own, maintaining the little state they thought necessary out of their own means, and allowing the income of Murkley, such as it was, to accumulate for their child: and all the parents of the wealthy young gentlemen whom Miss Margaret might have smiled upon as suitors for Lilias would have considered her poor. But to Mrs. Stormont she was an heiress and a person of importance. The revenues of Lilias, added to his own, would make Philip, if not a great man, at least one who had to be taken into account, who would be reckoned upon at an election, who might even stand for the county.

He was of a good family, and Lilias was of a better. They would supplement each other, and increase each other's consequence. In no other way was it likely that he could do half as well. He might get more money, Mrs. Stormont said to herself, but money was not everything. The last Stormont of the Tower married to the last Murray of Murkley would have a position which the duke himself must pay respect to. She had thought of this for years. When Lilias was a child she had been regaled with the finest gooseberries in the garden; little parties had been assembled for her, the first and the last strawberries reserved for her, with cream in which the spoon would "stand alone." Mrs. Stormont had never intermitted these delicate attentions. She stroked the girl's fair locks every time they met, and said, "I might have been your mother," with a laugh and a sigh. It had distressed Miss Margaret to see that these soft seductions had a great deal of effect upon the girl, and she had indeed been injudicious enough to do everything she could to push Philip's claims by a continual depreciation of them.

"That long-leggit lad," she had been in the habit of calling him, until Lilias had been roused to ask,

"Do you object to long legs, Margaret?"

"Me! object to long legs! No; but I like a head along with them," Margaret said.

"Oh! Philip has a nice curly head," cried Lilias.

This had happened when the girl was fifteen, when the General was still living to lead her into folly. After that she forgot and outgrew Philip Stormont. Her mourning and retirement made it easy for her sister to regain the reins which had slipped out of her hands, and establish her own more rigorous system. And then the young people had arrived at an age when it is no longer possible to make arrangements for them, when they begin to settle for themselves. Philip grown-up had showed no inclination to carry out his mother's wishes. He had gone away for some years. He had come home quite independent, making his own engagements. He had grown into an habitué of the manse, not of the castle. And Margaret had shut her little sister up, letting her go nowhere. This made at last a crisis in the history of the parish.

Mrs. Stormont lived a somewhat lonely life in her Tower. In winter especially it was a long walk for people who did not keep carriages. The remoter county people paid ceremonious calls, just as many as were due to her, and Mrs. Seton, never to be discouraged in the discharge of her duty, bravely climbed the cliff about once a fortnight. But these visits Mrs. Stormont did not esteem. As anxious as she was to find her son a fitting mate in Lilias, so anxious, she could not but allow, other people might be to advance the interests of their children. Philip would be but a bad match for Lilias, but he was an excellent one for Katie Seton. The one mother comprehended the tactics of the other. Therefore, when the minister's wife came to call, there was a sort of duel between the ladies—an encounter from which cordiality did not ensue. The only ground on which they were unanimous was in denouncing the pride of Margaret Murray in withdrawing her young sister from the society of her neighbours, and that ambitious project she had for taking her to London. Mrs. Seton had been powerless in all her attempts to have the embargo removed.

"You know what my little bits of parties are," she said, "just a few friends to tea—and, if the young people like to have a little dance after, I would not stop them; but no preparations—just the table drawn away into a corner—"

"Oh! you do yourself injustice," said Mrs. Stormont; "I consider those little parties very dangerous. I can understand very well why Margaret will not let Lilias go."

"Dangerous!" cried Mrs. Seton. "Dear me, what could put such a word into your head? My visitors are all very young, that is the worst of them. No, no, I should say it was the best. They are so young, they have nothing in their heads but just the dancing. Oh! perhaps you will be meaning Philip? Well, you should know best. I don't pretend to fathom what's in a young man's mind; but I see no signs of anything else but just a little natural pleasure. I was wild about dancing in my own day. And so is Katie after me. I cannot say a word to her. It's just like myself in my time."

"Oh! I think I have heard that," Mrs. Stormont said.

Now it was very well known that the minister's wife in her day had been a little person full of flirtations and naughtiness; and there was a good deal of significance in the tone in which the other lady spoke. But Mrs. Seton was clothed in armour of proof, and knew no harm of herself.

"I will never deny it," she said. "I was at every dance I could hear of. And Katie would be just the same, only that there are no dances—except the bit little things, which are not to be called dances, which we give ourselves. I will take her to the Hunt Ball when she is old enough; but it is not the like of that a young creature wants. She wants just her fun and a little movement; and to have something to talk about among her friends. Oh! the chatter they will keep up when two or three of them get together. You would think my little tea-parties were grand balls, nothing less."

"I consider them far more dangerous than your grand balls," said Mrs. Stormont. "The young men, when they go to the Hunt Ball, are on their guard; but he must be a very suspicious person who would take such precautions for a tea-party at the manse."

"It would be quite out of the question: precautions!" Mrs. Seton cried. "Two or three boys and girls thinking of nothing but what a bonnie waltz that is, or whose steps go best together."

She laughed, but Mrs. Stormont did not laugh. She sat very upright in her chair, and went on with her knitting without the relaxation of a feature.

"I am thinking," she said, after a pause, "if I keep well, of seeing a little company myself."

"Dear me! that will be a great pleasure to the young people to hear of."

"Oh, I'll not enter into competition with you," said Mrs. Stormont, coldly. "But Philip is not just in the boy and girl category. It's for his sake that I think it's necessary to see a few of my old county friends."

Mrs. Seton, though she was piqued, was equal to the occasion.

"That's quite a different thing, to be sure," she said, "from the parish. I may not be very quick in the uptake, but of course I can see that."

"On the contrary, I would say you were very quick in the uptake," said Mrs. Stormont; "there is nobody but knows it. It is not the same as just the neighbours in the parish; but I need not say that the clergyman, especially when he's respected like Mr. Seton, and his family are always included."

"That's very kind," said Mrs. Seton. "If it is to be soon, however, I'm afraid we will not have the pleasure; we are going to pay some summer visits, my husband and me, and I think we'll take Katie with us. It's time she were seeing a little of the world."

"Bless me! at sixteen, what does a girl want with seeing the world?" Mrs. Stormont cried.

"There is never any telling," said the minister's wife. "It's sometimes a great advantage to be made to see that a parish or even a county is not all the world. But," she added, rising with great suavity, "if we do not see it, we'll hear about it, and I'm sure I hope it will be a great success."

"She hopes nothing of the sort," said Mrs. Stormont, when her visitor was gone. She lived so much alone that she would sometimes say out in very plain language, confident that nobody could hear her, the sentiments of her mind. "She hopes nothing of the sort; she would like to hear that my cakes would not rise nor my bread bake, and that everybody was engaged."

When, however, a little time had elapsed, and Philip's mother had recovered her temper, she modified this expression. For Mrs. Seton was not an ill-natured woman. She liked to be first—who does not? She liked to feel herself a social personage sought by everybody. When she was neglected or threatened with neglect, she knew how to show "a proper pride;" but she wished no harm to her neighbours or their entertainments. And at the present moment the Stormonts were very important to her. She thought she saw a proposal in Philip's eyes. Poor lady! she was not wiser than another, she was not aware it had been made and accepted. She did not know that her little Katie, whose flirtations she considered of so little consequence, was holding a secret of such importance from her. She was very quick-witted in such matters, and would have found out any other girl in a moment; but to think that Katie was deceiving her was impossible to her. She thought she had it all in her own hands; sometimes she confided her feelings to her husband, who was very helpless, and did not know anything about it.

"Things have gone just far enough," she said to him, "with that lad Philip Stormont—just far enough. Unless he is going to speak, he has no business to hang about our house morning, noon, and night. He must see that we are not people to be trifled with, Robert. I am not going to put up with it if it goes too far."

"I hope, my dear," said the minister, with an air of distress, "that you don't want me to interfere; I understand nothing about it. I never spoke to a man upon such a subject in my life. I really could not do it. You must not ask me to interfere."

Mrs. Seton looked at him with a contemplative air of wondering contempt.

"Of all the frightened creatures in this world, there is nothing like a man," she said; "a hare is nothing to you. Interfere!—do I ever interfere with your sermons? I was silly to say a word, but there are times when a person cannot help herself, when there is just a necessity to speak to somebody. And I have not Katie to fall back upon. No, no—don't you be frightened. I hope I have more sense than to ask you to interfere."

The minister was relieved, but still not quite easy in his mind.

"I hope nobody will do it," he said. "I'd like to horsewhip the fellow that behaved ill to my Katie; but I would not say a word to him, I would—"

"Just you hold your tongue, Robert," Mrs. Seton said. "Am I likely to compromise Katie? Just you write your sermons, and leave the bairns to me. We are both best in our own departments."

To which sentiment the minister yielded a silent assent. He was altogether overwhelmed with alarm at the thought of having any negotiation to manage of such a delicate kind. And Katie, after all, was a child; and women have a way of giving such exaggerated importance to everything. But he watched his wife with a little anxiety for some time after. He found her, however, when he saw them together, on the best possible terms with Philip Stormont, and he congratulated himself that the cloud had blown over, and that there would need to be no interference at all.

"Your mother tells me she's meditating some parties," said Mrs. Seton, when she saw the young man. "Oh, no, no, not our kind. I hope I know better than to think of that. Me, I never venture on more than a tea-party, and, though you do us the honour to come, and the ladies from the Castle, the rest are just parish neighbours. But, so far as I understand from Mrs. Stormont, it is the whole county that is coming. Is it to be a ball? I said to your mother we would probably be away, Mr. Seton and myself, and that I thought of taking Katie; but I am not sure that I will keep to that, if it is going to be a ball."

"I don't know anything about it," said Philip. "My mother thinks we should do something, as people have been so kind to me; but nobody has been so kind as you have been, and, if you are away, it must be put off till you come back—unless you send Katie—"

"My dear Mr. Philip," said Mrs. Seton, "it is not that I'm a punctilious person: and you have known Katie all her life: but, you see, she is now grown up, and at the first opportunity I am going to bring her out. Yes, I allow it is very early—sixteen and a half—but the eldest daughter, that always counts for something. And, in the family, it would be ridiculous if you called her anything but by her name; but I must ask you, before strangers, to say Miss Seton, or even Miss Katie. It's more suitable when a girl grows up."

Philip stared with his mouth open, as well as his eyes. Nobody could say this was interfering. It was different from the brutal method which asks a man what are his intentions: but all the same he felt himself pulled suddenly up, when he was fearing nothing. He answered, faltering, that in that respect and every other he would of course do what Mrs. Seton thought right, but—

"Oh, yes," she said, with perfect good-humour, "of course you will do just what I please, but—I am acquainted with your buts, you young folk—you forget that I was once young myself. No, Philip, Katie is very well for the house, but it does not do for the world. What would you think in the middle of your grand party, with all the county there, as your mother says—that is, if we are asked, which I am not taking for granted—"

"There shall be no party in any house I belong to, where you are not asked the very first," Philip said.

"Well, that is a very nice thing to say. It is just what it is becoming and nice for you to say, having been so much about our house. But what would people think, if you were to be heard with your Katie here and Katie there in the middle of all the fine county ladies? What would they say? You see, I am obliged to think of all that."

"I don't know what they would think," said Philip, with what Mrs. Seton called afterwards, "a very red face." "I don't know what they might say—but I know what I should tell them, if any one of them ventured—"

Mrs. Seton put up her hand to stop him. She would indeed have liked very much to hear what he would have told them, if any one had ventured—But, after all, she had no mind to betray him into a hasty statement. She put up her hand, and said,

"Whisht, whisht! You may be sure nobody would venture. I will tell you what they would say. They would say that Mrs. Seton's a silly woman not to notice that her daughter is grown up, and to make other people take notice of it too. So you see, after all, it is myself I am thinking of," she concluded, with a laugh.

Philip retired, feeling much discomforted, after this conversation. His secret had not weighed upon him before. He meant no harm. There was a certain enjoyment in the mystery, in the stolen meetings, and secret understanding. He did not mean anything dishonourable. But as he listened to this unexpected address, and found himself placed on the standing-ground of one who had known Katie from a child, but henceforward must learn to respect her as a young lady, a curious shame and sense of falsehood came over him. As if he were a stranger! as if he had nothing to do with her! while all the while Katie was—All the interference in the world could not have convinced the young man like this. Was it possible that he would have to make believe; to call his betrothed by the formal name of Miss Seton? His imagination was not lively, but yet he was capable of figuring to himself his mother's party at the Tower, with Katie present amid the crowd of guests, and he, the master of the house, obliged to reserve his attentions for those who were entitled to them, and incapable of distinguishing her. Mrs. Seton had overlooked this, clear-sighted as she was. She had spoken as if the risk were that he would distinguish Katie over-much, and rouse the surprise of all the fine people by too familiar use of her name. Alas, if that had been all! But Philip knew better what his fate would be. He would be occupied with very different duties; his work would be all laid out for him—whom he was to dance with, to whom he was to devote his attentions. He would not be able to approach Katie, perhaps, till the end of the evening after he had paid his devoirs to all the greater people present.

Poor Philip's heart grew sick as he thus realized his position. If he could but prevail upon his mother to give up her plans!—failing that, he was obliged to confess with bitterness that it would be far better if Katie would go away visiting with her parents. He would not care for the ball were she absent, that was true; but, Heaven help him! what was he to do were she present?—how explain to her that he must abandon her?—and, still more, how explain to her mother, who expected something so different? Katie might pardon for love's sake, and because of his protestations and explanations, his apparent neglect—though Katie, too, was very high-spirited, and would ill be able to brook the slight. But her mother, how could she be mollified, how brought to understand it?—she who was so confident of her own great kindness to him and his indebtedness to her, and only afraid lest his extreme intimacy should appear too much. Poor Philip! his very soul sank within him as he anticipated his mother's party. Was it, perhaps, with some consciousness of all these promising elements of a quarrel that Mrs. Stormont's plans had been laid?

CHAPTER XXI

But Mrs. Stormont was not a person whom it was easy to move from her purpose. She was a serious woman, little addicted to balls, but, when she had determined upon this frivolity, it became to her a piece of business as incumbent upon her, and to be undertaken as conscientiously, as any other duty. If she foresaw in her sober and long-sighted intelligence the embarrassment it was likely to bring into her son's relations with the Setons, this was merely by the way, and not important enough to rank with her as a motive. She glimpsed at it in passing as an auxiliary advantage rather than contemplated it as worth the trouble she was taking in itself. Her motives were distinct enough. She said to the world that her object was to return the civilities which had been paid to her son, than which nothing could be more natural. She owned to herself another and still stronger motive, which she prepared to carry out by a visit to Murkley as soon as her project had fully shaped itself in her mind. If she could succeed in bringing out Lilias at this entertainment, and making it the occasion of her introduction into society—if, amid the gratification which this preference of his house above all the other houses of the district must give Philip, she could place before her son's eyes a young creature far more lovely than Katie, as well as more gently bred and of higher pretensions, and re-knit the old bonds of childish intimacy between them, and convince both that they were made for each other, Mrs. Stormont felt that all the trouble and the expense, which she did not like, but accepted as a dolorous necessity, would not be in vain. This was her aim, if she could but carry it out.

As she thought over the details, she felt, indeed, that the minister's family, who had given themselves the air of being Philip's chief friends, would no doubt on such an occasion find their level. Mrs. Seton, who had it all her own way in the parish, would in the society of the county be put in her right place. And as for the little thing, who was not worth half the trouble she was likely to give, she would get her fill of dancing—for she was a good dancer, there could be no doubt on that point—but she would not have Mr. Stormont to dance attendance upon her, as no doubt she would expect. This would be a sort of inevitable revenge upon them, not absolutely intentional—indeed, beyond any power of hers to prevent—but which naturally she would have done nothing to prevent, even if she had the power. She caught sight of it, as it were, by the way, and was grimly amused and pleased. They would not like it; but what did that matter? It would let them see what was their proper place.

This, however, which to Mrs. Stormont was but one of the gratifying details of her plan, bulked much more largely in the eyes of Philip. He did the best he could to turn her from the ball altogether.

"It will be a great expense," he said, with a face as long as his arm. "Do you think, mother, it is really worth the while?"

"Everything is worth the while, Philip, that will put you in your proper place."

"What is my proper place, if I am not in it already without that? There is no more need for a ball to-day than there was a year ago."

"Then the less I lee, when I say it's needed now," said Mrs. Stormont, who loved a proverb. "Being wanted a year ago, as you confess, it is indispensable by this time. I am going to begin with Murkley; they are our nearest neighbours, and the oldest family in the county. If Margaret will but bring Lilias, that of itself will be worth all the cost. The prettiest girl in the whole neighbourhood, and so much romance about her. I would dearly like if she took her first step in the world in this house, Phil. It was here she first learned to walk alone, poor bit motherless thing; and her first step was into your arms."

Philip laughed, but the suggestion was confusing.

"I hope you don't intend that performance to be repeated now," he said.

"I would have no objection for my part," said his mother. "You might go farther and fare worse—both of you. Murkley marches with your lands, and if anything of the kind should come to pass—"

"I wish, mother, you would give up calculations of that sort."

"I never began them," said Mrs. Stormont, promptly. "I say you may go farther and fare worse. You can drive me to Murkley, if ye please, in the afternoon, and pay your respects to the ladies."

"Can't Sandy drive you, as usual?" said her son, with a lowering brow.

"Oh, for that matter, I'm very independent. I can drive myself," said Mrs. Stormont, who went on the safe principle of making her own arrangements.

She lamented a little over Philip's churlishness when he left the room, reminding herself how different it had been when he was a boy, with a maternal complaint which is too common to require repetition. But she was too wise a woman to be tragical on this subject. A mother, even when she has but one child, must harden herself in such matters. She rang for Sandy, and ordered her little carriage without any sentimentality.

"Will I clean myself, and go with ye, ma'am," asked Sandy, "or will Mr. Philip?"

"We must not depend upon Mr. Philip," said Mrs. Stormont, with a smile. "Gentlemen have so many occupations. You will just be ready at three o'clock, in case I want you."

And at three o'clock, accordingly, the sturdy old pony felt in his imagination the flashing of Sandy's whip, and set off at a steady pace down the hill towards Murkley. They crossed in the big ferry-boat, to which they were all accustomed, and which the pony regarded as an every-day matter. Understanding all about the boat, probably he would have felt a bridge to be something more alarming. The day was fine, the river shining in the sun, the trees in their deepest summer wealth of shade.

"Is that the English gentleman that came over to lunch with your master?" Mrs. Stormont asked.

"I'm no that sure, mem, that he's English," Sandy replied.

"I'm astonished that he's still about. I thought he was a tourist, or some of those cattle. What is he doing so long here?" the lady asked, peremptorily.

"He's nae fisher," replied Sandy, with a slight shake of his head—implying at once a certain stigma upon Lewis' morals, and a deeper shade of mystery as to his object.

The young man himself was seated on the river-bank, with a sketch-book before him. He was surrounded by a group of children, however, and was evidently making very little progress with his sketch. There was a look of indolence about him which disturbed these critics.

"He's doing nothing," said Mrs. Stormont.

"I canna make out that he ever does anything but tell the bairns stories," said Sandy.

Such a phenomenon was rare at Murkley, where everybody had something to do. Had he been fishing however unsuccessfully, both mistress and man would have been satisfied. But in the absence of that legitimate occupation Lewis was a vagabond, if not a semi-criminal, meditating mischief, in their eyes.

The appearance of Mrs. Stormont's carriage was very welcome at Murkley in the languor of the afternoon. Something in the sense that she "might have been their mother" gave a softness to her manners in that place. She kissed even Margaret and Jean with a certain affectionateness, although they could not have been more than step-daughters to her in any case.

"And where is my bonnie Lily?" she said. There could not be a doubt that she loved Lilias for herself, besides all her other recommendations. She took the girl into her arms, into the warm enfolding of her heavy black-silk cloak. "Now, let me see how you're looking," she said, holding her at arm's length. "My dear Margaret, we'll have to acknowledge, whether we will or not, that this bit creature is woman grown."

"I have not grown a bit for two years," said Lilias. "I am more than a woman, I am getting an old woman; but Margaret will never see it."

"And what is the news with you?" said Miss Jean.

"Well, my dears," said Mrs. Stormont, "I have some news, for a wonder, and I have come to get you to help me. I am going to give a party."

Lilias uttered a soft little cry, and put out her hands towards Margaret with a gesture of appeal.

"A—ball," said Mrs. Stormont, with deliberation, making a pause before the word.

Lilias jumped to her feet. She clapped her hands together with soft vehemence.

"Oh, Margaret, oh, Margaret!" she cried.

"That is exactly what I mean," the elder lady said. "I meant to have approached the subject with caution, but it's better to be bold and make a clean breast of it. That is just what it is, Margaret. You see, everybody has been very kind to Philip, yourselves included. And I want to give an entertainment, to make some little return. But I am not a millionnaire, as you know, and I'm very much out of the habit of gaieties. There is just one thing my heart is set upon, and that is to have the Lily of Murkley at Philip's ball."

There are some things that even the most judicious cannot be expected to understand, and one of them is the manner in which persons who are most important and delightful to themselves may be regarded by others. That her son was neither a hero nor a genius Mrs. Stormont was very well aware. She had said to herself long since that she had no illusions on this subject. There was nothing wonderful about him one way or another. He would no doubt turn out a respectable member of society, like his father before him. "You are very well off when you can be sure of that; plenty of women just as good as I am are trysted with fools or reprobates," Mrs. Stormont said to herself: and Philip was neither the one nor the other. If he was not devoted to his mother, he had never yet gone against her or openly opposed her decisions, and with this she had learned to be content, and even to glorify herself a little, comparing her position with that of old Lady Terregles, who had been obliged for very good reasons to leave her son's house. But, reasonable as she was, there was one natural weakness which Mrs. Stormont had not got free of. It had not occurred to her that it could be anything but a recommendation of her ball to everybody about that it was Philip's ball. To say that it was for him seemed to be the way of attracting everybody's interest. She thought, in the unconscious foolishness which accompanied so much excellent sense, that there was much less likelihood of overcoming Margaret's scruples if she had claimed Lilias for her party on the ground of her own old affection: to ask this privilege for Philip's ball was the most ingratiating way she could put it. She expected with confidence the effect this statement would have upon them. Philip's ball: not for her sake—that might not be motive enough—but to confer distinction upon Philip. Poor Mrs. Stormont! It would have been some consolation to her had she known that Philip had been the object of Margaret's chiefest alarm for a long time past. But she did not know this; and when she looked round upon the ladies and saw the blank that came over their faces, it gave her a pang such as she had not felt since the first lowering of her expectations for Philip—and that was long ago. But Lilias herself did not show any blank. The girl had begun to execute a little dance of impatience before Margaret, holding out supplicating hands.

"Oh, will you let me go? Oh, Margaret, let me go! I will be an old woman before you let me see a dance. Oh, just this once, Margaret! Oh, Jean, why don't you speak? Even if I am to go to Court, the Queen will never know. And besides, do you think she would take the trouble to find out whether the girls that are present had ever been at a dance before? Do you think the Queen has the time for that? And she's far too kind, besides. Margaret, oh! will you let me go?"

Lilias, it is needless to say, being Scotch, was not skilled in the management of her wills and shalls; but there were no critical ears in the little company to find her out.

"I will be sixty before I ever see a dance, and what will I care for it then?" she added, sinking into plaintive tones.

But Margaret sat behind without saying a word. It is needless to add that Miss Jean had already put on a look as suppliant as that of the petitioner herself; instead of backing up her stronger sister, she went over to the side of youth without a struggle. But Margaret sat in her big easy-chair, with her feet elevated upon a high footstool—a type of the inexorable. And, as so often happens, it was upon the innocent one of the three, she who could derive no benefit from any yielding, that she turned her thunder.

"Jean," she cried, "I wonder at you! How often have we consulted upon this, and made up our minds it was best for the child to keep steady to her lessons till the time and the way that we had fixed upon for the best? Has anything happened to change that? I am not aware of it. Every circumstance is just the same; but you pull at my sleeve and you cast eyes at me as if I was a tyrant not to change at the first word. I understand Lilias, that is but a child, and thinks of nothing but diversion; but I am surprised at you!"

"Oh! Margaret," Jean said, but she did not venture on anything more.

"My dear Margaret," said Mrs. Stormont, "I would always respect a decision that had been come to after reflection, as you say. But, dear me, after all it's not so serious a matter. If a girl had to be kept out of the world till she's presented, as Lilias says, I suppose that would be a reason. But you know better than that. And I may never live to give another dance, though you will have plenty of them, my dear, long before you are sixty. And it will never be just the same thing again for Philip. Think what friends they've been all their lives. When I think they might have been brother and sister," she added, with a laugh, "if I had been left to my own guiding!—and Philip has always had that feeling for her. Bless me, Lilias, if that had taken place, you would have been no heiress at all. So perhaps it is as well for you I am not your mother," Mrs. Stormont said.

At this Lilias paused in the midst of her excitement to consider so curious a question. It opened up speculations, indeed, for them all. To have had a male heir had always been supposed to be the thing upon earth which would have been most blessed for the Murrays, and the elder sisters in past years had often sighed to think how much better it would have been had Lilias been a boy. But the idea that Philip Stormont might have been that heir-male was confusing and not agreeable. They felt a sort of half resentment at the suggestion. A young man like that, who was just nobody, a mere "long-leggit lad." Had the long-leggit lad been their own, no doubt the sisters would have represented him to themselves as the most delightful of young heroes: for even our own detrimentals are better than the best possessions of other people. But as a supposition it did not please them. To have had no Lilias, but Philip Stormont instead! Certainly Mrs. Stormont had been unfortunate in her modes of recommending her son. The presumption of supposing it possible that Philip could ever have been a Murray was scarcely less than that of believing that carefully constructed system could be broken through in order that Lilias might go to Philip's ball. What was Philip, that they should thus meet him upon every side? Mrs. Stormont did not quite fathom the cause of the sudden cloud which fell upon her friends. It could not, she said to herself, be her joke about Philip—that was just nonsense, she had no meaning in it. It was just one of the things that people say to keep up the conversation. But she had to retire without receiving any final answer to her proposition. She had indeed to congratulate herself that there was no final answer, for this left ground for a little hope; but, whether or not Lilias was eventually permitted to accept the invitation, Mrs. Stormont left Murkley with an uncomfortable feeling that her present visit had been a failure. She had gone wrong somehow, she could not exactly tell how. Something about Philip had jarred upon them, and she had been so anxious to present Philip under the best possible light! It was not often that she failed in making herself welcome, and the sensation was disagreeable. It was this failure, perhaps, which prompted her to tell Sandy to drive to the manse, perhaps with a slight inclination to indemnify herself, to make the people there suffer a little for the mistake she had made. She was so sure that Mrs. Seton had been injudicious about Katie, that she felt confident in her own power of being disagreeable at a moment's notice. It was not, however, with any intention of this kind that she stopped Sandy at the garden door, and went round by that way, instead of driving formally round the little "sweep," and reaching in state the grand entrance. Most of the visitors of the manse entered by the garden. Had she been walking, neither she nor any one else would have thought of any other way.

But it was an unfortunate moment. Somebody was playing the piano in the drawing-room. "And, if that is Katie, she must have been having lessons, for I never heard her play like that before: and, no doubt, dear lessons," Mrs. Stormont added to herself, "though there are six of a family, and boys that should be at college." She was a little jaundiced where the Setons were concerned. She came up to the glass door, and tapped lightly; whereupon there was a stir in the room, not like the placid composure with which people turn their faces towards a new visitor when they have been doing nothing improper. There was a confused sound of voices: one of the younger girls came in sight from behind the piano, and advanced with a somewhat scared face to the door which Mrs. Stormont had opened. Having thus had her suspicions fully aroused, she was scarcely surprised to see stumbling up from a chair, in a corner which retained a position of guilty proximity—noticed too late to be remedied—to another chair, her very son Philip who had already spoiled one visit to her, and of whom she believed that he was engaged in some necessary duty about the estate several miles off. Philip's face was flushed and sullen. Of all things in the world there is nothing so disagreeable as being "caught," and perhaps the sensation of being caught is all the more odious when you have the consciousness of doing no wrong. Katie, more rapid than her lover, was standing at the window with innocent eyes regarding the flowers. To jump up from Philip's side had been the affair of an instant with her. She came forward now, but not without a certain faltering.

"Mamma has just gone to the nursery for a moment; but I will tell her you are here," Katie cried. As for Philip, he stood like a culprit, like a man at the bar, and frowned upon his mother.

"Oh! Philip!" she said, "so you are here."

"Why shouldn't I be here?" the young man replied. He thought for the moment, with the instinct of guilt, that his mother had come on purpose to find him out.

All this time there was, as Mrs. Stormont afterwards remembered with gratitude, "one well-bred person" in the room, which was the stranger of whom Sandy had doubted whether he were English. English or not, he was a gentleman, she afterwards concluded, for he went on playing, not noisily, as if to screen anything, but as he had been doing when she came through the garden, and asked herself could that be Katie who played so well. Lewis had perception enough to know that this unexpected arrival would not be pleasant to his friends. He, who had stumbled into their secret before without any will of his, was aware of the whispering of the lovers in the corner, which he saw out of the corner of his eye with a wistful sort of sympathy. He had put his music between himself and them to afford at once a cover to their whisperings and a shelter to himself from the sight of a happiness which he thought never would be his. When the mother came in, startled, irate, yet self-subdued, his quick sympathy perceived that this was no moment to stop to emphasize the situation more. He had a vague perception of the half-quarrel, the sullen, too ready self-defence, the surprise which was an accusation. His heart took the part of the lover as a matter of course. The old lady was jealous, ill-tempered, full of suspicions. What wonder, he thought, that Philip, out of the offensive atmosphere at home, should take refuge here?

Mrs. Seton came bustling in a moment after, full of apologies. "I had not been out of the room a moment—not a moment. But this is always what happens. The moment you turn your back somebody appears that you would wish to have the warmest welcome. But I hope it's not too late. And I am so glad to see you, Mrs. Stormont. I hope you are not walking this warm afternoon. No, no, you must not sit down there; let me give you this comfortable chair, and I've told Katie not to wait, but to send for the tea at once. You will be all the better, after your drive, of a cup of tea."

"I am afraid," said Mrs. Stormont, "that I've disturbed you all. It is a stupid thing coming in at a side door. I am sure I don't know what tempted me to do it. Another time I will know better. I have just disturbed everybody."

She tried not to look at Philip, but his eyes were bent upon her under cloudy brows.

"You have disturbed nobody," cried Mrs. Seton. "We've just been sitting doing nothing, listening to the music. Mr. Murray is so kind; he just comes in and plays when he pleases, and it is a privilege to listen to him. There is my little Jeanie sits down on her little stool by his feet, and is just lost in it. She has a great turn for music: and I am sure it makes an end to work for Katie and me—we can do nothing but listen. Play that little bit again, Mr. Murray. I really forget what you called it—the bit that begins," and she sang a few bars in a voice that had been very good in its day. "Let Mrs. Stormont hear that; she will understand the way you keep us all just hanging upon you. He's so unassuming," she added, turning to the visitor, whose aspect was less sweet than the music, "so modest, you would never know he had such a gift. But he has taken kindly to us—I'm sure I don't know why—and comes in almost every day."

"No wonder he comes when he has such listeners," said Mrs. Stormont. "And, Philip, are you finding out that you have a turn for music too?"

"Oh, Mr. Philip, he comes with his friend," said Mrs. Seton. "Listen, now, that's just delightful! I let my stocking drop—where is my stocking? Music is a thing that just carries me away. Thank you—thank you, Mr. Murray; and, dear me, Katie is so anxious not to lose anything, here she is back already with the tea."

Katie came back with a little agitation about her, which the keen spectator observed in a moment, not without a little pang to perceive how prettily the colour came and went upon her little countenance, and how her eyes shone. Katie felt guilty, very guilty. There was a throb of pleasure in her heart to feel herself in the position of the wicked heroine. She was frightened and subdued and triumphant all at once. To see the mother watching who was suspicious, and angry, and afraid—actually afraid of Katie—made her heart beat high. She made all the haste she could to speed on the maid with the tea, under cover of whom she could go back to the arena of the struggle. It is needless to say that the music did not exercise a very great influence over Katie. It had veiled her whispering with Philip, so that not even her mother took any notice of it. And Mrs. Seton, though she was very tolerant of a little flirtation, was not in the secret, and would have certainly stopped anything that appeared very serious in her eyes.

Now that they were all put on their guard, the fact was that Mrs. Stormont was much mystified, and unable to assure herself that she had found out anything. No one can found an accusation on the fact that a girl grows red or a young man black and lowering at her appearance. Such evidence may be quite convincing morally, but it cannot be brought forth and alleged as a reason for action.

"If there was nothing wrong, why did she blush and you look so glum?" she asked afterwards.

"I don't know what you call looking glum," said Philip; "perhaps it is my natural look."

Alas! his mother was also tempted to say, it was. For the last three months he had been often glum, easily offended. He was only a little more so when vexed. And Katie blushed very readily; she was always blushing, with reason and without reason. The only certainty that Mrs. Stormont arrived at was that the stranger was "a fine lad;" and she invited him to her ball on the spot, an invitation which Lewis accepted with smiling alacrity. That was all that came for the moment of Mrs. Stormont's mission to Murkley.

CHAPTER XXII

But Mrs. Stormont's visit was far from being destitute of results. It caused a great many discussions and much agitation at Murkley, where Lilias was in the greatest commotion all the evening, and could scarcely sleep the whole night through. If it was not necessary, as Mrs. Stormont had hinted, to be absolutely in a state of innocence, unacquainted with all balls and parties, and every sort of dissipation, before the Queen would admit you to the drawing-room, why then, oh! why might not she go to Philip's ball?

"I was sure the Queen would never mind," Lilias said. "If it was for nothing else, she is far too kind; unless she was obliged for etiquette; and if she is not obliged—"

"Oh, my dear, the Queen is the fountain-head—how could she be obliged? She is never obliged to do this or that. Whatever she does, that is the right thing," cried Jean, shocked by the girl's bold words. Margaret was quite as loyal, but not quite so confident. She shook her head.

"There is nobody that has a greater respect for her Majesty than me; but, nevertheless, I cannot but think there are things she has to make a point of just for the sake of good order. Mrs. Stormont is no judge—she is not in the position; her Majesty would be little likely to take any trouble about small gentry of that kind; but the Murrays are not small gentry, and your mother was Lady Lilias Abernethy— that makes all the difference. You would be inquired about where an ordinary person would not, and there's an interest about a motherless girl. The Queen, who, they say, forgets nothing, will remember your mother, and that you never had that advantage; her heart will be sore for you, poor thing: and if it comes to her ears that Lilias Murray has been seen by everybody dancing at all the small country balls and dances—"

"Now, Margaret!" cried Lilias, jumping to her feet, "how could the Queen hear that, when it would be only one, only one at the most?"

"One would be just the beginning," said Miss Margaret. "When you had been to Mrs. Stormont's ball (for it is nonsense to call it Philip's), everybody else that was going to give a dance would be after you, and they would say, with reason, if she went to Stormonts, you cannot refuse to let her come to me; or else if you go to no other place, worse will be said, and it will go through the country that there is Some Reason why you should go there and nowhere else."

"Some reason!—but what reason could there be?" cried Lilias, appalled by this solemnity, and, in spite of herself, growing pale.

"They would invent some story or other," said her sister. "You see, there is nothing stands by itself in this world—one thing is always connected with another, so that ye can never just do a simple action without taking into account what comes after and what has gone before."

Miss Margaret enunciated this alarming doctrine in the evening, with the light of the lamp falling upon her face and the widespread whiteness of her newspaper, and showing against the dark background the scared looks of her two companions, one of whom listened with a gasp of alarm, while the other made a mild remonstrance.

"Margaret! you will frighten the poor thing out of her life."

"Is it true, or is it not true?" said Margaret. "You have lived long enough, Jean, to know. There is always," she added, with a little sense of success which is seductive, "a little of the next morning and the night before in every day."

Now Lilias had a lively mind, and, though she had been struck by the first statement, this repetition took away her alarm. Her reverential attitude towards her sisters prevented her from making any demonstration, but she was no longer cowed.

"To be sure," she said, "in a ball you are asked ever so long before, and it is sure to last till next morning. I see now what you mean."

"Oh, if that is all," said Jean, relieved.

"Whether that is all or not, it is time for bed," Miss Margaret said, which is always a good way of evading an argument with a young person. But she was somewhat severe upon her sister when they were left alone. "Do you not see," she said, "that all this is just to get Lilias for that long-leggit lad of hers? If it had been any other person I would have consented at once; but Philip Stormont! It would be like falling into a man-trap just outside your own gate."

"But you were just the same, Margaret—I'm not blaming you, for I am sure you have your reasons—about the little bits of tea-parties at the manse that could harm nobody."

"And where there was just the same danger," said Margaret. "Not that I would have any fear of Philip Stormont if there were others to compare with him; but, where there's nobody else, any young man would be dangerous. I want her when she goes from here to be fancy free."

"But there will be plenty to compare with him; there will be the best in the county—for Mrs. Stormont is much respected," said Jean. "And even at the manse, you forgot, Margaret, there was that young Mr. Murray."

"The lad that plays the music," said Miss Margaret, with a smile. "I would not hurt your feelings, Jean: but a young man that has nothing better to do than play the piano—"

"Oh, Margaret!" Miss Jean said.

She was wounded by so much ignorance and prejudice. She went away softly, and lighted her candle with a sort of quiet dejection, shaking her head. A young man that had such a gift! Yet Margaret, though she scoffed at Philip as a long-leggit lad, thought more of him than of the young musician. Her own profound respect for Margaret's superior judgment made it all the harder to bear. And Miss Jean was aware that Margaret expressed the general sentiment, and that there was nobody about who would not esteem the quality of him whose highest gift was to stand up to his waist in the water catching trout, far above that of the man who drew her very soul out of her breast with such strains as she had never heard before. She could not argue in favour of the more heavenly accomplishment. How could she speak of it even, to those who were insensible to it, and Margaret, who was so much cleverer than she was? The sense of helplessness and inability to explain herself, yet of a certain humble, natural superiority, and happiness in her own understanding, filled her mind.

Margaret, whose heart had smote her for wounding her sister, stopped her as she was going out, candle in hand.

"You must just set it down to my ignorance, if I have vexed you, Jean; and you will remember that I was ill enough pleased to see your friend (as we know nothing about him) in the company of Lilias the other day; so I'm meaning no disrespect to him."

"He is not my friend, Margaret—any more than yours, or any person's," said Jean, with gentle deprecation.

"I will not allow that," said Margaret, with a smile.

It was something of an uneasy smile, between ridicule and indignation, but Jean had not the smallest conception what its meaning was. She went upstairs with her candle somewhat consoled, but yet feeling that her favourite had scant justice, and grieved that Margaret, and even Lilias, should be incapable of the pleasure which was to herself so great. Both so much more clever than she was, and yet indifferent to, almost contemptuous of, music! Miss Jean shook her head as she went up the dark oak staircase with the candle, and her shadow stalking behind her, twice as large as she, nodded its head too, with a dislocated bend, upon the darkness of the panelled walls.

Next morning, however, Margaret astonished them all by a decision which went entirely against all the arguments of the night.

"I have been thinking," she said, as they sat at breakfast. "There are a great many things to be taken into account. You see, it is in our own parish, at our very doors. The horse-ferry is troublesome, but still it is a thing that is in use both day and night, and there is no danger in it."

"Oh, no danger!" cried Jean, who divined what was coming.

"It was you I was thinking of, to make your mind easy; for you are the timorous one," Miss Margaret said. "Lilias there, with her eyes leaping out of her head, would wade the water rather than stay at home, and, for my part, I'm seldom afraid. So it's satisfactory, you think; there's no danger, Jean? Well! and, for another thing, if we were to refuse, it might be thought there was a reason for it. That's very likely what would be said. That there was an Inclination, or something that you and me, Jean, had occasion to fear."

"It would never do to give anybody a chance of saying that, Margaret," said Jean, with dismay.

"That is what I have been thinking," Miss Margaret said.

And then Lilias jumped from her chair again, with impatience and wild excitement.

"Oh, will you speak English, Margaret, or Scots, or something that one can understand! What do you mean about Reasons and Inclinations? Is it philosophy you are talking—or is it something about the ball?"

"You are a silly thing with your balls. You don't know your steps even. You have never had any lessons since you were twelve. I am not going to a ball with a girl that will do me no credit."

"Me—not know my steps! And, if I didn't, Katie would teach me. Oh, Margaret! will I go after all?"

And Lilias flung herself upon her sister's neck, and spilt Miss Margaret's tea in the enthusiasm of her embrace. The tea was hot, and a much less offence would have been almost capital from any other sinner; but when Margaret felt the girl's soft arms about her neck, and received her kiss of enthusiasm, her attempt at fault-finding was very feeble.

"Bless me, child, mind, I have on a clean collar. And you'll ruin my gown: a purple gown with tea spilt upon it! Is that a way of thanking me, to spoil my good clothes? There will be all the more need to take care of them, for you'll want a new frock, and all kinds of nonsense. Sit down—sit down, and eat your egg like a natural creature. And, Jean, you must just give me another cup of tea."

"I will do that, Margaret; and, as for the dress, it will be better to write about it at once—"

"The dress is not all; there will be shoes, and gloves, and flowers, and fans, and every kind of thing. If you had waited till the right time, we would have been in London, where it is easy to fit out a princess; but I must just write to Edinburgh."

"She is a kind of a princess in her way," said Miss Jean, looking fondly at the young heroine.

Lilias was touched by all these tender glances, though she felt them to be natural.

"I only want a white frock," she said, with humility. "I want to go for fun, not for finery."

Miss Jean nodded her head with approval.

"But there is your position that we must not forget," she said.

"You are too innocent," said Miss Margaret, "you don't know the meaning of words. You shall just have a white frock. What do you think you could wear else?—black velvet, perhaps, because of your position, as Jean says? But there are different kinds of white frocks. One kind like Katie Seton's, which is very suitable to her father's daughter, and another—for Lilias Murray of Murkley. You may trust that to me. But it's a fortnight off, this grand ball, and if I hear another word about it betwixt this and then, or find it getting into your head when you should be thinking of Queen Elizabeth—"

"I will think of nothing but Queen Elizabeth," cried Lilias, clasping her hands with all the fervour of a confession of faith. And she kept her word. But, nevertheless, when Miss Jean was taking her little stroll in the Ghost's Walk, in the hush of noon, when studies were over and Margaret busy with her account-books, she felt a sudden waft of air and movement, a soft breeze of youth blowing, an arm wound round her waist.

"Oh! Jean," cried a soft voice in her ear, "will it come true?"

"My darling, why should it not come true? It is just the most natural thing in the world. I am never myself against a little pleasure; but Margaret has always," said Miss Jean, with a little solemnity, "your interest at heart."

"And you too, Jean—and you too."

"But I am silly," said Miss Jean. "I would not have the heart to go against whatever you wanted. I am just a weak-minded creature. The moment you wish for anything, that is just enough for me. But you have a great deal of sense, Lilias, and you can see that would never do. Now Margaret takes everything into consideration, and she has the true love to deny you when it is needful—that is true love," Jean said, with moisture in her eyes.

Lilias, who was responsive to every touch of emotion, acknowledged this with such enthusiasm as delighted her sister.

"But it is far nicer when she is not always thinking of my best interests. It is delightful to be going!" she cried. "You have been at a hundred balls, and you know how to behave. Tell me what I am to do."

This appeal was embarrassing to Miss Jean, who, indeed, had not been at a ball for a great many years, and understood that things were greatly changed since her day. For one thing, waltzes were looked but coldly on in those past times, and now she understood they were all the vogue. Jean was far too delicate in mind to suggest to her little sister that the waltz had been considered indelicate in her own day. It was the fashion now, and to put such a thought into a young creature's head, she said to herself, was what nobody should do. But she said, with a little faltering,

"What you are to do? But, Lilias, it is very hard to answer that. The gentlemen will come and ask you to dance, and all you have to do is just to—"

"To choose," said Lilias. "I know as much as that."

"Yes," said Jean, a little doubtfully, "I suppose you may say you have to choose; but you would not like to hurt a gentleman's feelings by giving him a refusal. I don't think that is ever done, my dear. You will just make them a curtsey and give them a smile, and they will write down their name upon a card."

"What! everybody that asks?" cried Lilias, "whether I like them or not?" and her face clouded over. "There will be sure to be some that are disagreeable, and there are some, Katie says, that cannot dance. Will I be obliged to curtsey to them, and smile too? But I will not do it," Lilias said, with a pout. "I do not see the good of going to a ball if it is like that."

"It is not just perfection, no more than other things," said Jean; "but most of the young men will, no doubt, be very nice, and you would not like to hurt their feelings."

Upon this Lilias pondered for some moments, with a countenance somewhat overcast.

"It is always said that a lady has to choose," she said; "but if it is only to say yes whoever asks you—"

Jean shook her head. She could not resist the chance of a little moralizing.

"My dear," she said, "with the most of women, I'm sorry, sorry to say it, it comes to very little more."

Lilias looked at her old sister with keen, unbelieving eyes. She ran over in her mind, in spite of herself, all that is said of old maids in books, and even in such simple talk as she had heard; her mind revolted against it, yet she could not forget it. She wondered in her heart whether this might account for so strange a version of the prerogative of women. She did not believe Jean's report. She raised her fair head in the air with a little fling of pride and power. She was not disposed to give up that stronghold of feminine imagination. A girl must have something to believe in to make her confront with composure the position that is allotted to her. If she is to give up all active power of choice, she must at least have faith that the passive one, the privilege of refusal, is still to be hers. She thought that Jean, in her old maidenhood, in her sense, perhaps, of failure or inacquaintance with the ways of more fortunate women, must be mistaken in her judgment. That she herself, Lilias, should have no greater lot in the world than to sit and smile, and accept whatever might be offered to her, was a conception too humbling. She smiled, not believing it. Jean was good, she was unspotted from the world, but perhaps her very excellence made her slow of understanding. Lilias concluded her thoughts on the subject by giving her old sister a compassionate, caressing look.

"It is you that never would hurt anybody's feelings," she said. But she did not ask any more questions. She concluded that it would be better, perhaps, on the whole, to trust to instinct and her own perception of the circumstances as they occurred. And then there was always Katie to fall back upon—a young person of much more immediate experience and practical knowledge than could be expected from Jean.

Miss Jean was conscious on her side that she had not satisfied the girl's curiosity, or given the right answer—the answer that was expected of her—and this troubled her much; for she said to herself, "Where is she to get understanding if not from Margaret or me?" Her first idea was to refer Lilias with humility to Margaret, but in this she paused, reflecting that Margaret had never "troubled her head" with such matters, that she had always been a masterful woman that took her own way, and preferred the management of the house and the estate to any sort of traffic with gentlemen or other frivolous persons. Margaret, then, perhaps, after all, would in this respect be a less qualified guide than herself, though it was a long time since she had entered into anything of the kind. And Jean, besides her tremulous eagerness to direct Lilias so that as much of the pleasure and as little of the pains that are involved in life should come to her as possibly could be, was not without a natural desire to teach and convey the fruits of her experience into another mind. She walked along in silence for a short time, and then she resumed the broken thread of her discourse.

"My dear," she said, "you may think my ways of knowing are small: and that is true, for Margaret and me have had none of the experiences of married women, or of the manners of men, and the commerce of the world. But you always learn something just by looking on at life, and, indeed, they say that the spectators sometimes see the game better than those who are playing at it. But there is just the danger, you know, that when we say what we've seen, it may be discouraging to a young creature who is just upon the beginning of life, and thinks all the world (which is natural) at her feet."

"I am sure," said Lilias, half offended, "I don't think all the world at my feet."

"When I was like you," said Jean, "I thought it was all before me to pick and choose, but you see that little has come of it: and many a girl has thought like me. It is very difficult not to think so when you start out upon the road with everything flattering, and the sun shining, and the heart in your bosom just as lightsome as a bird."

"Am I like that?" said Lilias, half to herself, and a conscious smile came upon her face. She was conscious of herself for the moment, of the lightness with which she was walking, the ease, the freedom, the easily-diverted mind, the happy constitution of everything. She had no thought of own beauty, or any special excellence in herself, for her mind had been rather directed to the wholesome consideration of her defects than of her advantages; but as she walked there, all young and light by her elderly sister's side, for the first time that conscious possession of the world and heirship of all that was in it became apparent to her. She felt like a young queen; everything in it was hers to possess, all the beauty of it and the pleasure—indeed, it was all in her, in the power she had to enjoy, to see, and hear, and admire, and love: her young fresh faculties all at their keenest—these were her kingdom. She could not help feeling it. It came over her in a sudden rush of sweetness and perception.

"Perhaps it is so—I never thought of it before," she said.

"Ah, but it is so, Lilias; and I hope, my darling, you will have your day, and get the good of it; none of us have more than our day. It is not a thing that will last."

To this Lilias answered only with a smile. She was not afraid either of not having her day, or that it would not last. She required to look forward to no future. The present to her was endless; it extended into the light on either hand. It was as good as an eternity. She smiled, confident, in the face of Fate. Jean walking beside her with her faded sweetness and no expectation any longer in her life, did not effect in the smallest degree the mind of her younger sister. Jean was Jean, and Lilias Lilias. How the one could develop out of the other, how the warm stream of living in herself could ever fall low and faint, and trickle in a quiet stream like that of her sister, she was all unable to understand. She smiled at the impossibility as it presented itself to her, but neither of that, nor of any failure in her opportunities of enjoyment, had she any fear.

CHAPTER XXIII

"Refuse?" said the experienced Katie, a little bewildered by the question. "Oh, but you could not want to refuse. It would not be civil. If you have an objection to a gentleman, you can always manage to give him the slip. You can keep out of his way, or say you're tired, or just never mind, and get another partner, and pretend you forgot."

"Then Jean is quite right; and you have no choice. You must just accept, whatever you think?" said Lilias, pale with indignation and dismay.

"I don't know what a gentleman would think, if you refused him," said Katie. "It is a thing I never heard of. You would make him wild. And then he would not understand. He would just gape at you. He would not believe his ears. He would think it was your ignorance. And the others would all take his part; they would say they would not expose themselves to such an insult. Nobody would ask you again."

"As for that, it is little I would care," cried Lilias throwing her head back. "It is as much an insult to a girl when they pass her by and don't ask her; and must she never give it them back? They have their choice, but we have none."

"Oh, yes," said Katie, "it is easy to say, what would I care? But when the time comes, and you sit through the whole evening and see everybody else dancing—"

At this Lilias gave her little friend a look of astonishment and disdainful indignation, which frightened Katie, though she could not understand it. No one could be more humble-minded, less disposed to stand upon her superiority. But yet that superiority was undoubted, and the idea that Lilias Murray of Murkley could sit neglected had a ludicrous impossibility which it was inconceivable that any one could overlook. Had a little maid-of-honour ventured to say this to a princess, it could not have been more out of character. The princess naturally would not condescend to say anything of that impossibility to the little person who showed so much ignorance, but it would be scarcely possible to refrain from a glance. Lilias ended, however, so ridiculous was it, by a laugh, though still holding her head high.

"If that is the case, it must be better not to go to balls," she said. "For to think that a gentlewoman is to be at the mercy of whoever offers—"

"Oh, but, Lilias, I never said you couldn't give him the slip!" cried Katie, who did not know what she had said that was wrong. "Or, if your mind is made up against any gentleman, you can always say to the lady of the house, 'Don't introduce so-and-so, or so-and-so.'"

"I was not thinking of myself," said Lilias, almost haughtily. "But, if a girl is asked," she added, after a pause, "what does that mean, if she may not refuse? The gentleman has his choice; he need not ask her unless he pleases—but she—she must not have any choice—she must just take everybody that comes! one the same as another, as if she were blind, or deaf, or stupid!"

"Oh, Lilias!—but I never said it was so bad as that! And when I tell you that you can always find a way to throw them over. You can say you're tired, or that you made a mistake, and were engaged before they asked you; or you can keep your last partner, and make him throw over his, which is the easiest way of all—but there are dozens of ways—"

"By cheating!" said Lilias, with lofty indignation. "So Jean was right after all," she said, "and I am the silly one! I never believed that ladies were treated like that—even when they are young, even when—"

Here Lilias paused, feeling how ungenerous was the argument, as only high-spirited girls do.

"If gentlemen were what it seems to mean," she said, with her eyes flashing, "it would not be only when ladies are young and—it would not be only then they would give that regard to them! And it should be scorn to a man to pass by any girl, and so let her know he will not choose to ask her, unless she has a right to turn too, and refuse him!"

"Oh, Lilias, that is just nonsense, nobody thinks of that," said Katie. "If you take a little trouble, you need never dance with a man you don't like. If you see him coming, you can always get out of the way, and be talking to somebody else; or say your card's full, or that you're afraid you will be away before then—or a hundred things. But to say No!—it would be so ill-bred. And then the gentlemen would all be so astonished, they would not expose themselves to such a thing as that. Not one would ever ask you again."

"That is what we shall see!" said Lilias.

Katie was so truly distressed by a resolution so audacious and so suicidal that she spent half the afternoon in an endeavour to persuade her friend against it. She even cried over Lilias' perversity.

"What would you say?" she asked. "Oh, you could not—you could not be so silly! They will just think it is your ignorance. They will say you are so bashful, or even that you are gauche."

Katie was not very clear what gauche meant, and the word had all the more terrors for her. The girls were walking in the Castle park, between New Murkley and Old Murkley, when this conversation went on. It was a way that was free to wayfarers, but the passers-by were very few. And Margaret had loosened a little her restrictions upon Lilias since the memorable decision about the Stormont ball had been come to. What was the use of watching over her so jealously, wrapping her up in blue veils, and keeping her from sight of, or converse with, the world, when in a little while she was to be permitted a glimpse of the very vortex, the whirlpool of dissipation—a ball? The blue veil accordingly was thrown back, and floated over the girl's shoulders, making a dark background to her dazzling fairness, her light locks, and lovely colour. And both form and face profited by the stir of indignation, the visionary anger and scorn which threw her head high, and inspired her step. These were the very circumstances in which the lover should appear: here were the heroine and the confidant, the two different types of women, not the dark and fair only (though Katie was not dark, but brown, hazel-eyed, and chestnut-haired), but the matter-of-fact and the poetic, the visionary and the woman of the world. And opportunities such as these are not of the kind that are generally neglected. It was no accident indeed that brought Philip by the little gate that opened from the manse garden into the path in which he knew he should find Katie. And perhaps it was not exactly accident which led to the discovery of Lewis when they neared the end of their walk, the great white mass of New Murkley—about which the young man was wandering, as he so often was, thinking many an undivined thought. He was there so often that, had any one thought on the subject, it might have been with the express object of finding him that the party strayed that way; but Lilias, at least, was entirely innocent of either knowledge or calculation, so that, so far as she was concerned, it was pure accident. He was walking with his back to them, gazing up at the eyeless sockets of the windows, when they came in sight. Lilias had been reduced to an embarrassed silence since the appearance of Philip. Her knowledge of their secret overwhelmed her in their presence. She thought they must be embarrassed too. She thought they must wish to get rid of her. She had not the least idea that to both these young persons she was a defence and protection, under cover of which they could enjoy each other's company, yet confront the world. While they talked undaunted—or rather, while Katie talked, for Philip was of a silent nature—Lilias walked softly on, on the other side, getting as far apart as she dared, drooping her head, wondering what opportunity there might be to steal away. She was not displeased, but somewhat startled at the outcry of pleasure Katie made on perceiving the other—the fourth who made the group complete.

"Oh, Mr. Murray—there is Mr. Murray; but I might have known it, for he is always about New Murkley," Katie cried. And Lewis turned round with friendly looks, which glowed into wondering delight when he saw the shyer figure lingering a little behind, the blue veil thrown back. Just thus, attended by her faithful guardians, he had seen her first. He recollected every circumstance in a moment, as his eyes went beyond Katie to her companion in the background. He remembered how Miss Margaret had stepped forth to the rescue; how he had been marched away, and his thoughts led to other matters. He had but just glimpsed then, and he had not comprehended, that type of beautiful youth in the shadow of the past. He had asked himself since how it was possible that he had passed it over? It had been like a picture seen for an instant. When he saw her now again, he felt like a man who has dreamed of some happiness, and awoke to find that he had lost it: but the dream had returned, and this time he should not lose it. He received, with smiling delight, the salutations of Katie, who hailed him from afar, and stood with his hat in his hand, while Lilias responded shyly but brightly to his greeting. She was pleased too. It was deliverance to her from the restraint which she felt she was imposing upon the lovers. And the friendly countenance of the stranger, and his confused looks, and the aspect of Jean at her own appearance before him, and of Margaret when he followed her into the dining-room, had created an atmosphere of amusement and interest round him. It had been all fun that previous meeting, the most delightful break in the every-day monotony. This made it agreeable to Lilias, without any other motive, that she should see Lewis again. She dared not laugh with him over it, for she did not know him sufficiently, nor would she have laughed at anything which involved Jean and Margaret in the faintest derision; but the sense of this amusement past, and the secret laughter it had given her, made the sight of him very pleasant. And then he was pleasant; not in the least handsome—unworthy a second glance so far as that went—totally unseductive to the imagination—so entirely different from the beau chevalier, six feet two, with those dark eyes and waving locks, who some time or other was to appear out of the unseen for Lilias. Never at any time could it be possible that so undistinguished a figure as that of Lewis should take the central place in her visionary world; but he had already found a little corner there. He was like, she thought, the brother she ought to have had. The hero whose mission it was to save her life, to be rewarded by her love, stood worlds above any such intruder; but this beaming, friendly countenance had come in as a symbol of kindness. Lilias had perceived at once by instinct that he and she could be friends.

"Lilias," cried Katie, "you must talk to him about Murkley. He is always here. I think he comes both night and day. You ought to find out what he means, if he has seen a ghost, or what it is. And you are fond of it too."

Lilias looked with a little surprise at the stranger. Why should he care for Murkley?

"You think it is strange to see such a great big desolate house in such a place."

"I think—a great many things that I do not know how to put into words: for my English, perhaps, is not so good—"

"Are you a German, Mr. Murray?" asked Lilias, shyly.

The end of the other two was attained; they had turned aside into the woods, by that path which led down to the old quarry and the river-side, the scene of so many meetings. Lilias had no resource but to follow, though with a sense of adventure and possible wrong-doing. She was relieved that Katie and Philip were at last free to talk as they pleased, and she was not at all alarmed by her own companion; still the thought of what Margaret might say gave her a little thrill, half painful, half pleasant.

"I am English," said Lewis; "yes, true English, though no one will believe me—otherwise I am of no country, for I have lived in one as much as another. I have a great interest in Murkley. If it were ever completed, it would be very noble; it would be a house to entertain princes in."

"That is what I think sometimes," said Lilias; "but, then, it will never be completed. All the country knows our story. We are poor, far too poor. And, even if it were finished, it would need, Margaret says, an army of servants, and to furnish it would take a fortune. So it would be long, long before we arrived at the princes." She ended with a laugh, which, in its turn, ended with a sigh.

"But you—would like to do it?—that would amuse you—"

"Oh! amuse me! It would not be amusement. It would be grand to do it! They say it would be finer than Taymouth. Did you ever hear that?"

"It is like the Louvre," said Lewis, "and that was built for a great king's palace. It is like the ghost, not of a person, but of an age. I think your ancestors must come and walk about and inspect it all, and hold solemn councils."

"But my ancestors knew nothing about it," said Lilias. "Oh! not that; if they come it will be to make remarks, and say how silly grandpapa was. If ghosts are like people, that is what they will be saying, and that they knew what it would end in all along, but he never would pay any attention. I hope he never comes himself, or he would hear—he would hear," cried Lilias, laughing, "what Margaret calls a few truths."

"Do you think he was—silly?" Lewis asked. What right had he to be so émotionné, to feel the moisture in his eyes and his voice tremble? What could she think of him if she perceived this? She would think it was affectation, and that he was making believe.

"I think I am silly too," Lilias said. She would not commit herself. She had heard a great deal about the old Sir Patrick, and she was aware that he had disinherited her; but he, too, was in her imagination a shadowy, great figure, of whom something mysterious might yet be heard, for all Lilias knew. Strange stories had been told about him. He had dabbled in black-arts. He had done a great many strange things in his life. Perhaps even now a mysterious packet might arrive some day, a new will be found, or some late movement of repentance. He might even step out from behind a tree in the Ghost's Walk, or out of a dark corner in the library, and explain with a dead voice, sounding far off, what he had done and why. This suppressed imagination made Lilias always charitable to him. Or perhaps she was moved by a kind of fascination and sympathy for one who had made his imagination into something palpable, and built castles in stone as she had done in dreams.

Lewis looked at her very wistfully.

"The princes you entertained would be noble ones," he said, "not only princes for show."

"Oh, how do you know, Mr. Murray? Do you think I am such a—fool? Well! it would be like a fool to dream of that, when there is next to no money at all; you might forgive a child for being so silly, but a woman grown-up, a person that ought to know better—"

He kept looking at her, with a little moisture in his eyes.

"I wish I were a magician," he said; and then, with one of his outbursts of confidence, which, having no previous clue to guide them, nobody understood—"What it would have been," he said, clasping his hands together, "if I had come here two years ago!"

Lilias looked at him with extreme surprise. She thought he had suddenly grown tired, as people so often do, of discussing the desires of others, and had plunged back thus abruptly into his own.

"If you had come here?" she said, with a little wonder. "Has Murkley, then, something to do with you too?"

He did not make her any reply; but, after a while, said, faltering slightly,

"I hope that—Miss Jean—is well. I hope it is not presumption, too much familiarity, to call her so."

"Oh, everybody calls her Miss Jean," said Lilias. "There is no over-familiarity. She is so happy with your music; she plays it half the day, and then she says she is not worthy to play it, that she is not fit to be listened to after you."

"I think," said Lewis, "that there can be no music that she is not worthy to play, not if it were the angel-music straight out of heaven."

"And did you see that, so little as you have known of her?" cried Lilias, gratefully. "Ah, then I can see what she finds in you, for you must be one that can understand. Do you know what Margaret says of Jean?—that she is unspotted from the world."

"And it is true."

The countenance of Lewis grew very serious as he spoke; all its lines settled down into a fixed gravity, yet tenderness. Lilias was altogether bewildered by this expression. He took Jean's praises far too much to heart for a stranger, yet as if they gave him more sadness than pleasure. Why should he be sad because Jean was good? An inclination to laugh came over her, and yet it was cruel to laugh at anything so serious as his face.

"And she has had her patience so tried—oh! dear Jean, how she has had her patience tried, her and Margaret, with me—me to bring-up! I have been such a handful."

Lewis was taken entirely by surprise by this leap from grave to gay. He was taken, as it were, with the tear in his eye, his own mind bent on the solemnest of matters, and she knowing nothing, amused by that too serious aspect, made fun of him openly, turning his pensiveness into laughter! He looked at her almost with alarm, and then he smiled, but went no further.

"It is that he will not laugh at Jean—no, nor anything about her; and what a thing am I to do it!" Lilias cried out within herself, with a revulsion as sudden into self-disgust. And then they both became very grave, and walked along by each other's side in tremendous solemnity, neither saying a word.

"Are you, too, so fond of music?" Lewis asked at length.

Lilias gave him a half-comic look, and put her hands together with a little petition for tolerance.

"It is not my fault," she said, softly. "I have not had time to understand."

Her penitence, her appeal, her odd whisper of excuse disarmed Lewis. His solemnity fled away; he forgot that he was to his own thinking the grave and faithful partner of Miss Jean, assuring himself that he had got in her the noblest woman, and pushing all lighter thoughts aside; and became once more a light-hearted youth by the side of a light-hearted girl in a world all full of love, and mirth, and joyfulness. He laughed and she laughed in the sudden pleasure of this new-found harmony.

"You do not care for it," he said; "you like it to make you dance, not otherwise."

In cold blood this state of mind would have horrified Lewis—in his present condition it seemed a grace the more, a delightful foolishness and ignorance, a defect which was beautiful and sweet.

"I think I should care if I knew better," said Lilias, trying on her part to approach him a little from her side, partly in sympathy, partly in shame of her own imperfection. "And as for dancing," she said, quickly seizing the first means of escape, "I know nothing about it. I have never been at one—I am going to one in a fortnight."

"And so am I," Lewis said.

"I am very glad; but you are different, no doubt. You have lived abroad, where they are always dancing. They have different customs, perhaps, there. It was not intended that I should go to any in the country. We are to spend the next season in London. But I was so silly (I told you I was silly) that I insisted to go, thinking it would be delightful. I don't at all wish to go now," said Lilias, drawing herself up with great dignity.

Lewis had been following all she said with so much devotion that he felt himself suddenly arrested too by this stop in the current of her feelings.

"Is it permitted to ask why?" he said. "I hope not because I am to be there?"

Lilias paused for a moment uncertain; then, "I am glad you are to be there, and I hope that we shall dance together," she said, making him a beautiful, gracious little bow like that of a princess, in her grace and favour according him the boon which he had not yet ventured to ask.

Lewis' hat was off in a moment, and his acknowledgments made with enthusiasm. He thought it the most beautiful and charming departure from the conventional, while she on her side thought it the most natural thing in the world. But at this moment the others turned back upon them in a tempest of laughter. Katie had recounted their recent conversation to Philip, and Philip had received it with all the amusement which became the occasion.

"Lilias," Katie cried, "Philip says he will be frightened to go to his own ball. If you say no to him, he will just sink down through the floor."

"You will never be so hard upon us as all that," said Philip, not quite so bold when he looked at her, but yet with another laugh.

Lilias blushed scarlet; the idea of ridicule was terrible to her as to all young creatures. She looked at them with mingled shame and pride and disdain and fear. Could there be anything more terrible than to be absurd, to be laughed at? She could not speak for a choking in her throat. And Lewis, who had not yet had time to replace his hat upon his head, or to come down to an ordinary level out of his enthusiasm of admiration and pleasure, felt Katie's quick eye upon him, and was discomfited too. But love (if it was love, alas!) sharpened his wits.

"It is a pity," he said, "that I do not understand the pleasantry, that I might laugh too. A stranger is what you call left out in the cold when you make allusions which are local. Pardon me if I do not understand. You are going to the river and the high-road?"

"Oh, not me!" cried Lilias. "Katie, you know I must not go this way; I meant to say so at once, but I did not like to disturb you. Good-bye. I can run home by myself."

"We are all coming," Katie said, somewhat sullenly. She had not meant any harm. A joke against Lilias was no more than a joke against any one else. One must have one's fun, was Katie's principle. But she was not aware of having done anything to call forth that violent and painful blush. Her own confidences were scarcely intended to be sacred, and she did not know the difference between her own easy-going readiness to take and give and the sensitive withdrawal of the other girl, who knew nothing about the noisy criticism of a family. She had intended to make use of the protection afforded by the presence of Lilias, to wander about all the summer afternoon in the woods, and be happy. Why Lewis should have interfered she could not tell. Could he not be happy too without meddling with other folk? Katie turned unwillingly and accompanied her friend along the unsheltered carriage road through the park towards the old castle.

"He had his hat off," she whispered to Philip. "Does he think she's a grand duchess, and that he must speak to her that way? They are just alike with their old-fashioned ways—or, at least, she is high-flown and he is foreign. But don't you tell anybody that, for you see she is angry. She did not mean me to tell it. She will be awfully angry if it goes further. I never thought of that; but, if you tell, I will never speak to you again."

"Toot! it is too good to keep," cried Philip. "There are just two or three fellows—"

"If you tell one of them," cried Katie, exasperated, "I will never, never—and you know I keep my word—speak to you again!"

While she thus made up for her inadvertent fault, Lewis walked slowly, and with a certain solemnity, by Lilias' side towards Murkley. He was suddenly stilled and calmed out of his excitement by the mere act of turning towards the old castle. He said, in a subdued voice, "I will go, if you will permit me, and pay my respects to Miss Jean. It is possible that she might wish for a little music:" which he said with a sigh, feeling in his heart that it was necessary to crush this dangerous sentiment in his heart, to flee from the dangerous bliss and elation that had filled his soul, and to establish himself steadily beyond any doubt in his more sober fate.

CHAPTER XXIV

They walked together very quietly towards the old house. The sound of the voices of Philip and Katie behind them seemed to save them from the embarrassment of saying nothing, and it seemed to Lilias that it was a very friendly silence in which they moved along. The fierceness of her anger died away from her, though she was still annoyed that Katie should have betrayed her, and Lilias felt a sort of repose and ease in the quietness of the young man by her side, who seemed, she thought, instinctively to respect her sentiment. She gave him credit for a sort of divination. She said to herself that she had known he would be kind, that he had such a friendly face, just like a brother. When they reached the door, she turned round to the others, saying good-bye, to the discomfiture of both; for Katie had promised her mother to have no meetings with Philip, and Philip knew that were he seen with Katie his reception at home would not be cordial. But Lilias confined herself to this little demonstration of displeasure, and allowed her little friend to follow her into the coolness of the old hall, which was so strange a contrast to the blaze of afternoon sunshine out of which they had come. Lilias led Lewis across to the drawing-room door. She gave him a smiling look to bid him follow her.

"I think Jean is here," she said; then added, softly, "I would come, too, to hear the music, but I must speak to Katie; and two of us would disturb Jean. It will make her more happy if she has it to herself."

Lewis did not make any reply. All the smiling had gone out of his face. He was glad to be allowed to go alone. He said to himself that he would have no more trifling, that it was unworthy of the lady whom he was approaching that he should go to her with regrets. He had no right to have any regrets, and their existence was a wrong to her. It might be that the vocabulary of passion was unnecessary at her calm and serious age, but the most tender respect and devotion she was well worthy of. It would be a wickedness to go to her with any other feeling. Lewis rose superior to himself as he went across the hall by the side of that wonderful creature, who had for the moment transported him out of himself. Let all that be over for ever. He did not even look at her, but composed his mind to what was before him, feeling a sudden calm and strength in the determination to postpone it no longer. Lilias even, all unsuspicious as she was, felt somehow the gravity that had come over him, which awakened again a little laughing mischief in her mind. Was it the music, or was it Jean that made him so serious? but she restrained the jibe that came to her lips.

Miss Jean was seated, as usual, in one corner of the large room, within the niche of a deeply recessed window, with her table, her silks, her piece of work. It was not yet the hour when Margaret retired from the manifold businesses that employed her. Margaret was not only housekeeper and instructress. She was the factor, the manager of the small estate, the farm, everything in one; and the universal occupation of Margaret had left the more passive sister time to grow ripe in the patience and sweetness of her less important rôle.

"Jean, here is Mr. Murray," said Lilias at the door.

She held it open for him, and stood smiling by as he passed in, watching the eagerness with which Jean rose to her feet, her little entanglement in her work, and startled anxiety to welcome her visitor.

"Oh, but I am glad to see you," Miss Jean said, holding out her hand. "I was afraid you had gone away—and left all that grand music. I was saying to-day where should I send it after you—but Margaret said you would never go without saying good-bye."

"I hope you did not think I could," said Lewis.

She smiled upon him with an indulgent look of kindness.

"I am aware," she said, "that young men will sometimes put off things—and sometimes forget. But I am very glad to see you, Mr. Murray. And have you had success in your fishing? But, now I remember, it was not for the fishing you were here—and, dear me, now it comes back upon me—you were thinking of settling near Murkley?"

Was it mere imagination that her voice was a little hurried and her manner confused? He thought so, and that she had felt the difference between the fervour of what he had said to her on his last visit and the interval he had allowed to elapse before repeating it. As a matter of fact, Miss Jean had never remarked the fervour, or had not taken it as having any connection with herself.

"I said then that it would much depend on you," he said.

"On the neighbours, and a friendly welcome—but you are sure of that," said Miss Jean. "Nobody but will be glad to see you. I give great weight myself to the opinion of a whole neighbourhood. It is not easy to deceive—and there is nobody but what is pleased to hear that you will stay among us."

"That was not what I meant," Lewis said; and then he made a pause of recueillement of serious preparation, that it might be made apparent how much in earnest he was.

But Miss Jean did not understand this: and though she was far too polite to suggest that, as music was his chief standing ground, he might as well proceed to that without further preliminary, yet she could not prevent her eyes from straying towards the piano, with a look which she was afterwards shocked to think was too significant. He caught it and answered it with a grave smile.

"After," he said, "as much as you please, as long as you will listen to me; but there is now something else, which I would say first, if I may."

"Indeed," cried Miss Jean, anxiously, "you must not think me so ill-bred and unkind. If you are not in the mood for it, I would not have you think of the music. I am very glad to see you," she added, lifting her soft eyes to him, "if you should never touch a note. You must not think I am a person like that, always trying what I can get—no, no, you must not think that."

"I think you," said Lewis, with a subdued and grave enthusiasm, "one of the most beautiful spirits in the world."

Miss Jean looked up with a little start of amazement. She looked at him, and in her surprise blushed, rather with pleasure than with shamefacedness. Nothing could be further from her mind than any notion that this was the speech of a lover. She shook her head.

"It is very kind and very bonnie of you to say that. I am fond that young folk should like my company. It is just one of my weaknesses. You would not think that, perhaps, if you knew me better; but I'm pleased—pleased to be so well thought of, not because I think it is true, but because—well, just because it is pleasant, I suppose; and then it is fine of a young lad like you to be so kind," said Miss Jean, smiling upon him with a tender approval.

Lewis had heart enough to understand this most delicate of all the pleasures of being beloved, this approbation and sense of moral beauty in an affection so disinterested, which filled Miss Jean's virginal soul with sweetness. Her eyes caressed him as his mother's eyes might have done, for a mother, too, is doubly happy in the love bestowed upon her because it is so good, so fine, so seemly in her children. Lewis understood it, but not at this moment. There was in him something of the feeling of a desperate adventurer and something of a martyr, and the curious excitement in his veins gradually rendered him incapable of perceiving anything but his own purpose, and such response to it as he might obtain.

"That is not what I mean," he said, clearing his throat, for his voice had become husky. "It is not anything good in me. It is that I think you the best, the most good and sweet. I have known no one like you," he added, with fervour. Of all things that he had encountered in the world, it seemed the most difficult to Lewis to make this proposal, and to speak of something that could be called love to this soft-eyed woman, looking at him with tender confidence, as if she had been his mother. How was he to make her understand? It was he who was red and embarrassed, not she, who suspected nothing, who had no idea in her mind of any such possibility. Her smile turned into a gentle laugh as she listened quite attentively and seriously to what he said. She shook her head, and put up her hand in gentle deprecation.

"No, no," she said, "you must not go too far. I will take a little flattering from you on the ground that it's friendship and your good heart, but you must not give me too much, for that would be nonsense. But since you like me (which gives me so much pleasure), I will be bold with you, and bid you just play me something," said Miss Jean, "for I think you are a little put about, and there is nothing like music to set the heart right; and afterwards you will tell me what the trouble is."

"It is no trouble," he said. "You look at me so sweetly—will you not understand me? I am quite lonely—I have nobody to care for me—and when I came here and saw you, it seemed to me that I was getting into a haven. But you will not understand! I am of far too little account, not worth your thinking of," cried Lewis—"too trifling, too young, if I must say it; but if you could care a little for me, and give me a right to love you and serve you, it would make me too happy," he said, his voice faltering, his susceptible soul fully entering into and feeling the emotion he expressed; "and if it would give you any pleasure to be the cause of that, and to have somebody near you who loved you truly, who would do anything in the world to please you—"

Miss Jean sat gazing at him with a bewildered face. Sudden lights seemed to break over it from time to time, then disappeared in the blank of wonder and incredulity. She was giving her mind to it with amazement, with interest, with a kind of consternation, trying to make out what he meant. One moment there was a panic in her face, which, however, gave place to the faint wavering of a smile, as if she represented to herself the impossibility of any meaning that could alarm her. Her attention was so absorbed in trying to find out what it was that, when his voice ceased, she made no effort to reply. She drew a long breath, as people who have been listening to an orator do when he comes to a pause; but she was so unable to comprehend what he could be aiming at that she was incapable of speech.

"I would live where you pleased," said Lewis; "I should do what you pleased. I know enough to fulfil all your wishes, there could be no failure in that. There is no worthiness in me, and perhaps you will think me unsuitable, a nobody, too young, too unimportant, that is all true; but, if devotion could make up for it, the service of my life—"

"Mr. Murray," said Miss Jean at last, interrupting him, putting out her hand to stop him, "wherefore would you do all this for me? What is it you are wanting? It must be just my fancy, though I am sure my fancy was never in that way—but you seem to be making me an offer, to me that might be your mother. It cannot be that, it is not possible; but that is what it seems."

"It is so," said poor Lewis, overwhelmed with such a sense of his own youngness, triflingness, insignificance, as he had never been conscious of before. "It is so! I want nothing better in this world than that you should let me love you, and take care of you; and if you would overlook my deficiencies, and be my—"

"Oh, hush, hush!" cried Miss Jean, her face growing very pale. She sat for a moment with her hands clasped together, the lines of her countenance tremulous with emotion, "you must not say that word—oh! no, you must not say that word. There was a time when it was said to me by one—that would be gone almost before you were born."

If Lewis had been suddenly struck by a thunderbolt he could not have been more startled, his whole being seemed arrested; he was silent, put a stop to, words and thoughts alike. He could do nothing but gaze at her, astonished, incapable even of thought.

Now whether it was simple instinct, or whether it was a gleam of genius unknown in her before (and the two things are not much different), Miss Jean, as soon as she perceived what it meant, which it was so difficult to do, perceived the way out of it in a moment. Her first words closed the whole matter as effectually, as completely, as if it had never been.

"You would never hear of that," she said. "How should you? I was but very young myself; at an age when that is natural. He was a sailor and a poor man. My father would never hear of it, and perhaps it could not have been; it is not for me to say. But the Lord had settled that in His great way, that puts us all to shame. It is my delight and pride," said Miss Jean, her soft eyes filling with something that looked like light rather than tears, "that it was permitted to him to end his days saving life, and not destroying it. There were seven of them that he saved. It is a long time ago. You know grief cannot last; it is just like a weed, it is not a seed of God; but love lasts long, long, just for ever. There are few people that mind, or ever take thought about him and me. But just now and then to a kind heart like you, and one that understands, it comes into my head to tell that old story. You would scarcely be born," Miss Jean added, with a smile that seemed to Lewis ineffable, full of the tenderest sweetness. He was entirely overcome. He had not been used to the restraints which Englishmen make for themselves. His eyes were full and running over. He leaned forward to her, listening, with a kind of worship in his face. He had forgotten all the incongruous folly of his suit as if it had never been, without being ashamed or wounded, or feeling any obstacle rise up because of it, between him and her. She had opened her tender heart to him in the very act of showing that it was closed and sacred for ever and ever. How long that moment lasted they neither of them knew. But presently he came to himself, feeling her soft, caressing hand upon his arm and hearing her say, "You will go and play me something, my bonnie man, and that will put us all right."

"My bonnie man!"—he had heard the women calling their children so. It seemed to him the most exquisite expression of motherhood, of tender meaning and unspeakable distance, that he had ever heard in his life. He went away like a child to the piano, and sat down there, hushed and yet happy, his heart quivering with sympathy, and affection, and ease, and peace; and Miss Jean folded her soft hands in her lap, and gave herself up to listening, with that look of entire absorption and content which he thought he had never seen in any other face. The music wafted her away out of everything troublous and painful, wafted her feelings to a higher presence, into some ante-chamber where chosen souls can hear some notes of the songs of the angels. He had played Beethoven to her and Mozart on the other occasions, now he chose Handel, filling the silent room with anthems and symphonies of heaven. He watched her lean back, her eyes growing dim with a silent rapture, till it became apparent that all the circumstances of common life had gone from her, and that her soul had lost itself in that world of exquisite sensation and perfect peace.

This was the end of Lewis's first attempt at wooing. Before he had done, Miss Margaret came in, who made him a sign to go on, and listened very respectfully, with great attention and stillness, making not a movement that could disturb her sister, or the performance. When it was over, she said it was beautiful, and that he must stay and take a cup of tea; and presently Lilias and Katie joined the party, two fair young creatures full of what is considered the poetry of life. Miss Jean had resumed her table-cover by this time, and sat among her silks, puzzling a little which to choose, very undecided and vacillating, between a yellow-brown and an orange red for one of the shades of her carnation. Lilias and Katie both gave advice which was authoritative, wondering how there could be any question as to which was the best.

"It is your eyes that are going," Lilias said, in thoughtless impatience.

"My dear, I suppose it must just be that," said Miss Jean. She was exactly as she always was, returned into all the little details of her gentle life, and not one of them was aware into what lofty regions she had been wandering. She spoke without the slightest embarrassment to Lewis, and looked up with all her usual kindness, quite matter-of-fact and ordinary, into his face. "You will not be long of coming back," she said, with a smile.

He felt too much bewildered to make any reply; the change from that wonderful interview in which he had been raised from earth to heaven, in which his heart had beat so high, and his life had hung in the balance, into the calm scene of the drawing-room with its tea-table, the lady who said that last thing was just beautiful, and the airy talk of the girls, was so bewildering that he could not realise it. He had been obliged to rouse himself up, to act like an ordinary denizen of the daylight, to laugh and listen even to Katie, as if that strange episode had never been; but when he went away he went back into it, and could not think even of Lilias. With what a strange gravity as of despair he had gone away from the side of Lilias to make this attempt which he thought honour and good faith made necessary, feeling all the while that in doing so he was giving up the brighter happiness, the more natural life, that had been revealed to him. But, after that interview with Miss Jean, Lilias herself had seemed tame. He did not wish to stay in her presence, to behold her beauty; he wanted to get away to think over the strange scene that had passed. He made his way through the park, not thinking where he was going, as far as New Murkley, then through the woods to the old quarry and the waterside, and during all this round he thought of nothing but Miss Jean and her story, and the way in which she had put him from her without a word of refusal, without a harsh tone, putting him away, yet bringing him closer to her very feet. He was refused, and that by a woman who, in comparison with himself, was an old woman, who permitted him to see that his suit was as folly to her; that she did not and would not give it a moment's consideration; and yet he was not affronted nor offended, nor did he feel the smallest shade of bitterness.

It all seemed astonishing to Lewis. Was it the difference of English ways and manners, or was it individual? But he could not make it clear to himself which it was. He walked round by the water-side and into the village that way, not to distract himself, but to have more time to think it over. His heart had been so deeply touched that he was still quivering with its effect. Everything seemed to have changed to him. He had believed last time he went by this way that his life was to be spent henceforward in a state of voluntary renunciation. He had meant to give up all that was warmest and sweetest in it, to content himself with a subdued and self-restrained well-being. Now all that was over, the situation changed, and he might hope like any other man to have what all men coveted. And yet he was not exhilarated. His mind had not leapt back to the thought of Lilias, as would have been so natural. Lilias seemed to have faded into the background; he scarcely thought of her at all. Happiness seemed to have become a thing secondary, almost an inferior item in the history even of the heart.

The landscape was very still in the afternoon quiet. The children were all at school, except the funny little parti-coloured group which belonged to the ferryman, little creatures like chickens, with lint-white heads and round, red cheeks, who were always on the very edge of the river, in risk, as it seemed, of their lives, but to whom nothing ever happened, except an occasional shrill cry of the mother from the cottage, or deep bass objurgation of the ferryman himself. They should all have been drowned a dozen times over, but were not. The big boat was making its way across with a farmer's shandry-dan upon it, reflected in the clear brown of the rushing water. Just within the shadow of the high cliff above which was crowned by the tower of the Stormonts, Lewis saw a fish leap half out of the water, with a gleam and splash. This sufficed to do what even Lilias had not done, to turn the current of his thoughts. He had not been able to get back to any consideration of his changed prospects and regained freedom, but the flash of the trout struck some accidental chord. With a half-laugh at the curious importance of this new subject, he crossed the broad opening of the village street, and went along the bank to Adam's usual nook opposite the cliff. There Adam was posted, as usual, one foot advanced to give him a firmer standing ground, his arms thrown high, a fine athletic image, against the brown water and the green leaves. Lewis went and stood by him for a time without saying anything. He felt a certain ease and sense of deliverance in the quiet scene, where there was enough to occupy the eye and a certain superficial mind, which occasionally takes the place of the real one, and to make thought unnecessary. His deeper cogitations dropped like a falling wind, and he watched with an amused interest the movements so wary, and skilful, the deep silence, and absorbed excitement of the fisher. It was only when the trout was landed and Adam took breath, that Lewis ventured to speak.

"That is a fine fellow," he said.

"Nothing to speak of," said Adam, throwing the silvery creature on the grass, with a certain contempt. "Lord, to think of a' that time wared upon a brute that will scarce make a mouthful a-piece for twa-three hungry men!"

"The brute, as you call it, would willingly have let you off."

"Oh, ay, sir, that's true enough. It's just as little sensible o' the end o' its being as you and me. The creatures o' God are a' alike, so far as that goes."

"Do you think, then, that the end of its being is that mouthful a-piece? I would rather think of the river, where no doubt poor Mrs. Trout and the little ones are expecting your victim home."

Adam shook his head with a short laugh.

"Ceevilization," he said, "stops on the land, Mr. Murray. Thae kind of regulations gi'e little trouble in the breast of Tay. That's just an ordinance of Providence, I would say; for, if there was any natural feeling among the brute creation, every river, and every moor, and a' the wild places of the earth, would be naething but just a moanin' and a mournin'."

"That is not a pleasant thought for you slaughterers of your fellow-creatures. I have my conscience clear," Lewis said with a smile.

Adam looked at him with a mild contempt, but made no remark. Then he said,

"Did you ever hear the sheep on the hill-sides when their lambs are ta'en from them? Oh, but yon's heart-breakin'. They're nothing but the inferior creation, and if they've hearts or no, I canna tell; but it's certain they have nae souls. For a' that, when I hear thae puir beasts, nothing will come into my head but just the Scripture itsel', which nae doubt was made for higher uses. Rachel weepin' for her children, and would not be comforted. It makes a man silly to hear them—when he has ony thought."

"There was once a saint in Italy," said Lewis, "that was not of your opinion about the animals. When he was tired of preaching to men, he preached to the birds or the fishes. The birds made a great noise one day in the middle of his sermon to the men, and he stopped and rebuked them, bidding them be silent till their turn came."

"And what came of that?" said Adam, quickly, looking up with a glance of interest. He was ashamed of it apparently, for he followed it up with a low laugh. "He would be one of thae craturs in the Middle Ages," he added, in a lower tone.

"The story says that the swallows, and the sparrows, and all the rest settled upon the roof and among the pinnacles of the cathedral, and everything was still till the sermon was over."

"And syne they had their turn?" Adam said, with the same low laugh. He was a little moved by the story. "It's a very bonnie fancy. Burns might have made a poem about it, if he had ever heard it. He was one that had a real pitiful heart for dumb creatures too. Do ye mind that, when he's lying in his bed warm and safe, and hearing the wind brattle at the windows, and like to take off the roof, 'I think upon the oorie cattle,' he says. Man, that's come into my head mony's the night! but the kye and the yowes, they're a kind o' human beasts, and the birds are like bairns, mair or less; but I canna get ony sentiment about the trout. There's nae feeling in them. They'll fight for their lives, but no for one another; and nae sort of sense in them that ever I heard."

"There was another saint that preached to the fishes—but I don't know the result," said Lewis. "No doubt it was meant to show the people that these were their fellow-creatures too."

"I like none of your explanations," said Adam, with a half-angry glance. "If the man that preached to them didna believe in them, he was just a dreamer, and the swallows would never have bud still for him, ye may take my word. Na," said Adam, "I'll say nothing about miracles—but, when there's a real true feeling, that has an awfu' grand effeck. Just a man that looks in your face, and believes in ye. That's a kind of inspiration. Bird, or beast, or, waur than ony, a contradictious human creature—ye'll no escape the power o' that."

Lewis said nothing. His eyes flooded silently with tears. They did not fall, not because he was ashamed of them, like an ordinary Briton, but because the emotion in his brain seemed too still for that demonstration. His heart filled, like his eyes, with a sacred flood of tenderness. He had not escaped the power of that. It made him sad with exquisite sympathy, and happy with such a sense of the beauty of truth and faithfulness, and a constant heart, as in all his life he had had no comprehension of before.

CHAPTER XXV

Miss Jean returned to her work after tea. It was her time for taking her walk, either with her sister, if Margaret had any inclination that way, or by herself, in the contemplative stillness of the Ghost's Walk. But this afternoon she sat still over that carnation which was never ending, with its many little leaves and gradations of colour; the carnation in the glass which she was copying had twice been removed, and perhaps it was the little apology with which she thought it necessary to account for her departure from her usual habit of taking a little relaxation at this time of the day, that aroused Miss Margaret's suspicion.

"I think I must just finish this flower. I have been a terrible time at it," Miss Jean said.

"Ye may well say that," said her sister; "it will never be done. You will come back and work at it to frighten Lilias' grandchildren after we are all in our graves."

"I will never do that," said Miss Jean firmly, "whatever I may do."

"There is no telling," said Miss Margaret. "I have often thought, if there were any ghosts, that a poor thing in that condition might just wander back to its old dwelling and hover about its old ways, without a thought that it might be a terror to those that behold it. It would not be easy to conceive that kindly folk in your house would be frightened at you."

"But, Margaret, how would a blessed existence that had passed into the heavens themselves come back to hover about earthly howffs and haunts? Oh, no, I cannot think that. To do a service or to give a warning, you could well understand; but just to wander about and frighten the innocent—"

"It is not a subject I have studied," said Miss Margaret, "though there's Lady Jean out there in the walk has had a weary time of it, summer and winter, if all tales be true. The music this afternoon must have been very moving, and you and your musician, you have grown great friends. I would have said you had both been greeting, if there could be any possible reason for it."

Jean's head was bent over her work, but Margaret kept her keen eyes fixed upon her. It was not a look which it was easy to ignore.

"It was Handel," said Miss Jean, softly; "there are some parts that would just wile your heart out of your breast, and some that are like the thunder rolling and the great winds. Friends, did you say? Oh, yes, we are great friends; and we were greeting together, though you may wonder, Margaret. He was telling me of his own affairs: and somehow, before ever I knew, I found that I was telling him about mine: and we both shed tears, I will not deny, he for my trouble, I am thinking, and me partly for his."

"And what was his, if one might ask?" Miss Margaret said.

"Mostly the troubles of a young spirit that has not learned to measure the world like you and me, Margaret, and that has little sense of what is out of his reach and what is in. And me, I was such an old haverel that I could not keep myself to myself, but just comforted him with telling him. He is a fine lad, Margaret; I never saw one that was more ready to feel."

"More ready, perhaps, than was wanted," cried Margaret, who could not divest herself of a little indignation and alarm.

"It's not easy to be too ready with your sympathy," said her sister, mildly. "Few folk are that."

Margaret was silent, wondering much what had passed. She stood at the window pretending to look out. She was perhaps a little jealous of the love of her life's companion. Had she known nothing of Lewis' intentions, there was indeed no indication to warn her that Jean's calm had been thus disturbed. She had expected some flutter in her sister's gentle spirit. She had expected perhaps a little anger, a few tears, or, what would have been worse, an exaggerated pity for the young man, and a flattered sense of power on Jean's part. Not one of these sentiments was visible in her. An anxious eye could see some traces of emotion: and that she had been much moved was certain, or she would not have "comforted him by telling him," as she had said. Margaret, who was excited and uneasy, was almost jealous that, even by way of crushing this young man's presumptuous hopes, Jean should so far have admitted him into her confidence as to tell him her own story; even that was a great deal too much.

"I would like to know," she said, "what right a strange lad could have, that is not a drop's blood to us, to come with his stories to you?"

"Poor callant!" said Miss Jean, "he has no mother. It was perhaps that, Margaret."

"Was he looking for a mother in you?" cried Margaret, sharply. If she had detected a blush, a smile, a movement of womanly vanity still lingering, there is no telling what Miss Margaret would have been capable of. But Jean worked on at her carnation in her tremulous calm, and made no sign. Perhaps it was the last sublimated essence of that womanly vanity which made her so tender of the young intruder. She would not hand him over to ridicule any more than to indignation. It was perhaps the first secret she had ever kept from Margaret; but then it was his secret, and not hers.

"He did not just say that, or perhaps think it," said Miss Jean; "he may have thought I would be affronted, being a single person: but that was what he meant."

"I hope you will never encourage such folly," said Margaret. "It is a thing that always ends in trouble. You are not old enough to be a man's mother, and it is very unbecoming; it is even not—delicate. You, that have been all your life like the very snowdrift, Jean!"

Jean raised her mild eyes to her sister. They were more luminous than usual with the tears that had been in them. There was a look of gentle wonder in their depths. The accusation took her entirely by surprise, but she did not say anything in her own defence. If there was any reproach in the look, it was of the gentlest kind. It was perhaps the first time in her life that Jean felt herself Margaret's superior. But she did not take any pleasure in her triumph. As for Margaret, her suspicion or temper could not bear that look. She stamped her foot suddenly on the floor with a quick cry.

"I am just a fool!" she said, turning all her weapons against herself in a moment—"just a fool! There's not another word to say."

"You were never that, Margaret."

"I have just been that all my life, and I will be so to my dying day!" cried Margaret, vehemently; and then she laughed, but not at her own want of grammar, of which she was unconscious. "And you are just a gowk too," she added, in her more usual tone.

"That may very well be, Margaret," said Miss Jean, returning to her carnation; and not a word more was said between the sisters of this curious incident.

But it was a long time before Margaret dismissed it from her mind. She watched Jean and all her movements, with many attempts to discover what effect had been produced upon her. But Jean went about her gentle occupations just as usual. The one departure from her customary routine was the omission of that evening walk. No doubt such a thing had happened before without attracting any notice; and if she were more still and silent than usual during the evening, where could there be a more natural explanation of that than in the fact which she had confessed that she had told her own story to her visitor? Not for nothing are those doors of the past opened. However entirely the sorrow that is long over may dwell in the mind, there is an agitation, a renewal of the first acuteness of the pain in the retelling of it. Miss Margaret said all this to herself, and fully accounted for any little change which her keen inspection found out in the demeanour of her sister; but, indeed, had it not been for that close watch, there was no change. She had not been disturbed in the calm of her spirit—perhaps she had not quite realised what Lewis meant. Afterwards it was certain, when she thought it over, she rejected altogether the hypothesis which had been forced upon her by his words, and said to herself that she must have taken him up altogether wrong. What motive could he have in speaking so to her? She was old, she was without money or any recommendation, and it was not as if he had known her long, to grow fond of her, as will happen sometimes without thought or premeditation on either side. She thought to herself that it was very fortunate she had not been betrayed into any expression that could have shown her mistake, for it must have been a mistake. And how fortunate that it had blown over so easily, for they were better friends than ever, and the sweet-hearted lad had wept actual tears for her trouble. The Lord bless him for it! Miss Jean said, with gratitude and tender pleasure. And then she fell to thinking how wonderful it was that you will sometimes unbar your secret heart to a stranger when you could not do it to those you see every day. How strange that was, with a confusing sort of sense in it, that in the dimness of this world, where you can only see the outside, those that were made to be the dearest of friends might never find each other out. But that was too deep a thought for Miss Jean, who returned to her carnation, and worked away a bit of musing into it in little broken half-suggestions, which never made themselves into words, but which made her life far more full and sweet, as she sat there and patiently worked the silken flowers into a piece of stuff not half worth the trouble—than anyone knew or suspected. Margaret would be a little impatient of its long duration sometimes, and even of the stooping of Jean's head, as she sat against the light in the window, with her basket of silks and the carnation in the glass.

This episode, however, was lost in the stir of the preparations for Lilias' first appearance in the world. Needless to say that no idea of the possibility of any incident in which she herself was not the central figure ever crossed the mind of Lilias. Her sisters were her guardians, the chief upholders of the little world of which she herself was the interest and living centre. That anything apart from herself should happen to them was as impossible as that everything should not happen to her, standing as she did upon the threshold of life. A natural conviction so undoubting would have closed her eyes even if there had been anything to see; and there was nothing, save in Miss Margaret's anxious fancy. She was the one of the party who was disturbed by the visit of Lewis. When he came back, as he did very soon, it is impossible to describe the restless anxiety of Margaret. She would have liked to see from some coign of vantage what they were doing; she would have liked to overhear their talk. Her impatience was almost irrestrainable while she sat and listened to Lilias reading. What was Queen Elizabeth to her? It was right, no doubt, that the child should be brought up in right views. But what if in the mean time all that mysterious scene which had passed downstairs out of her knowledge should be gone over again, and Jean, always too gentle, be this time over-persuaded? So restless did she become that Lilias at last paused in her reading.

"You are tired, Margaret; you are anxious about something. What is it?" the girl said.

"Me—anxious—what should I be anxious about? I am thinking of your dress, if it was right to have it silk—muslin would have been better at your age; and then there is Jean no doubt just taigled with that young lad, and not able to get him off her hands."

"Oh, as for Jean, do you not hear the piano, Margaret? You may be sure she is perfectly happy: for, you know, Mr. Murray is a great performer. Mrs. Seton says so, and she knows about music."

"I am sick of Mrs. Seton and her great performers. Murray! who knows even if he is a Murray? He cannot tell who he belongs to. If he was come of any Murray that has ever been heard tell of, he would know that—"

"I daresay," said Lilias, boldly, "there are a great many Murrays, very nice people, that have never been heard tell of—"

"Lilias!" said her sister, in dismay. "It is a great deal you can know about it," she added, with a somewhat angry laugh. Her mind was more easy when she heard the piano. Nothing of importance could be talked about while it went on in full force.

"I don't know very much, Margaret; but everybody is allowed to think," said the girl; "and old families, like old clothes, most surely wear out. I am not sure that it is such an advantage to be old. If I were a new man, I think I would be proud of it. It would be all my own doing; or, if I were a new man's daughter, it would be grand to think that it was all from my father, him and nobody else. That would be something to be proud about."

"Money," Margaret said, laconically, and with an accent of disdain.

"Money! Oh, but I did not mean money."

"Do you know what you meant?" said Miss Margaret, scornfully. "What does a new man, as you call it, make but money? For honours, you must have time and opportunity. In these days it is a quack medicine, or a new invention for taking work out of poor men's hands, or the grand art of selling water for milk, and carrion for meat, and the sweepings of the house for honest cloth. It's that that makes a new man; and it would be a great credit and honour, no doubt, to be his daughter."

"Margaret, you know that is not what I meant," cried Lilias, indignant. "I was not thinking of the people that are only rich. I was thinking—"

"I well understand that you know nothing about it; and how should you? But one thing of this age is that the babes and sucklings just think themselves as wise as Solomon in all his glory. I cannot hear if that piano is aye bumming. Bless me, what a waste for a young man that might be on the hill-side—or he might be in the colonies making corn grow for the good of man—or taming down the savages in Africa."

"He could not be on the hill-side, if you mean shooting, Margaret, for you forget it's only July—"

"He might be doing many better things than sitting at a piano at his age, deluding an old maid."

"Margaret!" cried Lilias, springing up with flashing eyes. "Is it my Jean you are calling that?"

"Well! and what else is she? or me, either, for that matter. Just two old maids: and, for anything we know, you may be a third yourself, more likely than not, unless you take the first that offers—which was what neither her nor me were allowed to do."

"I will never take the first that offers," cried Lilias, indignantly. "What is the matter with you, Margaret? Music is always called such a fine thing in books. If we do not care for it, perhaps it is our fault; and Jean is so fond of it, which shows it must be good."

There had been a lull in the sound of the piano which had called forth Margaret's outburst. She was more charitable as it went on.

"If you are going to read your book, Lilias," she said, "go on with it: but, if you are going to argue, just put the other away first. For my part, I think it is about time for the tea."

And when she went downstairs everything was re-assuring. The music was tranquil, and Miss Jean quite calm, not even excited and ecstatic, as she had been on previous occasions. The perfect composure of the atmosphere smoothed Miss Margaret down in a moment, and, as so often happens after a false alarm, she was more gracious, more gay than usual in the relief of her mind.

"Jean," she said, "you must mind that Mr. Murray is a young man, and wants diversion—not to be kept close to a piano on a bonnie summer afternoon, when everybody that can be out, is out, and enjoying this grand weather. I would not say but what music was a great diversion too—but we are old, and he is young."

"I have had my fill of sunshine," said Lewis, "and sketched everything there is to sketch within a mile or two. And I have no piano. I hope you are not going now to turn me away."

"So you sketch too? Yes, I heard it before no doubt, but I had forgotten. You are a very accomplished young man. In our day, it was the young ladies that learned all that; the boys were packed away into the Army, or the Navy, or to India, and never had any time. It was the girls of a family—"

"But oh, Margaret! if you will think what kind of music and drawing it was! 'Rousseau's Dream' upon the piano, and a painted flower upon cardboard. I think shame when you speak of it. A real musician, and a true artist, is very different—"

"I don't merit those fine titles," said Lewis, with a laugh. "I understand what Miss Margaret means. The thing to do for me is to turn me loose upon New Murkley, and let me decorate those great rooms. I have a little turn that way. I have seen the great palaces of that architecture, and I have studied. I should be no more idle, if you would permit me to do that."

"Decorate the rooms! But that would be worse still than being idle," said Margaret. "For it would be work for no use. If no miracle happens to the family, so far as I can see, Lilias will just have to pull down that fool's palace, or sell it, one or the other. You need not cry out. What would you do with it, you silly thing, with no money to keep it up?"

"I will never sell it," cried Lilias, with flashing eyes.

"That would be the best; for we might get some new rich person, one of the men you admire, Lilias, to give a sum of money for it. And you might build a wall between it and us, and we would be none the worse. Pulling it down would be a waste, though it would be more comfortable to one's feelings; for you would get nothing but the price of old materials for that big castle that we have looked at all our lives. But, any way, to decorate a house that is doomed, and not a window in it to keep out the weather—"

"It might be made into a hospital," said Miss Jean. "That has always been my notion, Margaret. We can make no use of it ourselves, and it would be a heartbreak to sell it, and Lilias would never like to pull down such solid bonnie walls. I doubt even if it would be right."

"Why should it not be right, you veesionary? It is her own at least, to do as she pleases—if once she were of full age, and nothing can be done before that."

"But, Margaret, there's more in it—solid bonnie walls that took a long time to build, and a good warm steady roof, and all the grand, big rooms, though there's nothing in them—and when you consider the poor sick folk and the helpless bairns that have no shelter! I'm not clear in my mind that it would be a lawful thing," Miss Jean said.

"Did I not say she was a veesionary?" said Margaret. "We would have had no shelter to our own heads, let alone help for the poor folk, if I had not been here to look over the house. We are just an impracticable race. One has one whimsey, and one another. The thing has been built for a fancy, and our fancies will keep us from getting rid of it. I am not sure that I am heartwhole myself. I would not like to see a pickaxe laid upon it. We will have to make up our minds before Lilias comes of age. But, one way or another, Mr. Murray, you will see that decorations are not just our affair. We are meaning to be—in town for the next season," she added, with the solemnity which such a statement demanded. "And afterwards our movements may be a little uncertain, not knowing what that may lead to. It is just possible that we may come no more to Murkley till Lilias is of age."

Lewis made no reply. He had to receive the intelligence with a bow; it was not his part to criticise, or even to regret. He had come fortuitously across their path, and had not even standing ground enough with them to venture to say that he hoped the friendship might not end there. To Miss Jean, had he been alone with her, he could have said this, but not under Margaret's keen, all-inspecting eye. It was with a mixture of pain and pleasure that he felt himself in the background, listening to what they said. The very termination of his plans in respect to Miss Jean detached him, and made him feel himself a stranger in the midst of this little company of women, to which he had attached himself so completely in his own thoughts. So long as that question was unresolved, Lewis had felt, even with a sort of despairing acquiescence, that he was one of them, though they did not know it, with a certain concern in all their family arrangements, and hold upon them. Now this visionary right had gone altogether, and he knew that he was of no importance, nothing to them one way or another. It chilled him to feel it, and yet there was no doubt that it was so, and that he could expect or look for nothing else. He sat by for a while in silence, with a sort of smile, while they proceeded to talk of other things. Now and then Miss Jean would make an effort of kindness to bring him into the current, but he felt that he had nothing to do with that current. He was outside; he felt even that he ought to go away, and that it was rude not to do so; but at the same time it was difficult for him to issue forth from the charmed circle. Once gone, it seemed to Lewis that he could scarcely have a pretence for coming again.

At last he got up to go away.

"You will come again soon?" said Miss Jean.

"Bless me, Jean," said Margaret, "you must think Mr. Murray has little to do that he will come day after day at your bidding; though we are always glad to see him, I need not say," she added, with some ghost of cordiality.

He felt himself standing before her as if she had been his judge, and looked at her somewhat wistfully; but there was no encouragement in Margaret's face. Lewis felt that the hand she gave him made a gesture of dismissal. He walked to the door sadly enough. It seemed to him that, his first attempt having ended in failure, there was no further opportunity left him by which to approach the family which he had so unwittingly wronged. He felt abashed and humbled by his failure. To have been accepted by Miss Jean, although that would have been to separate him from all brighter hopes, would have been far better than this. Then at least he would have had some means of reparation. Now it seemed, as he turned his back upon them, as if he were turning his back also upon the honest wish which had brought him here, the generous desire that had been his leading principle ever since he had heard of old Sir Patrick's rightful heirs. Lewis was exceedingly cast down and troubled. He thought, as he went slowly across the old hall, that in all probability he would never be admitted to it again.

There was no servant to open the door to him, none of the usual urgency of politeness by which one of the ladies themselves, if Simon were out of the way, would accompany a visitor to the threshold. It was one sign of their dismissal of him, he thought, that he was to let himself out without a word from anyone. As he put his hand, however, reluctantly upon the door, Lewis was suddenly aware of a skim and flutter across the oak floor and the old Turkey carpet in the centre of the hall, and, looking up, perceived with a start and flush Lilias herself, and no other, who had darted after him from the open door of the drawing-room. It lasted only a moment, but he saw it like a picture. The girl in her light dress, dazzling, with her fair head and smiling countenance bent towards him: and beyond her, in the room within that open door, Margaret standing in an attitude of watchfulness, keenly listening, intent upon what passed. Lilias had flown after him, indifferent to all remonstrance. Her sweet voice, with its little trick of accent, and the faint cadence in it of the lingering vowels, had a touch of gay defiance in its sound.

"You are not going away," she said—"you are to be at the ball—you are not to forget. And perhaps we shall dance together," she said, with a smile, offering him her hand.

What was he to do with her hand when he got it? Not shake it and let it drop, like an ordinary Englishman. He had not been bred in that way. He bowed over it and kissed it before Lilias knew. He would have kissed her slipper had he dared, but that would have been an unusual homage, whereas this was the most natural, the most simple salutation in the world.

It took Lilias altogether by surprise. No lip of man had ever touched her hand before. Her fair face turned crimson. She could not have been more astonished had he kissed her cheek, though the astonishment would have been of a different kind. She stood bewildered when this wonderful thing had happened, looking at her hand almost with alarm, as if the mark would show. She was ready to say, "It was not my fault," in instinctive self-defence. And yet she was not offended or displeased, but only startled. What would Margaret say? what would Jean say? or should she tell them? To end this self-discussion, she fled upstairs suddenly to her own room, and there considered the question, and the incident which was the strangest that ever had happened to her in all her life.

CHAPTER XXVI

The night of the Stormont ball was as lovely and warm as a July night could be so far north. It was, it is scarcely necessary to say, full moon, country entertainers taking care to secure that great luminary to light their guests home, though in this case it was scarcely necessary, for no one intended that anything less than daylight should see them leave the scene of the festivities. The commotion was great in the old house, where every servant felt like one of the hosts, and the house was turned upside down from top to bottom with an enjoyment of the topsy-turvy which only a simple household unused to such incidents can know. Mrs. Stormont had spared no expense; there were lanterns hung among the trees, along the whole length of the avenue; there were lights in every window; even on the top of the old tower there was a blaze which threw a red reflection on the water, and was the admiration of the village. To see the ladies of Murkley cross in the great ferry-boat in their old-fashioned brougham, which was scarcely big enough to hold the three, and the Setons after them, wrapped up in cloaks and "clouds," was a sight that filled all Murkley with pleasure. "And they'll come back like that at three or four in the morning. Eh, bless me! but they maun be keen of pleasure to gang through a' that for't," the elderly sceptics said; but they were pleased to see the ladies in their fine dresses all the same. Miss Jean had a silver-grey satin, a soft, poetical dress that suited her; but Miss Margaret, notwithstanding the season, was in velvet, with point-lace that a queen might have envied. As for Lilias, it was universally acknowledged that the ball-dress which had come for her from London "just beat a'." Nothing like it had ever been imagined in Murkley. We have read in an American novel—where such glories abound—an account of a lovely confection by Mr. Worth, called the "Blush of Dawn," or some other such ethereal title, by which an awed spectator might see what a fine thing a ball-dress could be; but English narrative is not equal to the occasion, and the dress of Lilias was white and virginal, as became the wearer, and afforded no such opportunities to the historian. These two parties were the only ones that crossed the ferry. Peter the ferryman was aware that their coming back might abridge his rest, and was not over-gracious.

"It'll be fower in the mornin' or sae, or ye come back?" he said to old Simon on the box of the brougham.

"Me! I'm coming back to my supper and my bed," said the other; "but fower is late for the leddies. I would say atween twa and three," which made Peter grave.

"One man's meat is another's man's poison," he said to himself. The manse party would certainly not return till four at the earliest, so that he had the comfortable prospect of being up all night, "and none o' the fun," not even a dram to keep him warm: for even a July morning, between two and four, is a chilly moment so far north. The high-road was in a cloud of dust with the carriages that came rolling along from all quarters in the soft twilight; for, though in July the days have shortened a little, the skies were still shining clear at nine o'clock, and the lingering reflections of the sunset scarcely passed away.

Mrs. Stormont and her son were both dressed and ready, standing in the handsome old gallery, where the dancing was to be. She was in her widow's dress, which so many ladies in Scotland never abandon, and which, notwithstanding all the abuse that has been levelled at it, is like a conventual garb, very becoming to a person with any natural claim to admiration. Her rich black silk gown, her perfectly plain, spotless cap with the long white, misty pendants like a veil behind, made Mrs. Stormont, who might have been buxom in gay colours, into a dignified, queen-dowager personage of imposing appearance. She was giving a final lecture to Philip, who was nervous in the prospect, and felt the dignity of the position too much for him.

"You will mind," she said, "my dear, that, when you give us a grand party like this, it is not altogether just for pleasure like those silly bits of dances you go to at the manse."

"You may be sure, mother," said Philip, ironically, "that there is no chance of forgetting that."

"I hope not, Philip. It's a return for favours received, and also it's a claim for your proper position in the county, a claim you must never let down; and Philip, my man, you will mind, will you not, to pay a great deal of attention to Lilias Murray? I consider her the queen of the ball. There will be a great curiosity about her, because she is so young, poor thing, and because nobody knows much about her, and her position is so very peculiar. As often as you can spare from duty to other people you will dance with Lilias, Philip. You have very little occasion, I can tell you, to make a face at that. Better men than you would be glad of the chance."

"That may very well be, and I hope they will take it," said Philip. "I am not going to make a fool of myself, I can tell you, dancing every dance with any girl—if she were Cleopatra!" Philip cried. Why he should have chosen Cleopatra as his type of womanhood nobody could have guessed, and himself least of all.

"That is right, my man, that is just what I desired to hear," cried his mother. "Of course, you must ask all the principal ladies, and mind you begin with the countess, and make no mistake. The quadrilles are for that. If I see you sitting out, as you call it, with Katie Seton or any other cutty, when you should be doing your duty—"

"I wish you would not be violent, mother," Philip said.

His mother had to pause, to gulp down the excitement which such an apprehension raised in her, and which just the moment before the arrival of the guests was doubly inappropriate, before she spoke. She had not time to be angry. She laid her hand on his arm, just as the bell clanged into the echoes announcing the first arrival.

"My dear boy," she said, almost with tears in her eyes, "mind that the Murkley lands march with Stormont, and, though they're not very rich, it's a grand old family, and two littles would make a muckle in such a case."

She put her hand upon his shoulder, but Philip twisted himself away from her touch. He had heard all this before, and he was not at all disposed to listen now.

"I think I had better go down to the hall and receive them as they arrive," he said.

His mother looked at him divided between admiration and suspicion.

"Well, that is a very good idea," she said. "It will have a nice effect if you lead the countess up the stairs yourself instead of leaving it to the servants, and you may do the same to Margaret Murray, or any important person, but don't you waste your time upon the common crowd: and, above all, Philip—" He gave his shoulders an impatient shrug, and was gone before she could say more. Poor Mrs. Stormont shook her head. "It will be to get a word with that little cutty out of my sight," the poor lady said, "and that scheming woman, her mother!" she added to herself, with a movement of passion. She could have been charitable to Katie—but a manœuvring mother, a woman that would stick at nothing to get a good marriage for her girl! that was what Mrs. Stormont could not away with, she said in her heart.

It is needless to say that she had divined Philip's meaning with the utmost exactitude. To get a word with Katie was indispensable: for, if he was rather more in subjection to his mother than was for his comfort, Philip was in subjection to Katie too, and just as much afraid of her. By good luck he fell into the midst of the group newly arrived from Murkley, which was followed almost immediately by the Setons. They were almost the first, and the young master of the house was at liberty to stand among them, and talk while the elder ladies took tea.

"The light on the Tower has a great effect, and so have the lamps in the avenue. Do you call it an avenue?" Miss Margaret said, graciously, yet with a betrayal of her sense of the inferiority which perhaps was not so well-bred as Margaret usually was.

"It's just like fairyland," cried Mrs. Seton, much more enthusiastic. "Yes, yes, just like the decorations you read of in the newspapers when some grand person comes of age. The lamps among the green are just beautiful, and an avenue is far more picturesque, if it's not so imposing, when it mounts a hill-side."

While they were talking, and Miss Jean was giving a last tender touch to the roses on Lilias' bodice, Philip ventured to Katie's side.

"If I seem to neglect you, Katie, will you understand?" he said.

"Oh, yes, I will understand," said the little cutty, with a toss of her pretty head, "that you are just frightened to speak to me; but I'll get plenty of others that will speak to me."

Philip in his despair was so wanting in politeness as to turn his back upon the elders and more important people.

"If you go flirting about with Murray and Alec Bannerman you will just drive me desperate," he said.

"What would your lordship like me to do?" said Katie. "Sit in a corner and look as if I were going to cry? I will not do that, to please anybody. I have come to enjoy myself, and, if I cannot do it in one way, I will in another."

"Oh, Katie, have a little pity upon me, when you know I cannot help myself," the unfortunate lover said.

"I will make everybody believe that there's nothing in it," said Katie, "your mother and all. And is not that the best thing I can do for you?"

She was radiant in mischief and contradiction, inexorable, holding her little head high, ready to defy Mrs. Stormont and every authority. Poor Philip knew she would flirt to distraction with every man that crossed her path while he was dancing quadrilles with the dowagers, and doing what his mother thought his duty. But at that moment among a crowd of new arrivals came the countess herself, and Katie had to be swept away by the current. Amuse herself! She might do it, or anyone else might do it: but as for the hero of the occasion, poor fellow, that was the last possibility that was likely to come to him. He walked through the quadrille with the countess, looking like a mute at a funeral, and as, fortunately, she was a woman of discretion, she gave him her sincerest sympathy.

"I think you might have dispensed with this ceremony," she said. "But don't look so miserable, it will soon be over."

"I miserable! Oh, no; though I confess I don't care for square dances," Philip said.

"Nobody does," said the lady, "but still you should show a little philosophy. Who is that little espiègle that is laughing at us?"

She laughed in sympathy, being a very good-natured woman, but Philip did not laugh; for of course it was Katie, radiant with mischievous smiles, upon the arm of Mr. Alec Bannerman, with whom she was to "take the floor" at once, as soon as this solemnity was over. By the glance she gave him, touching the card which swung from her fan, he divined that she had filled up that document, and had not a dance left: and for the rest of the melancholy performance the countess could not extract a word from him. Of his two tyrants, Katie was the worst. There was no telling the torture to which she subjected him as the evening went on. She was an admirable dancer; as airy as a feather, adapting herself to everybody's step, or in the intervals of the dances, during the other quadrille, which absolutely put Philip's sanity in danger, teaching her own in a corner to an intending partner. And her flirtations were endless.

"Katie?" said Mrs. Seton. "Oh, don't ask me anything about Katie! She has never once sat down all the night. No, no, not a sight of her have I had, the little monkey. She would just dance, dance till the day after to-morrow, if there was no stop put to her. I am just obliged to submit, for I cannot go running after her all down this long gallery, and she knows where to find me, if such a thing happened as that she had no partner, which is but little likely," Mrs. Seton said.

"I was coming to see if I could get her partners," said Mrs. Stormont. "For not being out, or in society, as I understood—"

"I am sure you are very kind: but nobody need give themselves any trouble about Katie," said Mrs. Seton.

It was "not very nice" of Philip's mother to be displeased and angry when she heard this; for as she took the trouble to separate Philip from her, she ought to have been glad that the girl, even if she was a "little cutty," should have others to amuse her: but Mrs. Stormont was not pleased. She felt injured by the popularity of the foolish little thing who had come between her son and herself.

Lilias enjoyed her first ball in a much more modest and subdued way. She stood by the side of her sisters, whose anxiety about the perfect success of her début was great, surveying the scene around her with a smile. She made the old-fashioned curtsey which they had taught her to the young men, who came round with eagerness, not only to do their duty to the old family tree, but to secure the hand of the heroine of the evening, the girl who had piqued the curiosity of the county more than anyone had done before for generations, and who was at the same time the prettiest creature, the beauty of the assemblage. Lilias made her pretty curtsey to them, and gave each a smile, but she said,

"I do not mean to dance very much. I am not used to it. You must not think me uncivil. Thank you very kindly. No, I wish to look on, and see the others. It is so pretty. If I were to dance, I should not see it."

Some of the suppliants were entirely discomfited by this novel reception; they retired in offence or in dismay; but those who were more discerning exercised a little diplomacy, and from time to time, "the

Lily of Murkley," as Mrs. Stormont, for the greater glory of her entertainment, had called the girl, was led forth by a gratified partner, to the envy of the others. Her success in the obstinacy of her determination not to accept everybody, gave a little excitement of triumph to Lilias. She was pleased with herself and with everybody. As for the sisters, there can be no doubt that this singular behaviour brought on them a momentary cloud.

"I see Katie Seton dancing every dance," Miss Jean said, with an air of trouble.

She looked wistfully at the partners whom Lilias sent away. And even Miss Margaret for the first moment was disappointed. The idea that anyone could imagine her child, her little princess, to be neglected, fired her soul, and it was all she could do to restrain herself when Mrs. Seton came bustling up to interfere.

"Dear me! dear me!" cried that energetic woman, "do I see Lilias without a partner? I could not believe my eyes. No, no, you'll not tell me that the young men are so doited; there must just be some mistake. No doubt there is some mistake. They are frightened for you two ladies just like two duennas. A girl should be left to herself for a little. But just let me—"

"You'll observe, if you will wait for a moment," said Miss Margaret, with dignity, "that Lilias does not just dance with everybody. It is not my pleasure that she should. I am not one that would have a girl make herself cheap."

"But not because she looks down upon any person," cried Miss Jean, eagerly, "because she is not just very strong, and we insist she should not weary herself, as it is her first ball, and she is not used to it."

Thus they took upon themselves the blame: while Lilias stood smiling by, and from time to time accepted the arm of a partner more fortunate than the rest, leaving her sisters in a flutter which it was difficult to conceal.

"Now what could be the reason of her choosing him?" Miss Jean whispered, in a faltering voice.

"Oh, just her ain deevil," cried Miss Margaret, moved out of all decorum. "I think the creature will just drive me out of my senses."

"But she has good taste," said Miss Jean, wistfully, "on the whole."

This action upon the part of Lilias changed to them the whole character of the evening. They would have liked that she should have been like Katie, besieged by partners. The partners, indeed, had besieged her, but the company was not aware of it, and it was possible that other people besides Mrs. Seton might suppose it to be neglect.

This was not the only way in which Lilias signalized herself, though fortunately it was only a few who were conscious of what she did. She was dancing with Philip Stormont, whom, with a sense of the obligations of a guest, she did not refuse, at the lower end of the gallery, far away from the inspection of the greater ladies of the party. Poor Philip looked very glum indeed, especially when Katie, at a height of gaiety and excitement, which betrayed some sentiment less happy below, came across him. He had never danced with Katie the whole evening through, and as her enjoyment grew, his countenance became heavier and heavier. Poor Philip was too far gone to attempt any semblance of happiness; he turned round and round mechanically, feeling, perhaps, a little freedom with Lilias, an emancipation from all necessity to talk and look pleasant.

"Look at Philip Stormont revolving," Katie said to Lewis, with whom she was dancing; "he is like a figure on a barrel organ. I suppose he is tired, poor fellow. Perhaps he has been fishing all day, Mr. Murray. You admire him for fishing all day: and you have been doing nothing but playing the piano. I am sorry for Lilias; he is dragging her about as if she were a pedlar's pack. Let us go round and round them," cried that spiteful little person, pressing her partner into a wilder pace.

"You must not be cruel," said Lewis; "you will be sorry to-morrow if you are cruel."

"Cruel!" cried Katie—"he never asked me till it was far too late. Was I going to wait for him—he that has always come to us as long as I can recollect?—and he never asked me. I want to show him the difference," Katie cried.

Next moment she begged her partner to stop, that she was out of breath. The poor little girl was too young to be able to keep the mastery over herself all the evening. The tears were very near her eyes as she laughed in Philip's face, who had come ponderously to a stop also close to her.

"I hope you are enjoying your ball," she said, maliciously. "It is a beautiful ball, and you have danced with all the best people,—you would, of course, in your own house," Katie cried.

Philip was beyond speech; he heaved a sigh, which nearly blew out the nearest lights, and cast a pathetic look at her.

"Oh, yes, I have seen you; you have been enjoying yourself," Katie cried, and laughed. "I am quite ready, Mr. Murray."

Upon this Lilias darted in, clapping her hands softly together as they do in childish games.

"We will change partners," she cried. It seemed to Lewis that he had bounded suddenly into the skies when she laid her hand on his shoulder. "Quick, quick, that they may not stop us," Lilias said.

And Lewis was not reluctant. They flew off together, leaving the other two astonished, confused, looking at each other.

"I suppose we may as well dance," said Philip, and then he poured forth his heart. His little tormentor was taken by surprise. "Oh, what a wretched night!" said poor Philip. "I have been wondering whether it would ever be over, and, now that I have got you, it is against your will. I will never forget Lilias Murray for it all the same. That's what a good girl will do for you—a real true, good girl, by Jove, that does not mind what anybody thinks."

"And I am a bad girl, I suppose?" said Katie, held fast in his arm, and carried along against her will, yet with a thrill of pleasure which had been absent from all her previous merry-making.

"Oh! I don't know what you are," cried the angry lover. "You are just you; there is nobody else. Oh! Katie, how are we to get out of this? I cannot go through such another night. If I had not got you, what would have happened to me?"

"Nothing," cried Katie, almost sobbing, determined to laugh still at all costs; "you would just have gone to your bed and had a good night's rest."

"I think I would have gone to the bed of Tay," cried poor Philip.

She laughed upon his shoulder till he could have beaten Katie, until he suddenly found the sound turn to crying, when Philip grew frightened and abject. He took her downstairs, as soon as she had recovered a little, to have some tea, and caught up the first shawl he could find and wrapped it round her, and led her out into the flower-garden, where the night odours were sweet from the invisible flowers, and the tower threw a deep black shadow, topped by the glare of the light which rose red and smoky against the shining of the moon. There were various other pairs about, but they kept in the moonlight. Philip and Katie felt themselves safer in the dark, and there lingered, it is needless to say, much longer than they ought.

"Are you shocked at my behaviour, Mr. Murray?" said Lilias. "Should I not have done it? Perhaps I should not; but they were so unhappy. And I thought you would never mind. I do not think I would have done it if it had not been you."

"That is the best of all," said Lewis.

"What is the best of all? It was taking a liberty—I am very conscious of that; but Jean says you are full of understanding. And you saw, didn't you, as well as me? Why should people come between other people, Mr. Murray? If I were Philip's mother—you need not laugh—"

"What should you do if you were Philip's mother?" he said.

"I would never, never stand between them. How can she tell she might not be spoiling his life? You read that in books often. Philip is not the grand kind of man who would die for love—"

"Do you think that would be a grand kind of man?"

"Oh, don't you? I would like to live among that kind of people. It would be far finer, far simpler, than the common kind that die just of illnesses and accidents like beasts. I would like to die by my heart."

"I don't think Mr. Stormont will die."

"No, he is not good enough," said Lilias, "he is afraid of his mother. I am a little afraid of Margaret, too; but I would not do an ill thing, I think, even if she wanted me. To be sure, she never would want me. Do you know, I have had my way to-night; I have just refused the people I did not like. Katie dared me to do it, and Jean said I must not do it; but I did it—I was determined I would: and Margaret knew nothing about it, so she could not forbid me," said Lilias, with a laugh.

"That was very prudent, when there is only one you are afraid of, not to let her know."

"I did not keep it from her on purpose," said Lilias, half-offended. "Mr. Murray, do you see that they have gone away downstairs? I am afraid they may be silly now they are together. Don't you think we should go too?"

"I will do whatever Miss Lilias pleases," said Lewis, "and go where you like best. After this you will give me one other little dance—just one; that was like heaven."

"Heaven!" cried Lilias, scandalized. It seemed profanity to her innocent ears. "That will be the way," she said, somewhat severely, "that people permit themselves to speak abroad? I have always heard—But I am sure you did not mean it. It was very nice. I suppose, Mr. Murray, you dance very well?"

"I am not the judge," said Lewis laughing, but confused in spite of himself.

"Neither am I," said Lilias, calmly, "for I have never danced much with gentlemen. But you do not bump like most; you go so smoothly, it was a pleasure. But I wonder where Katie is? Doesn't it seem to you a long time?"

"It is only a moment since we have been together," Lewis said.

"Do you think so? Oh! I am afraid a great many moments—even minutes. Look! Mrs. Stormont is beginning to be uneasy—she is looking for Philip. Oh! come before she sees—"

They hurried downstairs, Lilias leading the young man after her, with a guiding hand upon his arm. The great hall door was standing open, the freshness of the summer night coming in, close to the house a dark belt of shadow, and beyond the shadow, and beyond the shrubberies and garden paths clear in the moonlight. It could only have been by instinct that Lilias penetrated round the corner to the lonely spot in the darkness where the two lovers had betaken themselves, and where Katie, after her hysterical outburst, had become calm again and recovered command of herself. The darkness, and the moonlight, and the soft noises and breathings of the night, and the neighbourhood of the other pair, mounted into the head of Lewis. He scarcely knew what he was doing. He said in a whisper, "Do not interrupt them. Wait here a little," not knowing what he said.

Lilias did not object, or say a word. She took the rôle of sentinel quite calmly, while he stood by her, throbbing with a thousand motives and temptations. His own conscious being seemed arrested, his reason and intelligence; bold words came into his mind which he wanted to whisper to her—he bent towards her, in spite of himself approaching her ear. How was it that he said nothing? He could not tell. His heart beat so fast that it took away his breath. Had he not been so entirely transported out of himself he must have spoken, he must have betrayed himself. He felt afterwards, with a shudder, as if he had been on the edge of a bottomless pit, and had been kept on firm standing-ground not by any wisdom of his, but by the rapture of feeling which possessed him. He had kissed her hand in her own house without any hesitation or sense of timidity, but he did not do it now. He did not even touch with his own the hand that lay on his arm. He was in a sort of agony, yet ecstasy. "Wait a little, wait a little," was all he said. And Lilias took no fright from the words. She did not know how near she was to some confession, some appeal, that would have startled her at once out of her usual freshness and serenity. They stood close together, like two different worlds, the one all passion and longing, the other all innocent composure and calm. But by degrees Lilias became impatient of waiting.

"You are kinder than I am," she whispered, "Mr. Murray. It is a little cold, and Mrs. Stormont will be looking everywhere for Philip. We must not stand any longer, we must try to find them. Do you see nothing?"

"Nothing," said Lewis, with a gasp of self-restraint. His face seemed nearer to her than she expected, and perhaps this startled Lilias. She gave a sudden low cry through the stillness.

"Katie! are you there? Katie! are you there?"

CHAPTER XXVII

Mrs. Stormont felt that all was going well. Philip had not shown any great degree of gaiety, but he had done his duty like a man. The countess, after that duty-quadrille, had come and sat down beside her, and praised her son in words ever pleasant to a mother's ear.

"He did not pretend to like it," she said; "but he did his duty nobly. Now I hope he will enjoy himself: I have no objection to stand up with such a nice young fellow, but I think, dear Mrs. Stormont, that in the country we might dispense with these formal quadrilles that all the young people hate."

"Perhaps I am an old-fashioned person," said Mrs. Stormont; "but it could be nothing but a pleasure to Philip."

The countess shook her head, and said he was a fine young fellow that a mother might well be proud of.

"He is dancing with Ida now, which is more to the purpose," she said.

Now Ida was her ladyship's niece, and for a moment it occurred to Philip's mother that perhaps she had come to a conclusion too quickly in respect to Lilias, and that her son, with all his attractions, might have done better. She had the good sense, however, to perceive that Lady Ida was altogether too great a personage for the Tower of Stormont: but this did not lessen her satisfaction in the good impression produced by her boy. And her confidence increased as the evening went on. She saw him taking out Lilias, dazzling in her fair beauty and white robes, and thought with natural pride that they made a lovely couple: he so dark-haired, brown, and manly, and she so fair. In all her progresses among her guests, her intimate conversations with one and another, Mrs. Stormont had always one eye directed towards Philip. He was very dutiful, and did all that she had pointed out to him as right and proper to do. And he kept away from the Setons. Her heart rose. Here it was evident she had succeeded in doing the right thing at the right time. She had separated him from the manse people, and that little cutty, and she had put him in the way of better things. Naturally he would contrast little Katie with Lady Ida, or even with Lilias, and he would see how he had been taken in. All this went on to perfection till after supper, when, dancing having begun again with double energy, the evils above recounted took place quite out of sight of the anxious mother. Her vigilance had slackened. She had scorned to fix upon her son that all-seeing regard. She had even begun a little to enjoy herself among her old friends independent of him, with old recollections and many a scrap of individual biography. She had seated herself between Miss Margaret and Miss Jean, and, well-pleased, was receiving their congratulations upon the success of everything, when it suddenly occurred to her that amid all the mazes of the dancers Philip was not anywhere visible. She watched with increased anxiety for a time: but after all he might have taken down some lady for refreshments, or to get a breath of fresh air after the dance.

"They will catch their death of cold," she said, "those thoughtless things! I have little doubt my Philip is away into the moonlight with some of them, for I cannot see him."

"Bless me! it will be our Lilias," said Miss Margaret.

"Oh, I'll run and see that she has her cloak," cried Miss Jean, starting to her feet, but both the elder sister and the mother protested against this extreme care.

"They must just take their chance," said Miss Margaret. "We cannot be always after her."

"And my Philip will take care of that," said Mrs. Stormont.

But after this alarm, the eyes of all were busy, watching for the truants. A vague uneasiness was in Mrs. Stormont's mind. If it was Lilias, as the other ladies said, then all was well: but the mother of a man recognizes a perversity in that article which is never to be calculated upon. It was possible they might be mistaken. It was possible—who can tell what a young lad is not capable of? It was very consoling, very re-assuring, that Lilias was invisible as well as Philip, but a hundred terrors shook the anxious mother's bosom whenever, through the circles of the dancers, she saw a dress more white than usual, a blonde head, like that of Lilias, reveal itself; and there were of course many fair-haired girls. At last her suspense got too much for her. She left the sisters, under pretence of speaking to another old friend, but once free stole towards the door, and out upon the wide old staircase, which was full of sitters out. Mrs. Stormont escaped with difficulty from the too-zealous cavaliers, who were anxious to take her down for the cup of tea she professed to be in search of. She could hardly get free from their importunities. The door was wide open; the chill that comes before dawn was stealing in, but even when she looked out, shivering, from the threshold some officious person insisted on talking to her.

"Yes, yes, it is a fine night, and the moon is just beautiful—but, for my part, I think it's very cold, and I wish those incautious young creatures would not wander about like that, with nothing on them. If I could see Philip, I would send him out to beg them to come in."

She stood on the step, drawing her shawl round her, looking out with great anxiety into the gloom. It was just trembling on the turn between darkness and light: ten minutes more would have betrayed to her what was taking place under the shadow of the bushes—the change of partners once more in the little group at the corner of the house. But it is impossible to tell what a bound of relief Mrs. Stormont's sober heart gave when suddenly, coming forward into the light, she beheld the welcome figure of Lilias, all white and fair, leading rather than being led by Philip. There was a look which was half-shame and half-mischief in Lilias' eyes. She was a conscious deceiver, yet enjoyed the rôle. Her eyes were shining, dazzled with the light, as she came out of the darkness, a blush upon her face, a little shrinking from the gaze of the happy mother, who was so thankful to make sure that it was Lilias.

"Oh, my dear child," she cried, "is that you? and what do you mean, you selfish loon, by keeping her out in the cold?"

As she addressed him with this abusive expression, Mrs. Stormont laid her hand caressingly upon Philip's other arm. He had not looked so happy all the evening. She turned and went in with him, ordering her son to get his bonnie lady something to warm her after stravaighing like that in the dark. Poor lady! she did not see little Katie, her heart fluttering in her throat, who stole in after, and hurried off to her mother, while the mistress of the feast had her back turned. Lewis took her back to Mrs. Seton very gravely, and Katie was frightened for once in her life, but presently, finding no harm come of it, shook herself free of all unnecessary tremors, and was flying over the floor with Alec Bannerman, who had been looking for her everywhere, as he was telling her when Mrs. Stormont came into the room radiant. That lady went back to the sisters, nodding her head with satisfaction.

"It was just as we thought," she said. "They were out for some fresh air, the monkeys! Fresh air!—it was like December! But I'm glad to tell you my boy had the sense to put a shawl upon her, and they're safe now in the tea-room, where I bade him give her some wine or something to warm her. So now your minds can be at ease."

How much at ease her own was! She left them to seat herself beside another county lady, whose sons, poor soul, were wild, and gave her a great deal of trouble: and there discoursed, as women sometimes will, upon the perfections of her Philip, not without a gratified sense that the other sighed over the contrast. But Margaret and Jean were not so much relieved as Mrs. Stormont.

"It is not like our Lilias," Margaret said. "I hope she will not learn these unwomanly ways. Out in the dark with a long-leggit lad like yon Philip, that his mother thinks perfection—I am disappointed in her, Jean."

"It will have been some accident," said Jean, cast down, yet faithful.

"Accident!—how could it be an accident? I hope it is not the appearance in her of any light-headedness. I would shut her up for the rest of her life if I thought that."

"How can you think so, Margaret?" cried Jean, indignantly. "There are no light-headed persons in our family."

"But she is of her mother's family as well as ours," said the elder sister, seriously. "You can answer for your own blood, but never for another. Have you been out too, Mr. Murray? There is a breath about you of the caller air."

"That is a pretty word, the caller air," said Lewis. "It is just upon dawn, and the birds will soon be singing; but I think it is too cold for the ladies to go out. They are very brave not to mind."

"Brave!—I call it foolhardy; and, indeed, if it's on the turn of the dawning, as Mr. Murray says, I think, Jean, we should be making our way—"

"Margaret," cried Lilias in her ear, "I have got it upon me! Now I am going to dance every dance. It is just a sort of a fever, and, when you take it, it must run its course. Was this the dance you asked me for?" the girl said, turning and holding out her hand to Lewis. Her eyes were shining, her face full of animation, the thrill of the music in her frame.

Lewis was so much entranced gazing at her that he scarcely realized the boon she was offering him. Did she mean to turn his head? She who had refused half the people in the room, and now gave herself to him with this sweet cordiality. The sisters sat and looked at each other when the pair floated away.

"It is because she thinks him a stranger, and a little out of his element," said Jean, ever ready with an apology.

"A stranger! He is just a beautiful dancer. Very likely he would be clumsy in a reel; but nobody dances reels nowadays. And as for those round dances (which I cannot say I approve of), he is just perfect. I don't wonder Lilias likes to dance with him. But I hope she will not just put things into his head," Margaret said.

"Oh, no," said Jean—"I don't think she will do that."

It was not till two hours later, in the lovely early daylight, that the Miss Murrays left the Tower. Though there was not much room in the brougham, they sat close to take Mrs. Seton and her daughter into it, Katie, much subdued, sitting on Miss Margaret's velvet lap, upon the point lace which was almost the most valuable thing she possessed. The elder ladies talked a little, moralizing upon the perversity of human nature, which sent them home like this in their finery on the bonnie bright morning, when working folk were going out to their day's darg.

"If they would have the sense to begin early, as you do at your little tea-parties," Miss Margaret said, graciously.

"But oh! we must make allowances for a ball. Yes, yes, there are so few of them in the county we may make allowance once in a way for a ball—and a grand ball, too, we must all admit; and the young people all enjoyed themselves just uncommonly," cried Mrs. Seton.

When they were in the ferry-boat, Lilias desired to be allowed to get out of the carriage, and, with their fleecy white wraps about their heads, the girls went to the bow of the boat and stood in the fresh light looking out upon the silent river, which lay in that ecstasy of self-enjoyment, brooding upon all its shadows, and reflecting every gradation of light, which Nature is possessed by in hours when man is, so to speak, non-existent. The birds sang as if they had never known before what delight there was in singing, and were all trying some new carols in an enthusiasm of pleasure, breaking off and beginning again as if they had never sung them before this day. And the shadows were all made of light, as well as the illuminations, and everything was glorified in the water which reproduced the bank and the foliage and every sleeping cottage. There was a little awe in it, it was so bright, so limpid and serene. Lewis, who was crossing with them, leaned over the side of the boat, and did not even speak when they approached him: and when Katie began her usual chatter, though even that was subdued, Lilias stopped her with a movement of her hand.

"They are all at their prayers," said Lilias. She spoke, not quite knowing what she meant; for it is doubtful whether this is enough to express that supreme accord and delight of Nature in her awakening, before she has begun to be troubled by her unruly inmate, man.

But Katie was not to be restrained for long. She acquiesced for the moment, her little soul being influenced for about that space of time. Then she got her arm round that of Lilias, and drew her aside.

"It is very bonnie," said Katie, "but I must speak to you. You never came home from a ball in the morning before, or you would not be so struck with it. It's always like this except when it is raining. Lilias, oh! I want to tell you; I will never forget what you did to-night, nor Philip either. He is just silly about it. He says that's what a good girl will do for a friend. I was just at the very end of what I could bear—I would have been hysterical or something. Fancy, bursting out crying in a ball-room! I believe I would have done it; I could not have put up with it a moment longer. That was why we went out upon the grass; it was very damp," said Katie, looking at her slippers. "I don't know what mamma will say when she sees my shoes."

"I wonder," cried Lilias, half disgusted, "that you can think about your shoes."

"I am not thinking about them—I am thinking what mamma will think. But, Lilias, that's not what I was going to speak of. We will never, never forget it, neither him nor me." (This is perfectly good grammar in Scotch, which was Katie's language, though she was not aware of it.) "And, Lilias, do you think you would, just out of kindness, keep it up for a while, like that?"

"Keep it up?—like what!" Lilias was bewildered, and looked in Katie's face for an explanation.

"Oh, surely you know what I mean. It would be no harm; I am the only person it could hurt, and it is I that am asking you to do it. Oh! Lilias, it is only to make Mrs. Stormont believe that it is you that Philip is after, and not me."

"Katie, are you crazy? Me that Philip is—after! Oh! how can you say such vulgar things?"

"Why should it be vulgar?" said Katie, growing pale at this reproach; "it is true. Philip has been after me as long as I can remember. What would you have me say—in love? Oh! but to say that just gives you a red face—it makes your heart jump. It sounds like poetry."

"And so it should, Katie; if it does not sound like poetry, it cannot be true."

"It is very well for you to say that; in the first place, you have no one—after you; at least, not as yet. And then you are a grander person than I am. It might suit you to talk of love, every day, but it would not suit me—oh, no! But that does not alter the thing; or, if you like to change the word, I am sure I am not heeding: if you will only, only— Oh! Lilias, for the sake of friendship, and because we all knew each other when we were little things—if you would only let Mrs. Stormont think that he was in love with you!"

A flush of somewhat angry pride came over the face of Lilias. She drew her arm away from Katie's clinging grasp, which scarcely would consent to be detached.

"I don't know what you mean. I think you must want to insult me," she cried.

"What good would it do me to insult you?" cried Katie, reproachfully. "Instead of that I am just on my knees to you. Oh! don't you see what I mean? We want to gain a little time. If she does not consent, nobody will consent, nor even mamma, and never, never papa. They will not go against his mother. And Philip is very dour: he would quarrel with her, if it came to a struggle. That is what I am frightened for. If she thinks it is you, she will never stop him from coming. She will be so pleased, she will do whatever he likes, and we will be able to meet almost every day, and no suspicion. Oh! Lilias, what harm would it do you?" cried Katie, clasping her hands.

Lilias was taken entirely by surprise. Her action in the midst of the dance had been quite unpremeditated. She had been struck by sudden pity to see Philip so dark and gloomy, and little Katie, in her excitement, so near to self-betrayal. She looked with dismay now at the little pleading face, so childish, yet occupied with thoughts so different from those of a child. To think the elder ladies, Katie's mother, her own sisters, should be so near and so little aware what was passing.

"How could I pretend anything like that?" she said. "I would be ashamed. I could not do it. And what would it come to in the end?"

"It would all come right in the end, if we only could have a little time," said Katie. "Oh, Lilias, here we are at the shore. Just say yes, or I will break my heart."

"Why should you break your heart?" Lilias said, looking with dismay and trouble upon the little countenance just ready to dim itself with weeping, the big tears just gathering, the corners of the mouth drooping.

But next moment the boat grated on the shore. Lewis came forward to give them his hand. The brougham, with a little plunge and roll, came to land, and Mrs. Seton's voice was heard with its habitual liveliness and continuance.

"No, no, we'll not give you that trouble. We will just run home, Katie and I; it is no distance. No, no, I could not let you put yourself about for me, and Lilias in her satin shoes. Katie's are kid, and will take no harm. We are quite used to it; it is what we always do. Good night, or, I should say, good morning; and many thanks for bringing us so far. Katie, gather up your frock, we will be home in a minute," Mrs. Seton said. "No, no, Mr. Murray, there is no need for you either. In a minute we will be at our own gate."

Lilias stood in the clear morning light, looking after them as they hurried away, neglecting the call of her sisters and the attitude of Lewis, who stood waiting, holding open the door of the brougham. The still morning, the village street, without a creature moving, the sleep-bound look of the cottages, and the two figures disappearing like muffled ghosts into the lane which led to the manse, was like a story to the girl—a story into which she had stumbled somehow in the middle of it, but in which she was about to play a part against her will. She shivered a little with the excitement and bewilderment, and also because this fresh, clear, silvery air, so still, yet tingling with the merry twitter of the birds, was a little chill too.

"Lilias, Lilias, do not stand there. And the poor horse just dropping with sleep, and Sanders too."

"And you will catch your death of cold," added Miss Jean.

But it was Lewis holding out his hand to help her into the carriage who roused Lilias. He looked at her with an admiring sympathy, so full of understanding and appreciation of her difficulty, as she thought, that it brought her back to herself. Had he heard what Katie had been saying? Did he know the strange proposal that had been made to her? She looked at him with a question and appeal in her eyes, and she thought he answered her with a re-assuring look of approval and consolation. All this was imagination, but it gave her a little comfort in her bewilderment. He put her into the carriage with a touch of her hand, which seemed to mean more than the mere little unnecessary help. It did mean a great deal more, but not what Lilias supposed; and then the slumberous old horse and old Sanders, scarcely able to keep his eyes open upon the box, got the old vehicle into motion again, and Lewis, too, disappeared like a shadow, the only one upon the silent road. Margaret and Jean looked like two ghosts, pale in the light of morning.

"Well, that is one thing well over—but as for sleeping in one's bed at this hour, with all the birds singing, it is just impossible," Miss Margaret said.

CHAPTER XXVIII

Next morning Katie appeared at the old castle before Lilias had woke out of her first deep sleep. They had gone to bed after all, notwithstanding that Margaret pronounced it impossible, and even the two sisters were an hour late for breakfast. But it was now noon, and Lilias' windows had not yet been opened. Katie, who was, in comparison, well used to dissipation, contemplated her friend's privileges with admiration.

"Mamma will always make me come down to breakfast," she said, plaintively. "She just never minds. She says balls are all very well if they are never supposed to interfere with next day; and the consequence is I just feel as if I were boiled," said Katie.

"You are looking just as usual," said Miss Margaret.

Katie pouted a little at this re-assuring statement, but afterwards recovered, and begged leave to be allowed to carry up the cup of tea which was being prepared for the darling of the house.

"You may come with me," said Miss Jean; "but I must go myself, for I am afraid she may have got a cold after all the exposure last night."

Katie went upstairs after Miss Jean, with various reflections upon the happiness of Lilias.

"I was exposed just the same. Oh! much more," cried Katie to herself, "but nobody thinks I can ever take cold."

What differences there were between one girl and another; Mrs. Stormont would give her little finger if Philip would marry Lilias, and would not hear of Katie, though she was Philip's choice. These things were inscrutable. And the luxury of Lilias' room, the tray set down by her bed-side, the soft caution of the awakening, and Miss Jean's low tones, "I have brought you your breakfast, Lilias." Katie thought of her own case, called at seven as usual, in the room she shared with two little sisters, plagued by half a dozen appeals. "Oh, will you tie my hair, Katie! Oh, will you fasten my frock!" when her eyes were scarcely open. This it is to be an only child, an heiress, a lady of high degree. And, when Lilias opened her eyes and saw Katie beside her, her look of alarm was unquestionable. She jumped up from among her pillows.

"Is anything wrong?" she said.

"I just came," said Katie, "to talk over the ball. I thought you would want to talk it all over. When it is your first ball, it is not like any other. But we got home quite safe, and opened the door and were in bed without waking anyone. And I was up to breakfast as usual," Katie said.

"Lilias is not used to such late hours," said Miss Jean. "She never was up so late in all her life, and neither Margaret nor I have seen the early morning light like that for years—except in cases of sickness and watching, which is very different. It was a great deal finer than the ball, though at your age perhaps it is not to be expected that you should think so."

Katie opened her eyes wide, and gave Miss Jean a puzzled look. To be sure there were many agitations in her little soul that did not disturb a middle-aged existence. She was anxious to get rid of the elderly sister to pour out her heart to the young one who could understand her.

"Don't you think it was a very nice ball?" said Katie. "I never sat down once, and it was not too crowded, either. Oh! I like when you have no more room than just enough to get along. I don't mind a crowd. It makes you feel it's a real ball, and not just a little dance. Mr. Murray dances beautifully. Didn't you think so, Lilias? I saw you, though you refused so many people; and you danced three times with him, including—" Here Katie paused, with a blush and a sudden recollection of the presence of Miss Jean.

"Did I?" cried Lilias, with a look of great surprise. "I did not think of it. I suppose that is what you call wrong, too, to dance with some one that is nice to dance with, instead of just taking anyone that comes?"

Lilias was somewhat proud of having carried her point. Her evening had been triumphant, in spite of her daring exercise of her right of choice.

"My dear," said Miss Jean, mildly, "everything depends upon the meaning you have. The like of Mr. Murray will never harm you; he is not thinking of any nonsense. And he is a stranger; he has nobody belonging to him."

Katie gave a little cough of dissent. It was all that she permitted herself. And Miss Jean did not leave the room till Lilias had taken, which she was nothing loth to do, the dainty little breakfast that her sister had brought her. This represented the very climax of luxury to both the girls, and Jean looked on benignant with a pleasure in every morsel her little sister consumed, which the most exquisite repast could not have given her.

"Now I will leave you to talk about your dances," she said; "but, Lilias, Margaret will like you to be up soon, and ready for your reading. We like you to have a good sleep in the morning, but not to be idle all day." She gave them a tender smile as she went away. "Now you will just chatter nonsense—like two birds in a bush," she said. She could remember faintly, from her old girlish experiences, the talk about this quadrille and that country dance, for waltzes had scarcely penetrated into the country in Miss Jean's day, and about the new figures, and the new steps, and how So-and-so was a stupid partner, and So-and-so an amusing one. She thought she knew exactly the sweet nonsense they would rush into, like two birds, she said, in the headlong twitter of domestic intercourse crowding their notes and experiences together, as the birds had done that morning, till the listeners felt as if they were eavesdropping. It would be like that, not much reason in it, one scarcely stopping to listen to the other, each full of her own reminiscences, a sort of delightful gibberish—but so sweet!

Instead of this, Katie ran to the doors, when Miss Jean departed, to see that they were all closed, and then rushed back and took her seat upon the bed, where Lilias was sitting up among her pillows, her fair locks streaming about her shoulders.

"Oh, I have so much to say to you, Lilias," Katie cried, and threw herself upon her friend and kissed her. "I should have hated to think of last night if it hadn't been for you. Oh! Lilias, you are just going to be our salvation."

"How can that be?" said Lilias. "I did not mean anything. Oh! Katie, never think about that any more. It was just a silly impulse—I did not mean it."

"But when I ask you," said Katie—"and when you know it will be so important for Phil and me—and when you see the power you have, and that only you can do it—oh! Lilias, you will not turn your back upon me—you will stand our friend?"

"I should not turn my back on anyone," said Lilias; "but what am I to do, and how can I stand your friend? Just let me alone, Katie, please. I am too ignorant—I don't know about these sort of things. Philip and you should not be like that when everybody objects. I am sure I would not vex Margaret and Jean, not for any man."

"That is all you know," said Katie, shaking her head. "That just means that you do not know the man. When your time comes, you will just carry on like the rest. And nobody said a word about Philip and me till it was too late. We were let to be together as much as we liked; he was for ever at the manse, and nobody said a word. If mamma was against it, she might have told me; but just to step in at the last and say, 'We'll not allow it,' and never a word of warning before, that is cruel," Katie said, with an angry flash from her eyes. "And now they think they can just part us as if we were two sticks!"

Lilias could not deny that there was reason in what was thus said.

"But you should have told your mother, Katie, before—"

"Told my mother!—do you think you can tell your mother all the nonsense that is said to you? Most part of it is just nonsense. I would think shame. When they speak of love and things like that, either you laugh, or—or—you put faith in it," Katie said. "It would not be fair to tell when you just laugh, and, when you believe, you think shame."

Katie's little countenance, flushing and glowing, her little head shaken from time to time as she delivered these words of wisdom, her eyes full of many experiences, gave weight to what she said.

"But, Katie, you are younger than I am," said Lilias, "and where did you find out all that? It is Latin to me."

"It is being in the world," said Katie, with great gravity. "You see, I am the eldest, and I was brought out very early, perhaps too early, but mamma did not think so. She always said, 'Her sisters will just be on her heels before we know where we are,' and that was how it was. But I am not so young—I am seventeen," said Katie, drawing herself up with the air of a woman of thirty. Her own private opinion was that a woman of thirty was approaching decrepitude, and no longer likely to interest herself in matters of the heart.

"I shall not be eighteen till August, and your birthday is—"

"Oh, what does it matter about a month or so?" said Katie. "I am far, far older than you are: and if I were only six, that does not make it any easier; for here is Philip and me that they are wanting to separate, and we will never, never give each other up. And, Lilias," she added, dropping into tender confidence after this little outburst, "there is nobody that we put our faith in but you."

Lilias turned her head away from her friend. She was touched by the appeal, and she felt, as every girl would feel, a thrill of pleasure in being believed in, and in the idea of being able to help. Who does not like to be a guardian angel, the only deliverer possible. But along with this there came a shiver of alarm. How could she undertake such an office, and what would Margaret say?

"I told you in the ferry boat," said Katie, "but you were sleepy."

"Me! sleepy! when it was all so beautiful!"

"When you are up all night," said the young philosopher, "you never heed whether it is beautiful or not. But, any way, you did not understand. You were terrified, and then you thought it would bring you into trouble, and then—"

"I never thought it would bring me into trouble," cried Lilias, indignant. "I was not thinking of myself, and I was no more sleepy—! But to do something that is not true, to pretend—to cheat, for it would be cheating—"

"It would be nothing of the kind," said Katie, indignantly. "Do you think I'm asking you to go to Mrs. Stormont and tell her that Philip is in love with you? Oh! Lilias, don't be angry. It's just this. Let him come here sometimes—Miss Margaret would not mind; and then if you will come out with me for a walk in the afternoons? Oh! Lilias, it is not so much to do for a friend. It is quite natural that, when he sees you much, he should like you best. If he had never come to our house when he did, if he had never met me, if there had been no Katie at all," said the girl, with pathos; "of course it would have been you that Philip would have thought of. There would never have been another fancy in his mind; he would have loved you, and all would have gone well. Oh! what a pity," she cried, "what a pity that ever, ever there was a Katie at all!"

"You are the silliest little thing in the world," cried Lilias, starting up in her white night-dress, with her hair floating about her. "All would have gone well? Oh! you think I would have taken Mr. Philip Stormont? You think Margaret would have let me? Was there nothing to do but for him to take a fancy to me? Oh! that is just too much, Katie; that is more than I can put up with," she cried, with a spring on the floor. "Will you go away, please, and let me get up?"

Katie was prudent, though she was offended, and she was determined to gain her point.

"I will go into the library and wait there," she said. "But oh! Lilias, why will you be so angry with me?"

"I am not angry, if you would not speak such nonsense," Lilias cried.

"I will not speak nonsense, I will say nothing to displease you; but oh! Lilias, what will happen to me if you turn your back upon me?" said the girl.

She went away so humbly, with such deprecating looks, that Lilias not only felt her anger evaporate, but took herself severely to task for her sharpness with poor little Katie.

"After all, she is a whole year younger than me, whatever she says," Lilias said, sagely, to herself, "and a year makes a great difference at our age." Then her heart softened to Katie; if anything she could do would smooth over her poor little friend's troubles, what a hard-hearted girl she would be to deny it—

"Me that does nothing for anybody, and everybody so good to me!" Lilias said in her heart. It began to seem to her a kind of duty to take upon her the task Katie proposed. If it did them good, it would do nobody harm. If Margaret got a fright and thought that she—she, Lilias Murray of Murkley—was going to fix her choice upon Philip Stormont, it would serve Margaret right for entertaining such an unworthy idea. "Me!" Lilias cried, with a smile of profound disdain. But for Katie it was all very well. For Katie it was entirely unobjectionable. Philip was just the right person for her, and she for him. Lilias made as short work of any romantic pretensions which the Stormonts might put forth as her sister could have done. What were they, to set up for being superior to the minister's daughter? The Setons were well born, for anything Lilias knew to the contrary, and the others were but small lairds, not great persons. Perhaps Mrs. Stormont's favourite claim upon her as one who might have been her mother had irritated the temper of the daughter of Lady Lilias Murray. She had a scorn of the pretensions of the smaller family. Katie was "just as good," she declared to herself. All this process of thought was going on while Lilias went through the various processes of her toilet. When she went into the book-room, which was sacred to her studies, and found Katie there, she gave her little friend a condescending kiss, though she did not say much. And Katie, who was very quick-witted, understood. She did not tease her benefactress with questions. She was ready to accept her protection without forcing it into words.

And no doubt, in the days that followed, Margaret and Jean were much perplexed, it might even be said distressed. Philip Stormont began to pay them visits with a wearisome pertinacity. When he came he had not much to say; he informed them about the weather, that it was a fine day or a bad day, that the glass was falling, that the dew had been heavy last night, with many other very interesting scraps of information. But, when he had exhausted this subject, he fell to sucking the top of his cane. He was very attentive when anyone else spoke, especially Miss Margaret, and he looked at Lilias, perhaps as Katie had instructed him to look, with a gaze which indeed was more like anxiety than anything else, but which might do duty as admiration and interest with those who did not know the difference. To the outside spectator, who knew nothing about the conspiracy entered into by these young people, it would indeed have appeared very evident that Philip had been converted to his mother's opinion by the apparition of Lilias at the ball. And indeed the beauty of Lilias, like her position, was so much superior to that of Katie that nobody could have been surprised at the young man's change of opinion.

It might have been thought very natural too, that, after his early flirtations with the minister's daughter, whose mother brought her far too much forward, his fancy should have turned legitimately in a higher direction as his taste improved. Mrs. Stormont heard of her son's proceedings with the liveliest delight, giving God thanks indeed, poor lady, in her deceived heart that He had turned her boy's thoughts in the right direction, and given her this comfort when she needed it most. And she also applauded somewhat her own cleverness in having seen the right means for so desirable an end, and secured the début of Lilias at Philip's ball, an event which connected their names, and no doubt would make them feel themselves more or less bound to each other. Mrs. Stormont felt that little Katie was routed horse and foot, and also that poor Mrs. Seton, whom she considered a designing woman and manœuvring mother (entirely oblivious of her own gifts of that kind), was discomfited and thrown out, a thought almost as sweet to her mind as that of Philip's deliverance. And it would be wrong to say that Mrs. Seton herself did not feel a certain sense of defeat. When she met Philip going up the village towards the castle, the smile and banter with which she greeted him were bitter-sweet.

"I am really glad to see that you are finding some entertainment at Murkley," she would say. "I have so often been sorry for you with nothing to occupy you. Yes, yes, whatever women may think, a young man wants something to amuse him; and the ladies at the castle are most entertaining. Miss Margaret has just an uncommon judgment, and dear Miss Jean, we are all fond of her; and as for Lilias, that speaks for itself. Yes, yes, Mr. Philip, with a face like that, there is nothing more to say."

Philip listened to all this with wonderful composure. He secretly chuckled now and then at the ease with which everybody was taken in. "Even her own mother," he said to himself, with the greatest admiration of his Katie. Deception looks like a high-art to the simple intelligence when it is exercised to his own advantage, and even the highest moralist winks at the artifices with which a couple of young people contrive to conceal their courtship. It is supposed that the supreme necessity of the end to be obtained justifies such means: at least that would seem to be the original cause of such a universal condonation of offence.

Miss Margaret did not share Mrs. Stormont's sentiments. She had always been afraid of this long-leggit lad. He was just the kind of well-grown, well-looking production of creation that might take a young girl's eye, she felt, before she had seen anything better: and she blamed herself as much for permitting the ball as Philip's mother applauded herself for contriving it. Margaret was very far from happy at this period. The more Philip talked about the weather, and the more minute were the observations he made about the glass rising, or the dew falling, the more she looked at him, with a growing consternation, wondering if it were possible that Lilias could be attracted by such qualities as he exhibited.

"He is just a gomeril," she said, indignantly.

"Indeed, Margaret," Jean would say, "he is very personable, there is no denying that."

"He is just a great gowk," growing in vehemence, Miss Margaret said.

But, in fact, her milder, less impassioned statement was, after all, the true one. His chief quality was that he was a long-leggit lad, a fine specimen of rural manhood. There was nothing wrong, or undersized, or ill-developed about him. He had brain enough for his needs. He was far from being without sense. He had a very friendly regard for his neighbours, and would not have harmed them for the world. There was nothing against him; but then Lilias was the apple of the eye to these two ladies, who were entirely visionary in their ambition for her, and in all the hopes they had set on her head. That she should make a premature choice of one of whom all that could be said was, that there was nothing against him, was a terrible humiliation to all their plans and thoughts.

And in the afternoons, while July lingered out, with its warm days and rosy sunsets, the month without frost, the genial heart of the year, Lilias' walks were invariably accompanied by Katie, who, liberated as she was from visitors at home by Philip's desertion, ran in and out of the castle at all hours, and was the constant attendant of her friend. Philip would join them in their walks, which were always confined to the park, almost every day, and Lilias, at one moment or other, would generally stroll off by herself to leave them free. She got a habit of haunting New Murkley very much during these afternoon walks. She would wander round and round it, studying every corner, returning to all her dreams on the subject, peopling the empty place with guests, hearing through its vacant windows the sound of voices and society, of music and talk. How it was that those half-comprehended notes which entranced Jean and had established so warm a bond of union between her and the young stranger at Murkley should always be sounding out of these windows, Lilias could not tell, for she had professed openly her want of understanding and even of interest. But, notwithstanding her ignorance, there was never a day that in her dreams she did not catch an echo, among all the imagined sounds of the great house, from some room or other, from some corner, of Lewis Murray's music. Perhaps it was that she met himself so often about this centre of her lonely wanderings.

Generous though Lilias was, and ready to sacrifice herself for the advantage of her friends, it is not to be supposed that when she left those two together to the mutual explanations and consultations and confidences which took so long to say, she herself found much enjoyment in the solitude even of her own words, with the sense in her mind all the time that for the sake of the lovers she was deceiving her sisters, whom she loved much better, and in a lesser sense helping to deceive Katie's parents and Philip's mother, all of whom were more or less under the same delusion. It did not make Lilias happy; she fled to her dreams to take refuge from the questions which would assail her, and the perpetual fault-finding of her conscience. When Lewis appeared she was glad, for he answered the purpose of distracting her from these self-arraignments better even than her dreams; yet sometimes would be vexed and angry, disposed to resent his interest in the place as an impertinence, and to wonder what he had to do with it that he should go there so often and study it so closely, for he had always his sketch-book in his hand. She was so restless and uncomfortable that there were moments when Lilias felt her sense of propriety grow strong upon her, and felt disposed to treat the young man haughtily as an intruder, just as there were other moments when his presence was a relief, when she would plunge almost eagerly into talk, and betray to him, only half consciously, only half intentionally, the visions of which her mind was full. There got to be a great deal of talk between them on these occasions, and almost of intimacy as they wandered from subject to subject. It was very different from the conversation which Lilias carried on with her other companions, though she had known them all her life—conversations in which matters of fact were chiefly in question, affairs of the moment. With Lewis she spread over a much wider range. With that curious charm which the mixture of intimacy and new acquaintance produces, the sense of freedom, the certainty of not being betrayed or talked over, Lilias opened her thoughts to the new friend, whom she scarcely knew, as she never could have done to those whom she had been familiar with all her life. It was like thinking aloud. Her innocent confidences would not come back and stare her in the face, as the revelations we make to our nearest neighbours so often do. She did not reason this out, but felt it, and said to Lewis, who was at once a brother and a stranger, the most attractive conjunction—more about herself than Margaret knew, or even Jean, without being conscious of what she was doing, to the great ease and consolation of her heart.

But one of these afternoons Lilias met him in a less genial mood. She had been sadly tried in patience and in feeling. Mrs. Stormont had paid one of her visits that day. She had come in beaming with triumphant looks, with Philip in attendance, who, in his mother's presence, was even less amusing than usual. Mrs. Stormont had been received with very cold looks by Margaret, and with anxious, deprecating politeness by Jean, who feared the explosion of some of the gathering volcanic elements; and Lilias perceived to her horror that Philip's mother indemnified and avenged herself on Jean and Margaret by the triumphant satisfaction of her demeanour towards herself, making common cause with her, as it were, against her elder sisters, and offering a hundred evidences of a secret bond of sympathy. She said "we," looking at Lilias with caressing eyes. She called her by every endearing name she could think of. She made little allusions to Philip, which drove the girl frantic. And Philip himself sat by, having indeed the grace to look terribly self-conscious and ashamed, but by that very demeanour increasing his mother's urbanity and her triumph. Lilias bore this while she could, but at last, in a transport of indignation and suppressed rage, made her escape from the room and from the house, rushing out into the coolness of the air and silence of the park, with a sense that her position was intolerable, and that something or other she must do to escape from it. So far from escaping from it, however, she had scarcely got out of sight of the windows when she was joined by Katie, whose fondness and devotion knew no limits, and who twined her arm through that of Lilias with a tender familiarity which made her more impatient still.

The climax was reached when Philip's steps were heard hurrying after them, and Lilias knew as if she had seen the scene, what must have been the delight of Mrs. Stormont as he rose to follow her, and what the dismay and displeasure of Margaret and Jean. She seemed to hear Mrs. Stormont declare that "like will draw to like" all the world over, and to see the gloom upon the face of her mother-sisters.

"Oh! Lilias," Katie cried, "here he is coming; he can thank you better than I can; all our happiness we owe to you."

Lilias turned blazing with quick wrath upon her persecutor.

"Why should you be happy," she cried, "more than other people—and when you are making me a liar? Yes, it is just a liar you are making me!"

"Oh, Lilias, you are just an angel!" cried Katie, "and that is what Philip thinks as well as me."

"Philip!" cried Lilias, with a passion of disdain. She cast a look at him as he came up, of angry scorn, as if his presumption in forming such an opinion was intolerable. She drew her arm out of Katie's almost with fury, pushed them towards each other, and walked on swiftly with a silent step of passion which devoured the way. She was so full of heat and excitement that when she reached the new house of Murkley, and almost stumbled against Lewis, who was standing against a tree opposite the door, she gave a start of passion, and immediately turned her weapons against him. She cast a glance of angry scorn at the sketch-book in his hand.

"Are you here, Mr. Murray?" she cried, "and always your sketch-book, though I never see you draw anything. I wonder what you come for, always to the same spot every day; and it cannot be of any interest to you."

Lewis, who had not been prepared for this sudden attack, grew red with an impulse of offence, but checked himself instantly.

"You have entirely reason," he said, with his hat in his hand in his foreign way. "I do nothing; I am not, indeed, worth my salt. The sketch-book is no more than an excuse; and it is true," he added, "that I have no right to be here, or to claim an interest—"

There is nothing that so covers with discomfiture an angry assailant as the prompt submission of the person assailed, and Lilias was doubly susceptible to this way of putting her in the wrong. She threw down her arms at once, and blushed from head to foot at her own rudeness.

"Oh, what was I saying?" she cried—"what business have I to meddle with you, whether you were sketching or not? But it was not you—it was just vexation about—other things."

His tone, his look (though she was not looking at him), everything about him, expressed an indignant partisanship, which went to Lilias' heart.

"Why should you have any vexation? It is not to be borne!" he cried.

Lilias was so touched with this sympathy that it at once blew her cloud away, and made her feel its injustice more than ever, which is a not unusual paradox of feeling.

"Oh, what right have I to escape vexation?" she said. "I am just like other people." And then she paused, and, looking back, saw the two figures which she had abandoned in such angry haste turning aside into the woods. They cared nothing about her vexation, whoever did so. She laughed in an agitated way, as though she might have cried. There was no concealing her feelings from such a keen observer. "I suppose," she said, "that you are in the secret too?"

"I am in no secret," said Lewis, and his eyes were full of indignation; "but that you should be made the scapegoat—oh, forgive me! but that is what I cannot persuade myself to bear."

"Ah!" said Lilias, "how nice it is to meet with some one who understands without a word! But I am no scapegoat—it is not quite so bad as that."

"It ought not to be so at all," Lewis said, with a touch of severity that had never been seen in his friendly face before.

Lilias looked at him with a little alarm, and with a great deal of additional respect. And then she began to defend the culprits, finding them thus placed before a judge so much more decided than herself.

"They don't think I mind—they don't mean to hurt me," she said.

"But they do hurt you—your delicate mind, your honour, and sense of right. It is much against my interest," said Lewis, "I ought to plead for them, to keep it all going on, for otherwise I should not see you, I should not have my chance too; but it is more strong than me. It ought not to be."

Lilias did not know what to answer him. His words confused her, though she understood but dimly any meaning in them. His chance, too!—what did he mean? But she did not ask anything about his meaning, though his wonder distracted her attention, and made her voice uncertain.

"It is not so bad for me as it would be for them," Lilias said.

And then his countenance, which she had thought colourless often and unimportant, startled her as he turned towards her, so glowing was it with generous indignation. She had used the same words herself, or at least the same idea, but somehow they had not struck her in their full meaning till now.

"Why should they be spared at your expense? But you have no hand nor share in it," he said. "We must bear our own burdens."

"But, Mr. Murray," said Lilias, "what should you think of a friend that would not take your burden upon her shoulders and help you to bear it?" The argument restored her to herself.

"I should think such a friend was more than half divine," he said.

Lilias knew very well that she was not half divine, and Katie's declaration that she was an angel roused nothing but wrath in her mind; nevertheless she was curiously consoled in her troubles by this other hyperbole now.

CHAPTER XXIX

"This will never do," said Miss Margaret to Miss Jean.

They were sitting together with very serious faces after the triumphant departure of Mrs. Stormont, who had declared with a countenance full of smiles that to wait for Philip would be nonsense, since "when these young creatures get together there is no telling when we may see them again." The ladies had listened with grave looks, presenting a sort of blank wall of disapproval to their visitor's effusiveness, and when she had been seen to the door with stern politeness and cleared, as it were, out of their neighbourhood, they had returned and sat down for a few minutes without speaking, with many thoughts in their hearts.

"No," said Miss Jean, deprecating yet decided. "It is very natural, no doubt, on her side; but to expect you to be pleased with it—"

"Pleased with it! What is there to be pleased with?" cried Miss Margaret. "It is just a plot and a conspiracy—that is what it is, and Lilias has no more to do with it than you or me."

"If I thought that, Margaret—"

"If you just apply your mind to it, you will soon see that. She could not put up with that woman's petting and phrasing. If we had not brought her up to politeness, she would have said something. She just flew off when she could bear it no longer. And then that long-leggit Philip—if it had not been a look from his mother, he would not even have had the spirit to go after her. That woman is just a—"

"Oh! whisht, Margaret. I would not call her that woman; long-leggit or not, he is just her son, and she thinks much of him. Very likely," said Jean, "she thinks it would be a grand thing for Lilias if—"

"The impertinence of her is just boundless!" Margaret said; "but we cannot let ourselves be beaten and put out of all our plans, and our bonnie Lilias turned into just a common country laird's wife—not for all the Mistress Stormonts and all the long-leggit loons in Scotland!"

When Miss Margaret was excited, it was her habit to take advantage of a few strenuous words of what she would have called "broad Scots." She was no more Scotch perhaps at these moments than in her most dignified phraseology, to a southern ear; but to herself the difference was intense, and marked a crisis. It was as if she had sworn an oath.

"No, no, Margaret," said Miss Jean, soothingly—"no, no; we will never do that."

"And how are we to help it if we sit with our hands in our laps?" Miss Margaret cried. She got up in her excitement and began to pace through the room, which was such a home of quiet, with its brown wainscot and the glimmer of its many windows, that this agitation seemed to disturb it as if it had been a living thing. Jean followed her sister's movements with anxious eyes.

"Oh! Margaret," she said, "I am not afraid but you will think of something. If it was only me, it would be different; but, so long as there is you to watch over her—"

"What can I do, or anybody, if they will not be watched over, these young things?" Margaret said, sitting down as suddenly as she had sprung up. And then there was a moment of profound silence, as if the very walls were relieved by the cessation of that thrill of human movement. They had seen a great deal worse, these old walls, bloodshed and violence, and struggle and tumult; they seemed to treat with contempt, in their old-fashioned experience, a mere question about the managing of a silly little girl, or even her wooing, which was less important still.

Lilias was of opinion that she had already put up with quite too much annoyance on the subject when she got home. She had taken with great docility and sweetness the disapproval of Lewis, and been grateful to him for taking her part; but when Katie fell upon her with tears and kisses, and Philip, standing by with confused looks, sucked his stick, and murmured an assent to the praises and entreaties poured upon her, Lilias had not been able to withstand the importance of the position and the benedictions of the lovers. What should they do without her? She herself was not disinclined, when it was thus put before her, to recognise the necessity for her help, and that without her they must be ruined altogether; such a catastrophe, she felt, must be averted at all hazards. "It would just be my death," Katie said, weeping; "and oh, Lilias, we have been brought up together all our lives, and how could you see me perish like that?" Philip did not count for much in the matter. He was not unwilling perhaps that there should be a question of some one perishing for his sake, but he wanted to enjoy his walks and talks with Katie. Lilias, however, was altogether subdued by the idea of a funeral procession, and all the black hat-bands tied up by white ribbons. She felt that if Katie were to perish, it would be murder on her part. She yielded, notwithstanding her sense of wrong, and the disapproval of Lewis. After all, he had nothing to do with it—nobody had anything to do with it. If she chose to make herself a shield for the loves of Katie and Philip, it was her own business. Even Margaret had no right to interfere. But Lilias felt she had enough of it when she went home. She did not want to hear even the names of the people whom she was thus serving at so great a cost, and the remembrance of the scene with Mrs. Stormont and all her caresses was odious to her. She put it severely out of her mind. She resolved that for no inducement would she be present when Mrs. Stormont paid another visit, and that Philip should never be permitted to accompany his mother to the castle. These things she would insist upon, and then nothing so disagreeable as this past afternoon could happen again.

She stole in, a little breathless, and desirous of getting to her room unperceived. The result of so much agitation was that she had lingered longer than usual. There had been Lewis in the first place, who had a great deal to say, and then the lovers, from whom she had broken away in anger, had taken a long time to reconcile her. It was late, accordingly, when she got in, and by the time she had changed her dress, and was ready to appear in the drawing-room, it was very late, and her sisters were both waiting for her. They did not say anything at that moment, but contemplated her with very serious looks during their evening meal. Even old Simon perceived that something was coming. He showed his sympathy to "little missie" by offering her everything twice over, and anxiously persuading her in a whisper to eat.

"It will do you good, missie," he said in her ear; "you're taking nothing." He even poured out some wine for her, though she never took wine, and adjured her to drink it. "It will just be a support," he said.

These signs were not wanted to show Lilias that a storm was brewing. She was a little frightened, yet plucked up a courage when she heard Margaret clearing her throat. After all, she had done nothing that was wrong. But the form which the assault took was one which Lilias had not foreseen. They returned to the drawing-room before a word was said. By this time it was quite evening, the sunshine gone, and a twilight much more advanced than that out of doors lay in all the corners. Except the space in front of the windows, the room, indeed, was almost dark, and the bare walls seemed to contract and come close to hear what was going to be said.

"Lilias," said Miss Margaret, "Jean and I have been consulting about many things. You see, this is rather a dear place, there are so many tourists; and especially in the autumn, which is coming on, and the meat is just a ransom. Even in a little place like Murkley there are strangers, and Kilmorley just eats up all the provisions in the country."

Lilias' heart, which had been beating high in anticipation, sank down at this in her bosom with a delicious sense of relief and rest. There was nothing to be said then on any troublous subject, for who could be excited about the tourists and the price of meat? She was glad she had not taken the wine, for there could be no need for it—evidently no need.

"I don't know anything about that, Margaret," she said. "I wish there was no meat at all."

"Yes, you are just a perverse thing about your eating," said Miss Margaret—"we all know that."

"And it is not good for you, my dear; it keeps you delicate," said Miss Jean.

"Oh!" cried Lilias, springing from her chair, "was that all you were going to speak to me about? And even Simon saw it, and brought me wine to drink to do me good; and it is only about the price of meat and provisions being dear! What do you frighten people for, if it is nothing but that?"

If Lilias had been wise, she would have perceived by Margaret's serious looks and the wistful sympathy in Jean's face that she was far as yet from being out of the wood; but, after the little bound of impatience which was habitual to her, she calmed down immediately, and made them a curtsey.

"I don't know what is dear and what is not dear," she said.

"Ah," said Margaret, shaking her head, "but if you were to marry a poor man, or into a struggling family that have more pretensions than they have money, you would soon have to change your mind about that. You would have to study what was dear and not dear then. You would have just to spend your life in thinking what he would like, and what they would put up with, and the price of butter, and how many eggs your hens were laying. I'm not averse to such things myself, but how the like of you would win through it—"

"I suppose," said Lilias, "when there is need for it, there is nobody who cannot do that?"

"Oh, Lilias, that is far from being the case, my dear," said Miss Jean. "It takes a great deal of thought, just like other things. Margaret there has just a genius—"

"It was not me we were speaking of," said Margaret. "I don't wish you to be exposed to that. It is a hard life for any young girl; and you have been bred with—other thoughts. I don't wish you, Lilias, to be exposed to that."

"You speak as if I wished it," said the girl. "Do I want to be poor? What I want is to be rich, rich! to have a great fortune, and finish the house, and fill it with people, and live like a lady—"

"You might do that without being rich," said Miss Jean, softly, which was a sentiment quite inappropriate to the occasion, and at which Margaret frowned.

"Well, that is a digression," the elder sister said. "We cannot tell whether you are to be rich or poor—we must just leave that in the hands of Providence; but in the mean time, not just to be ruined and over-run with those tourist cattle, I was thinking, and Jean was thinking, that if we were to retire a little and economize, and save two or three pounds before we go to London—to Gowanbrae."

"To Gowanbrae!" said Lilias, wondering, scarcely comprehending.

"My dear," they both said, together, "it will be far better for you. You will never be free of engagements here," Margaret went on, "after that unfortunate weakness of mine about letting you go to Mrs. Stormont's; and then, you know, we can face the winter quietly, and get all our things together for the season. And—what is it, Lilias? What is it, my pet? What is it, my dear? Oh, Jean, you said true. It is breaking her heart."

"Margaret! you will never be hard upon our darling—even if you cannot approve—"

Here Lilias, who had flung herself upon her elder sister, with her arms round her neck, sprang apart from her again, clasping her hands together with the impatience of a child.

"What is it you are saying about me?" she said. "Breaking my heart! when I am just like to dance with joy? Gowanbrae! that is what I want, that is exactly what I want. Oh, yes, yes, let us go, let us go to-morrow, Margaret. That will put everything right."

They sat in their high-backed chairs, looking at her like two judges, yet not calm enough for judges, full of grave anxiety yet tremulous hope. Margaret put up her hand to check Jean, who showed an inclination to speak.

"Not a word," she said, "not a word. Lilias, this is more serious perhaps than you think. All our plans and all our thoughts are for you. It's your good we are thinking of. But don't you trifle with us. When you say that, is it out of some bit quarrel or coolness? or is it to cheat your own heart? or is it a real conviction that it is for your safety and your good to go away?"

Lilias stamped her foot upon the floor. She clenched her hands in a little outburst of passion.

"Oh! you are just two—Oh! what are you making such a fuss about? It is neither for a quarrel nor for safety (safety! Am I in any danger?) nor for any other silly thing. It is just because I want to go. Oh, Gowanbrae! We have not been there for two years. I like it better than any place in the world. That was what I was pining for all the time, only I could not remember what it was!"

"It was just a little change she was wanting, Margaret," Miss Jean said.

Margaret did not make any immediate reply. She kept her eyes upon Lilias as a physician keeps his finger upon a pulse.

"You will get your wish then," she said. "This takes away the only doubt I had; and now we're all of one mind, which is a wonderful blessing in a house. As soon as the washing is done, and the things ready, we'll start; for that will just give them time to put up the curtains, and put everything right."

This was a somewhat dry ending to so emotional a discussion, but Miss Margaret, who was not fond of scenes, considered it best to restore everything to its matter-of-fact basis as quickly as possible.

"Go away, and play some of your music," she said to her sister, in an undertone, "and don't just carry this on, and put nonsense into people's heads." She took up her stocking, which she had dropped. "Bless me," she said, "how much shorter the days are growing, though we are only in July. Gowanbrae is just beautiful in the autumn, and warm for the winter. Your old castle, Lilias, is grander, but there is more sun in the south country."

"Margaret, if you will make comparisons, I shall have to stand up for Murkley," cried Lilias. "But I like the one just as well as the other, winter and summer."

"Which is all that is necessary," said Miss Margaret, nodding her head. "Now take your book or something in your hands to do, for I cannot bide to see a young person sitting idle. It's not becoming either in young folk or old; and work is best, in my opinion; for doing nothing but reading books just bewilders the brain," Miss Margaret said.

Nevertheless, it was with a book in her arms that Lilias stole into the window, where Miss Jean usually sat with her work. She took the book, but she did not read. It was now dark enough to conceal from the quick eyes of Margaret how far she was carrying out her injunction, and Lilias was in so considerable a commotion of mind that she was glad to retire into her own thoughts. Jean's music made no very strong appeal to either of her listeners. She sat in the further part of the room in the dimness, scarcely perceptible, and filled the silence with soft strains which formed a sort of accompaniment to thought, and did not interrupt it. Miss Margaret in the middle of the room, with such light as remained centering in her face and the hose upon her hand, sat motionless in her high chair. She had allowed her stocking to drop upon her lap; though she had made that protestation against idleness, she was herself doing nothing. Perhaps she was listening to the music, for now and then she would say, "That is a very bonnie thing you have just been playing," or, "What was that? for I liked it, Jean." She said this, however, night after night, at the same place, so that it is to be feared she did it purely out of sympathy, and not from any appreciation of the "bonnie thing" of which she desired so often to know the name.

The soft shadows gathered over the group thus composed. Lilias in the window, her profile showing against the light, sat in a hush of relief and calm, never stirring, half conscious only of the dim background, of Margaret in the chair, and Jean at the piano; other pictures were before her eyes. Katie all in tears, hearing with consternation the news of this unlooked-for change; Philip sucking his cane; Lewis—Ah! she could not but wonder a little what Mr. Murray would think of it. He would be glad, no doubt; he would approve; he would think it a good thing that she should go away, and no longer be a screen to the lovers. Then Lilias wondered a little, with a faint sense of mingled amusement and—no, not regret. Why should she regret or care at all about it? He was Jean's friend, not hers. But it was not possible not to be moved by a question or two in respect to him. Would he go to New Murkley as often, would he stand with his sketch-book in his hand never drawing a line, would he take as much interest in it all when she was no longer there? A faint smile woke about the corners of her mouth. Nobody could see it to ask what she was smiling at. To such a question she would have answered, "Nothing;" and it was nothing, only a vague, amused wonder in her own mind. He would be glad she was going away, but—The road through the park and the grass-grown spaces round the great empty house, would no one at all linger about them now? Not Katie, who could no longer have the excuse of coming to her friend; nor Philip, whom no doubt his mother, much disappointed, would keep a closer hold upon than ever. But Lilias did not care so much about them. What would the other do, who was a stranger, who took such an interest in the vacant palace? The smile continued upon her face; perhaps, though she said "No, no!" vehemently to herself, there was a slight sensation of regret, a little blank in her heart. She wondered whether it would all come to an end? whether, when the fishing was over (but he did not care for the fishing), he would disappear and be seen no more? or whether he would turn out to be somebody, and to have a real interest in Murkley? He might be, not the Australian cousin, but perhaps a son of that superseded benefactor, secretly inspecting his cousins before he disclosed the link of kindred; he might be—But here Lilias turned back again, quite illogically, breaking her self-argument off in the middle, to repeat all these wonderings from the beginning. Would he drop out of their knowledge when they left Murkley? would they ever see him again? what would happen? But why should anything happen? No doubt he would just go away when it began to grow dull in Murkley, and be seen no more. Lilias had a consciousness that it would grow very dull in Murkley when she herself went away, and perhaps it was this that made her, after the first moment of pleasure with which she had heard of the proposed change, feel something that it would be wrong to call sadness—a little blank, a subdued sensation of regret, not for herself, as if she were leaving anything, but for the others. And of course it would be the stranger, he who had no other thing to amuse him, who would feel it most.

The news of the revolution and radical change of all the conditions of life which had thus been decided upon reached the stranger with the utmost promptitude and distinctness. Miss Margaret herself was not aware of having revealed it to anyone but her confidential maid when it came like a thunderbolt upon Lewis, something which it had not entered into his mind to fear. He had been engaged all the morning in finishing a sketch of New Murkley which he meant to offer—to Lilias, if permitted—if not, to her sisters, and which he had hoped would bring about some new rapprochement, some further step in the intercourse which had as yet so little sanction from the heads of the house, and which he was almost nervously anxious to reveal; for even his own chance meetings with Lilias, which had followed in the train of the other imprudent business to which she had given her protection, troubled the young man's conscience and aroused his prejudices, although against himself. He was as anxious to get the sanction of authority for these meetings, and even to betray himself, as Philip was to shelter in the slender shadow of Lilias and keep his real wooing secret. This had kept him from his usual morning saunter by the river-side, and, when Adam arrived late for his dinner with a basket of trout, Lewis, who had heard Janet's not very amiable greeting of her husband from the open window, went down to see the results of the fisherman's morning work. It was not very great, and Janet stood with a disproportionately large ashet[1] in her hand, which she seemed to have chosen from the biggest in her possession, while Adam took from his basket deliberately one by one a few small fish. She greeted each as it appeared with a little snort.

[Footnote 1: A dish, from the French assiette.]

"Well, that was worth the trouble! Eh, but that's just grand for a day's work! It shows the valley o' a man to see that."

"Ye talk about the valley o' a man that ken nothing about it," said Adam, "the smawller they are they gi'e the mair trouble whiles. But here is ane that was a dour ane," he added, after a pause, producing at last a fish of reasonable size. "He's taken me maist of my mornin'. Up the water and down the water he's tried a' the ways o't. A fish is a queer beast: it has nae sense o' what's possible. Would you or me, Mr. Murray, think life worth leevin' with a hook through our jaws? though I will not say but there are human creatures that gang through it little better off."

"Some would be a' the better for a hook through their jaws; it would keep them from havering," said Janet, tartly.

"Deil a bit. No if it was a woman, at least, wha will haver till her last breath, if she had all the lines in Tay grippit to that souple jaw o' hers. But you would think," said Adam, dropping into his usual tranquil strain after this outburst, "that a trout, gey high up as I have heard in the awquatic organizations, would have the sense to ken that a glancing, darting thing like a fishing-line with a far cleverer cratur at the other end o't—"

"Eh, but the troutie would be sair deceived! ye mean a blind, blundering cratur that a bit thing like this can lead a bonnie dance up the water and down the water, as you say yoursel'. Fishes maun ha'e their ain thochts like the rest o' us, and ye mightna be flattered if ye heard them, for a' you think so little o' their opinion."

"The inferior creation," said Adam, calmly, "have a' their bits o' blasphemies against man, who is their lord and master; but nobody could think little o' the opinion, if ye could get at it, of a cratur that had such a warstle for its life. Think o' a' the cunning and the cleverness, and what you would ca' calculation, and its wiles and its feints to draw aff your attention. Na, I canna have a gallant beast like that put into a frying-pan in my house."

"Then, Mrs. Janet," said Lewis, always courteous, "you will put it in a basket and send it to the castle, and I will tell the ladies that it is a hero, or a great general, to be eaten tenderly."

"My poor young gentleman," said Janet, with a sort of compassionate contempt, "whatever you have to send to the Misses, you must send it soon, soon! for a' is settled and packit, and they're starting for the south country."

"The south country!" said Lewis, in dismay. The announcement was so sudden that it bewildered him, and, once more deceived, he thought of Italy. "But why—what is the matter? What has happened?" he cried; "they are not poitrinaires. Ah, I forgot, it is something else you mean by the south."

"I mean just their ain house, that is near Moffat, a bonnie enough place, but no like Murkley. I thought, sir, you would have heard," said Janet, fixing her eyes upon him. She had become greatly devoted to her lodger, but human curiosity is stronger even than affection, and she was anxious to know how he would take this blow which, she felt sure, would crush all his hopes.

And, indeed, Lewis grew a little pale; his surprise was great, a sickening disappointment came over him; but yet, along with it, a certain relief. His mind had been greatly disturbed by the existing position of affairs. He had a passing sense that he was glad in the midst of his downfall. Janet could not comprehend how this was.

"It must be very sudden," he said, moistening his lips, which the sudden shock had made dry: and he grew pale, and his face lengthened; but nevertheless he had a smile which contradicted these signs, so that the keen observer at his side was at a loss.

"The mair need to lose no time with the trout," said Adam; "and, besides, it's always best caller from the water. Janet, have ye a basket? I'll take it up mysel'."

"Oh, ay, onything that means stravaighin'," said Janet, bitterly. "Just gi'e a glance round ye, my man, and see if ye canna capture a basket for yersel'."

But these passages of arms amused Lewis no more. He walked upstairs very gravely into his parlour, where his sketch stood upon a small easel. Would there not be time even to finish it? His face had grown a great deal longer. This was an end upon which he had not at all calculated: and somehow an end of any kind did not seem so desirable as it had done an hour ago, when none seemed likely. The reign of Philip and Katie, after all, was not, perhaps, so much harm.

CHAPTER XXX

It was curious how the aspect of everything had changed to Lewis when he walked up the now familiar way to the old Castle of Murkley through the sunshine of the July afternoon. It was still full summer, but there seemed to him a cloud in the air—a cloud too subtle to show upon the brightness of the unsympathetic blue, but which indicated storm and change. The trees were almost black in the fulness of their leafage, dark green, no tender tints of spring lingering among them, as there had still been when he first came to the little village on the river-side, and first saw those turrets sheltered among the trees. What a difference since then! The unknown, with all its suggestions, had disappeared; he was aware what he was likely to meet round every corner. But the excitement of a life in suspense had only been intensified. When he came to Murkley, with the virtuous intention of bestowing himself and his fortune upon one of old Sir Patrick's disinherited granddaughters, there had been no very entrancing expectations in his mind. He had not thought of falling in love, but of accomplishing his duty. That duty he would have been happy to accomplish under the gentle auspices of Miss Jean. He would never have grumbled at the twilight life he should have spent with her; no such radiant vision as Lilias had ever flitted across his imagination, nor had he expected, in case his suit should be rejected (a possibility which at first, indeed, he had not taken into account), to return with anything less agreeable than that calm sense of having done his duty which consoles a man for most small disappointments. But now all this was changed. In the case he had supposed beforehand, a refusal would have been an emancipation. He would have felt that he had done all he could, and was now free to enjoy unfettered what he had felt the justice of sharing, should they please, with one of the natural heirs. But Lewis felt now that the whole question had been opened, and did not know where he might find himself, or what he might feel to be his duty if he failed now. It had been easy to put all that aside when he knew that Lilias was near him, that he had the same chance as all her countrymen, and was free to speak to her, to exercise what charms he might possess. Every decision was stopped naturally, every calculation, even, until it appeared whether in this supreme quest he might have good fortune. But when she should be gone, what would happen? When she should be gone, the glory would be gone out of everything. Murkley would turn into a dull little village, full of limited rural people, and his own life would appear as it was, a mere exotic, without meaning or rule. There was a meaning in it now, but then there would be none.

He walked up the village-street with that suddenly elongated countenance, feeling that everything was crumbling about him. The children with their lintwhite locks, the fowls sheltering beneath the old cart turned up on the roadside, the slow, lumbering figures moving about across the fields and dusty roads, struck him for the first time with a sense of remoteness. What had he to do among them? It was impossible to imagine anything more entirely unlike the previous tenor of his life, and if he failed—if he did not succeed in the suit which, as soon as he thought of it, seemed to him preposterous, what would his life become? Whatever it was, it would be very different from Murkley, and any existence that was possible there. Accordingly it was not only his love that might be disappointed, but his life, which probably would entirely change. Very few men have this to contemplate when they think of putting their fortune to the touch, unless it is those men who take up marriage as a profession, a class fortunately very few.

The ladies were all in, Simon said. He had made an alteration in his appearance which revealed a high sense of the appropriate. He had an apron upon his person, and several straws at his feet, which he stooped to pick up.

"You'll excuse us, sir, if we're not just in our ordinary," Simon said. "You see we're packing." A hope that he would be the first to tell it, and that explanations might be demanded from him, gave vivacity to Simon's looks. But he relapsed into gravity when Lewis, with that long face, gravely replied that he was very sorry, and that it must have been a sudden resolution. "Things is mostly sudden, sir," said Simon, with a dignified sense of superiority, "in a lady's house. Miss Jean is in the drawing-room, but Miss Margaret is up the stair."

Lewis stood, with his heart beating, under the old man's calm inspection.

"I am going to see Miss Jean," he said, "but afterwards will you ask, Simon, if Miss Murray will grant me an interview. There is something—I wish to ask her."

"Lord bless us!" said Simon, "you'll no be meaning—"

And then he stopped short, eyeing Lewis, who stood half angry, half amused under this inspection. The old servant's eyes had a twinkle in them, and meant much, but he recollected himself in time.

"You'll be meaning Miss Margaret," he said. "I'll allow it's ridiculous, with the two leddies here; but the one that is Miss Murray according to all rights is Miss Lilias—for she is Miss Murray of Murkley, and the other two leddies, they're just the Miss Murrays of Gowanbrae. That was, maybe, the General's fault: or, maybe, just his wisdom and far-seeingness; for he was a clever man, though few saw it. Old Sir Patrick, the old man, he was just the very devil for cleverness," Simon said.

This did not sound like a servant's indiscretion, but the somewhat free opinion of a member of the family, which was how Simon considered himself. He made a little pause, contemplating Lewis with a humorous eye, and then he said,

"I'll take ye to Miss Jean, sir, and then I'll give your message to Miss Margaret. I will say in half an hour or three-quarters of an hour, that they may be sure not to clash."

"That will do very well," said Lewis, not knowing why it was that Simon twinkled at him with so admiring an eye.

The old servant smote upon his thigh when he had introduced the visitor into the drawing-room.

"If one will not do, he'll try the other. But, Lord save us, to tackle Miss Margaret! Eh, but yon's a lad of spirit," Simon said. For the little episode of the devotion of Lewis for Miss Jean had not passed unobserved by the keen eyes of the domestic critics. They understood what had happened as well as Lewis, and considerably better than Jean did, though with consternation, not knowing what the young man's object could be. No doubt he had thought that she was the one that had the siller, they concluded, but his desire to have an interview with Miss Margaret convulsed the house with wonder.

"Miss Margaret will soon give him his answer," said the cook, indignant. "I would have turned him about his business, if it had been me, and tellt him our ladies werena in."

"Would you have had me file my conscience with a lee?" said Simon; and then he added, with a chuckle, "I wish the keyhole was an honest method, or I could get below the table. I would sooner see them than ony play."

"She will send him away with a flea in his lug," said the angry cook.

Meanwhile Lewis, unsuspecting that his designs were so evident, went into the drawing-room, where Miss Jean sat as usual. She gave him her usual gentle smile.

"Come away," she said, "Mr. Murray. I am very glad to see you. I should have sent for you, if you had not come. For it will not be much longer I will have the pleasure—We are going away from Murkley for a time. It is sudden, you will think, but that is just because we have kept it to ourselves. Murkley is just a terrible place for gossip," Miss Jean said.

There was a little pause. It was one of those crises in which there is much to say, but no legitimate means of saying it. "I am very sorry," said Lewis. Miss Jean, on her side, was much embarrassed, for somehow it seemed to her that she had acted unkindly, and forgotten the claims of this young man who threw himself in so strange, yet so trusting, a way on her consideration. The events of the former interview, in which there had been so much agitation, she had never formally explained to herself. The shyness of her sweet old-maidenhood had eluded the question. She had never asked herself what he meant, or why it was that she had taken the extreme step of narrating to him the history of her own love. She had done it by instinct at the moment, and the doing of it had agitated and occupied her mind so much that she scarcely thought of Lewis. But she had retained a warmer kindness for him, a sense of having more to do with him than the others had, and she felt now as if she had deserted him, almost betrayed his trust in her.

"You see," she said, a little anxiously, "we are not just free agents, Margaret and me. There is always Lilias to think of. What is good for her is the thing we are most guided by: and we think a change will be good for her."

"And I am sure you are quite right in thinking so," said Lewis, hastily. It was a thing he had no right to say. He reddened with embarrassment and alarm when he had thus committed himself, and said, hurriedly, "Everything, of course, must give way to that."

"You have thought her looking—pale? That is just what we have been thinking, Margaret and me. And what is a very good thing is, that she's fain, fain to go to Gowanbrae herself. That is our little place in the south country, Mr. Murray. I am sure that if you were—passing that way at any time, Margaret would be very glad to see you." Jean said this, however, with but a half-assured air, and continued, hurriedly, "It would be taking much upon ourselves to say you would perhaps miss us: for you have many friends already in this country-side, and this house is a very quiet house for you to find pleasure in; but it vexes me just to cease to see you when we were beginning to know you."

"I will come to—the south country—with pleasure," said Lewis; then he added, seeing her hesitation, "We shall meet, perhaps, in town."

"That will be the surest," said Miss Jean, brightening; "we will be there by March, from all Margaret says. So far as she can hear, that is the time when the drawing-rooms begin. If you are in London, that will just be a great pleasure to look forward to, Mr. Murray. Dear me! to think of meeting you among strangers, and hearing you play, and all as if we were still at Murkley, in a great, vast, terrible place like yon London! And where shall we hear of you? You will have a club, or something. But, after all, what can that matter?" Miss Jean added, with gentle dignity; "you will always be able to hear of the Miss Murrays of Murkley; and you will tell me where I can hear good music, that is one thing I am looking forward to."

"Are you too busy? or may I play to you now?" he said.

"Oh, no, I could never be too busy," said Miss Jean, "and, as a matter of fact, I have nothing to take me up. Margaret is just a woman in a thousand. She thinks nobody can do a thing right but herself. I would be sitting with my hands before me but for this work that they all laugh at. And never, never could I be too busy for music," she said, with a little sigh of satisfaction, turning her face towards the piano. Lewis was in that condition of suspense in which a man, with his mind all directed to the near future, is scarcely conscious what he is doing in the present. There had been a moment before in which his heart had beat very anxiously in this same room, but with a very different kind of anxiety from this. There lay before him then no dazzling possibility of happiness, but now the hurry and tumult in all his veins was moved by the knowledge that everything which was most beautiful in life was before him. He did not expect that he was to get it. He had no hope that Miss Margaret would open the doors of the house or the arms of the family to him. But the mere idea of declaring himself, of making the attempt, made his heart beat. It was almost certain, indeed, that he would be rejected, but he had learned now to know that no such injustice could be final. After Margaret, there was another tribunal. Parents might frown, yet it was always possible in England that the maiden herself would smile. He felt that, be the answer what it might, when he opened his lips this day he would open up the supreme question of his life. And yet, with this ferment in his being, he went to the piano to play to the gentle listener who was never too busy for music. He himself, though he was an enthusiast in his way, was too busy for it now; he could not hear the sounds that came out from under his fingers for the strong pulsations that beat in his heart and made every other sound indifferent to him. In consequence of this, it happened to Lewis to do what all artists have to do sometimes, whether man or woman, seeing that life is more urgent than art. He played with his hands not less skilfully, not less smoothly than usual, but he did not play with his soul, and of all people in the world Miss Jean was the most sensitive to the difference. She loved music not for its technicalities, or for its execution, or for the grammar and correctness of its construction. She loved it for the soul of it, by instinct and not by purpose, and the fine dissatisfaction that arose in her when she felt it came to her from his fingers only is more than can be said. A veil of bewilderment came over her face. Was it her own fault? was her mind taken up with the excitement of the journey, the cares which she shared with her sister respecting Lilias? Miss Jean placed herself at the bar with a sort of consternation. But it was not she who was to blame. Had she received it as usual with serene satisfaction and delight, he would have continued for some time at least, anxious and excited though he was; but when the support of her faith was withdrawn, this became impossible. He stopped abruptly when he came to the end of the movement he was playing, broke into a wild fantasia, and finally jumped up from his seat after a great jar and shriek of outraged chords, holding out his hands in an appeal.

"Pardon!" he cried, "pardon! I cannot play a note—it is too strong for me, and you have found me out."

"You are not well," she said, with ready sympathy, "or there is something wrong."

"There is this wrong," he said, "that I think all my life is going to be settled to-day. You, whom I have always revered and loved since I first saw you, let me tell it to you. Oh! not the same as what happened the other day when you stopped my mouth. I do not know what you will think of me, but it was not falsehood one way or another. I had scarcely seen her then. I have asked Miss Margaret for an interview, and this time it is for life or for—no, I will not be fictitious, I will not say death: for that is not how one dies."

"An interview with Margaret?" Jean repeated after him. She grew a little pale in sympathy with his excitement. "My poor lad, my poor lad! and what is that for?"

But she divined what it was for. For a moment it startled her indeed. That gentle sense of property, of a sort of possession in him, which was involuntary, which was the merest shadow of personal consciousness, disturbed and bewildered her for a moment. Was this what he had meant all along? It gave her a little shock of humiliation, not that he should have changed his mind, but that she should have mistaken him. How glad she was that she had stopped him at once, that she had prevented all compromising words; but yet the possibility that she had been so ridiculous as to mistake as addressed to herself what was meant for Lilias, did touch Miss Jean's mind for a moment with a thrill of pain; the next she was herself again.

"It is Lilias you mean?" she said, in a low and tremulous voice.

He made no reply except with his eyes, in which there was an appeal to her for pardon and for help. He was too deeply moved and anxious, fortunately, to realize the ludicrous element in the situation, and, in his confusion and sense of guilt yet innocence, had no ridiculous admixture of the comic in his thoughts. Perhaps people are slow to see the humour in their own case: and Lewis had absolute trust in the patroness whom he addressed. Even had he supposed her to have a feeling of wrong in this quick transference of his suit, he would have opened his heart to her all the same. But he had no reason to suppose that Miss Jean could have any sense of wrong. She shook her head in reply to his look of confusion and appeal.

"She is just the apple of Margaret's eye," she said.

"And I am—no one," said Lewis.

"You must not say that; but you are not a great man. And Margaret thinks there is nobody good enough for her. I would not mind so much myself; you are young, and have a kind, kind heart. But you have said nothing to her?"

"What do you take me for?" said Lewis, with gentle indignation. Only a few words had been said, and his former attitude towards Miss Jean had not been one that would have seemed to make his present confidences natural: but the fact was that he had utter confidence in her, and she a soft, half-maternal compassion and sympathy for him which had ranged her on his side in a moment. They were born to understand each other. All that was confusing and embarrassing had blown away from the thoughts of both. They sat together and talked for some minutes longer, forgetting everything else in this entrancing subject; then she sent him away, bidding God bless him, to the more important interview which awaited him. Miss Jean dried her eyes, in which tears of sympathy and emotion were standing, as she closed the door upon him. It was a thing to stir the heart in her bosom. The first lover of Lilias! To think that little thing newly out of the nursery, who had been a baby but the other day, should have entered already upon this other stage of existence! Miss Jean sat down in her window again and mused over it with a tremor of profound sympathetic feeling in her heart. Bless the darling! that she should have come to this already. But then, what would Margaret say? He was not an earl nor a duke, but a simple gentleman. Even when you came to that, nobody knew what Murrays he was of; was there any hope that Margaret would yield her child to such a one? Miss Jean shook her head all alone as she sat and mused; her heart was sore for him, poor young man! but she did not think there was any hope.

As for Lewis, he walked to the library, in which Miss Margaret awaited him, with a sort of solemnity as men march to hear their sentence from the court-martial that has been sitting upon them. He had not much more hope than Miss Jean had, but he had less submission. He found Margaret seated in a high-backed chair of the same order as that which she used in the drawing-room—a commanding figure. She had no knitting nor other familiar occupation to take off the edge of her dignity, but sat expecting him, her hands folded upon her lap. She did not rise when he came in, but gave him her hand with friendly stateliness.

"Simon tells me you were wanting to speak to me, Mr. Murray. It is most likely our old man has made a mistake, and you were only coming to say good-bye."

"He has made no mistake," Lewis said; "there is something I wanted to say to you, to ask you. It is of the greatest importance to me, and, if I could hope that you would give me a favourable answer, it would be of importance to you too."

"Indeed!" she said, with a smile, in which there was some haughtiness and a shade of derision. "I cannot think of any question in which our interests could meet."

"But there is one," cried Lewis, anxiously. "And you will hear me—you will hear me, at least? Miss Murray, I once said something to you—I was confused and did not know—but I said something—"

"Not confused at all," said Miss Margaret. "You made your meaning very clear, though it was a very strange meaning to me. It was in relation to my sister Jean."

The young man bowed his head. He was confused now, if he had not been so then. All that Miss Jean's gentle courtesy had smoothed over for him he saw now in Margaret's smile.

"I hope," she said, pointedly, and with the derision more apparent than ever, "that the answer you got then was of a satisfying kind."

"I got no answer," said Lewis, with a little agitation. "Your sister is as kind as heaven; she would not let me put myself in the wrong. The feeling I had was not fictitious; I would explain it to you if I dared. She forgave me my presumption, and she stopped me. Miss Murray, it is a different thing I have come to speak to you of to-day."

"I am glad of that," said Miss Margaret—"very glad of that; for I may say, since you have thought better of it, that it was not a subject that was pleasing to me."

Lewis rose up in his excitement; the little taunt in her tone, the sternness behind her smile, the watchful way in which her eyes held him, all made him feel the desperate character of the attempt he was making, and desperation took away every restraint.

"It is very different," he said—"it is love. I did not intend it—I had never thought of it—my mind was turned another way—but I saw her by chance, and what else—what else was possible? Oh! it is very different. Love is not like anything else. It forces to speak, it makes you bold, it is more strong than I—"

"You are eloquent," said Miss Margaret. "Mr. Murray, that was very well put. And who are you in love with that can concern us of the house of Murkley, if I may ask the question? I will hope," she said, with a laugh, "that it's not me you have chosen as the object of your affection this time."

He looked at her with a pained look, reproachful and wistful. It did him more good than if he had spoken volumes. A little quick colour, like a reflection of some passing light, gleamed over Miss Margaret's face.

"Mr. Murray," she said, "if that is your name, which you say yourself is not your name—who are you, a stranger, to come like this to ladies of a well-known family? I am not asking who is your object now. If I seemed to jeer at you, I ask your pardon. I will say all I can—I will say that I believe you mean no harm, but rather to be honourable, according to what you think right. But I must tell you, you are not, so far as I know, in the position of one with whom we could make alliances. It is kindest to speak it plain out. It is just chance that has thrown us in your way, and you take impressions far too seriously," she added, not without kindness. "There was my sister Jean, you know; and now it is another. This will blow over too, if you will just wait a little, and consider what is befitting."

She rose up from her high chair. She was more imposing seated in it than standing, for her stature was not great. Lewis knew that this was intended to give him his dismissal, but he was too much in earnest to take it so easily.

"Let me speak one word," he said. "If I am not great, there is at least one thing—I am rich. What she wishes to do, I could do it. It should all be as if there had been no disinheriting. To me the family would be as great an interest, as great a desire, as to her. Her palace of dreams, it should be real. I would devote myself to it—it should be a dream no longer. Listen to me, I could do it—"

"What you say is without meaning to me, Mr. Murray," Miss Margaret said, with stern paleness. "It is better that no more should be said."

"Without any reference, without any appeal? how do you know," he said, "that she might not herself think otherwise—that she might not, if only for the sake of her dream—"

"A gentleman," said Miss Margaret, "will never force his plea upon ladies when he sees it is not welcome. I will just bid you farewell, Mr. Murray. We shall very likely not meet again."

She held out her hand, but he did not take it. He looked anxiously in her face.

"Can I say nothing that will move you?" he said.

"I am thinking not, Mr. Murray. When two persons disagree so much as we do upon a business so important, it is best to wish one another good-bye. And it is lucky, as you will have heard, that we are going away. I am offering you my hand, though you do not seem to see it. I would not do that if I thought ill of you. Fare-you-well, and I wish you every prosperity," Miss Margaret said.

He took her hand, and gave it one angry pressure. It was what he had expected, but it hurt him more than he thought. The disappointment, the sadness of leaving, the blank wall that seemed to rise before him, made Lewis sad, and made him wroth. It did not seem to him that he deserved so badly of Fate. He said "good-bye" almost in a sullen tone. But when he reached the door he turned round and looked at her, standing where he had left her, watching his departure.

"I must warn you. I do not accept this as final," he said.

CHAPTER XXXI

The house of Gowanbrae was not an old historical house, like the castle of Murkley. It had no associations ranging back into the mists. It was half a cottage, half a country mansion-house, built upon a slope, so that the house was one story higher on one side than on the other. The ground descended from the back to a wooded dell, in which ran a sparkling, noisy burn, like a cottage girl, always busy, singing about its work as it trickled over its pebbles. The view from the higher windows commanded a great sweep of country, long moorlands and pastures, with here and there a comfortable farm-steading, and a group of carefully cultivated fields. The noble Tay sweeping down into its estuary was not more unlike the burn than this modest, cosy villa was unlike the old ancestral house, with its black wainscot and deep walls. The grandfather of Margaret and Jean had built it with his Indian money when he came back after a lifetime of service in the East—hard, and long, and unbroken, such as used to be, when a man would not see his native country or belongings for twenty years at a stretch. This old officer's daughter had not been a sufficient match for the heir of Murkley, but it was a fortunate circumstance afterwards for Margaret and Jean that their mother's little property was settled upon them. Everything in the house was bright but homely. It had always been delightful to Lilias, to whom Gowanbrae meant all the freedom of childhood, open air, and rural life. She was not the lady or princess there, and even Margaret acknowledged the relaxation of state which this made possible. But when the little family travelled thither on this occasion, the charm of the old life was a little broken. Not a word had been said to Lilias of Lewis' proceedings. She was told drily in Jean's presence by Miss Margaret, who gave her sister a severe look of warning, that Mr. Murray had called to say good-bye, but that it had not been thought necessary to call her.

"You have seen but little of him," Margaret said.

Lilias did not make any remark. She did not think it necessary to tell how much she had seen of Lewis, and, to tell the truth, she did not think it certain that an opportunity of saying good-bye to him personally would not be afforded to her. But, as a matter-of-fact, there was no further meeting between the two, and Lilias left Murkley with a little surprise, and not without a little pique, that he should have made no attempt to take his leave of her. She had various agitating scenes with Katie to make up for it, and on the other hand an anxious visit from Mrs. Stormont, full of excitement and indignation.

"What can take Margaret away at this moment? it is just extraordinary," that lady said, in the stress of her disappointment. "For I cannot suppose, Jean, my dear, that you have anything to do with it. Dear me, can she not let well alone? Where could you be better than at Murkley?"

"We are both fond of our own house," Jean said, with gentle self-assertion.

"Bless me!" cried Mrs. Stormont, "are you not just the same as in your own house? I am sure, though it belongs to Lilias, that Margaret is mistress and more."

"—And Lilias is fain, fain to get to Gowanbrae. She was always fond of the place—and we think her looking white, and that a change will do her good."

"Oh! I am very well aware Margaret will never want for reasons for what she does," cried the indignant mother.

Meanwhile Katie was sobbing on Lilias' shoulder. "He says he will go away. He says he cannot face it, his mother will just drive him out of his senses; and what is to become of me with nobody to speak to?" Katie cried.

"Oh! Katie, cannot you just wait awhile?—you are younger than I am," said Lilias, in desperation.

"And when I think that we might just have been going on as happy as ever, if it had not been you forsaking us!" cried Katie.

Lilias was too magnanimous to defend herself. She treated the departure as a great ordinance of Nature against which there was not a word to be said. But when the last evening passed, and nowhere in park or wood did there appear any trace of the figure which had grown so familiar to her, to say a word or look a look, it cannot be denied that a certain disappointment mingled with the surprise in Lilias' heart. She could not understand it. Though Margaret thought they had seen so little of each other, there had been, indeed, a good deal of intercourse. Lilias was very sure it had always been accidental intercourse, but still they had met, and talked, and exchanged a great many opinions, and that he should not have felt any desire to see her again was a bewilderment to the girl. She did not say a syllable on the subject, by which even Miss Jean concluded that it was of no importance to her, but, as in most similar cases, Lilias thought the more. She looked out with a little anxiety as her sisters and she drove to the station in their little brougham. They passed on the road the rough, country gig which belonged to the "Murkley Arms," which Adam was driving in the same direction.

"Are you leaving the country too, Adam?—all the good folk are going away," Miss Margaret said, as they passed.

"It's no me, mem, it's our gentleman. He's away twa-three days ago, and this is just his luggitch," said Adam.

"Dear me, when the season's just begun!"

"The season is of awfu' little importance to a gentleman that is nae hand at the fishing, nor at naething I ken of, except making scarts upon a paper," said Adam, contemptuously. He was left speaking like the orators in Parliament, and only half of this sentence reached the ears of the ladies as they drove on. This was all Lilias heard of the young man who had been the first stranger with whom she had ever formed any friendship: which was the light in which she thought she regarded him. She had never talked so much to anyone who was not connected with her by some tie of relationship or old connection, and that very fact had added freshness and reality to their intercourse. It had been a new element introduced into her life. Why had he gone away without any reason? He had said nothing of any such purpose. On the contrary, they had talked together of the woods in autumn and the curling in winter, all of which he had intended, she was sure, to make acquaintance with. Why had everything changed so suddenly in his plans as well as in theirs? It did not seem possible that there should be any connection between the one and the other; but a vague curiosity and bewilderment arose in the girl's mind. But it did not occur to her to ask Jean or Margaret for information. He was Jean's friend: it would have been natural enough to ask her where he had gone, or why he had left Murkley? But she did not, though she could not explain to herself any reason why.

And the question was one which returned often to her mind during the winter. The nearest post-town was several miles off, and there were no very near neighbours, so that by times when the roads were bad or the weather wild, they were lonely in Gowanbrae. Of old, Lilias had never known what it was to have time hang heavy on her hands. She had a hundred things to do; but now insensibly her childish occupations had fallen from her, she could scarcely tell how. She missed the park, she missed the river-side. She missed, above all, the great, vacant, unfinished palace, with its eyeless windows staring into the gloom. Her dreams seemed now to have no settled habitation, they roamed about the world, now here, now there, wondering about a great many things which had never excited her curiosity before. It seemed to Lilias for the first time that she would take to travel, to see new scenes, to make acquaintance with the places spoken of in books—indeed, she turned to books themselves with a feeling very different from anything she had felt before. Till now they had been inextricably associated with lessons. Now lessons, though she still continued a semblance of work under Margaret's eye, seemed to have floated away from her as things of the past, and Lilias began to read poetry eagerly, to dive into the mysteries of sentiment which hitherto had only wearied her. She was growing older, she thought, and that was the reason. Pages of measured verse which a few months before her eye had gone blankly over in search of a story now became delightful to her. Things that even Margaret and Jean turned from, she devoured with avidity. She became familiar with those seeming philosophies which delight the youthful intelligence, and liked shyly and silently to enter, in her own mind, into questions about constancy and the eternal duration of love, and whether it was possible to love twice,—a question, of course, decided almost violently in the negative in Lilias' heart. No one knew anything of those developments, nor were they in any way consciously connected with the events of the summer. Indeed, no change had taken place officially in the character of Lilias' dreams. The hero of six feet two, with his hair like night, and his mystical dark eyes, had not been dethroned—heaven forbid!—in favour of any smiling middle-sized person, with a complexion the same colour as his hair. No such desecration had happened. The hero still stood in the background, serene and magnificent; he saved the heroine's life periodically in a variety of ways, always at the hazard of his own. He had never been amusing in conversation; it was not part of his rôle; and when she thought of another quite insignificant individual occupying an entirely different position, who would talk and smile, and tell of a hundred unknown scenes, beguiling away the hours, or play as no one had ever played in her hearing, Lilias felt that the infidelity to her hero was venial. It was indeed an effort on her part to think not less but more of her friend on this latter account, for, as has been said, "the piano" was not a popular attribute of a young man in those days in Scotland. People in general would have almost preferred that he should do something a little wrong. Gambling, perhaps, was excessive, but a little high-play was pardonable in comparison. Music was a lady's privilege—the prerogative of a girl who was accomplished. But Lilias forgave Lewis his music. She resorted to his idea in those dull days somewhat fondly, if such a word may be used, but not with love—far from it. She had never thought of love in connection with him. That was entirely an abstract sentiment, so far as she was aware, vaguely linked to six-feet-two and unfathomable eyes.

The whole house was a little out of joint. They had come to Gowanbrae when they had not intended to do so, for one thing. All their previous plans had been formed for Murkley, and various things were wanting to their comfort, which, under other circumstances, would have been supplied. For instance, there were new curtains and carpets wanted, which Miss Margaret must have seen to had they intended from the first to winter there, but which, with the prospect of a season in London before them, could not be thought of. The garden was to have been re-modelled under the eye of a new gardener, and a new greenhouse was to have been built during their absence; but they had returned while these improvements were in course of carrying out.

Gowanbrae, in fact, was better adapted for summer than for winter. When the hills were covered with snow, the prospect was melancholy, and down by the burn, though it was lovely, it was damp in the autumn rains. The broad drive in the park between old Murkley and new, had always supplied a dry and cheerful walk, and even the well-gravelled road by the Tay was sumptuous in comparison with the muddy roads wending by farmsteadings over boggy soil towards the moors. Indoors, to be sure, all was cheerful, but even there disturbing imaginations would enter. Miss Jean would spend hours playing the music which Lewis had left with her, and which was a little above her powers. Her pretty "pieces," the gentle "reveries" and compositions that were quite within her range, the Scotch airs which she played so sweetly, were given up, with a little contempt and a great deal of ambition, for Mozart and Beethoven; and the result was not exhilarating. When Margaret said, "I would far rather hear your Scotch tunes," Jean would smile and sigh, with a little conscious pride in her own preference of the best, and play the "Flowers of the Forest" or "Tweedside" with an air of gentle condescension, which made her sister laugh, and took the charm out of the pretty performance, which once had been the pride of the house. As for Lilias, she was more indulgent to these reminiscences of the past. It did not trouble her, as it might have done had her ear been finer, to hear the stumbling and faltering of Jean's fingers in her attempt to render what the practised hands of the other had done so easily. On the contrary, in the long winter evenings, when the house was shut up by four o'clock, Lilias, with her book of poetry, whatever it might be—and her appetite was so large that she was not so fastidious as perhaps she ought to have been—half-buried in a deep easy-chair by the fire, would catch, as it were, an echo of the finer strain as her sister laboured at it, and liked it as it linked itself, broken yet full of association, with the other kind of music she was reading. Sometimes, when Margaret was absent, there would be a little colloquy between the pair.

"That is bonnie, Jean. Play just that little bit again."

"Which bit, my darling?—the beginning of the andante?"

Miss Jean had learned from Lewis to speak more learnedly than was natural.

"Oh, what do I know about your andantes? Play that—just that little flowery bit—it's like the meadows in the spring."

"I wish Mr. Murray, poor lad, could have heard you call it that."

"Why is he a poor lad? I thought he was very well off. You always speak of him in that little sighing tone."

"Do I, my dear? Oh, he is well enough in fortune—but there are more things needed than fortune to make a young man happy."

Upon which Lilias laughed, yet blushed as well—not for consciousness, but because she was at the stage when the very name of love brings the colour to a girl's cheek.

"He must have a story, or you would not speak of him so. He must be in love—"

"He is just that: and little hope. I think of him many a day, poor lad, and with a sore heart."

"Did he tell you? did he say who it was? Is it anybody we know? Tell me, tell me the story, Jean!"

"Not for the world. Do you think I would break his trust and tell his secret? And whisht, whisht; Margaret is not fond of the name of him," Jean would say; while Lilias dropped back into her book, and the "Andante" was slowly beaten out of the old piano again.

This was all Miss Jean dared to do on behalf of Lewis; but she had a great many thoughts of him, as she said. She had imagined many situations in which they might meet again, but as the time drew nearer it occurred to her often to wonder whether he would find it so easy as she had once thought to find the Miss Murrays of Murkley in town. Margaret had been receiving circulars from house-agents, communications from letters of lodgings, counsels from friends without number—from all which it began to become apparent to Miss Jean that, big place as Edinburgh was, it was nothing to London. Would they be so sure to meet as he had thought? He did not know London any more than they did, and there rose before Miss Jean's eyes a melancholy picture of two people vainly searching after each other, and meeting never. Naturally as the year went on, they talked a great deal on this subject. Margaret decided at last that to take lodgings would be the best, as the transportation of servants to London would be an extensive matter, besides their inacquaintance with the ways of town: while, on the other hand, she herself shrank from the unknown danger of temporary London servants, if all was true that was said of them.

"Though half of it at least will be nonsense," Miss Margaret remarked. "You would think they were not human creatures to hear what is said in the papers; in my experience, men and women are very like other men and women wherever you go."

"And do you think it will be so very big a place that without an address—if such a thing were to happen," said Miss Jean—in her own opinion, with great astuteness—"you would not be able to find out a friend?"

"Your friend would be a silly one indeed if she went about the world without an address," said Miss Margaret; but after a moment she added—"It would depend, I should say, whether she was in what is called society or not. When you are in society you meet every kind of person. You cannot be long without coming across everybody."

"And shall we be in society, Margaret?" said Lilias, unexpectedly interposing.

"My dear," said Miss Margaret, "what do you suppose we are going to London for?—to see the pictures, which are no such great things to see when all's done; or to hear the concerts, which Jean may go to, but not me for one? Or perhaps you think to the May-meetings, as they call them, to hear all the missionary men giving an account of the way to save souls. I would like to be sure first how to take care of my own."

"We must see all the pictures and go to the concerts; and the play and whatever is going on, of course?" said Lilias. "Yes, I know society means something more. We are going into the world, we are going to Court. Of course that must be the very best society," the girl said, with her serious face.

"Well, then, there is no need for me to answer your question," said Miss Margaret, composedly. "Society is just the great object in London. It is a big place, the biggest in the world; but society is no bigger than a person with her wits about her can easily, easily learn by headmark. I understand that you will meet the same people at all the places, as you do in a far smaller town."

"Then in that way," said Miss Jean, with a little eagerness, "you could just be sure to foregather with your friend, even though he had no address?"

"And who may this friend be," said Miss Margaret, "that you are so anxious to meet?"

"Oh, nobody!" said Miss Jean, confused. "I mean," she added, "I was just thinking of a chance that might happen. You and me, Margaret, we have both old friends that have disappeared from us in London—"

"And that is true," Miss Margaret said. The words seemed to awaken old associations in her mind. She sighed and shook her head. "Plenty have done that," she said. "It is just like a great sea where the shipwrecks are many, and some sail away into the dark, and are never heard of more."

Under cover of this natural sentiment, Miss Jean sailed off too out of her sister's observation. She had given a sudden quick look at Lilias, and it had occurred to her with a curious sensation that Lilias knew what she meant. It was a momentary glance, the twinkling of an eye, and no more; but that is enough to set up a private intelligence between two souls. Jean felt a little guilty afterwards, as if she had been teaching her young sister the elements of conspiracy. But this was not at all the case. She had done nothing, or so very little, to bring Lewis to her mind that it was not worth thinking of. Nevertheless, it was a great revelation to her, and startled her much, that Lilias understood. No, no, there was no conspiracy! Margaret herself could not object to meet him in society; and, if they did not succeed in this, Jean had no notion where the young stranger, in whom she took so great an interest, was to be found.

Thus, with many a consultation and many an arrangement, often modified and changed as time went on, the winter stole away. It seemed very long as it passed, but it was short to look back upon, and, after the new year, a gradually-growing excitement took possession of the quiet household. From Simon, who, the other servants thought, gave himself great airs, and could scarcely open his mouth without making some reference to the memorable time when he was body-servant to the General, and had been in London, and seen the clubs and all the sights, or uttering some doubt as to the changes which might have passed since that time; to Miss Margaret, upon whose shoulders was the charge of everything, there was no one who did not feel the thrill of the coming change. The maids who were not going were loud in their declarations that they did not care, and would not have liked it, if Miss Margaret had asked them—but they were all bitterly derisive of Simon, as an old fool who thought he knew London, and was just as proud of it as if it were a strange language.

"You could not make much more fuss if it was to France you were going," the women said.

"To France! As if there was onything in France that was equal to London, the biggest ceety in the world, the place where you could get the best of everything; where there were folk enough to people Scotland, if onything went amiss."

"And what should go amiss? Does the man think the world will stand still when he's no here," the maids said.

"Aweel, I do not know what ye will do without me. But to let the ladies depart from here, alone in the world, and me not with them, is what I could not do," Simon said.

Miss Margaret was almost as deeply moved by the sense of her responsibilities. Many of them she kept to herself, not desiring to overwhelm the gentle mind of Jean, or to frighten Lilias with the numberless difficulties that seemed to arise in the way. The choice of the lodgings alone was enough to have put a feebler woman distraught altogether, and Margaret, who had never been in London, found it no easy task to choose a neighbourhood which should be unexceptionable, and from whence it would be a right thing to produce a lovely débutante. When we say that there were unprincipled persons who recommended Russell Square to her as a proper place of residence, the perils with which Margaret was surrounded may be imagined. It was almost by chance that she selected Cadogan Place, which is a place no lady need be ashamed of living in. It was Margaret's opinion ever after, pronounced whenever her advice was asked as to the ways and means of settling in town, of which her experience was so great, that this was a matter in which advice did more harm than good.

"There is just one thing," she would say, with the conscious superiority of one who had bought her information dearly, and understood the subject au fond, "and everything else is of little importance in comparison. Never you consult your friends. Just hear what the business persons have to say, and form your own opinion. You know what you want yourself, and they have to give—but friends know neither the one nor the other."

This was severe, but no doubt she knew what she was saying. For two months beforehand her mind was occupied with little else, and every post brought shoals of letters on the subject. You would have thought the half of London was stirred with expectation. To Miss Jean it seemed only natural. She was pleased that the advent of Margaret should cause so much emotion, and that the way would be thus prepared for Lilias.

"Of course it will be a treat for them to see Margaret; there are not many people like Margaret: and then, my darling, you, under her wing, will be just like the bonnie star that trembles near the moon."

"I hope you don't mean that Margaret is like the moon," said Lilias, recovering something of her saucy ways since this excitement had got into the air.

She laughed, but she, too, felt it very natural. There was no extravagance of pride about these gentlewomen. They were aware indeed of their own position, but they were not proud. It was all so simple: even Lilias could not divest herself of the idea that it would be something for the London people to see Margaret in her velvet with all her point lace, and the diamonds which had been her mother's. There was, however, another great question to be decided, which the head of the house herself opened in full family conclave as one upon which it was only right that the humbler members of the family should have their say.

"The question is, who is to present us?" Miss Margaret said. "Her aunt, my Lady Dalgainly, would be the right person for Lilias. But I'm not anxious to be indebted to that side of the house."

"Would it not be a right thing to ask the countess?" said Miss Jean.

It had already been decided that one Court dress was as much as each property could afford, and that Jean was not to go; a decision which distressed Lilias, who wanted her sister to see her in all her glory, and could scarcely resign herself to any necessity which should make Jean miss that sight.

"The countess would be the proper person," said Margaret; "but blood is thicker than water, and suppose she had not you and me to care for her, Jean, where could she turn to but her mother's family?"

Here Lilias made a little spring into the centre of the group, as was her way.

"I have read in the papers," she said, "all about it. Margaret, this is what you will do: the countess will present you—for who else could do it?—and then you will present me. I will have no other," cried Lilias, with a little imperative clap of her hands.

"Was there ever such a creature? She just knows everything," Miss Jean cried.

CHAPTER XXXII

The spring was very early that year. It had been a severe winter, and even on the moors the leap of the fresh life of the grass out of the snows was sudden; but when the ladies found themselves transported to the fresh green in Cadogan Place, it is impossible to say what an exhilarating effect this revelation had upon them. The elder sisters, indeed, had visited London in their youth, but that was long ago, and they had forgotten everything but the streets, and the crowd, and the dust, an impression which was reproduced by the effect of the long drive from Euston Square, which seemed endless, through lines of houses and shops and flaring gaslights. That continuity of dreary inhabitation, those long lines of featureless buildings, of which it is so difficult to distinguish one from another, is the worse aspect of London, and even Lilias, looking breathless from the window, ready to be astonished at everything, was chilled a little when she found nothing to be astonished at—for the great shops were closed which furnish brightness to an evening drive, and it seemed to the tired women as if they must have travelled half as far through those dreary, half-lighted streets as they had done before over the open country. But with a bright morning, and the sight of the opening leaves between them and the houses opposite, a different mood came. Miss Jean in particular hailed the vegetation as she might have greeted an old friend whose face she had not hoped to see again.

"Just as green as our own trees, and far more forward," she said, with delight, as she called Lilias next morning.

With the cheering revelation of this green, their minds were fully tuned to see everything in the best light; but it is not necessary to enter into the sight-seeing of the group of rural ladies, all so fresh and unhackneyed, and ready to enjoy. Margaret preserved a dignified composure in all circumstances. She had the feeling that a great deal was expected from her as the head of the family. The excitement which was quite becoming to the others would to her have seemed unbecoming, and, as a matter of fact, she made out to herself either that she "remembered perfectly," or, at least, was "quite well aware from all she had heard" of the things which impressed her sisters most profoundly. The work she had in hand was far more important than sight-seeing, which, however, she encouraged in her sisters, being anxious that Lilias should get all that over before she was "seen," and had become an actual inhabitant of the great world. Margaret had made every arrangement in what she hoped and believed was the most perfectly good style. She spared no expense on this one episode of grandeur and gaiety. All the little savings of Gowanbrae went to swell the purse which she had made up for the occasion. Old Simon, the old family servant, who had seen them all born, gave respectability to the little open carriage which they had for fine days alternatively with the brougham, by condescending to place himself on the box. He was not very nimble, perhaps, in getting up and down, but he was highly respectable, and indeed, in his best "blacks," was sometimes mistaken by ignorant people for the head of the party. Simon, though he liked his ladies to know that he was aware it was a condescension, in his heart enjoyed his position, and laid up chapters of experience with which to keep respectful audiences in rapt attention both at Murkley and Gowanbrae. He made common cause with Lilias in her eagerness to see everything. When Miss Jean held back, afraid that so much curiosity might seem vulgar, Simon would take it upon himself to interpose.

"You'll excuse me, mem," he said, "but Miss Lilias is young, and it's my opinion a young creature can never see too much. We are never seventeen but wance in our lives."

"Dear me! that is very true, Simon," Miss Jean would say, and with a little air of reserve, as if she herself knew all about it, would accompany the eager girl, who sometimes called Simon forward to enjoy a warmer sympathy.

"Look, Simon; that armour has been in battle. Knights have fought in it," Lilias would say, her eyes dancing with excitement, while Miss Jean stood a little apart with that benevolent smile.

Simon examined everything very minutely, and then he said,

"I'm saying naething against the knights, Miss Lilias, for I'm not one that believes in mere stature without sense to guide it; but they must have been awfu' little men. I would like to see one of those fine fellows on the horses, with half a dozen of them round him," Simon remarked. Lilias was somewhat indignant at this depreciation of the heroes of the past, yet still was able to smile, for Simon's devotion to the sentries at the Horse Guards was known. He thought at first they were not real, and, when their movements undeceived him, was for a long time disposed to think they were ingenious pieces of mechanism. "Thae men!" he had said. "I canna believe it! That's what ye call an occupation for a rational being! Na, na; I canna believe it." But he would walk all the way from Cadogan Place in the morning before breakfast to see these wonders of the world. And he acknowledged that St. Paul's was grander than St. George's in Edinburgh, which showed he had an impartial mind. "But, if ye test them by the congregation that worships in them, it is we that will gain the day—and is that not the best beauty of a kirk?" Simon said. These were days when popular sermons and services were unthought of. But this history has no space for the humours of this new exploration of London sights. It would be difficult to say which of the party enjoyed them most: Lilias, all eagerness and frank curiosity, or Miss Jean, holding back with that protesting smile, asking no question lest she should show an ignorance which did not become her position as the head of the party, or Simon, who never forgot his rôle of critic and moralist. But, while they all enjoyed themselves, Miss Margaret sat in her parlour much more seriously engaged. She had everything to contrive and to decide, and Lilias' dress and all the preliminaries of her introduction to settle. For herself, what could be more imposing than her velvet and all that beautiful lace? The only thing that was wanted was a longer train. The countess had been very ready to undertake the presentation, and had asked the party to dinner, and sent them cards for a great reception. She was very amiable, and delighted to see the Miss Murrays in town.

"And as for your little sister, she ought to make a sensation. She ought to be one of the beauties of the season," the countess said.

"No, no; that is not to be desired for so young a thing. She is just a country girl," said Miss Margaret, half-hoping that the great lady would protest and declare it impossible that a Murray of Murkley should be so described; but the countess, who was but slightly occupied with Lilias, only smiled graciously and shook hands warmly, as she dismissed her visitors. When they had left her noble mansion, Miss Jean, mild as she was, on this occasion, took upon her to remonstrate.

"You must not speak of Lilias so," she said. "If you will think for a moment, she has just a great deal of presence for so young a person, and Lady Lilias' daughter. People are too civil to contradict you. I would not call her just a country girl."

Margaret gazed at her sister with something of the astonishment which Balaam must have felt on a certain remarkable occasion. "I would not say but you are right," the candid woman said.

The Drawing-room was in the beginning of May. Lilias was greatly interested in all the preparations for it. She was put into the hands of a nice old lady who had been a great dancer in her day to be taught her curtseys, which was a proceeding that amused the girl greatly. She persuaded her instructress to talk, and learned with astonished soul a great many things of which she had no idea, but fortunately no harm: which was the merest chance, the sisters having given her over in the utmost confidence to her teacher, not suspicious of anything injurious that youth could hear from a nice old woman. These lessons were as good as a play to the girl, and sometimes also to the spectators as she practised her trois obeisances. To see her sink into the furbelows of her fashionable dress, and recover herself with elastic grace and without a sign of faltering, filled even Margaret with admiring wonder. The elder lady's majestic curtsey was a far more difficult proceeding, but even she condescended to practise it, to the delight of Lilias and the admiration of Miss Jean, throned all the time in the biggest chair, and representing Her Majesty.

"I would just bid you kneel down and make you Lady Margaret on the spot, if it was me," Jean said.

"My dear, you are just a haverel: for it is men that have to kneel down and be made knights of—and you would not have me made a Sir, I hope?" said Margaret, with a laugh.

"I must say," said Miss Jean, "that there is injustice in that. Your forefathers have been Sirs far longer than Her Majesty's family has been upon the throne, and why should there be no trace of it left to give pleasure, just because you and me—and Lilias too, more is the pity—were born women?"

"I have yet to learn," said Miss Margaret, drawing herself up, "that a title would make any difference to a Murray of Murkley; we are well enough known without that."

"Oh! but, Margaret, you should be my lady," cried Lilias, springing up and making curtseys in pure wantonness all round the room. "Miss is not suitable for you. Mistress would be better, or Madam, but my lady best of all. I think Jean is a wise woman; and if the queen—"

"You are a grand judge of wisdom," said her sister. "Jean and you, you might just go in a show together, the female Solomon and the person that explains the oracle; but you will just go to your bed, and take a good rest, for it will be a fatiguing day to-morrow. You will have plenty to do looking after your dress, and remembering your manners, without taking it upon you to give your advice to Her Majesty, who has been longer at the trade than you."

"To-morrow!—is it really to-morrow? Oh!" cried Lilias, "when I come before her I will forget everything: and what will she say to me?" This made the elder sister look a little confused, but she had herself but little idea what the royal lady would do in the circumstances; and the safest plan was to send Lilias to bed.

Next morning it was a sight to see the two débutantes. Miss Margaret had a train of velvet sweeping from her shoulders that made her look, Lilias declared, like Margaret of Anjou, though why this special resemblance was hit upon, the young lady declined to say. As for herself, in clouds of virgin white, it seemed to her sisters that nothing had ever been seen so lovely as this little lily, who would, however, have been more aptly termed a rose, with the colour of excitement coming and going upon her cheeks, her eyes like dew with the sun on it, her dazzling sweetness of complexion. Perhaps her features were not irreproachable, perhaps her little figure wanted filling out; but at seventeen these are faults that lean to virtue's side. She was dazzling to behold in that first exquisite youthful bloom, which is like nothing else in the world. When she came into the room where they were awaiting her, she made them a curtsey to show her perfection, her face running over with smiles. And then Lilias grew grave, a flutter came to her child's heart. Her eyes grew serious with the awe of a neophyte on the edge of the mysteries of life.

"When I come back I will be a woman," she said, with a little catch of her breath.

"No, no, not till you are one-and-twenty, my darling," cried Jean, who did not always know when to hold her peace.

"I shall be a woman," Lilias repeated. "I shall be introduced to the world—I shall be able to go where I please—"

"There may be two words about that," said Margaret, interfering; "but this is not a time for discoursing. So just you gather up your train, Lilias, and let us go away."

Miss Jean went downstairs after them; she watched them drive away, waving her hand. She thought Margaret was just beautiful notwithstanding her age. "But, after all, forty is not such an extraordinary age," Jean said to herself; and, as for Lilias, words could not express what her sister felt. The Court must be splendid indeed, and a great deal of beauty in it, if two ladies like that were not observed. She took out her table-cover, which had been much neglected, and sat down at the window and arranged her silks as of old. There was no carnation now for a pattern, but indeed she was done with that flower. When a woman has seen her best-beloved go forth in full panoply to conquer, and feels the domestic silence close down upon herself, there is, if she is the kind of woman, an exquisite repose and pleasure in it. The mother who comes out to the door to watch her gay party go away, and, closing it again with all their pleasure in her mind, goes back to the quiet, either to work for them or to wait for them, has her share both real and vicarious, and doubles the pleasure. She goes with them along the way, she broods over their happiness at home. Miss Jean, who was this kind of woman, had thus a double share, and worked into her flowers the serene and delicious calm, the soft expectation, the flutter of an excitement out of which everything harsh was gone. She could not help thinking that it would be a real pleasure to Her Majesty, who had girls of her own and a kind heart, to see such a creature as Lilias just in the opening of her flower. The Queen would be glad to know that General Murray had left such representatives, though, no doubt, she would be sorry there was no son. Jean felt too, modestly, that it was always possible, seeing Margaret and Lilias, and admiring them as she must, that Her Majesty might graciously ask whether there was no more of a family, and command that "next time" the other sister should be brought to see her. "But, oh, she would be disappointed in me!" Miss Jean said to herself. All these thoughts kept her amused and happy, so that she wanted no other entertainment. She even forgot Lewis and the confidence which had so touched her heart. She thought it so likely that some young duke, some glorious lord in waiting, would clasp his hands together and say, in the very presence chamber, "Here, by God's word, is the one maid for me." Lewis had floated from her mind, which was beguiled by higher things.

When the carriage drove up to the door, she rushed downstairs to meet the victorious pair. Lilias was the first to appear, a little crushed and faded, like a rose that has been bound into a bouquet and suffered from the pressure: but that did not matter, for everybody knows there is a great crowd. But the face was not radiant as it had been, Miss Jean could not but perceive. There was a great deal of gravity in it. The corners of the mouth were slightly, very slightly turned the wrong way. She came in quite seriously, calmed out of all her excitement. Margaret followed with the same serious air.

"Well, my darling!" Jean cried, running forward to meet the girl.

"Oh, it has all passed very well," Margaret said over Lilias' head.

Jean drew them into the little dining-room, which was on the ground floor, to hear everything.

"And were the dresses beautiful, and the jewels? and was Her Majesty looking well? and what did she say to you?" cried the eager spectator.

"You will just make Lilias take some wine, for the child is like to drop with tiredness; and as for me, before I say a syllable, I must get rid of this train, for it weighs me to the earth," said Margaret.

"My darling," cried Jean, throwing her arms about Lilias, "something has happened!"

Upon which Lilias burst into a laugh, which, compared with the extreme gravity of her face, had a somewhat rueful effect. It was a laugh which was not mirthful and spontaneous as the laughter of Lilias generally was, but produced itself of a sudden as by some quick impulse of ridicule.

"No," she said, "Jean, that is just the thing, nothing has happened;" and then the rueful look melted away, and a gleam of real fun came back.

"Dear me! dear me! something has gone wrong. You never got to the drawing-room at all?"

"Oh yes," cried the girl, "and all went off very well, didn't you hear Margaret say?"

"Well, then, my dear, I don't understand," Jean said, puzzled.

"It is just that that was all," said Lilias, with her laugh. "It all went off very well. Everything was quite right, I suppose. Me that thought it was the great, beautiful court itself, and that we would see everybody, and that it would be known who you were, and everything! I said to Margaret, 'Is that all?' And I think she was quite as astonished as me, for she said, 'I suppose so.' And then we waited, and at last we got the carriage, and we came away! Now that I think of it, it was awfully funny," said Lilias, with tears, which were no doubt tears of merriment, but which were also tears of vexation, in her eyes. "To think we should have thought of it for months and months, and got such dresses, and played such pranks with Madame Ballerina—all for that!"

"But, my dear," said Miss Jean, always consolatory, "it is not only for that, it is for everything. It is just the beginning, you know. You will see better society, and you will be asked to more places, and, if ever you go abroad, they say it is such an advantage, and—Besides, my darling, it is your duty to your sovereign," Miss Jean added, with a little solemnity.

Upon this Lilias laughed more and more.

"Oh," she cried, "that is just the thing, Jean! I saw my sovereign yawn. I am sure she did. I was so astonished. I noticed everything, but the queen saw nothing to be surprised at, she has gone over it so often. I am sure I saw her yawn, though she concealed it. Could there nothing be invented," cried Lilias, with a liveliness in which there was a sparkle of annoyance and passion, "that would be better than that? And this was what we came to town for," she said, sitting down upon her pretty train and her flowers, which were all tumbled. The laugh went out of her face. "It is so funny," Lilias said, as grave as a judge, "when you think upon it; so little, and yet so much."

"And did Her Majesty say nothing then about papa? She would not know it was you, that must have been how it was. There are many Murrays, you know. You will see the name even over shops. And never asked where you were staying, or said that she would see you again—?"

"Jean," said Miss Margaret, appearing suddenly in a dressing-gown, "what nonsense is that you are talking? Did anybody ever suppose that the queen was to make remarks, and ask questions, with crowds of women in their best gowns just ready to eat you to get past? It all went off very well," she said, seating herself on the sofa. "Lilias, I just cannot bide to see you at this hour of the day in that ridiculous dress. I've taken off mine, and thankful to get rid of it. A girl of your age can stand a great deal, but you are far nicer, to my opinion, in your natural clothes. As I was saying, it went off just extremely well. We got through really without so much crushing as I expected, and the dresses were beautiful, and diamonds enough to make the sun think shame of himself. No doubt it is just a little ridiculous, as Lilias says, to see the ladies in all their finery in the daylight; but then it is the custom. You can put up with anything when you know it is the custom. People like us that just go once in a way, we never get into the way of it; but for those that go often, you know, they just never mind. And of course it was a beautiful sight."

"It must have been that," cried Jean, seizing hold upon this certainty; "you will call it to mind, Lilias, when it's long past, and it will always be a pleasure to think of. It must have been a wonderful sight."

"As for expecting," continued Margaret, "that it would be an occasion for rational intercourse, or anything like making acquaintance either with the Court or Her Majesty, I could have told you from the beginning that was nonsense. Just think of such crowds of women, one at the back of another, like birds in a net. It would be out of the question to think of it. Now, Lilias, go and get your things off, and, if you are tired, you can lie down a little—"

"Yes, my dear, you must just lie down a little—it will do you good."

"Jean and Margaret," cried Lilias, jumping up, "do you think I am old, like you? What am I to lie down for?—and besides, you never lie down, that are old. It is only me you say that to. I will go and take my things off, and then I will take Susan and go out, and look in at all the vulgar shops, and see the common folk, for I think I like them best."

"I am afraid, Margaret, the poor child is disappointed," said Jean, when Lilias had gone away.

"It will be because you have been putting things into her head, then," said Margaret; "everything went off just as well as possible. You are surely later than usual with the tea? My back is just broken with that train. It is really as warm as a summer day, and to go dragging about miles of velvet after you is something terrible. She made her reverence as well as you could have desired, and looked just as bonnie. I cannot say as much for Lady Ida, though she is nice enough; and oh, but that dress is dreadful for women that have lost their figures, and are just mountains of flesh, like so many of these English ladies. When I see them, I am just thankful I never married. Husband and bairns are dear bought at that cost. Where are you going? Now, Jean, just sit and listen to me, and give me my cup of tea. There is Susan to take care of Lilias."

"But if the poor thing is disappointed, Margaret? I am sure, for my part, I expected—"

"And if you expected nonsense, will that do Lilias any good to let her see it?" cried Margaret, testily. "When she comes to herself, she will see that we have all been fools, and those that have the most sense will say nothing about it. That is the part I am intending to take. When you think of it, there could be nothing more ridiculous. When you speak to Lilias, you must just laugh at her. You must say that a drawing-room means nothing—it is just a formality. It means that you have come into the world, and that you are of the class of people that are beholden to pay their duty to the queen. That is all it means. I cannot tell," said Margaret, with irritation, "what other ridiculous idea the child has got into her head, or who put it there. Will you give me my cup of tea?"

Lilias came down after awhile in her ordinary dress, and with a countenance divided between mirth and melancholy.

"I thought I should feel a different person," she said, "but I am just the same. I thought the world was going to be changed, but there is no difference. All the same, I am a woman. I never can be sent back to the school-room, and made to refuse parties, and stay at home, and give up all the fun, now."

"All the fun is a vulgar expression," said Margaret. "It is just to take you to parties and give you pleasure that we have come here."

"Ah, but there is more than that. I am not going to be taken, but to go. I am grown-up now. It is curious," said Lilias, with a reflective air, "how you understand things just by doing them. I was thinking of something else; I was not thinking of this; and, of course, it turns out to be the most important. All this time I have been your child, yours and Jean's—now I am just me."

"So long as you do not carry it too far, my dear."

"I will carry it just as far as I can go," cried Lilias, with a laugh. She rejected the tea, out of which Margaret was getting much comfort, and ran upstairs again, where they could hear her at the piano, playing over everything she knew, which was not very much. The sound and measure were a little ease to her excitement. By-and-by Miss Jean was allowed by Margaret to get free, and, going upstairs, found Lilias standing with her forehead pressed against the window, looking out. There was not very much to see—the upper windows opposite across the light green foliage, a few carriages passing under the windows. When she heard some one coming into the room behind her, the girl broke forth suddenly.

"What are we here for in this strange place? I don't want to go to parties; they will just be like seeing the Queen. What has that to do with us? We may fancy we are great people, but we are only little small people, and nobody ever heard of us before."

"Lilias, my love," said Jean, with her arms round her little sister, "you must not say that."

"Why shouldn't I say it when it is true? To see all these grand ladies, and none of them knew us. Oh yes, Margaret had known them—two or three—but they had forgotten her and she only remembered them when she heard their names. But when we are at home everybody knows us. What is the use of pretending that we are great people like these? When we are at home we are great enough—as great as I want to be."

"Your nerves are just a little upset, my darling, and you are disappointed (and little wonder)."

"I am not disappointed—that is, I can see it was foolish all through; and I have no nerves; but I have made a fool of myself, and I could kill myself," cried Lilias; "and everybody—"

"Whisht! whisht! my bonnie dear. Put on your hat, and we will go out. Margaret is resting, and I have got some little things to do."

After a while this simple project delivered Lilias out of her trouble; to walk about in the air and sunshine, to see the other people, so many of them, going about their business, to watch the movement of the living world, even to go into the shops and buy "little things" here and there, a bit of ribbon in one, some gloves in another, a pretty bit of china Miss Jean had set her heart on, was enough to restore her to her usual light-heartedness. Nothing very tragical had happened, after all.

CHAPTER XXXIII

It was after this that the experiences in society began. The countess gave them a dinner, which was very kind and friendly, and at which they met various country friends. Indeed it was an entertainment which had a whiff of the country about it altogether, a sort of rural air; some of the gentlemen who were posted here and there about the table to talk the talk of the clubs and give the other convives a sense of being in London, got together after the meal was over and talked in the doorway between the two drawing-rooms with mutual commiseration.

"I suppose all this is on account of Bellendean," they said. Bellendean was her ladyship's son, and was intended to stand for the county on the next opportunity. "It is like the Georgies," these gentlemen said. "It is like running down into the country."

"The country!" said another, "where could you find any country like that? Not within five hundred miles."

The countess smiled upon this pair as she passed among her guests, and said, very low, "Talk to them— you are not doing your duty." The gentlemen from the clubs followed her with mute looks of despair. In this way a great lady does her devoir to her county without much hardship. At least, three of the more important guests believed the party to be made for them, and were surprised, and even a little more than surprised, to find themselves among their country neighbours. "Who would have thought of seeing you?" they said to each other. To Lilias it was delightful to find these old friends. She sympathized in the countess's very effusive regret at Bellendean's absence. "How sorry he will be," his mother said. Bellendean was believed to be engaged to Lady Ida, his plain relation. He was very good about it, and did his duty manfully; but to have put a pretty little creature like that in his way would have been madness, his mother felt. So that she entertained her rural neighbours alone, with the aid of the gentlemen from the clubs, who were all quite safe from bread-and-butter beauties, though they admired her complexion and said to each other, "Jove! where does the girl get her bloom from?"

"It does not come out of Bond Street," said the countess.

Miss Margaret was very stately in this party. She saw through it, and was indignant with Jean and Lilias for enjoying themselves. Two or three engagements sprang out of it, very pleasant, but somewhat humiliating to the head of the family, who had come to London in order to be beyond the country, and give Lilias experience of the great world. There were two or three little dinners, one in a hotel, and the others in other lodgings of similar character to those in Cadogan Place, and many proposals that they should go to the play together, and to the Royal Academy to see the pictures, proposals which it was all Margaret could do to prevent the others from accepting. She gave a couple of little parties herself to the rural notables. But all these did not count, they only kept her out of society, in the true sense of the word. Margaret was as proud a woman as ever bore a Scottish name, which is saying much; but it seemed to her that she would almost have stooped to a meanness to get an entry into the upper world which she felt to be circling just out of her reach, and from which now and then she heard echoes dropping into the lower spheres. It was not for herself she desired that entry. And almost wrathful contempt grew upon her as she heard the chatter of society, the evil tales, the coterie gossip, the inane vulgarities which, to a visionary from the country expecting great things, made the first impression of town in many cases the most distressful of disappointments. For herself, she longed for the serene quiet which, if it was sometimes dull, was at least always innocent, and where the routine of every day contented the harmless mind. Here an uneasy discontent, an ambition which she felt humiliating, a constant strain of anxiety which was mean and contemptible, filled her being. She wanted to know people who had no claim upon human approbation but that of knowing a great many other people and giving parties. She was unhappy because she was not acquainted with ladies in the fashionable world, and men who went everywhere. When Jean and Lilias, seated upon chairs by her side looking on at the passing crowds of Vanity Fair in Rotten Row with all the delight of people from the country, saw and hailed and exchanged joyous greetings with other people from the country passing by, Margaret's soul was filled with irritation and annoyance. These were not the acquaintances she desired. It vexed her to be exposed to their cordiality, their pleasure at sight of anybody they knew. Jean too was delighted to perceive in the crowd what she called "a kent face;" but Margaret's heart was wrung with envy, with unsatisfied wishes, and with a profound contempt for herself which underlay all these. She took the greatest trouble, however, to find out people of any pretensions to fashion whom she had ever known, to recall herself to their recollection, she who at home considered it her due to be courted and sought out by others. While she sat in the crowd and listened to the strangers about her talking over their amusements, her heart burned within her. "I saw you at Lady Dynevor's last night. Did you ever see such a crowd! As for dancing, it was out of the question:" or, "Are you going to the duchess's concert to-morrow? Mamma has promised to go if we can get away soon enough from the Esmonds', where we dine:" or, "We have promised just to look in at the French Ambassador's after the opera." She felt the muscles of her face elongate, and a watering in her mouth. She looked at these favoured ones with wistful eyes. She did not form any illusive vision to herself of the charm of society, or suppose it to be eloquent and brilliant and delightful, but she wanted to be in it, in the swing, as the slang expression was, not merely making little parties with friends from the country, fraternizing with known faces, going to the theatres and the sights. These were not Margaret's object; her heart sank as she saw the weeks passing, and felt herself to make no advance.

The countess's dinner had been a disappointment—almost, in the excited state of Margaret's feelings, had seemed an insult; but there was the greater gathering in prospect, the reception, at which all society was expected to be present, and to which she looked forward with a half-hope that this might realize some of her expectations, yet a half-certainty of further disappointment and offence. Lilias had got a new dress for the occasion, to her own surprise and almost dissatisfaction, for she was somewhat alarmed by Margaret's bounties; and Jean, though not without a little tremor lest the countess should recollect that she had worn it at Mrs. Stormont's ball, and indeed on several other occasions, put on her grey satin. Margaret was in black silk, very imposing and stately, with her beautiful lace. The three sisters were a fine sight as their hostess came forward to greet them at the door of the beautiful rooms, one within another, which, what with mirrors and a profusion of lights, seemed to prolong themselves into indefinite distance. The rooms were not very full as yet, for the ladies had come somewhat early, and the countess was very gracious to them. She admired Lilias, and kissed her on the cheek, and told Jean, who beamed, and Margaret, who was not quite sure that she was not offended, that their little sister was a credit to the North.

"If you keep in this room, you will hear who the people are as they come in," she said, with an easy assumption of the fact that they knew nobody.

They took their places accordingly at a little distance, the two elder ladies seating themselves until they were almost buried by the crowds that streamed in and stood all about them in lively groups, standing over them, talking across their shoulders as if they were objects in still life, till Miss Margaret rose indignantly and formed a little group of her own with Jean, who was a little bewildered, and Lilias, who eyed the talkers round her, half frightened, half wistful, with a great longing to have some one to talk with too.

"We may as well go into the next room," said Margaret; "there will perhaps be some more rational conversation going on there;" for it is impossible to describe how impatient she was growing of the duchess's concert, and dear Lady Grandmaison's Saturdays, and all the other places in which these fine people met each other daily or nightly. "To hear who they are," said Margaret, "might be worth our while, if they were persons that had ever been heard of; but when it is just Lady Tradgett, and Sir Gilbert Fairoaks, and the Misses This or That, it is not over-much to edification."

"And you cannot easily fit the folk to their names," said Miss Jean.

"They are just as little attractive as their names are," said Miss Margaret; "and what does it matter, when it is a name that no mortal has ever heard tell of, whether it has Lady to it or Sir to it?—or Duke even, for that matter; but dukes are mostly historical titles, which is always something."

"But it is a beautiful sight," said Miss Jean, "though it would be more pleasant if we knew more people."

"I cannot think," said Margaret, with a little bitterness, "that we would be much made-up with the acquaintance of the people here. So far as I can judge, it is just the rabble of society that comes to these big gatherings. It is just a sight, like going to the play."

"There is Lady Ida," said Lilias. "I hope she will come and speak to us. But I would rather go to the play, if it is only a sight."

"Oh, my dear, it is just beautiful," said Miss Jean. "Look at the flowers. The cost of them must have been a fortune—and all those grand mirrors reflecting them till you think every rose is double. And the diamonds, Lilias! There is an old lady there that is just like a lamp of light! and many beautiful persons too, which is still finer," Miss Jean added, casting a tender glance upon the little figure by her side, which she thought the most beautiful of all.

"Oh, Miss Murray, I am so glad to see you," said Lady Ida. "We were afraid you must have been caught by some other engagement; for no one minds throwing over an evening invitation. Yes, there are a great many people. My aunt knows everybody, I think. It is a bore keeping up such a large acquaintance, but people always come, for they are sure of meeting everybody they know."

"But that is not our case, for we are strangers—" began Miss Jean, thinking to mend matters.

Her sister silenced her by a look, which made that well-intentioned woman tremble.

"Being so seldom in town," she said, "it is not my wish to keep up an indiscriminate acquaintance. In the country you must know everybody, but in a place like London you can pick and choose."

This sentence was too long for Lady Ida, whose attention wandered.

"How do you do?" she said, nodding and smiling over Lilias' shoulder. "Ah, yes, to be sure, that is quite true. I suppose you are going to take Lilias to the ball everybody is talking of—oh, the ball, the Greek ambassador's?"

"Dear me, you have never heard of it, Margaret!" Miss Jean said.

"Oh, you must go! Lilias, you must insist upon going," Lady Ida cried, her eyes going beyond them to some new comers who hurried forward with effusive greetings. "You have got your tickets?" were the first words she addressed to them.

"Oh, so many thanks," said the new people. "We got them this morning. And I hear everybody is going. How kind of you to take so much trouble for us."

Miss Margaret, somewhat grimly, had moved away. Envy, and desire, and profound mortification were in her soul.

"If you cannot speak to the purpose, you might at least hold your tongue," she said to Jean, with unwonted bitterness.

Lilias followed them forlorn. She was dazzling in her young bloom. She was prettily dressed. Her sweet, wistful looks, a little scared and wondering, afraid of the crowd, which laughed and talked, and babbled about its pleasures, and took no notice of her, were enough to have touched any tender heart. And no doubt there were a number of sympathetic people about to whom Margaret and Jean would have been much more interesting than the majority of the chatterers, and who would have admired and flattered Lilias with the utmost delight. But there was nobody to bring them together. Lady Ida, in the midst of a crowd of her friends, was discussing in high excitement this great event in the fashionable world. The other people were meeting each other daily in one place or another. Our poor country friends, after the brave front they had put upon it at first, and their pretence of enjoying the beautiful sight—the flowers, the lights, the diamonds, the pretty people—began to feel it all insupportable. After a while, by tacit consent, they moved back towards the door.

"But the carriage will not be here for an hour yet, Margaret," Jean said.

"Then we will wait for it in the hall," said Margaret, sternly.

"Are you really going away so soon?" cried the countess, shaking hands with them. "I know! you are going to Lady Broadway's, you naughty people. But of course you want to make the best of your time, and show Lilias everything."

It was on Jean's lips to say, in her innocence, Oh no, they knew nothing about Lady Broadway: but fortunately she restrained herself. They drove home very silently, no one feeling disposed to speak, and when they reached the stillness of Cadogan Place, where they were not expected for an hour or two, and where no lamp was lighted, but only a pair of glimmering candles upon the mantel-piece, Miss Margaret closed the door, sending old Simon peremptorily away, and made a little address to her sisters.

"It appears," she says, "that I have been mistaken, Lilias. I thought the name of Murray of Murkley was well enough known to have opened all the best houses to us wherever we went, and I thought we had old friends enough to make society pleasant; but you perceive that I have been mistaken. I would have concealed it from myself, if I could, and I would have done anything to conceal it from you. But that is not possible after to-night. My heart is just broken to have raised your hopes, and then to disappoint them like this. But you see everything is changed. Our old friends are dead, or out of the way, and it's clear to me that those fashionable people, that are just living in a racket night and day, have no thought for any mortal but just themselves and their own kind. So there is nothing for it but to confess to you, Lilias, that I have just made a mistake, and proved how ignorant I am of the world."

"Oh! Margaret, not that—it is just the world that is unworthy of you," cried Jean, whom her sister put down with an impatient wave of her hand.

And now it was that Lilias showed her sense, as was often remarked afterwards. She gave her little skip in the air, and said, with a laugh,

"What am I caring, Margaret? Ida was never very nice. She might have introduced the people to us. If it had been a dance, it would have been dreadful to stand and see the rest enjoying themselves; but when it was nothing but talk, talk, what do I care?"

"It was a beautiful sight," said Jean, taking courage. "I am very glad to have seen it, though I had never spoken to any person. And we were not so bad as that. There was the countess and Lady Ida, and that old gentleman who trod upon my train, and that was very civil, besides—"

"Besides that we did not want them a bit, for there are three of us, and what do we care?" cried Lilias, throwing her arms round Margaret, who had dropped, overcome by disappointment and fatigue, into a chair.

Thus there was a little scene of mutual tenderness and drawing together after the trial of the evening, and Margaret retired to her room with a relieved heart, though she had felt an hour or two before as if, after having made her confession, she must drop the helm of the family for ever and slip into a secondary place. No one, however, seemed to see it in this light. Lilias and Jean had vied with each other in professions of enjoyment. They liked the Row, they liked the park, they liked going to the shops, and to see the play. If Margaret would not make herself unhappy about it, they would be quite content without society. They soothed her so much that she gave the helm a vigorous push before she went to rest that very night; for even while the others were speaking, and protesting their indifference to all the delights of the fashionable world, her thoughts had leapt away from them to speculate whether, after all, it might not be possible to show the countess and Lady Ida that their good offices were not necessary, and that without them Margaret Murray in her own person had credit enough to get tickets for the great ball. She said to herself that her cards were not played out yet, that she still had something in her power.

Lilias, for her part, was half-disposed to cry after her demonstration of pride and high spirits. As Jean helped to undress her, which she loved to do when she had the chance, the girl changed her tone.

"What is the use of all my pretty things, if we go nowhere?" she said. "Oh, I should like one ball, just to say I have been at a real ball in London. It would be dreadful to go back again, and, when Katie comes asking how many dances we were at, to say not one. Oh!" cried Lilias, clasping her hands, "I will tell fibs, I know I will, for it would be terrible to confess that."

"My darling!" cried Miss Jean. "Oh, I wish there was any way to get you asked to this grand one that all yon people were talking about. I am sure I would give a little finger if that would do any good."

"But your little finger would do no good," said Lilias, ruefully. "I see now that you never asked that fairy to my christening, as you ought to have done: and she has never forgiven it. But never mind, I must just tell Katie a good big one, for I will not have her pitying me. If it is a little bigger than a fib, it will only be a lee, and that is not so dreadful, after all."

"You must not tell even a fib, my darling—it is never right."

"No, it is never right," said Lilias, with a comical look, kissing her sister, who was now busy, smoothing out and folding the creamy, foamy white draperies in which Lilias had stood about the countess's rooms, not unremarked, though unfriended. What was the use of all these pretty things if they went nowhere? Miss Jean's thoughts were busy with the same problem that occupied her elder sister. It was too impossible to be considered a hope; but if she herself—she who was always the second and far inferior in every way to Margaret—if only she could find some way!

Thus those wonderful prognostications of glory and success with which Miss Margaret had persuaded Lilias to give up the little dissipations of the country, and in which she herself had entertained a faith so calm and assured, came to nothing. Lilias, though in Margaret's presence she took it so nobly, had a great many thoughts upon the subject after she had smiled sleepily and received Miss Jean's good night as if from the very borders of sleep. When Jean went out of the room on tiptoe, Lilias woke up and began to think. She looked down from those heights of experience on which she at present stood, upon herself in the happy vale of her ignorance in Murkley, with a little envy, yet a great deal of contempt. What a little silly thing she had been, expecting to go to Court in the way people write of in books, and to be one of the fine company about the Queen! Lilias reflected with amazement, and even with an amusement which was more droll than pleasant, that had it been suggested to her that she would certainly be invited to Windsor Castle, she would have accepted the incident as quite probable. Margaret had even spoken of the post of maid-of-honour. Lilias laughed a small laugh to herself in the dusk. She had believed it all, it had seemed to her quite natural; but never—never could she be such a simpleton again. One may be silly once, but when enlightenment of this sort comes, she said to herself, it is for ever!—never—never could she be deceived again. And then gulping down something in her throat, and drying her eyes hurriedly under cover of the dark, she declared to herself that it was far better to know, and that even the pain of it was better than the credulous foolishness with which she had taken everything in. In any case it was best to know. If Margaret had made such a mistake, it was not much wonder that she, Lilias, should have been deceived. Lilias recalled Lady Ida's look over her shoulder, the warmth of her greeting to the people who had got the tickets, who were in the world, and felt once more a sensation of hot resentment and indignation darting over her. And yet, perhaps, even that was not so bad as it seemed. When Katie Seton was taken by her mother to the county balls, the great ladies, even Margaret herself, would not encourage the intrusion. To be sure, Katie could not be left standing unnoticed, for she knew everybody just as well as Lady Ida did. But London was very different, London was the world, and it was evident that it was not Lilias' sphere. She saw all the foolishness of the idea as she lay thinking, throwing off the coverings and back the curtains to get as much air as possible in the little, close, London room. She said to herself: Oh! for Murkley, where there was always air enough and to spare, and wide, peaceful horizons, and unfathomable skies, and people who had known her from her cradle. That was far better than standing smiling at nothing, and trying to look as if she liked it, among hordes and hordes of unknown people who stared but never took any trouble to be kind to the strangers. "If I were them," cried Lilias, regardless of possibilities, "and saw strangers standing that knew nobody, it would be there I would go! I would not just stare and think it was not my business. I would make it my business!" She remembered so many ladies who looked as if they must be nice, and girls like herself surrounded with acquaintances and admirers. "Oh!" Lilias cried to herself, her eyes flashing in the dark, "if it had been me!" She would not have let another girl stand forlorn while she was enjoying herself. And Margaret and Jean, whom everybody could see were so far above the common! Perhaps it was because they were English—she said to herself, almost with a pleasant flash of enlightenment—that they were so little kind. But, then, the countess was not English. It was London that made them heartless, that made them think of no one but themselves: at home it could not be so. Then Lilias assured herself once more with lofty philosophy that, though it might not be very pleasant, it was well to have found out at once, so that there might be no further question about it, what a stranger had to expect in the world. No such thing could ever happen at home. The thing for herself and her sisters to do was to turn their backs upon this heartless society, indignant, dignified, valuing it as it deserved, and return to their native scenes, where everybody honoured them, where they were courted when they appeared, and regretted when they went away. The worst wish that Lilias could form was that some of these same young ladies whose looks she could remember anywhere, she thought, should appear in the country, knowing nobody: and then what a gracious revenge the Murrays would take! Margaret would not even wait for an introduction, she would let nobody stand there forlorn in the crowd, and Lilias herself, proudly magnanimous, would prefer them to all the little attentions which on Tayside could never fail. This thought gave a warmer desire to the longing of her disappointment to get home.

But, as she was going to sleep, lulled by this anticipation, two regrets sprang up within her mind, retarding for at least five minutes each her slumbers—one was the thought what a pity to have so many pretty things and never to go anywhere where they could be worn; the other was a keen, acute, stinging realization of Katie, and the many questions that little woman of the world would ask her. "How many balls were you at?" Lilias almost skipped out of bed in her impatience. "But I will not own to it. I will tell her a fib rather. I will almost tell her a lee," Lilias cried to herself. A lee was perhaps worse than a fib; but it was not supposed to be so harsh a thing as a lie—at least upon Tayside.

CHAPTER XXXIV

Next morning some further incidents occurred which disturbed Margaret, just recovering from the discomfiture of the preceding night, and plunged her into fresh anxiety. It was Jean that was the cause of one of these as of so many of her annoyances since they came to town—Jean, who could not contain her pleasure when amid all these crowds of unknown people she saw "a kent face." She had got so much into the way of doing this, and was so delighted with everybody that looked like home, ministers with their wives who had come up for a holiday after the Assembly, and little lairds, and professional persons of all classes, that, when it was possible, her sister had contrived to leave Jean at home when they went into the Row for their usual walk. But on this occasion it had not been possible to do so, and scarcely were they seated under their favourite tree, when Margaret with dismay heard the usual explosion.

"Oh! Lilias, just look—it is certainly him; though I never would have thought of seeing him here."

"Whom do you mean by him?" said Margaret. "And for goodness sake, Jean, where everybody is hearing you, do not exclaim like that. You will just be taken for an ignorant person that knows nobody."

"And I'm sure they would not be far wrong that thought so," said Jean. "Yes, I was sure it was him: and glad, glad he will be to see us, for he seems not to have a creature to speak to. Dear me, Philip," she said, rising and stretching out her hand through a startled group who separated to let the friends approach each other, "who would have thought of seeing you here!"

Philip Stormont's face lighted up.

"I was looking for you," he said, in his laconic way. He had been strolling along with a vague stare, looking doubly rustic and home-spun and out of place; he had the very same cane in his hand with the knob that he used to suck at Murkley. "I knew you were here, and I was looking for you," he said.

"And have you just arrived, and straight from Tayside? and how is your good mother and all our friends?"

"My mother is away: and I've been away for the last three months," said Philip; "I've been out in the Mediterranean. There was little doing at home, and she was keen for me to go."

"And now I suppose you have come to London to go into all the gaieties here?" said Margaret, for the first time taking her part in the conversation. She looked somewhat grimly at the long-leggit lad. He was brown from his sea-voyaging, and too roughly clad for these fashionable precincts. "This is just the height of the season, and you'll no doubt intend to turn yourself into a butterfly, like the rest of the young men."

"I am not very like a butterfly now," said Philip, suddenly awakened to the imperfections of his dress.

"Oh! but that is soon mended," said Miss Jean, always kind; "you will have to go to your tailor, and you will soon be as fine as anybody."

Philip grew fiery red with sudden shame and dismay. He cast a glance at Lilias, and read the same truth in her eyes. Except Jean, who had first found him out, nobody was very glad to see him in his sea-going tweeds. It had not struck him before. He muttered something about making himself decent, and left them hurriedly, striding along out of sight under the trees. Miss Margaret smiled as he disappeared.

"Well," she said, drawing a long breath, "that is a good riddance; and I wish the rest of our country friends were got rid of as easy. I think you might remember, Jean, that to entertain the like of Philip Stormont is not what we came to London for."

Jean was magnanimous. She had it on her lips to say something of the failure so far of their expedition to London, but it died away before it was spoken. As for Margaret, she had forgotten the downfall of last night. Her mind was labouring with schemes for advancement. All her faculties were nerved to the struggle. But, alas! what are faculties when it is friends you want? To repulse Philip was a matter of instinct; but to open the doors of the great houses was another affair. And, even when that was done, all was not done; for what would be the good of taking Lilias to a great ball unless there was some prospect of getting her partners when she was there? Margaret had determined that she would accomplish both—but how? To see a worthy human being struggling in the face of difficulties is a great sight, especially when he (or she) struggles not for himself, but for those he loves. Nothing can be more entirely true, or indeed more completely a truism; but when the difficulties are those of getting an invitation to a ball, and, when there, partners for your charge, the world may laugh, but the struggle is no less arduous. A mother in such a case gets contempt, if not reproach, instead of any just appreciation; but a sister may perhaps secure a gentler verdict. Such love was in the object, if it was not otherwise very worthy; and if there was much pride too, it was of so natural a kind. She shook off Philip as she would have shaken off a thorn that clung to her dress; but still he was another element of discomfort. She wanted no long-leggit lad to attach himself to her party, and less now than ever—for who could tell what effect the contrast between the indifference of the world and the devotion of her old playfellow might have upon Lilias if once, she said to herself, he was out of those ridiculous tweeds, which he ought to have known better than to appear in. Margaret made the signal to her party to rise from their chairs after this little incident. She had a suspicion that the people about were smiling at the encounter with the rustic. But indeed the people about were concerned with themselves, and paying little attention to the ladies from the country. Everybody knew them to be ladies from the country, which of itself was an irritating circumstance enough.

They got up accordingly with great docility and joined the stream of people moving up and down. And now it was that another encounter, more alarming and unexpected still, brought her heart to Margaret's mouth, and moved both the others in different ways with sudden excitement. As they moved along with the tide on one hand, the other stream coming the other way, an indiscriminate mass, in which there were so few faces that had any interest for them, suddenly, without warning, wavered, opened, and disclosed a well-known countenance, all lighted up with animation and eagerness. There was no imperfection of appearance in the case of this young man. He was walking with two or three others, and there was in his eyes nothing of that forlorn gaze in search of acquaintances which distinguished the rural visitor. He had been, perhaps, too dainty for Murkley, but he was in his element here. He came up to the three ladies, taking off his hat with that unusual demonstration of respect which had amused them amid the less elaborate salutations of the country. His appearance froze the blood in Margaret's veins. She felt that no compromise was possible, that her action must be stern and decisive. She turned and gave Lilias a peremptory look, then made Lewis such a curtsey as filled all the spectators with awe. She even dropped her hand by her side and caught hold of the draperies of Lilias to ensure that the girl followed her. Lilias had almost given her little skip in the air for pure pleasure at the sight of him, when she received that look and secret tug, more imperative still. She put out her hand as she was swept past with an "Oh, Mr. Murray!" which was half a protest: but she was too much astonished to resist Margaret. Jean, left behind, in her surprise and delight, greeted the stranger with a tremulous cry.

"Oh, but I am glad to see you!" she said.

But, when she saw that Margaret had swept on, she made an agitated pause. Lewis took her hand almost with gentle violence.

"You must speak to her—you have always been my friend," he said.

"Oh, yes, Mr. Murray, I am your friend," said Miss Jean, following with her eyes the two figures that were disappearing in the crowd; "but what am I to do if I lose Margaret?"

Her perplexity and distress would have amused a less tender observer.

"We will go after them," he said, "and, if we miss them, cannot I see you home?"

"But that would be taking you from your friends," said Miss Jean, with wondering eyes and much-divided wishes. As, however, even in this moment, she was already separated from Margaret, there was nothing to be done but accept his companionship.

Jean was in a ferment of excitement and anxiety. It was what she had wished and hoped for—it was delightful—it filled her with an exhilarating sense of help and satisfaction; but, at the same time, if it should turn out to be going against Margaret! How difficult it is in such a terrible, unlooked-for crisis to know exactly what to do! She did what her heart desired, which is the most general solution.

"They will probably turn at the end, and then I can go back to them," she said. "And why should Margaret object? for you have always been my friend."

"Yes," said Lewis, "you will recollect it was you I knew first in the family: and I was always supposed to be your visitor. What pleasant hours those were at the piano! Ah, you could not be so cruel as to pass me, to treat me like a stranger. We are in each other's confidence," he said, looking so kindly, tenderly at her, with a meaning in his eyes which Miss Jean understood, and which delivered her at once out of her little flutter of timidity. She answered him with a look, and became herself once more.

"It is so indeed," she said. "We have both opened our hearts to one another, though I might be your mother. And glad, glad I am to see you. I feel a little lost among all these people, though it is very interesting to watch them: but I am just most happy when I come upon a kent face. And have you been long in London, and have you friends here? Without that there is but little pleasure in it," Miss Jean said, with a suppressed sigh.

Then Lewis began to tell her that he had been in town for a week or two, and had gone everywhere looking for her and her sisters; that he had found abundance of friends, people whom he had met abroad, who had known him "in my god-father's time," he said.

"I think I know almost all the diplomatic people, and they are a host; and it is wonderful to find how many people one has come across, for everybody goes abroad."

Jean listened with admiration and a sigh.

"There are few," she said, "of these kind of persons that come in our way, either at Murkley or Gowanbrae."

Something in her tone attracted his attention, especially to the sentiment of this remark, and Lewis was too sympathetic to be long unacquainted with its meaning.

"No doubt," he said, "it is a long time since you have been here: and you find your old friends gone, and strangers in their place."

"That is just it," said Miss Jean. "It has been perhaps a little disappointment—oh, not to Lilias and me, who are delighted to see everything, and never think of parties and things—but Margaret will vex herself about it, wanting the child to enjoy herself, and to see all that's worth seeing. You will understand the feeling. There is some great ball now," she added, with vague hopes for which she could not account to herself, "which everybody is speaking of—"

"It is perhaps the Greek ball? Is she going?" cried Lewis, eagerly. "Ah, that will be what you call luck—great luck for me."

"I cannot say that she is going—if you mean Margaret," said Miss Jean, trembling to feel success within reach. "It is not a thing, you know, that tempts the like of us at our age—but just for Lilias. Well, I cannot say. I hear people are asking for invitations, which, to my mind, is a wonderful way of going about it. I do not think Margaret, who is a proud person, would ever bring her mind to that."

"She shall not need," said Lewis. "Would she go? Would you go? Dear Miss Jean, will not you do this for me? They are my dear friends, those people. They know me since I was a boy. They will call at once, and send the invitation. If I were not out of favour with your sister, I would come with my friends. But not a word! Do not say a word! It will all pass as if we had nothing to do with it, you and I. That is best; but in return you will see that Miss Lilias saves for me a dance, two dances perhaps."

"Poor thing!" said Miss Jean, "my fear just is that she will have all her dances to spare; for we do not know many people, and the people we know are not going—and it is perhaps just a little unfortunate for Lilias."

"That will not happen again," cried Lewis, with a glow of pleasure. "I am not of any good in Murkley, but I can be of some use here."

In the mean time Lilias, very much disappointed, was demanding an explanation from her sister.

"It was Mr. Murray, Margaret! I would have liked to speak to him. He was always nice. And you liked him well enough at Murkley. He was dressed all right, not like poor Philip. Why might not I stop and speak to him? I had to give him my left hand, for you pulled me away."

"There was no need for giving him any hand at all. He is just a person we know nothing about—what his family is, if he belongs to anybody," Miss Margaret said.

"But we know him," said Lilias, with that perfectly inconclusive argument which sounds so powerful to the foolish speaker, but which in reality means nothing.

Margaret was full of irritation and annoyance, and a sense of danger to come.

"What does that matter?" she cried. "Him! We know no harm of him, if that is what you mean. But his belongings are unknown to me, and with a man of his name, that cannot but harm. If it was one of your English names, it might just be any ignoramus: but there is no good Murray that has not a drop's blood, as people say, between him and Murkley. I will have no traffic with that young man."

"But he came to us at home!" said Lilias, in great surprise, "and I saw him—often."

"Where did you see him, you silly thing? Twice, thrice, at the utmost!"

"Oh, Margaret! I used to see him with Katie. Katie was always about the park, you know; and he was so fond of the new castle, and always making sketches—"

Margaret looked at her with severe eyes. And indeed Lilias, who had revealed perhaps more than was expedient, coloured, and was embarrassed by her observation, though she indignantly declared to herself that there was "no cause."

"So you saw him—often?" the elder sister said. "This is news to me—and the more reason we should see nothing of him now; for a young man that will thrust himself upon a girl's company when she is out of the protection of her friends—"

"Margaret!" cried Lilias, with a flash of indignation. "Are you going to leave Jean behind?" she added, hastily, in a voice of horror, as Margaret, instead of turning back at the end of the walk, hurriedly directed her steps homeward, crossing with haste and trepidation the much crowded road.

"Jean must just take the risk upon herself. It is no doing of mine. She will tell him no doubt where we are living, and the likelihood is he will see her home. But mind you," said Margaret, turning round upon the girl with that little pause in her walk to emphasize her words, which is habitual with all eloquent persons, "I will not have that young lad coming about us here. There must be no seeing—often, here— no, nor seldom either. I am your guardian, and I will not be made light of. He is not a person that I consider good enough for your acquaintance, and I will not have it. So you must just choose between him and me."

"Margaret!" cried Lilias again, in consternation.

Her mind had been agreeably moved by the sight of Lewis. He was more than a kent face, he was a friend: and indeed he was more than a friend. Whatever might be her feelings towards him, on which she had not at all decided, Lilias had a very distinct idea of what his feelings were towards her, and, let theorists say what they will, there is nothing more interesting to a girl than the consciousness that she is—thought of, dreamed of, admired, present to the mind of another, even if she does not permit herself to say beloved. The sight of him had brought back all those vague pleasures and embarrassments, those shynesses, yet suddenly confidential outbursts, which had beguiled the afternoon hours at Murkley. How friendly he looked! how ready to listen! how full of talk! and how his face had lighted up at the sight of her! He was very different from Philip sucking his stick, not knowing what to do, and from the young men of society, who stared, inspecting the ladies as if that impertinence was a certain duty. Lewis had expanded with pleasure. He had detached himself from his friends in a moment. The sun had shone full upon his head as he stood uncovered, eager to speak. He was not handsome. He was not even tall or big, or in any way imposing. As for the hero of whom Lilias had dreamt so long, Lewis was not in the smallest degree like that paladin; there need be no alarm on that subject. But he was a friend, and to be swept away from a friend in this desert place where there were so few of them, was at once a pain and an injury. What did Margaret mean? Lilias felt herself insulted by the suspicion expressed, which she was too proud to protest against. Her indignant exclamation, "Margaret!" was all that she would condescend to. And they walked homeward through the streets, which Margaret, in despite and alarm, had hastily chosen instead of returning by the park, without saying a word to each other. It was the first time that this had happened in Lilias' life. Her heart grew fuller and fuller as she went home. Was Margaret, the ruler, the universal guide, she who up to this time had been infallible, was she prejudiced, was she unkind? When they reached the house, they separated, neither saying a word. But this was intolerable to Lilias, who by-and-by ran down to Margaret's room, and flung herself into her sister's arms.

"I cannot bear it! I cannot bear it! Scold me, if you like, but speak to me, Margaret," cried the little girl.

It was a very small matter, yet it was a great matter to them. Margaret took the girl in her arms with a trembling in her own strong and resolute figure.

"You are the apple of my eye, you are the light of my eyes," she said, which was all the explanation that passed between them. For Lilias was awed by the solemnity of her sister's rarely-expressed love. It thrilled her with a wonderful sense of something too great for her own littleness, an undeserved adoration that made her humble. It did not occur to her that great tyrannies are sometimes the outspring of such a passion. On the contrary, she felt that in the presence of this, her little liking for a cheerful face was as nothing, too trifling a matter to be thought of; and yet there was in her mind a little hankering after that pleasant countenance all the same.

It was some time later before Jean returned, and there was in her a wonderful flutter of embarrassment and delight, and of fictitious composure, and desire to look as if nothing had happened, which filled Lilias with curiosity and Margaret with an angry contempt for her sister, as for an old fool, who was allowing her head to be turned by the attentions of that young man. That young man was the name Lewis took in the agitated mind of the elder sister. He was not even a long-leggit lad, a member of a well-defined and honourable caste, which it is permissible to women to be foolish about. Did the old haverel think that it was really her he was wanting?—Margaret asked herself: with a disdain which it wounded her to entertain for her sister.

"He would say he had been just wearying to see you," she said, when Jean entered late for luncheon, and with her hair hastily brushed, which the wind had blown about a little under her bonnet. Jean was not too old to indulge in hairdressing, in fringes and curls on her forehead, had she so chosen, and indeed the wind would sometimes do as much for her as fashion did for others, finding out unexpected twists and fantasies in her brown locks. She had smoothed herself all down outwardly, but had not quite succeeded in patting down those spiritual signs of a ruffling breeze of excitement which answer to the incipient curls and secret twists in the hair.

"He said he was very glad to see us all, poor lad! It was a great disappointment to him, Margaret, when you just sailed away like that—without a word."

"I hope," said Miss Margaret, "that I am answerable to nobody for the choice I make of my friends, and this young man is one that gives no satisfaction to me."

"Oh, but, Margaret—" cried Miss Jean, in eager remonstrance.

"I am laying down no laws for you—you are your own mistress, as I am mine; but I will have none of him," Margaret said, decisively.

This sudden judgment had a great effect upon the gentler sister.

"Oh! but, Margaret," she repeated, again looking wistfully at the head of the house. Then her anxious eyes sought Lilias. "I am sure," she said, "that one more respectful or more anxious to be of any use—"

"And what use do you expect a lad like that to be?" cried Margaret, with high disdain. "I hope the Murrays of Murkley will be able to fend for themselves without help from any unknown person," she added, with lofty superiority.

Jean looked at her with a glance in which there was disappointment, impatience, wistfulness, and something else which Lilias could not divine. There was more in it than mere regret for this ignoring of Lewis' excellencies. There was—could it be possible?—a kind of compassion for the other side. But this was so very unlikely a sentiment to be entertained by Jean for Margaret that Lilias, secretly observing, secretly ranging herself on Jean's side, felt that she must be mistaken. But Jean was not herself; she was so crushed by this conversation that she became silent, and said no more, though it was evident that there came upon her again and again an impulse to talk, which it was scarcely possible to restrain. Something was on her lips to say, which she had driven back almost by force. A concealed triumph was bursting forth by every outlet. When she sat down to her work, secret smiles would come upon her face. A quiver was in her hands which made her apparent industry quite ineffectual. She would start and look at Lilias when any sound was heard without. Once when Margaret left the room for a moment, Jean made a rush at her little sister and kissed her with an agitation to which Lilias had no clue.

"Just you wait a little; it will come perhaps this afternoon," cried Miss Jean in her ear.

"Do you expect Mr. Murray, Jean? Oh! Margaret will not be pleased," Lilias cried, in alarm.

Jean shook her head violently and retreated to the window, where, when Margaret returned to the room, she was standing looking out.

"Dear me! can you not settle to something?" said Margaret. "I have no nerves to speak of, but to see you whisking about like this is more than I can put up with. The meeting this morning has been too much for you."

"Oh, how little you know," cried Jean, under her breath—and this time there was no mistaking the compassion, the reproachful pity in her eyes; but then she added—"Perhaps I am a little agitated, but it is to think you should be so prejudiced—you that have always had more insight than other folk."

"If I have had the name of more insight, cannot you believe that I'm right this time?" said Margaret.

Jean, standing at the window looking out, did nothing but shake her head. She was entirely unconvinced. When, however, Margaret announced some time after that she had ordered the victoria, and was going out to make some calls with Lilias, this intimation had a great effect upon Jean. She turned round with a startled look to interpose.

"Dear me, you are not going out again, Margaret! and me so sure you would be at home. You will just tire yourself, and Lilias too: and if you remember that we are going to the play to-night. There are no calls surely that are so urgent as that."

"Bless me!" said Margaret, taken by surprise, "what is all this earnestness for? You are perhaps expecting a visit from your friend; but in that case it is far better that Lilias and me should be out of the way."

"I am expecting no visit from him. I had to tell him, poor lad, that it would be best not to come; but I wish you would stay in, Margaret: I think it is going to rain, and you have just an open carriage, no shelter. And you can never tell who may call. You said yourself that when you went out in the afternoon you missed just the people you most wanted to see."

"I am expecting nobody to-day," said Margaret; "and, if anybody comes, there is you to see them."

"Me!" cried Jean, with a nervous tremor. "And what could I say to them? What if it should be strangers?"

"I hope you have a good Scots tongue in your head," said Miss Margaret, somewhat warmly perhaps. But Lilias lingered to console the poor lady, whose look of alarm and trouble was greater than any mere possibility could have produced.

"Oh! my darling, try to persuade her to stay at home; but mind you do not say a word," cried Jean in the ear of Lilias, holding her two arms. "I think there may perhaps be—some grand people coming. And how could I speak to them?"

"What grand people?" the girl cried.

"Oh, hold your tongue—hold your tongue, Lilias! I would not have her suspect—but who can tell what kind of people may be coming? Something always happens when people are out; and then this ball—"

"Margaret," cried Lilias, "don't go out this afternoon. Jean thinks that people may be calling—somebody who could get us tickets—"

"Oh! not me, not me," cried Jean, putting her hand on the girl's mouth. "I never said such a thing. It was just an imagination—or a presentiment—"

"Well," said Margaret, with her bonnet on, "Jean is just as able to receive the finest company as I am. She is looking very nice, she has a little colour. To be silly now and then is good for the complexion; she is fluttered with the sight of her young friend—is it friend you call him, Jean?"

"What could I call him else?" cried Jean, with dignity. "I will never call a man more, as you well know; and besides, I might be his mother. And why should I call him less, seeing he has always been so good to me, and one that I think much of? But I am not expecting Mr. Murray, you need not be feared for that. It is just a kind of presentiment," Miss Jean said.

CHAPTER XXXV

Miss Jean sat down to her work at the window when the others went out. There was a balcony full of flowers which prevented her from seeing anything more distinct than the coming and going of the carriages, but that was enough to keep her in a flutter of awed and excited expectation. Lewis had said that his friends would call at once, and the idea of receiving a foreign lady, a foreign ambassadress, who perhaps did not speak English, made Miss Jean tremble from the lace of her cap to the toe of her slipper. She tried to remember the few words of school-book French which lingered in her mind; but what if the lady spoke only Greek? In that case, their intercourse would need to be carried on by signs: or, since she was an ambassadress, she would perhaps carry an interpreter with her. Jean did not know the manners and habits of such people. To be left to encounter such a formidable person alone was terrible to her. And what would so great a lady think if she came in expecting Margaret, whom no doubt Lewis would have described, and found only Jean? "We saw nobody but a homely sort of country person,"—that was what she would say. But the case was desperate, and though, when the moment actually arrived, and an imposing carriage and pair dashed up with all the commotion possible to the door, and the knocker resounded through the house, Miss Jean's heart beat so loudly in her ears that it drowned the very knocker, yet still there was a sort of satisfaction in thus venturing for the sake of Lilias, facing such an excitement for her benefit, and obtaining for her what even Margaret had not been able to obtain.

Simon, creaking along the passage in his creaking shoes, seemed to tread upon Miss Jean's heart. Would he never be ready? She waited, expecting every moment the door to open, the sweep of silken draperies, or perhaps—who could tell?—the entrance of a resplendent figure in costume other than that of fashion; for Jean was aware that Greece was in the east, and had been delivered in her youth out of its subjection to the Turks, and that the men wore kilts, and the women probably—These were long before the days of the dual dress, and the idea filled her with alarm. She put away her work with trembling hands, and stood listening, endeavouring to calm herself and make her best curtsey, but in a whirl of anxiety lest Simon should not say the name right or else be unable to catch it. But when, instead of this extraordinary ordeal, she heard the clang, the stir, the glittering sound of hoofs and wheels and harness, and became aware that the carriage had driven away, Jean came to herself quite suddenly, as if she had fallen to the ground. It was a relief unspeakable, but perhaps, also, it was a little disappointment. She dropped back upon her chair. To go through so many agonies of anticipation for nothing is trying too. And Simon came upstairs as if he were counting his steps, as if it was of no consequence!

"I told them you were in, Miss Jean, but they just paid no attention to me: and I do not think you have lost much, for they were too flyaway, and not of your kind. I hope there's cards enough: and this big letter, with a seal as large as Solomon's," said Simon.

She took them with another jump of her heart. The envelope was too big for the little tray on which he had placed it; it was half covered with a great blazon. The cards were inscribed with a name which it taxed all Jean's powers to make out. She was so moved that she made a confidant of Simon, having no one else to confide in.

"It's an invitation," she said, "for one of the grandest balls in all London."

Simon, for his part, looked down upon the magnificent enclosure without any excitement, with a cynical eye.

"It's big enough to be from the Queen," he said, "and it will keep ye up to a' the hours of the night, and the poor horse just hoasting his head off. You'll excuse me, Miss Jean, but I cannot help saying rather you than me."

"I should have thought, Simon," said Miss Jean, reproachfully, "that you would have had some feeling for Miss Lilias."

"Oh! I have plenty of feeling for Miss Lilias; but sitting up till two or three, or maybe four in the morning is good for nobody," Simon said.

Miss Jean could not keep still. As for work, that was impossible. She met Margaret at the door, when the little victoria drove up, with a countenance as pale as ashes.

"God bless me!" cried Margaret, in alarm, "what has happened?"

Jean thrust the cards and the envelope into her hands.

"You will know," she said, breathless, "what they mean better than me." Miss Jean salved her conscience by adding to herself, "And so she will! for she understands everything better than I do."

"What is it, Margaret?" said Lilias.

The ladies had been engaged all the afternoon in a hopeless effort of which Lilias was entirely unconscious; they had gone to call on a number of people in whom the girl, at least, felt no interest, but to whom Margaret had condescended with a civility which her little sister could not understand—The countess, who was too much occupied to pay them any attention, and Lady Ida, who thought quite enough had been done for the country neighbours, and was inclined to show that she was bored; and the wife of the county member, who was on the other side in politics, and consequently received the Miss Murrays with respect but coldness, and some dowagers, who had almost forgotten Margaret, and some new people who were barely acquainted with her—Why did she take all that trouble?

"You are bound," Miss Margaret said, "when you are in London just to keep up everybody. You never can tell when they may be of use."

"Is it to make them of use that you are friends with people?" Lilias had asked, with wonder. But they were of no use. How was it possible? And, even if they had been likely to be so Margaret's heart had failed her. She was not used to such manœuvres. She came back in very low spirits, feeling that it was impossible, feeling impotent, and feeling humiliated not so much because of her impotence, as for a contempt of her own aim. Between the two her heart had sunk altogether. To think it possible that she, Margaret Murray, should be going from door to door in a strange place, seeking an invitation to a ball! Was such ignominy possible? She was angry with herself, angry with the world in which trifles were of so much importance, angry with that big, pitiless place, which had no knowledge of the Murrays of Murkley, and cared for neither an old race, nor a lovely young creature like Lilias, nor anything but just monstrous wealth and impudence: for that was how Margaret put it, being disheartened and disappointed and disgusted with herself. And coming in, in this state of mind, to meet Jean, pale as a ghost, what could she think of but misfortune? She expected to hear that Murkley Castle had been burnt to the ground, or that their "man of business" had run away. Poor Mr. Allenerly, who was as safe as Edinburgh Castle standing on a rock! but panic does not wait to count probabilities. When the big envelope was thrust into her hand she looked at it with alarm, as if it might wound her. And to think, after all this mortification, disgust, and terror, to think of finding, what at this moment looked like everything she desired, in her hand! For the time, forgetting the frivolous character of the blessing, Margaret was inclined to believe with a softening and grateful movement of her heart that it had fallen upon her direct from heaven.

And during the rest of the afternoon no other subject was thought of. When the ladies assembled over their tea in delightful relaxation and coolness after the fuss and flutter of their walks and drives, and those afternoon calls, which had brought nothing but vexation, the little scene was worthy of any comedy. The delight of Lilias, which was entirely natural and easy, had no such impassioned character about it as the restrained and controlled exultation which showed in Margaret's quietest words and movements. Jean, who was still pale and trembling with the dread of detection and the strain of excitement, by-and-by began to regard, with a wonder for which there were no words, her sister's perfect unconsciousness and absence of suspicion. To associate this envied distinction with Jean or anything she could have done, or with the slight person whom she had declined to have anything to say to in the morning, whose overtures she had negatived so sternly, never entered Margaret's thoughts. In the happiness and calm that came over her after the first ecstasy, she indulged, indeed, in a number of speculations. But, after all, what so natural as that the lady with the wonderful name, which none of them ventured to pronounce, had heard that the Miss Murrays of Murkley were in town, and perhaps had them pointed out to her somewhere, and felt that without Lilias the ball would be incomplete.

"It might be the countess, but I can hardly think it, or she would have let fall something to that effect," Margaret said; "and as for Mrs. Maxwell, they are just in a sort of House-of-Commons circle, and know little about fashion. But I am not surprised for my part: for, after all, family is a thing that does tell in society, and I have always felt that what was wanted was just to have it known we were here. Yes, it is a great pleasure, I do not deny it—though if anybody had told me I would have been so pleased to get an invitation to a ball at my age—"

"It is not for yourself, Margaret."

"—But I am not surprised. The wonder has been the little attention we have received: but I make little doubt we'll have even too much to fill up our time now it is known we are here. And, Lilias, you must remember I will not allow too much of it, to turn your head."

Lilias did not make any reply. She was studying the face of Jean, who was very intent upon Margaret, following her looks with wondering admiration, and half-struggling against her better knowledge to believe that her sister must be in the right after all.

"You see," said Margaret, discoursing pleasantly and at her ease, as she leant back in her chair, "we are all apt to judge the world severely when we are not just getting what we want. I confess that I was in a very ill key the other night. To be in the middle of a large company all enjoying themselves, and acquainted with each other, and to know nobody, is a trial for the temper. And as I am a masterful person by nature, and perhaps used to my own way, I did not put up with it as I ought. And if I had left town in a pet—as I had a great mind to do—the impression would just never have been removed. But you see what a little patience does. Indeed I have remarked before this that, when you see everything at its blackest, Providence is just preparing a surprise for you, and things are like to mend."

"If one can say Providence, Margaret," said Jean, a little shocked, "about such a thing as a ball!"

"Do you think there is anything, great or small, that is beneath that?" Margaret cried; but she felt herself abashed at having gone so far. "I am not meaning the ball," she said. "What I am meaning is just the recognition that we had a kind of a right to look for, and the friendship and understanding which is the due of a family long established, and that has been of use to its country, like ours. I hope you do not think that beneath the concern of Providence—for the best of life is in it," she added, taking high ground. "Little things may be signs of it: but you will not say it is a little thing to be well thought upon and duly honoured among your peers."

To this Jean listened with her lips dropping a little apart, and her eyes more wide open than their wont, altogether abashed by the importance of the doctrine involved, not knowing how to fit it into her own ideal of existence, and half-tempted to confess that it was by her simple instrumentality, and not in so dignified a way, that the event had come about.

"But, Margaret—" she said.

"My dear, I wish you would not be always so ready with your buts. You are just becoming a sort of Thomas, aye doubting," Margaret said. "But, Jean—if you are going to the play, as you are so fond of, we will have to be earlier than usual—and, in that case, it is time to dress: though I am so tired, and have so much to think of, that I would rather stay at home."

"There will be your ticket lost," said Jean, though in her heart she was almost glad to have a little time out of Margaret's presence to realize all that had passed on this agitating day.

"You can send it to Philip Stormont," said Margaret, moved to unusual good humour, "and take him with you. To look for your carriage and all that, he will be more use than old Simon. No, it is true I have no great opinion of him. He is just a long-leggit lad. He has little brains, and less manners, and his family is just small gentry; but still he's maybe a little forlorn, and in a strange place he will look upon us as more or less belonging to him."

"Oh, Margaret!" cried Jean, almost with tears in her eyes, "that is a thing I would never have thought of. There is nobody like you for a kind heart."

Margaret said "Toot!" but did not resent the imputation. "When you find that you are thought upon yourself, it makes you more inclined to think upon other people. And I'll not deny that I am pleased. To think you and me, Jean, should be making all this work about a ball! I am just ashamed of myself," she said, with a little laugh of pleasure.

But Jean did not make any response. She sent off old Simon to the address which Philip even in the few moments they had seen him had found time to give, and went upstairs to prepare in the silence of bewilderment, not able to explain to herself the curious self-deception and mistake of the sister to whom she had always looked up. She had been afraid of being seen through at once: her tremor, her excitement, her breathless consciousness, all, Jean had feared would betray her yet: Margaret had never observed them at all! She was glad, but she was also bewildered on her sister's account, and half-humiliated on her own. For to have been suspected would have been something. Not to have even been suspected at all, with so many signs of guilt about her, was so wonderful that it took away her breath. And, tenderly respectful as her mind was, she felt a little ashamed, a little to blame that Margaret had been so easily deceived. Her satisfaction in her delusion abashed Jean. She saw a grotesque element in it, when she knew how completely mistaken it was. Lilias, who had been questioning her with her eyes without attracting much attention from Jean, whose mind was busy elsewhere, followed her upstairs. If Margaret did not suspect the secret with which she was running over, Lilias did. She put her arm round the conspirator from behind, making her start.

"It is you, Jean," she whispered in her ear.

"Oh! me, Lilias! How could it be me? Do I know these kind of foreign folk?"

"Then you know who it is, and you are in the secret," Lilias said.

Jean threw an alarmed glance towards Margaret's closed door.

"You are to keep two dances for him," she whispered, hurriedly; "but if I had thought what a deception it would be, Lilias! It just makes me meeserable!"

"I hope you will never have anything worse to be miserable about," said the girl, with airy carelessness.

"Oh! whisht, whisht!" cried Miss Jean, "it would go to her very heart," and she led the indiscreet commentator on tiptoe past Margaret's door. Lilias sheltered herself within her own with a beating heart. To keep two dances for him! Then it was he who had done it. It did not occur to Lilias that to call any man he was dangerous and significant. She had not a doubt as to who was meant. Though she had not been allowed to speak to him, scarcely to look at him, yet he had instantly exerted himself to do her pleasure. Lilias sat down to think it over, and forget all about the early dinner and the play. Her heart beat high as she thought of the contrast. She had no knowledge of the world, or the way in which girls and boys comport themselves to each other now-a-days, which is so different from the way of romance. To think that he should have set to work to procure a gratification for her, though she had been made to slight him, pleased her fancy. Why did he do it? It could not be for friendship, because she was not allowed to show him any. Was it—perhaps—for the sake of Jean? In the unconscious insolence of her youth, Lilias laughed softly at this hypothesis. Dear Jean! there was nobody so kind and sweet; but not for such as Jean, she thought, were such efforts made. It would have disappointed her perhaps a little had she known that Lewis was entirely capable of having done it for Jean's sake, even if he had not had the stronger inducement of doing it for herself. But this did not occur to her as she sat and mused over it with a dreamy smile wavering upon her face. She did not ask herself anything about her own sentiments, or, indeed, about his sentiments. She only thought of him as she had done more or less since the morning in a sort of happy dream, made up of pleasure in seeing him again, and of a vague sense that herself and the future were somehow affected by it, and that London was brighter and far more interesting because he was in it. To think of walking any morning round the street corner, and seeing him advancing towards her with that friendly look! It had always been such a friendly look, she said to herself, with a little flutter at her heart. The bell ringing for dinner startled her suddenly out of these thoughts, and she had to dress in haste and hurry downstairs, where they were all awaiting her, Philip looking red and sunburnt in his evening clothes. He was never a person who had very much to say, and he was always overawed by Margaret, though she was kind to him beyond all precedent. He told them about his voyage and the Mediterranean, and the places he had seen—with diffidence, drawn out by the elder ladies, who wished to set him at his ease. But Lilias was pre-occupied, and said little to him. She felt that she was on no terms of ceremony with Philip. She knew a great deal more about him than the others did. She had borne inconveniences and vexations for him such as nobody knew of—even now to think of his mother's affectionate adoption and triumph in the supposed triumph of her son brought an angry red on Lilias' cheek. All this made her entirely at her ease with Philip. There could be no mistake between them. She behaved to him as she might have behaved to a younger brother, one who had cost her a great deal of trouble—that is to say, that he might have been a gooseberry-bush or a cabbage-rose for anything Lilias cared. She took his attendance as a matter of course, and gave him the orders about the carriage with perfect calm. Philip on his part was by no means so composed. There was a certain suppressed excitement about him. He had been chilled to find that Lilias was not down when he came in, and feared for the moment that he was to go to the theatre with the elder ladies: but the appearance of the younger set this right. Lilias immediately decided in her own mind that some new crisis had occurred in the love struggle of which she was the confidant, and that it was his anxiety to speak to her on the subject which agitated Philip. She took the trouble to contrive that she should sit next to him, letting Jean pass in before her, and as soon as there was an opportunity, when Jean's attention was engaged, she took the initiative, and whispered, "You have something to tell me?" in Philip's ear.

He started as if he had been shot; and looked at her eagerly, guiltily.

"Yes—there's a good deal to tell you: if you will listen," he said, with something between an entreaty and a defiance, as if he scarcely believed that her benevolence would go so far.

"Of course I will listen," said Lilias; and she added, "I have not heard from her for a long time, Philip. Wasn't she very wretched about it when you came away?"

A guilty colour came over Philip's face. He had looked a sort of orange brown before, but he now became a dusky crimson.

"I don't know what you mean," he said, "by she," and stared at Lilias with something like a challenge.

Lilias, for her part, opened her eyes twice as large as usual, and gazed upon him.

"You—don't—know! I think you must be going out of your senses," she said, briskly, with elder-sisterly intolerance. "Who should it be but one person? Do you think I am some one else than Lilias that you speak like that to me!"

"Indeed," said Philip, growing more and more crimson, "it is just because you are Lilias that I am here."

This speech was so extraordinary that it took Lilias an entire act to get over its startling effect, which was like a dash of cold water in her face. By the time the act was over, she had made out an explanation of it: which was that the something he had to tell her was something that only a listener so entirely sympathetic and well-informed as herself could understand. Accordingly, as soon as the curtain had fallen, she turned to him again.

"Philip, I am afraid it must be something very serious that has happened, and you want me to interfere. Perhaps you have quarrelled with her—but you used to do that almost every day."

"There is nothing about her at all—whoever you mean by her," Philip replied, with angry embarrassment, and a little shrinking from her eyes.

"Nothing about Katie! Then you have quarrelled?" Lilias cried. "I had a kind of instinct that told me; and that is why you are looking so glum, poor boy."

If Philip was crimson before, he became purple now.

"I wish," he said, "that you would not try like this to fix me down to a childish piece of nonsense that nobody approved. Do you think a man doesn't outgrow such things?—do you think he can shut his eyes and not see that others—"

Philip had never said so many words straight on end in all his life, nor, if he had not been tantalized beyond bearing, would he have said them now. Lilias fixed her eyes upon him gravely, without a sign of any consciousness that she was herself concerned. She was very serious, contemplating him with a sort of scientific observation; but it was science touched with grief and disapproval, things with which scientific investigation has nothing to do.

"Do you mean to say that you are inconstant?" she said, with solemnity. "I have never met with that before. Then, Philip," she added, after a pause, "if that is so, everything is over betwixt you and me."

"What do you mean by saying everything is over?" he cried—"everything is going to begin."

She drew a little away from him with an instinctive movement of delicacy, withdrawing her cloak, which had touched him. She disapproved of him, as one of a superior race disapproves of a lower being. She shook her head quietly, without saying any more. If he were inconstant, what was there that could be said for him or to him? He was outside the pale of Lilias' charity. She turned round and began to talk to Jean at the other side. There had been a distinct bond between him and her; she had been Katie's friend, their confidant, and she had been of use to them. There must always be, while this lasted, a link between Philip and herself; but all was over when that was broken. Lilias was absolute in her horror and disdain of every infidelity; she was too young to take circumstances into consideration. Inconstant!—it almost made her shudder to sit beside him, as if it had been a disease—worse than that, for it was his own fault. She had read of such things in books, and burned with indignation in poetry over the faithless lover. But here it was under her own eyes. She looked at it severely, and then she turned away. She heard Philip's voice going on in explanation, and she made him a little bow to show that she heard him. She would not be uncivil, even to a person of whom she so thoroughly disapproved.

CHAPTER XXXVI

But there is no lasting satisfaction in this world. Margaret had no sooner received the invitation she longed for, the opportunity of introducing Lilias to a brighter and gayer circle than any that had been within their reach, than a sudden chill struck to her heart. A mother has many special anguishes and anxieties all of her own which nobody shares or even suspects, and Margaret had assumed the position of a mother, and was bearing her burden with susceptibility all the more intense that she had no right to it. Other women in society find a satisfaction in the civilities and attentions that are shown to themselves individually, but the mother-woman is so intent upon what is going on in respect to her belongings that she cannot take into account as she ought these personal solacements. It does not matter to her if she is taken in first to supper, and has all the ladies in the neighbourhood put, so to speak, under her feet, if, in the midst of this glory, she is aware that her girls are not dancing, or that her son is considered by some important maiden an awkward lout.

The poor lady with half a dozen ungainly daughters, who appears everywhere, and who is held up to so much ridicule, how her heart cries out against the neglect which they have to suffer! Her struggles to get them partners, her wistful looks at everybody who can befriend them, which are all ridiculous and humiliating enough, have a pathos in them which is heart-rending in its way. The cause of the sudden coldness which crept over Margaret, into her very heart like the east-wind, and paralyzed her for the moment, was not perhaps a very solemn one. It was no more than tragi-comic at the best; it was the terrible question, suddenly seizing upon her like a thief in the night, how, now that she had secured her ball, she was to secure partners for Lilias? Those who laugh at such an alarm have never had to encounter it. What if, after this unexpected good-fortune, almost elevated in its unexpectedness and greatness into a gift from heaven, what if it should only be a repetition of the other night? Visions of sitting against the wall all the night through, looking out wistfully upon an ungenial crowd, all occupied with themselves, indifferent to strangers, rose suddenly before her troubled eyes. To see the young men come in drawing on their gloves, staring round them at the girls all sitting expectant, of whom Lilias should be one, and passing her by, was something which Margaret felt no amount of philosophy, no strength of mind, could make her able to bear. She grew cold and then hot at the prospect. It was thus they had passed an hour or two in the countess's drawing-room, ignored by the fine company; but in a ball it would be more than she should be able to bear. She had scarcely time to feel the legitimate satisfaction in her good-fortune, when the terror of this contingency swooped down upon her. She had stayed at home with the intention of having a few peaceful hours, and thinking over Lilias' dress, and anticipating her triumph, when suddenly in a moment came that black horseman who is always at our heels, and who had been unhorsed for a moment by the shock of good-fortune—got up again and careered wildly about and around her, putting a hoof upon her very heart.

It is not to be supposed that Margaret was unconscious of the fact, which the simplest moralist could perceive, that to regard a frivolous occurrence like a ball with feelings so serious was excessive and inappropriate. Nobody could be more fully aware of this. She, Margaret, a woman not without pretensions, if not to talent, at least to the still more wonderful gift of capacity, that she should give herself all this fyke and trouble, and just wear her very heart out about a thing so unimportant! But who can regulate his feelings by such thought? Who can hold a fire in his hand by thinking on the frosty Caucasus? But all her self-reminders to this effect did nothing for her. Her scorn of any other woman who concentrated her being on such frivolity would have been as scathing as ever, but the fact remained that of all the many objects of desire in this world not one seemed to her at the moment half so important. Poor Margaret! her very goodness and piety added torments to her pain; for she had been so used to pray for everything she desired warmly that in the fervour of her heart she had almost formulated a new petition, before she bethought herself, and stopped abashed. "Lord send partners for Lilias!" Could any travesty of piety be more profane? Margaret checked herself with unmingled horror, yet returned to the subject unawares, and almost had uttered that innocent blasphemy a second time, so great was her confusion—a fact which was not without some pathos, though she herself, grieved and horrified, was unaware of this. The overwhelming character of this new care disturbed all her plans, and, instead of sitting tranquil enjoying her solitude and thinking over her preparations, Margaret hastened to bed on pretence of weariness, but in reality to escape, if possible, from herself. Pausing first to look at the cards which had been left in the afternoon, and which the delight of the invitation had made her neglect, she found the card of Lewis, and stood pondering over it for full five minutes. Simon, who had been summoned to put out the lamps, gave a glance over his mistress's shoulder, with the confidence of a rural retainer, to see what it was that occupied her. Margaret put the card down instantly. She said,

"Simon, I see Mr. Murray, who was at Murkley, has been here this afternoon."

"Yes, Miss Margaret," said Simon; "he has been here. He asked for you all, and he said he was glad to see me, and that I must be a comfort (which I have little reason to suppose); but maist probably that was just all blethers to get round me."

"And why should Mr. Murray wish to get round you?" said Margaret; but she did not wait for any reply. "If he calls again, and Miss Jean happens to be in, you will be sure to bring him upstairs; but if she is not in the house, and me alone, it will perhaps not be advisable to do that. You must exercise your discretion, Simon."

"No me, mem," said Simon. "I'll exercise no discretion. I hope I know my place better than that. A servant is here to do what he is bid—and no to think about his master's concerns; but if you'll take my advice—"

"I will take none of your advice," cried Margaret, almost angrily.

What contemptible weakness was it that made her give directions for the problematical admission of the stranger whom she had made up her mind to shut out and reject? Alas for human infirmity! It was because it had suddenly gleamed upon her as a possibility that Lewis might be going to the ball too!

When the momentous evening arrived, Lilias herself, though, with unheard of extravagance, another new and astonishing dress had been added to her wardrobe, did not quiver with excitement like Margaret. The girl was just pleasantly excited; pleased with herself, her appearance, her prospect of pleasure, and if with a little thrill of keener expectation in the recollection of "two dances" mysteriously reserved for "him," of whom Jean, even in moments of confidence, would speak no more clearly—yet still entirely in possession of herself, with none of the haze of suspense in her eyes or heart, of anxiety in her mind, which made her elder sister unlike herself. Margaret was so sorely put to it to preserve her self-control that she was graver than usual, without a smile about her, when, painfully conscious that she did not even know her hostess, she led her little train into the dazzling rooms, decorated to the last extremity of artistic decoration, of the Greek Embassy. A dark lady, blazing with diamonds, made a step forward to meet her: and then our three strangers, somewhat bewildered, passed on into the fairyland, which was half Oriental, half European, as became the nationality of the hosts. Even the anxiety of Margaret was lulled at first by the wonder of everything about her. They had come early, as inexperienced people do, and the assembled company was still a little fragmentary. The country ladies discovered with great relief that it was the right thing to admire and to express their admiration, which gave them much emancipation; for they had feared it might be vulgar, or old-fashioned, or betray their inacquaintance with such glories, if they ventured openly to comment upon them. But, after all, to find themselves, a group of country ladies knowing nobody, dropped as from the skies on the skirts of a magnificent London mob belonging to the best society, was an appalling experience, when the best was said; and they had all begun to feel as they did at the countess's party, before aid and the guardian angel in whom Miss Jean trusted, but whom even Lilias knew little about, who he was—appeared. They had not ventured to go far from the door, having that determination never to intrude into high places probably intended for greater persons, which turns the humility of the parable into the most strenuous exhibition of pride that the imagination can conceive. Nobody should ever say to Margaret, "Give this man place." She stood, with Lilias on one side of her, and Jean on the other, half a step in advance of them, and felt herself stiffening into stone as she gazed at the stream of new arrivals, and watched all the greetings around her. Every new group was more splendid, she thought, than the other. If now and then a dowdy person, or an old lady wrapped in dirty lace, appeared among the grand toilettes, the eyes of the three instinctively sought her as perhaps a sister in distress: but experience soon showed that the dowdy ladies were often the most elevated, and that no fellowship of this description was to be looked for. Dancing began in the large rooms while this went on, and, with a sensation of despair, Margaret felt that all her terrors were coming true.

"My darling," she said, turning to Lilias with a fondness in which she seldom indulged, "you must just think, you know, that this grand sight is like coming to the play. If it is just a sight, you will be pleased to have seen it—and, when there are so many people, it cannot be very pleasant dancing; and, my sweet, if by any sacrifice of money, or trouble, or whatever woman could do, I could have made friends for you, or gotten you partners—But it is just a beautiful sight—"

"I would rather have our parties at home," said Lilias, plaintively, looking with wistful eyes towards the doorway, through which an opening in the crowd permitted the sight now and then of the happy performers in that whirl of pleasure from which she was shut out. But she had a high spirit. She threw up her fair head, and would have performed her little skip upon the floor had there been room for it. "We are three Peris at the gate of Paradise, and that's too many," she said, with a laugh.

Margaret was in no laughing mood. Dignity, which was almost tragical, was in her whole person. The pose of her head, the stateliness of her aspect, were enough to have dismayed any applicant for favour. She began to eye the groups about, not anxiously as she had done at first, but defiantly, as if she scorned them for their ignorance of her.

"I cannot say that I am surprised," she said; "for I counted the cost—and I thought you would be better pleased to come and just see what like it was. And then we can go away when we please." Margaret added this forlorn consolation with a sigh. "What are you saying, Jean?" she asked, somewhat sharply; for her sister's voice reached her ear, not tuned at all in harmony with her own, but with a tone of exultation in it. It would be the music that pleased her, or some dress that she was admiring! Margaret, in her vexation and disappointment—though indeed she had expected to be disappointed—turned round upon her sister with rage in her soul. Lilias had turned round too, with perhaps sharper ears, and, before Margaret had recovered her composure, she found herself addressed in tones whose blandishments she had rejected, but which now, against her will, her heart beat to hear. There was the little strange accent, the inflection not like any one else's, which had always hitherto moved her to impatience—for why should a man pretending to be an Englishman, and calling himself by a good Scots name, speak like a foreigner? All this passed through her mind like a sudden flash of a lantern, and then she found herself looking at Lewis with her most forbidding aspect, a frown under her brow, but the profoundest anxiety in her heart.

"You are not in a good position here," he was saying, "and soon there will be a great crowd. May I take you to a better place?"

"Oh! we are in a very good place for seeing, Mr. Murray, I am obliged to you. We are not like friends of the house to take the best places. We are just strangers, and enjoying," said Margaret, in her sternest tones, "the fine sight."

"We are all friends of the house who are here," said Lewis, "and there is no place that would be thought too good for Miss Murray. You would like to see your sister when she is dancing: let me take you into the other room," he said, offering his arm, with a smile which even Margaret felt to be almost irresistible. She said to herself that it was French and false, "like all these foreigners," but this was a secret protest of the pride which was about to yield to necessity. She made a little struggle, looking at him with a cloudy brow. "Your sister—will like to dance," said Lewis.

And then Margaret threw down her weapons; but only after a fashion. She took his arm with proud hesitation and reluctance.

"You just vanquish me," she said, "with that word; but I am not sure it is quite generous. And, if I take advantage of your present offer, you will remember it is in pure selfishness, and alters nothing of what has passed between us. You will make nothing by it," she said.

He had the audacity to press her hand a little closer to his side with something like a caress, and he laughed.

"In pure selfishness," he said. "I accept the bargain. Nothing is altered, only a truce for reasons of state. But I must be free to act according to the same rule of pure selfishness too."

Margaret gave him another keen look. She was not sure that he was clever enough to mean what he was saying; but she did not commit herself by any further explanation. She said, "We will just stay where we can see what is going on, Mr. Murray. Lilias, who is a stranger here, does not expect to dance."

Lewis smiled. He led the ladies to a sofa, where there was room for Margaret, and introduced her to a lady in diamonds, who called him Lewis.

"Take care of Miss Murray," he said, "duchess;" and, leaving Margaret, approached Lilias, who stood demure behind her. Duchess! Margaret's head seemed to spin round. She sank down by the side of this new and magnificent acquaintance, who smiled graciously, and made room for her. It was like a transformation scene.

"He is your relation, I suppose," said the great lady, with benign looks.

"I cannot say that," Margaret answered, with a gasp of astonishment and dismay. "I do not even know what Murrays—"

"Ah! in Scotland one knows you are all related." Margaret's horror at this statement may be more easily imagined than described, as the newspapers say; but there was no pause to give an opportunity for the indignant explanation that rose to her lips. "But I forgot," the duchess said, "there is quite a romantic story. Anyhow, he is a dear boy. There is no family that might not be proud to claim him. And that pretty creature who is dancing with Lewis. She is your—niece?"

"My sister," said Margaret. "It is a long story. My father, General Murray of Murkley, married twice—"

"Ah! I knew you were related somehow. And that is your sister? You must feel quite like a mother to her. She is a most perfect little Scotch beauty—that lovely hair and that sweet complexion."

"And as good as she is bonnie," cried Miss Jean, who was standing beaming at the end of the sofa. The unknown duchess lifted her eyes with some surprise, and made her a small bow.

"I can very well believe it. I have a grandchild nearly that age, and she seems to me an angel. I could wish that she should never grow any older."

"Oh, no, madam," said Jean, whose heart responded to the eyes of the other, as Margaret, proud, suspicious, and dominant, could not permit herself to do. It seemed to Jean in her simplicity that some word of respect ought to be added when she spoke to a duchess. "They are more sweet than words can say," said the simple woman, "but we must not for any pleasure of ours keep them from living their life."

"Will not you sit down?" said the duchess; "it is very hard standing all the evening through, when you are not accustomed to it. You interest me very much. I am sure you have thought a great deal on the subject."

"My sister Jean," said Margaret, "has instincts that come to her like other people's thoughts. She is not very wise, perhaps. But, if you will allow me, Scotland is just the country where such ideas should not be encouraged, for our names being names of clans, are just spread among all classes, and—"

The duchess was much experienced in society, and never permitted herself to be bored, which is one of the first rules for a great lady. She suffered just that faintest shadow of indifference to steal over her face, which warns the initiated, and said, sweetly,

"I have heard of that—it must be embarrassing. I am going to have a little dance on the 17th—may I hope that you will bring your young sister to it? It is a great pleasure to see anything so fresh and fair: and Lewis may always command me for his friends," this gracious lady said. And then she turned and talked to Jean, and ended by arranging to convey her to a very recondite performance of classical music a few days after. She left her seat on the sofa by-and-by, seeing, as she said, some friends arrive whom she must talk to. But this was not the only incident of the kind which made the evening remarkable. In the course of these exciting hours Margaret and Jean made the acquaintance of several other distinguished personages who were giving entertainments, and who hoped they would bring their young sister. They did not like to venture far from the spot where all this had occurred, but they abandoned the sofa, with their sensitive fear of being supposed to take too much upon them, and stood for the most of the night, confused with all that passed, watching Lilias through every dance, following her with their eyes when she disappeared in the crowd. Jean was perfectly, ecstatically happy; though her unaccustomed limbs were trembling under her, she stood up heroic, and never complained since Margaret thought it right to stand lest they might be taking up somebody's place. Margaret's happiness was not so complete. She was able for a time to enjoy the consciousness that all her troublous thoughts had come to nothing, and that Lilias' succès was unquestionable. But, alas! there came with this the thought that it was all owing to Lewis. His friends had given the invitations; the young men who were contending for Lilias' dances were all friends of his. It was supposed that the ladies were his relatives, a family group whom he had brought up, all fresh and original, from the country. Thus the sweetness was encompassed with bitterness, and surrounded with embarrassment. How was she to keep her hostile position and receive such favours?—and, if she allowed Lilias to be won after all this trouble by a young man who had proposed for her in Murkley, what was the object of all the care and expenditure? But that hypothesis was impossible; it was not to be contemplated for a moment. Lilias to marry a plain Mr. Murray, a person who was nobody, whose very right to the name was doubtful—such a thing was not to be thought of. And, though he had so many friends, these afforded no indication as to the standing of his family, nor did anybody seem to know what his family was, or they would not—not even those inconsiderate persons in London, who, Miss Margaret said, "absolutely knew nothing" about families in Scotland—have thought of supposing that he was related to Murkley. Her enjoyment was marred by all these questions and thoughts, which kept her still alive and awake when, in the dawning, Lewis put them into their carriage—Lewis again—always Lewis. It was to Margaret he devoted himself; he had taken her to supper, he had paid every attention that a son or brother could have paid her.

"We are enemies," he had said—"generous enemies respecting each other. We will hob and nob to-night, but to-morrow I know you will not recognize me in the Row."

"I am far from sure that I am going to the Row—it is just a waste of time," Margaret said, with a literalness which it pleased her sometimes to affect. And Lewis laughed. He was himself somewhat excited, and his laugh had a nervous sound. He had been very generous, he felt. He had not tried to absorb Lilias; the utmost propriety had regulated all his actions; he had presented to her the most attractive people he knew; his behaviour had been almost angelic. He held Margaret's hand for a moment (he was so audacious) as she followed the others into the carriage.

"We are to go on the same rule as before," he said; "it is to be pure selfishness; but you will not refuse to accept other invitations for fear of meeting me."

"You are right about the principle, Mr. Murray," said Margaret, with seriousness, "but, as for your fine friends and their invitations, it will be time enough to answer them when I get them. Word of mouth is one thing—but more is necessary for Lilias." And then she bade him "good night," or rather "good morning," leaning out of the window of the carriage to prevent any interchange of glances. There was pure selfishness in that action, at least.

From this time the remainder of their season in London was almost too brilliant. Though Margaret was greatly subdued, and would take little pleasure in the thought that it was "the best people" to whose houses they went, and whose acquaintance they made, she yet did not refuse the invitations, and watched Lilias enjoying herself with a swelling heart. Lilias, for her part, had no arrière pensée. She enjoyed her gaieties with all her heart, and recovered from her awe, and set as small store by her partners and admirers as she had done at Murkley. She had "got out her horns again," Margaret said. She took little airs upon her, and refused the languid gentlemen who proposed themselves in tones which invited refusal. But even these languid gentlemen did not like to be refused, and woke up, startled and tingling, when they came into contact with this independent little beauty. For it had been decided that she was a beauty in the highest circles. At home she had only been a pretty girl; but, when fashion took Lilias up, she became a beauty out of hand. Let nobody be deceived, however, and think that her photograph was in the shop-windows or the newspapers. The professional beauty had not been invented in those days, nor indeed was she known till long after. There were not even any photographs to speak of, and books of beauty had died out. It was an unusually safe moment for the lovely face that did not want exhibition. She was the Scotch beauty, which was distinction enough. Her sweet complexion, her fair locks, too fair to be golden, the dazzling freshness of her altogether, were identified with her country in a way which perhaps neither Margaret nor Jean fully appreciated. They were both themselves brown-haired and rather pale, and they were of opinion that their own complexion was quite as distinctively Scotch, though not so beautiful as the other. When it became the fashion to praise her accent and her little Scotticisms, Margaret and Jean were much irritated. They were very much attached to their country, but they were fondly convinced that no shade of peculiarity or provincialism was to be found in Lilias, whose English they considered perfect, far more perfect than that generally spoken in London. When some unwise person spoke of the "whiff of the heather," the sisters took it as an offence. But, with this small exception, everything went to their wishes, and more than to their hopes. Margaret, who had prepared herself at least a dozen times to do final battle with Lewis, and show him conclusively, as she had threatened at first, that "he would make nothing by it," was almost disappointed that he provoked no explanation, and never indeed thrust himself upon them except in society, where he was their good genius. Was this a policy so astute that her simple wisdom was scarcely capable of understanding it? or was it that he had thought better of his suit, and meant to give up an effort so hopeless? This last supposition did not perhaps bring so much pleasure with it as Margaret would have wished. For in fact she had rather looked forward to the final battle and trial of strength, and did not feel satisfied to think that she was to be allowed to walk over the field.

CHAPTER XXXVII

"I do not ask what you are doing or how you are doing it—I am only asking if you are making progress, which is the great thing. No doubt they will be seeing everybody in London, and, though she is not to call a great heiress, she is a beautiful person—and an old castle in Scotland, though it's much the worse for wear, is always something. There's a romance about it. You may have one of those long-leggit English fellows against ye before ever you are aware."

Mr. Allenerly too identified the strapping youths who have nothing else in particular to recommend them as the long-legged order. Perhaps he had taken it from Margaret. He was in London, as he said, upon business, but also with a view to such sober-minded amusement as a play, a night or two in the House of Commons when a Scotch bill was in progress (which occurred sometimes in those days), and a dinner or two with Scotch members at their clubs. He had come to see Lewis before going to pay his respects, as it was his duty to do, at Cadogan Place.

"I am afraid I have made little progress," said Lewis. "Miss Margaret is as unfavourable to me as ever. I think she expects me to speak to her again; but what is the good? She has steeled her heart against me. We have seen a good deal of each other in society—and I do not think she dislikes me; but she will not give in, and what is the use of a struggle—"

"Then you are giving in? Do you mean to tell me that? throwing up your arms for two old maids—"

"I will not have my dear ladies spoken of so—I throw up no arms. If I do not succeed, it will not be my fault."

There was a faint smile about Lewis' mouth, a dreamy pleasure which diffused itself over his face, and seemed to dim his eyes, like a cloud just bursting, with the sunshine beyond it, and no darkness in it at all.

"I see, I see," said the lawyer, and he began to sing, in a jolly bass voice a little the worse for wear—

"He speered na her faither, he speered na her mither,
He speered na at ane of her kin,
But he speered at the bonnie lass hersel',
And did her favour win."

"That is the best road in the long run," Mr. Allenerly said.

"When it is successful," said Lewis, with a grimace which was partly comic and partly very serious. "Every way is the best way when it succeeds."

"But you have never told me how you got rid of the other: how you got out of that mistake you made. It was a terrible mistake that first try—"

Mr. Allenerly had a broad grin on his face. He had every respect for the Murkley ladies, whom he had known all their lives. They were considerably younger than he was, and he did not yet care to call himself an old man; but the joke of a proposal to Miss Jean was one which no masculine virtue could withstand.

"I did not get rid of her at all," said Lewis, with gravity, "if you will understand it, Mr. Allenerly, I am deeply attached to Miss Jean, and when you smile at my friend it hurts me. There is no room for smiling. She was more gentle even than to refuse, she prevented me. After I have told you my foolish presumption, it is right that you should know the end of the story: and that is, it makes me happy to tell you, that we are dear friends."

The lawyer kept eyeing the young man while he spoke, with a sarcastic look; and, though he was by no means sure that Miss Jean's position had been so dignified as was thus represented, he felt, at least, that Lewis' account of it was becoming and worthy.

"You speak like a gentleman," he said, "and I have always felt that you acted like a gentleman, Mr. Lewis. And, this being so, it just surprises me that in one thing, and only one thing, you have come a little short. You took pains to warn Miss Margaret that you were seeking her little sister, and that was well done; and you went away when she told you frankly she disapproved: which was also fit and right."

"Pardon," said Lewis, with a smile, "I was not perhaps so good. I went away when I heard they were going away. But always with the intention of using the English method whenever I should have the chance."

"What do you call the English method? It is no more English than Scotch," said the lawyer, with some indignation. "That is, 'speering the bonnie lass herse'? It is, maybe, the best way; but still having informed the parents, or those that stood in place of the parents, it would seem to me that what you owe them is a full confidence, not half and half. Being the real gentleman you are—"

"You think so? I am very glad you are of that mind. It perplexes me sometimes what is the meaning of the word. There are many things which gentlemen permit themselves to do. But you are more experienced than I am. You understand it."

"I hope so," said Mr. Allenerly, "and a real gentleman you have proved, if just not in one small particular, Mr. Lewis. I call you by the name you have most right to. You should have let Miss Margaret know who you are."

Lewis looked at him with a startled air.

"Do you think so?" he said. "But then there would have been no hope for me," he added, with simplicity.

"That should be of no consequence in comparison with what was right. You see," said the lawyer, with true enjoyment, "that is just the difference between your foreign ways and what you call the English method. We think nothing amiss here of a young man 'speerin' the bonnie lass hersel'.' It is natural, as, after all, she is the person most concerned. But what we cannot away with," said Mr. Allenerly, "is any sort of mystery, even when it's quite innocent, about a man's name or his position, or what we call his identity. There's no social crime like going under a false name."

Lewis' countenance had grown longer and longer under this address. He grew pale; there was no question on which he was so susceptible.

"But," he cried, with a guilty flush of colour, "it is not a false name. It was his wish, his last wish, that I should take it. If I wavered, it was because I was sick at my heart. I did not care. In such circumstances a false name—That is what cannot be said. It is a wrong," he said, vehemently, "to me."

"You may be justified in taking the name," said the lawyer, "but not in using it, which is what I complain of, with intention to deceive."

Never culprit was more self-convicted than Lewis. His courage abandoned him altogether.

"If this is so, then I am a—a thing which I will not name."

"You are just a young man not wiser than your kind, and that has made a mistake: and I think it has done more harm than good. Margaret Murray, she cannot get it out of her head that, being of no kent Murrays, no name that you could give her, you are not only no Murray at all, which is true enough, but just a sort of upstart, a deceiver—"

"Which is true also," said Lewis, looking at him with eyes that were very pathetic and wistful, "if she thought badly of me in what you call my false appearance, they all thought more badly of myself. Perhaps you did so also. They described me as a designing person, upstart, as you say, that wheedled an old man into making me his heir. Now that you know me, you know a little if that was true: but they thought so all of them. Should I have gone and said, 'Here am I, this deceiver, this cheat, this dependent that took a base advantage of his benefactor. Behold me, I have robbed you of your money. I have cajoled your father'!"

"I would not have done it quite in that way; it would have been unnecessary. I would have described it all without excitement. Excitement is always a pity. I would have explained, and let them see how a man's motives can be misrepresented, and how little you knew of what was going on. If you had done so, you would have been in a better position now."

Lewis paused long over this, pondering with troubled face. "You never," he said, "told me so before."

"I never had the chance. You had settled your mode of action, and were known to all the village before I ever heard you were in Scotland; and then what could I say?—I hoped you would perhaps give it up."

"I shall never give it up," cried Lewis, "till it is quite beyond all hope."

"Which you think it is not now? But, my young friend, just supposing that you are right, and that the young lady herself should decide for you, which she is no doubt quite capable of doing. In that case there would come a moment, you will allow, in which all would have to be explained."

The countenance of Lewis grew brighter; a little colour flushed over it.

"But then—" he said, and stopped: for he could not tell to another all the visions that had been in his mind as to the new champion he should have, the advocate whose mouth was more golden than that of any orator to those before whom his cause would have to be pleaded. Of this he would say nothing; but his abrupt breaking off was eloquent. Mr. Allenerly was opaque neither in one way nor the other; he had some mind and some feeling. He caught a portion of the meaning with which Lewis was musing over.

"I see," he said. "You would have some one, then, some one who would be very potent to stand your friend. I do not doubt the importance of that; but the straightforward way—"

Here Lewis sprang up from his chair with an impatience unusual with him. Mr. Allenerly paused till the quick movement was over, and then he continued, quietly.

"The straightforward way would be now, this very moment, to go and tell your story, and abide—whatever the consequences might be. You will have to do it one day. You should do it before, and not after, another person is involved."

In all his life Lewis had never had such a problem to solve. In the face of success so probable that, but for the reverence of true feeling, which can never be certain of its own acceptance, and his sense of the wonderfulness of ever having belonging to him that foundation of all relationship, the love which means everything, he would almost have ventured to be sure—was very hard to throw himself back again, to undo all his former building, to present himself under a different light, in the aspect of one not indifferent, but hated, not a stranger, but one who had done them cruel wrong. It seemed to him that even Jean would forsake him, that Lilias, just trembling on the point of throwing herself into his arms, would turn from him with loathing, would flee from him, rejecting his very name with horror. Was it possible for a man to risk all this? And for what? For mere verbal faithfulness, for the matter-of-fact truth which would in reality be falsehood so far as he was concerned, which would convey not a true, but an erroneous, representation of him to their minds. Never had he even thought of so violent a step, one that would open all the question again, and lose him all the standing he had gained. If it had been done perhaps at first—but, now that things had gone so far, why should it be done? The question was debated between the two men until the heart of Lewis was sick with undesired conviction. Mr. Allenerly, to whom it was a matter of business, and who was an entirely unemotional person, had, it need not be said, the best of the argument. He held to his point without swerving; he was very friendly, but a little contemptuous perhaps of the excitement and trouble of Lewis, concluding in his heart that it was his foreign breeding, and that an Englishman (but, to Mr. Allenerly, even an Englishman was tant soit peu foreign), if ever he could have fallen into such an unlikely situation, would have taken care at least not to betray his emotion. The conclusion, however, which they came to at last was that this one evening, almost the last before the ladies left town, and which Lewis was to spend in their company, should be left to him—an indulgence of which Mr. Allenerly did not approve; but that after this the matter should be left in the lawyer's hands, and he should be entrusted with a full explanation of everything to lay before Margaret. With this he went away grumbling, shaking his head, but in his heart very pitiful, and determined so to fight his young client's battles that Miss Margaret, were she as obstinate as a personage whom Mr. Allenerly called the old gentleman, should be compelled to yield; and Lewis was left to prepare for his last night.

His last night! His mind was in so great a state of agitation when Mr. Allenerly left him that he could not settle to anything. At last he had to look in the face an explanation which he saw now must be made, in case his hopes were realized, which he had always pushed from him as unnecessary, or rather had never thought of at all since the first days when he had been in dread of discovery, and when the mere consciousness of a secret had made him uncomfortable. But it was long since he had got over that. And all through he tried to console himself, he had told no lie. He had been rash even in his statements. Had any one put two and three together, he might have been unmasked at any moment. In the entire absence of suspicion, he had talked about his life abroad, his old godfather, from whom his name and money had come, as he would have done had he been assuming no disguise. And indeed he had assumed no disguise; but yet he had, as the lawyer had said, that intention to deceive which is the foundation of all lying. And now the end of all this had come; he had not thought of the explanation that must be made at the end.

He had thought of carrying away his bride like the Lord of Burleigh, with no clearing up of matters until perhaps he should bring her home to her own great palace all decked and garnished, and shown to her the realization of all her dreams. Alas! he saw now that this could not be. The heiress of Murkley could not be wedded so lightly. Was it possible that he had never realized the settlements, the laying open of all things, the unveiling of every mystery? Perhaps it was because he had not thought of anything material in respect to Lilias, of anything but the permission to love her and to serve her, the hope of having her for his own, his companion, the epitome and representative of all loves and relationships. This had been enough to fill all his being; he had thought of nothing more; behind there was the dark shadow of an interview with Margaret to throw up the glory of the sunshine; but he had thought that when he went to Margaret with the news that Lilias loved him, though she might struggle, it would be but a passing struggle. They would not resist the love, the wish of Lilias. There would be a painful interview, and it was likely enough he would have need of all his patience to brave the bitter things that Margaret would say. But what could they do against Lilias? They would give in; and Lewis would have done nothing dishonourable, he would only have done what was justified by the usages of the country, what was so far justified by Nature—what the best in England declared to be the best way. It had been his intention for a long time to risk the final question to-night. He had put it off that none of his proceedings might be hurried or secret. He had given Margaret full warning. When she declared that pure selfishness was to be her rule, he had claimed it also for his. She had no right to expect, after the severe repulse he had received at her hands, that he would go to her again—at least, until he had tried his fortune at first hand from Lilias herself. And he meant to do so on this last night.

It is scarcely possible not to stray into the conventional when such words are the text. They have been as fruitful of truism as ever words were. But truism and conventional phrases now and then gain a certain glorification from circumstances, and Lewis went to his ball that night with all that had ever been said on the subject buzzing in his mind. The last! it must bring a pang with it, even if it were to be followed by higher happiness—the last of all those meetings which had divided his life, which had been the points of happiness in it, the only hours in the twenty-four that were of any particular importance. How sweet they had been; sometimes, indeed, crossed by awful shadows of tall heroes, with languishing eyes, exactly like (though fortunately he did not know this) the hero of Lilias' dreams. These shadows had crossed his path from time to time, filling his soul with pangs of envy and hatred; but the tall heroes had come to nothing. Either they had obliterated themselves, having other affairs in hand, or Lilias had put them quickly out of their pain, and she had always turned back to himself with a smile, always been ready to welcome him, to look to him for little services. Was she, perhaps, too confiding, too smiling, too much at her ease with him altogether, considering him more as a brother than a lover? This fear would now and then cross his mind, chilly like a breath of winter, but next time he would catch a glance of her eyes which made his heart leap, or would see her watch him when he was apart from her, as she watched no one else. But this gave him an exhilaration against which prudence had no power. And now this was the last time, and it must be decided once for all what was to come of it. Something must come of it, either the downfall of all his dreams, or something far more delightful, happy, and brilliant than the finest society could give. He had looked forward to this climax since ever the time of the ladies' departure had become visible, so to speak. At first a month or six weeks seemed continents of time; but when these long levels dwindled to the speck of a single week, it had become apparent to Lewis that he must delay no longer. He would have liked to say what he had to say in the woods of Murkley, in some corner full of freshness and verdure, in the silence, and quiet of Nature. To say it in a corner of a ball-room, with the vulgar music blaring and the endless waltz going on, was a kind of profanation. But there was no help for it. He had waited till the last day, and he had arranged the very spot, the best that could be found in such a scene, the shade of a little thicket of palms in a conservatory where there was little light, and where only habitués knew the secrets of the place. It had been before his mind's eye for days and nights past. The cool air full of perfumes, the Oriental leafage, the shaded light, the sounds of revelry coming faint from the distance. He would take Lilias there under pretence of showing her something, and, when they had reached this innermost hermitage, what if the thing he had to show her was his heart?

So Lewis had planned. He had been full of it all the morning. It seemed to run into his veins and brim them over. It was not that he was planning what to say, but that the theme was so strong in him that it said itself over and over, like a song he was singing. And that Mr. Allenerly, and his trenchant advice, his disapproval, his suggestion that filled Lewis with panic, his almost determination not to leave the matter where it was, should fall upon him precisely at this moment, was like the very spite of fate. Had the lawyer appeared before, or had he come after, one way or other, it was over—there would have been no particular importance in him; but that it should happen now!—no interruption could have been more ill-timed. It checked his élan at the moment of all others when he wanted his courage. It chilled him when he was at the boiling point. Lewis did his utmost to throw off the impression while he dined and prepared for the crisis. He had chosen to dine alone, that nothing might disturb him, but the feverish anticipation which was in him was so much twisted and strained by the lawyer's ill-starred appearance, that he was sorry he had not company to deliver him from himself and the too great pressure of his thoughts.

At last the moment came. He felt himself to change colour like a girl, now red, now white, as he set out for the ball, late because his heart had been so early. He did not know how he was to get through the first preliminaries of it, the talking and the dancing, until the time should come when he could find a pretext to lead Lilias away. The programme was nearly half through before he got into the room, where, after an anxious inspection, he saw his three judges, his fates, the ladies of Murkley, all standing together. Lilias was not dancing; she was looking, he thought, a little distraite. He stood and watched her from the doorway, and saw her steal one or two long anxious looks through the crowd. The sisters, he thought, looked grave—was it that Allenerly had not respected their bargain, that he had gone at once to make the threatened explanation? Lewis lingered gazing at them in the distance, racking his soul with questions which he might no doubt have solved at once. All at once he saw the countenance of Lilias light up; her face took a cheerful glow, her eyes brightened, the smile came back to her lip. Was this because she had seen him? He could not help feeling so, and a warm current began to flow back into his heart. She seemed to tell her sisters, and they, too, looked, Miss Jean waving her hand to him, and even Miss Margaret more gracious than her wont. How often a little gleam like this, too bright to last, fictitious even in its radiance, comes suddenly over the world before a storm! He made his way towards them, ignoring the salutations of his friends. When he reached them, Margaret herself, who generally used but scant courtesy to him, was the first to speak.

"We thought you were not coming," she said, "and I fear you have not been well. You're looking pale."

"Dear me, Margaret, he is looking anything but pale—he has just a beautiful colour," Miss Jean said, giving him her hand.

And then he felt that Margaret looked at him with interested eyes—with eyes that were almost affectionate.

"I do not like changes like that," she said. "I am afraid you are not well, and all this heat and glare is not good for you."

It had the strangest effect upon Lewis that she should speak to him as if it mattered to her whether he was ill or well. Even with Lilias' hand in his, he was touched by it. His heart smote him that he was not fighting fair. Surely she was an antagonist worthy to be met with a noble and unsullied glaive. He could not help giving her a warning even at the last moment.

"You are very good to think of me," he said. "It is the mind, not the body. I have had a great deal to think of." Surely a clever woman could understand that. Then he turned to Lilias. "This is the dance you promised me," he said.

Nothing could be more audacious or more untrue, but she acquiesced without a question. She had scarcely danced all the evening. Some wave from his excessive emotion had touched Lilias. She scarcely knew that she was thinking of him, but she was preoccupied, restless. She had told the others that she was tired, that this last evening she meant to look on. How deeply she, too, felt that it was the last evening! There was thunder in the air—something was coming—she knew it, though she could not tell what it was. But, when he came to her, she remembered no more her previous refusal, her plea of being tired. She went away with him without a thought of what everybody would say, of the visible fact that she had rejected everybody till his approach. She ought to have known better, and indeed Margaret and Jean ought to have known better, and to have interfered. But they were simple women, notwithstanding their season in town, which had taught them so much; and they were moved by a sort of vibration of the excitement round them. Lewis affected them, though he was unaware of it, and though they had not known till this moment that any change had taken place in him, or any momentous decision been made.

The young pair danced a little, but he was not capable of this amount of self-denial.

"Do you want to dance very much?" he said. "Then let us go and find a quiet corner, and rest."

"That is what I should like," said Lilias, though she had said to her other suitors that she wanted to look on. "I am tired too. I never thought I should have had as many balls in my life."

"It is not the balls we have had—but the thought that this is the last which troubles me."

"Yes," said Lilias, "it is a little strange. So long as it has been; and then all to come to an end. But everything comes to an end," she added, after a moment. A more trite reflection could not be; but Shakespeare, they both felt, could not have said anything more profoundly and touchingly true.

"Come into the conservatory," he said. "It is cool; and there will be nobody there."

Lilias raised no objection. She liked the idea that there would be nobody there. She was quite ready to be talked to, ready to declare that quiet conversation was, in certain cases, preferable to dancing. It was because they had both danced so much, Lilias supposed.

Heaven and earth! He was so much disappointed, so much irritated, that he could have taken the young fellow by the shoulders and turned him out, when the tittering girl would no doubt have followed. To think that a couple of grinning idiots should have occupied that place, chatterers who had nothing to say to each other that might not have been said in the fullest glare of the ball-room. Lewis was annoyed beyond description. That secret corner commanded every part of the conservatory, though it was itself so sheltered. He could not walk about with Lilias, and tell her his tale under the spying of these two young fools, to whom an evident courtship would have been a delightful amusement. He was so disturbed that he could not conceal it from Lilias, who looked at him with a little anxiety, and asked,

"Are you really ill, as Margaret says?"

"I am not ill, only fretted to death. I wanted to put you in that chair, and talk to you. Does Margaret really take any interest whether I am ill or not?"

"Oh, a great deal of interest! She thinks it her duty sometimes to look severe, but there is no one that has a tenderer heart."

"But not to me. She never liked me."

"Oh, how can you say so!" Lilias cried. "She likes you—just as much as the rest."

Lewis was annoyed more than it was possible to say by the appropriation of his hermitage. And now the unexpected discovery that he was an object of interest to Margaret caught him, as it were, by the throat.

"As much—" he said, with a sigh, "and as little. Will any one remember after you have been gone a week?"

"I suppose," said Lilias, "that you will still be dancing, and dining, and driving about to Richmond, and going everywhere—for much longer than that, till the season is well over."

"I don't know what I may do," he said, disconsolately. "That does not depend upon me. But, if I do, it will be without my heart."

Lilias felt a great strain and commotion in her own bosom, but she achieved a little laugh.

"Do you always say that when people you know are going away?"

He was angry, he was miserable, he did not know what he was saying. Providence, if it was fair to connect those two idiots with any great agency, had prevented him. His programme of action seemed to be destroyed. He could not answer this little provocation with any of those prefaces of the truth which would so soon have brought everything to a crisis had they been seated together under the palms. He said, almost sharply, which was so unlike Lewis,

"You must go away; that is a little soil of society. You would not have said so at Murkley last year."

"Mr. Murray!" cried Lilias.

The tears came suddenly to her eyes. It was as if he had struck her in the melting of her heart. She made a gulp to get down a little sudden sob, like a child that has been met with an unexpected check. And then she said, softly,

"I do not think I meant it," with a look of apology and wonder, though it was he who ought to have apologized. But he did not; he pressed her hand close to his side almost unconsciously.

"Do you remember," he cried, "that lovely morning—was there ever such a morning out of heaven? The river and the birds just waking, and you standing in the bow—If it could but have lasted—"

"It lasted long enough," said Lilias, with an effort. "It began to get cold; and Katie whispering, whispering. You never said a word all the time."

Again he pressed her hand to his side.

"And I cannot say a word now," he said. "Let us go back and dance, or do something that is foolish; for to think of that is too much. And Margaret takes an interest in me! I wish she had not looked at me so kindly. I wish you had not told me that."

"I think you are a little crazy to-night," Lilias said.

Was there a touch of disappointment in her tone? Had she too thought that something would come of it? And the last night was going, was gone—and nothing had come. Heaven confound Allenerly and all such! And Margaret to take an interest in him! But for that lawyer, Margaret's interest would have encouraged Lewis. Now it achieved his overthrow. He was busy about them all the night, making little agitated speeches to one and another, but he did not again attempt to find the seat vacant under the palms in the conservatory. He gave up his happier plans, his hopes, with an inward groan. Whatever was to be done now, must be done in the eye of the day.

CHAPTER XXXVIII

Margaret was in the act of adding up her bills, and counting the expenses of the season, next morning, when Mr. Allenerly was shown into the room. She rose from her chair, and gave him a warm welcome; for he was not only their "man of business," but an old friend of the family. She asked after his belongings, and if Scotland stood where it did, as is the use of compatriots when they meet in a strange country, and then she said, though not without a certain keen glance of curiosity,—for the visit of your man of business may always have something important lying under it, however innocent it appears,—

"You will just have come to this great big Vanity Fair of a place to divert yourself, like the rest of us?"

"A little of that—and a little thought of business too. Lawyers have such an ill name that it is difficult to make the world believe we take sometimes a great interest in our clients, and like to look after them. But my diversion would never be like yours. I hear there has been nothing but triumph in your career."

"Triumph! That is another question. You must have a great deal of money, and not much sentiment, I should say, to make a triumph in London—but we were not thinking of anything of that kind. We have had some very pleasant society, and that is as much as we wanted."

"I know what that means," said Mr. Allenerly. "I have heard of Miss Lilias; that there is nothing talked about but the young Scots' beauty, and all the conquests she has made."

"Toot!" said Margaret; and then she melted a little. "Everybody has been very kind. And we have seen a great deal—more than I ever expected, such quiet people as we are. But as for triumph, that is a large word. Whatever it has been, it has not turned her head."

"There is too much sense in it for that," said the lawyer.

"The sense in a young person's head of her age is never much to be trusted to. But she just takes everything, the monkey, as if she had a right to it, and that is a greater preservation than sense itself."

"I am thinking," said Mr. Allenerly, "that, after having all those grandees at her feet, it will be ill to please her with a plain Scots lad."

Miss Margaret gave him another keen look, but, though she had a great deal of curiosity herself as to his meaning, she did not intend to satisfy his curiosity. She laughed, accepting the inference, though turning over in her mind at the same time the question what Scots lad the lawyer could be thinking of. Not long-leggit Philip, it was to be hoped!

"There is no hurry," she said, "for any decision of that kind."

"There is no hurry on her side," said Mr. Allenerly, "but on the other there is generally a wish for an answer. So that I was thinking—But you will stop me, if there is any absolute bar in the way of what I was going to take upon me to say."

He looked at her with much keenness of inspection too, and their eyes met like two rival knights, without much advantage on either hand.

"I can scarcely do that," said Miss Margaret, "till I know what it is you are going to say."

Mr. Allenerly was tolerably satisfied by these preliminaries. Had there been any approaching brilliant marriage for Lilias, it must have been somehow revealed to him. He said,

"I am going to refer to events in the past that were painful at the time. Things have come to my knowledge that have made me wishful to interfere. There is a person who was once, without any will of his, an instrument of wrong to this family."

"Dear me, that is a very serious beginning," Miss Margaret said.

"And it will be more serious before the end. I am not going to beat about the bush with you. You are too well-informed and have too much judgment to take up a thing hastily. You will remember, Miss Margaret, all the vexation and trouble there was about your grandfather's will."

"Remember it! I would have a short memory or an easy mind if I did not remember all about it. It is not three years since."

"That is true; and there was a great deal of vexation. Such a thing, when it arises in a family, just spreads trouble."

"I don't know what you call vexation—that's an easy word. It was just burning wrong, and injustice, and injury. There was nothing in it that was not hateful to think upon and bitter to bear. I wonder that any one who wishes well to the family should be able to speak of it in that way."

"And yet I have been one that has wished well to the family—for more years than I care to reckon," the lawyer said.

"Grant me your pardon, Mr. Allenerly! I try to put it out of my mind as a Christian woman should; but, when I think of it, I just lose my patience. Vexation! it was just a bitter wrong and shame all the ways of it, both to him that gifted it and us that lost it."

"That is all true—it is all true: and nobody would suspect me of making little of it. At the same time, Miss Margaret, I will own that there was one part of the story that I was deceived in. The young man that wrongously got this inheritance—"

"The favourite, the foreign swindler."

"That is just where we were deceived," cried the lawyer, hastily throwing up his hand as if to stop the invective. "The young man—Miss Margaret, if you will have a little patience! Am I one to be easily convinced, or without chapter and verse? You have called me a bundle of prejudice before now. I am fond of nothing foreign; an intriguer is just what I cannot abide. Well, but this young man was neither foreign nor a swindler. He was not to blame. I declare it to you, if it was my dying word—he was not to blame."

Miss Margaret got up, and began to pace the little room in great excitement. It was the little back room attached to the dining-room, and was very small. She was like a lion in a cage. She put up her hand, and turned away from him with an expression of resentment and scorn.

"That is a likely thing to say to me!"

"It is not an easy thing to say to you—you will grant that; but it is true. He was young, and had been taken by Sir Patrick from a child; he was an orphan and friendless. He knew nothing about the Murrays. He did not even know that his benefactor had any children. He gave up the best of his life to nursing and tending the old man. A woman could not have been kinder. He expected nothing; when he heard what had happened, that he was the heir, he thought it would at most be to all the nicknacks and the gimcracks. He was thunderstruck when he knew what it was. I was on the look-out for deceptions, and I thought this was one. I will not deny it, I was of your opinion. You are not taking any notice of what I say."

"On the contrary," said Miss Margaret, with a laugh of disdain, "I am taking the greatest notice of it. And how did you come to change your opinion? He must be a clever fellow, this person, to get over a Scotch writer too."

"It is not so easy to get over a Scotch writer, as you say," said Mr. Allenerly, wiping his forehead. "What got over me was just experience of the lad. I have had a great deal to do with him. What with letters and what with observation, I've come to know him. It is not that he's difficult to know. It was all in him at the first glance, but I could not believe it. I thought it was certain he must be a deceiver. But he is no deceiver. He is more simple than the generality. You will believe me or you will not believe me, as you please; but what I am saying is true."

"It would be impossible for me not to believe—that you are speaking what you think the truth—just as impossible," said Miss Margaret, "as it is to believe that this is the truth. Was the old man doited then? was he mad? had he lost every sense of what was due to those that came after him? Then why did not you, a man of the law like you, prove him so? This was what I never understood, for my part."

"He was neither mad nor doited, but knew what he was doing well, or, you may be sure, if there had been any proof—There was no undue influence; the young man did not so much as know what there was to leave, or if there was a will at all."

"This is a very likely story," said Margaret, with a grim smile, "and I acknowledge, at all events, that there is a kind of genius in making you believe it all."

The lawyer gave her a look of indignation and anger, but restrained himself with professional power.

"The General," he said—"you will forgive me, Miss Margaret: far be it from me to say a word to his disadvantage—but he was not what you would call a dutiful son. There was no question of that, you will say, at his age—which is true enough. And Sir Patrick had been long abroad, and none of you had ever gone near him, or showed any interest in him."

"How could we?" cried Margaret, roused to instant self-defence. "Was it our part? We were women, never stirring from home. If he had held up a finger—if he had given us the least invitation—"

"And, on the other hand, why should he?" said the lawyer. "He had a kind of son of his old age that had no thought but his comfort. Why should he put himself out of the way to invite his grandchildren, that cared nothing about him? If he had known you and your sister, or if he had seen that bonnie creature, Miss Lilias—"

"I am glad," cried Margaret, vehemently, "that we were never beguiled to travel all that long way and put ourselves and Lilias into competition with the wriggling creature you call the son of his old age—I am thankful for that with all my heart."

"Then you will pardon me for saying you are thankful for small mercies," the lawyer said, in an indignant tone. They paused, both eyeing each other for the moment with equal displeasure and breathing quick with excitement. "There seems but small encouragement," said Mr. Allenerly, with that air of compassionate resignation which is so irritating to an antagonist, "for the rest that I had to say; for, if you will not listen to the first part of my story, it is very unlikely that you will put up with the second."

"Oh, say on, say on!" said Miss Margaret, with an affectation of calm. She went into the next room through the folding doors, and brought back her knitting, and seated herself with a serene air of resignation in the one easy-chair which the room contained. "I would like to hear the whole," she said with a smile, "now that we are on the subject. It is a pity to miss anything. If I were what they call a student of human nature, it would be just a grand amusement. A clever man, and an Edinburgh writer, and a person of judgment, telling me what's neither more nor less than a fairy tale."

"It is God's truth," said Mr. Allenerly, sternly, "and I dare any man to prove me mistaken; but the rest, you are right, it is like a fairy tale. This young man, finding, after his first astonishment at being a rich man (he was astonished to be rich, but not that his old friend, his protector, his godfather, as he called him, had made a will in his favour, which was the most natural thing—)"

"His—what did he call him?" Margaret said, with a start, looking up.

"His godfather—that was the name of kindness between them."

A gleam of fierce light came over Margaret's face. She threw down her knitting and clasped her hands forcibly together.

"Ah!" she cried, in the tone of one upon whom a sudden light had been thrown; then she said, "Go on! go on!" with an angry smile.

"I say he was sorely astonished, overcome at first, and it took him a long time to accustom himself to it. He knew nothing about any relations, and, when he was told of their existence, you'll excuse me for saying that he would not believe in them—saying, as was quite natural, that nobody ever came near the old man, that he was quite alone in the world. But we have already discussed that question. I let him know, however, that it was true, and it made a great impression on him. For one thing, it wounded him in his love for old Sir Patrick: for, after hearing that, he could not regard him as just the perfect being he had supposed."

"That was a very delicate distress, Mr. Allenerly," Margaret said, with fine sarcasm.

"He had a very delicate mind, as you shall see," said the lawyer, equally caustic. "The second thing was that he conceived a grand idea of setting the wrong right. He heard that the heirs were all ladies, and his determination was taken in a moment—it was without any thought of pleasing himself, or question whether they were old or young—just to come to Scotland and offer himself to one of them."

Margaret rose from her seat with a start of energy. She flung her knitting from her in the fervour of her feelings.

"There is no need to say any more," she cried, vehemently, "not another word. I know who your friend is now. I know who he is. Lord in heaven! that I should have been one of the credulous too!"

"If you know who he is, there is the less need—"

"Not another word," she cried, putting up her hand, "not another word. To think that I should have been taken-in too! Oh! I see it all now. I might have thought what was the motive that made him so keen after one of us. Jean first, and, when that would not do, Lilias. Lilias! as if I would give my child, my darling, the apple of my eye, to a man of straw, a man of nothing, a man that has just her money and nothing more. And so that was what it was! and me trying to find out what Murrays he was come of. Man!" she cried, turning upon the lawyer with a movement which resembled the stamping of her foot in passion. "Oh, man! why did you let me be humbled so?"

"Miss Margaret!—is that all you will say?"

"What more is there to say? I am humbled to the dust—I am just proved a fool, which is a bitter thing for a woman to put up with. I have had him in my house. I have let him come and go. I have accepted favours at his hands. Lord!" cried Miss Margaret again, in passionate excitement, clasping her hands together, "it is all his doing. I see it now. It is just all his doing. It is he that brought these fine folk here. He got the invitations for us that he might meet her. He has been at the bottom of everything. And I—I have been a fool—a fool! and would never have seen through it till doomsday, and was getting to be fond of—Oh!" she cried, stamping her foot on the ground, unable to contain herself, "is this me, Margaret, that have always had such an opinion of myself? and now I am just humbled to the ground!"

"There is little occasion for being humbled—if you never do anything less wise—"

"Hold your tongue, sir," she cried; "oh! hold your tongue. It has been a scheme, a plot, a conspiracy from the beginning. I see through it all now. Mr. Allenerly, I beg your pardon. If I am ill-bred to you, it is just that there is more than I can bear!"

"Be as ill-bred as you please, if that is any ease to you; but, Miss Margaret, be just. You are a just woman. Oh! think what you are doing. You are not one to give way to a sudden passion."

"I am just one to give way to passion! What else should I do? Would you have me to take it like a matter of business, or, maybe, thank your friend for his good intentions," she cried, with a laugh of anger. They both belonged to a race and class which forbids such demonstrations of feeling; but righteous wrath is always exempted from the range of those sentiments which are to be kept under control.

While this interview was going on, Lewis was passing through a strange revolution, a sort of volcanic crisis such as had never happened in his life before. He had not been trained to thought, nor was that his tendency. He had all his life taken things as they came: au jour le jour had been his simple philosophy, a maxim which may be the most sublime Christianity or the most reckless folly. In his case it was neither, but rather the easy temperament of a simple nature, always able to reconcile itself to the circumstances of the moment, finding more or less enjoyment in everything that happened, and very little pre-occupied with its own personality at all. A prudent young man would have been concerned as to what was to happen to him after Sir Patrick's death, when his luxurious home would be broken up, and he himself, without profession or property, thrown upon the world; but Lewis had given the matter no thought at all, with an easy confidence of always finding bread and kindness, which both the circumstances of his life and the disposition of his friends had fostered. Afterwards, when he found himself Sir Patrick's heir and a man of fortune, he accepted that too with surprise, but an easy reconciliation of all confused matters, which, had he contemplated the subject in all its lights, would have been impossible. It was only by degrees that he woke to the other side of the question, the position of the despoiled heirs. Then, the reader of this history is aware, his resolution had been uncompromising. He had not thought of his own satisfaction at all. Having come to the decision that Sir Patrick's heiress, or at least one of Sir Patrick's heiresses, should have back the inheritance in the only way that occurred to him as practicable, he had set about it at once in the most straightforward manner possible. He had been ready to subordinate his own feelings, to consider only the question of duty. In every way that had seemed possible to him he had pursued this object. When it happened, in pursuit of this duty, that love stepped in, dazzling and bewildering, yet intensifying to the highest degree his previous purpose, it had been a boon from heaven, a blessing upon that purpose rather than a new object. It seemed to him another proof that he was born under a happy star, that the one woman in the world whom he desired to marry should also be the one in the world with whom it was his duty to share everything that was his. It was this that made all methods seem lawful to him, and had stirred him to the intention, which was contrary to all his prejudices, of obtaining, if possible, her assent to his suit, without the previous knowledge or even against the wish of her family—the English way—the way that Philip Stormont and Katie Seton, and indeed everybody about, thought legitimate. But now for the first time Lewis had been driven out of his easy philosophy. Mr. Allenerly's stern conception of honour, the new light upon the whole subject that had been thrown by the lawyer's lantern, had found those openings in the young man's mind which a new and deeper sentiment than any he had ever known had opened in him. The natural affections may be ever so warm and lovely without startling the soul into any new awakening. Full of friendship, full of kindness, he had been all his life more prone to serve and help than even to enjoy: but when a great primary passion, one of the elementary principles of life, goes down into the depths of innocent nature the effect is different. It is like the Divine life, when that enters into a soul, bringing not peace but a sword.

The year which had elapsed since he left Murkley had been a period of chaos and doubt. He had been without any ray of distinct guidance, looking vaguely to the chances of the future. Since he came to town and had seen Lilias again, his whole mind had been occupied in her service, in devising means for her entertainment and success, but also in securing opportunities for himself, and in conspiring with everybody who knew him, and would help him, for the glorification of his heroine. And in fact, during the most of this period, simple love had carried him away on its current. He had thought of no rational obstacles or difficulties, but only of herself. Her looks, her words, the way in which she took his arm, a glance surprised in the course of an evening, had occupied him to the complete exclusion of everything else. The approach of the critical moment when all must be decided had raised the whole being of Lewis into an atmosphere of passion. The crisis affected his mind as well as his feelings, and quickened his intelligence as it developed his heart. When that clear, cold lantern of good sense in Mr. Allenerly's hand flashed upon the confused scene, the light effected in an instant what previous months had not effected. He began to see that his own easy way was impossible. It would have been so much happier, so much less complicated! but it was impossible. He could not even, as has been seen, when the moment came, attempt to solve everything in that easy way. Sailing over the surface would do no longer. He had to go down into the heart of things, to question the depths, and see what answer was in them. He began to ask himself what was the question which he had skimmed over from the beginning, which he had so often attempted to settle by natural compromises, by pleasant expedients, as was his nature? When self is imperious in such a nature, necessity brings forth treachery and guile. But to Lewis self was never in the foreground, even in love, where self-will has a kind of justification, and indulgence has an air of duty; it was not his nature to put it forward, and truth was dear to him wherever he saw it. He began to think, almost for the first time in his life.

And the first result of this process is seldom a pleasant one. When he had put the ladies into their carriage on that last night, or rather morning—for the dawn was blue in the streets, and London was coming slowly into sight out of the darkness, with lamps burning unearthly in a light far more potent than theirs—Lewis put his hat on his head, and set out on a wonderful walk, which he remembered all his life. The market carts, all fresh and alive, and somewhat chilly with their start before the day; the carriages, with a jaded air, horses and people alike, white bundles of drapery huddled up within them, and their lamps flickering like impish eyes; the houses all asleep in long blank lines, closed to every influence; the Park lying dewy and still, without a speck of life upon it, gave a kind of unnatural background, familiar yet strange to his thoughts. It might have been the extraordinary character of these thoughts that had thus altered the aspect of the visible world, in itself so well known. He assisted at the spectacle of the great city's awaking, as he walked on and on; the parks always lying in the midst of the scene, shut up, and silent, and inaccessible, the early sun sweeping over them unbroken by any human shadow, in the midst of the growing life and motion, like a haven which was not to be attained, the always possible Eden, open to the longing vision, but guarded from the eager step, which tantalizes most existences. His mind got only more confused, a greater whirl of imperfect thinking was about him as he hurried along, receiving all these external objects distractedly into the ferment of his brain. It was full day, nearly six o'clock, when he got home, and threw himself on his bed unnaturally in the sunshine. But it was not to sleep. Thinking was so new a process to Lewis that he felt as if some new jarring machinery had been set up in his brain, and the whirl of the unaccustomed wheels made him giddy, and took away all consciousness of mental progress. He seemed to be in the same place, beating a painful round, with the whirl and the movement and confusion, but nothing else, in his bewildered brain. He must have slept, though he was scarcely aware of it, late into the morning. But when he was disturbed by the entrance of his servant, and sprang up suddenly into full consciousness and life, the first flash of self-recollection revealed to him a resolution formed and perfect. Where had it come from? Had the wheels been working while he slept, and ground it out? had something above earth whispered it to him out of the unseen? He was almost afraid, when he saw it looking him, as it were, in the face, a something separate from himself, a definite thing, resolved and certain. It was not there when he had come in; where had it come from? He sprang up into the consciousness of a new world, a new life, a changed order of things, as well as a new day.

When Mr. Allenerly came in about an hour after, Lewis met him with a pale and somewhat jaded aspect not inappropriate to a man who had been up all night, the lawyer thought, but also subdued and grave as of one whose reflections had not been of a happy kind. The lawyer came in, himself very serious, with the painful sense that his mission was to quash all the hopes and make an end of all the plans which the other had been making himself happy in forming. He sat down at the table on which Lewis' breakfast stood untouched, without a word. The sight of this partly reduced his sympathy for Lewis, for there was an air of dissipation about it which displeased his orderly mind. Perhaps, notwithstanding all the advantages of the arrangement, a young man who had not breakfasted at twelve o'clock was scarcely a fit husband for Lilias Murray, or one in whose hands her happiness would be sure. He sat down and looked at Lewis with a disapproving eye.

"You are very late," he said. "I will soon be thinking of my lunch; but I suppose you were up till all the hours of the night."

"I don't think I have slept at all," said Lewis, "I have been thinking. Stop and hear me first. I know by your face what you are going to say. But that has nothing to do with what I have made up my mind to. One way or other, it could have nothing to do with it. Our talk yesterday turned me all outside in. I never had thought it over from the beginning to the end before."

"You must form no rash resolution," Mr. Allenerly said.

"It is the least rash I have ever formed. I suppose I am not given to thinking. And, if it is wrong, it is you who have set me on this way," Lewis said, with a wistful sort of fatigued smile. "Now, before you say anything, have patience and hear me out."

CHAPTER XXXIX

There were many circumstances to add to the passionate annoyance and irritation with which Margaret became aware of the deception, as she conceived it, of which she had been the victim. She saw now a hundred indications by which she ought to have been able to make sure from the beginning who and what the stranger was: his sudden appearance at Murkley, a place calculated to attract nobody, which even "those tourist-cattle," who roused Miss Margaret's wrath, had left out, where nobody came but for the fishing; his anxiety to secure their acquaintance, to recommend himself to them, his suit to Miss Jean, so unlike anything that had ever come in the way of the sisters before, even his conversations, of which she recollected now disjointed scraps and fragments quite enough to have betrayed him. Twice over had he come to her to explain his wishes; the last time, she believed now (though that was a mistake), that he had meant to confess everything. And she would not listen to him. Well, that was all honest enough; it had not been a wilful attempt to deceive her on his part: but yet she had been completely deceived. How blind she had been! Had it not been plain to every eye but hers? Had the Setons suspected something? Had Jean known anything? Was it possible—Margaret started up and rang the bell with great vehemence. She was so little in the habit of doing this that it brought Simon rushing from below and Susan flying from above, and Miss Jean in consternation to listen at the head of the stairs.

"Is my sister ill?" Jean said, trembling with apprehension.

"She would like if you would go and speak to her, mem," said Susan, who had outstripped the heavier-footed man. Simon was standing ready to open the door for her into the little room in which Margaret was sitting.

"Is my sister ill?" she asked again.

"I reckon, mem, that something is wrong," Simon said, in his deliberate voice.

"There is nothing wrong with me," said Miss Margaret. "Sit down, sit down, and make no fuss, if you will not drive me doited: I am well enough. But there is a matter to be cleared up between you and me. Will you tell me frankly, Jean, eye to eye, what you know about this young Murray that has just been haunting our house?"

"About Mr. Murray?" said Jean, looking more guilty than ever criminal looked, innocent guilt faltering and ready to betray itself in every line of her face.

"Just about Mr. Murray. I have said always he was of no kent Murrays—were you in this secret all the time, you, my sister, the other part of me? Oh! Jean, was this well done? I can read it in your face. You were in his secret all the time."

"Margaret! what do you call his secret?" the culprit said.

She was of the paleness of ashes, and sat twisting her fingers nervously together, feeling her treachery, her untruth to her first allegiance, weigh upon her like something intolerable. Her very eyelids quivered as she stole a glance at Margaret's face.

"Do you mean his secret at Murkley," poor Miss Jean said, breathless, "or his secret—here?"

Margaret laughed aloud. The tones in this laugh were indescribable—wrath, and scorn, and derision, and underneath all a pitiful complaint.

"It is evident you are further ben than me, for I know of but one secret," she said, "but we'll take them in succession, if you please."

"Oh! Margaret," said poor Jean, trembling, "was there any harm in it? There was harm in me, perhaps, but what in him? For who could see Lilias and not be in love with her? And then, when he saw us in London just a little forlorn, and knowing so few folk, and him that had everybody at his beck and call—"

"Him that had everybody at his beck and call—Yes?—and then? He took pity upon us and—What are you meaning? Our friends in London," said Margaret, with dignity, forgetting how she had, by the light of Mr. Allenerly's statement, glimpsed the truth on this point as well as on others, "are persons we have met at other friends' houses in the ordinary way of society. There was nobody came to me from him, except just perhaps that old duchess who takes you to the music. Your friend's compassion, Jean, I think, might have been spared."

"Oh, Margaret!" faintly said the accused at the bar.

"What do you mean by 'Oh, Margaret'?—is it not true that I say? What did it advantage us, I ask you, that this young lad had everybody, as you say, at his beck and call?"

Jean gave a deprecatory, wistful glance at her sister, and said nothing—but it was the look of one that had a great deal to say: and there was that mixture of pity in it by which Margaret had been moved to a passing wonder before.

"What did he ever do," she repeated, scornfully, "when he saw us, as you say, forlorn in London, and knowing few folk? It is a pretty description, but I cannot recognize it as a picture of me," Margaret said, with a laugh of resentment. The conviction that had flashed upon her concerning their life in London had been intolerable, and she had pushed it from her. She was ready now to resist to desperation any suggestion that Lewis had served them in society, or been instrumental in opening to them so many fashionable houses. The consciousness in her mind that this was so, gave heat and passion to her determination to ignore it, and gave a bravado of denial to her tone. "All this," she added, "is nothing, nothing to the main subject; but, as we are on it, let us be done with it. What has your friend done for us I—I am at a loss to know."

Jean was in a terrible strait, and knew not what to do. She was divided between her desire to do justice to Lewis and her desire to save Margaret pain. She hesitated, almost prevaricated in her anxiety, but at last the story burst forth. The Greek ball, the beginning of all, Margaret had firmly believed all along, was a homage to the importance of the Miss Murrays of Murkley, a natural acknowledgment of their claims to be considered. She could not help remembering the change that had occurred in the aspect of affairs from the moment that Lewis had appeared on the scene, but the invitation for which she had wished so much, and the others that flowed from it, Margaret had endeavoured to believe were natural: at least the first—she had always clung to that. But when Jean's story, extracted in fragments, with many a protestation and many an unintended admission, fell upon her ears, the sudden disenchantment was terrible. To think that everything was his doing from beginning to end, that he, this upstart, this minion, this foreign favourite, should have been able to open the doors of fashion to those whom he had so injured and supplanted, whose chief enemy he was! Was it to humiliate them still more, to smite them down into deeper abasement, to triumph over them in every way? The pang which it gave Margaret was too bitter for speech. There had been an appeal made to him, and in his magnanimity—that easy magnanimity of the conqueror—he had responded to the appeal, and had taken compassion upon them. It was a bitter pill for a proud woman to swallow. Jean had appealed to him, and he had been kind—oh! these were the words. He had been kind to the poor country ladies, and no doubt presented them as originals, out of whom a little amusement could be had, to his fine friends. Margaret would not even tell her sister, with whom she was indignant beyond all possibility (she thought) of forgiveness, what she had heard this morning. Her mortification, her sense of having been tricked and cheated, was too great: the only thing she could think of was to turn her back upon this hated place with all its delusions.

"I am just sick of London," she said; "my very heart is sick. Get your packing done this afternoon. I will not spend another day here. I think we will go home to-night."

"To-night!" cried Jean, with dismay. To oppose a decision of Margaret was impossible, and she felt guilty, and wounded, and miserable, out of favour, out of heart. But yet to be obliged to cut off her little leave-takings, and not to see him, the cause of all this, the friend who had been so kind, so tender, so eager to carry out all her wishes, was very hard. And even to travel at night was alarming and terrible to Miss Jean: she thought the dangers of the way were doubled by the darkness, and that very likely there would be a railway accident. "It is very sudden," she said. "Oh! Margaret, I know you are ill-pleased at me. I am sorry—sorry! if I have done what was foolish, it was with a good intention; but will you change all our plans just for that, only for that?"

"Only for that!" said Margaret. "Only for what is burnt in on me in shame, and should on you still more, if you had the heart—to have been indebted to our enemy, to have sought the help of him, if there had not been another man in the world, that should have been the last—"

"Oh! Margaret," cried poor Miss Jean, "you are unjust. You are cruel. He is nobody's enemy. You may think him not good enough for Lilias,—for who would seem good enough for Lilias to you and me?—but an enemy he is none. Oh, no enemy, but a friend: or more like a son, a brother."

Margaret rose with a stern intensity of tone and look that made her sister tremble.

"Do you know who this friend is," she said, grimly, "this brother, this lover, this benefactor? His name is not Murray, but Lewis Grantley, a name you have heard before. He is your grandfather's heir. He has gotten the inheritance of Lilias. And now, seeing she is a lovelier thing even than the inheritance, this creature of nothing, this subtle serpent, this practiser upon an old man's weakness, would have her too."

Jean had risen also, with eyes full of horror, in the extremity of her astonishment. She lifted her arms, she opened her lips to cry out, but no sound came. She stood an image of dumb consternation and misery gazing at her sister. No doubt of Jean's innocence from all complicity in the secret could be entertained by any one who saw her. She stood dumb, staring at Margaret for some minutes. Then her breast began to labour with choking sobs.

"Oh! no, no. Oh! no, no—no, no," she ran on, unable to restrain herself. It was a protest which was pitiful, like the cry of a dumb creature unable to articulate. Hysterics were unknown in the family, and Margaret was alarmed. It subdued her anger in a moment, and relieved her own oppressed and excited mind by giving her a new subject of concern. She put Jean into the easy-chair, and brought her wine, and soothed her: in the midst of which process Lilias came into the room, all fresh and radiant, untouched by any darker knowledge.

"Just run away, my dear, Jean is not very well. I want her to stay quite quiet just for two or three minutes, and then she will come to you upstairs."

"But why should I run away? Let me take care of her, Margaret. How pale she is!" cried Lilias, in alarm.

"There is—no—nothing the matter with me," said Jean, tremulously, making shift to smile, and waving her hand to her darling. "I'll be better—in two or three minutes."

"Just run away, my dear," Margaret repeated: and Lilias, as she was told, ran away, in considerable alarm and uneasiness. But, after all, there was nothing so alarming in the fact that Jean was pale, and wanted to be quiet for two or three minutes, and the fear soon dissipated itself. When the door was closed upon her, the two sisters looked at each other: the shadow of anger that had been between them had passed away. It even brought them nearer together, this secret which was so momentous but which she, that young creature whom it was their happiness to guard from all evil, knew nothing of. Jean pressed Margaret's hand which held hers.

"You will not tell her?" she said.

"That is what we must see—and judge," said the elder sister. "We must think of it when you are better."

Margaret said I oftener than we. It was a pledge of renewed union and closer fellowship, which brought back Jean's smile.

And next morning they left London. It had not been intended that they should go away till the end of the week, and their abrupt departure was the occasion of various disturbances of other people's plans. The person whom it was chiefly designed to affect was Lewis, who, knowing as he did the crisis that had been reached, and occupied indeed with the still more extraordinary crisis in his own existence, was not affected by it at all. He had never, during all the intercourse of those six weeks, been invited to Cadogan Place. He had been admitted occasionally when he called, latterly almost always, and it had been supposed by all the ladies that he would come to bid them good-bye. But after the interview between Margaret and Mr. Allenerly there was an end to that intention, and it was only by chance he discovered their premature departure, which did not move him; for he had run through all the gamut of emotion, and nothing seemed now to matter. But as Lewis stood, more pensive than disappointed, gazing at the house, in the window of which once more hung the intimation that it was to let, and where a charwoman appeared at the door in place of Simon, some one else strode up, to whom it was, to all appearance, much more important. This was Philip Stormont, who, though he could not follow the ladies into the fashionable world, had hung about them whenever and wherever he could, following them to the park, turning up in all their walks, and attaching himself like a sort of amateur footman to the party. Lilias had been very cold to him for some time after that evening at the theatre, but by-and-by had slid into her old habit of a sort of sisterly indifference, thinking it not necessary to make much account of what Philip said or did. And her sisters were always "kind—enough," as Miss Jean said, to the young man whose lands marched with Murkley, their nearest county neighbour, whom they had known all his life. When it was fully apparent to them that Lilias was entirely indifferent to this long-leggit lad, they were very kind to him, though they gave him much good advice on the subject of going home. He had hung on, following their steps, without any clear explanation of the reason why, always postponing his departure until the time of theirs approached. When that date was settled, he speedily found out that it was important he should get home by the 26th, and it was settled that he should travel with them. But in the hurry of sudden departure no one had thought of Philip. He came "round," as he called it, to make the final arrangements, and to settle where he should meet them, just at the moment when Lewis, walking slowly past, looking up at the windows, had concluded within himself, in a sort of stupor of over-feeling which made the discovery almost unimportant to him, that they were gone. What did it matter to Lewis? They were as far from him in Cadogan Place as if they had been in Murkley. It made no difference; between him and them there was a great gulf fixed. And yet he would have liked to see her once more! but it made no difference—this was what he was saying to himself. To Philip, however, it made a very great difference. He went briskly up to the door, undismayed by a certain vacant air, and the ticket in the window. Indeed he had not observed these signs. And, when he was met by the charwoman with the news, his astonishment and indignation knew no bounds.

"Gone! Why, I was to go with them. Are you sure they are gone?" he said, with a dismay that was almost ludicrous. When he perceived Lewis a little way off, he hurried up to him. "Do you understand anything about this?" he said, with a sense of injured antagonism to everybody who could be supposed to be in the ladies' confidence. There had always been a jealous feeling in his mind in respect to Lewis, whose constant presence at all the fine places of which Lilias spoke, to which he himself had no way of procuring admittance, had given him a feasible ground of complaint. But a common grievance is a great bond. When Lewis had declared his ignorance, in a tone from which even his insensibility to further pain could not take a certain pathos, Philip, in the excitement of his feelings, obliged to talk to some one, seized upon his arm, and poured out his heart.

"They just play with a man," he cried, "these women! They don't care a bit what they do to you, so long as it doesn't touch themselves. I was to go with them. It was all settled. Our way was the same, as far as the railway goes—as far as the water-side, for that matter; for you remember how near we are. And here they are, off without a word, without a single word! not so much as to say, 'We are going sooner than we thought,' or anything like that—but no, not a word! I was coming to ask where I was to meet them, and if I should take the tickets, and so forth."

Lewis did his best to dissipate the victim's dilemma. He suggested a sudden change in their plans, a lost message, a mistake of one kind or another, till Philip was somewhat mollified. But in his heart he was not displeased to see another man suffer. That the ladies had been agitated by the revelation made to them, and had changed their plans, and forgotten their secondary engagements in consequence, soothed him and gave him a faint sensation of pleasure. Besides, it is never disagreeable to one man, whose heart is devoted to a certain woman, to see another man left in the lurch. So far as he was able to enjoy at all, Lewis enjoyed it, and this made him very amiable to the other, who was certainly not a successful rival, or likely to be so. He who had affected their minds so much as to make them alter all their arrangements at the last moment had no reason to be uncharitable to the man whose very existence they had evidently forgotten. And Philip, in his ignorance, took refuge in the sympathy of Lewis. He had not seen him much in the company of Lilias; they had revolved in different spheres, and had rarely come in contact, and, so far as Philip knew, Lewis was little more than an acquaintance of the ladies, who never invited him, and seldom talked of him. He had forgotten by this time the position of companion to Lilias which Katie and he had thrust upon the stranger at Murkley. All that stage of existence had faded away from Philip's thoughts.

"You see," he said, thrusting his arm through that of his sympathetic friend, "I came here at first with no will of mine. A man should be left free one way or other. If the mother is to have so much say as my mother has, the son should be free to go where he likes, and make his own way; but, as it is, I am neither laird nor loon, if you understand what that means. I have the name of being independent; but, if my mother were to take away her share and leave me with that house to keep up, where would I be? So I have to be guided by her in many ways, whether I will or not."

"I do not suppose that she is very hard to please," said Lewis, politely.

"Oh, I don't know about that! She has always had her own way, and she likes it. So do I, for that matter. But, you see, for years past there has never been but a craik about Lilias Murray. She was the only girl my mother would ever hear of: our lands march; and then the Murrays are a great family, and then—"

"Do you think it is right to talk of things so private to me?"

"Oh, you!—you are just the person to talk to them about. You are a stranger, you are an outsider; it cannot be any concern of yours. And then you know what an ass I made of myself last year," Philip said, reddening, and with an embarrassed laugh.

"I do not know about the ass," said Lewis, gravely; "I know—what was happening last year."

"Well, it comes to the same thing, you know. My mother would not hear of that—It is all very well for a fellow like you, that are independent, that never needs to think of pleasing anybody but yourself. But I can do nothing without my mother. As for marrying or that sort of thing, it would be out of the question. If she gave me up, I should be as poor as a church-mouse: so I am obliged to mind what she says. And then, if truth must be told, I got just a little tired of the affair itself."

"I don't think," said Lewis, disengaging his arm, "that it is quite comme il faut to say so."

"Com-eel—what do you mean by that? It began when I was too young to think of anything but the fun of it: and she liked the fun, too. It was a great joke to make a fool of everybody, and carry on behind their backs; but, when it comes to be serious, you can't go on like that."

"I don't think you can go on like that at any time," Lewis said, gravely.

Philip laughed.

"That is just your stiff, foreign way," he said; "you are always thinking harm—and there was no harm. Well, then, my mother insisted I was to go away, and, as there was a good opportunity to have a little yachting and see something of the world, I just consented. Absence makes a great difference, you know," he added, laughing again somewhat nervously. "I saw what an ass I had been making of myself. And then I heard from home that the Murrays were here, and that I had better stay and make myself agreeable. Now, you know, there's a great deal to be done in London that makes the time pass. So I just stayed, and made myself agreeable—as far as I could, you know—"

"Indeed it is not for me to know how far that is," said Lewis, with something between a jeer and a snarl: for it was not in flesh and blood to remain passive. "You are a dangerous fellow, no doubt, when you please."

"Oh, I don't know about that," said simple Philip; "it was a bore at first, but I couldn't help feeling that it was far the best way to get out of the other, you know. And that little Lilias has grown awfully pretty, don't you think?—whether it's the dress, or the way she's got of carrying herself, or having seen a little more of the world—"

Lewis would have liked to knock him down, but probably could not have done so, for the young Scot was much bigger and stronger than himself: and then, even if he could, he had no pretext for so doing, for there was no intentional disrespect in what Philip said.

"I never discuss ladies whom I respect—it is bad form," said Lewis, bringing forward a word which he had picked up, and generally found most effectual.

Philip reddened and grew serious all at once. He was one of the class who hold that vague but stinging accusation in special awe.

"It would be worse form, I think, to discuss ladies whom you do not respect," he said, very pertinently, but changing his tone. "Well," he said, "to please you, I will say nothing about that. I thought it a bore at first, but by-and-by it was different. And it is just the only way of coming out of the other business safe and sound; and it would be a fine thing for the property; and, to sum up all, the girl herself—"

Lewis raised his hand, for he felt that he could not bear much more.

"You mean that you fell in love, I suppose, since that is the English phrase," he said, with a slight inflection of contempt, which the ear of Philip was not keen enough to seize.

"Well, you may call it that, if you like," he said. "And I thought we were getting on very well—they all bully me, as if I were a small boy, and she too, but that's one way of showing that they consider me one of the family, you know. So I thought we were getting on as well as possible, and I wrote home word to my mother, and we were to travel together, which would have given us just the opportunity to settle everything before we got home: and that was what I wanted above all—"

Here poor Philip's face grew long once more, and the sense of the ludicrous which had been growing in the mind of his hearer—a sort of forlorn amusement to think of this little commonplace thread running smoothly through the tangled web of affairs—rose above the irritation and disdain, which were too serious for the occasion.

"Perhaps," he said, gravely, "it was the elder sisters. They might be afraid of you."

Philip turned upon him with a beaming face and gave him a blow of approval on his shoulder.

"Now that just shows," he said, "that you have an eye in your head. I always knew you were a clever fellow—it is just that. Margaret cannot abide me—my mother herself sees it. She has just held me at arm's length since ever I was that height; but, if Lilias takes to me, I will just snap my fingers at Margaret," cried the long-leggit lad, plucking up his courage.

Finally he made up his mind to follow them by the evening train, and pick them up at Stirling or Perth, where they would be sure, he thought, to stay for the night. And Lewis went home to his rooms, where also packing was going on, with a sense of exhaustion, through which faint sensations of amusement penetrated. He was sad as death, but, at the same time, he was worn out by a great mental conflict. At such a moment pain is deadened by its own excess. He was like a man newly out of a fever, not able to feel at all save in a muffled and ineffectual way: and it almost amused him to see Philip's self-complacency and confidence in "getting on very well." For such a rival he was not afraid.

CHAPTER XL

The ladies were very tired when they got home. It is a long journey from London to the north. They were late next morning, and still languid with the fatigue, and with the curious sense of having dropped out of another sphere which came after their strange London experiences. To come into the old house, and see everything unchanged, was very wonderful. It made the past look like a dream. To Lilias, above all, for whom life had sustained an entire revolution, there was something extraordinary, weird, and uncanny about the old existence, which seemed to wait for her here like a distinct and separate thing, receiving her once more into its bosom, going on with her as if the other had never been. As she lingered with Jean over the late breakfast from which Margaret had risen an hour before, she looked round upon the wainscot, with all those gleams of reflection in it which she remembered all her life, and the old pictures, and the furniture all in its place, with a sort of dismay.

"Do you think we have ever been away?" she said, with a scared look in her eyes. She was afraid of the stillness, which seemed to close over her, making all the colour and commotion of the past season, and all the new thoughts with which it had filled her mind, die away like things that had never been.

"That is just the feeling every time you make a change," said Jean, "for life is a very strange thing. I've sometimes thought it was never more than half-real at the best of times: and whiles you would like to put forth your hand and grip to feel if it is true."

This was beyond the experience of little Lilias; but there was a sensation of suspense and uncertainty in her mind which made her old sister's contemplative thoughts very congenial to her.

"It will turn out," she said, with a laugh, the sound of which half-frightened her, "that we have all been sleeping and dreaming. But no!—for now I remember. I am not so silly now as when I went away. London was very bonnie, but not grand like what I thought, and, oh, do you remember, Jean, about the Queen in the Court, what a fool—what a fool I was!" Lilias clapped her hands together in shame and self-impatience. "You should have told me," she cried.

"But, my dear," said Miss Jean, "I cannot affirm that I know any better, even now: for it was not me but Margaret that went with you to see Her Majesty. You are more experienced than I am. You have had a grand setting-out in the world, Lilias; none of our house for many a day has done what you have done. Even your bonnie young mother, though she was an earl's daughter—you have had, you may say, the world at your feet, my bonnie dear. And it has not turned her head either," said Miss Jean, smiling upon her with pride and happiness, "you are just our little Lilias all the same."

"The world at my feet! I wonder what that means?" cried Lilias, with a little scoff; but, after all, the suggestion was pleasant to her. She was silent a little, thinking, with a smile, of two or three acts of homage that had been done her, that had made the little girl aware that she was a woman in her moment of power. It pleased and flattered, and at the same time it amused her to recall those scenes in the brief and bright drama which seemed, as she looked back upon it, like something she had seen in the theatre, a curious, vivid, all-interesting performance, in which the chief character was herself: and yet not herself, a visionary creature, whose proceedings she, Lilias Murray, at home in Murkley, could gaze at from afar with wonder and amusement. She put her hands softly together, and said, "But if this is what it all comes to in the end!" But even as she said these words there came a delightful sense of expectation to her heart, and she laughed, knowing that this was not all it was coming to. Jean, for her part, gave a soft little sigh.

"When you are older, my darling," she said, "you will find a great soothing is always coming back. Home is just like an old friend holding its arms open to you, always waiting for you, aye ready, whatever troubles you may be in."

Lilias listened, smiling. It was not the aspect of home which pleased her fancy at the moment. Of all unrealities in the world nothing seemed so unreal to her as the idea that a refuge from trouble would ever be needful for the long young life that was in her heart and her thoughts. She looked at her sister with a loving pity, tinged with amusement too. It was natural that Jean should look upon it so. Dear Jean! with all her pretty, old-fashioned ways, the tranquillity of her gentle soul. She was in her element at Murkley, not in London. Lilias knew that the old table-cover, with all its silken flowers half done, would come out in another half-hour, and the basket of silks be set forth upon the little table: and that Jean, with her fine head relieved against the window, would look as if she had never moved from that spot. She laughed at the thought, which was sweet, comical, pleasant. For her own part she would sit down with a book in the other window and look back, and behold the performances of that other Lilias who had the world at her feet, and wonder—wonder and dream what was going to come of it all! as if in her heart she did not know very well what was going to come.

But, as they were preparing to go to the drawing-room to carry out this performance, a voice reached their ears from the hall with a somewhat excited, anxious tone in it.

"I could not have been more surprised if they had told me the Queen had come: for I expected you all to-morrow. And what have you done with my Philip?" Mrs. Stormont said. She came into the dining-room, followed by Margaret, and came forward to the table, holding out her hands with an air of joyous welcome under which there was a certain restlessness of anxiety. "Oh, fie! this is your London hours, still at breakfast when other people are thinking of their luncheon. But we must forgive you this time on account of your journey; and what have you done with my Philip?" she said again.

"Bless me!" said Margaret, "to think I should have been so far left to myself as to forget all about that. It is true Philip was to have travelled with us to-morrow; but circumstances made it more convenient for me to come away sooner, and I never let him know. But I dare to say," she added, "that he will not be ill-pleased; for to attend upon three women and their boxes is a trial for any man."

Mrs. Stormont shot a keen look at the speaker over the shoulder of Lilias, whom she was just then embracing with great fervour.

"Margaret is always severe upon men, as is perhaps natural enough," she said; "but I would have thought my bonnie Lily would have had more feeling. And so my poor lad is left to kick his heels at the railway station waiting for them that never come? I cannot thank you for that, Margaret. I think you might have had a little more consideration. There was perhaps something due to me—if Philip, poor man, was not grand enough to merit a thought—"

"Indeed I can assure you," cried Miss Jean, anxiously, "there was no want of thought. But, you see, we had serious business to attend to, and Margaret was very much taken up at the end, and we were just hurried away—"

Mrs. Stormont did not make any reply. It was evident that she was anxious underneath the offence, and full of uneasy thoughts. She drew Lilias into a chair by her side, and held her hand, and stroked it tenderly.

"And you have just had a great success, by all I hear. The Lily of Murkley has been blooming in the King's gardens. But I hope it has not turned your little head. For whatever strangers may say, there are no hearts so leal as those are at home."

"You must think me a very silly little thing," said Lilias, "if you suppose that would turn my head. It was never for us; it was just because of—" Here she caught Margaret's eye, and divined by something in it, and perhaps also by a rising something in her own breast which brought the colour to her cheeks, that her intended attribution of honour where honour was due was for the moment unnecessary. "Because of friends," she said, with hesitation and a blush. "Because of him, because of him!" she added to herself in her heart, with an indignant glance at Margaret.

If she were prevented from saying it out, all the more would she maintain it to herself.

"Good introductions," said Margaret, significantly, "are, as everybody knows, the half of the battle; and it would be strange if the Murrays of Murkley could not get that advantage. It is all very well over, I am glad to say. And Lilias has enjoyed herself, and we have all seen a great deal of company; but for my part I enjoy nothing so much as getting home."

"And what did you make of my Philip?" said Mrs. Stormont. "That is a crow I have to pick with you, Lilias; for he would have been home long ago, but for somebody that kept him hanging-on in town. 'I have put off for another day; for I'm going to a ball at Lady So-and-so's, where the Miss Murrays will be—' And then, 'I've put off a week; for I'm going to travel with the Murrays.' That is what his letters have been, poor fellow—and then to be left in the lurch at the end. Ye little fairy! If your head's not turned, I am afraid you have turned other people's heads," said Philip's mother, with a laughing flattery, which concealed much graver feelings.

Lilias was somewhat alarmed by this personal attack. She looked at her sisters for help, and it was Jean who came first into the breach.

"You need not be in any way uneasy about that; for Philip has plenty of friends," said Miss Jean. "We met him no doubt from time to time, and he was extremely kind in coming to see us; but he had always a number of friends—he was not depending upon us. I assure you it could not make that difference to him," she said, anxiously.

Mrs. Stormont confronted her with a superior smile.

"My dear Jean," she said, "do you think I was supposing my son had no friends, or was just depending upon his country neighbours for a little society? No, no, I am not such an ignoramus as that, though I have myself been little in London, and never was at the expense of a season: but I am not just so ignorant as that. There are other reasons that influence a young man, and one that has had every encouragement—"

"Encouragement!" Margaret said, whose eyes were full of the light of battle.

"Encouragement!" said Miss Jean, deprecating. "We were just kind, as was natural."

The mother returned the look of defiance, and took no notice of Jean.

"Indeed, my dear Margaret," she said, "I was not addressing myself to you. It is well known in the countryside what your ambition is, and that nothing less than a duke or a prince would please you, if you had any chance of getting them. I am speaking to Lilias, not to you, and I am not a person to stand by and see a young thing's heart crushed, especially one that might, had matters taken another turn, have been my own. Yes, my bonnie pet, it is you that I am speaking to; and you know you have given my boy a great deal of encouragement. You will not be persuaded by thoughts of a grand match, or by worldly inducements, or by the fear of man—or woman either—to turn against one—"

Here she stopped, perhaps with a sense of the rashness of this appeal. She was very tremulous and anxious, and as she looked round upon the three sisters, who had all been instrumental, as she thought, in disappointing her and scorning her son and leaving him behind, it was all the mother could do to restrain the flood of bitter words that came pouring to her lips. She stopped, however, hastily, and with a little agitated laugh.

"I am just taking the disappointment a great deal too seriously, you will say; but I am disappointed, you see. I looked for my Philip coming home happy and well pleased; and then to hear you were back before your time, and not a word from him!—But no doubt he'll be home to-morrow, and nothing changed. I am just going too fast; you will think nothing of it. I'm of an anxious nature, and it's my way."

The elder ladies accepted the apology, according to their different characters, Miss Jean eagerly agreeing that it was very disappointing when you were looking for your only son, and found nothing but strangers, and Miss Margaret receiving it stiffly with a dignity beyond words.

"For," she said, "though we might be glad of the company of any friend on a long journey, yet I never think it a good thing for women to put their fashes about luggage and so forth upon a man, unless he belongs to them. He is apt," she added, "to think more of it than it deserves—as if the women could have done nothing without him, which is not my way."

"No," said Mrs. Stormont, with a laugh which was in itself a confession of excitement; "you're one of those that like to be independent. But don't you copy your sister in that, Lilias, for it is a thing the men cannot bide. They would rather you were silly, and always clinging to them, than going your own gait in that bold manner. And though it may suit Margaret, who is done with everything of the kind, it is not the same for you."

Lilias had been watching the scene with anxious, half-amused eyes. There had always been little passages of arms between Margaret and Mrs. Stormont.

"Philip is not very clever about the luggage," she said. "He lost all his own things, you know. I told him I could do it better myself."

"And what did he say?" said the mother, beaming upon her. "Oh, nothing to say over again, I am sure, for he is not one for phrases, my Philip. And so you had your fill of dancing and every pleasure? Well, well! it is a grand thing to have your day: and now you've come back, Lilias, just as you went, you must not scorn your old friends. 'Sneer na British lads awa',' as Burns says."

"I hope she will sneer at nobody," said Miss Jean; "and two or three months in London is not such a terrible time. There are few changes in the parish, so far as I can hear. Old Mrs. Johnston at The Hillhead is gone, poor lady; but that was to be looked for at her age; and young Lauder married upon his housekeeper, which is a great pity, and must vex all his friends; and—"

"No," said Mrs. Stormont, still looking at Lilias; "there's little sneering in that bonnie face; but still hearing just one thing round you may give a warp to your mind, and you must remember, Lilias, that the grand folk in London, though they may be very smiling for a time, they just go their own gait, and think no more of a country girl, however she might be admired for the moment; but old friends are always safe—they never change."

"Old friends or new friends, I would not advise her to be dependent either upon one or the other," said Margaret. "It's best to stand on your own ground. Lilias, will you go and tell Simon about getting out the carriage, and bid him ask if we can have the horses, for there are some visits that we ought to pay. You will forgive me," she said, when the girl left the room, "for sending her away: for we must respect her simplicity at her age. She is thinking nothing, neither of British lads nor of any other. I am not one that likes to put such things in a girl's head."

Mrs. Stormont blushed with anger and annoyance.

"It is the first time," she said, "that I have been blamed with putting things that should not be there into a girl's head. But we all know about maidens' bairns—and since Lilias is to be the immaculate one that never thinks upon a lover—But, if that was your meaning, I wonder you ever took her to London, which is just the grand marriage market, if what everybody says is true."

"It was no marriage market, you may be sure," cried Margaret, growing red in her turn, "for any child of mine."

"Well, that is proved, no doubt," said the other, with the composure of successful malice, "since Lilias ye took her away, and Lilias ye have brought her back."

"Oh, what is the use," cried Miss Jean, breaking in anxiously, "of the like of us old friends casting out with each other about nothing? If Lilias were to be married, it would be a terrible day for Margaret and me."

"Oh, nobody will doubt that," cried Philip's mother. "After being mistress and more at Murkley, and keeping that little thing that she dare not say her soul's her own, it would be a terrible down-coming for Margaret—"

"Mrs. Stormont!" Jean exclaimed, in terror and dismay.

As for Margaret, who had been moving about setting various things in order, she came back at this to where the visitor was sitting, pale and red by turns, in great nervous excitement. Margaret was very composed, and smiled, though she was pale.

"I can make every allowance," she said, "for a disappointed mother."

She had the best of it, after all. She was able to regard with perfect calmness the heat and passion of the other, whose long-leggit lad had come so little speed.

"I am not the one to call disappointed," said Mrs. Stormont. "I am not a woman with ambitions, like you. It is not me that has made a great campaign, and nothing to show for it. But I would warn you just to mind what you are about, for to play fast and loose with a high-spirited lad—"

"Bless me!" said Margaret, in a tone which Jean herself could not but allow to be very irritating, "who may that be? There were two or three, I will allow, but they got their answer. Though I say it that should not say it, having brought her up myself, Lilias is very clear in her notions; she will never say no when she means yes, of that we may be sure."

"Well," cried Mrs. Stormont, rising hurriedly, "I can only hope you'll find things answer to your anticipations. It would be a terrible thing to go through the wood and through the wood, and take up with a crooked stick at the end."

"Or perhaps without a stick at all," said Margaret, with sarcastic gravity, "which has happened with both Jean and me, you were going to say."

"And so I was," said the angry woman—"you have just divined it; but that beats all, Margaret Murray. If you are going to doom that bonnie little thing to be an old maid like yourself, just that you may keep the management and power in your hands—"

"It is such a grand scope for management, and so much power—"

"It's just as much as you ever had the chance of. Oh, I can see through you. You just flatter her and stop the mouths of her friends with giving her every opportunity, that you know will come to nothing—I see through you like glass—and so keep her property in your hands, and make her an old maid like yourself. And to keep up the farce," cried Mrs. Stormont, "you'll keep one or two just hanging on, and give them every encouragement. But just see if she does not turn upon you one of these days, and choose for herself."

She hurried out, sending this shot after her from the door, and leaving, it cannot be disputed, a great deal of the smoke and confusion of a cannonade behind her. Even Margaret was confused, disturbed by that sudden perception of how her proceedings might appear in the eyes of others, which is so disenchanting. It is not a happy, though it may be an improving process, to see ourselves as others see us. Though she was so angry, she looked at her sister with a little dismay.

"The woman is daft," she said. "Who was it that encouraged that long-leggit lad of hers? Never me, I'll answer for that. I hope it was not you, Jean, that out of superabundant charity—"

"He came here more than you liked in the afternoons, Margaret, last year."

"And what of that?" cried the mistress of Murkley. "If it had been Donald Birnie, could I have turned him away from the door?"

"Donald Birnie knows his place," said Miss Jean, doubtfully; "but Philip is just very suitable; and his mother might think—"

"I cannot tell what you mean with your 'very suitable.' Would you like our Lilias to take up with the first long-leggit lad that comes to hand? I thought we were agreed upon that point, you and me."

"Oh, Margaret, I am saying nothing else! I was only thinking that it would not be so strange if his mother—And then there was always that little Katie here."

"Now that is what I would call very suitable," said Margaret, regaining her composure. This recollection freed her at once from a little fear that was beginning to creep upon her. "Katie! that would just be the best thing in the world for him; for the Setons are very well connected; and it would settle Philip Stormont, and make him steady, and be company to his mother. There could be nothing better," Margaret said.

But, unfortunately, this was not how the matter presented itself to those who were more immediately concerned. Mrs. Stormont went forth in haste and heat, which old Simon, as he opened the door, perceived with a chuckle, divining, with tolerable justice, the state of affairs; for Simon, an old family retainer, was just as determined as Miss Margaret that no long-leggit lad should carry off the young lady of Murkley. Mrs. Stormont went away very hurriedly, and in so doing encountered little Katie Seton hurrying towards the house. The very sight of the girl added to the soreness and sense of downfall which was in the mind of Philip's mother. She seemed to see Fate lowering upon her over Katie's head. What if she were destined to accept the minister's daughter for her son's wife after all!

"You are losing no time," she said. "Katie! you mean to hear all the grand news and see the grand dresses the first moment that it's possible. It is the best way."

"I am not so early as you, Mrs. Stormont," said Katie, who was pert, and not inclined to yield her own cause.

"You will allow there is a difference," the angry woman said. "My son was to have travelled with them; but he had a number of engagements, having so many friends in London, and he left them in the lurch, which gentlemen are too apt to do, even at the last moment. It is not pretty of them, but it's just their nature," said Mrs. Stormont. This was an arrow into Katie's heart as well as a forestalling of any report in respect to Philip's unsuccess which she might hear. Katie replied with a smile only, and went on to the house; but she had received the arrow. And Philip's mother felt that she had in some degree redeemed the fallen fortunes of the day.

CHAPTER XLI

"And was it all very grand, Lilias? and did the ladies wear their diamonds every day? and did you see the Queen? and what did she say to you? I've come to hear everything—everything!" cried Katie. She had taken off her hat and established herself in that corner of the book-room where so many talks had taken place, where Lilias had painted all the anticipatory scenes of grandeur which she intended to go through, and where she had listened to Katie's plans, and not refused her aid. It was a year since they had met, and Lilias, seated there, with a little mist of suspense about her, waiting for the next chapter in her life, had an air of dreamy development and maturity which made a great impression upon her friend. In other days Katie, though the youngest, had been the one that knew most of the world. She had been full of dances, of partners, of what this one and that had said, while Lilias had still no souvenirs. But all this had changed. It was Lilias now who knew the world. She had gone away, she had been in the secrets of society. She knew how duchesses looked, and what they put on. She had seen princes walking familiarly about as if they were but men. Was it this lofty experience which gave her that soft air as of a dream enveloping her, as if, to put it in Katie's way, she was thinking of something else, listening for somebody coming. Katie did not understand the change; but she saw it now, and it overawed her. Her eyes sought those of Lilias wistfully. There were other questions more important which she had to ask; but, to begin with, the general ones seemed necessary. She kept in her personal anxieties with an effort. For Katie had many personal anxieties too, and was rather woebegone and pale, not like the sprightly little girl of old.

"It was not nearly so grand as I thought—nothing is ever so grand as you think," said Lilias. "London town is just big—big—not grand at all, and men just look like men, and women like women. They are silly just like ourselves. It is not another world, as I once thought. It is quite the same. It was an awful disappointment," said Lilias, with a Scottish force of adjective which had not come to be slang in those days; "but it was just nice enough all the same," she added, condescendingly, after a momentary pause. "I thought I would just look at it all, and admire it; but you could not do that, you had just to take your part, as if you had been at home."

"Oh, I should not have cared to look at it," said Katie. "I would have liked to have my share."

"Except at the Countess's," said Lilias, with an involuntary laugh. "We stood there, and looked on. Lady Ida came and talked to us, and the Countess herself. And then we stood and stared at all the people. It makes me laugh now, but then it was like to make me cry. We were only country neighbours there."

"And what were you in the other houses?" Katie asked.

"I don't know. It was different—" Lilias paused a little, musing, with eyes full of a smile of recollection; then she said, suddenly, glad to have an outlet, "Guess whom we met in London—a gentleman—one that you know. And he knew everybody—and—" Lilias made another pause of grateful thought, then added, softly, "he was a great man there."

Katie clasped her hands together. To her Philip Stormont was a great man anywhere. Her little countenance flushed, then grew pale, and it could be seen how thin her cheeks had grown, and her eyes big and eager, as the colour melted out of her face. She did not say anything, but looked at Lilias with a wide-eyed, deeply meaning, reproachful look. Her poor little bosom heaved with a painful, long-drawn breath. Oh, how can you speak to me of him, her eyes seemed to say; and yet how anxious she was to hear!

"Can't you guess?" said Lilias, with a smile of content.

"I suppose—it could be but one person. But oh, Lilias, everything is so changed, so changed!" cried poor little Katie; and those caves, once soft circles in which her pretty eyes were set, seemed to contract, and fill with deep lakes of tears. She kept them back with a great effort, and produced a little pitiful smile, the best she could muster. "I am sure it isn't your fault," she said, magnanimously. "Tell me—all about it, Lilias."

"All about what?" Lilias paused too, to look at her in amazement, and a sort of cold breath came into her heart, chilling her in spite of herself. "I did not know," she said, with sudden spirit, waking out of her dream, "that Mr. Murray was of any consequence, Katie, to you."

Katie's countenance changed again in a moment from misery to gladness.

"Oh, Mr. Murray!" she cried. In the relief of the moment, the tears came dropping down her cheeks like rain, and she laughed in the sudden ease of her mind. "No, no consequence, no consequence at all," she cried. "I thought—I thought it must be—"

The eyes of the girls met, the one inquiring, almost with a gleam of contempt; the other shyly drawing back, denying the answer.

"I see," said Lilias, nodding her head. "No, I had not forgotten. I knew very well—But, dear Katie," she cried, with the unrestrained laugh of youth, "you could not think Philip—for it was Philip you thought of—could be a great man in London. Philip!" The idea brought with it a peal of laughter. "He may be very nice at home, but among all the fashionable folk there—!"

Katie did not laugh with her friend; on the contrary, she grew red and angry. Her tears dried, high indignation lighted up her face, but along with it a little consolation too.

"They say," said Katie, "that you were not always of that mind, Lilias, and that he was with you—oh, every day. They say he went with you to all the parties, and danced with you every dance. They say—I would like you to tell me true," cried the little girl. "Oh, you need not think I will break my heart! Whatever has happened, if you think I will make a work about it, and a fuss, and all that, you are just mistaken, Lilias! I hope I have more pride than that. If he likes you better than me, he is welcome, oh, he is welcome! And if you that were my own friend, that was like a sister—that was—"

Poor little Katie was choked with tears and excitement. She could not say any more. Her voice failed her altogether, everything swam and wavered in her eyes. Her own familiar friend had deceived her, her love had forsaken her. The bitterness of abandonment was in her heart. She had struggled hard to show what her mother called "a proper pride," and though it had hollowed out the sockets of her eyes, and taken the colour from her cheeks, she thought she had succeeded. But to hear Lilias, who had stolen him away, speak disdainfully of Philip, to hear him scoffed at, whom Katie thought the first and most desirable of human beings; it is impossible to say how hard this was. All the faculties of her soul rose up against it: and yet—and yet—She would not have let herself go, and suspend her proper pride so entirely, if there had not been beyond, as it were the sense of her despair, a rising gleam of hope.

"Who said that?" cried Lilias, in great astonishment and dismay. And then she drew Katie's unwilling form towards her. "Do you think so much about Philip still? Oh, Katie, he is not half good enough for you."

Katie flung herself out of her friend's grasp.

"I can put up with your treachery," she cried. "Oh! I can stand that; but to hear you insult Philip is what I will not, I will not bear!"

Upon which Lilias sprang to her feet also.

"I will say just what I please of Philip," she cried; "and who is to stop me? What am I caring about Philip? I just endured him because of you. He neither went with me to parties, nor danced with me, nor was with us every day. He is just a long-leggit lad, as Margaret says. If he was rich or great, or if he was clever and wise, or even if he was just kind—kind and true like some—But he is none of these, none of these, Katie, not half good enough for you; and me, what is Philip to me?" Lilias cried, with a grand disdain.

"Perhaps he has forsaken you—too," said Katie, looking at her with mingled wrath and relief and indignation. She was very wroth and wounded for Philip, but her heart, which had been so sore, felt cooled and eased as by the dropping of some heavenly dew. Her anger with Lilias was boundless. She could not refrain from that little blow at her, and yet she could have embraced her for every careless word she said.

Lilias looked at her for a moment, uncertain whether to be angry too. But then the absurdity of the idea that Philip might have forsaken her, suddenly seized her. She laughed out with a gaiety that could not be mistaken, and took her seat again.

"When you are done questioning me about Philip—" she said. "I would not have remembered Philip but for you. We forgot he was to have come home with us, and never let him know; and nobody remembered, not even Jean. But we have heard enough of Philip since we came home. His mother has been here, demanding, 'What have you done with my Philip?'" Lilias here fell into Mrs. Stormont's tone, and Katie, though still in tears, had hard ado not to laugh. "Just demanding him from Margaret and from me: and you next, Katie. As if we were Philip's keepers! He is big enough, I hope, to take care of himself."

Here Katie came stealing up to her friend, winding a timid arm about her neck.

"Oh! Lilias, was it all stories? and are you true, are you true?"

"Is that what has made you just a little ghost? And why did you never write and tell me, when I could have put it all right with a word?"

"Oh, what could I say?" cried Katie. "A girl must have a proper pride. Would I let you see and let him see that I was minding! Oh! no, no! and his mother every time we met her, and every time mamma met her, always, always on about Philip and you. She told us all the places he went with you—every place, even to the Queen's Court: and there was his name in the Times—for she got it on purpose, and sent it over the water to papa: and she said he always contrived to get an invitation wherever you went."

Lilias smiled with high disdain.

"Many people would have liked to do that," she said, "for we went to the grandest houses, where Philip Stormont, or even the Murrays of Murkley, who are very different, would never set a foot. Oh! it was no credit of ours—we just had—a friend—"

"A friend! And that was the gentleman you meant, not him; and it was a person I knew? I cannot guess it, for I don't know any person who could be a friend to you. But just it was not—him? That is so wonderful, I cannot think of anything else; for all this time I have been thinking and thinking, and trying not to think, and then just thinking the more."

Lilias smiled upon her, a gracious, but half-disdainful, half-disappointed smile. Katie could think of nothing but this. She had no sympathy, no interest, in what had happened to her friend. It hurt Lilias a little: for there was no one else whom she could speak to of that other who was so much more important than Philip. She was wounded a little, and retired into herself in lofty, but gentle superiority. She could have told things that would have made her little companion admire and wonder. But what did Katie care except about Philip, a country youth who was nobody, a rustic gentleman that gaped and was helpless in the brilliant world? Lilias felt a great superiority, but yet a little check and disappointment too. It seemed to her that her little companion had fallen far behind her in the march of life, that Katie was only a child, crying, sobbing, unable to think of anything but one thing—and a little nobody, too. She herself had gone a long way beyond her little rural companion, which was quite just—for was not Lilias a whole year older, besides her season in town? So she allowed herself to be tolerant and indulgent. Was it not natural? So young and little, and only one thing in her head—Philip, and no more. Lilias put away her own interrupted history with a proud self-denial. She would not betray it to any one who was not worthy of that confidence, although her heart ached a little with the solitude of it and the need of speech. But surely it was but for a day or two that it could be allowed to continue, this solitude of the heart? She went out in the afternoon with Katie for a walk, and went to New Murkley with many a thought. But New Murkley was overflowing to Katie with images of Philip, and Lilias moved along abstracted, always with a little sense of disdainful wonder and toleration for one who could think of nothing but Philip, though on the verge, had she chosen, of far greater things.

When she returned to her sisters afterwards, she found these ladies in a state of great perturbation and distress. Jean was sitting, with her bonnet still on, too much agitated to think of her work. Margaret was walking up and down the drawing-room, also in her outdoor dress, and carrying on an indignant monologue. The entrance of Lilias discomposed them both. They had not expected her, and, as Margaret did not perceive her at first, Jean gave a little exclamation of warning.

"Margaret, it is Lilias!" she cried.

And Margaret, in her walk up and down, turned round and faced her, with a look of annoyance which it was impossible to conceal. She was heated and angry, and the interruption aggravated her discontent. She said,

"Well, what about Lilias? It's all Lilias so far as I can see, and we seem just fated to have no more peace in our lives."

"Is it I that am taking away your peace, Margaret?" Lilias said. She had come in with a kind of lofty sadness and longing, her heart full, and no relief to it possible; her life waiting, as it seemed, for a touch from without—a something which could not come of her own initiative. It was not enough to trouble her as with a sense of dependence, but only to make her sensible of an incompleteness, an impotence, which yet was sweet.

"There are several persons, it appears, from whom ye have taken away the peace," said Margaret. "The countryside is just ringing with it from all I hear. When was it that you gave so much encouragement to that long-leggit fellow, Philip Stormont? I have heard of little else all the time I have been out, and Jean will tell you the same thing. They say he went to every place with us in London (I told you not to take him to the theatre, Jean), and that it's all settled between him and you."

"Margaret, I would not speak like that to Lilias that knows nothing about such things."

"Just hold your peace, Jean; if she does not know about them, she'll have to learn. When a man wants her to marry him, she'll have to hear about it, and make her own decision." Margaret's conscience, perhaps, upbraided her at this moment, for she made a perceptible pause, then resumed, with increased impatience: "It may be true, for anything we can tell. You gave him great encouragement, they say, before we went from here—was that true? for I've many a thing to think of, and I cannot call all these bits of nothings to mind."

"Oh, Margaret, how can ye upbraid our Lilias, that is as innocent as an infant? Encouragement, as they call it, was what she never gave any lad. Encouragement, say they?—that just means a forward person that knows what a gentleman is meaning, and helps him on. Lilias, my dear," said Jean, "you'll just run away. Even to hear the like of that is not for you."

"Is it Philip Stormont again?" cried Lilias. "I think you are very unkind, Margaret; you ought to take my part, instead of scolding me. What am I caring about Philip Stormont? I wish he was—no, I don't wish him any harm—I don't care enough about him," cried the girl angrily. "What is it now?"

"She knows there is something, Jean."

"And how could she help knowing, Margaret, when his mother was at her this morning with that very word in her mouth? Encouragement!—it's just his mother's doing, everything about it; he would never raise that cry himself."

"Himself!—he has not enough in him," said Margaret. "But, Lilias, whatever you have done, you will have to bear the blame, and it must just be a lesson to us all. In the first place, they were all for congratulating us, every person we met. Bonnie congratulations! I think the world is out of its wits. To wish us joy of wedding the heiress of Murkley upon a bonnet-laird like Philip Stormont! The old Murrays would just turn in their graves, but all this senseless canailye wishes us joy."

"Oh, whisht, Margaret! the people just meant very well; no doubt they had many a private thought in their mind, but they would think it was well to put the best face upon it."

"And, when they saw we knew nothing of it, what does the minister's wife do but reads me a lecture on the sin of crossing young folk in their affections! I am the kind of person, you will say, to be lectured by

Mrs. Seton and Mrs. Stormont, and all the rest," said Margaret, with a laugh of scorn; but it was not indifferent to her. There was a slight nervous tremor about her person, which betrayed a vexation almost more serious than her words conveyed. "I am not finding fault with you, Lilias. I well believe you meant no harm, and never thought you could be misconceived; but I would mind upon this in the future if I were you. Meet with nobody and walk with nobody but those that belong to you, or that are like yourself. If you do that, you will give no handle to any ill-disposed person. My dear, I am not finding fault."

"It sounds worse than finding fault," said Lilias. "It sounds as if you thought I had been—Oh!" she cried, with a little stamp of her foot, "unwomanly!—you will not say the word, but I know that is what you mean. And it is not so—it never was so. It was not for me, it was for—"

Here Lilias stopped in her impetuous self-defence, stopped, and blushed crimson, and said, more impetuously still, but with a tone of humility and self-reproach—

"I am just a traitor! It is true—I am a false friend."

"That was what I said, Margaret," cried Jean, "you will mind what I said."

Of this Margaret took no notice, neither of the interrupted speech of Lilias, but continued to pace about the room with a clouded brow. She asked no further explanations; but she had many thoughts to oppress her mind. The Countess had been one of those who had wished her joy. That great lady had stopped her carriage, in which Lady Ida sat smiling, and, with a certain air of triumph, had offered her congratulations.

"I always thought there was something between them," she had said, "and two such charming young people, and in every way so suitable—"

"Your ladyship seems to forget," Margaret had said, trembling with wrath, "that the Murrays of Murkley have been in the county before any other name that's worth counting was heard of, and were never evened with the small gentry, so far as I know, till this day."

"Oh! my dear Miss Murray, that is quite an antediluvian view to take," the Countess had said, and had driven off in great glee, accepting none of the angry sister's denials. There was something underneath that made this very galling to Margaret. Young Lord Bellendean had been one of those that had been at the feet of Lilias, and this was the reason of his mother's triumph. It had its effect upon Margaret, too, in a way which was not very flattering to young Bellendean. She had not been insensible to the pleasure of seeing the best match in the countryside refused by her little sister. Lord Bellendean, too, was one of the class which she described as long-leggit lads; but a peerage and great estates make a difference. Lilias had never shown any inclination towards their noble young neighbour; but the refusal of him would have been gratifying. And now his mother, with this story of Philip, would turn Bellendean effectually away. This was the chief sting of the discovery she had made. But even to Jean she had not betrayed herself. She was aware that perhaps it was not a very elevated hope, and that her mortification would have but little sympathy had the cause of it been revealed. This was in the foreground of her mind, and held the chief place among her disturbed thoughts. But it was not all. She could not flatter herself she had got rid of Lewis Murray by turning her back upon him. Thus she stood as in the midst of a circle of masked batteries. She did not know from which side the next broadside would come. It was indispensable for her to be prepared on every hand.

CHAPTER XLII

Philip Stormont did not return home for a week, during which period Lilias had ample reason to share her sister's annoyance. She was received wherever she appeared with congratulations and good wishes, though it was a very daft-like thing, the village people thought, for young folk, who had known each other all their lives and might have spoken whenever they pleased, to go away up to London, and meet in strange houses there before they could come to an understanding.

"No true! hoot, Miss Lilias! It must be true, for I had it from the leddy hersel'," was the reception her denial got: and there was not unfrequently a glance aside at Katie, which showed the consciousness of the speaker of another claim. It was a curious study in human nature for the neighbourhood, and, though it was perhaps cruel, the interest of the race in mental phenomena generally may have accounted for the pleasure mingled with compassion with which one after another offered in Katie's presence their good wishes to Lilias, keenly observing meantime the air and aspect of the maiden forsaken.

"It'll no have been true about Miss Katie and him, after all," Janet, at the 'Murkley Arms,' announced to her husband, "for she took it just as steady as a judge."

"Oh, ay, it was true enough; but men are scarce, and he's just ta'en his pick," said Adam.

"My word, but he's no blate," said Janet, in high indignation. "Two of the bonniest and best in a' the countryside for Philip Stormont to take his pick o'! I would soon learn him another lesson. And it's just a' lees—a' lees from beginning to end."

"In that case," said Adam, with philosophic calm, "I would not fash my thoom about it, if I were you." But the philosophy was more than Janet was capable of. She bade him gang aff to his fishing for a cauld-hearted loon, that took nae interest in his fellow-creatures.

"It's naething to you if a young thing breaks her bit heart," Janet said; and she added, with a sigh, "No to say that I had ither views for Miss Lilias mysel'."

Perhaps it was some glimmer of these "ither views," some implication of another name, never mentioned, but understood between them by a subtle feminine freemasonry, which made Lilias insist so warmly to Janet upon the falsehood of the common report. The girls went on to the manse after this explanation, Lilias walking with great dignity, but with a flush of offence and annoyance on her face.

"I wish he would just come back, and let them see it is all lies," Lilias cried.

Katie dried a furtive tear when they got within the shelter of the manse garden. Would Philip, when he came, show that it was all lies? or was he minded, like his mother, to make it true? And, if he put forth those persuasive powers which Katie felt so deeply, could Lilias resist him? These questions kept circling through Katie's brain in endless succession. "It would maybe be better if he never came back," she said, with a sigh.

Mrs. Seton was in all the bustle of her morning's occupations. She came into the drawing-room a little heated, and with some suppressed excitement in her eyes. Katie's mother was not entirely in Katie's confidence, but she knew enough of her child's mind to take an agitated and somewhat angry interest in the news of Lilias' supposed engagement. Perhaps indeed she was not without a guilty sense of intention in her former hospitality to Philip, which turned now, by a very common alchymy of the mind, into an angry feeling that she had been kind to him, and that he had been very ungrateful. She came in with a little bustle, unable to chase from her countenance some traces of offence.

"Well, Lilias, so you have come to be congratulated," she said. "I am sure I wish you every prosperity. Nobody will doubt that we wish you well, such great friends as you have always been with Katie, and all the old connection between us and Murkley." Here she kissed the girl on both cheeks sharply, conveying a little anger even in the kiss. "But I think, you know, you were a little wanting—oh! just a little wanting, I'll not say much—considering all the intimacy, not to write at once and let Katie know—"

"I would like to hear what there was to let Katie know," cried Lilias, with indignation. "And why you should wish me prosperity? You never did it before. I am just as I always was before; and as for Philip Stormont," cried the girl, "he is nothing to me. Oh, yes, he is something—he is a great trouble and bother, and makes Margaret angry, and everybody talk nonsense. I wish he was at the other end of the world!" Lilias cried, with a little stamp of her impatient foot upon the floor.

"Dear me!" said Mrs. Seton, "but this is very different from what we heard. No, no, it must be just a little temper, Lilias, and Margaret's scolding that makes you turn it off like this. I can well understand Margaret being angry," said the minister's wife, with a gleam of satisfaction. "Her that thought nobody too grand for you; but there is no calculating upon young folk. Here is Lilias, Robert; but she is just in an ill way. She will have none of my good wishes. She has quarrelled with him, I suppose. We all know what a lovers' quarrel is. Yes, yes, she'll soon come to herself. And it would be a terrible thing, you know, to tell a fib to your clergyman," Mrs. Seton said, with an attempt at raillery; but she was anxious in spite of herself.

"Miss Lilias," said the minister, who had come in, and who was more formal, "will have little doubt of our good wishes in all circumstances, and especially on a happy—"

"Oh, will you hold all your tongues!" cried Lilias, driven out of recollection of her good manners, and of the respect she owed, as Mrs. Seton said, to her clergyman. "There's no circumstances at all, and nothing happy, nor to wish me joy about. I am no more engaged than you are," she said, addressing Mr. Seton, who stood, interrupted in his little speech, in a sort of consternation. "I am not going to be married. It is all just lies from beginning to end."

"Oh, my dear, you must not say that. It is dreadful to say that. If we are really to believe you, Lilias—"

"You need not believe me unless you like. You seem to think I don't know my own concerns. But it is all lies, and nothing else," cried Lilias, with a glow of momentary fury. "Just lies from beginning to end."

"Dear, dear me!" said Mrs. Seton. "My dear, we will not press it too far. But perhaps you have refused poor Philip, and he cannot make up his mind it has been final. If you are so sure of it on your side, it will perhaps just be a mistake on his."

"Oh, I wish I had refused him!" cried Lilias, setting her small teeth. "I wish he had asked me, and I would have given him his answer. I would have said to him, I would sooner marry Adam at the inn, I would sooner have little Willie Seton out of the nursery. Oh, there would have been no mistake!"

"But, my dear Miss Lilias, why this warmth?" said the minister. "After all, if the young man wanted you to marry him, it was a compliment, it was no offence. He is a fine young fellow, when all is said; and why so hot about it? It is no offence."

"It is just a—" Here Lilias paused, receiving a warning look from Katie, who had placed herself behind backs, but how gave a little furtive pull to her friend's dress.

"Margaret is very angry," she said, with dignity, "but not so angry as I am. To be away a whole year, and then, when I am so glad to come home, to have this thrown in my face! It is not Philip's fault, it is just Mrs. Stormont, who never would let me alone—and oh! will you tell everybody? You may say out of politeness that it is a mistake, but I say it is all lies, and that is true."

"Whisht, whisht, whisht, my dear!" cried Mrs. Seton. "If you are sure you are sincere—No, no; me doubting! I would never doubt your word, if you are sure you are in earnest, Lilias. I will just tell everybody with pleasure that some mistake has happened—just some mistake. You were old friends, and never thought what meaning was in his mind; or it was his mother who put a wrong interpretation. Yes, yes; you may rely upon me, Lilias: if you are sure, my dear, if you are quite sure that you are sincere!"

Lilias went home alone, in high excitement and anger with all the world, holding her head high, and refusing to pause to speak to the eager cottagers by their doors, who had all a word to say. This mode of treatment was unknown at Murkley, and produced many shakings of the head, and fears that London had made her proud. The wives reminded each other that they had never approved of it. "Why can they no bide at hame? It was never the custom in the auld days," the women said. But Lilias made no response to their looks. She went through the village with an aspect of disdain, carrying her head high; but, before she came to the gates of the old castle, she became aware of Mrs. Stormont's pony-carriage leisurely descending towards the river. With still stronger reason she tossed her head aloft and hurried on. But she was not permitted to escape so easily. Mrs. Stormont made her preparations to alight as soon as the girl was visible, and left her no possibility of escape. She thrust her hand through the unwilling arm of Lilias with confidential tenderness.

"It was you I was looking for," she said. She had not the triumphant look which had been so offensive on her previous visit. Her brow was puckered with anxiety. "My bonnie Lily," she said, "you are angry, and I have done more harm than good. What ails you at my poor laddie, Lilias? Who have we thought upon all this time but only you? When I took all the trouble of yon ball, which was little pleasure to me at my time of life, who was it for but you? Do you think I was wanting to please the Bairnsfaithers and the Dunlops, and all the little gentry about, or even the Countess and Lady Ida? I was wanting to please you: and my Philip—"

"He was wanting to please Katie Seton," said Lilias, with an angry laugh; "and he was quite right, for they were fond, fond of each other."

"Oh, my bonnie pet, what a mistake!" cried Mrs. Stormont, growing red. "Katie Seton! I would not have listened to it for a moment! The Setons would never have been asked but just for civility. Philip to put up with all that little thing's airs, and the vulgar mother! Oh! my darling, do not you be deceived. What said he in London? Was there ever a word of Katie? You would not cast up to him a folly of his youth now that he's a man, and all his heart is set on you?"

"Even if it was so," cried Lilias, "my heart is not set on him; I do not like him—Oh! yes, I like him well enough. He is just a neighbour; but, Mrs. Stormont, nothing more."

"Lilias, Lilias, you don't know what you are doing! Oh! my dear, just think a little. He has never come home; he has taken it sore, sore to heart that you left town like that, and never let him know. How do I know what my boy is doing, left by himself, with a disappointed heart, among all yon terrible temptations? Oh, my lovely Lily, whom I have petted and thought much of all your life, one word from you would bring Philip home!"

"I cannot send him a word," cried Lilias. "Oh, how can you ask me, when, wherever I go, everybody is at me wishing me joy; and, though it is all lies, they make me think shame, and I don't know how to look them in the face; but I am not ashamed—I am just furious!" Lilias cried, with burning blushes. "And then you ask me to send him a word—"

"To bring him home! He is everything I have in the world. Oh! Lilias, you would not be the one to part a mother from her only son; you would not be so hard-hearted as that, my Lily. If he has been wanting in any way, if he has not been so bold in speaking out—"

It was all that Lilias could do to contain herself.

"Do I want him to speak out?" she cried. "I do not want Philip at all, Mrs. Stormont. Will you believe what I tell you? If you want to get him home, let him come back to Katie."

"Put Katie out of your mind," said Mrs. Stormont, sharply. "There is no question of Katie. It is just an insult to me to speak of her at all."

Upon which Lilias threw her head higher still.

"And it is just an insult to me," she cried—"oh, far, far worse! for I am little and young, and not able to say a word, and you are trying to force me into what nobody wants. And Margaret will scold me as if it were my fault."

"You are able to say plenty for yourself, it appears to me," said Mrs. Stormont; and then she changed her tone. "Oh, Lilias, I have always been fond, fond of you, my bonnie dear. I have always said you should have been my child; and now, when there's a chance that you may be mine—What ails ye at my Philip? Where will you find a finer lad? Where will ye get a better son, except just when he loses his judgment with disappointment and love? Oh, my bonnie Lily, he will come back—he will come to his duty and his mother, if you will only send him a word—just a word."

This conversation was interrupted in the strangest way by the sudden apparition of a dog-cart driven at full speed down the road, which Lilias had vaguely perceived approaching with a little flutter of her heart, not knowing at any minute who might appear out of the unseen. When it drew up suddenly at the roadside for a single moment the light wavered in her eyes. But she came to herself again at once as Philip Stormont jumped out and advanced to his mother, whose evident relief and pleasure at the sight of him touched Lilias' heart. The poor lady trembled so that she could scarcely stand. She could do nothing but gaze at her son. She forgot in a moment the half-quarrel, the pathetic plea which she was urging with Lilias. "Oh, my boy, you've come back!" she said, throwing herself upon him. Lilias was far too young to fathom what was in the mother's heart, but she was touched in spite of herself. The change in Mrs. Stormont's face, the disappearance of all the curves in her forehead, the melting of all the hard lines in her face, was like magic to the watching girl. A little awe seized her of the love that worked so profoundly, and which she had made so little account of. It was true love, though it was not the form of true love of which one thinks at eighteen. She withdrew a little from them in the first moment of their meeting with natural delicacy, but did not go away, feeling it would be somewhat cowardly to attempt to escape.

As for Philip, when he had greeted his mother, he turned from her to Lilias with a countenance by no means love-like.

"You played me a pretty trick," he said. "Lucky for me that I went to Cadogan Place first. I might have been at the station now kicking my heels."

"Not for a week, I hope."

"I might have been there all night: and thinking all the time that something must have happened. I did not take it kind," said Philip. His mother was holding his arm, and already making little demonstrations upon it to stop him in these ill-advised complaints; but Philip paid little attention. "I wonder how you would have liked it yourself to be left in the lurch without a word!"

"We were all very sorry," Lilias said, with an air of penitence, and then she added, "when we remembered," with an inclination to laugh, which was all the stronger because of the gravity of the situation a few moments past.

He was somewhat travel-worn, covered with dust, and bearing marks of the fact that he had left London the night before, and had not paused long upon the way. His looks, as he regarded Lilias, were not those of a lover, and as she said the last words he coloured high with not unpardonable resentment.

"I can well believe that you took little pains to remember me at all," he said.

"Oh! Philip, how I have wearied for you," said his mother, anxiously, making a diversion. "We were speaking of you, Lilias and I: and I was going to send a message—"

"You are always so impatient," cried Philip, "pursuing a fellow with telegrams as if he were a thief! Yes, I waited a day or two. There was something I wanted to see. You can see nothing while that confounded season is going on. But I'm tired, mother, and by your leave I'll get home at once."

"You'll excuse him, Lilias," cried Mrs. Stormont, once more with anxiety; "he'll pay his respects to you at a more fitting moment. Yes, my dear boy, certainly we will go home; you can drive me back—"

"I've got a dog-cart from Kilmorley," said Philip; "and a better beast than yours. I'll just go on in that. I'll be there half-an-hour before you."

He took off his hat carelessly to Lilias, who was looking after him almost with as much astonishment as his mother. The two ladies looked at each other as he drove away. Poor Mrs. Stormont, after her agitation and joy, had grown white and troubled. She gazed at Lilias wistfully with deprecating eyes. The situation was ruefully comic, but she did not see it. To have compromised the name of Lilias for Philip's sake—to have compromised Philip by pleading with Lilias: and then to have it proved by both before her eyes how useless were her pains—so broadly, so evidently that she could not pretend to disbelieve it, was hard. She said, quickly, as if with an attempt to convince herself, "He is wearied with his journey; he is dusty, and not fit for a lady's eye." But after that the situation was too strong for her; for a moment there was humility in her tone. "My dear, perhaps I have made a mistake; I will do what I can to put it right," she said. Then the inalienable instinct of defence awoke again. "It is just that he is turned the wrong way with all these slights and disappointments, to be taken up one moment and cast away the next. He'll have taken an ill notion against women. Men are always keen to do that. It's their justification; and there is no doubt," she continued more briskly, nerving her courage, "whatever you may say now, that he got a great deal of encouragement at one time, Lilias. And now he's just turned the wrong way," Mrs. Stormont ended with a sigh, slowly mounting into her pony-carriage. Her old servant sat there motionless as he had sat through all this conversation. "I hope you may never repent your handiwork," she said.

CHAPTER XLIII

There is something in the unchangeableness of rural scenery, and in the unaltered method and order of a long established and carefully governed household, which gives the sensitive spirit, returning to them after great changes have passed over itself, a sort of shock as of pitiless permanence and a rigid machinery of existence which must triumph over every mere vicissitude of happiness or unhappiness.

After the little incidents of the first days, which after all had had little to do with her own personal history, the absolute unchangedness of Murkley, not a leaf different, every branch drooping in the same line, the same flowers in the garden, the same arrangement of the flower-vases to which Jean was so glad to get back (for she had never been able to arrange the London bouquets to her own satisfaction in those terrible glass things in Cadogan Place), conveyed to Lilias a sense of some occult and secret power of passive authority in existence itself, as separate from any individual will or wish, which appalled her. London and all those wonderful scenes—the lights, the talks, the dances, the intoxication of flattery and delight which had mounted to her head—were all gone like a phantasmagoria. But life, which had been waiting for her just as of old, which had been going on just as of old, while she was flitting through that dream-world, had now taken her in again steadily to its steady routine which admitted no thought of change. It appalled her for the moment; her feet came down, with a power of gravitation over which her impulses seemed to have little or no influence, into the self-same line, upon the self-same path. She tried to laugh sometimes at what everybody called the force of habit, but she was frightened by it. She had acquired a great deal of experience in those six weeks of the season; her memory was full of scenes which flashed upon the inward eye whenever she was by herself, or even when she sat silent in the old rooms where Jean and Margaret were so silent too. And when some one called her, or something from the outer world came in, Lilias felt a momentary giddiness, an inability to arrange her thoughts or to be quite sure where she was, or which was real, the actual world or that other in which the moment before she had been. Her head seemed to turn round when she was spoken to. To feel herself surrounded by a smiling crowd in rooms all splendid with decoration, flowers, and lights, and fine pictures, with music and flattering voices in the air—and then to look up and see Jean's head somewhat paler than usual against the dark wainscot, and Miss Margaret's voice saying, "If you will put on your hat, Lilias, we will go out for our walk—" Which was true? She faltered as she rose up, stumbling among the real. She was afraid of it: it seemed to her to be a sort of ghost of existence from which she could not escape.

And in other respects there was no small agitation in the inner consciousness of Lilias. She had felt that there was much in the air on that last evening which never came to anything. The atmosphere of the place, in which neither he nor she had cared to dance, had tingled with something that had never been said. All those weeks, when she had seen him so often, had produced their natural effect upon the girl. She had never deceived herself, like Margaret, as to the many houses that had suddenly been thrown open to them. Lilias had not forgotten how it had been at the Countess's reception. She remembered the immediate alteration of everything as soon as Lewis had appeared. She had not been allowed to speak to him in the Row, but immediately after all the doors had been thrown open as by magic. She knew very well that this magic was in his hand. And how was it possible for her to believe that it was merely "kindness," as she at first thought? It was kindness, but there was something more. She saw not only the tenderness, but the generosity of his treatment of her with wonder, almost with a little offence at the magnanimity which she found it so difficult to understand. Lewis had brought to her everybody that was best and most attractive. She had looked again and again into eyes, bent upon her with admiration, that might have been the eyes of the hero of her dreams. Six-foot-two of fine humanity, in the Guards, in the Diplomatic Service, or, better still, in no service at all, endowed with the finest of English names and possessing the bluest blood, had exhibited itself before her in the best light again and again. We do not pretend to assert, nor did Lilias believe, that these paladins were all ready to lay their hearts and honours at her feet; but there was one at least who had done so, without even moving her to more than a little tingle of gratified vanity and friendly regret. But from all these tall heroes she had turned to middle-sized Lewis, with his eyes and hair of no particular colour. She had always been aware when he was in the most crowded room. Everybody had talked to her about him, believing her to be his relation. They had all met him abroad; they had all some grateful recollection of his services when they were ill, or where they were strangers; they poured forth praises of him on all sides, till Lilias felt her heart run over. Above even the attractions of six-feet, had been the enthusiasm in her mind for the good and true. She did not indeed want this enthusiasm to turn her thoughts to that first friend, as she had called him in her heart, the first companion who had been of her own choice and discovery, and whose absence had made to her a wonderful blank, of which she felt the effect without fully realizing the cause. But she realized the cause very well now: and felt the day blank indeed in which he had no share.

Also she knew by instinct that something was to have been said to her on that last evening. Was it merely his disappointment at finding his favourite nook under the palms in the conservatory already occupied, which prevented it being said? or was there some other cause? When they left London so abruptly, two days before the appointed time, without seeing Lewis, Lilias had been somewhat disturbed and wistful. She had wondered at it, however, without being greatly cast down: there was no fear, she thought, but that he would soon follow. He would come after them to Murkley. What he had to say would be more fitly said under the shadow of the great house, about which he too, like herself, had dreamed dreams: he could not stay away, she felt sure. And as for Margaret's opposition, that did not appal the young heroine greatly. All it meant was that Margaret wanted a prince of the royal blood for her child, and not even he unless he were handsome and gallant, a youth to please a lady's eye. Lilias felt a little humorous sympathy with Margaret: she felt that it would be hard for herself to give up the idea of a hero. Lewis was not like a hero. He was like a thousand other people, and nobody could identify him, or say, "who is that?" as the owners of great dark eyes, and dark hair, at the top of six-feet-two of stature, are ordinarily remarked upon. Lilias laughed as this thought crossed her mind, and, with a little sympathetic feeling, was sorry for Margaret. For herself she had ceased altogether to think of the other, and she was not afraid that her sister would stand out against Lewis. There would be a struggle: but a struggle in which the happiness of a beloved child is at stake is decided before it has begun. So on the whole, after finding this phantom life more ghostly because there was no Lewis in it, she reflected that when he came it would bloom into reality; and she was satisfied to bear it for a little—until the better time should come.

But when day followed day, and the better time did not come, a curious blight, like the atmospheric greyness which agricultural people call by that name, crept slowly over her, she could scarcely tell how. The earth looked as if a perpetual east-wind were blowing, yet as if there was no air to breathe; the skies were all overcast, the trees seemed to dry up and grow grey like everything else: and a certain air of consciousness, a perception that this was so, seemed to come into the house. Lilias perceived vaguely, as she went about with a heart growing heavier and a dull wonder which went through everything, that everybody was sorry for her. Why were they sorry for her? Jean said, "My poor darling!" and petted her as if she had been ill. Old Simon even put on a look of sympathy. In Margaret's eyes, there was something the girl had never seen there before. Anger, compunction, pity—which was it? All of these feelings were in it. Sometimes she would turn away as if she could not bear the sight of Lilias, sometimes would be so tender to her that the girl could have wept for herself. Why? for Margaret had never made an exhibition of the adoration with which she regarded her little sister, and it was only at some crisis that Lilias was allowed to suspect how dear she was. They studied all her little tastes, watched her steps, devoted themselves to please her: every one of which indications showed Lilias more and more that they were aware of something of which she was not aware, some reason why she should be unhappy. And she became unhappy to fulfil the necessities of the position. There was something which was being hid from her; what was it? Was it that he was only amiable and kind after all, and had merely wished to be serviceable, without any other feeling? But, if that was so, Margaret would be glad, not sorry; and how could they know that this would make any difference to her, Lilias? But, if not that, what could it be? And every day for many days she had expected to see him, when she walked down to the water-side, or wandered about New Murkley. She had thought that she would meet him round every corner, that Adam at the 'Murkley Arms' would be seen with his cart going for "the gentleman's" luggage, and Janet hanging the curtains and selecting the finest trout. It seemed so natural that he should come back. It seemed so certain that he must somehow seek the opportunity of telling that tale that had been left untold.

And as the time passed on, day following slowly after day, and he came not, Lilias felt that some explanation was necessary. There must be an explanation. What was it? That Margaret had sent him away? Margaret's eyes looked as if she had sent him away. Was it possible that he could have taken his dismissal from any one but herself? Then it was that Lilias had hot fits and cold fits of suppressed unhappiness. Sometimes she would be angry with Margaret for rejecting, and with Lewis for allowing himself to be rejected, and then would fall into a dreamy sadness, saying to herself that it was always so, and that this was the way of the world. But of all these troubles she said not a word, being too proud to signify to any one that her heart was engrossed by one who had not given her his. There were moments indeed in which she was tempted to throw herself upon Jean's sympathetic bosom: but then she recollected that Jean's story, such as it was, had been one of mutual love, whereas hers could only be that of an unfortunate attachment, words which made Lilias flame with resentment and shame. No, she must just pine and wait until he made some sign, or shake it all indignantly off, and make up her mind to think of it no more.

This was the state of affairs one afternoon when the next event in this history occurred. They were all seated together in the drawing-room, Jean, as usual, working at her table-cover, Margaret from behind her book casting wistful looks now and then at Lilias, who for her part was seated in one of the windows, in the recess, with her head relieved against the light, doing nothing. She had a book, it is true, but was not looking at it; her mind had turned inward. She was pondering her own story, which was more interesting than any romance. Margaret gave many glances at her as she sat, with her delicate profile and her fair locks, against the afternoon light. The post was late, and Simon brought the bag into the drawing-room, moving them all to a little excitement. Margaret opened it and took out its sole contents, a large blue envelope containing a bulky enclosure.

"There is nothing for either of you," she said, "but something of the nature of business from Mr. Allenerly for me." Then the little flutter of disappointed expectation calmed down, and silence fell again over the room, broken only by the sound of the torn paper and breaking seal, as Margaret opened her parcel. It was a law-document of some sort, bulky and serious. Margaret looked at it, and gave a sharp, sudden cry, which startled the others. The crackling of the paper as she unfolded it seemed to make a noise of disproportionate importance in the stillness of the room; for a law-paper, what could that mean but mere business and money? it could affect nobody's well-being. But the paper, they saw, trembled in Margaret's hands. She could not contain herself as she turned it over. She burst forth into strange exclamations.

"It is only just: it is only right: it is no more than ought to be done: it is the right thing: no more—" But after a while, she added, as if the words were forced from her—"It is not everybody that would have done it. I will not deny him the praise."

"What is it, Margaret? What is it?" Jean said.

Margaret made no immediate reply. She turned over the pages, which were many, with hands that shook, and much crackling and rustling of the paper.

"I cannot read it," she said; "I cannot see to read it. It makes my head go round. Oh, no, it is no more than justice—it is just the right thing; no more—no more—"

"Margaret, it is something far, far out of the ordinary, or you would not cry out like that."

"Yes, it is out of the ordinary; but then the first thing, the wrong doing, was out of the ordinary. This is no more—oh, not the least more—than he ought to have done from the first."

She was so much agitated that her voice shook as well as her hands, and Jean got up, throwing aside her work, and came to her sister's side. Lilias rose too, she did not know why, and stood watching them with an interest she could not explain to herself. Matters of business were not of any interest to her generally. All the law-papers in the world, in ordinary circumstances, would not have drawn her for a moment from a book, or out of the dreamy moods which she called thinking. But she rose now, full of an indefinable anxiety. When Jean had looked anxiously over her sister's shoulder, peering at the paper with wondering eyes for a few minutes, she too cried out with a quavering voice, and threw up her hands.

"What does it mean? What does it mean, Margaret? That he wills it back to her, is that what it says?"

"More than that! There's the letter that explains. He gives it back, every penny of the money, as he received it. It is a great thing to do. I am not grudging him the praise."

"Grudging him!—it is everything he has—it is all his living. Margaret! You will not let her take it—everything he has?"

"Jean, be silent—he had no right to a shilling. It was hers by nature and every law. I will not deny that, as soon as he saw his duty, he has done it like a man."

"His duty?—but it is everything! and he was son and daughter both to the old man. It is all his living: and neither you nor me ever thought what was our duty to our father's father. Margaret! Oh! it is more than justice this—more than justice! You will not let Lilias strip him of every shilling that he has!"

This impassioned dialogue, quick and breathless, gave Lilias a kind of half-enlightenment, kindling the instinct within her. She came forward with a quick, sudden movement.

"If it concerns me, what is it?" she said.

"There would have been no need to tell her, if you could but have held your tongue," cried Margaret to Jean, vehemently, "and now she will insist to hear all."

"It is her right to hear everything," cried Jean, as eagerly. The gentle woman was transformed. She was turned into a powerful opponent, a determined champion. Her face was pale, but she was firmer than Margaret herself.

"What is it?" cried Lilias, coming forward. It seemed to her that she was on the edge of some great change, she could not tell what. Her steps were a little uncertain, her looks a little wild. Strange fancies and tremors touched her mind, she anticipated she knew not what. She put out her hand for the papers. "If it concerns me, will you let me see it?" she said.

"You would not understand," said Margaret, with a quiver of her lips. "It is a law-paper; it is what they call a deed of gift. It is giving you back, Lilias, all your old grandfather died possessed of. It is a wonderful thing. He it was all left to—was perhaps not so ill a person as we thought—"

"Ill!—he was never ill—he is just honour itself," cried Miss Jean, "and righteousness and truth."

"I'm not grudging him his due. The person's name is Lewis Grantley that was your grandfather's companion, and got all his money. His conscience has troubled him. I will say nothing against him. At the last he has done justice and given it all back."

"Is it only about money, then, after all?" Lilias said, with a disappointed tone; then she looked again upon her sisters, in whose agitation she read something further. "There is more than that!" she cried.

"Jean, will you hold your tongue! Do you understand what I am saying to you, Lilias? All your grandfather's money, which has rankled at our hearts since ever he died. Money!" said she—"it's a great fortune. It makes you a great heiress—it restores the Murrays to their right place—it makes wrong right. It is more than money, twenty times more; it's family credit, it's restoration, it's your fit place. By the time you come of age, with good guiding—listen to me, Lilias—you'll be able to have your palace, to reign like a princess, to be just a queen in your own country. Is it wonderful if it goes to my heart? It is more than money—it is just new life for the family and for you."

"And in the mean time," said Miss Jean, who had been kept down almost by physical force, Margaret grasping her by the arm and keeping her back—"in the mean time, he that gives it—which he has no right to do, for it was willed to him and intended for him by the man that owned it all, and who was just as well able to judge as any of us—he will go out into the world penniless; he will have to earn his bread, he does not know where; he will have to give up everything that makes life pleasant. And he has not the up-bringing for it, poor lad. He has lain in the soft and drunk of the sweet all his life. It will be far harder to him to give up than for us to do without it, that have never had it. If you hear the one side, you must hear the other, Lilias."

Lilias, thus suddenly elevated into a judge, gazed at them both with eyes in which wonder soon gave place to a higher sentiment. It had never happened to her in her life before to be appealed to thus. Margaret took up the word almost before Jean had finished. They contended before her unconsciously like two advocates. She drew a chair towards her, and sat down facing them, listening, a strange tumult of different feelings in her mind. By this time the meaning of what Margaret had said had begun to penetrate her intelligence. A great fortune, a palace restored, a reign like a princess—Lilias was not insensible to such hopes; but what was all this about a man who would go out friendless upon the world?

"Stop a little," she said, "Margaret and Jean." The crisis had given to Lilias an extreme dignity and calm. "There is one thing that I have first to hear. The man that you are speaking of, that has done this, who is he? Do I know him?" Lilias said.

They both returned the look with a sort of awe, and both were afraid. They could not tell what might come of it; they had known her from her cradle, and trained her to everything she knew, and yet, in the first great emergency of her life, they neither of them knew what she would do. They looked at her taking her first step alone in the world with a troubled wonder. It was beyond them; they tried to influence the new adventuress amid all these anomalies of existence, but, having said what was in them of their own, were silent, afraid to reveal the one fact upon which all hung, the one thing that must decide all. They did not know how she would take it; they had no clue to the mysteries of that heart which had opened into womanhood before their eyes, nay, under their wings, taking warmth from them. Then Margaret spoke.

"It is right and fit," she said, "that Lilias should be the judge. I would have taken it in my own hand, and saved her the pain and the problem; but sooner or later she would have to know. Lilias, the man that is your grandfather's heir is one that we are all acquainted with. He came among us, I will not say with treachery, with what he thought a good meaning. I will allow him all that. We thought very ill of him, me in particular. I believed him a lickspittle, a creature that had fawned to the old man, and got round him. Perhaps I was altogether mistaken: I will acknowledge to you that I was mistaken in many things. And now he has at last seen what was the root of the whole matter—he has seen that from beginning to end the inheritance was clearly yours. I am not denying that it is a great thing to do. Now that he sees it, he gives it you back out of—I will allow it—a good heart. Here is the gift to you."

Lilias waved the paper away; her voice was hoarse and weak.

"You don't say who it is. Oh! what do I care for all that? Who is he, who is he, this man—"

"You must have divined it. He is just the young man you have known, both here and in London, under the name of Murray, to which I always said he had no right."

Upon this Lilias jumped up in a sudden access of excited feeling; her blue eyes flashed, her fair hair shone against the light behind her like a nimbus. She said not a word, nor left time for such in the lightning speed of her movements, but, snatching the paper suddenly out of Margaret's astonished hands, tore it across and yet across with the action of a fury. Then she flung the fragments into her sister's lap, and stamped her foot upon the ground.

"How dares he, how dares he," she cried, "send that to me! Oh! it is to you, Margaret! and you would traffic in it; but it must come to me in the end. Send him back his rags, if you please, or put them in the fire, or do what you like with them. But never, never more," cried Lilias, "let them be named to me! Me take his money from him!—I would sooner die! And if you do it, Margaret," she cried, advancing closer, shaking her little fist in her sister's face, "if you do it, I will just disown it the moment I am old enough. Oh, how dared he, how dared he send that to me!" Then the height of her excitement dropped, her tone changed, she began to cry like a child. "So that is what he has been doing, that! instead of coming—and me that wanted him so!" Lilias cried, piteously, her lips quivering. She who had been a dignified judge of the highest morals, and an impassioned actor in one of the gravest difficulties of life within the last ten minutes, sank down a little sobbing girl, struck with the keen barb of a child's disappointment, that infinite sharpness of despair which is to last for ever. To think that he should have been occupied with matters like this and not come to her! She was barely eighteen. The great and the small were still confused in her mind. "And me that wanted him so!" she repeated, with that little piteous quiver of her lips, and a sob coming at intervals.

The two ladies sat and gazed at her without a word to say. They exchanged a look. If there was a little subdued triumph in the soft eyes of Jean, they were not for that the less bewildered. Lilias had solved the whole question, not by the tearing up of the paper, which was so easily renewed again, but all unconsciously by that childlike, piteous complaint. Margaret, in the look which she cast upon her sister, acknowledged it as much as Jean did. There was nothing more to say.

CHAPTER XLIV

"MY DEAR SIR,

"Your packet and enclosure were duly received by me, and I think it right, having perhaps misjudged the young man, to begin by telling you that I am now willing to allow I may have been prejudiced, and that there was more to be said than I thought perhaps upon his side of the question. We are all very dour and set upon our own way in this family. Ladies like my sister Jean and me have many lessons to bring down our pride, besides the gift of a judgment not so swayed by personal circumstances as a man's. But Sir Patrick had ever had his own way, and it had no doubt become a law to him. And it may be as you say, that we that were his nearest kin made little effort to gain his confidence. We were led to believe it would have been of little use. In all that, it is just possible we may have been mistaken; and, though I cannot for a moment allow any justification of his unnatural act in passing over Lilias (though unacquainted with her, which is the only excuse, but that too was his own blame), yet I will avow that to make some provision for a companion that had been so attentive, as I am informed Mr. Grantley was, giving up his entire time to him, was no more than what was just. You will see that in admitting so much as this, I am going far, farther than I ever thought to do; but his action in the matter being so honourable, and you speaking so well of him, I am ready to make this concession. The deed you enclosed to me is no more than justice, according to my sentiments. I honour the young man for having strength of mind to do it, but I think it was his duty to do it, and my only surprise is that, being capable of that sacrifice now, he should not have done it sooner, and thus remedied the wrong before further harm could arise. Few persons, however, divine just the right moment for an effort of this kind, and I am very willing for my part to give the young man his due.

"There is, however, I am grieved to say, some difference of opinion in this respect among us, always so united as we have been: and it is in accordance with a desire on the part of my sisters that I have to request you will inform Mr. Grantley that his deed is inadmissible, but that we all think it might be possible to come to some better understanding by a personal interview. If, therefore, he will come here when it is convenient to him, we will receive him. He will be stopping in London, no doubt, till the end of the season; but, having so many friends, we cannot but think it more than likely that he will be coming North to the moors about the 12th or sooner. He will no doubt find his old quarters in the 'Murkley Arms' at his disposal, and a personal conference would redd up many matters that we cannot allow to remain as they are. You will therefore have the kindness to represent this to him. I retain the paper in the mean time, but a glance at it, with the commentaries that have been made upon it in this family, will let him see at once that it is a thing which we could never accept nor think of. You will perhaps say to him, in sending this message, that I Margaret Murray of Gowanbrae (not of Murkley), respect his reasoning and approve his action, which I should in all likelihood have accepted without further comment, if it had been me only that was concerned. But I will not go against the sense of the family, and I desire that he should be acquainted with our determination.

"I hope you are returned in good health, and none the worse for your London diversions. It seems to me that I have long arrears of sleeping to make up, which is hard to do, seeing no person can sleep more than the time they are used to, whatever the occasion may be. You will make our compliments to Mrs. Allenerly and the young people, who, I hope, are all in good health and giving you satisfaction.

"I remain, my dear Mr. Allenerly,

"Your faithful servant,
"MARGARET MURRAY (of Gowanbrae)."

Miss Margaret was, on the whole, pleased with the construction of this letter. She smiled somewhat grimly to herself as she re-read her sentence about the deed and the commentaries upon it. The one emphatic commentary upon it was that of Lilias, and nothing could be more conclusive. It lay torn in six pieces in Margaret's desk. It was impossible to express an opinion more decisively. There had been a pause of consternation after Lilias' self-betrayal. But the look the sisters exchanged over her was one in which volumes were expressed. Margaret's eyes were dim with trouble and astonishment. To her, as to so many parents and caretakers, the young creature who had grown up at her side was still a child. She had been vaguely alarmed about her, afraid in the abstract lest she should love unwisely, prepared in the abstract for suitors and "offers." But it had not occurred to her that it was possible for Lilias, unassisted, uncompanioned, to leap by herself into the greatest of decisions, and to entertain anything like a passion in that youthful bosom. In some mysterious way, her fears had never settled upon Lewis at all. She had seen her child surrounded by other and more brilliant competitors for her favour. He, discouraged, no doubt, by her own refusal to consider his claims, had been too generous, too magnanimous, she thought, for a lover. And they had parted with him without any harm done. Lilias had been cheerful enough on the journey, not like a girl who had left her heart behind. She had not drooped even when they reached home, though something dreamy, something languid, had appeared in her. Margaret had been entirely re-assured in this respect. But in a moment all this fabric of consolation went to the winds. She looked at Jean with wonder and dismay unspeakable, and met her eyes in which there was a subdued satisfaction mingled with surprise. But there was no time to resent that glimmer of triumph. The chief thing was that not the faintest possibility remained between them of doubt or uncertainty. Without a conflict the question was decided. Margaret might struggle as she pleased, it was a foregone conclusion. The eyes of the sisters said to each other, "This being so, then—"

There was no more to be said. Even Margaret, who would have stood to the death under any other circumstances, felt the arms drop out of her hands. What could be done against Lilias, against that sob, so ungrammatical, so piteous? "And me that wanted him so!"

Long and troubled were the conferences held between Margaret and Jean thereafter. One of the questions discussed was whether Lilias herself should be called and examined on the subject, but this both decided was a thing not to be done.

"To open her heart to you and me when they have never opened their hearts to one another," Miss Jean said. "Could we ask it, Margaret?"

"You think you are further ben in such subjects than I am," said Margaret. "But who thinks of asking it? Would I profane her thoughts, the infant that she is? No me! Deep though I regret it, and hard though I take it, she shall never think shame to look me in the face, whatever happens."

"It is not just that she would think shame," said Jean, the better informed.

But this expedient was rejected unanimously. They sat together till late in the night discussing the subject in all its branches. It is curious how easy of acceptance a decision becomes which may have been resisted and struggled against with might and main, as soon as it is seen beyond all question to be inevitable. Margaret on that morning would have declared that a marriage between Lilias Murray and her supplanter was a thing she would die to prevent. But, after her little sister's self-betrayal, the impossibility shifted and changed altogether, and Margaret found that the one thing which she would die to prevent, was not Lilias' marriage, but Lilias' unhappiness. The change was instantaneous.

"This being so, then—"

It was all over. There was no longer any ground upon which to struggle and resist.

As for Lilias, she escaped to her room as soon as she had come to herself and realized what had happened. The girl was two or three different creatures in these days. She was a child ready to cry, ready to commit herself on a sudden provocation, and a woman able to stand upon the edge of the new world which she contemplated with an astonished comprehension of its loftiness and greatness, and to meet its higher requirements with a spirit as high. She felt able to judge in her own small person, with an ideal sense of youthful detachment from all sophistications, the greater question, and at the same time unable to bear the smallest contrarieties without a burst of superficial emotion, anger, or despair. Her development was but half accomplished. Nobody understood this, neither did she herself understand it. She escaped from the observation of her sisters with a sense of impatience, which did not for some time deepen into the sense of having betrayed herself. That indeed scarcely came at all. There was so much else to think of. She went to her own room, and threw herself down upon the sofa, with her heart beating and her head throbbing, every pulse sounding, she thought, in her ears in the excitement that possessed her. So that was what he had been doing! Not lingering, as disappointment had begun to picture him, in London among his fine friends, dancing, talking, as if Lilias had never been; but employing his time, his thoughts, in transferring to her his fortune, all he had in the world. Lilias tingled with impatience, with a desire to clench her small fist in his face, as she had done to Margaret, and ask him how dared he, how dared he! While underneath, in her growing soul, there diffused itself that ennobling satisfaction in the consciousness of a nobleness in him, which enables women to bear all the strokes of fate, the loss of their heroes, of their sons, joyful that their beloved have done well. By degrees this higher sentiment swallowed up everything else in her. She sat up, and put back her ravelled hair, and held her head high. There had been an injustice, and, at the cost of everything he had, he had set it right. He had gone beyond all duty, all necessity, and despoiled himself of everything, not, the letter said, "for love, but for justice." She was a girl in love, and it may be supposed would rather have believed that her lover had done something partially wrong for love than altogether right for justice; but those who think so have no knowledge of the ideal of youth. Her heart swelled and rose with this thought. She felt that happiness, that glory of approval which is the very crown of love. The colour came to her cheeks. She jumped up with that elastic bound which was natural to her, and stood in the middle of the room with her head high, smiling at him through the distance and the unknown, approving him. At that moment she felt with pride that the tie between them was not a mere empty liking, a natural attraction towards youth and pleasant qualities, or that still less profound but more enthralling charm of beauty, which so often draws two young creatures together. Lewis had no beauty. There were hundreds of others more gifted than he; but which of them all could have done this, "not for love, but for justice!" She began to go deep into it, this great action, and to set it forth and enhance it to herself in every way. He had but to have come to her, to have spoken to her as he had meant to do (she knew) that evening, when those two nobodies, those two fools, had taken possession of the corner under the palm-trees, and she would have accepted him, and this justice would have been done in a roundabout way, not for justice, but for love. But when it came to the point (oh! yes, oh! yes, it was something more than the foolish couple under the palms) his mind had felt that this was inadequate, he had shut his mouth in spite of himself and given over his hopes, and determined that it must be justice and not love. The other would have been the happier way: all this waiting, and suspense, and the separation, and those lingering days without him would have been spared; but this was the better! Lilias felt herself grow taller, grander, in her approval of everything; he had done what was right, not what was pleasant. The growing weariness, the gathering doubt, the film which had seemed to be rising between them, were all made desirable, noble by this issue. He would not have made her suffer, oh, not a day's suspense, if he could have helped it; but it was inevitable, it was better thus—

And now—Lilias caught her breath a little, and laughed for pleasure, and blushed for shy shamefacedness. She would have liked to write herself, and send him the torn up deed, and say, "What folly! is not thine mine, and mine thine?" but she remembered with a blush that she could not, that it would be "unwomanly," that word with which Margaret had scared her all her life, that she must wait now till he came to set everything right. The waiting brought a little pang with it not altogether to be chased away. "Of course he will come at once," she said to herself. But when there is distance, and separation, and all the chances of the unknown between you and the person whom you love, the "of course" has always a quaver in it. This was all. Her happy excitement, her satisfaction, her triumph in his excellence, would have made her perhaps too confident of every blessedness, but for this one faint note of uncertainty which just trembled through it, and made it perhaps more exquisite, though Lilias did not think so. The waiting, which she thought the only pain in the matter, was the perfume, the flavour of the whole.

Next day, Margaret wrote to Mr. Allenerly the letter above recorded; by the time she did so, her mind had worked out the subject. She had grudged the great match which it had always been on the cards that Lilias might make; but, at all events, it was not a long-leggit lad who had taken her eye, to be a disappointment and vexation to all her future life.

"He is not a fool," she said, "that is a great thing, for a fool is the most unmanageable of all the creatures on this earth; and he has plenty of resources, he will not be on her hands for ever: and he must have a kind nature, or he would never have taken such care of yon old man. And he cannot be much heeding about money for its own sake; and he must have a strong sense of justice. And on the whole, though I have set my face against him, I have always liked him," Margaret said, with a sigh.

"He has just the tenderest heart and the best disposition that ever was," cried Jean.

"Oh! yes, no doubt you will speak well of him: for he is in love with you too," said Margaret.

"Oh! Margaret, that is what I like in him—he has no jealousy, as small creatures have. He is just as fond as he can be of those that like her best. He is in love with us all three."

Upon this Margaret shook her head.

"Not with me—that would be beyond nature—for I have scorned him and denied him."

"Nevertheless," said Miss Jean, with the firmness that necessity had developed in her, "he is in love with us all three."

The next morning there was a very different kind of scene in Mr. Allenerly's office, where the excellent writer read Miss Margaret's letter with a grin that was somewhat cynical.

"They may try as they like," he said to himself, "they will not get him now. I said he was hasty, I said he was premature, but he would not be guided by me." He stretched out his hand for the newspaper which lay on one side of his table with his morning letters, and ran his finger down a line of small paragraphs: then shook his head when he had found the one he wanted, and, drawing his paper towards him, replied at once as follows:—

"MY DEAR MADAM,

"Your communication I would have had much pleasure in forwarding to my client, Mr. Lewis Grantley, sometimes calling himself Murray, but I regret that that is not now in my power. You will easily understand that, after despoiling himself of everything he had, it was no longer possible for him to live like a gentleman, doing nothing, in an expensive place like London. His friends were all very kind, but he has a great deal of sense for so young a man, and saw that in that there was nothing to trust to. So he took advantage of his opportunities, and struck when the iron was hot. He had little difficulty in getting an appointment as secretary to Sir Andrew Morton, the new Governor of the Pharaway Islands. He was in good spirits, comparatively speaking, and said the Governor was an old friend, and that he had every hope of getting on well and enjoying the post—which I make no doubt he will, being one of the people that always fall on their feet: which no doubt is greatly due to his being of a very friendly kind of nature himself.

"It is a long voyage, and he did not expect to arrive till September; but, any way, I will forward to him your letter, and he will no doubt reply in good time. The appointment was either for two or three years. It was strongly on his mind to go to Murkley before he left, but there were delays about preparing the deed, for which I, I am afraid, am partly responsible, and I discouraged him, remembering that you would not hear of it. I imagine, by the tone of your letter, that you may have more or less changed your mind; but, unfortunately, it is too late.

"If I hear anything of Mr. Murray during his voyage, I will let you know. I am none the worse, I thank you kindly, for my London diversions. I avoided late hours and hot rooms, which play the mischief with the constitution. My wife warmly reciprocates your kind messages, and I remain, my dear Miss Murray,

"Your obedient servant to command,

"A. ALLENERLY."

This letter fell like a thunderbolt on Murkley. They had anticipated not only no such obstacle, but no obstacle at all. They had thought that Lewis would arrive by the next train, throwing aside all his engagements, too happy to be called upon to appear before them and explain all that he intended and wished. Margaret for a time was absolutely silenced by the news; it fell upon her like a stone. Fortunately she was alone when it came, and was not besieged by the anxious looks of the others, which would have been more than she could bear. After she had fully realized it, she sent for Jean and communicated the news to her.

"It will kill Lilias," Jean said.

"Lilias is not such a poor creature," cried Margaret, though her very soul was quaking. "My poor Jean, I do not want to put you in mind of your trouble—but you did not die."

"Ah! but it was different, very different," said Jean. "You cannot put me in mind, Margaret, of what I never forget. It was settled between us, and we understood each other; that takes the bitterness out of it."

"Some people would say that put the bitterness into it," said Margaret.

"Ah! but they would be ignorant folk; we were belonging the one to the other; now Lilias, poor thing! has nothing to lean upon. She is just nothing to him. If he were to die—"

"God forgive you for such thoughts! He is a young lad, and healthy, and well-conditioned. Why should he die?"

"Others have done it before him," Miss Jean said; "but, living or dying, she will feel that there is nothing in it. She has no right to him nor he to her. It will just kill her."

"Hold your tongue, Jean, hold your tongue," Margaret cried in dismay.

In the mean time there was no appearance of anything killing Lilias. She had come out of the dreamy state of expectation that had been growing upon her into a cheerful energy. On this particular morning she was as sunny as the day. She had been seen to look at the list of trains, but it was too soon as yet to expect that he could come from London. She did not speak of him or make any reference to what she looked for; but when their daily walk led through the village, Lilias lingered opposite the 'Murkley Arms' with an intuition which unhappily brought its own fulfilment. Adam, with his creel over his shoulder, came up as usual with his slow, lumbering tread, and Margaret was too much interested in the trout not to cross the road to look at them. He was turning them over for her inspection when Janet appeared at the door as usual. Lilias thought that she had always been fond of Janet; she said to herself that it was for that reason she had been anxious to assure her that all the fable about Philip Stormont was untrue. She was glad now to see her honest face, and it made her heart beat to think that perhaps Janet might have some news. She responded to her "Good day, Miss Lilias," by holding out her hand, an honour which the good woman received as if this little country girl had been a princess, curtseying as she touched it and making her little compliment.

"I am aye blithe to see ye passing; and ye are no looking white and shilpit, as I feared, but just in grand health, and like a rose after your season in London. Miss Margaret has always taken such good care of you. Lady Eeda she is just like a ghost. They've come hame, maybe you'll have heard."

"Lady Ida stays longer and goes out more than we did," said Lilias; "but everybody," she added, with a little natural wile, "is leaving London now."

"Oh ay, we'll soon be in August, and you'll no keep the gentlemen after that," said Janet, with true appreciation. "It makes more stir in the countryside, but it's little it does for us, and I'm wae, wae for my gentleman that was here in the last year; ye may mind upon him, Miss Lilias. I never could tell what brought him here. It wasna for the fishing, for he was no hand at that, but as pleasant-spoken and as good-hearted a lad as ever stepped. There was one of his portmanteaus aye left here, and I hoped to have him back; but we had word to send it to him a week since."

"And is that why you are wae? But perhaps there may be no occasion for it, Janet," said Lilias, with a smile. "We saw him in London, and I think he meant to come back."

"Eh, Miss Lilias, that would have been a good hearing; but maybe you do not hear that he has lost his siller, poor lad—some o' thae banks, I suppose," said Janet. "It's a braw thing to have nae siller and nae trouble with the losing o't."

"I think that is a mistake too," said Lilias, her fair face glowing with pleasure. "He has not lost so much as he thought."

"Well, Miss Lilias, no doubt you'll have ways of kennin'. I only judge by his letter, and that was very doun. My heart was wae for him when I read it, and they sailed yesterday. I hope he got his things in time."

"Sailed!—yesterday!" Lilias echoed, with a wondering face.

"And, losh me!" cried Janet, "they say it's away among the cannibals. If they sent the sodgers to shoot them down, I would think nothing o't—for them that feed upon their neighbours' flesh, Lord bless us!

they're fit for nothing better—but a fine, peaceable young gentleman, with none of those warlike ways, what would they pit the like of him forrit for, just to fa' a victim—"

"Lilias, it is time we were going home," said Margaret, turning round quickly and surveying the blanched countenance and wondering eyes aghast of her companion.

"Ye are just frichtening the ladies," said Adam; "there's nae mair danger among the cannibals than at hame. They're no cannibal now; do you think that could last, in the face of steam-engines and a' that, and advancin' civileezation and British rule? But the ladies they have mair sense. There's no such things now-a-days. We a' eat ane anither, but it's in a mair modest way."

"I have no more time to speak to you, Adam; but ye'll just take that trout up to the cook; and come away, Lilias—you have walked too far, your face is just the colour of wax," said Margaret, anxiously drawing her sister's arm within her own.

"It is not the walk—did you hear that, Margaret?"

"Did I hear what? I just heard that woman Janet havering, as she always does."

"She said he sailed yesterday." Lilias made a pause and looked into her sister's face. "Is it true?"

"Where would he sail to, I would like to know?" Margaret said; then, with a sudden pressure of the girl's arm, "And supposing it were true? It was what I would have done in his place, if it had been me."

Lilias' young figure swayed upon her arm, the light went out of her eyes. She walked on mechanically for a few minutes, sustained by Margaret, not seeing where she went. In those minutes everything was dark to her, the out-door world, the inner horizon. Blackness came up without and within, and covered earth and heaven. First disappointment, and that terrible prolongation of suspense, the hope deferred that maketh the heart sick; then an overwhelming sense of uncertainty, of insecurity, of the earth failing beneath her feet. All had seemed so easy before. To tear a piece of paper, to write a letter, what more simple? But perhaps now what had seemed so easy might be impossible—impossible! He might never have loved her, he might never come back at all; it might be all a delusion. Lilias did not swoon or lose consciousness; on the contrary, she remembered everything, saw everything in the darkness like a horrid dream; her heart throbbed, her blood all rushed to the brain to reinforce it, to give strength for the emergency; all round her there was nothing but blackness. The sun was shining full upon her, but where she was it was night.

All that Margaret saw outside was that Lilias said nothing, that she clung to her arm, that she stumbled a little in walking, as if she did not see any little obstacles in the way, and hurried on as if she were pursued, bending her head, her feet twisting with a sort of headlong impulse. She did not know what to think; she said, with a quaver of profound anxiety in her voice,

"My darling, where are you going so fast, Lilias, my bonnie dear?"

These words penetrated the gloom, and brought Lilias in some degree to herself. The darkness quivered and opened up. She slackened her steps, leaning still more closely on her sister's arm, and gradually the common day came back in widening circles, and she began to see the light and the trees. The crisis had been terrible, but her heart already rallied.

"What do you say—about going fast? Do you mean the ship?" she said.

"My bonnie dear!" was all Margaret's reply. And she held the girl up with her strong arm, half carrying her, and hurrying her on the road towards home. Margaret thought she was going to faint and fall, not seeing that she was in fact recovering from the blow.

"Do not hold me so tight, Margaret; you are hurting me. Yes, I was walking fast—I forgot: for I want to be home, home. Oh! never mind me, Margaret; I am just a little giddy, but I am better." Lilias freed her arm almost with impatience. "Why should you support me? Has anything happened to me?" she said.

Then Margaret, who was always mistress, sank into humility.

"My darling, I don't know that anything has just—happened; but you are not strong, and you are worried. I would like to get you home."

"I am going home," said Lilias, with dignity.

There was so much noise in her head still, as if all the wheels of her being were working and turning, that she had not much power of speech. But she walked with a certain stateliness, rejecting all aid. And Margaret, who had been sovereign all her life and directed everybody, accompanied little Lilias in the height and greatness of her passion, without saying a word, with a pathetic humility, wondering at her as the people of Camelot wondered at Elaine.

CHAPTER XLV

The following winter was very dreary and long. It began early; the 12th itself, the beginning of the season, the day of days in the North, rained from morning to night. It never ceased raining through all the shooting season. The rain ran into every crevice, into the holes in the rocks, which were usually as dry as the sun could make them, and the heather grew out of a bog, and the foot sank in the treacherous greenness all over the moors. There was little encouragement to tourists, and not much to sportsmen, and women were kept indoors and exhausted all their resources, and quarrelled, and were miserable. If there had been perpetual bickering in the old Castle of Murkley, there would have been nothing surprising in it. The ladies were not happy; they were in a state of painful suspense and uncertainty. They neither knew what the future was, nor when it should cease to be the future, and become an astonishing present, changing all their life. In the strange and dreary days which had succeeded their discovery of Lewis' departure, there had been a kind of pause in existence altogether. The unaccustomed contrariety of events, the impossibility of doing anything but waiting, the inclination to upbraid each other, the uneasy desire at heart to blame somebody, was like a stimulating poison in all their veins. They stood, as it were, at bay against fate, and in the silence, and with the keen perception they had that nothing could be done, were tempted to turn their arms against each other, and make themselves thoroughly miserable. There was a moment indeed when this seemed inevitable. Margaret had only the impatience of unhappiness to warrant her in assailing Jean, but there was a certain reason in the instinctive impulse with which the others turned upon Margaret, murmuring in their hearts that it was she who was in fault. She it was (though neither of them knew how entirely it was she) who had sent the hero of their thoughts away. But for her, the dilemma might have been met with natural ease, and the problem solved. It was she who had stood in every one's way. Her pride, her hard-heartedness, her ambition for Lilias, even the temporary obtuseness and self-conceit (that such epithets should ever have been applied to Margaret!) which prevented her from seeing as the others did what Lewis had done for them, had brought matters to this crisis. It was her doing from first to last. She was herself fully aware of this, and the consciousness was as irritating as it was terrible. She alone had ordained her child's unhappiness, had taken the responsibility upon herself. When Lilias was seen wandering about her old haunts, trying to accomplish her old duties with a pale and abstracted countenance, retiring within herself, she who had been so simple and child-like, and crushed under the weight of an uncertainty which made her heart sick, Margaret was nearly beside herself. She irritated the suffering girl by her anxious solicitude. She would scarcely allow her the solace of quiet, the last right which a spirit in trouble has, of at least reconciling itself to its trouble unobserved, and without interruption. Margaret pursued Lilias with anxious questions what ailed her? though she knew so well, to the bottom of her heart, what the ailment was. Had she a headache? What was the matter that she could not eat her dinner? Why did it weary her to walk?

"I must get the doctor to you," Margaret said, devoured by alarm lest the delicate spirit should affect her slight body, and harm come of it before their eyes.

"Oh, if you would but let her alone! Can you not see that it's the heart that ails her, and nothing else?" Miss Jean would say.

"Hold your peace about hearts. Do you think I am not as unhappy about what has happened as any person; but I am not going to stand by and see her digestion a wreck as well as—" And Margaret would almost weep in misery, in impatience, in impotence, till poor Jean's heart was almost broken with the impossibility of binding up her sister's, and making her believe that all would be well. For to this, after a while, her desire to upbraid Margaret turned—a desire to console and soothe her. It was her fault, poor Margaret! that was the issue at last to which Jean's sympathetic passion came.

Lilias, who was the most deeply involved, went through an alarming crisis; for some days she said nothing, averted her looks, shut herself up as much as possible, would accept no comfort, nor open her heart to any one. And in this moment, when the girl suddenly found herself before the impossible and understood that nothing—nothing which any one could do could change the fact, could break the silence, could make it possible for her to have any communication with him to whom she had so much to say—that even a hundred chances might arise to keep her from any communication with him for ever, a cloud of utter darkness, and of that sickness of the heart which accompanies the blank of disappointment, took possession of her being. It was against all the habits of her life. Hitherto she had but appealed to Margaret, and all had gone right. Even in the present case there had been an end of all opposition, as soon as it had been made apparent to Margaret what was in her heart: and for a moment it had appeared as if everything was to be well. But not Margaret nor any one could pierce the silence of the seas, and bring back a reply. No one could stop the ship swiftly speeding to the other side of the world. No one could shorten the inevitable time, blank and dark and eventless, which must pass before any word could be heard across those silent seas. And who was to speak the word? And how could any one answer for it, that Lewis, repulsed and sent away, would listen, or that he would undo all his plans, and come? or that he had not changed his mind? He had never said those final words which cast down all walls between two hearts. Lilias had been sure he meant to say them; but he had not done so. And who could tell now if they ever would be said? and who could invite him to say them? To write to him would be to do so. In the retirement of her own room she had written to him again and again to tell him how she had treated his paper, and what she thought of it, her admiration, her pain, and her impatience of his "justice." But not one of those letters ever found its way to the post. What were they, when she looked at them again, but invitations, every one? She tore them to pieces, as she had torn the deed, and at last recognized with such a schooling of her heart as is inconceivable at first to the young disciple of life, the unaccustomed sufferer and unwilling learner, that she could do nothing, that there was nothing to be done but to wait, the hardest expedient of all.

Thus it was Lilias, the youngest, the softest, the one whom the others would have died to save, who had to bear the worst, and to bear it in most loneliness of spirit. After a while the others consulted over it, and in their anxious watch over her, and mutual discussion of every aspect of her face and mind, found a sort of occupation in their distress. And both of them secretly sent out a messenger, a letter—an effort to confront the impossible, and overcome it, which brought them immediate consolation. Lilias could neither write, nor could she, in her shy and delicate youth, unveil her heart to her sisters, or communicate the absorbed and endless preoccupation with which her thoughts were centered on this one subject. She "thought shame,"—which is different from being ashamed—which is the reverence, the respect which a pure nature has for the new and wonderful passion that is in her veins, as well as her shrinking from a subject which she had never learned to discuss, and which, till it had been made into reality by communication with the person beloved, is beyond disclosure. They talked to each other about her, but Lilias could not talk to them or to any one, any more than she could write to him. She was dumb. She could do nothing, say nothing. Sooner or later, in one way or another, almost every woman has to go through this ordeal. Poor little Lilias met it unprepared.

It is wrong to say, however, that the letters which were sent were sent secretly. Margaret, when she recovered from her abasement as the cause of all this trouble, and began to recollect again that she was the head of the family, made no mystery of her proceedings. It is possible that even Lilias knew, though she had no positive information. Margaret wrote, inclosing to Lewis his torn deed, and commentary on the facts of the case.

"You would have done well to see us before you put the ocean between us, with such a grand question as this to settle," she wrote. "I know not for how long you are to be absent, or what may be your mind as to other matters, but I would press, as far as it may be allowable, the necessity of personal explanations before any other steps are taken."

It was thought by Margaret's audience, now consisting of Jean alone, that this letter was very dignified, very moving, and certain to effect its purpose.

"He will be back by the next ship after he gets that," she said.

"How can we tell," said Margaret, "what his engagements may be? He may not be able to leave his post. He has now gotten himself a master; and who can tell if he will be able at any inducement, to set himself free?"

"There is nobody that could resist that," Miss Jean said; but, notwithstanding her confidence in Margaret's letter, she herself, all secretly and trembling at her own boldness, trembling too with a sense of guilt at the falsity of it, the treachery to her sister, the idea of taking any step which she could not disclose, "took up her pen," as she described it, and wrote a long letter too, a letter which was full of details, and far more touching than Margaret's. But it was not so dignified, perhaps, nor was it at all ambiguous in its phrases, but said, "come home" in so many words, and promised all that heart of lover could desire.

And then a great pause fell upon the agitated household. It was to a distant, newly-established colony that Lewis had gone, and in those days there were not steamboat services to all the world, to shorten time and distance; nothing but a sailing ship was likely to carry his letter all the way, and not for a long time could any answer be expected. It has almost gone out of our habitudes now to wait weeks or months for an answer, and even then this old penalty of separation had been much modified; but still there was a long time to wait before they could hope for any response, and the autumn days closed down darkly over the house which had been interrupted in all its innocent habits by the invasion of this new life. Margaret made a speech to her little sister upon the expediency of resuming all the occupations of old.

"You are but a young thing yet," she said, "and history is just an endless subject. How are you to get through life, when you come to be our age, if you know nothing about the thirty years' war, or the French Revolution? You will just look out all your books, Lilias, and we will begin on Monday. There is little use in starting anything at the end of the week."

To this Lilias assented without objection; but that Monday was very slow in coming. Who could settle down to read history with a girl to whom a message would come in the middle of a lesson that Lord Bellendean in the library was "Fain, fain to see her, and would not take an answer from me," a commission which Miss Jean brought upstairs, breathless, one of the first mornings on which this duty was attempted.

"What is Lord Bellendean wanting?—it will be me he is wishful to see," Margaret said, rising up at once.

"Oh, Margaret, you know very well what the lad is wanting; but he will not take his answer from us. I was just greatly flustered, and I said I would let you know, but nothing will serve him but to see Lilias," Miss Jean said.

And, after the interview was over, is it to be supposed that a young creature who had just refused a prospective coronet could settle down again to the thirty years' war? Lilias took Lord Bellendean with great composure, but it was not to be expected that she could go so far as that. This was a very great event, as may be supposed. It crept out somehow, as such events do, all the village being aware that the young lord had driven to Murkley all alone that August morning, abandoning even the grouse, and that he had not even stayed to luncheon, but drove back again in an hour, looking very woebegone.

"She will have refused him, the wilful monkey; that is what comes of training up a girl to think so much of herself," Mrs. Seton said, with a countenance of awe. It took away her breath to think of such a wilful waste of the gifts of Providence. "If I thought any child of mine would show such conceit, it would break my heart—yes, yes, I am sure it would just break my heart. Conceit!—what could it be but conceit, and thinking far more of herself than she has any right to think? Would she like the Prince of Wales, I wonder?" cried the minister's wife.

"Let us hope she'll not be one of those that go through the wood and through the wood and take up with a crooked stick at the end," said Mrs. Stormont, grimly.

It was somewhat comforting to the latter lady to know of Lord Bellendean's discomfiture, too. But she, like Mrs. Seton, felt that the self-importance of the Murrays was almost beyond bearing. Who did they want for Lilias?—the Prince of Wales, as Mrs. Seton said; but he was a married man.

Thus Lilias lost the sympathy of her neighbour. Philip Stormont had shown symptoms of a desire to return to the position of hanger-on which he had occupied in town, but his mother, once so eager, no longer encouraged this wish.

"You will get nothing but slights and scorns from these Murrays," she said to her son. "Let them be; they are too grand for the like of us."

"It was all your doing, mother," said Philip, "that I ever went near them at all."

"It might be all my doing," said Mrs. Stormont, "but it was not my doing that you let yourself be left in the lurch and made a fool of by a parcel of women. If you have no proper pride, I have some for you. There's Lady Ida, that is a far finer girl than Lilias Murray, there's no comparison between them; the one is but a country girl, and the other is a titled lady: and young Bellendean has not behaved as he ought. If I were you, Philip, a strapping, personable young man—"

Philip did not stop to ask what his mother's inference meant. He went down in the rain to the river, and pondered the whole business among the boulders in the bed of Tay, up to his knees in the brown rushing water. Here Philip reflected that women were no judges, that he would have none of Lady Ida, who would expect a man to be always on his knees to her, and that, though Lilias was a pretty creature, there was still as good fish in the sea as ever came to the net. He reflected, too, with some warmth of satisfaction, that he was a personable man, as his mother had said, and need not be afraid of showing himself anywhere, and that there was no hurry; for though girls must make their hay while the sun shines, poor things, as for a man, he could wait. This course of reflection made him respond with careless good-humour to the greeting of the minister, who called to him from the river-side to ask what sport he was having.

"Not bad," Philip replied. "I thought I had lost the knack of it, but it's coming back."

"Little doubt but it would come back," Mr. Seton said, and they had a talk about the habits of the fish, and the bait they preferred, and all their wily ways, which was refreshing to Philip, and in which Adam Bennet, who was in his usual place, took part.

"They're just as cunning as the auld gentleman himsel'," Adam said. "They would make grand lawyers, they're that full of tricks and devices; but tak' them when they're no thinking, and they'll just bite at onything."

"My wife would like some of your trout, Adam, for to-morrow," the minister said; "and talking of that, Stormont, there's some nonsense going on in the evening among the young folk; no doubt they will be glad to see you."

"I'm afraid," cried Philip across the rush of the river and amid the patter of the rain, "that I have an engagement."

"Well, well," said the minister, good-humouredly nodding at him from under his umbrella as he went on, "just as you please—just as you please."

This was all that passed; and it was not a thing that could be called an invitation, as Mrs. Seton said afterwards. "No, no; not an invitation: just one gentleman to another, which is as different as possible. We'll be glad to see you, or my wife will be glad to see you; just the kind of thing that Robert says to everybody, for he's far too free."

But it disturbed Philip in his fishing more than he could have imagined possible. It came into his mind in the morning as soon as he woke, it accompanied him in his thoughts all day.

"There is some dancing or nonsense going on at the manse, I hear—or was it last night?" said Mrs. Stormont at dinner, secure in the confidence that no invitation had come for her son. "I am very thankful that they have seen the uselessness of it, and given up asking you, Philip."

"Oh! I can go if I like," Philip said.

"But you have too much sense to mix yourself up with their village parties," said his mother.

To this Philip made no reply. His pride was touched at once by the suggestion that he was not asked, and by the idea that his good sense had to be appealed to. This is always an offensive idea. He did not go up to the drawing-room after dinner. In spite of himself, the contrast between the dull warmth of the fireside, where his mother sat with her book and her knitting, and the lively scene on the other side of the water, struck him more and more forcibly. Mothers are all very well in their way, but they pall upon the sense of young men. He went out to the door, and the fresh, damp night air, as it flew in his face, seemed to carry upon it a far-off sound of the music. To be sure, this was impossible, but it mattered little to Philip; he heard it all the same, he knew the very waltz which at that moment Mrs. Seton would be playing. What need to follow all the steps of the short and half-hearted straggle? They were in full career of gaiety in the manse drawing-room, when Philip strayed in, half-afraid of the reception he might receive.

"Oh! Mr. Philip, is this you? You are just a great stranger," cried Mrs. Seton. "But there is Alice Bairnsfaither not dancing; you are just come in time."

CHAPTER XLVI

The days were very long in Murkley that winter. It was not a brisk, frosty winter, with ice and skating and curling, and all the cheerful activities with which the strong and young set winter at defiance. Everything of the kind, every attempt at pleasure out of doors, melted away in the rain. The roads were deep in mud, the fields were sodden, the river almost in flood, the skies so laden and so low that you could almost have touched them, with your hand—so, at least, the country folk in their bold phraseology, described them. Jean's table-cover was almost done. She was able to sit at it, she said, as she never had been before. There was little variety in the life of the ladies at Murkley. There had never been much variety in their life; though, now that Lilias was acknowledged to be "out," it might have been supposed that their engagements would have increased. But this was not the case. Lilias had signalized herself by closing two houses in the country upon them at once. Murray was a name which was not now pronounced before the Countess, who was gayer than usual, and gave several parties, as Margaret firmly believed, for the sole purpose of making it appear that the sisters were shut out.

"But I never blame her, poor woman; for no doubt it was a great mortification," Margaret said, with proud triumph.

And the break with Mrs. Stormont had never been healed. Philip indeed had returned to his old friendliness, as he had returned to other bonds, but his mother stood out. Thus they were shut up a little more than usual to their own resources, and Lilias, if she had taken advantage of her opportunities, ought to have known all about the thirty years' war. It was a long, long time before any reply came to their letters, and, when it arrived, it was not satisfactory. Lewis had been travelling with his chief. He was so engaged to his chief that he could not get free to answer in person, as he would have wished. He answered Margaret by the intimation that, in case he should die in the mean time, he had left everything by will to Lilias, which was an arrangement which could not be found fault with, though he hoped to find some other immediate solution when he came home. Even his letter to Jean was subdued and sad in tone. He seemed unable to believe that she was right in the confidence of her hopes; he thought his good-fortune had forsaken him, and that it was contempt, not tenderness, which had made Lilias tear up his offering. "She would not take even her right from my hands." Miss Jean wept much over this epistle. She avowed that she ought to have understood the perversity of man.

"When you think it is all just plain and easy, and nothing to do but to enter upon your happiness, it is just then that they will turn the wrong way," she said. They were all somewhat humiliated by the non-success of the overtures, which they had expected to be received with enthusiasm. Lilias, who did not know all, felt the discouragement fall back upon her with a sudden sense of failure and shame, which gave an altogether new aspect to life. It seemed to her that she had been offered and rejected; her pride sprang to arms, and all the force of her nature rallied in self-defence. When Margaret addressed her little conclave on the subject, Lilias, with fire in her eyes, would scarcely hear her speak.

"It is possible," Margaret said, "that there is some mistake in the whole matter. We, perhaps, did not understand him at the first, and perhaps we may not understand him now."

"What does it matter?" cried Lilias, with passion. "Who is it you are wanting to understand? Oh! will you just forget about it, and never let us say a word on the subject any more!"

"This was what I was going to say," said Margaret, firmly. "It may very well be that a mistake has been made; but it's not for our dignity or for our peace of mind to dwell upon that. We will just consider this a closed chapter, Lilias. There has no harm been done. The young man meant well, it was in his mind to do justice. He had my approval, as ye all know. And no doubt but it was a great effort. For a man to give up all his living and everything he has, is never a small matter. You will mind that even the young man that our Lord loved had not the strength of mind to do that. It is just an extraordinary thing to the credit of the lad that he did find it in his heart to do it. But when his sacrifice was thrown back upon him, which was what Lilias in a manner forced upon me to do—"

"I am glad I did that! I am glad—glad I did it," Lilias cried.

"Well—I am saying nothing against that. When he has got it thrown back into his bosom, he very likely thinks he has done all, and more than ought to be required, and there's just an end of it. I have not a word to say concerning Mr. Grantley. He has done all—and more—that honour could require. But now we're done with him, and that chapter closed."

"Oh! Margaret, bide a little," cried Jean. "Oh! Lilias, listen to your own heart; is there nothing there that speaks for him? He is under engagements: he cannot just hurry away, and leave his duty. Give him a little time, and let him speak for himself."

"I agree with Margaret," said Lilias, hotly. "It is Margaret that is right. There has been too much about it—too much! and now that chapter is closed."

"It is for the best that it should be so," Margaret said.

"Oh! Margaret, you were always hard upon him! What have you ever done but discourage him and put him away? And now will this be for ever—will you just reject him without a hearing?" Jean cried. Margaret gave her a look in which there was at once judgment and warning.

"There is no hearing," said Margaret, "there is nothing but just to put him out of our lives and all the thoughts he has raised. That chapter is closed," she said, with great dignity and gravity. It was a decision against which no further protest could be made.

And indeed there was a long time in which this seemed a final decision. The chapter was to all appearance closed. Even Jean, hard though she found it, was obliged to hold-in all demonstrations of sympathy, to leave Lilias to herself. And Margaret, putting real force upon her inclinations, such as no one appreciated, left her to herself. Jean was coerced by her elder sister, and obeyed with a mute protest, with tearful, appealing looks, with a continual lifting up of her testimony to earth and heaven, against the fate which she could not resist. But Margaret had no one to coerce her, no one to protest against. She was her own tyrant, more hard to herself than to Jean. She resisted the impulse to take her little sister into her bosom, to soothe and caress her, to weep over her, to open up to her all the secret hoards of her own love and tenderness. Margaret, whom they all thought so severe, so contemptuous of sentimentality, had too much reverence for the child of her adoration to intrude into her little sanctuary of pain, and innocent shame, and wounded affection. It was better for Lilias that no eye should penetrate into that refuge—her mother-sister heroically shut the door, and stood longing, wistful, without. In the mean while the household, for no one out of the household knew anything of the matter, was very hard upon Margaret. Old Simon declared to the cook that the pride of her was just more than any person could put up with.

"She'll see that bairn buried afore her een, or she let her wed the lad she likes," Simon said.

"And wha is the lad she likes?" the maids asked in chorus, all but Susan, who held her tongue, and looked all the knowledge she possessed. Upon which old Simon bid them go all to their work for a set of idle taupies that had no eyes in their heads.

"But I'll never forgive Miss Margaret, if harm comes of it; and what but harm can come of it?" the oracle of the kitchen said.

The wet winter was succeeded by a wistful and doubtful spring, and then by summer gay as northern summers sometimes are, with long days, all monotonous and feelingless, such as oppress the heart. If the year had been specially arranged to look longer than ever year looked before, it could not have been more successfully done. It lingered and dragged along, never gracious nor genial, a tedious, unfruitful year. And the same change which had come over the seasons, seemed to have come over the life of Murkley. There were no longer the little varieties of old; just as the winter's frost, and brisk March winds, and the caprices of April, and the disappointments of May were all lost in one fretful dulness, so the little impatiences and mock quarrels, the little routine of work and play, the little entertainments and hopes of the past, all seemed to have dropped into one settled rule, rigid and immovable, in which no relaxation or variety was. What she did one day, Lilias did the next, unwavering, shutting herself up within herself. She could not have borne it, had she said a word. The sense of having come to nothing, the defeat and failure of her whole independent existence, cut short and ended off, overwhelmed her both with trouble and shame. That any man could have it in his power to turn all her brightness and hopes, all her youthful gaiety and adventure, her delightful beginning, her innocent triumph, into a mere episode suddenly broken off, having no connection with the rest of her life, was a thing intolerable to her; nor could she endure to think that whatever happened to her in the future must be like a second life, another beginning; rather, much rather, she would have had nothing happen to her at all, but relapse into the dimness for ever. This indeed was what Lilias thought she had done. But yet now and then a sudden gale of expectation, a stirring of life, would breathe over her—as if all were not ended, as if something must still be coming. There were days in which she felt sure that something would certainly come: after which she would rise up and slay herself in shame and indignation, asking herself if she could be so poor a creature as still to wish him to return. But all this passed in silence; and the shame of those relentings, of those renewed disappointments, of those involuntary hopes and awakenings, were to herself alone. Thus the year went on. It had passed the meridian, and the long evenings were beginning to "creep in" a little, soothing somewhat the spirits wearied with this greyness of living. It was a good thing, whatever happened, to be rid of those endless days. Nothing so beautiful when the heart is light, or even moderately tranquil and at ease, but, in suspense or waiting, they were intolerable. Lilias told herself that she was not in suspense any longer, that there was nothing to wait for; but still she was glad when the long days were over, when autumn began to whiten the fields, and a little fire to glimmer in the dark wainscoted rooms. By the end of August that was natural in Murkley. The house in the evening looked more cheerful with the glow of the ruddy fire, and when sometimes, with a sudden perverse fit, she would steal out in the twilight after dinner, the lights gleaming in all the windows gave her a certain pleasure to see. They looked warm, and the world so cold; they were bright, and it was so dim. What did she know about the world, this nursling of love and tenderness? Nothing at all: only that her first venture in it had turned, as it seemed, into bitterness, and it was the privilege of her youth to generalize, and to adopt as her own experience the conclusions of world-worn men.

She had done this one evening early in September; the year had run round, and all her anniversaries were over: the time of his sacrifice, the time when she had given it back to him, the woeful day of his departure, all were past. It ought to be all over, she said to herself bitterly; what a servile thing it was to dwell upon every incident in this way, to keep thinking of them when it was clear he thought of them no more. Lilias began to take herself to task. She had taken a plaid from the hall and flung it round her; the evening was closing, the road through the park towards New Murkley was entirely deserted, no step but her own upon it, no fear of interruption. She began to say to herself as she went along that all this was unworthy; that, since the first chapter of her life had been broken off, she must let it break, and begin again; that it was like a slave to cling to the past, to bind herself to a recollection, to let all her life fade into a shadow. As she came in sight of the old visionary palace, with its vacant windows staring into the twilight, there came into her head the bitter fancy of associating herself with it. It was an emblem of her existence, she said to herself—unfinished: all ambitiously framed for life, life on a grand and beautiful scale; but never to be lived in, an empty memorial of what might have been, a house for dreams and nothing else, a place where never fire would be lighted, nor any sweet tumult of living arise. Oh! it was like her, her great deserted palace, her strong-built emptiness. Lilias stood and gazed at it, rising majestic against the greyness of the sky, her eyes flooding with tears, a poignant and sudden pang in her heart. Could any resemblance be more close? This old house was her fortune, all she had in the world;

and she was like it. There was a mockery in it, yet sympathy; a vacant place, where no shelter was, a vacant life, in which there never would be any warmth of human interest. The greyness of everything about, the shadow-trees softly waving in the night wind, the faint clouds scarcely rounding against the cloudless sky, the mass of building all still and vacant, everything combined to enhance the effect. The two lakes of silent passion in her eyes blurred everything, and made that effect still greater. The old house in the distance, with its glimmers of ruddy light in all the window, had nothing in it so congenial with her mood. Her castle was like herself, empty and cold, an abode of dreams and nothing more.

Nevertheless, it gave Lilias a little thrill of alarm to see something more upon the broad steps, all overgrown with weeds and grass, that led to the never-opened door. Though she had been in her own consciousness but now so tragic a figure surveying the tragic desolation of her great house, yet she was in reality only a girl under twenty, in the grey evening, almost dark, out of hearing of any protector, and out of sight of her home. Some one moved upon the steps, and came slowly down and towards her. She was too proud to turn round and fly, but this had been her first thought. If it should turn out a neighbour, all was well; but if it should be a stranger, a vagrant, a wandering tramp, perhaps! Half for pride and half for fright, Lilias could not turn her back upon this unknown; but she stood and waited to see who it was, holding up her dress with her hands, ready for instant flight.

He came slowly forward through the dusk; her heart beat with alarm, with wonder, with displeasure, for no stranger had any right to be here so late. But no suspicion of the reality touched her mind. Many times she had expected vainly, and often, often felt that round the next corner, at the next turning, he might come. But this expectation was far from her mind to-night, nor was there light enough to see him as he came nearer and nearer. He stopped when they were within a few paces of each other.

"You are afraid of me, but I am no stranger. Ah! you do not know me?" he said.

Then there rang through the silent woods and the grey night a wonderful cry. Lilias was not mistress of herself; the whole world went round and round with her, the great house behind him seemed to move, to break into unequal outlines, to crash together and fall. Her voice sounded like something independent of her, a wild creature crying out in the night. She threw out her hands wildly to grasp at something, she did not know what, to hold by and sustain herself. There was nothing near her except him. He was trembling too. He took her hands into his without any presumption or mistake of her meaning.

"I have frightened you," he said. "It is to do more harm, always more harm, that I come. But lean upon me, you know that I mean no evil—it is not to take any advantage."

Lilias did not hear what Lewis said. She heard his voice, that was enough. She discovered that it was he with a revulsion of feeling which there was nothing in her to withstand.

"Oh! where have you been so long—so long? and me that wanted you so!" she cried.

POSTSCRIPT

(Which is scarcely necessary.)

Inside the lighted windows which threw so cheerful a gleam upon the soft darkness of the night outside, Margaret and Jean were seated, with their heads very close together, bending over a letter. They were reading it both together, with great agitation and excitement. The faces of both were flushed and eager; there was a controversy going on between them. Nothing more peaceful than this interior, the little fire burning brightly, the lamp on the table, the wainscot reflecting the leap and sparkle of the burning wood, but nothing more agitated than the little group, the faces so like each other, so close together, lighted up with all the fire and passion of civil war.

"She is beginning to forget him," Margaret said. "I will send him his answer to-night, and she need never know. Why should the little thing be disturbed again? She has had a terrible year, but it is all over, all over now."

"All over now he has come. In no other way will it ever be over."

"Oh! hold your peace with your romance, Jean. It was always sore, sore against my will to entertain the thought of him—and now that she has got over it—"

"She will never get over it," said Miss Jean. "Oh, Margaret, have ye no mercy in you? Will you let her heart break just for a prejudice, just for—"

"Do you call it a prejudice that the man should be a gentleman, that his father before him should have been a gentleman?—"

"I care nothing for his father before him," exclaimed Jean, with the energy of passion. "He is as true a gentleman as ever stepped. I call it just a prejudice—"

"Hold your peace, Jean. Break her heart! when I tell you she is mending, mending day by day. Her peace shall not be disturbed again. I will write to him that it is too late. He is gentleman enough for that, I allow; that he will go away, that he will do nothing disloyal to me—"

"Would you have him disloyal to her?" Miss Jean cried. "No, Margaret! I have done your bidding many a day, but I will not now. If you write and bid him go, I will write and bid him stay. He will judge for himself which of us knows best."

Margaret rose to her feet with an indignant gesture.

"Will you defy me—me, your own sister?" she said.

"Oh! Margaret, do not break my heart!—but I will defy all the world for Lilias," cried Miss Jean. "She is more than my sister, she is my bairn; and yours too—and yours too!"

"It is for that," cried Margaret, with something like a sob, "that I will just defend her to the death."

"Is it defending her?" cried the other, "to break her heart?"

"There is no question of breaking hearts," said Margaret, hurriedly controlling herself, and taking up the letter; "but, Jean, for God's sake, not a word, for here is Lilias at the door."

Neither of them remembered, in the excitement of the moment, that the sight of them standing up to receive her, with the traces of their struggle in their looks, must have shown Lilias, had there been no other indication, that something extraordinary had happened. But that mattered little, as the reader knows. Lilias came in smiling, her eyes dazzled with the lights, her fair locks jewelled with the dews. She kept Lewis behind her with her hand.

"I have brought somebody to see you, Margaret and Jean," she said.

Margaret let the letter fall from her hand. It was the final throwing down of her arms before triumphant Love and Fate.

Margaret Oliphant – A Short Biography

Margaret Oliphant Wilson was born on April 4th, 1828 to Francis W. Wilson, a clerk, and Margaret Oliphant, at Wallyford, near Musselburgh, East Lothian.

She spent her childhood at Lasswade, near Dalkeith, Glasgow before moving to Liverpool.

Her youth was spent in establishing a writing style so much so that, in 1849, she had her first novel published: Passages in the Life of Mrs. Margaret Maitland based on the Scottish Free Church movement. It met with some success and was a good start to her career.

Two years later, in 1851, her third book Caleb Field was published. It was also now that she met the publisher William Blackwood in Edinburgh and was asked to contribute to his well-received Blackwood's Magazine. It was to be a lifelong endeavor. Over the course of the relationship she would have well over 100 articles published.

In May 1852, Margaret married her cousin, Frank Wilson Oliphant, at Birkenhead, and they settled at Harrington Square, Camden, London. He was an artist working primarily in stained glass. With the marriage she became Margaret Oliphant Wilson Oliphant.

Their marriage produced six children but three tragically died in infancy.

When her husband developed signs of the dreaded consumption (tuberculosis) they moved, on the advice of doctors, to warmer climes. In January 1859 it was to Florence, and then to Rome where, sadly, he died.

Margaret was naturally devastated but was also now left without support and only her income from her writing. She returned to England and took up the task of supporting her three remaining children by her literary activity.

By now she was being published both as an established novelist and regularly in Blackwood's Magazine, amongst several others. Her incredible and prolific work rate increased both her commercial reputation and the size of her reading audience.

Against this her domestic life continued to be tragic, full of sorrow and disappointment.

In January 1864 her only remaining daughter, Maggie, died and was buried in her father's grave in Rome. Her brother, who had emigrated to Canada, was shortly afterwards involved in financial ruin. Margaret generously offered a home to him and his children, adding another demand to her already heavy responsibilities.

In 1866 she settled at Windsor to be closer to her sons, who were being educated at near-by Eton School. That year, her second cousin, Annie Louisa Walker, came to live with her as a companion-housekeeper. Windsor was now to be her home for the rest of her life.

Her literary career for three decades was one of constant delivery and success. Whether she wrote historical works or across several genres in fiction: domestic realism, historical, romance or supernatural she was successful.

For more than thirty years she pursued a varied literary career but family life continued to bring problems.

The literary ambitions she wished for her sons were unfulfilled. Cyril Francis, the eldest, died in 1890, leaving a Life of Alfred de Musset, which was later incorporated in his mother's Foreign Classics for English Readers. The younger, Francis, who she nicknamed 'Cecco', collaborated with her in the Victorian Age of English Literature and won a position at the British Museum, but was rejected by Sir Andrew Clark, a famous physician. Cecco died in 1894.

With the last of her children now lost to her, she had but little further interest in life. Her health steadily and inexorably declined.

Margaret Oliphant Wilson Oliphant died at the age of 69 in Wimbledon on 20th June 1897. She is buried in Eton beside her sons.

At her death, Margaret was still working on Annals of a Publishing House, a record of Blackwood's Magazine with which she had enjoyed such a successful relationship.

Her Autobiography and Letters, which present a thoughtful picture of her domestic anxieties, was published in 1899. Only parts were written with a wider audience in mind: she had originally intended the Autobiography for her son, but he died before she could finish it.

Opinions on Oliphant's work are split, with some critics seeing her as a 'domestic novelist', while others recognize her work as influential and important to the Victorian literature canon. Critical reception from her contemporaries is also divided. John Skelton took the view that Oliphant wrote too much and too quickly. Writing a Blackwood's article called 'A Little Chat About Mrs. Oliphant', he asked, "Had Mrs. Oliphant concentrated her powers, what might she not have done? We might have had another Charlotte Brontë or another George Eliot." However not all of the contemporary reception was negative. The esteemed M. R. James admired Oliphant's supernatural fiction, concluding that "the religious ghost story, as it may be called, was never done better than by Mrs. Oliphant in 'The Open Door' and 'A Beleaguered City'. Mary Butts lavished praise on Oliphant's ghost story 'The Library Window', describing it as "one masterpiece of sober loveliness".

More modern critics of Oliphant's work include Virginia Woolf, who asked in 'Three Guineas' whether Oliphant's autobiography does not lead the reader "to deplore the fact that Mrs. Oliphant sold her brain, her very admirable brain, prostituted her culture and enslaved her intellectual liberty in order that she might earn her living and educate her children."

Whatever the merits of their cases Margaret Oliphant has been shamefully neglected in modern years. She is now becoming more widely recognised as a leading writer of her day.

Margaret Oliphant – A Concise Bibliography

A canon of more than 120 works, including novels, travel books, histories, and volumes of literary criticism.

Novels
Margaret Maitland (1849)
Merkland (1850)
Caleb Field (1851)
John Drayton (1851)
Adam Graeme (1852)
The Melvilles (1852)
Katie Stewart (1852)
Harry Muir (1853)
Ailieford (1853)
The Quiet Heart (1854)
Magdalen Hepburn (1854)
Zaidee (1855)
Lilliesleaf (1855)
Christian Melville (1855)
The Athelings (1857)
The Days of My Life (1857)
Orphans (1858)
The Laird of Norlaw (1858)
Agnes Hopetoun's Schools and Holidays (1859)
Lucy Crofton (1860)
The House on the Moor (1861)
The Last of the Mortimers (1862)
Heart and Cross (1863)
Salem Chapel (1863)
The Rector (1863)
Doctor's Family (1863)
The Perpetual Curate (1864)
Miss Marjoribanks (1866)
Phoebe Junior (1876)
A Son of the Soil (1865)
Agnes (1866)
Madonna Mary (1867)

Brownlows (1868)
The Minister's Wife (1869)
The Three Brothers (1870)
John: A Love Story (1870)
Squire Arden (1871)
At his Gates (1872)
Ombra (1872
May (1873)
Innocent (1873)
The Story of Valentine and His Brother (1875)
A Rose in June (1874)
For Love and Life (1874)
Whiteladies (1875)
An Odd Couple (1875)
The Curate in Charge (1876)
Carità (1877)
Young Musgrave (1877)
Mrs. Arthur (1877)
The Primrose Path (1878)
Within the Precincts (1879)
The Fugitives (1879)
A Beleaguered City (1879)
The Greatest Heiress in England (1880)
He That Will Not When He May (1880)
In Trust (1881)
Harry Joscelyn (1881)
Lady Jane (1882)
A Little Pilgrim in the Unseen (1882)
The Lady Lindores (1883)
Sir Tom (1883)
Hester (1883)
It Was a Lover and his Lass (1883)
The Lady's Walk (1883)
The Wizard's Son (1884)
Madam (1884)
The Prodigals and Their Inheritance (1885)
Oliver's Bride (1885)
A Country Gentleman and His Family (1886)
A House Divided Against Itself (1886)
Effie Ogilvie (1886)
A Poor Gentleman (1886)
The Son of His Father (1886)
Joyce (1888)
Cousin Mary (1888)
The Land of Darkness (1888)
Lady Car (1889)
Kirsteen (1890)
The Mystery of Mrs. Biencarrow (1890)

Sons and Daughters (1890)
The Railway Man and His Children (1891)
The Heir Presumptive and the Heir Apparent (1891)
The Marriage of Elinor (1891)
Janet (1891)
The Cuckoo in the Nest (1892)
Diana Trelawny (1892)
The Sorceress (1893)
A House in Bloomsbury (1894)
Sir Robert's Fortune (1894)
Who Was Lost and is Found (1894)
Lady William (1894)
Two Strangers (1895)
Old Mr. Tredgold (1895)
The Unjust Steward (1896)
The Ways of Life (1897)

Short stories

Neighbours on the Green (1889)
A Widow's Tale and Other Stories (1898)
That Little Cutty (1898)
The Open Door (1918)

Selected Articles

Mary Russel Mitford (Blackwood's Magazine, Vol. 75, 1854)
Evelin and Pepys (Blackwood's Magazine, Vol. 76, 1854)
The Holy Land (Blackwood's Magazine, Vol. 76, 1854)
Mr. Thackeray and his Novels (Blackwood's Magazine, Vol. 77, 1855)
Bulwer (Blackwood's Magazine, Vol. 77, 1855)
Charles Dickens (Blackwood's Magazine, Vol. 77, 1855)
Modern Novelists—Great and Small (Blackwood's Magazine, Vol. 77, 1855)
Modern Light Literature: Poetry (Blackwood's Magazine, Vol. 79, 1856)
Religion in Common Life (Blackwood's Magazine, Vol. 79, 1856)
Sydney Smith (Blackwood's Magazine, Vol. 79, 1856)
The Laws Concerning Women (Blackwood's Magazine, Vol. 79, 1856)
The Art of Caviling (Blackwood's Magazine, Vol. 80, 1856)
Béranger (Blackwood's Magazine, Vol. 83, 1858)
The Condition of Women (Blackwood's Magazine, Vol. 83, 1858)
The Missionary Explorer (Blackwood's Magazine, Vol. 83, 1858)
Religious Memoirs (Blackwood's Magazine, Vol. 83, 1858)
Social Science (Blackwood's Magazine, Vol. 88, 1860)
Scotland and her Accusers (Blackwood's Magazine, Vol. 90, 1861)
The Chronicles of Carlingford (Blackwood's Magazine 1862–1865)
Girolamo Savonarola (Blackwood's Magazine, Vol. 93, 1863)
The Life of Jesus (Blackwood's Magazine, Vol. 96, 1864)
Giacomo Leopardi (Blackwood's Magazine, Vol. 98, 1865)

The Great Unrepresented (Blackwood's Magazine, Vol. 100, 1866)
Mill on the Subjection of Women (The Edinburgh Review, Vol. 130, 1869)
The Opium-Eater (Blackwood's Magazine, Vol. 122, 1877)
Russian and Nihilism in the Novels of I. Tourgeniéf (Blackwood's Magazine, Vol. 127, 1880)
School and College (Blackwood's Magazine, Vol. 128, 1880)
The Grievances of Women (Fraser's Magazine, New Series, Vol. 21, 1880)
Mrs. Carlyle (The Contemporary Review, Vol. 43, May 1883)
The Ethics of Biography (The Contemporary Review, July 1883)
Victor Hugo (The Contemporary Review, Vol. 48, July/December 1885)
A Venetian Dynasty (The Contemporary Review, Vol. 50, August 1886)
Laurence Oliphant (Blackwood's Magazine, Vol. 145, 1889)
Tennyson (Blackwood's Magazine, Vol. 152, 1892)
Addison, the Humorist (Century Magazine, Vol. 48, 1894)
The Anti-Marriage League (Blackwood's Magazine, Vol. 159, 1896)

Biographies
Edward Irving (1862)
Francis of Assisi (1871)
Count de Montalembert (1872)
Dante (1877)
Cervantes (1880)
Life of Sheridan in the English Men of Letters series (1883)
John Tulloch (1888)
Laurence Oliphant (1892)

Historical & Critical Works
Historical Sketches of the Reign of George II (1869)
The Makers of Florence (1876)
A Literary History of England from 1760 to 1825 (1882)
The Makers of Venice (1887)
Royal Edinburgh (1890)
Jerusalem (1891)
The Makers of Modern Rome (1895)
William Blackwood and his Sons (1897)
The Sisters Brontë. In: Women Novelists of Queen Victoria's Reign (1897)